The Complete Poems of
HUGH MacDIARMID

Hugh MacDiarmid was the pseudonym of Christopher Murray Grieve, who was born in 1892 in Langholm, Dumfriesshire. He attended school there where he was taught by the composer F. G. Scott, an important influence and later collaborator. He planned to become a teacher but abandoned this for journalism which gave him scope for the expression of his left-wing politics. During the First World War he served in the R.A.M.C. (1915–19), after which he worked as a journalist in Montrose and later in London and Liverpool. After a breakdown in health he retreated to a croft on Whalsay, in the Shetlands, where he lived in poverty. He worked as an engineer on the Clyde during the Second World War, afterwards settling at Biggar, Lanarkshire, where he and his second wife lived in a small cottage without indoor sanitation or electric light. In 1934 he joined the Scottish Communist Party but was expelled in 1938 because of his continued membership of the Scottish Nationalist Party, which he had helped to found in 1928. Awarded a Civil List Pension for his services to Scottish literature, he also received an honorary doctorate from Edinburgh University, the Fletcher of Saltoun Medal and the Foyle Poetry Prize.

Hugh MacDiarmid brought about a renaissance in Scottish culture and is now acknowledged as a great poet. During the twenties he began his attack on the existing cultural situation in Scotland, which he believed was provincial, out of touch with the mind of Europe and its own past. His aim was to resurrect the Scottish tradition that had petered out with Burns, and his early volumes, such as *Sangschaw*, contain some of the most vigorous poems written in Scottish. As the poet Tom Scott writes, 'It was clear at once that a poet of genius had arisen, using Scots with a new power, vitality, subtlety of thought, and grasp of diction and idiom.' However, MacDiarmid's dictum was 'Not precedent, but innovation' and he also sought to assimilate the distinctive attitudes and techniques of the Modern Movement into a truly contemporary Scots poetry. His output was prodigious but for many years his work was largely unavailable. *The Complete Poems of Hugh MacDiarmid* (published in two volumes) represents the definitive collection of his work.

Hugh MacDiarmid died in 1978

THE COMPLETE POEMS OF
HUGH MacDIARMID

VOLUME II

Edited by
Michael Grieve and W. R. Aitken

Penguin Books

Penguin Books Ltd, Harmondsworth, Middlesex, England
Viking Penguin Inc., 40 West 23rd Street, New York, New York 10010, U.S.A.
Penguin Books Australia Ltd, Ringwood, Victoria, Australia
Penguin Books Canada Ltd, 2801 John Street, Markham, Ontario, Canada L3R 1B4
Penguin Books (N.Z.) Ltd, 182–190 Wairau Road, Auckland 10, New Zealand

First published by Martin Brian & O'Keeffe Ltd 1978
Published with corrections and an Appendix
in Penguin Books 1985

Made and printed in Singapore by
Richard Clay (S.E. Asia) Pte Ltd
Set in Bembo

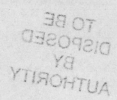

CONTENTS

VOLUME II

In Memoriam James Joyce (1955)

Three Hymns to Lenin (1957)

The Battle Continues (1957)

The Kind of Poetry I Want (1961)

From *Collected Poems* (1962)

Poems to Paintings by William Johnstone 1933 (1963)

From The Company I've Kept (1966)

From A Lap of Honour (1967)

Early Lyrics (1968)

From *A Clyack-Sheaf* (1969)

From *More Collected Poems* (1970)

From *Selected Poems* (1970)

From *The Hugh MacDiarmid Anthology* (1972)

Dìreadh (1974)

Appendix

IN MEMORIAM JAMES JOYCE

From A VISION OF WORLD LANGUAGE

(1955)

Our community of insight
  Makes it fitting
That I should link with this book
  As dedicatees
  My two old friends,

JOHN TONGE and JAMES H. WHYTE

Experts in, and enthusiasts of,
World Literature whether as conceived,
  Not very dissimilarly,
By Goethe, Gorki, or myself,
And in Scotland among the exceeding few
Competent receivers of all Joyce gave
And transmitters thereof because possessed
  Of a due sense of operative form;

And PRINCE DMITRY MIRSKY

A mighty master in all such matters
Of whom for all the instruction and encouragement he gave me,
I am happy to subscribe myself here
The humble and most grateful pupil.

The real goal of progress is then on the one hand a total lived experience of the whole of the real, and on the other such a deeply rooted fixation of spirit that, thanks to it, man can by the function of comprehension and by spiritual initiative acting through it, make the entire universe his own.

COUNT HERMAN KEYSERLING

Tatra visvam bhavaty ekanīdam. (When the whole world meets in one place. Sanskrit; motto of Rabindranath Tagore's Visvatharati [i.e. International University]).

Vers toutes les traditions réunies.

SAINT-BEUVE

To purify the dialect of the tribe.

MALLARME

The true unity of languages is not an Esperanto or Volapuk or everyone speaking French, not a single language, but an all-embracing language, an interpenetration of all languages.

VLADIMIR SOLOVYOF

Languages, grammars, all the ramifications of philology opened to him as if a magic hand had revealed the realm of words, English and foreign, and led along the paths of philology, steep and stony for most of us, full of colour and harmony for him. He always remembered this sudden sense of inner revelation, of blissful release, as one of the happiest moments of his life. – Mezzofanti himself would have scratched in a match with Harold Williams. This gift of tongues was not an end in itself. Sir Samuel Hoare rightly recognised that it was 'the evidence of a wonderful sympathy with human nature in all its forms' – a sympathy that 'unlocked' for him the secrets not only of the tongues but of the hearts of many peoples.

Written of the late HAROLD WILLIAMS

Ogni voce in tuo suono si ritrova
e in ogni voce sei
sparso, quando apri e chiudi i fori alterni.
Par quasi che tu sol le cose muova
mentre solo ti bei
nell' obbedire ai movimenti eterni.
(Every voice in thy music is found
And in every voice art thou diffused.
When thou openest and shuttest the alternate stops
It seems almost as if thou alone dost move all things,
While thou art only taking delight
In obeying the eternal motions.)

D'ANNUNZIO: Laudi III, Il Fanciullo

. . . did I not need
A language by itself, which would exceed
All those which are in use.

LORD HERBERT OF CHERBURY

Yes, Joyce's work does, indeed, contain all the erudite sophistication natural to the end of a vast Æon of spiritual evolution; but it can hardly be called degenerate, for it also reeks of the harshly-obscure, jarringly-obscene, jeeringly-blasphemous filthily agglutinate birth pangs of life being born afresh.

JOHN COWPER POWYS

I REMEMBER how you laughed like Hell
When I read you from Pape's 'Politics of the Aryan Road':
'English is destined to become the Universal Language!¹
The vibratory effect of English correctly spoken
(Which has somewhat of a nasal intonation)
On the Pineal Gland is unique,
And a necessary factor in the evolution of humanity.
I have yet to find any creative effect from Esperanto or Ido.
The creative effect of European languages
Can be demonstrated in that the vibrations
Produced in speaking these languages
– One and all – have direction.
I have not found any vibratory direction in Esperanto.
– Force without direction is Chaos.'
We who are concerned with 'the living whole
Of all the poetry that has ever been written,'
And the *sodaliciis adstricti consortiis*
Of all the authors who have been, are, or will be,
We remember Jacint Verdaguer whose *Atlàntida* and *Canigó*
Did for Catalonia what Mistral's *Mirèio* did for Provence,
And the Italian, Marco Girolamo Vida,
Who duly figured in Chalmers' collection of *British Poets*
(Trust the English to appropriate all they can!)
An odd fate for an Italian rhetorician
Who wrote Latin verse in defence of Greek poetics!
And let us not forget Doughty's pregnant prototype,
Richard Stanihurst,² who thus describes the Muse
I am, as will appear, concerned with now –
'Fame, the groyl³ ungentil, than whom none swifter is extant:
Limber in her whisking: her strength in journey she trebbleth,

---

¹ 'The English language is very good, but only for discussing in "smoking rooms," while sitting on an easy chair with legs outstretched on another, the topic of Australian frozen meat, or, sometimes, the Indian question. It is like the dish which is called in Moscow "Solianka," and into which everything goes except you and me, in fact everything you wish, and even the "after dinner *Cheshma* of Scheherazade."'

(*Cheshma* – veil.)   Gurdjieff: *All and Everything.*

² 1547–1618.   ³ A person ever on the move.

First like a shrimp[1] squatting for feare, then boldlye she roameth
On ground prowd jetting: she soars up nimblye to skyward;
The earth, her dame, chauffing[2] with graund Gods celical anger,
Littered this leveret, the syb,[3] as men sundrye rehersed,
To the giant Caeus, sister to swad[4] Encelad holden.
Furth she quicklye galops, with wingflight swallolyke hastning.
A foule fog[5] pack paunch: what feathers plumye she beareth,
So manye squint eyeballs shee keeps (a relation uncoth),
So manye tongues clapper, with her eyes and lip labour eevened.
In the dead of night-time to the skyes shee flickereth, howling,
Through the earth shade skipping, her sight from slumber amooving'
(And did he not anticipate Gerard Manley Hopkins too?
'Much like as in cornshuks singed with blasterous hurling[6]
Of southwind whistling: or when from mountain a rumbling
Flood rakes up furrows, ripe corn, and tillage of oxen.
Down tears it windfalls, and thick woods sturdily tumbleth.
The crack rack crashing the unwitting pastor[7] amazeth')
Porson with his *exquisita sermonis Attici perceptio*,
Rolfe with his tyrianthine style, diaphotick verse,
Orchidaceous vocabulary, and his archellenisms,
Argute, deaurate, investite, lucktifick, excandescence,
Galbanate, effrenate, dicaculous, pavonine, torose,
Hybristick, gingilism – Rolfe whose mantelpiece held
A card inscribed *Verro precipitevolissimevolmente*,
Hardy with words like lewth, leazes, dumble-dores,
Spuds, cit, wanzing, and his trained architect's use
Of adze, cusp, ogee, and the like: and, again,
Fantocine, junctive law, foresightlessness,
Meredith's specialised philosophical vocabulary,
'Yaffles on a chuckle skim,'
'Heaven a space for winging tons,'
Uttering a secret language as if in the belief
That it was a universal speech, yet even if
A secret language it contains a body
Of thought and intuitions worth unravelling.

---

[1] A wizened person.   [2] Moved with anger.
[3] The relation.   [4] Clownish.
[5] Corpulent.   [6] Commotion.   [7] Shepherd.

Davidson, too, with his angry cry
'Our language is too worn, too much abused,
Jaded and overspurred, wind-broken, lame, –
The hackneyed roadster every bagman mounts';
Patmore with 'shaw,' 'photosphere,' 'prepense-occulted,' 'draff,'
Thompson calling that the time had come
To raise a banner (but not raising it himself)
– 'I who can scarcely speak my fellows' speech' –
Against the Praetorian cohorts of poetry, whose prescriptive aid
Every aspirant to the poetical purple invokes!
And on to Doughty and Hopkins – then the younger men
(Name after name after name comes to me now
As a climber night-bound on a high wind-swept pass
Sees the world recreated peak by peak at dawn
And instinctively rises to his feet in homage
As, *parvis componere magna*, those who sit and wait
Rise at their Sovereign's coming)
Who go back to Langland's homely Anglo-Saxon verse;
Doughty, by far the greatest of them all,
Infinite in his awareness and charity,
Harbinger of the epical age of Communism,
Writing of ogival arches, traps, and basalt,
But equally ready when it comes to the pasterns of a horse,
The tilts of a camel-litter,
The nombril of a shield,
The burdon of a pilgrim:
Knowing that squirrel's *drey* is better than squirrel's *nest*,
Making language at once more rich and more precise,
And passionate for naming particular things
And particular parts of things,
So he writes of a *shive* of wood, *shivers* of silex,
Of a *gripe*, a *thrave*, and a *strike* of corn
And likes to use words for parts of the body
Like *shanks*, *chine*, *neckbone*, and the older
Halse, *weasand*, *chaps*, and *barme*
(And so, like Browning's Karshish – Arabic, *qāhash* –
Picker-up of learning's crumbs,
On to T. S. Eliot's line

'Bewray the repricon, outstent the naze'
And myself with my Ecclefechan Gongorism,
And even Spender's 'the narcine torpesce.'
Since ecdysis is never complete
Language like the Andean Indian character
Is always prepared to conjoin the incongruous
And marry the incompatible into a polycladous tradition
Multiradicate in the distant past)[1]
– I delight in all these and hundreds more
As one of the 'funny ones,' a race which includes
Any creature unlike his fellows
And sensitive of his unlikeness,
Any misfit, any lunatic, any deformity, hobbledehoy.
Mystic, criminal, beggar, saint,
Or persecuted or martyred unfortunate,
A race for which I have boundless sympathy and love
– Not only am I, as a 'funny one,'
In particular sympathy with the 'funniness'
Of these great spirits, but also I recognise in them
That prophetic, sooth-saying, magical, Logos-uttering quality
Which I know to make them not merely 'funny ones,'
Liable to the cruel persecution of 'normal' persons,
But also the salt of the earth, –
Ivar Aasen, Elizabeth Elstob, Rabelais, Browning, Meredith, Remizov,
Gjergj Fishta and Avetik Isaakyan,[2]
And William Barnes and his sixty languages,
(Browning with his 'to talk as brothers talk
In half-words, call things by half-names, no balk
From discontinuing old aids') – words like the fortune-telling table
Whereby things not yet discovered are foreknown to Science
– As Meldelyev predicted scandium, germanium and polonium,
As astronomers have foretold where a planet should be
And the telescope later has found it – as blue roses

---

[1] 'Allergic? I don't know where you pick up these words, I really don't. It's not what I call education. Words!'

[2] Gjergj Fishta, Albanian poet, 1871–1940. Avetik Isaakyan, Armenian poet, born 1875, of whom Alexander Blok wrote: 'Isaakyan is a poet of the first class, perhaps of a talent more brilliant and unusual than any poet in the whole of Europe.'

Can never be found, but peas with yellow blossoms
And haricot beans with red blossoms will yet be found,
Guests not yet arrived – whose places await them.
(At the table Moseley revised – the table at which
Between aluminium and gold, masurium, rhenium and illinium
Have taken their places – not without question still –
While 85 and 87 – alabamine and virginium –
Are still in dispute,
New places have been requisitioned
For Fermi's 9 and 94,
And whether the neutron is itself an element,
Lower than hydrogen,
And to be distinguished therefore as No. 0,
Is now in fierce debate.)
Or like the Shemhameporesh which gives magical creative power
(I might have joined the *Imyaslavtsy*[1] once)
To the man who can articulate it,
(*Aum;* the support of the meditation
According to Shri Sankaracharya,
Or, as declared in the Mundakopanishad's text itself,
'The bow by means of which
The individual self attains the universal self')
– We know that total speech is impossible, of course,
Like a too big star that therefore could transmit no light,
Like the dumbness finally desired by Tyutchev and Pasternak.
We only seek the full unobstructed light
Of the speech of our own star – the speech of all mankind.
Vendryes' linguistic introduction to History,
Stohr's 'Algebra der Grammatik'; Brøndal's
Logico-syntactical system; Jespersen's analytic syntax
(Proceeding from the basis of a particular language
And thus given a peculiar orientation from the start,
Syntax like idiom being socially conditioned)
And Carnap's logical syntax of language.
'Philosophy is to be replaced by the logic of science,
For the logic of science is nothing other

---

[1] Glorifiers of the name, ascribing a sacred or even sacramental significance to the name of God.

Than the logical syntax of the language of science'
And Alan Gardiner's exposé of de Saussure's typical 'circuit of speech'[1]
His contemplation of the possibility of a sentence of a single word
In which he is in sharp conflict with the eminent John Ries,
His pairs of terms, . . . locutional and elocutional, congruent and
    incongruent,
And the indispensable distinction between language and speech;
And Kostes Palamas and all the μαλλαιροί,[2]
Carco the Toulouse-Lautrec of speech, and Stramm,
Jenner, the first Grand Bard of Cornwall, and that
Most gallant youth, Charles Henderson, and all
The members of the Tyr Tavas movement, and Padraic O'Conaire,
(And R. L. Stevenson's Joseph Finsbury
'With a polyglot Testament in one hand
And a phrase-book in the other,
Groping his way among the speakers of eleven European languages,'
– Joseph discoursing in the Tregonwell Arms
To the inmates of the public bar
On nine versions of a single income,
Placing the imaginary person
In London, Paris, Baghdad, Spitzbergen,
Bassorah, Heligoland, the Scilly Isles,
Brighton, Cincinnatti, and Nijni-Novgorod
– Only an Englishman yet much to my liking
And one I resemble a little in a way perhaps
– For the authors I love best are they
Who have lived, knocked about in the world,
Had a thousand adventures of every sort,
And penetrated every kind of milieu,
Feeling, watching, taking stock the whole time;
Men for whom writing was first and above all
A pleasure, men who, when they sat down to write,
Had merely to let their pens run freely,
So great was the pressure of memory
And the weight of the thousand living images

[1] *The Theory of Speech and Language*, by Sir Alan H. Gardiner.
[2] 'The Hairy Ones.' Reference to the movement for the liberation of modern Greek, in which Palamas and Alexander Pallis were the chief protagonists.

That dwelt with them. Most writers today
Remind me of somebody who talks about love
Without ever having known it outside of marriage.
There is much to be said today for reviving
The poetical method of Jalal ud-Din Rumi
Who made use of every kind of anecdote
And allowed his pen to run on unchecked
With every idea, every fancy, every play on words
Which suggested themselves to him
– And not attempting the impossible task
Of creating original forms of expression
For 'unknown modes of being,'
Illimitable abyss of unquiet speculation!
It is safer to keep to the surface of things
And maintain our discussion in terms
Of the individualised mentality
From which escape seems so difficult).
(I agree with the Swiss littérateur:[1]
'Let us regard modern poetry
As one of the signs of the times
In which men formerly read
The fate of their century . . .
To maintain it has little influence
Today is to be blind to the fact
That since romanticism,
And especially from 1912 to 1927
Poetry has often performed
The function of the looker-out aboard ship.
It is true it may have few readers
And sometimes discourages readers;
Nevertheless it registers the slightest change
In the atmosphere, and makes the gesture
Others will imitate and develop,'
Even as Migliorini's chapter on 'Innovazioni grammaticali
e lessicali dell' italiano d'oggi'
May appear to cover an almost ludicrously diminutive field

[1] Marcel Raymond, in *From Baudelaire to Surrealism* (Wittenborn, Schultz, 1947).

Compared with the daring innovations of modern America,
Nevertheless as Pancrazi said in *Corriere della Sera*
The young writers to a greater or lesser degree
Have broken away from time-hallowed standards
And are making for a suppler style
– And all this here, everything I write, of course
Is an extended metaphor for something I never mention.)
And, above all, my great master, Shestov, with his supreme τόλμα
His glorious insistence on 'the words that are swallowed up,'[1]
His indeflectible concern with τὸ τιμιώτατον
Plotinus's 'what matters most.'
And my own kinsmen, Lindley Murray, the father of English
    Grammar,
And Alexander Murray, who studied the languages
Of Western Asia and North-East Africa and Lappish
And wrote the 'History of European Languages,'
And others of my contemporaries living still
(Most cunning dealers in *zaumny* and *skaz*
And workers in dialect and slang,
Multilinguists and grammarians and philologists,
Orismologists, sematologists, semasiologists,
And epeolators all),
Diaskeuasts of the Omnific Word,
That heroic genius, Antonio Gramsci,
Studying comparative linguistics in prison,
For, as he said in his *Lettere dal Carcere*,
'Nothing less! What could be more
Disinterested and *für ewig*?'
Valéry's *Poésie et Pensée Abstraite*,
Paulhan's *Les Fleurs de Tarbes*
And *Jacob Cow The Pirate* or *Whether Words Are Signs*,
Parain's *Traité sur la Nature et les Fonctions de Langage*,
Francis Ponge's *Le Parti-pris des Choses*,
And Sartre's *Aller et Retour*
And *Recherches sur la Langage*,
(Countless references, all close as a Cumnock hinge)
And Stalin, the Georgian, and all

[1] Job VI. 2 and 3.

The languages and literatures of the U.S.S.R.
In days when from the teratoma cyst of omnitude
The surgeon of clear thought is taking away
Millions of crude forms of infant life.

Welcome then, Joyce, to our *aonach*[1] here,
Here where alone we can live
(We who know, *pace* Middleton Murry, that nothing matters
Save 'the poetry of a fanatic' and feel ourselves
What Valéry calls 'invaded by fanaticism;
Suffering the overwhelming progress of a decisive spiritual conquest'
Where nothing matters save Implex and Noösphere).
(I have spoken elsewhere of 'the lies by which we live,'
The ubiquitous irresponsibility, the general atimy,
L'énorme bêtise, the Thyestean banquet of clap trap,
The monstrous superstructure almost everyone erects
On an incredible ignorance of even the barest facts,
– An ignorance people cannot *believe* they can have,
Assuming that they are entitled to their own opinions
And never doubting they have sufficient sense to go by –
The 'economic behemoths,' the leviathans
That have men, unconsciously, at their mercy.
Germane to this poem, and most amazing instance perhaps
Of the lengths to which malicious misrepresentation goes
And the *suppressio veri* that accompanies it everywhere
Is the great question of Sinus Tone Production,
The production of vocal tone in the various
Sinuses of the head and face and not by means of the vocal cords.[2]
Such a colossal superstructure has been built
On the false foundation of the vocal cords theory
That the truth has no chance of recognition,
– Doctors, singing masters, vocalists, and all concerned
Are inextricably caught in the network of falsity.
Yet many are the hints in the precepts and methods
Of the old masters of singing that point to the truth –

[1] Scottish Gaelic, meaning (1) a solitary place, (2) a place of union, cf. Latin: unicus, single; unire, unite, – both from unus, one.
[2] Vide *Sinus Tone Production* by Ernest George White (London, 1938).

They *felt* what was the nature of the problem of voice production,
In the stress they laid upon 'head-resonance' [dans la masque].
That this degenerated into the characteristic 'French' nasality
Is neither here nor there; and the old Italian *maestro* was right
[Making due allowance for his temperamental exaggeration]
Who cried to his pupils: 'Never the throat! Always the nose!
If I had Two Noses I would use them!'
He had a true instinct for the vital locale
Of the matter in singing; but despite the cases cited
In recognised standard text-books of throat-surgery,
Of people with excised vocal cords being taught
Not only to speak but to sing, and ample medical evidence thereof,
There is no chance of credence or attention being given
To a body of evidence too damningly destructive
Of the conventional 'vocal cord' theory for even
The deliberate blindness and obscurantism of an interested orthodoxy
To deny – no chance of the truth winning through
And being accepted and acted upon – though here and there
A man has the courage to proclaim it, notably
The Italian laryngologist, Marafioti.
Yet everywhere, what is demonstrably false
Continues to be taught in spite of the proven and established truth,
For, as Ernest Newman says, give a lie a good start
And it is practically impossible for truth to overtake it.)
As for the eyes' elaborate arrangements with crossed and uncrossed
  fibres
(So it is with most Scots, whereas in more highly developed man
A quarter of all fibres are direct)
For overlapping the fields of vision and centring the sight,
For focussing both eyes on varying distances,
For adaptation of scotopic vision in the dark
Or for perceiving colour vibrations,
Space fails me to indicate them here,
But – probably through the comparatively small group of optic
  fibres,
Dispatched to the pulvinar in the lateral nucleus of the optic thalamus, –
The eyes can pull the whole body about and adjust
Hands, trunk, and position of head

For the purpose of preparing the frame and active muscles
For instantaneous motor action in connection with sight.[1]

Scotland has not developed or has lost
That provision or allowed it to become atrophied.
It cannot move its own members about
But is hypnotically controlled from London.
Scotland has nothing clear in its own mind.

Ah, Jenny Lind, I will write a poem one day
('Voices drop away like rose-leaves')
About the world's great singers, about you
And Grisi – O gracious, golden Grisi,
As Adalgisa in Bellini's *Norma*
Or in her *Casta Diva* or in the famous Polacca
Son vergin vezzosa in *I Puritani*
Or, the cavatina on, the melting voice
In mazes running, – and Malibran,
In the duet from *Andronica*,
'Vanne, se alberghi in petto,'
And executing a fearful shake
On the high B flat,
And doing it again when the audience encored
Though she knew it would kill her
– And dying, in fact, within ten days
And only twenty-eight years old.
How could I fail to sing of such feats
Who am a connoisseur of the human voice,
And of all turns of language from the 'fu' po'
As the old Scotswoman called the *faux pas*
To the ἅπαξ λεγόμενα of wise-cracking journalists;
Concerned at one moment with the whole of *Weltliteratur*
And equally concerned the next with Vogul,
The smallest of the Finno–Ugrian language group,
Spoken by only 5000 people,
And have spent many of my happiest busman's holidays

[1] 'That the eye is necessary to sight seems to me the notion of one immersed in matter.' – J. S. Mill.

In books like Leonard Bloomfield's *Language*,[1]
Happy as most men are with mountains and forests
Among phonemes, tagmenes, taxemes,
Relation-axis constructions,
The phrasal sandhi-type and zero-anaphora?
(What? Complaint that I should sing
Of philological, literary and musical matters
Rather than of daffodils and nightingales,
Mountains, seas, stars and like properties?
– As if human nature and the human mind
And everything that specially appertains thereto
Were not infinitely the greatest miracles
And most important matters in the world
– Anything else of any consequence only
In its bearing thereon!)

(Do not mistake me. For well I know
'The more a poet can open himself to the world.
The more he can embrace life directly,
The better poetry he is likely to write.'
Only I am dealing particularly
With literature here,
Not with 'How to make poultry pay,'
'The Language of Monkeys,' 'Military Discipline'
– And was not *poppysmos* originally a clucking noise
To entice animals before it became
An invocation to the divine powers
For aid in battle? –
'The Training of a Young Polo Pony,'
Or with telling a ship's cook where to find
The heart and liver of a porpoise
Rather than with the *Amattoren Uzta of Mayi Ariztia*
Or Wiro[2] or the Venetian dialect '*poesie giustiniane*'[3]
Or the fifty-two *Dvaapadesát Horkych Balad Vecneho Studenta
Roberta Davida*,[4]

---

[1] Published London, 1935.
[2] Giles' name for the hypothetical original Aryan tongue and its speakers.
[3] e.g. the *canti popolari* of Leonardo Giustinian.   [4] Prague: Fr. Boróvy, 1937.

That Villonesque work the author dared not continue.
Yet what I have just said
Involves me in no contradiction
If I go on to agree, as I do,
That 'to cut a man off from the world of sense
As we have it in land and sea
And their living contents
Would be to separate him
From the springs of the mind's life.
Even to insist on the alienness
Of external nature to ourselves
Is misleading. "The interest of man,"
We are told, "is man,
Not natural history but human history."
So interpreted man ceases to be man.
Mere internality spells mere externality.
Human history in the fertile sense
Is not the history of the human species
But the story of the universe of experience.')

For this is the poetry I want – the Racinian purpose
(Remembering Péguy's remarkable disquisition too
On Racine's use of the world 'cruel'!)
Of following with mathematical exactitude
The movements of a mind
Actuated by an assumed purpose
– One can picture the dramatist
Contemplating a new tragedy
Picking up his well-worn *Tacitus*, and reading.
He finds the passage he has been
Turning over in his head, runs through it,
Puts down the volume and thinks.
Hour by hour he must have thought,
Moving the little puppet figures in his mind
In logical evolutions, watching the effect
Of each one's development upon all,
Calculating stresses and strains
In the manner of an engineer

– So versed in mental analysis that he gives
The impression not of wondering what would be
The movement of a certain mind in given circumstances
But of knowing. He did not wish his audience
To recognise familiar feelings in the characters
And to see something of themselves upon the stage,
But to give them the opportunity
Of a difficult intellectual pleasure
As they followed the struggles of minds
Dominated by given passions.
In short, a high classical poetry
– An exacting intellectual undertaking,
The expression to a far greater extent
Of thought and reason than of emotion,
And fully understanding
The sources of its emotions and ideas,
– Trying to see the whole of life reasonably,
Adopting a detachment whence I can judge
Man with unbiassed, impersonal calm,
And lay my finger on the sores of humanity,
– Cultivating deliberately an intensely analytical view of life;
And a poetry not only stating or advocating these principles
But activated by them at every point,
And not with that classical formalism which is now
Most of all incompatible with such a purpose;
Following the letter but without the spirit
(The conventional appearance of reasonableness
Utterly devoid of the reality).

And enjoying like a voyage down the Clyde
An excursion among the American-Indian languages,
The Algonquian, Athabascan, Iroquoian, Muskogean and Siouan
    groups
With the possible addition of the Uto-Aztecan;
Groups further divided
Into about sixty separate tongues,
And especially rejoicing in the chapter
On Form-Classes and Lexicon, where he once more explodes

The ridiculous tradition of the peasant or working man
Only using a few hundred words,
Whereas he really uses more than Shakespeare
– A work of amazing erudition by a writer who seems
Equally at home in primitive Chinese,
Pre-Irish, Samoan, Sumerian, and Tagálog.
What if others think we've gone stone winnick,
Bung bughouse, you know,
Mad, raving, potty, dippy?
We take in the whole range from Worthington English
To Lichtenberg's catalogue of 150 synonyms
For 'he is drunk' – 100 in High German
And the rest in dialect.
For it is in literature as it is in mountaineering
Inevitable when once all the great ridges and faces
Have been conquered by 'fair means'
New piton techniques must be evolved
For the creation and solution
Of new climbing problems.

And just as any hard-scrabble cowman can tell you
No matter how hungry a slat-ribbed old cow gets
She isn't licked till she lies down, so
With every language, dialect, usage of words,
Even any sort of gobbledygook,
The mode despised, neglected or rejected
May become the corner stone of a miracle of expression.
But whatever language we use
We must command its *Wesen* at its deepest,[1]
That element that cannot express itself
More than dimly in man's everyday life,
For in the aesthetic experience
Instead of language meaning the material of experience
– Things, ideas, emotions, feelings –
This material means language.

Once again we seek to heal the breach
Between genius and scholarship, literature and learning,

[1] i.e. the 'salt' or 'Tzimus.'

(These two which share the knowledge
Of a broken unity of the human spirit,
Which to genius appears
Mainly a moral and personal disaster
To be mended by intuition, by divination,
But to the second, equally conscious
Of the discontinuity of tradition,
Of the accidents of time, language, place and race
That hinder sympathy and understanding,
Presents itself as an intellectual trouble
To be solved by piecing together
Minute particles of evidence)
Which, since consummate learning is far more rare
Than genius, has led to the ridiculous condition
That the world, which holds out both hands to genius,
Is unhappy in the presence of scholarship
Often contemptuous, sometimes even resentful,
Siding naturally with the spiritual valour
Which dashes itself to pieces
On the unbreachable walls which fence Truth,
But having little sympathy
With the slow and cautious movement of learning.
Yet we all know now the world might get on better
If it ceased to produce great men of action;
Speculative genius is a mixed boon too.

We are for the very opposite then
Of these radio variety programmes
– Many programmes but no variety.
Radio variety with sound all–important
Should depend upon the happy madness of the word.
Alas, it seems afraid of that genuine nonsense
Which should be at the core of vaudeville.
Programmes do not fizz up spontaneously,
They imitate each other. They are anxious,
Mechanical, cut–to–pattern. They have
Their careful continuity, talkative compères,
Synthetic jollity, their imitations of Hollywood film stars

(Always the same ones), their pseudo-American accents,
Their strident songs, their Audience Participation.
Everything appears to be mass-produced, stencilled.
It is rare to find a programme
That is just uninhibited nonsense,
Nonsense presented with gusto and style and flourish,
And the proper slightly off-the-edge gravity
By comedians who do not rely
Upon self-conscious catchphrases
Or some odd approximation
To the accents of Michigan or Arkansas,
We will away with all this parish pump humour,
These feeble topicalities, 'Hiya chum' accents,
And battering-ram bands –
And everything *lo cursi*, [1]
Public opinion and all its wretched manifestations,
(As Valéry said: 'Tout ça, tout ça, vous savez
– La psychologie, la photographie, la théologie –')
The dividing line between the folk and the vernacular arts
Is never vague to us. We know
The moribund vernacular art of to-day
Is characterised by energy,
Vitality replacing technique, selection, and taste,
(Stopping short before consideration is applied)
So that, though the aesthetic level is necessarily lower
The original impulse remains more clear,
Complex (favouring a 'nice rich debased baroque
And the overlaying of one decoration by another')
Unsubtle (aiming at 'being like,' uninterpretatively)
And leaning towards disquiet and sometimes terror
Because it is the expression of an illiterate or simple way of life.

We have the privilege – or the great misfortune – to be present
at a profound, rapid, irresistible, and total transformation of all the
conditions of human activity and of life itself. [2]

[1] Slang word current in Cadiz as applicable to that which, though middleclass
and poor, aspires to be regarded as exquisite. Not quite equivalent to *possidon io*
(Portuguese), meaning condition of artificial gentility.
[2] Paul Valéry, in his address of July 1953, to the Collège de Sète. In this

So, like him, we cry '*l'honneur des hommes: Saint Langage*'
Knowing even in the case of an excellent translation,
How the original French has the ring of Venetian glass
But the English of Waterford;
Papiemento, mixture of half the languages on earth,
The construction *Apo Koinou* in the Germanic languages,
Notando Jabavu and her native Xhosa;
And comment on the collapse of statecraft,
The special nature of French vowels,
The cultural significance of the Rhine,
The status of Paris as the 'capital of criticism,'
The ethics of dictatorship,
The white grapes of Thoméry –
Our object to counter in however small a degree
The general falling-off of first-hand intellectual effort;
For this decline, we realise, is far more dangerous
Than many an obvious disaster.

Hence this *hapax legomenon* of a poem, this exercise
In schablone, bordatini, and prolonged scordatura,
This *divertissement philologique*,
This Wortspiel, this torch symphony,
This 'liberal education,' this collection of *fonds de tiroir*,
This – even more than Kierkegaard's
'Frygt og Baeven' – 'dialectical lyric,'
This rag-bag, this Loch Ness monster, this impact
Of the whole range of *Weltliteratur* on one man's brain,
In short, this 'friar's job,' as they say in Spain
Going back in kind
To the Eddic 'Converse of Thor and the All-Wise Dwarf'

---

connection it is true of Joyce, as was said by and of another poet: ' "I will not leave a corner of my consciousness covered up, but saturate myself with the strange and extraordinary new conditions of this life." This willingness – and ability – to let himself be new-born into the new situation, not subduing his experience to his established personality, is a large part, if not the whole secret, of the character of his best work. It was his exposure of his whole personality that gave his work its quality of impersonality.'

'For there is nothing covered that shall not be revealed; neither hid that shall not be known.' (Luke XII. 2.)

(Al-viss Mal, 'Edda die lieden des Codex Regius,' 120, 1 f)[1]
Existing in its present MS form
Over five centuries before Shakespeare.
You remember it?

Let the only consistency
In the course of my poetry
Be like that of the hawthorn tree
Which in early Spring breaks
Fresh emerald, then by nature's law
Darkens and deepens and takes
Tints of purple-maroon, rose-madder and straw.

Sometimes these hues are found
Together, in pleasing harmony bound.
Sometimes they succeed each other. But through
All the changes in which the hawthorn is dight,
No matter in what order, one thing is sure
– The haws shine ever the more ruddily bright!

And when the leaves have passed
Or only in a few tatters remain
The tree to the winter condemned
                    Stands forth at last
        Not bare and drab and pitiful,
But a candelabrum of oxidised silver gemmed
By innumerable points of ruby
Which dominate the whole and are visible
Even at considerable distance
As flame-points of living fire.
That so it may be
With my poems too at last glance
Is my only desire.

All else must be sacrificed to this great cause.
I fear no hardships. I have counted the cost.
I with my heart's blood as the hawthorn with its haws
Which are sweetened and polished by the frost!

                    [1] Text, G. Neckel, Heidelberg, 1914.

See how these haws burn, there down the drive,
In this autumn air that feels like cotton wool,
When the earth has the gelatinous limpness of a body dead as a whole
While its tissues are still alive!

Poetry is human existence come to life,
The glorious energy that once employed
Turns all else in creation null and void,
The flower and fruit, the meaning and goal,
Which won all else is needs removed by the knife
Even as a man who rises high
Kicks away the ladder he has come up by.

This single-minded zeal, this fanatic devotion to art
Is alien to the English poetic temperament no doubt,
'This narrowing intensity' as the English say,
But I have it even as you had it, Yeats, my friend,
And would have it with me as with you at the end,
I who am infinitely more un-English than you
And turn Scotland to poetry like those women who
In their passion secrete and turn to
Musk through and through!

So I think of you, Joyce, and of Yeats and others who are dead
As I walk this Autumn and observe
The birch tremulously pendulous in jewels of cairngorm,
The sauch, the osier, and the crack-willow
Of the beaten gold of Australia;
The sycamore in rich straw-gold;
The elm bowered in saffron;
The oak in flecks of salmon gold;
The beeches huge torches of living orange.

Billow upon billow of autumnal foliage
From the sheer high bank glass themselves
Upon the ebon and silver current that floods freely
Past the shingle shelves.
I linger where a crack willow slants across the stream,

Its olive leaves slashed with fine gold.
Beyond the willow a young beech
Blazes almost blood-red,
Vying in intensity with the glowing cloud of crimson
That hangs about the purple bole of a gean
Higher up the brae face.

And yonder, the lithe green-grey bole of an ash, with its boughs
Draped in the cinnamon-brown lace of samara.
(And I remember how in April upon its bare twigs
The flowers came in ruffs like the unshorn ridges
Upon a French poodle – like a dull mulberry at first,
Before the first feathery fronds
Of the long-stalked, finely-poised, seven-fingered leaves) –
Even the robin hushes his song
In these gold pavilions.

Other masters may conceivably write
Even yet in C major
But we – we take the perhaps 'primrose path'
To the dodecaphonic bonfire.

They are not endless these variations of form
Though it is perhaps impossible to see them all.
It is certainly impossible to conceive one that doesn't exist.
But I keep trying in our forest to do both of these,
And though it is a long time now since I saw a new one
I am by no means weary yet of my concentration
On phyllotaxis here in preference to all else,
All else – but my sense of sny!

The gold edging of a bough at sunset, its pantile way
Forming a double curve, tegula and imbrex in one,
Seems at times a movement on which I might be borne
Happily to infinity; but again I am glad
When it suddenly ceases and I find myself
Pursuing no longer a rhythm of duramen
But bouncing on the diploe in a clearing between earth and air
Or headlong in dewy dallops or a moon-spairged fernshaw

Or caught in a dark dumosity, or even
In open country again watching an aching spargosis of stars.

Let us arise,
We whose 'calf-country' is *Siksha*,
The science of proper pronunciation, and the grammar of Panini.
Beyond all grammars for originality of plan
And for analytical subtlety – Panini
Fabled to have *seen* rather than composed
This 'natural history of the Sanskrit tongue'
In Sūtras which are perfect miracles of condensation,
The maximum abridgement being effected by the coining
Of an arbitrary symbolical language,
The key to which must be acquired
Before the rules themselves can be rendered intelligible.
– The closing *Sūtra* shows the consummate brevity attained.
It reads merely 'a a', which is said to mean
'Let short *a* be held to have its organ of utterance
Contracted, now we have reached the end of the work
In which it was necessary to regard it as otherwise.'
– Grammar regarded as we should regard the natural sciences,
Something to be studied and elaborated for its own sake
– And so on to Kātāyana's Vārttikas
Or 'supplementary rules and annotations'
And to Patanjali's Mahabhashya or 'great commentary'
And to the hundred and fifty grammarians and commentators
Who followed in the footsteps of that great triumvirate,
Each criticising or commenting on his predecessors –
Kaiyata, Vamanan, Bhattoji-dīkshita,
To Madhyama-kaumudī, the laghu-kaumudī of Varada-rāja,
Vopadeva – we know them all
And every detail of their works
Even as in our own Europe we know
How what was once the dialect of Burgos
Was acquired by Aztecs, Mixteks, Zapoteks,
Aimaras, Quechuas, Araucanians, Guaranies and Tagálogs,
And we know the clear, well-balanced Castilian,
The explosive concentration of Portuguese and Extremenan,

The thin pliancy of Galician,
The soft vigour and luminousness of Valencian and Mallorcan,
The bitter and sincere harshness of Catalan,
Even as we know Greek, from Homer to modern Greek,
Including the Koine and the dialects, ancient and modern,
And rejoice over how κάμνω found in Homer
In the sense of 'make' survived in popular speech
For 3000 years, though it did not get into books.
And how the third plural οντι is used in Cos
Where also survives the Doric form πόκα
And in Astypalaea the true aspirate survives
As t-th (like pot-hook) for Θ

Even as we know how
Costa i Llobera's *Pi de Formentor*
Is not Catalan but Majorcan,
Not Majorcan but of Pollensa,
Not Pollensan but a specific pine-tree
Hanging in verdure over the rocks by the sea,
And have understood the need of definitely fixing the meaning of
    a word,
Now so important, once in fairly common use
Both in Jewish and Christian literature
Down to the eleventh century A.D.
And to that end have traced the usages
In 'The Oracles of Papias,' Sophocles' Greek Lexicon
Josephus, Philo, Clement of Rome, Polycarp, Irenaeus,
Noting the cunningly concocted plausibilities
With which heretics have misled the minds of the simple
And all the distortions of those who have proved
Incompetent exegetes of noble utterances,
And so tried to trace the exact meaning of this word
Whether in the form of τὰ λόγια or τὰ λόγια τοῦ θεοῦ
Or τὰ λόγια αὐτοῦ, or κυριακά
Or τὰ λόγια αὐτοῦ, or ἐκείνου
Or, lastly, as θεῖα λόγια and ἱερὰ λόγια

Even as we know that in B.C. 500
The Chinese symbol meaning 'moon' was pronounced 'ngiwpt'

But in Peiping to-day is read 'yueh', 'ut' in Canton,
'Ngwok' in Foochow, and 'yö' in Shanghai,
While the Japanese read it as 'gestu'
And it is called 'saran' in Mongolia
And 'biya' in Manchuria,
While in Tibet, Korea, Annam, and other places
Still other sounds are attached to it
But in each case the meaning is perfectly clear
And its use through many centuries by the literate sections
Of so many linguistically different peoples
Surely proves there must be something in it,
Quite aside from its sound,
That is universally accessible;
Loving to trace back the doctrine of *amor intellectualis Dei*
To its fountain-head,
To find a 13th-century anticipation
Of the Pound-Eliot *olla podrida* of tongues
In the *descort* of Raimbaut de Vaquieras,
Or, brooding over the world history of the dance,
Review with the mind's eye all the forms,
Passecaille, chaconne, sarabande,
The dances of the Dinka, the Naura, the Nilotic Nanda,
The Toba of the Gran Chaco,
To the maxixe, tango, charleston,
Shag and big apple, and, *en route*,
Rejoice, in a philological parenthesis,
To analyse the Hebrew verb *rakad*
And find thence that King David *skipped*
Rather than *danced* before the Ark.
The Russian *Trepak* and the Georgian *Lekuri*,
The French *Bourée* and Spanish *Fandango*,
The dizzy *Moldavanesca* with its circular movements,
The slow *Hora* languid as the strains of the Moldavian *doina*,
The men's fiery *Ciocarlia* dance, the *Coasa suite*,
And the charming Tadjik *Non-Boza*.
(Compare the dance passages in Dynnik's *Skazanniya o*
    Nartakh
And in Dozon's *Bulgarski Narodni Pesni*)

Even as we delight in the letter of Aristeas
Which contains less than 2000 words
(All listed in Wendland's *Index Verborum*)
Of which more than 500 are various forms
Of twenty-eight words only;
– Apart from the interest of its contents
This short treatise is of unique value to men like us
Because it contains no fewer than thirty-two hapax legomena
And thirty-seven other words which can be described as rare.
We who have sat with Kurds in their appalling cellars,
With Kazaks in their round igloo-like huts,
With Persians in their earth-floored hovels,
And talked with Uzbeks, Tadjiks, Tartars,
We, who know intimately *meddah*, *karagöz*, and, above all
Orta oyunu, that imitation of peasants and of all
The various nationalities composing the Ottoman Empire,
Are coming now to the *orta oyunu* of all mankind.

And even as we know Shelta, Hesperic Latin, and Béarlagair na Sāer,
(Knowing them as a farmer surveying his fields
Can distinguish between one kind of crop and another
At a stage when that is a mystery to the unskilled eye
– Knowing that wheat has a deeper green,
Barley a twisting blade that gives it a hazy look,
Oats a blue, broad blade.
The beans blossom, and the cloverfields also,
Now the valley becomes clothed as with diverse carpets
– Red clover, white clover,
The silver blue of beans,
And occasionally
The wine-glow of a field of trefolium).

Even as we know
The Cretan Mantinades (or Chattismata as Cypriots call it),
The 'poe etarides' going on for hours at fairs and rural banquets,
Instantly improvised pendeca-syllabic couplets
(Much like *puirt a beul* at Hebridean ceilidhs
Or like the Welsh pennillion)

Each one capping its forerunner to a ritual tune;
Or the similar performance of two Basque Bersolaris
Involving, with more than Finnish *sisu*, the whole being,
All the senses at once, and not merely
A St. Vitus' dance of head, shoulders and arms,
Like the top dissection of a chicken;
Or, best of all, Valéry's *nuit de Gênes*,
The painful and ecstatic awareness
Of language as the central mystery
Of the intellectual life, the great obsession
With language and the point of consciousness.

Or even as we know
Schweitzer and Cappelletti on the Cimbric language[1]
Of the last descendants of the old Lombobards;
Tibetan influences on Tocharian;
Glottalized Continuants in Navaho, Nootka, and Kwakiutl,
A doctrinal dissertation on the Takelma language;
Studies in the language of the Kharosthi documents
Written in a variety of Indian Prakrit
Used as the administrative language
Of Shan-Shan or Koraina in the third century A.D.;
A practical introduction to Ruq'ah script;
And Pirandello's treatise in German on the Sicilian dialect,
Laute und Lautentwicklung der Mundart von Girgenti.

And rejoicing in all those intranational differences which
Each like a flower's scent by its peculiarity sharpens
Appreciation of others as well as bringing
Appreciation of itself, as experiences of gardenia or zinnia
Refine our experience of rose or sweet pea.

Or even as, in the Shetland Islands where I lived,
I know, in the old Norn language, the various names
Applied to all the restless movements of the sea

[1] Tautsch (Lehrbuch des Cimbrischen Dialekts von Giazza) Bolzano, Ferrari –
Auer 1945. Die Herkunft der Zimbern (Jahrbuch für vergl. Volkskunde: Die
Nachbarn, Band 1) Göttingen: Vandenhock and Rupprecht.

– *Di*, a wave; *Da mother di*, the undulations
That roll landward even in calm weather;
Soal, swell occasioned by a breeze,
Trove, a short, cross, heavy sea,
Hak, broken water, *Burrik*, a sharp sea or 'tide lump,'
Bod, a heavy wave breaking on the shore,
Brim, sound of sea breaking on the shore,
Especially when land could not be seen, as in a fog,
Brimfooster, sea breaking on a sunken rock or *baa*,
Faxin, a *baa* threatening to break,
Overskud or *votrug*, broken or spent water or backwash,
Gruttik, ebb-tide, *Grinister*, ebb during spring tide,
Draag, the drift of a current,
Sokin or *Saagin*, short period of still water between tides,
Snaar, a turn or whirl in a current,
Roost, a rapid flowing current,
And the several names applied to the sea bottom
Flör, maar, jube, graef and *ljoag*

Or like the differences between the writers
Of one province and those of another in Italy
– The Venetians, as Raffaello Barbiera has pointed out,
Have an expansive and brilliant note; the Lombards
Are more prone to reflection and to brooding
Over the eternal tears of mankind; the Piedmontese
Have been noted for their fervour of patriotic and liberal enthusiasm,
The Neapolitans, again, burn with the fire of extemporisation
And sing of their flaming mountain and of their sunlit seas . . .

We commend two passages – as clues to possible method.
The first is this from Mallarmé:
'To evoke in a deliberate shadow the unmentioned object
By allusive words, never direct words,
Which may be reduced to an equal silence.
That means an attempt very near creation.'

The other is from a book on Buddhism:
'It would be possible to write a learned book

On Buddhism which should recite
The various facts with scholarly exactness
Yet leave the reader at the end
Wondering how intelligent and spiritual men and women
Of our day could really be Buddhists.
One must seek to avoid this effect
And try to enable the reader to understand
A little *how it feels to be a Buddhist.*
To give the feelings of an alien religion
It is necessary to do more than expound
Its concepts and describe its history.
One must catch its emotional undertone,
Enter one's way into its symbols, its cult, its art,
And then seek to impart these not merely
By scientific exposition
But in all sorts of indirect ways.'
The way is the way of Rozanov's *Solitaria*
Or Kierkegaard's dialogues of 'indirect impartation.'
There is urgent need for a new humanism.
(And to that end we must have a language
As personal as Chinese calligraphy
– When a Chinese calligrapher 'copies'
The work of an old master it is not
A forged facsimile but an interpretation
As personal within stylistic limits
As a Samuel or Landowska performance
Of a Bach partita
– A language in which it is easy to see
The bibulous genius of the inspired monk, Huai Si,
The cultured and carefree personality
With the tastes of an antiquarian of President Yu,
The rather effeminate grace of Chao,
The obstinate resolution of Huang, the rare energy,
The consummate control, of Wang Shi-Chih,
The ostentatious vulgarity of the Emperor Chien Lung,
And, in the plump and chirpy strokes of Su Tung-po,
The loose flesh and easy manner of a fat person.)
The real humanity of the humane is departing from the world.

I am troubled by the tendency in science to-day
For the law to be derived from limited groups of observations
Rather than from the wide generalisations of understanding.
And I am haunted by the masses
In our great industrial centres,
Greedy for productivity and neglecting fertility.
The fertility and potential abundance of life
Is a gift so strange to their minds that they feel in themselves
No responsibility towards it – they hold it something
That rises of itself, not an achievement
Which nothing but adequate effort can keep alive.

. . . While the Sicilians, though passionately attached to their beautiful
      island,
Are yet wont to philosophise concerning Nature in general
And are filled with a revolutionary spirit – it was they
Who began the great European movement of 1848 –
And the Tuscans, Emilians, and Romans must be classed together
For they inherit the majestic traditions of Rome
And the ancient purity of the language.
The Venetians are Betteloni, Boito, Fogazzaro and Zardo,
The Lombards, Arnaboldi, Fontana, Ada Negri,
The Piedmontese (by birth or residence) De Amicis, Graf, and Ferrero,
The Neapolitans Milelli, D'Annunzio and Perroti,
The Sicilians, Capuana, Rapisardi, and Fleres,
While to the Central contingent belong
Carducci, Chiarini, Nencioni, Gnoli, Panzacchi,
'Stecchetti,' Mazzoni, Marradi, Pascoli, and Bacchelli,
– But most I love Fontana's '*Bambann*' in the Milanese dialect,
Fucini's '*Poesie (di Neri Tanfucio)*' in *vernacolo pisano*,
Graf's '*poems cast in steel*' – his 'acqueforti indimenticabili'
Boito's 'curiosité pittoresque du vocabulaire,'
Mazzoni's predilection for the bizarre and recherché
And his translation of music into poetry
As in his '*Cori della Vita*' from Beethoven,
Capuana's '*Semiritmi*,' and the '*Diva Natura*' of Bacchelli
Who believed with me that the poetry of the age
Should be brought into conformity with its scientific spirit.

And, above all, Karl Kraus[1]
And his *Die Dritte Walpurgisnacht*
– Kraus whose thinking was a voyage
Of exploration in a landscape of words
And that language German
– For, while an English writer or speaker
Over long stretches of his verbal enterprise
Is protected by the tact and wisdom
Of linguistic convention, his German counterpart
Risks revealing himself as an idiot
Or a scoundrel through the ring and rhythm
Of his first sentence. Had Hitler's speeches
Been accessible to the West in their unspeakable original
We might have been spared the War
For the War was partly caused
By Hitler's innocent translators
Unavoidably missing in smooth and diplomatic
French or English the original's diabolic resonance.
Only German, in all its notorious long-windedness
Offers such short cuts to the termini of mankind.
It was Karl Kraus who knew them all.
He examined the language spoken and written
By his contemporaries and found
That they lived by wrong ideas,

[1] Vide *Times Literary Supplement*, 8th May, 1953. Compare David Urquhart's *The Effect of the Misuse of Familiar Words on the Character of Men and the Fate of Nations*.

As Mr. Terence Prittie says: 'For a time, for a very short time (after the German defeat in World War II), Germans talked about *Die Niederlage* – "defeat." Then this word was changed for *Der Zusammenbruch* – "the collapse," fortuitous as it sounds. This in turn became *Die Überrollung* – the "rolling over and grinding down." Out of such apparently harmless play with words will, maybe, spring a new myth of the German people under Hitler as the outpost of western culture, stemming the Red Flood, installing a fine "New Order" in Europe.'

Cf. the incontrovertible proof of Balzac's anglophobia as displayed by his use of English words and his strange mismanagement of some of them, which nevertheless is not nearly so barbarous as his devastatingly accurate phonetic imitations of Englishmen, and especially Englishwomen, speaking French. For no doubt, the average British traveller leads the world in murdering the French tongue; no doubt whatever that all the music and magic would vanish from Racine if declaimed by an Englishman and thus transcribed by Balzac: *Lei jour n'aie pas plous pour kè lei faound de mon quer* !

Listening to what they said he discovered
The impure springs of their actions.
Reading what they wrote he knew
They were heading for disaster.
The linguistic structure of a diplomatic correspondent's report
Revealed more of the political situation
Than the conference so reported.
The diplomats may have had reason to be optimistic
But portents occurred in their reported speeches
– Wrong subjunctives and false inflections.
The hopes of the world
Proclaimed in manifestoes of good will
Came to grief at the barrier of a misplaced comma
And the highest expectations of mankind
Were frustrated by the verbal alliance with a cliché.
'The German language,' as he said,
'Is the profoundest of all languages,
But German speech is the shallowest.'

What was the inspiration of his vast productivity?
The answer is Hamlet's: 'Words, words, words!',
And the commas between them
And the deeds they beget
And the deeds they leave undone;
And the word that was at the beginning,
And, above all, the words that were at the end.
These were printed in newspapers.
Hence newspapers were one of his main themes;
And the men who wrote them,
And the things about which they wrote:
Society, law-courts, sex and morality,
Literature, theatre, war, commerce,
In brief the whole world that is called into being
By a headline, organised by a leading article,
And sold by an advertisement.
But his contrast-theme was the words
That make up a drama by Shakespeare
Or a poem by Goethe.

Thus his theme behind the themes
Was the culture of Europe,
Its glory, its betrayal, its doom.
Exploring the labyrinths of contemporary verbiage
Karl Kraus never lost the thread,
His purpose 'to show the very age and body of the time
His form and pressure.'

Karl Kraus had an unfailing ear
For two kinds of sound: the common talk of the town
He satirically reproduced with amazing precision
And the language of prophecy he discerned
As the whispered accompaniment that, seemingly supporting
The trivial chat, suddenly forced it
Into a key of ultimate significance.
Oppressed by the confusing chorus of apparent triviality,
All the seething sciolism of the conventional world,
His ear was tuned to the pitch of the Absolute.
People gossiped about a War; he heard them
Lament the loss of their souls; at every street corner
Acts of high treason were committed.
The shouts of the newspaper boys
Announcing in mysterious vowels the latest edition
Became monstrous threats to man's spiritual safety,
Or cries of anguish from the lowest deep.
This metamorphosis of the commonplace[1] will forever remain
One of the greatest achievements in the German language,
For the technique Karl Kraus employed,
If technique it was, was literal quotation;
The contrast was obtained
Not by a portentous raising of the voice
Or the use of prophetic diction
But simply by creating another context for the trivial.
He took the frivolous seriously, and discovered

[1] Cf. 'A rhythm of simplification may be at work in our vocabularies: the inner balance of certain important words may be changing rather rapidly: the long winter of the cold war may, more slowly, be thickening our words and our minds, as wool thickens with the north wind.'

The situation was desperate. His invention consisted
In assuming the existence of natural states of culture
And self-evidently correct norms of conduct;
For example – that modesty befits the mediocre –
And instantly mediocrity was seen
To have risen to demonic heights
From which it ruled the world.[1]
He assumed that the prominent German writers and journalists
Of his time wrote in the German tongue
And the German tongue answered back
Saying they were illiterates.
He dealt with the practice of the law-courts
As though they were based on moral convictions,
With the theatre as though it were concerned
With the art of drama,
With journals as though they intended
To convey correct information,
With politicians as though they desired
The promotion of communal prosperity,
And with the philosophers as though
They were seekers after Truth.
The satirical effect of these inventions
Was annihilating.

His more important poetry is detached from his satire
Meeting it only at the source of their common inspiration,
The mystery of language.
A first and superficial judgment
May class the poetry as 'Epigonendichtung'
And that is what, in a particular sense,
He called it himself. Its forms, metres, rhythms and rhymes
Are traditional. It is determined
By the history of German poetry
From Goethe to Liliencron, yet bypasses the poet
Whose genius was to direct, and misdirect,

---

[1] The mediocrities of this world are our masters, Nature abhors the appearance of a beacon light, and therefore arranges that Shakespeare falls for Anne Hathaway and Goethe for his cook.

Distinctively modern trends – Hölderlin.
He had to remain outside Kraus's poetical orbit
For, with Hölderlin's later and greatest poems,
Poetry leaves its articulate German tradition,
Achieving the miracle of speechlessness
Bursting into speech.
If Goethe had the gift of his Tasso
To say what he suffered
And say it at a level of realisation
Where others would be silenced by agony,
Then Hölderlin sought,
And often miraculously found,
The word with which silence speaks
Its own silence without breaking it.

(Silence supervening at poetry's height,
Like the haemolytic streptococcus
In the sore throat preceding rheumatic fever
But which, at the height of the sickness,
Is no longer there, but has been and gone!
Or as 'laughter is the representative of tragedy
When tragedy is away.')

Short of miracles surpassing that miracle
From Hölderlin's poetry the way leads
Either to silence itself or to poetic mischief,
The verbose stammer of those who have never learned
To speak or to be silent,
Or the professional ecstasies of souls
That, only because they are uninhabitable,
Are constantly beside themselves.

So beyond all that is heteroepic, holophrastic,
Macaronic, philomathic, psychopetal,
Jerqueing every idioticon,
Comes this supreme paraleipsis,
Full of potential song as a humming bird
Is full of potential motion,

When, as we race along with kingfisher brilliance,
Seeking always for that which 'being known,
Everything else becomes known,'
That which we can only know
By allowing it to know itself in us,
Since 'determinatio est negatio,'
Suddenly 'chaos falls silent in the dazzled abyss.'
Ciò che lo mio intelletto non comprende
'Thin, thin the pleasant human noises grow
And faint the city gleams.'
(O poet, hold thy peace and be content!)
Like the amount of material never heard at all
In the six *dumky* of Dvořák's Opus 90,
Possibly a third of the music never heard at all
Yet the *Trio* is one of his most remarkable works
Though I doubt if any performance
Can realise all that's implicit in the score.
Or like Monsieur Teste who 'dies without confessing,'
Or Olivier Messiaen's *Antienne du silence*
(*Pour le jour des Anges gardiens*)
Or the blanks and spaces in Mallarmé's *Coup de Dés*
Showing the retractions, prolongations, flights of the thought,
'L'attente, le doute, la concentration étaient choses visibles
Ma vue avait affaire à des silences
Qui auraient pris corps,'
Or like Hindemith questioning the importance
Or even the relevance, to music, of sound itself.
Sound shrinks to nothingness and musical composition
Becomes an abstract philosophical activity,
So we become intolerant of lesser music,
Idle tinkling, uncontrolled and unskilled composition,
And our minds are opened to music
Using symbols that are yet unknown to us,
Wrapped in strange sounds we must first learn to decipher.
Even so, Conscience calls the self of *Dasein*
Out of the state in which it is lost
In the 'one like many.' The caller
Is unfamiliar to 'oneself' in its everydayness

And speaks in the uncanny mode of silence
To call the self back into the silence
Of the 'existent' potentiality of being.

But Kraus's poetry is the poetry of speech.
He never allows his genius
To busy itself in regions beyond
The beginning that began with the word.
But there he is at home
And at his 'Ursprung'! He is identical
With one of the '*Zwei Läufer*' who, in his poem of that name,
Compete for the prize; one, coming from Nowhere,
Reaches his goal, while the other,
Starting at the beginning, the Ursprung.
Dies on the way, humbly,
And yet triumphantly attaining his end:
'Und dieser, dem es ewig bangt
ist stets am Ursprung angelangt.'
But make no mistake! Kraus did not commune
With St. John of the Cross.
He had no access to mysticism
And as for psychology,
'I combine in myself a great capacity
For psychology with the still greater capacity
To disregard a psychological state,'
He said, and 'Psychoanalysis is the disease
Of which it pretends to be the cure.'
It was Nietzsche who defined mysticism
As the marriage between scepticism
And the craving for the transcendent.
Karl Kraus was free of both.
His Ursprung was the force that is expressed
In the highest forms of human culture.
In apprehending them his vision
Was never unsteadied by scepticism.
They were self-evidently true.
If they had the blessings of language,
That language he believed could say everything

Worth saying, and deceive no one
Who spoke it faithfully. He knew not
The suspicion that there might be
'A deeper truth' beneath what we thus say with truth
– The presistent suspicion of transcendentalism
As well as psychology.
The suspicion itself was suspect to him
And with his contemporary world
He had little difficulty in showing
That it rose like a miasma
From the corruption of language.

The unity of thing and word,
Of feeling and its articulation,
Which is the essence of poetry,
Has in Karl Kraus's verse
A distinctly erotic character.
He was in love with language,
But not in the manner of those promiscuous affairs
With sounds so liberally encountered
In the society of symbolists.
His passion aimed at a more real possession
– The body and soul of words.

It is the limitation of the satirical faith
That its emphasis is on a world
Whose heart is not safe from total corruption.
Satire ends at the very point
Where hatred of the world's abuses
Becomes irrelevant, because the world itself
Has ceased to be lovable.
This point is reached when absurdity
Gains control of that plane of experience
At which men form their idea
Of order and normality;
When right and wrong lose their names.
That there was a comma missing
In the nation–wide appeal, 'Deutschland erwache!'

Is a satirical observation wasted
On a humanity that, in its universal sleep,
Was oblivious, even of its main clauses.
Commas no longer mattered
In the face of such a full stop.

It was the end of Kraus's satirical world
When Hitler came to power.
In 1919 he said of *Die Letzten Tage der Menschheit*
That its satirical inventions and exaggerations
Were merely quotations of what was said and done
In those years of war. Hitler's Germany
Reversed the situation; her words and deeds merely quoted
And by quoting exaggerated beyond belief
The satirist's inventions.
Where the truth of facts took on the shape
Of inflated lies, truth became truly unspeakable.
Kraus realised the defeat of satire.
'Mir fällt zu Hitler nichts ein,'
Was his shatteringly nonchalant formula
For an agony of the spirit,
For, also, his contempt of those
Who urged him in Vienna satirically to fiddle
While in Berlin the Reichstag burned.
In 1933, the four pages of *Die Fackel*
Printed his short poetic declaration of silence,
'Ich bleibe stumm,' ending
With 'Das Wort entschlief,
als jene Welt erwachte.'

Has the curtain fallen on the third Walpurgis night?
If so, the electrician must have blundered
For the auditorium is still in darkness.
Or have we insensibly passed into the fourth?
The terrifying race between the material
And its realisation seems still in progress.
It may even be in the material's very nature
That it will forever resist

The attempt to raise it to a sphere
Which permits its artistic contemplation.
For it is more than material;
It is in itself perversely realised art,
The *ne plus ultra*
Of an infernal spiritualisation of the real.
Indeed it 'took place,'
But the place it took was a world
Too densely populated with real demons
To leave any room for the liberating effects
Of the artistic imagination.

It was a world that had acquired
An incommensurable perfection of its own,
Inexpressible in terms of a contrast
With, say, that of Goethe,
While the first and second Walpurgis nights
Were Goethe's inventions, the third
Consisted in matter-of-fact reality
Frustrating human imagination
By a total exhaustion and perversion of its resources.
– If the book's ultimate realisation
Is the impotence of language
In the face of the event,
This abdication is announced
With a power of words wholly inaccessible
To those never overpowered and speechless.

But in this poem at least I will leave
Thoughts of these difficulties
As no more than the dark green glossy leaves of black bryony
Which strike an exotic note in our hedgerows
– Even though this poem itself may rather seem to most
An impossible display of *Epipogium aphyllum*
And the only bird in it – a Bermudan Cahow!
(Or, others may think, a dense forest of trees
Like the *Sterculia rubiginosa*, or *Tangisong Burong*,
Said to 'make the birds weep!')

Or, again, as in Spain the virile Aragonese
Display their local spirit in 'La Jota,'
The slow tempo of which speaks of the Arab influence,
While the energetic agitation running through the music
Manifests the almost brutal spirit born
Of the rocky mountains and the torrents of the Ebro;
The soul of Andalusia is shown in the gay rhythm of guitars,
While the methodical and industrial character of the Catalans
Needs the *Sardana's* ponderous equilibrious rhythm
In the repetitive parts of which one can almost hear
The thunder of machines; and so the tempo
Of the '*Zortzico Guernicako Arbola*'
Is in keeping with the land and spirit of the Basques,
And so in turn I recognise in its due place
The '*Segadores*,' the '*Himno de Riego*,' and '*El Pasodoble*'[1]
– A diversity of music, revealing as inspiring
While Hitler's Germany had but '*Horst Wessel*'
And Fascist Italy its '*Giovanezza*'
Or, again, as I found at Yale University
A Norwegian studying anthropology,
A Portuguese East African studying education,
A Fijian studying nutritional problems,
A Chinese studying chemistry,
And a Turk studying Hittite;
And the eating of a meal in the dining hall

[1] As Jaime Pahissa says Manuel de Falla, working in his last years on 'L'Atlàntida' was 'realising his ambition of combining the music of the different regions of Spain into one work' – a pointer to what may yet be achieved, not in music only but in poetry too, in respect not of the various regions of one country merely, but of the whole world. In a poem like this, full of references and cross-references,

'. . . Like the way in which the Pada text
Is converted by a process of euphonic combination into the Samhita
Or like the more than six-score synonyms of gamati he gives
Which include all forms and varieties of motion,
Or like Fred Astaire, who has combined
All forms of dancing into one perfect whole . . .'

readers may complain that just to confuse them there are many references which are not significant, just as in Busoni's 'Arlecchino' the last section of the piano Sonatina ad Usum Infantis is so liberally quoted – without reason, save perhaps that Busoni just happened to like the tune. It must be admitted that there *are* elements in this poem hardly susceptible of any other conclusion.

Resolved itself into a vertical exploration
Of the fields of human knowledge
Or a horizontal one of the races of mankind.

My concern is not to be more Darwinian than Darwin and to read
Into the physical universe all those qualities of life and mind
Which are then said to 'emerge' (but is this
The proper use of that equivocal term?) from it.
But with the shrewd analysis of the space-time network
As the distinctive character of human consciousness
And of language as the instrument
For the progressive articulation of the world
In spatial and temporal terms.

Ranging from the phonetic and tonal structure of Efik, say,
To Óndra Łysohorsky's poems in the Lach dialect of Silesia,
'Spiwajuco Piaść,' half-way between Czech and Polish;
Dorn's 'Chrestomathy of the Pushtu and Afghan Tongues,'
And, above all, Scottish Gaelic, Irish, and Manx,
Welsh with its two groups of dialects, Cornish,
And Breton with its four dialects – Trcgorois,
Leonard, Cornouaillais, and Vannetais;
Celtiberian *viriae* corresponding to Gaulish *virolae*
Whence come the French *virole* and the Irish *ferenn*,
Or Spanish *gurdus*, Gallo-Roman *gurdunicus*,
Welsh *gwrrd*, French *gourd* (numb), or, again,
For Cisalpine Gaulish μανιάκης, we find
Irish *muince* and Old Welsh *minci*; and *sasiam*,
The name for rye among the Ligurian Taurini,
Is the same as the Brythonic word for barley,
Welsh *haidd* and Breton *heiz*.
For we have fallen into none of those springes and snares
Donne warns about in detaching sentences from Scripture,
But understood throughout the organic nature of communication,
And the relations of words to a whole, and of that whole
To the whole of our mind and personality.
And we rise from the variety of ways in which the sounds

Usually written *ss* and *s* were written – the spellings which hesitate
Between *s, ss, ds, d, sd, st,*
To a perfect appreciation of *cynghanedd*
– *Cynghanedd lusg, cynghanedd draws, cynghanedd groes,* and
   cynghanedd sain –
And the arts of *gair llanw*[1] and *tor ymadrodd,*[2]
Never grudging the time we spend,
Like Jenny Lind's whole morning
With 'Zersplittere' on a high B flat,
Or the Leeds sopranos' successful wrestling
With Beethoven's 'in gloria Dei patris' on high A.

Indulging to the full all the love of my people –
Gwyr y gogledd[3] for accomplished eloquent speech[4]
(Is fl- really like 'moving light' in any way
In which sl- or gl- is not?
What resemblance and natural connection can there be
Between the semantic and phonetic elements in a morpheme?)
Until 'I wish writing need not sound like writing'
And we make it sound so unlike writing
Readers may not see what is meant at first, but, looking harder,
Be not abashed not to have understood at once, as water
May not seem transparent to the observer, but has
A perspicuous opacity in which the fish swims at ease,
Like 'There is no doubt of what is a masterpiece
But is there any doubt of what a masterpiece is?'
Or 'No one knowing me knows me – and I am *I* I,'
'An audience never proves to you that you are you,'
And the root meaning, as contrasted with the meaning in use,
Is like the triple painting on projecting lamellae
Which, according as to whether one stands in front
Or at the right or at the left, shows a different picture;
And in a real writer's experimenting there can be
An effect of originality, as one can achieve

[1] 'Filling-in phrase' (in Welsh poetics).
[2] 'Break in the sense' (in Welsh poetics).
[3] Welsh; meaning 'the men of the North.'
[4] Actually, of course, in Scotland, it is as one writer says 'still necessary to talk Polish, particularly if you are a woman and want an affair.'

A kind of Venetian needlepoint by fitting into each other
Two pieces of hackneyed pattern of peasant edging.

We are no farther from the 'centre of things,'
No farther from the 'great warm heart of humanity'
Or 'the general good,' no less 'central to human destiny'
When alone with a work of scholarship
That can only appeal to perhaps one person per million
Than when one with the crowds in the streets
In any of the great centres of population,
Or in a mile-long cinema queue, or
In a two-hundred-thousand spectatorate
At Twickenham or Murrayfield or Ibrox
Or reading a selection of to-days' newspapers
Rather than Keller's *Probleme der englischen Sprache und Kultur*,
Or Heuser's *Die Kildare-Gedichte: die ältesten
mittel-englischen Denkmäler in anglo-irischer Überlieferung*,
Or Esposito's articles in *Hermathena*
On the Latin writers of mediaeval Ireland,
Or Curtis on *The Spoken Language
Of Mediaeval Ireland*, or Heuser on the peculiar dialect
Of English spoken less than a hundred years ago
– Direct descendant of the language of the Kildare poems –
In the baronies of Forth and Bargy in County Wexford
And often (wrongly) described as a mainly Flemish speech.

We must know all the words, even as in chess
(All the words – although we know the tendency
Of men's words to be all of one size and weight,
All the phrases in which excite the same emotion
– That of a woodchuck eating a carrot!) [1]
Despite the great difficulty of reducing the mass
Of available material to system, Spielman and Znosko-Borovsky
Have laid the foundations of a science of combination
By classifying its types and devising

[1] Cf. . . . 'these languages are compiled by people, or rather "grammarians," who are in respect of knowledge of the given language exactly similar to those biped animals whom the esteemed Mullah Nassr Eddin characterizes by the words: "All they can do is to wrangle with pigs about the quality of oranges." ' – Gurdjieff, *All and Everything*.

Some sort of terminology, still weak in giving guidance
On the marks of a position in which the moment has arrived
To look for a swift decision by combinative play
(Which under the conditions of time-limit is apt to be
The player's most urgent problem. He hopes his patient pursuit
Of a strategic plan will be crowned
By some sudden foray to seize a decisive advantage
And has not had time to examine the chances
Of such a foray at every move. What he needs is to acquire
A kind of subconscious faculty for recognising the positions
In which a combination ought to be discoverable.
For cultivating that faculty perhaps
Dr. Euwe's book is the best yet written
Not only classifying the combinations and illustrating them from play
With examples exhibiting each device in its purest form,
But, having given the demonstration of each combination in action,
Returning to deduce from it the strategical considerations on the board
That must be present to give that type
Of combination the prospect of success).

Even so, as Schopenhauer says, all previous philosophy
Revolves about certain fundamental ideas which always return,
For which all we need is not a new philosophy
But a history of philosophy written
In accordance with the historical-materialist method
– But *how* they return, out of what causes,
In what form, and under what circumstances,
To determine this requires an ever more precise
Scientific instrument – the object of *our* quest, my friend.

There lie hidden in language elements that effectively combined
Can utterly change the nature of man;
Even as the recently-discovered plant growth hormone,
Idole-acetic acid, makes holly cuttings in two months
Develop roots that would normally take two years to grow,
So perchance can we outgrow time
And suddenly fulfil all history
Established and to come.

Loathing all Imperialisms, colour-bars, and class-distinctions
And, equally, the classic seeking the final average
And the romantic seeking the final variation,
I seek a ground where my personal vision seizes
The individual who is of a certain race and no other
(Ultimately the means of seizing any individual
Of any race, and every individual of every race),
The point where science and art can meet,
For there are two kinds of knowledge,
Knowing about things and knowing things,
Scientific data and aesthetic realisation,
And I seek their perfect fusion in my work.
– That key position Leonardo da Vinci
Seems to Paul Valéry to have captured,
From which he could advance with equal confidence
Into any province of art or science
(Close to – almost indistinguishable from –
That other great landmark in spiritual geography
When imagination, which is what 'providence' uses
In order to get men into reality, into existence,
Has helped them as far out as they are meant to go
– *That is* where reality, properly speaking, begins).

A language, a poetry, in keeping with the new quantum mechanics
(The non-intuitive handling of data, introduced by Heisenberg;
The translation of the matrix calculus
Into operational and 'Poisson brackets' methods;
And, finally, the new 'wave mechanics' of de Broglie, Schrödinger,
      and others
Giving a perfect translation into intuitive methods)
Which 'deals with a world of *absolute individuals*
And therefore our languages must be such as to reflect
Such individuality. With the newer quantum mechanics
The old "discontinuity" resolves itself
Into an essential *individuality*,
Perfectly foreign to the older theories.'

A poetry in keeping with the human nervous system,
– The human-natural-history fact of the inherent circularity

Of all physiological functions which in any form
Involve human 'knowing' – lack of understanding of which,
Disregard of these structural, semantic issues,
And consequent restriction to cruder animalistic patterns,
Necessarily pathological and regressive for man,
Has made poetry hitherto a poetry to which
Poetry henceforth must compare as modern astronomy
Compares to astrology; increasingly getting away
From the 'magic word' which represents
Only a minor yet very complex manifestation
Of Aristotelian semantic reactions of identification,
And, naturally, exhibits also
The reversed natural order in evaluation.
The present status of the white race
– Leaving out of account for the moment
Other races the structure of whose languages
And their semantic reactions may be relatively unknown to us –
Is such that a majority of our self-imposed difficulties
Is due to the lack of scientific structural analysis
Which lack makes it impossible
To control or regulate physiologically and adequately
The semantic evaluation through education.
Under such conditions, everything based
On arguments involving the 'is' of identity
And the older elementalistic 'logic' and 'psychology'
Cannot possibly be in full accordance
With the structure of the nervous system.
This, in turn, affects the latter and results
In the prevailing private and public un-sanity.
Hence unrest, unhappiness, nervous strain,
Irritability, lack of wisdom, and absence of balance
Instability of our institutions, the wars and revolutions,
The increase of 'mental' ills, prostitution,
Criminality, commercialism as a creed,
The inadequate standards of education,
The low professional standards of lawyers, priests,
Politicians, physicians, teachers, parents, and even of scientists
– Which, in the last-named field, often lead

To dogmatic and anti-social attitudes
And lack of creativeness.
Nescis, mi fili, quantilla prudentia mundus regatur.

The old animalistic, fallacious generalisations
Have been, and are,
The foundations of our 'philosophies,'
'Ethics,' 'systems,' and, naturally,
Such animalistic doctrines must be disastrous to us.
Neurologically we have built up conditions
Which our nervous systems cannot stand;
And so we break down,
And, perhaps, shall not even survive.
The poet of the future is able to compare,
Evaluate and relate, revise and adjust
His private experience and observations
With the *translated* experiences from higher abstractions
Of many more individuals. The *translation* is indispensable
Because the reactions of both levels are entirely different,
And comparable only when they are on one level.
Creative work has begun.
So we must get rid of all semantic blockages.
Above all, the old 'unknowable' becomes abolished
And limited to the simple and natural fact
That the objective levels *are not* words.
(The so-called 'unknowable' was the semantic result
Of identification, of semantic unbalance,
Which posits for knowledge
Something 'beyond' knowledge.
But has such a postulation any meanings
Outside of psychopathy? Of course not,
As it starts with a self-contradictory assumption,
Which, being senseless, leads to senseless results!)
Specific differentiation, generation after generation
Of distressed existences with extinction looming at the end.
Either we take hold of our destiny or, failing that,
We are driven towards our fate.
Cyclopean prejudices, innate misconceptions,

Oceans, mountain barriers, limitless space,
The protean blind obstructions of nature
Within us and without, will not prevail
Against the crystallising will, the ordered, solvent knowledge,
The achieved clear-headedness of an illuminated race.
Amidst the fear and lassitude and ugly darkness
Of our world today I can believe *that*,
Believe that the specific man in us
Has the power to assimilate, utilise, over-ride and fuse
All our individual divergencies.

Metaphysical and empirical language communities,
With a continuous interweaving of threads between them,
Between inner, mobile, emphatic, and therefore
Untranslatable language forms, crossed by countless
Isophones, isolexes, isorhemes, and outer, rigid,
Metaphorical forms – all external language communities,
All the systems and structures of language usage,
Existing and resting on the bosom of linguistic thought,
Which envelops, carries, and fructifies them
Like the ocean the Earth!

Language moving about freely, revelling to its heart's content,
In its nominal and verbal wealth, unable to pledge itself
To the logos as it does in mathematics, or become
A substitute for it as often as it likes, but nevertheless
In the service of the logos and bound to serve it
– But only as Faust served his 'master' *'auf besondere Weise.'*
It strives hard and often errs, but remains
Conscious of the right way – in its
'Dunkeln Drange sich des richten Weges wohl bewusst.'
A relation of love, not that of a contract,
Since the logical and scientific thinker can only
Contemplate, express, communicate, and represent
His knowledge if he loves it. – Understanding unites
With contemplative and creative thought in the Platonic *eros*
Provided we regard it philosophically and not
Historically, or, still worse, mythically; and, in this embrace,

The logos, which would otherwise be something general,
Something that stands alone in the world,
Becomes ours;
Allen gehört was du denkst; dein eigen ist nur, was du fühlst.
Soll er dein Eigentum sein, fühle den Gott, den du denkst.[1]

Language,
Accomplishing what it pleases, traversing all things,
By subtlety of nature; rising to colossal dimensions,
Or standing on the tops of the filaments of a flower,
Or rising to the solar sphere on a sunbeam,
And commanding the three worlds,
Avagahate, perlustrat, embrasse,
Dives down into, has business with, apprehends,
Presenting the whole of being in the intellect
As a lamp reveals objects – capable, then,
Of rising to the heaven of Indra or other celestial abodes,
Or of descending to the vilest human forms
Or even to the bodies of beasts and reptiles
– All the way from Brahma to a stock.
As the horrific fabric of a thunderstorm vanishes
(Like any *universale fantastico* we reduce)
As it had never been and the sun floods all
(How splendid and how fearful the explosion of force,
Yet how slight, how petty almost, any direct issue!
The heavens seem split by the jagged fissures of dazzling light,
The crash is as the fall of a mountain,
The immense drops of rain, if not of hail, come down like bombs;
But even this pageant seems unsubstantial,
The fabric even of this storm baseless;
And the sun sets on a peaceful earth, a quiet sky),
So in the speech to which all our efforts converge
Vanish all the complications of human life
Before the exultant note of universal joy.
The Mature Art – alone with the Alone.
No voice not fully enfranchised,

[1] Everyman has thy Thought; only things felt are thine own. If thou wouldst make him thine, feel thou the God thou hast known.

No voice dispensable or undistinguishable
Like a man who needs uses words from many dialects
To say what he has to say as exactly and directly as possible.

Where the Paneubiotic Synthesis is grasped in its totality,
Omnilateral aristology obligatory on everybody,
Each having five hundred ethnohistorians within reach,
A thousand philosophies, and being well acquainted
With the universal masterpieces of literature and the fine arts,
And enjoying the perfect vitality that only comes
Through mastering the synthesis and duly welcoming
All the higher thought-currents of love.

With, ever just beyond, the stillness of light into which
Vanish the multitudinous waves of speech,
Ever just beyond,
For is perfection desired
Or an average of imperfection
Such, for instance, as makes
A tutti of twenty strings
Playing together
Distinguishable from one violin
Magnified twenty times?

Able to dispense at any moment with the elaborate
Apparatus our Western tradition provides
Of universals, particulars, substances, attributes, abstracts,
Concretes, generality, specificities, properties,
Qualities, relations, complexes, accidents, essences,
Organic wholes, sums, classes, individuals,
Concrete universals, objects, events, forms, contents, *et al*.
And, like Mencius, get along without any of this
And with nothing at all definite to take its place
– In no danger of thinking this machinery (or some part of it)
Necessary; not only convenient for our traditional type of thinking
But inevitable for all thought and correspondent to or valid for
The structure of any possible universe.
'And, after all, a generation which is cheerfully becoming

More and more self-, sex-, race-, and world-conscious
Should not complain if it is required to become word-conscious also.'[1]
And in such word-consciousness may be found
The solvent for most other problems.
I look with confidence to a future when, no man content
To be cut off from another by a mere difference in language or habit
    of thought,
– All prejudices, pet theories, linguistic habits, tastes
For particular brands of logical machinery, emotional dishonesties,
    abandoned –
Peoples of a hundred traditions will be freely in contact with one
    another.
(The only alternative, if utter chaos is to be avoided,
A regimentation in simplified standardised meanings
– By broadcasting perhaps – that would be disastrously wasteful.
And Heaven only knows what ideological escamotage !)

All poetry lost in the *guorguolacadas*,
As Dom João de Castro[2] might have written,
Of some fantastic Ogpufbi world of Basic Grunters
(What threatens ethnography we agree
Is to be darkly stifled
Under a clotted jumble of facts
Like sociology in America
Where a horrible mixture of 'applied sociology'
And its theoretical justification
Has utterly buried the meagre theory,
Giving birth to a malignant tumour
Of half-educated people. Our ideal ethnological method
May be fairly called the ecological one.)

    [1] Vide I. A. Richards: *Mencius on the Mind. Experiments in Multiple Definition*.
    [2] See J. Gerson Da Cunha's 'Materials for the History of Oriental Studies among the Portuguese' in Vol. 2 of the *Atti del IV Congresso Internazionale degli Orientalisti tenuto in Firenze nel Settembre 1878*, published in 1881, and Gomez Rodeles's *Imprentas de los Antikuas Jesuitas en las Missiones de Levante durante los Siglos 16 al 18*, with its references to the presses at Goa, Vaipicota, Rachol, Punicale, Ambalacata, and Angamala y Cranganor in India, Macao in China, and the press in Japan.

Even those who are the leading advocates
Of Basic English to-day, though they may claim
To be familiar with all the proposals
For a neutral auxiliary language,
Artfully dissemble their knowledge
And give no inkling of the grand-scale demonstration
Esperanto has been carrying on for half a century.
And never mention De Wahl's 'Occidental'
Or Peano's 'Interlingua,'
Far more significant
Than Jespersen's 'Novial'
And omit any reference to the very thorough, scholarly work
Done over a number of years by the staff
Of the International Auxiliary Language Association.
On the other hand, Professor Richards, for example,
Betrays, or rather displays,
The magnificent insularity
Which is the pride of the Anglo-Saxon mind.
He is aware of the problem and states it lucidly:
'It (a common language) must be clear from any threat
To the economic, moral, cultural, social or political
Status of any person or any people.
It must carry no implications
Of intellectual, technological, or other domination.
No one learning the world language
Must have any excuse
For even the least shadow of a feeling
That he is submitting to an alien influence
Or being brought under the power of other groups.'
Then he proceeds to propose exactly
What he himself so definitely condemned,
For the adoption of English as the supra-national language
Would imply the acknowledgment of Anglo-Saxon supremacy.
The proof of this is that all the arguments adduced
By Professor Richards and his colleagues
Are all based on our manifold superiorities:
We are richer, more numerous,
More civilised, more virtuous than the rest!

– All dreams of 'imperialism' must be exorcised,
Including linguistic imperialism, which sums up all the rest.
The best policy would be to apply
The method of Basic, not to English,
But to the vast international vocabulary which already exists.

The result would be neutral enough:
For although purely 'Western'
It would not be associated with any political power.
This is where every man belongs
Who is truly a philosopher and a world citizen,
Not a chauvinist in 'orthological' clothing.

A Sanskrit *sūtra* in Pags-pa letters;
Lorimer's Grammer of Wasiri Pashto;
Documents in Uighur, and the whole marvellous story
Of the rediscovery of Soghdian,
Lingua franca from the Caspian Sea
To the Gulf of Pechili
From the first to the eighth centuries of our era
Yet so entirely ceasing to be the speech of men
That its very existence had been forgotten;
The Mahavyutpatti,[1] Vambéry's Cagataische Sprachstudien;
A polyglot list of birds in Chinese, Turki and Manchu;
Pamva Berinda (the dictionary of Slavonic Russian
With Jewish, Greek, and Latin words
Gorky felt he *must* read, but never did);
The history of the Six Writings by Tai T'ung;
The three dialects of Albanian,
Cheg, Tosk, and Chimariot;
And the word *Kabikaj*, constantly recurring
In manuscripts from India, and said to be
An invocation to the King of the Cockroaches
Or an Angel concerned with the repression
Of exuberant cockroaches and other insects
Which destroy books.

[1] The Sanskrit vocabulary of all the technical terms of Buddhism, with a Tibetan translation and English renderings added by the great Hungarian scholar, Csoma de Körös.

Experiments with that odd metre, the teliambus,
And conjectures toward a completion
Of Callimachus's *Coma Berenices*
Which Catullus rendered, and Scaliger tried
But with less knowledge than's available now;
It is unnecessary to insist minutely
On Richardson's derivations from K'ung-Fu-Tsze
Or Po-Chü-I, though influences have been chased out
Of the Sage of the Middle Kingdom to Voltaire;
But on the subordination of clauses in Greek
Contriving an adequate illustration
Of the development of 'syntaxis' from 'parataxis,'
Or in an account of the classic dances of Japan
Making it clear that *Nihon-Buyo*
Cannot rightly be called classic, being based
On the *Dengaku* and *Nō* performances,
'Rustic,' and comparatively popular forms
Which in the course of the Kamakura and Muromachi periods
Replaced the ancient classical and ritual performances
Till in and through them mimetic posturings
Gradually developed into lyrical drama;
And so on to Sholom Jacob (Mendele Mocher Sephorim
Abramovitch, Reb Mendele – three geniuses in one man;
The Giant, the Genius, the Pyramid!)
First consummate literary artist in Yiddish – creator
Of a polished literary language
Out of the common witticisms
And legends of the vernacular
Current among the people.
Is it possible for any one man to do more?
He practically created a new language,
Reinvigorated another,
Portrayed a whole civilisation
In all its minutest detail,
Became the grandfather, the source of inspiration,
Of a whole galaxy of writers,
Gave dignity to the humble
And hope to the unfortunate

Of a whole people. –
And the Saadiah Gaon who is still of living interest to us
Though he wrote in a language we no longer know
And for a civilisation that is already dead;

And Concalves Dias and his 'Dicionario da Lingua Tupi';
Or, again,
Ferreira de Castro's *A Selva*
And Euclides da Cunha's Os Sertôes
Written *com cipó* (with a liana stalk)
In a new vernacular Portuguese,
Vigorous and rooted in the Brazilian soil,
Knotty and tangled as the scrub-forest of the backlands,
The *caatinga* where we followed Conselheiro's jagunços
Till the last defenders of Canudos fell;
And José Hernández's *Martin Fierro*
Derived in verse and manner
From Argentine popular poetry
And appealing to peasants and workers,
As much as to intellectuals and littérateurs;
And Homburger on the Negro–African languages,[1]
To appreciate the underlying unity and peculiarities of these
And for the pleasure of seeing our knowledge
Of one particular idiom in a wider perspective.
The poet, Franz Tamayo, forming a new army,
New industries, a new education, and reading
Greek and Latin as well as most modern languages,
And Domingo Faustino Sarmiento, teacher,
Journalist, writer, President of the Argentine Republic,
Whose scope as an essayist ranges
From philology to architecture, and from
The criticism of a historical play on Cromwell
To a spirited analysis of such Paris types
As the *modiste* and the *flâneur*;

[1] To enable us to acquire an adequate background to what knowledge we have
of all the great African Empires which attained a level of civilisation equal to any
in the world, and such wise and humane rulers as Mansa Musa, Askia the Great,
Soni Ali, and many others in the great chronicle of negro achievement.

And Taroa Taketomo on the 'Tanka,'
Free from English poeticisms
Dissonant from the Japanese spirit;
And asking ourselves now and again perhaps
(Though with little sympathy with the advocates
Of Novial or Hogbosh or Basic Bantu –
Our discussion of these matters need be no more
Unfriendly than a United Nations meeting!)
Whether the aesthetic is right after all
For which the simple constitutes the very climax
Of admirable achievement, when in living Nature,
From the point of view of success and fitness
It is the complicated which is that climax.[1]

And on to Sequoyah the Cherokee Indian
Who, alone, created a written language for his people;
Johannes Scotus Eriugena, John the Celt as he called himself,
Who, almost alone in Western Europe then,
Contrived to learn Greek, and created
A vast philosophical vision of the spiritual world
No thinker of today could equal;
The term קץ in the Dead Sea Scrolls and in Hebrew Liturgical Poetry;
Edward Sapir on the Navaho Indians;
Amos Tutuola, the Yoruba writer,
Who has begun the structure of new African literature;
Paul Bohannan on the Tiv of Central Nigeria;
The metaphysical system, so complex and yet so tidy,
Of the Dogon of French West Africa;
Nahuatl, Mazatec, and Tarāhumara;
Shirokogoroff's *Psychomental Complex of the Tungus*;
(If that line is not great poetry in itself
Then I don't know what poetry is!)
And my fellow-Scot, Gibb,[2] with his classic
History of Ottoman Poetry which to him meant
The so-called *divan* poetry, written in close imitation
Of the classical Persian poets, in the same metres,

[1] *Vide* Sir Charles Sherrington's *Life's Unfolding* (1943).
[2] E. J. W. Gibb (1857–1901).

On the same themes, almost in the same language,
For Persian words and construction are often more obtrusive here
Than Latin syntax and vocabulary in Milton
Or Sir Thomas Browne; before the Hungarian scholar,
Kúnos, revealed an old and rich tradition
Of popular poetry in Turkey,
Written in imparisyllabic lines,
Without either quantity or accent,
Intensively studied in Turkey today,
Where few readers can now enjoy
The old court poetry, and deeply influencing
The technique of modern poets.

Concerned, I repeat, with the shrewd analysis of the space-time
      network
As the distinctive character of human consciousness
And of language as the instrument
For the progressive articulation of the world
In spatial and temporal terms. Not retaining
The naive or 'copy' theory of language and creating
An artificial difficulty about space. As speech flows in time,
As it *is* time, there is no difficulty in its expressing
Temporal ordering, but how can the fugitive
Express or translate the static ordering of things in space?
The answer takes us beyond the theory that language
Reduplicates or reconstructs a pre-existently given world
And leads in the direction of the theory outlined
In Cassirer's masterly discussion of speech
In his *Philosophie der Symbolischen Formen*
In which the temporal as well as the spatial functions
Are exhibited as underived, or properly creative, functions
Through which speech actually shapes and extends our experience;
Not reproductions of the given
But conditions of anything being given
And of its progressive elaboration,
'The supreme organ of the mind's self-governing growth'[1]

[1] *Vide* 'Notes Towards an Agreement Between Literary Criticism and Some
of the Sciences,' by Dr. I. A. Richards in *Confluence*, March 1954.

'How can you get on in London without such words as *Tyib*, *mafish*,
   inshallah, and *wakri*'

— WM. HOLMAN HUNT TO WM. BELL SCOTT

'But ,when he pleas'd to shew't, his speech
In loftiness of sound was rich;
A Babylonish dialect
Which learned pedants much affect;
It was a party-coloured dress
Of patch'd and pyball'd languages:
'Twas English cut on Greek and Latin
Like fustian heretofore on satin.
It had an odd promiscuous tone,
As if h' had talk'd three parts in one;
Which made some think when he did gabble,
Th' had heard three labourers of Babel;
Or Cerberus himself pronounce
A leash of languages at once.

— *Hudibras*, I. i.

Have we not travelled all over
What the Arab geographer Al-Aziz
Called Daghestan's 'Mountain of Languages,'
Kumyk, Avar, Lezghin, Lak,
Darghin and Tabasaran?
— All powerfully developed now
Under the Soviet regime,
All used in the schools
And in newspapers, magazines, and radio broadcasts,
Where thirty years ago ninety per cent.
Of the population were illiterate,
Poverty-ridden, hungry, ravaged by disease,
And to-day all radiant with new life
And great creative developments
In every aspect of arts and affairs.

O I too will sing the Korean Tsui Si-syan's song,
The Peoples of the World are One
But I'd like best to do it

As mieters[1] like the Clyde Valley Stumpers do
With the aid of a washboard, a jam jar,
And two kazoos.

Always with Janáček's delight
In 'melodies of human speech';
Relishing the *Glagolitic Mass* all the more
Because the musical accentuation of it
In accordance with modern Czech pronunciation
Is incorrect and the text slightly corrupt,
Or *The Diary of One who vanished*
Because it too was based on a newspaper report.

I am even more interested of course
In Nikos Skalkottas' *Five Dances*
And other music, much of it in the twelve-note system
And an even more complicated system of his own.

Yes, I will have all sorts
Of excruciating *bruitist* music,
Simultaneist poems,
Grab-bags and clichés, newspaper clippings,
Popular songs, advertising copy,
And expressions of innocence,
And abstract sounds – taking care
That one of them never turns out to be
Merely the Rumanian word for *schnapps*;
And all dada, merz, fatagaga.

Even as before you would cross a desert
You ought to know all the different breeds of camels,
Sabayyehs or *raguabils*, *oonts*, *arregans*.
Or even as, if English stone for Scottish buildings
Is proposed, with prompt particularity,
Since, of course, I cherish every τοπισμός
Ask why the excellent Earnock and Auchinlee freestones
From Blantyre and Cleland respectively,

¹ Current Dutch slang for terrific 'turns.'

The red sandstones of Ballochmyle,
Locharbriggs or Corsehill,
The fine-grained honey-gold Leoch stone from Dundee,
Whitsome Newton from the Borders
Or Braehead stone from Fauldhouse
Should not be preferred.

And greatly I love to hear a girl
Back from three years at school
Say to her father in fluent Greek
'Morning, old lad: like your eggs fried or boiled?
Going to be cursed hot to-day
But thank Heaven I've nothing to do
But grill ἡλιάζω on the lawn
And smoke καπνίζω a handful
Of cigarettes σκιρτεῖν or χειροπηδᾶν'
– All in Plato's or Xenophon's style and vocabulary,
Only borrowing from the modern language
The few words necessary
For purely 20th century things,
And wish I might be found so speaking too
fhios dom fhéin some fine day
Tho' I appreciate Euripides' use
Of archaic diction too,
But alas I can speak no Greek
And am now too old to learn
And nil leiyeas ogam air.

Virgil salutes him, and Theocritus;
Catullus, mightiest-brained Lucretius, each
Greets him, their brother, on the Stygian beach;
Proudly a gaunt right hand doth Dante reach –

For this is the kind of poetry I want,
Wandering from subject to subject
And roaming back and forth in time
Yet always as essentially controlled
As a *saeta* or a flamenco song.

As a poet I'm interested in religious ideas –
– Even Scottish ones, Wee Free ones even – as a matter of fact
Just as an alcoholic can take snake venom
With no worse effects than a warming of the digestive tract.

To fules the spirit seems to be active
When the senses alane are really spry
Even as the mune appears to move
When it's nocht but the clouds ga'en by.

Once one's attuned to the elemental
One's banished by the superficial for ever.

We must respond maximally
To the whole world we can,
Even as in building houses you can have
Gurjun, Mengkulang, and East African camphorwood
For ceiling joists; external door frames
Made from Chumprak, Afrormosia, or Berlinia,
Draining boards of Merawan or Thingan,
And floor-boards of some soft-woods, and most hardwoods,
If easy enough to work,
Such as Geronggang, Nongo, or Dalli,
Seeing everything too under various aspects
As who might tour the various festivals
Of the Athenian theatre,
– The Lenaea, the Anthesteria,
The rural Dionysia, the city Dionysia.

Remembering how the same red takes on
Different properties according to its use
In distemper, tempera, fresco or oil
And to the manner of its application each case,
And that a 'volume' may change
As it assumes shape in marble, bronze or wood
– And, in short, that life in general,
Not only mental life,
Is conditioned by sensory stimuli,

Some forms of life persisting with a minimum
Of stimuli from their environment
And, unlike the artist, most human beings,
And almost every human being in some respects,
Being like some of the lowest forms of animal life
– Tapeworms and other parasites –
Whose receptive, and primitive motor, apparatus
Just permits them, at an early phase of their existence,
To migrate to an appropriate site
In an internal organ where they live
The remainder of their existences
With their sensory apparatus degenerate and superfluous
– Unaware of matter, life, mind, and society
As a series of levels of organisation,
None of which are reducible to lower levels
But none of which are in the least inscrutable. . . . [1]

If we think that any feature of our language and
Thought is absolutely necessary, this is nearly
Always because we have not made the effort of
Imagination needed in order to project
Ourselves outside our habits. A language is
A form of life; but there are many forms of li fe.

All the world's languages as I see them then
– For this is my favourite *Raum der Rühmung* –
Are like the Albani polyptych of Perugino,
– How cool in its warmth,
With its space continuous through the various panels,
Felt through beautiful arches,
Stretching to enchanted distances,
Evoking freshness and fragrance,
Bringing back to us those rare moments
When, new to life,
In the early hours of a summer morning,
For an instant we tasted of Paradise.

[1] Cf. Joseph Needham's *History Is On Our Side*; Henri Focillon's *The Life of Forms in Art*; Henri Piéron's *La Sensation, Guide de Vie*.

Or even as we know the Brahui language, closely allied
In grammatical structure to the far-off Dravidian tongues
Of Southern India, and with a small core of Dravidian words
'Expressing the fundamental and elementary concepts of life,'
Though, in general vocabulary, polyglot in the highest degree
With elements derived from Arabic, Persian, Balochi,
Pashto, Sindhi, Jatki, Urdu, and even English;
Or even as we know the special Palace language of Siam,
The 'language of their own' (R. L. Stevenson tells us)
The nobles in Samoa use,
Covering the primary interests of life,
The separate languages for men and women
In the West Indies, Africa's swarms of secret languages,
And on to 'the Glynnese language'
And all such family jargons;

Or even as we know Slovanské Spisovné Jazyky V
Dobé Pritomné,[1]
And Ratna, the Mandaean vernacular,
Or even as we know Burushaski and Werchikwar,
– Burushaski, possessing no literature and no history
(Irrelate as Moschatel in the world of flowers)
Spoken by so small a population in Hunza and Nagir,
Yet appearing to form an isolated linguistic relic of the past,
Like Basque, for which no connection has yet been shown
With any other family of languages
(Though, unlike Basque, its detailed study is now made possible,
Thanks to Lieut.-Col. Lorimer and Professor Morgenstierne,
By Instituttet for Sammenlignende Kulturforskning,
And we can delight in a difficult phonetic structure,
And a grammar which with its four gender classes
Its intricate pronominal prefixes and infixes,
And its complicated verbal system, vies in complexity
With that of any other language in the world).
Going all the way from Shanghai *pai hua*
To the *wen-li* which is read, not spoken;
Or abruptly shifting American-accented English

[1] The Slavonic Written Languages at the Present Day.

To an accented multi-tonal *kuo-ya*
Flavoured by the patois *erhs* and *nay-guh's*
Yet avoiding the harsh growling tones
And rhythms resulting from them
As befits a *hsiu ts'ai*, a man of flowing talent

(For unlike you, Joyce, I am more concerned
With the East than the West and the poetry I seek
Must be the work of one who has always known
That the Tarim valley is of more importance
Than Jordan or the Rhine in world history).

And with ever, at the back of our minds
Leibniz's *De Arte Combinatoria*,
'A general method in which all truths of the reason
Would be reduced to a kind of calculation.
At the same time this would be
A sort of universal language or script
But infinitely different from all those projected hitherto,
For the symbols and even the words in it
Would direct the reason
And errors, except those of fact, would be
Mere mistakes in calculation.'
Or again (as he wrote to Huygens)
'A new characteristic,
Entirely different from algebra
Which will have great advantages
For representing exactly and naturally to the mind
And without figures,
Everything that depends upon the imagination.'

And on to Patrick Geddes's 'thinking graphics,'
Those folding squares of paper on which
He juggled words like algebraic terms
To gain a clearness of idea impossible
To get through prose exposition alone.
– A completeness of thought,
A synthesis of all view points,
No one brain could otherwise grasp.

Geddes worked out in this way
A description of living
That included or could include
Every act and fact,
Dream and deed,
Of all mankind on this planet,
Revealing more on one sheet of paper
Than whole volumes of science or philosophy.

And so on, delighting in 'hohlraum'[1] oscillators,
Veiled allelomorphic transitions such as liquid helium
Exhibits around a certain low temperature,
Simple numerical multiples of the Riemannian ζ function,
Black-body radiation, direct observation
In the case of crystal lattices,
Evaluation of the integral by the German *Sattelpunktsmethode*,
Entropy transactions, adiabatic relations,
The Richards effect, the Dulong-Petit law,
The Pauli exclusion principle,
– And on to Cantor on the theory of sets,
The Dedekind 'cut,' the spinal cord of analysis,
'The essence of mathematics resides in its freedom,'
And so to Schrödinger's *Statistical Thermodynamics*
Designed to develop briefly one simple unified standard method
Capable of dealing, without changing the fundamental attitude,
With all cases (classical, quantum, Bose-Einstein, Fermi-Dirac, etc.)
And with every new problem that may arise.

On towards the calculus of ideas then,
While handling a simple logarithmic progression
Translated into a delicate spiral of lucite
Or three-dimensional forms
Based on more complicated formulas
– Playing with a twenty-four sided polygon,
A cardioid design, a catacaustic curve,
And all Jekuthiel Ginsburg's paraphernalia,

[1] Hohlraum – an 'ether-block' considered as the seat of electro-magnetic field events.

Plastic, lucite, alabaster, marble, mahogany,
The endless joys of *Scripta Mathematica*,
Recalling that when young ferns unfold in springtime
They are seen as logarithmic spirals,
When light is reflected under a teacup
A catacaustic curve is spotted,
And so on
    Through all creation's forms forever.

So how can one write or think of writing even
Without a set of all the known 49 hypothetical curves
– The littus, the chordel, the logarithmic spiral,
Epicycloid, hypocycloid, calculus hook, cardioid and all –
Done in intersecting string areas?
Or lacking the trained fingers that can make
A sennit, a pudding fender, a cringle,
A Spanish Fox or a Turk's head?
Though we meet the disapprobative cold fish-eyes
Of to-day's reading public and are made to feel
Like Salvador Dali discussing Surrealism with Sitting Bull!

Mass-formels in the Mathematics of Psychology;
Techniques which deal with fluid flow
In orifices, nozzles, and venturi tubes;
Olaf Rudbeck on the relation between
                      Finnish and Hungarian
And his *Atland eller Manheim* written in
                      Latin and Swedish

Or the *Krio* of the Mende of Sierra Leone:
Schopenhauer's 'excellent Csoma' of Székely race,
(Lying now where a rose-bush and weeping willow
Bend over his white marble monument
Facing the Himalaya mountains at Darjeeling)
Nicholas Revay with his *Elaboratior Grammatica Hungarica*,
And John Sajnovics' *Demonstratio Idioma Ungarorum et Lapponum*
    idem esse;

Julian visiting the Bashkirs on the banks of the Gama
And subsequent visitors to the Ostyak,
The Mordvinian, Cheremiz, Votyak, and Zyryan;
Paul Hunfalvy, Joseph Budenz, Gabriel Szarvas,
Arminius Vámbéry, Zsolt Béothy, and Kālmān Mikszāth of Palócz
    race,
Dobrentei's *Régi Magyar Myelvemlélek*
And Dobrovsky's *Institutiones linguae Slavicae veteris*
And *Ausführliches Lehrgebäude der böhmischen Sprache*,
– Ah, good it has been even for a moment to lift
The heavy silk curtains and look
(A rich egocentric bulimian vision that makes me feel a super
    Cyril Connolly)
Through the porphyry-framed windows of the palace of Buda
– A lover of Plato and Plotinus once again
In the 'land of the four rivers'
As five centuries ago at King Matthias' Court
And thirteen centuries before that
In Marcus Aurelius's near the banks of the Granua[1] –
And good to handle from the carved bookcases
With crimson silk draperies, the books, all bound in silk,
The workmanship of whose silver clasps and corners
Is splendid as the miniatures to be found inside
Which display the rich imagination of the Renaissance
Blended with that of antiquity,
Graceful garlands of flowers and fruit,
Cupids riding on fawns or playing with rainbow-coloured butterflies,
Tritons and nymphs sporting, and, as a border,
Antique gems, and delicate climbing plants with golden flowers,
And remember again how I travelled with Janus Pannonius
(John Csemiczey) when he was still *le delizie del mondo*
To Florence, and went with him and Vespasiano
To see Cosimo de Medici, Poggio, and Argiropolis;

Yet always wheresoever we may range,
While rejoicing in such new discoveries
As the Goad, the female Shriek,

                    [1] Garam.

The Garble with an Utter in its claws,
Most partial to those we were familiar with first
Which almost never come completely from behind anything.

The World of Words

Words alone are certain good.
W. B. YEATS

The philosophy of the Middle Ages was the work of men who were ignorant of nature, but learned the Latin grammar. Neglecting the verbs, they tried to describe the universe in terms of substantives and adjectives, to which they attributed an independent existence under the name of substances and accidents or attributes. Modern physicists are engaged in a somewhat similar attempt to describe it in terms of verbs only, their favourite verb at the moment to undulate, or wiggle.

J. B. S. HALDANE

Easy – Quick – Sure – The exact word
You want – when you want it.
Elusive words easily captured and harnessed.
New ideas spring to your mind.
Your imagination is stirred by this simple
But wonderful Idea and Word Chart.
It puts words and ideas at your finger tips,
It will enable you to open the flood-gates of the mind
And let the torrent of drama and tragedy –
Human strife, flaming love, raging passion,
Fiendish onslaught, splendid heroism –
Flow from your pen, leap into type
And fly to your readers, to grip them and hold them
Enthralled by the fascinating spell of your power.
Gilbert Frankau says: '. . . it is
The best adjunct I have so far discovered.'

We have of course studied thoroughly
Alspach, English, and the others who have written
On 'Psychological Response to Unknown Proper Names,'
Downey on 'Individual Differences In Reaction to the Word-in-Itself,'
Bullough on 'The Perceptive Problem
In the Aesthetic Appreciation of Single Colours,'

Myers on 'Individual Differences in Listening to Music,'
And Eleanor Rowland on 'The Psychological Experiences
Connected with Different Parts of Speech,'
Know Plato in 'Cratylus' on the rhetorical value
Of different classes of consonants, and Rossigneus's
'Essai sur l'audition colorée et sa valeur esthétique,'
Jones on the 'Effect of Letters and Syllables in Publicity,'
Roblee and Washburn on 'The Affective Value of Articulate
     Sounds,'
And Givler on 'The Psycho-physiological Effect
Of the Elements of Speech in Relation to Poetry,'
Downey on 'Emotional Poetry and the Preference Judgment,'
Ribot's 'L'Imagination Créatrice' with its distinction between
The plastic versus the diffluent imagination,
And pondered the differences in imagination related
To variations in psychical temperament and differences in imaginal
     type,
And recorded reactions as to the degree of tolerance or liking
For the exciting or for the depressive emotions
And the varying delight in novelty or familiarity
Of art stimulus; and know Sterzinger's findings
In 'Die Gründe des Gefallens u. Massgefallens am poetischen Bilder'
As to the relative significance in aesthetic enjoyment
Of empathy (Einfühlung) and substitution of meaning
(Unterschiebung) as it occurs in the metaphorical consciousness.
Kroh's 'Eidetiker unter Deutschen Dichtern,' too
And Martin's exhaustive study of imaginal traits,
'Die Projektionsmethode und die Lokalisation visueller und anderer
     Vorstellungsbilder,'
And, of course, the 'Vergnügliches Handbuch der Deutschen Sprache'
Parts of which might well have been written
By Edward Lear and Wilhelm Busch
With occasional advice from Lewis Carroll
– Yet a mine of information about German life and habits
Standing on a foundation of solid linguistic erudition
With chapters on the distinction between the spoken and the written
     language,
On various sources of slang and colloquialisms,

– Sporting, technical, nautical, and so forth –
On preciosity and affectation,
On the vulgar errors and muddled and slipshod thinking
To which most folk must plead guilty,
On provincialisms,
On the Berlin and Viennese dialects,
And a host of other subjects.
Carr on 'The Visual Illusion of Depth,'
Titchener's 'Experimental Psychology of the Thought Processes,'
Henry Cowell on 'The Process of Musical Creation,'
And Jaensch's distinction between the Tetanoid or 'T-type'
And the Basedowoid or 'B-type' of eidetic image.
And, above all, Groos's contributions to aesthetic theory
'Die optischen Qualitäten in der Lyrik Schillers,'
'Die akustischen Phänomena in der Lyrik Schillers,'
'Psychologisch-statistische Untersuchungen
Über die visuellen Sinneseindrücke
In Shakespeares lyrischen und epischen Dichtungen,'
Stahlin's 'Zur Psychologie und Statistik der Metaphern,'
Downey's 'The Psychology of Figures of Speech,'
Groos's 'Das Anschauliche Vorstellen beim Poetischen Gleichnis,'
Pluss's 'Das Gleichnis in Erzählen der Dichtung,'
Which concludes that the value and purpose of a poetic comparison
Are not to be found in the arousal of a visual image
But in the creation of a 'Gesamtvorstellung'
Common to both the principal and subordinate object.
Muller-Freienfels's 'Psychologie der Kunst,'
Bullough on 'Psychical Distance,'
And are learned in all manner of hypnagogic images,
Verbal reflexes, visual onomatopoeia,
Word-physiognomy, colour associations, tactile values,
The psychological experiences differentiating
Noun-consciousness from verb-consciousness,
And the adjective state of mind from the adverb.
The psychomotor effects of different sound-combinations,
The fact that poetry is largely tonal and that the sounds of poems,
Especially those of lyric poetry, yield of themselves
A mood comparable to that of the original poem.

Even when torn from their positions and their rhetorical anchorage
('Name the lyric poets and you have named those
Not only whose lines metathesize best, but also
Those who will produce in these tappings
As recorded in the graphs on the smoked drum
The finer form quality of the curve of motor discharge.')
Acoustic terms in Schiller are twice as frequent as in Goethe
And seven times more frequent than in Shakespeare's sonnets.
The following order represents the success with which
Images of a given kind were aroused
Through direct suggestion – auditory 46.8 per cent.,
Olfactory 39.3, cutaneous 35.5, organic and pain 30.7,
Gustatory 14.2 – certain auditory images
Are particularly easy to arouse – the sound of rain
And of the bugle-note; the sighing of the wind;
The rush of wings; the noise of the surf;
The tolling of a bell are imaged without difficulty.
– Shelley's preoccupation with odour,
Keats' penchant for cutaneous experience,
The fact that Poe induces an optical-kinaesthetic reaction
Much more frequently than a posture or a movement reaction,
Swinburne's tonal vision, Poe's phonism of the night,
Blakes' visions, and Keats' 'dazzled lips'
Are due to individual idiosyncrasies,
Where Swinburne's organic toning of phrases
Poe's kinaesthetic analogies, Keats' tactual imagery,
And Shelley's odour and auditive similes
Are literary and imaginative in significance,
Coleridge's miraculous memory, his 'optical spectra,'
His flair for words, his active intellect
'Applying curb and rudder to the streaming associations.'
The goal is that of pure beauty, and in quest of it
All experience, whether one's own or that recorded
By other adventurous spirits, is laid under contribution,
As well as dominant epochal concepts
That pattern the blending ideas.
Images interlocking through multitudinous associations
And coalescing through magical identities,

Musical words shadowing and haloing the images,
All unwinding with the precision of a chain of reflexes,
Restoring memories deep-buried in the debris of forgotten days,
Or information that never before entered the focus of consciousness.
And we are fully aware in ourselves and others
Of archetypal patterns stamped upon the physical organism
Or inherited in the structure of the brain,
Primordial images, psychic residua
Of numberless experiences of the same type,
A priori determinants of individual experience.
The need for the capture of objects complete,
By the assimilative imagination,
Of some inner factor – the stir within us
Of larger systems of feeling,
Of memory, of ideas, of aspirations.
And we are rich in verbal cruces
Drawn from the whole field of world literature
– The gap in Athena's speech which, as Verrall says,
Aeschylus could no more have filled than Dante could have told
The words of the song sung by the angelic host
That witnessed the meeting with Beatrice,
The song of which he can only report
'I understood it not, nor here is sung,
The hymn which then that people sang,
Nor did I endure its melody outright.'
And along with these that stock problem of the Gluck critic
– The aptness of the famous *Che Farò* in *Orfeo*.
Critics have thought it strange that Orpheus should
At this ineffable moment sing an aria at all,
And that this aria should be in C major
And might as well express the opposite meaning,
Express joy or sorrow. But let a phrase of Goethe's
Be remembered as explaining everything:
'And although men be stricken dumb in woe
A God did grant me words to tell my sorrow.'
It is devoid of pathos because it transcends all expression.
Only the singer is left to speak here and to speak
As purely and perhaps inflexibly as possible.

And the very mysterious line in the Rubáiyát,
'U danad u danad u danad u –'
'Breaking off something like our wood-pigeon's note
Which she is said to take up just where she left off.'
Rilke's debate whether he should write in German or Russian.
The conflict in Jakob Wassermann between his conscious ambition
To be a 'bürgerlich' German writer and the influence
On himself, and on the people round him, of his Jewish race.
The archaic elements of regional vocabularies
In the writings of Unamuno, who sunk his roots
Deep in the intra-history of his people.
Whether in Hardy's Dynasts the 'y' is long or short?
He got it from the 'Magnificat' the Greek version.
The Greek 'u' is short. Bridges' remark,
'If you ever read through a man's poems to find out
How often he uses the letter z you will end
By making some real discoveries about his poetry.'
– And on to the Indian science of proper pronunciation,
The laws of euphony peculiar to the Veda,
The knowledge of letters, accents, quantity,
The right use of the organs of articulation,
And phonetics generally – Haug on 'The Vedic Accent,'
Goldstucker on Panini; Muller's, Whitney's and Weber's
Translations of the four Pratisakhyas,
Colebrooke's essay on Sanskrit and Prakrit metres.
'A Hindu poet may proceed to any length he pleases
Within the limits of a thousand syllables to the half-line.'
The Dandaka metre (of which a specimen occurs
In the drama called Malati-madhava, Act V)
Offers more than any other
An almost incredible capacity of expression.
It will admit, indeed, of the stanza extending
27 x 4 to 999 x 4 syllables.
(Even as in Gower's *Confessio Amantis* the stories vary
In length from a mere mention in a single line
To the romance of Apollonius of Tyre in about 2000;
Even as, in modern angling, size D line
May vary from thirty-seven thousandths

To forty-five thousandths at the thickest part
[A matter of no moment perhaps to the average fisherman
Content to buy a tapered cast on the shopman's word
With no more than a glance at the thick end and the thin
But of vital concern to those who bring
The application of intelligence and intense concentration
To my favourite sport – who look over the sections
When they buy a rod to make sure
That the leaf marks in the bamboo are well staggered,
Calibrate a 'leader' [cast] with a micrometer,
Know the importance of proper taper in line and cast,
And are thoroughly posted in the Solundar Theory,
Problems of conservation, niceties of fly-dressing, etc.])
And then, of course, there is the Vedan-gas-Nirukta,
Or exposition of difficult Vedic words.
In the Nirukta-parishishta the 'four defined grades
Or stages of speech' are said to be explained
By the Rishis as meaning the four mystic words[1]
Om, bhuh, bhuvah, svar; by the grammarians
As denoting nouns, verbs, prepositions, and particles;
By the ritualists as the humns, liturgical precepts,
Brahmanas, and ordinary language; by others
As the speech of serpents, birds, reptiles and the vernacular;
By the spiritualists as the speech
Of beasts, musical instruments, wild animals, and soul.

We are familiar with the phenomena of psychic epilepsy,
Of Grübelsucht, the metaphysical mania, and all the rest
In relation to derangements of the senses,
Gestaltungsvermögen, Tiefenanschauung,
Wahrnehmungsvermögen, Seelenblindheit,
Hirnsehschwäche, strange freaks of verbigeration,
'Unknown tongues' . . .

'Such, in truth,' says Renan, 'is the richness of the resource
of the human mind that there is absolutely nothing in common
between Chinese and Sanskrit, the two languages which differ most,

[1] Referred to in Rig-veda I, 164, 45.

save one thing, the end to be attained, that is, the expression of
thought. Chinese attains this end as well as the grammatical
languages, but by entirely different means.'

The sudden fluent speech of mutes
Under unusual stimulus or emotion
As in the case detailed by Dr. Adriani
In 'Relazione Statistica Clinica del Frenocomio
di S. Margherita di Perugia
per gli Anni, 1874-1875-1876.'

Dr. Wigan tells of a case of the sudden excitation of speech
Almost as wonderful as the well-known story of the son of Croesus.
Much other material of a like sort
We have perpended in Adolf Kussmaul's
'Die Störungen der Sprache; Versuch einer Pathologie der Sprache,'
And of course we know the amazing disparity
Between the power of thinking
And the power of expressing thoughts
In the case of my countryman, John Hunter.[1]
'One of the few intellectual defects traceable in him
Was the great inequality of his powers
Of language and thought. In every mind
Thoughts and words are so interwoven
That each shares always the qualities of the other.
Thoughts and words are like mutual reflectors;
If either of them distorts an object placed between them,
The other cannot but receive the distorted image
And reflect it. Or each is, alternately,
Master and servant. Now, thought employs words
For its expression, and, then, these same words
Take part in directing the next thoughts.
If either be defective or erroneous,
The other suffers. Hunter was a great master of facts,
And in plain and customary English
He could with great power
Collect, compare, arrange, and construct

[1] John Hunter, 1728-1793, the great surgeon and anatomist.

Whatever could be made from them;
But he was not a master of words.
His large, strong mind did not in anything
Show that subtlety which,
Whether in thinking or writing,
Can accurately employ
Many words of scarcely different meanings
– A quality which is very necessary
For the consideration of abstract ideas,
And in which a defect is a hindrance,
Not only to the expression of thoughts,
But to the process of thinking.
Hunter's thinking power, strong as it was by nature,
Was hindered and baffled by its weak associate.'
And of course we have read
Tamburini's 'Contribuzione alla Fisiologia
e Patologia del Linguaggio,'[1] and
Wilks' 'Notes from the History of My Parrot.'
And on thought without words, and the relation of words to thought,
We are familiar with Helmholtz's 'Handbuch der Physiologischen
    Optik,'
Dufour and others, born blind from early infancy,
Suddenly put in possession of sight by surgical operations
Showing that a man of full intellect cannot distinguish
Distance by sight alone – know how the longer most people live
The less they are inclined to examine objects in all their parts,
Hence if they look at them from a new point of view
They often see something in old familiar things
They had not noticed before – the colours of a landscape
Appear with more brilliancy and clearness than usual
When one views it lying on the side
Or turning the head upside down.
As Itard says, in proportion as man advances
Beyond the period of his infancy,
The use, the exercise of his senses
Becomes every day less universal.
In the first stage of his life

[1] *Origine de Langage* (Paris, 1856).

He wishes to see and touch everything;
His senses are directed to all objects,
Even those which have no apparent connection with his wants.
As he becomes older, objects strike him
Only as far as they happen to be connected
With his appetites, his habits, or his inclinations;
Often there is only one, or two, of his senses
Which awakens his attention.

So we have read Bridgman, Lancelot Hogben, Thurman Arnold,
Jerome Frank, Alfred Korzybski, Ogden and Richards,
Taking from Korzybski at least a notion
Of the utility of semantics as an instrument
For extirpating pernicious thinking and emotional reactions,
A real understanding of 'the *is* of identity,'
And a demand for 'a language whose structure
Corresponds to physical structure,'
And from Ogden and Richards
Their discussion of levels of abstraction,
Their diagram explaining the relations
Of symbol (word), reference (meaning),
And referent (thing meant),
And their four-fold analysis of meaning
Into the item presented for attention,
The speaker's feeling towards the item,
His tone towards the hearer,
And his intention.
And we have read all that is to be read
On Mirror-Writing and its relation[1]
To left-handedness and cerebral disease
– Bianchi's 'Changes in Handwriting in Relation to Pathology,'

[1] Michael Tippett in his essay on Schönberg, 'Moving Into Aquarius,' says: 'So in Joyce's *Finnegans Wake*, as if to make quite sure we shall understand nothing, the very words are dismantled and reassembled. The immense book goes round in a huge circle: We end where we began. It would be quite as proper to read it backwards. In the Lyric Suite of Alban Berg, one of the fast movements is written in an exact mirror form. Would it do the same for us in this piece if it were played backwards – or upside down? Probably. Take it or leave it.'

'Peretti über Spiegelschrift,'
Buchwald and Erlenmeyer,
The change from right-hand to left-hand writing
In the MS. of the 'Codex Atlanticus' of Leonardo da Vinci
In the Ambrose Library at Milan.
All that bears on man distinguished from other animals
As $\mu\acute{\epsilon}\rho o\psi$, or voice-dividing,
And all the evidence bearing on Sir William Hamilton's
'Pluribus intentus, minor est ad singula sensus.'
By Charles Bobbet the mind is allowed
To have a distinct notion of six objects at once;
By Abraham Tucker only four;
By Destutt Tracy six again.
'Consciousness is proportioned to change
And fades with invariability of impression.'
Thoughts unassociated with words soon
Die away from the memory – even intense feelings,
When never expressed, are soon forgotten.

(So Gobineau contended that while Europeans
Can only believe one thing at a time
Most Orientals possess the faculty
Of stringing one thing after another –
Taking nothing from the old
While adding to the new.
Ah! China! a people 'among whom
Revelations are impossible,'[1]
Of all the literary devices we need
Today and in the foreseeable future
Surely the most important is the *tien kou*;
C'est une façon subtile (et prudente),
Exquise (et difficile) de dire
Ce qu'on n'a pas dit, de montrer
Ce qu'on n'a pas montré –
L'usage systematique du *tien kou*
Dans l'art poétique chinois.)

[1] Balzac's *L'Interdiction* (p. 292).

Of course, as Galton long ago established,
People can think of things
Without having images of them,
Can think clearly and effectively
Though they image but poorly,
And can image clearly,
Without their thinking being good.
No thinking consists entirely of images
And some thinking contains no images at all.
When a subject, posed with a question,
Has thought out the answer
What else can he always recollect
To have been going on in his mind
During his occupation with the problem?
Various things are reported to have been experienced
Such as feelings of muscular strain,
Emotions of bafflement or relief,
Vocal or sub-vocal mutterings, etc.
But these were also often reported missing.
One experience is generally present
Though dwindling in intensity down to vanishing point
As the ponderings improved in facility,
Something vaguely called the *Bewusstseinslage*,
A hardly describable waft
Of consciousness or awareness – of what?
The world of Baroque in whose court ballets
Vast spectacles are constructed only
To disintegrate suddenly in flame and thunder,
Change, inconstancy, disguise, movement,
The vision of an impermanent world,
And the ebb and flow of the interior life
With Bernini's Circe and the Peacock
The symbol of it all.
Thought – psychons analogous
To the photons of a sunbeam!

For it's no use employing a medium
Simultaneously given to producing

Effects we know nothing of
On countless other planes,
In addition to the few we envisage
On the planes within our purview.

Mistral, Carl Spitteler, these are my friends
And Rubén Darío, Vasile Alecsandri, Uys Krige,
Otokar Březina, Jens Peter Jacobsen, Paavo Cajander,
Svatopluk Cech, Arne Garborg, Jaroslav Vrchlicky,
Rasmus Effersoe, and Ceiriog who wrote of himself
Carodd eiriau cerddorol, carodd feirdd,[1]
Cesare Pascarella, and Carlo Salustri,
And, of course, Al Capp, opening great new vistas
In these days of the monstrous decline of fun!
These, and thousands upon thousands of others
(Many in the flesh too, Chaim Bialik, Theodor Daubler,
Dòmhnull Mac na Ceàrdaich, Yeats, AE, Dylan Thomas,
Sturge Moore, T. S. Eliot, Austin Clarke, Fred Higgins,
Gogarty, Montale, Surkov, Marshak,
Mulk Raj Anand, Harindranath Chattopadhyaya,
Of many different nations and languages –
And high among them the Catalan singer, Maria Manent,
Reaping 'La Collita En La Boira.'[2]
With, in his obscure harvesting, such magical things
As the songs 'Amigueta, el turmell' and 'Pomera daurada' –)
I think there should be a soul-show
Compulsory for everybody
At least once a year.

So many people are persuaded
They have a lovely soul
Hidden away somewhere
– They don't know just where –
Of which as matters stand
They can vouchsafe no proof
While appearances, by which they say

[1] He loved musical words, he loved poetry.
[2] i.e. *The Harvest in the Mist* (published Barcelona: La Revista, 1921).

We shouldn't judge, are all against them.
That would be their chance,
And our chance, who simply don't believe them,
To call their bluff
And settle the matter once for all.

And think of the embarrassment
Of certain Royal Personages
And Great Divines and other V.I.P.s
Who when it came to the push
Found they'd mislaid theirs!

Yes, I think there should be a soul-show
Compulsory for everybody
At least once a year,
Like a short-arm inspection in the Army,
Though hardly so attractive, of course. –

Then sing your song in praise of life
And acclaim the great creative plan
And all the ups and downs that chart
The graph of every human span.

One thing sticks out. You must agree
Poetry apart, as life you scan,
The whole thing's due, in human terms,
To woman taking a rise out of man. –

There is no language in the world
That has not yielded me delight
(Ranging lightly from Mackay on the various forms of the Gaelic
      story –
Comh-abartachd eadar Cas-Shiubal an t-Sléibhe agus A' Chailleach
      Bheurr –
To the 218 plots of Kotzebue
And Somdeva's Katha Sarit Sagara [Ocean Streams of Story]
And the way Stesichorus learned his method of handling
Some of his stories from the Hesiodic epic

And owed his form to Dorian choral poetry.
I have known all the *Shihp'in*[1]
Even as I know that the elephant's paws
Are like the *lishu* style of writing,
The lion's mane is like the *feipo*,
Fighting snakes write wonderful wriggling *ts'aoshu* ('grass script'),
Floating dragons write *chuanshu* ('seal characters'),
The cow's legs resemble *pafen*[2]
And the deer's *hsiak'ai*[3]
And that the *wen* or literary beauty of all things
Arises from their nature – those that fulfil their nature
Clothe themselves in *wen* or beautiful lines,
Therefore *wen*, or beauty of line or form,
Is intrinsic and not extrinsic)
With exact appreciation of
Its poets' various sleight,
Even as I rejoice in the virgins
Advancing slowly for the parodos,
Sliding gently into the famous processional anapaests,
Pacing the rhythmic movement of the emmeleia.
– The long choric ode to Venus Anadyomene,
The trochaic hymn to Artemis,
And on to the final kommos, gathering
The harmonies and rhythms, which have crossed and recrossed
      each other
In subtle interchange throughout the poem,
In one vast symphonic summary,
And the whole purport and beauty of the drama is disclosed,
As that of all language in my vision now.

And so, in a *coup d'oeil*, I gather here
Mayakovsky's disregard of the unstressed syllables
And break with tonico-syllabic verse
(*Mayakovsky dlya Golosa*[4]),
Pasternak's weird metaphorical jumps,

[1] Personalities of poetry.
[2] Comparatively stout and symmetrical writing.
[3] Elegant 'small script.'   [4] Mayakovsky for the voice.

Tikhonov's predilection for the ballad form,
Selvinsky's punctuation of words with full stops and queries
And the mixture of Latin characters with Russian,
Bezymensky's splendid amusical bombast, rich with vulgarisms,
Rilke, Valéry, Soffici, Stefan George –
(And, most of all, those, untranslated into English,
For lack of whom the perspective of poetry
In that language is hopelessly inadequate,
– Kostes Palamas, Endre Ady, Amado Nervo,
Alexander Blok, Holger Drachmann, Antonio Machado –)
But most I delight in *cywyddau brud*,
Deliberately riddling and obscure,
In dexterous *dyfalu*, tours de force
Like Dafydd ab Edmund's untranslatable beauties,
Magical melodies in the metre *cywydd deuair fyrion*
And all subtle distinctions between
Geuwawd and *gwawd*,[1]
And the causes that strew poems like Pantycelyn's
With words like *analeisio*, *leflo*, and *disapwyntir*,
And, rhymed by the spoken pronunciation,
Such typically South Wales rhymes as *bur-hir*,
And the singularly subtle and haunting rhythm
Of a poem in free metre
Like the *Clegyr* of Iorwerth Peate.
(Ah, in the Gaelic countries still – in Ireland
And Scotland and Wales – the poor man
Is seldom poor in spirit or address.
No matter how 'low' you look there
You find something aristocratic in him.
He can be as mean about money
Or as money-grubbing as anyone else
But lack of money does not spell poverty of spirit.
He responds to quality. He understands quantity
No less than others, but, possessing quality himself,
He salutes it in others. The English working man
Has far more civic virtues and less murder in his heart,
But he has no such poetry in his soul,

---

[1] *Geuwawd*, false song; *gwawd*, true song.

He does not respond to quality,
He is unintelligent – he is not interested
In the world outside himself. Aristocracy of spirit
Makes no appeal to him whatever, while he has
An unholy reverence for aristocracy of wealth.)

Ah, Joyce, this is our task,
Making what a moving, thrilling, mystical, tropical,
Maniacal, magical creation of all these oppositions,
Of good to evil, greed to self-sacrifice,
Selfishness to selflessness, of this all-pervading atmosphere,
Of the seen merging with the unseen,
Of the beautiful sacrificed to the ugly,
Of the ugly transformed to the beautiful,
Of this intricate yet always lucid and clear-sighted
Agglomeration of passions, manias, occult influences,
Historical and classical references
– Sombre, insane, brilliant and sane,
Timeless, a symbol of the reality
That lies beyond and through the apparent,
Written with the sweeping assurance, the inspired beauty,
The intimated truth of genius,
With natures like ours in which a magnetic fluidity
That is neither 'good' nor 'bad' is forever
Taking new shapes under the pressure of circumstances,
Taking new shapes, and then again,
As Kwang makes Confucius complain of Laotze,
'Shooting up like a dragon.'
But, taking my life as a whole,
And hovering with the flight of the hawk
Over its variegated landscape,
I believe I detect certain quite definite 'streams of tendency'
In that unrolling map,
Moving towards the unknown future.
For one thing I fancy the manner I have allowed
My natural impulses towards romance and mysticism
To dominate me has led to the formation
Of a curious gap or 'lacuna'

Between the innate and almost savage realism,
Which is a major element in my nature,
And the imaginative, poetical cult
Whereby I have romanticised and idealized my life.
In this realistic mood I recognise
With a grim animal acceptance
That it is indeed likely enough that the 'soul'
Perishes everlastingly with the death of the body,
But what this realistic mood, into which
My mind falls like a plummet
Through the neutral zone of its balanced doubt,
Never for one single beat of time can shake or disturb
Is my certain knowledge,
Derived from the complex vision of everything in me,
That the whole astronomical universe, however illimitable,
Is only one part and parcel of the mystery of Life;
Of this I am as certain as I am certain that I am I.
The astronomical universe is *not* all there is.

So this is what our lives have been given to find,
A language that can serve our purposes,
A marvellous lucidity, a quality of fiery aery light,
Flowing like clear water, flying like a bird,
Burning like a sunlit landscape.
Conveying with a positively Godlike assurance,
Swiftly, shiningly, exactly, what we want to convey.
This use of words, this peculiar aptness and handiness,
Adapts itself to our every mood, now pathetic, now ironic,
Now full of love, of indignation, of sensuality, of glamour, of glory,
With an inevitable richness of remembered detail
And a richness of imagery that is never cloying,
A curious and indescribable quality
Of sensual sensitiveness,
Of very light and very air itself,
– Pliant as a young hazel wand,
Certain as a gull's wings,
Lucid as a mountain stream,
Expressive as the eyes of a woman in the presence of love, –

Expressing the complex vision of everything in one,
Suffering all impressions, all experience, all doctrines
To pass through and taking what seems valuable from each.
No matter in however many directions
These essences seem to lead.

Collecting up all these essences,
These intimations coming willy-nilly from all quarters,
Into a complex conception of all things,
An intricately-cut gem-stone of a myriad facets
That is yet, miraculously, a whole;
Each of which facets serves its individual purpose
In directing the light collected from every side outwards
In a single creative ray.
With each of these many essences culled
From the vast field of life some part of one's own
Complex personality has affinity and resembles
When climbing on to the ice-cap a little south of Cape Bismarck
And keeping the nunataks of Dronning Louises Land on our left
We travel five days
On tolerable ice in good weather
With few bergs to surmount
And no crevasses to delay us.
Then suddenly our luck turns.
A wind of 120 miles an hour blows from the East,
And the plateau becomes a playground of gales
And the novel light gives us snow-blindness.
We fumble along with partially bandaged eyes
Our reindeer-skin kamiks worn into holes
And no fresh sedge-grass to stump them with.
We come on ice-fields like mammoth ploughlands
And mountainous sécracs which would puzzle an Alpine climber.
That is what adventuring in dictionaries means,
All the abysses and altitudes of the mind of man,
Every test and trial of the spirit,
Among the débris of all past literature
And raw material of all the literature to be.
But all language? A glare like that of an arc-lamp,

D

No self-deceptions, no quaint hiding-places now,
No groove to get into where one
Can move automatically. Every instant demanding
A new concentration of one's powers,
Breaking completely with all ready-made, mechanical, conventional
        conceptions
Of the conglomerate experience of life, accepted gratefully by
        laziness and fear,
No shred left us in common now
With those who mistake blind eyes for balanced minds,
Who practise, in Disraeli's words,
'The blunders of their predecessors.'
People to whom experience means nothing,
Whose strength is the strength of cast-iron, not steel,
Whose souls exist in a state of sacred torpidity,
Prostrated before cold altars and departed gods,
Whose appeal to commonsense is only an appeal
To the spiritual sluggishness which is man's besetting sin.
And in the present unexampled crisis our deadliest peril.

All language!
Not like Valéry with an occasional doling out
Of a word like '*pur*' used as the chemists use it,
Nor finding the touchstone of poetry
In the correct management of the mute 'e'!
– And here I think of Chaucer's inconsistency
In his pronunciation of the final 'e' –
(Though there *is* all the difference in the world
Between whisky and whiskey, of course!)
And (without recourse to the *Dictionnaire des Idées Reçues*
And the *Sottisier*, that Siberia of the human spirit,
The ghastly miles stretching endlessly on every side)
Have all mankind like a few friends at the fireside!
My muse 'needeth no simple man' – no 'review of all the sciences
As they appear to two lucid enough minds
Of a mediocre, simple order' . . . or a few million such minds,
'*Pas de monstres et pas de héros,*'
Not overhung with the 'weight of all the world'

But only with a vast panoply of knowledge
That seems more and more fantastic,
Tired Jobs, agèd eagles, Bouvard and Pécuchet,
Coping with the immense florilegium of nonsense they have compiled
As a result of their search, i.e. with Flaubert's *Sottisier*
Brought up to date by H. L. Mencken and Gerald Barry.
Nor yet such of the indices that must serve as guides
To monetary management by credit control as are yet perhaps
Not fully appreciated by even the acutest economist,
Nor the analogues of such indices in any sphere of life.
Her sensitive finger requires in all connections
The equivalent of the Frenchman's ingenious device
Of the milled edge, to prevent clipping of coins – or wings!
As only that which aspires to a *caoin*, an edge,
Like a melody tends to the infinite,
Or, as Jammes said, 'Man is horribly complicated.
He should be at pains to simplify himself
Until he comes to the slender tapering line
Like the crest of a mountain as seen in the evening,'
– *Le mot juste*, to which the whole universe 'gives'
As Schubert in 'Der Einsame' after having in the first stanza
Played ducks and drakes with the poet's form to secure
Complete licence for his own self-evolving melody
In the second stanza makes his musical form
'Give' to the sense of the words – since the vocal melody
Of the first stanza can be played on a violin
And not lose a shred of its beauty or its musical meaning
But the vocal line of the second stanza
Would have no meaning at all on a violin.
It is broken up into ejaculations
To which meaning and justification are given by words alone.

In these days of ballyhoo, rubber-stamp minds, diabolical clichés,
When universal lies have mankind in their death-grip
And endless impotent and disloyal vility of speech
And the effect of the misuse of familiar words
On the character of men and the fate of nations,
'Verbomania, The Pathology of Language,'

('eine Art Jardin d'Acclimatation für die grösseren Arten von Lügen,
die man bei uns noch nie gesehen hatte, und ein Palmenhaus
von Übertreibungen und eine kleine, gepflegte Figuerie falscher
    Geheimnisse.'
Or, as the *Atma-bodha* calls them, *avidya-vikshepán*);[1]
Everywhere the *Diktatur der Lüge*,
In a world of which indeed the sightseer can only say
'Is tric a bha na loingis mhór a' crìonadh
'S na h-amair-mhùin a' seoladh,'[2]
Threatens to destroy the whole of civilisation
– In these days nevertheless of the revival and extension
Of Taal, Frisian, Faroese, Irish Gaelic, and a thousand more,
When the *diganta* lifts in Bengali poetry
Though MacAulay, the Englishman, would have prevented it forever,
And of the heightened *lasciveté parfumée* of the best of the *motêng*
    Chinese poets
I praise you then, Joyce, because you too
Were – like all Gongorists – one of those altruists
(However their conscious motives may be mixed)
Risking contemporary misunderstanding, personal obloquy even,
For the sake of enriching the inheritance
Each administers in his generation.
– Like not schussing straight
But in fast swinging traverses under good control
Swaying now into a perfect christi,
Going down the side of the bowl in a lovely rush
With the powder curling below our knees
And only the ski points showing!
– The sense of pure delight and spiritual deportment,
One's element running pure,
Precision, crispness, and grace – just the right dose
Of delicate perfumed sentiment, in a word
That style and breeding almost extinct to-day,
Measuring all the changing baffling situations of life
According to settled standards and sure convictions,

---

[1] Avidyá-vikshepán, 'the projections of ignorance.'
[2] Scots Gaelic saying, literally: ''Tis often that were the big ships a-foundering and only the pots of piss continuing to sail.'

Giving the sense of a scorn,
Largely, but not always completely, veiled,
For all other minds, personalities, and even events,
A mind that on every issue that presents itself
Opens and shuts smoothly and exactly
Like the breech of a gun
Or like a production of the *Marriage of Figaro*
Which lets Mozart's unquenchable radiance
Work through without hindrance all the time . . .
To rise from the corruption that goes draining away
Into the slobbered mud of a marish waste
Slow-heaving as it perishes into nothingness,
Filth and eternal oblivion – the way of escape
From the limitations which the learned, the wise,
Would lay upon the soul, binding it
In the laws of its own desires – the way of the spirit
He revealed, to honour whom we must glorify ourselves
By sending forth once more the reverberating, seven-thundered
Asseveration of the great Jehovah – I AM.
I have spoken elsewhere of the master swordsman, *amaiseach*,
(Forward in counter swift as the dart of a snake's tongue,
Every pass in prime or carte, in tierce or second,
Quintz or parade de point volante
– 'Bottes,' parries, simple feints, bindings, coupes, and flanconades,
Thrusts in quinte and lunges parried cercle,
The eyes of a cat and a knowledge of the art
– Guard, lunge, methods of advancing and retiring –
Approaching the uncanny and partaking
Of the speed of lightning).
Eireachdas lann – the fine play of blades,
His sword (*lann trìchlaiseach*) ricasso (to let his finger rest on the blade);
And of the *gìomanach* – a masterly fellow in anything,
Gìomanach a'ghunna, the masterly marksman,
I mean the quality that Mencius calls *Jen* -
'The heart of a man,' 'being a man,' which is 'like archery
Because when we miss the mark we come back for self-examination.'
It is the miracle of literature, of culture, of the Celt,
In that it is at once the bow and the mark,

The inspiration and the aim. 'In the beginning was the Word.'
The Word is also 'the last of life for which the first was made.'
– Here, indeed, is the bending of Ulysses' bow.
The arrow is called *paitāmaham astram* in the *Rāmāyana*
And described as having the wind for its feathers,
The fire and the sun for its point, the air for its body,
And the mountains Meru and Mandara for its weight.
It has the convenient property of returning
To its owner's quiver after doing its work.
So too archery in the traditional Japanese sense
Is not a sport, not even an art.
It is a spiritual discipline with the aim
Of hitting not a material but a spiritual goal,
'So that fundamentally the marksman aims at himself
And may even succeed in hitting himself.'
The bow and arrow are merely the means
Of achieving a state of spiritual enlightenment,
Wherein the bow, arrow, marksman, and target,
As well as everything else in the universe,
Become one. The problem of hitting the target
Thus becomes entirely secondary.
It is merely something which invariably happens
Once the correct spiritual state has been reached.[1]

> *Where there are no graves, there can be*
> *No resurrection.*   NIETZSCHE

I rejoiced when from Wales once again
Came the ffff-putt of a triple-feathered arrow
Which looked as if it had never moved.[2]

But now the bowman has fitted one more nock
To his string, and discharged the arrow straight up into the air
Partly as a gesture of farewell, partly of triumph,
And beautiful! – I watched the arrow go up.
The sun was already westing towards evening

[1] See *Zen in the Art of Archery*, by Eugen Herrigel.
[2] With acknowledgments to T. H. White, *The Sword in the Stone*. The reference here is to the author's friend, Dylan Thomas.

So, as the arrow topped the trees
And climbed into sunlight,
It began to burn against the evening like the sun itself.
Up and up it went, not weaving as it would have done
With a snatching loose, but soaring, swimming,
Aspiring towards heaven, steady, golden and superb.

Just as it had spent its force,
Just as its ambition had been dimmed by destiny
And it was preparing to faint, to turn over,
To pour back into the bosom of its mother earth.
A terrible portent happened.
A gore crow came flapping wearily
Before the approaching night.
It came, it did not waver, it took the arrow,
It flew away, heavy and hoisting,
With the arrow in its beak. I was furious.
I had loved the arrow's movement,
Its burning ambition in the sunlight,
And it was such a splendid arrow,
Perfectly-balanced, sharp, tight-feathered,
Clean-nocked, and neither warped nor scraped.

I was furious but I was frightened.
It is a very old and recurring portent in our history.
We remember the story of Valerius Corvus[1]
(Ah, would my bowman had been saved like Valerius
By a crow which hid him from the foe with its wings!)
And the famous episode in the great Irish epic of Ulster,
The *Táin Bó Chuailgne*,[2]
In which the goddess Morrigu attacks Cuchulainn,
Who scorned her love,
In the form of a crow.
(A like episode is depicted on one of the decorated faces
Of an Etruscan alabaster vase in the Florence Museum,[3]

[1] Livy. VII, 26 (the campaign of 345); Dio Cass., fr. 34.
[2] The Cattle-Lifting of Cooley.
[3] Minali. *Studi e materiali di archeologia e numismatica.*

Among scenes of the Trojan War.)
The crow is not a mere flight of fancy.
It is the creature which stands for battle
And the gods and goddesses of war.

But the crow cannot quench the light
With its outstretched wings forever
Nor break the law of gravity
Nor swallow the arrow.
We shall get it back. Never fear!
And how I shall rejoice when the War is over
And there comes from Wales once again
The fff-putt of a triple-feathered arrow
Which looks as if it had never moved!

Do not forget the scene at the court of King Drupada
When the hundred sons of Dhrita-rashtra strained every nerve
In vain to bend the enormous bow
While Arjuna 'with one vigorous effort braced the string;
Quickly the shafts were aimed; they flew;
The mark fell pierced.' Or the like scene in the *Odyssey*.
The bow I speak of is a greater Gandiva
'An archer shoots an arrow which may kill
One man, or none; but clever men discharge
The shaft of intellect, whose stroke has power
To overwhelm a king and all his kingdom.'
'Darts, barbed arrows, iron-headed spears,
However deep they penetrate the flesh,
May be extracted; but a cutting speech
That pierces, like a javelin, to the heart,
None can remove.' (No wonder the Indians had stanza-forms
Such as the *kadga-bandha*, a stanza shaped like a sword,
The *dhanu-bandha*, shaped like a bow,
And the *go-mutrika*, like a stream of cow's urine!)
The best wood is yew – *not* English yew,
For that's too flabby, but Spanish or Italian yew
Is grown at such an altitude it has to fight
For its existence, and the wood is better.

Alas, there's little of it and it's ill to get
For various reasons. So we must rule out yew
Unless we get it from the United States.
Oregon yew is a beautiful wood, light, steady, and sweet,
With a fine cast, equal to any bow wood ever used.
Then there's Osage orange, another fine, tough, springy American
    wood
Almost as good as yew. And degame, or lemonwood,
A wood like lancewood, from Cuba and South Africa.
Hickory's another bow wood, but it's sluggish
And soon loses its cast. They make steel bows in Sweden
And these have advantages, for they do not fire
Or 'go down,' but they lack the sweetness of the true bow wood.
The string is of hemp, shoemakers' flax thread, or Irish linen thread.
The arrow is of Baltic pine, that is, varnished deal.
It is footed with a beefwood nock with, on the other end,
A metal pile, shaped like a bullet.
The arrow has three turkey feathers,
Taken from the same side of the bird.
This ensures that the arrow turns in flight
Like a bullet.

'Of that king-slaying arrow, was their strife;
Fledged with what fowl's wing, nocked was, in what sort,
Ashen, or birch, the stele, or river reed;
Of bronze or bone, or subtle flint, the head.'
Yet here even I have forgotten the dance at times
– The stomp, the jive, 'gutbucketing,' and the 'hot' and 'swing' music,
Desperately attempting to count *entrechats* and *fouettés*,
Speculating vaguely on what I missed in Nijinsky and Karsavina,
And have had to go at times, like the hare
That 'limp'd trembling through the frozen grass,'
Amid the haunting swarm of half-things dissolving each into each,
Changing and intermixing monstrously in a fluctuating putrescence.

How shall I word what I needs must say
To carry conviction against the Niagara of official lies?
When there is no longer anything one can do,

And even passive resistance has lost all meaning!
Yet I cannot join the ubiquitous impotent opposition
Or take an easy protective coloration and close my eyes
And give no sign of what is in my heart.
I stand for things which transform all the 'best of mankind'
Into no better than the half-illiterate
Dull-eyed, vacant-faced talesmen at the Scottsboro trial.
Our purest stock!
What has brought about their degeneracy
(Maddened by economic fear.
Structural alarm, cultural fear, blind fear)
With the boys in the dock better-mannered, better-dressed,
Infinitely more generous, more honest, more intelligent,
Hatefully intelligent, their hair slicked with anti-kink grease?
– All the most vital evidence for the defence debarred,
Human nature apparently constitutionally incapable of hearing it,
Or the 'tongues of men and angels' of expressing it!

So for me beauty is not the seeking for a conventional ideal,
Nothing is done by premeditation, everything by necessity,
Order and harmony do not lead to the decorative as in Italy,
The expression of an ardent inner life is not my sole aim as in Spain,
The senses and the matter do not predominate as in Flanders,
But mind, heart, and the senses unite
In giving expression to all the beauty of life,
There need be no *Torschlusspanik* anywhere.
I find inexhaustible riches in the life of everyday.
Nothing is ever commonplace to me that is imbued with life.
The artist imitates the Creator and tries to achieve unity.
Back to the eager appetites of the Renaissance! Back
To the 'best that has been thought and felt in the world,'
Back to John Keats first looking into Chapman's Homer,
Back to Karl Marx reading Aeschylus through every year!
Poems like the development in the first movement of the Appassionata
Where the terrific speed and duration of temperament replaces the
　　　content.
A poetry so flexible it includes death;
'I am not sure,' said Whitman, 'but the last

Inclosing sublimation of race or poem is
What it thinks of death. After . . . the pervading fact
Of visible existence, with the duty it devolves,
Is rounded and apparently completed
By suffusing through the whole and several
That other pervading invisible fact, so large a part
(Is it not the largest part?) of life here.'
I too to whom consciousness is exquisitely precious,
For whom the creative imagination of man is a constant theme,
Do not look upon death as an enemy, but gently and firmly
Have made that largest part of life an accepted part.
(For who among the thousand millions of the so-called living
Are not dead in comparison with some hundreds
Of the so-called dead who are more alive than they were
In their lifetimes, many of them becoming
Ever more and more alive
Not with the 'animation' of the Zombies of 'Heaven,'
Still-born foetuses of the Second Birth,
[For what is the Christian Heaven
But an Eventide Home
For *mantequeros* (*anglice*, butter-ghosts)
And decerebrated rats?]
                – But cleansed
Of all the atrocities of human intercourse,
Save their own quintessential communication,
Starlike to the dirt of the 'consciousness,'
The little – the all-but-naught – they have of that,
Of the many, the all-too-many,
The innumerable meat without minds.)

Bien (*dit M. Teste*). *L'essentiel est contre la vie.*

Civilised living is bound up with values
Unaffected by the destruction of *ce qui ferme*
Because the only *résistance au temps*
Relevant to them is a resistance
Having nothing to do with survival in time.
The objects of an endeavour acceptable

In the light of these values are alone
Invulnerable to the decay of time
Or the disappointment of imperfection;
By their means alone may we approach
The ideal of self-possession and self-coincidence
And become 'changed into ourselves by eternity.'

It is death that most of all reveals love
In its aspect of *résistance à la durée*
– Liberation from devouring time, the true
Durability in the domain of the timeless –
Because the function of death is, more than all else,
To mark off that which is timeless
From that which is merely living.
The things least conditioned by life
Are also least frustrated by death.
Love is indeed one of these
Finding (as it does) a sort of crown in death
Because it needs no realization
In a cycle of renewal[1]
Here or anywhere else.
(Out of the mouths of babes – and Sucklings!)
Out of the intensity of consciousness of individuality
The individuality itself seems to dissolve
And fade away into boundless being,
And this not a confused state
But the clearest of the clear,
Where death is almost a laughable impossibility,
The loss of personality seemingly no extinction
But the only true life.

Excessus mentis, alienatio mentis
Like those great South Sea Island snails,
Bigger than a man's fist, crawling over one's fingers,
No part of them moving,
Yet with everything in motion.

[1] Vide *Paul Valéry and the Civilized Mind*, by Norman Suckling.

While as a Scottish **Borderer**
I still take an unholy delight
(Like the man who could not be a good philosopher
Because cheerfulness was always breaking in)
In occasional ascholic invasions
Of the autotelic,
Yet, continually tempering my judgment
With new understanding,
Not denying the autonomy of new work
Even as I declare its human value,
I know that in the final artistic
– The highest human – vision
There is neither good nor evil,
Better nor worse,
But only the harmony
Of that which is,
The pure phenomenon
Abiding in the eternal radiance.

The vision is in no sense dynamic or prophetic.
It is a vision of understanding, not creation;
Of some vast wisdom deepening into twilight,
The glimmering light of intuition
Fading into mental complication;
Typical perhaps of the kind of psychism
That breaks out at the end of a dispensation,
But it is not the 'scream of Juno's peacock,'
There is a fragrance of sweet death about it,
Of anointment for a pagan burial;
And we wonder, after all, if the author
Has not found some ingenious way
Of winding his mind up in its own cocoon;
That may be his own self-criticism, indeed,
As in the last stanza of the Epilogue:
'Such thought – such thought have I that hold it tight
Till meditation master all its parts,
Nothing can stay my glance
Until that glance run in the world's despite

To where the damned have howled away their hearts
And where the blessed dance;
Such thought, that in it bound
I need no other thing,
Wound in mind's wandering
As mummies in the mummy-cloth are wound.'

Ah, Joyce, thus we who are still confined
To mortal life are faced to-day
With a world that is barely within
The limits of present human comprehension,
A world in which logic and causality,
Our three-dimensional modes of thought
And our two-dimensional modes of speech
Are at most very imperfect instruments.
For beyond the four dimensions of space-time
There is the fifth dimension, individuality,
Characterised by rhythm, elasticity, intensity,
Here empty space as well as the space-time continuum disappear.
The individual discontinuum
Becomes established as the physical principle
Of this world, and the five-dimensional aspect is introduced.
Homogeneity, causality, probability disappear.
In a universe without emptiness events do not happen
Because other events happened before.
Within its five dimensions
Forces influence each other elastically.
There is no logic,
No determinate sequence,
Only tendencies.
Even the subject-object antithesis
Is only an approximation.
Life is an element like other elements.
It is an organisation with its own special rhythm,
Particularly elastic, but otherwise
Much less of a miracle
Than is the fact of matter at all.
It is the element of adaptation

And all parts of living beings
Are integral components of it.
All most of us can know of it yet
Is that five hundred to a thousand generations ago
Through some overcoming of inertia,
A loosening of connections in the nervous centre,
There was a general development
Of the power of conscious reflection.
A true step of evolution took place.
The new species of man was marked among other things
By the loss or degeneration
Of many important instincts
Such as nutrition and reproduction.
These now require intelligent guidance.
The power of conscious reflection
Is still only at an early and comparatively rudimentary stage,
But we are committed to it;
It is an irreversible specialization,
And, judging by the incredible number of our nerve cells.
There is already ample room for its development.[1]
We are literally at the opening of a new era,
The events of which no one can foresee
Because they are strictly indeterminate,
We must aim at producing
The most intensely organized individual
In proper balance with a society
Itself in proper ecological balance;
The recognition of our responsibility
In promoting these values
Is the first essential;

[1] Professor H. J. Muller, in *Out of the Night* (1936), says that we now have the scientific means to create a society when men like the great philosophers, poets, and scientists in our history will no longer be, as they have always been hitherto, very rare exceptions, but the rule; the time when the earth will be occupied by 'a race of people all of whom come up to the level of what we now call "genius".'

Of course there are things the biologists don't know yet. It is very difficult to say what are bad genes, and as another Scottish writer recently pointed out, some genes believed to be bad, may prove otherwise, like the 'sickle cells' in the blood which were regarded as bad, but which, in African negroes are related to their resistance to malaria.

We must put all our reliance in the intellect
And develop it in everybody;
The demand for intellectual leadership to-day
Far exceeds the supply.
Variation must be encouraged
Rather than suppressed. –

'The last long wain wends slow away,
And we are free to sport and play.'[1]

Even as in a description of rain,
Falling on Rouen and the surrounding hills,
Flaubert flattens out every image,
Removes every salient word,
Docks every 'original' idea,
Until what is left is what anybody
Might have said about the scene
– Though nobody, of course, but Flaubert
Could have said it![2]

St'īm'ra di'lša, a st'īme aga di'lša
(If you're a piper, have your own pipe)
That gloy's nīd-el tarsp, he's tāp min'úrt
(That man's not dead, he's alive now)
Klisp'n thalósk, soon be ludhus thôrī stūrt the grenôg
(Day is breaking, light will soon be coming through the window)[3]

Speech. All men's whore. My beloved!
Elle est nue – sans défense.
Hated as women hate a woman who,
They feel, assails some secret privilege

---

[1] Sir Walter Scott: *The Heart of Midlothian.*
[2] Flaubert, 'a man who by his entirely new and personal usage of the *passé léfini*, the *passé indéfini*, of the present participle, of certain pronouns, of certain prepositions, has almost as much renewed our vision of things as Kant did with his Categories, with the theories of Knowledge, and of the Reality of the External World.' – Proust, *A propos du Style de Flaubert.*
[3] Shelta, *vide The Secret Languages of Ireland,* by Professor R. A. S. MacAlister.

They are entitled to – destroys
The very foundations of their existence.
The demands she makes are for the supreme desires of men.
In herself, and with the particular form of lure she has,
She foils the far-reaching purposes of nature,
Threatens the whole psychological relation of the sexes,
By which women call men in to the herd,
Rouses that by which, through the deceits of their emotions
Men reach out to those things which are beyond their grasp,
– The embodiment of every vital desire
That gives them consciousness of being;
Not lust but exhilaration.
They are roused to exalted visions of themselves.
She will never belong to any man.
It is a freed slavery they give her.

Ah, my queen slender and supple,
In a delightful posture
As free from self-conscious art
As the snowcap on a mountain!
– An absorbing attachment of the spirit,
Not a sexual relationship as that is generally understood,
But an all-controlling emotion
That has no physical basis.
Love resolved into the largest terms
Of which such emotions are capable,
The power of the spirit beneath that exquisite tremulous envelope
Possessing moral courage to a rare degree
Which can keep her steadfast in the gravest peril,
And a dignity so natural and certain
That it deserves the name of stateliness.
Death cannot intimidate her.
Poverty and exile, the fury of her own family,
And the calumnies of the world
Are unable to bend her will
Towards courses she feels to be wrong
– Imparting with every movement, every look,
Some idea of what the process of literature could be,

Something far more closely related
To the whole life of mankind
Than the science of stringing words together
In desirable sequences.

The Snares of Varuna

THE world is fast bound in the snares of Varuna
– 'Cords consisting of serpents,' according to Kulluka
(*Pasaih sarpa-rajjughih*). The winkings of men's eyes
Are all numbered by him; he wields the universe
As gamesters handle dice. These are the unexampled days
Of false witness – a barbarous regime which gives power over life
        and death
To an oligarchy of brigands and adventurers,
Without security from vexation by irresponsible tyrants,
Without protection of the home against the aggression of criminal
        bands,
Without impartial justice, without dignity.
We are denied all the deepest needs of men who do not wish
To sink to the level of the beasts – condemned
To a life deprived of its salt.

Already, everywhere,
The speed-up, the 'church work,' the lead poisoning,
The strain that drives men nuts.
The art of teaching fish by slow degrees
To live without water.
Men cheaper than safety
– Human relations have never sunk so low.
'The meaninglessness of the individual
Apart from his communal framework,'
The men in power who are worth no more
Than an equal number of cockroaches,
Unconcerned about values,

Indifferent to human quality
Or jealous and implacably hostile to it,
Full of the tyranny of coarse minds and degraded souls;
The abominable clap-trap and politicians' rhetoric,
The tawdry talk about the 'King' and 'the King's lieges'
And 'the Government' and 'the British people';
The concentration camps, the cat o' nine tails,
The law more lawless than any criminal,
The beatings-up by the police,
The countless thuggeries of Jacks-in-office,
The vile society women, infernal parasites,
The endless sadism, Gorilla-rule,
The live men hanging in the plaza
With butcher's hooks through their jaws
– And everywhere the worship of 'efficiency,'
Of whatever 'works' no matter to what ends,
The general feeling that if a thing
'Runs like a machine' it is all right
– That there can be no higher praise;
Mechanical authoritarianism,
A Lord Lloyd thinking 'the whole method of conference
Adverse to efficient government'
– Those (as Leonard Woolf has said)
Who question the authority of the machine,
Who claim the right to do what they want
And to be governed by themselves,
Condemned as rebels and extremists
Against whose claims to freedom of soul
It is the primary duty of all loyal citizens
To vindicate the machinery of law and order
– Against the claims of
Aminu Kano in Nigeria,
Cheddi Jagan in 'British' Guiana,
Liam Kelly and the Fianna Uladh in Northern Ireland.

But if, as could be, ninety per cent.
Of human drudgery were abolished tomorrow
And the great masses of mankind given

Ample incomes and freed for 'higher things'
They could no more live than fish out of water,
They could not sustain life on that level
– On any level worthy of Man at all.

The ancestors of oysters and barnacles had heads.
Snakes have lost their limbs
And ostriches and penguins their power of flight.
Man may just as easily lose his intelligence.
Most of our people already have.
It is unlikely that man will develop into anything higher
Unless he desires to and is prepared to pay the cost.
Otherwise we shall go the way of the dodo and kiwi.
Already that process seems far advanced.
Genius is becoming rarer,
Our bodies a little weaker in each generation,
Culture is slowly declining,
Mankind is returning to barbarism
And will finally become extinct.

'Let us endure and see injustice done.
It is but for an indefinite period.'
Already in every connection
The bulk of our people
And above all our ruling class
(Utterly unscrupulous neurotics for whom
Betrayals, lies, and murders are merely
The natural tools of existence)
Are unconscious of inescapable facts
– Everywhere there is class blindness,
Fantastic miscalculations of statemanship,
Atrocities unequalled
In the long history of trickery and deceit.
Countless millions whose mental condition should be obvious
To any village constable across the street
Labouring under the crassest delusions
In an increasingly desperate and catastrophic
Condition of world affairs,

With a suicidal contempt, a Gadarene stampede
Against good will, intelligence, and honour.
A determined cancer of filth destroying all
The constructive elements in our race,
And the only hopeful element
Evidences here and there in quarters
Where even that was hardly to be hoped for
Of suddenly awakened, and therefore bewildered, panic.
Bren guns, Devoitine fighters,
Pylons and petrol pumps,
Tinned frogs, more laws,
More licences, more verbots,
More inspectors,
More and redder red tape
In every phase of life.
But *everywhere*!

Above all I rejoice that we are not
All 'Joan Thompson's bairns'
But that there are many, perhaps countless,
Psychologically incommensurable,
Even mutually incomprehensible, types
(Can any human being ever understand another?
The great Gods, Work, Money, Government,
May require and secure conformity,
But all finally good considerations require
The accentuation of such differences
To the Nth degree.)[1]
Of human beings – sanguine, mercurial,
Jovial, phlegmatic, melancholic, saturnine,
Stockard's 'linear' and 'lateral' types,
Sheldon's classification in terms
Of somatotonic, viscerotonic, and cerebrotonic.
The person who, if he went mad,
Would be a manic depressive, cannot comprehend

[1] The author is in complete disagreement with the social theory of Talcott Parsons and its implications concerning limits to the range of variation of which human society is capable.

The potential victim of schizophrenia.
It is all but impossible for the melancholy man
To enter the universe inhabited by the choleric.
Some people are so clear sighted they can see
The moons of Jupiter without a telescope;
In some the sense of smell is so keen that,
After a little training, they can enumerate
All the constituent elements in a perfume
Composed of fifteen to twenty separate substances;
Some people can detect minute variations of pitch
To which the majority of ears are deaf . . .
Ah, types of mind and body,
(Do not talk to me about likemindedness,
Brotherhood of man, democracy, or any such rot)
The Pyknic, the Asthenic, the Dysplasias,
The *Breviligne*, and all the others,
Or shall we gather in a schizophrenic group
The hebephrenes, paraphrenes, and pre-psychotic schizoids
Or go on to consider the syntonics,
The cyclothymes, the schizothymes . . .?
'Now by the two-headed Janus,
Nature hath framed strange fellows in her time.'
'I, the Lord, try the heart, I try the reins.'
'What care I for the limbs, the thighs, the good proportions of a man?
Give me the spirit.'

We must look at the harebell as if
We had never seen it before.
Remembrance gives an accumulation of satisfaction
Yet the desire for change is very strong in us
And change is in itself a recreation.
To those who take any pleasure
In flowers, plants, birds, and the rest
An ecological change is recreative.
(Come. Climb with me. Even the sheep are different
And of new importance.
The coarse-fleeced, hardy Herdwick,
The Hampshire Down, artificially fed almost from birth,

And butcher-fat from the day it is weaned,
The Lincoln-Longwool, the biggest breed in England,
With the longest fleece, and the Southdown
Almost the smallest – and between them thirty other breeds,
Some whitefaced, some black,
Some with horns and some without,
Some long-wooled, some short-wooled,
In England where the men, and women too,
Are almost as interesting as the sheep.)
Everything is different, everything changes,
Except for the white bedstraw which climbs all the way
Up from the valleys to the tops of the high passes
The flowers are all different and more precious
Demanding more search and particularity of vision.
Look! Here and there a pinguicula eloquent of the Alps
Still keeps a purple-blue flower
On the top of its straight and slender stem.
Bog-asphodel, deep-gold, and comely in form,
The queer, almost diabolical, sundew,
And when you leave the bog for the stag moors and the rocks
The parsley fern – a lovelier plant
Than even the proud Osmunda Regalis –
Flourishes in abundance
Showing off oddly contrasted fronds
From the cracks of the lichened stones.
It is pleasant to find the books
Describing it as 'very local.'
Here is a change indeed!
The universal *is* the particular.

(And in a poem like this, of course
Dealing with Plato and the East,
One must range the library[1]

[1] See *The Alexandrian Library* by Edward Alexander Parsons (London, 1952), especially with regard to the loss of the invaluable 'Pinakes' of Callimachus, a *catalogue raisonné* in one hundred and twenty volumes, of the contents of the library and therefore of all ancient literature; and also the references to the five great librarians, who were also chancellors of the University, dynamic figures who

Of an Epicurean contemporary of Cicero,
Philodemos, whose works were brought to light
More than a century and a half ago
In the lava that covered Herculaneum
Though it is only recently
That a narrative of the death
And of the last sayings of Plato
With a Chaldean guest,
And the polemic of Philodemos's master,
Epicurus, with Aristotle, have been reconstructed
– A polemic full of very instructive allusions
To the instructions received
By Aristotle and Plato,
And containing also a reproach
Made to the Academia by Epicurus,
That of being perverted
By the influence of the East.
To these we must join
The letters of Plato himself
And also a letter
Of his successor, Spensippos,
To the King of Macedonia,
Philippos, father of Alexander.
The authenticity of those documents,
For a long time disdained as false,
Is recognised to-day and one finds there,
In the relations between the Platonic School
And many Oriental personalities,
Indications which, surprising as they may seem,
Must be taken into serious consideration.
Not only that in the form,
And especially the introduction, of his Dialogues
Plato imitated the dialogues
Of the Buddha with his disciples
In Indian literature,

---

catalogued the enormous collection, translated it, assessed it, annotated, purified,
and amended the classics – laying the foundation of that exact science whose
accents and punctuation we employ today.

But the masterly work of Rudolf Hirzel
On the story of philosophical dialogue in Greece shows
That the question is infinitely more complicated
And that during a long literary production
Plato constantly perfected his manner
Without leaving out
The hypothesis of such a borrowing.
And after considering orphic texts
In interpreting the great myth
At the end of the 'Republic' of Plato
We must proceed to consider
Some of the philosophical romances
Of Herakleides Pontikos
– Especially the history of the legendary 'Empedotimos'
Whom Herakleides represented going to hunt
With his comrades and then during the heat of noon,
While he was left alone,
Suddenly seeing Pluto and Proscrpine appear.
In the dazzling light which surrounds these divinities
Spontaneous visions shcwed to the hero
'The whole truth about the soul.'
He would have, among others, perceived
Three doors and three ways leading
– Quite as in the vision of Er –
The one to the gods of Heaven,
The others to Tartarus.)

The influence of Plato's and Aristotle's metaphysics
Over scholastic and modern logic
Has, on the whole, been unfortunate.
We cite the dilemma of the *Meno*
And the Aristotelian definition of 'learning'
As 'generated by pre-existing knowledge,'
Not only because of the obvious ultimacy
Of these famous passages, but also
Because Plato's appeal to 'mythology' at this point
Betrays his suspicion
Of the proximity of sheer mystery,

While even Aristotle's less timorous dip
Into the 'delusively clear waters,'
With its wavering between the 'higher' and 'lower' νοῦς
And its hesitant identification of the latter
With αἴσθησις and ἐπαγωγή, reveals
A subtle consciousness of the same significance.
The metaphysical quarrel between Plato and Aristotle
Regarding the status of the hypostatized universal
Involves no disagreement within logic.
To proceed from these beginnings to argue
That Aristotle's limitations as a mathematician
Availed nothing to save him from falling
Into Plato's undue emphasis upon static unity
Or consenting to Plato's expulsion
Of the temporal and contingent
From the realm of the fully knowable.
Along these lines the wilderness of epistemology
May be made to blossom like the rose
Even if it is not made clear,
Granting all or most of the conclusions so reached,
Where a place remains for any kind of logic
Among the towering forms of Science, Phenomenalism and
        Psychology,
Unless perhaps it lies in discharging
The humble function of a species
Of philosophical Exchequer and Audit department.

The difficulty here is maximally the same
As that with which Thurman Arnold deals when he says:
'Definition is ordinarily supposed
To produce clarity of thinking.
It is not generally recognised
That the more we define our terms
The less descriptive they become
And the more difficulty we have in using them.'[1]

[1] *The Folklore of Capitalism* by Thurman W. Arnold (Yale University Press, 1937).

Hence it is here to the Nth degree
As it is with Mozart – All those
Who have really appreciated Mozart
Will admit that at one time or another
They have felt certain Mozart masterpieces
As one would feel a still, bright, perfect, cloudless day.
Such a day has no meaning, none of the suggestiveness,
The 'atmosphere,' the character, of a day of cloud or storm.
Such a day does not provoke or in the faintest degree
Suggest one mood rather than another.
It is infinitely protean.
It means just what you mean.
It is intangible, immaterial,
Fitting your spirit like a glove.
Then suddenly there will pass through you a tremor of terror.
A moment comes when that tranquillity,
That perfection, take on a ghastly ambiguity.
That music still suggests nothing, nothing at all;
It is still just infinitely ambiguous.
Then you may remember the phrase of a German critic
Who wrote of the 'demoniacal clang' of Mozart.
Then you look at a genuine portrait of Mozart
And – you see a straight jutting profile,
With a too-prominent nose
And an extraordinary salience of the upper lip,
And for an instant you feel as if you have had a revelation.
But that revelation escapes you
As suddenly as it came
And you are left face to face with a mask
Whose directness and clarity is completely baffling.
Pushkin's Salieri who wanted
To poison Mozart was right.
He should have poisoned Pushkin too.

Like Stifter (*Seelenfrieden-Stifter* they punned)
Whom Nietzsche (!) commended and in whom
What seemed natural harmony and simple purity
Is now seen as concealing a bitter struggle,

Profound and terrible behind the idyllic facade,
– Stifter engaged throughout his life
In an unconscious and piecemeal process
Of self-destruction – a manic depressive psychotic
Revealed in this gentle creature,
This pious *Heimatdichter*, intent above all
To hide the authentic reaction of his self to the world.
Feeling all is blind and senseless chaos
And so, that his inner life, threatened by evil,
Must be kept holy, buried alive in 'the simple life.'
Stifter, trying to eliminate all
The demonic elements from his world
And substitute for them the *Sanftes Gesetz des Seins*,
Only to have the demonic re-enter his work
In the subtle and uncanny disguise
Of simplicity and innocence.[1]
So the American angler is right who tells how,
First fishing in England with the dry-fly,
He lost fish by striking too soon and too hard.
He deems this due to the difference between
English and American conditions; in our chalk streams
Every movement of the fish is seen
While in America, though their rivers
Are apparently clear enough, they have not
The 'gin' clearness of which so much has been written.
But it is not only the American visitor
Who loses the best fish by striking too soon.
It requires 'iron nerves' for all fishermen,
English or others, to hold their hands
When the great nose of a four-pounder
Slowly rises to the fly. So Pushkin is clear enough
But he can't be caught. There is a genius
In literature too like the Zambesi crocodile
That keeps its powerful jaws wide open
What time a bird hops about in the gape

[1] Eric Lunding: *Adalbert Stifter*. Studien Zur Kunst und Existenz (Copenhagen, 1952). Curt Honoff: *Adalbert Stifter*. Seine dichterischen Mittel und die Prosa des XIX (Düsseldorf, 1952).

Picking food from between the teeth.
The bird is never injured. The crocodile
Appreciates its service as a toothpick.[1]

(Moreover as I have often told
My angling friend Norman MacCaig
If I went fishing I could not be content
With salmon or brown trout.
My heart would be set on an oar-fish,
'King of the Herrings,' with its long tapering tail,
Continuous scarlet dorsal fin,
Scarlet erectile crest, and pelvic fins,
Placed far forward, transformed
In long slender oar-like blades.
And then[2] I'd have dorado,
The golden fish of the Alto Paraná,
The giant wels or sheat-fish which runs
To 600 lb in the Volga,
The African tiger-fish,
'The fiercest fish that swims,'
Sail-fish, marlin, wahoo, tarpon, tuna,
Sword-fish in New Zealand, and the great mako shark,
And largest of the true giants of the sea,
Largest of living animals indeed,
The blue rorqual . . . and even then
I'd remember with Herman Melville
That behind Leviathan
There's still the kraken,
And no end to our 'ontological heroics.'
And MacCaig has laughed and said
'Let me see you catch anything yet
Big enough not to throw in again.')

[1] Cf. Herodotus (II 68).
[2] *Vide* Goethe: *Dichtung und Wahrheit*, p. 385. 'Weil meine Empfindung wie mein Urteil nicht leicht etwas völlig ausschloss' (Because my way of feeling, like my judgment, was not prone to exclude anything completely).

The Meeting of the East and the West

'WILT thou unite in one name heaven and earth?
Then I name you, Shakuntala, you, and all is said'
Goethe wrote – and that is my concern too,
And as I view it here in its entirety again
I am confronted with a gigantic maze
Of faulty knowledge, indirections, and distortions of all kinds,
Remembering how Anton von Pforr translated the Panchatantra
Into German, not from the original Sanskrit, but from a Latin version
Itself derived from Hebrew, Arabian, and Pahlavi renderings;
How the Dutchman Roger's 'Open Door to the Hidden Paganism,'
With its prose translation of 200 maxims
Of the Sanskrit poet Bhartrihari, was long the chief source
From which the West drew its knowledge of the religion and
    literature of the Hindus
Influencing even Goethe and Herder. One of the chief sources
On which the 18th century relied was a translation of the 'Ezour
    Veda,'
Supposed to be a commentary to the Vedas,
In which Christian occidental monotheism was taught,
But in fact a forgery used by missionaries for the purpose of
    conversion.
Actual investigation of Indian literature only began
At the end of the 18th century – Sir Charles Wilkins,
Sir William Jones, Sir Henry Thomas Colebrooke,
H. H. Wilson, Anquetil Du Perron (who translated the Upanishads
From the Persian versions of Sultan Darashekoh).
Herder expressed his love for the 'tender Indian Philosophy
Which cannot but ennoble mankind'; Goethe
In his letter to the French Sanskrit scholar, Chézy,
Tells, in 1830, how 40 years earlier
He 'could not be quiet until I studied it profoundly
. . . Felt myself drawn to the impossible undertaking
. . . I grasp only the inconceivable impression made upon me
Of the most subtle wisdom of life, of the purest moral endeavour,

Of the most dignified majesty, and most earnest contemplation of
   God;'
At the same time he remains nevertheless 'Lord and master of his
   creation,
So that he may dare to employ vulgar and laughable contrasts,
Which must be regarded as necessary connecting links
On the organised form.' Schiller shared Goethe's high idea
Of the Shakuntala. Of other Indian poems
Goethe especially admired the Meghaduta and the Gitagovinda
And treated Indian subjects in 'Der Gott und die Bayadere'
And the 'Pariah-trilogy,' while, as the Prologue on the Theatre
   shows,
The Indian drama influenced his 'Faust' technically.
Goethe himself did not know Sanskrit. Still
It attracted him so much that he made attempts
In writing in Devanâgâri, still to be seen in the Goethe-Archive.

Friedrich Schlegel learned Sanskrit, aided by Alexander Hamilton,
And the result of his study was his epoch-making treatise
'Über die Sprache und Weisheit der Indier:
Ein Beitrag zur Begründung der Altertumskunde,'
Throwing light on hitherto totally obscure fields of remotest antiquity.
Thanks to his amazing power of entering into totally different literary
   ideas
August Wilhelm Schlegel became the real founder
Of Sanskrit philology on German soil. At the same time
– Giving to linguistics what A. W. Schlegel gave to literature –
Franz Bopp studied Sanskrit in Paris and went on
To give comparative philology the rank of a science,
Not making the similar sound of words, which might be a matter
   of chance
Or caused through its origin, the base of his investigations,
But investigating the flexion and the whole build of words,
In fact, the whole formation of the language.

Lassen, Weber, Roth, Boehtlingk, Max Müller,
Buehler, Keelhorn, Oldenberg, and countless others
Have since continued the work of Schlegel and Bopp.

Humboldt had a fine understanding for the individuality of Indian
    ideas,
Shown especially in his treatise on the Bhagavad-gita,
'Perhaps the profoundest and most sublime work the world has ever
    known.'
Friedrich Rückert earned immortal fame by his congenial and perfect
Translations from the Sanskrit – above all in the 'Gitagovinda'
Where he not only gives a true version of the original text,
But recreates the rhythm and the plays on words and rhymes
In perfect imitation till no wish is left unsatisfied.
According to Paul Deussen, Kant may be said
To have 'given the scientific basis for the intuitive doctrines of
    Shankara'
(Stcherbatsky calls attention also to similarities between lines of thought
Of Kant and later Buddhistic thinkers like Chandrakirti).
Fichte in his essay 'Anweisung zu einem seligen Leben'
Comes near to the Advaita doctrine most amazingly
– So much so that Otto[1] has even attempted to give
Whole passages of Fichte in the language of Shankara.
There are parallels to Indian philosophy in Hegel too,
Especially regarding his dialectics and that
Of the great Mahayana teacher, Nagarjuna.[2]
(But these parallels are really no more
Than mere coincidences of particular results
Arrived at from totally different starting points
– Of Nagarjuna Hegel knew nothing,
And all he had heard of Indian philosophy
Made no impression on him at all.)

Schelling's interest for India on the other hand
Was very lively, especially in his later life
When he worked on his 'Philosophie der Mythologie und
    Offenbarung'
And placed the Upanishads higher than the Biblical books,
Holding that the latter 'can in no way be compared
As regards real religious feeling with many others

[1] R. Otto: *Westöstliche Mystik* (Gotha, 1926).
[2] See Stcherbatsky: *The Conception of Buddhist Nirvana* (Leningrad, 1927).

Of former and later times, especially the sacred writings of India.'
Schopenhauer acknowledges a powerful stimulation from India,
Reading the Upanishads in the Latin translation
Made by Duperron from the Persian 'Oupnekhat.'
His praise of the 'Oupnekhat' is well-known: –
'We breathe Indian air and original, spontaneous existence . . .
Every line is so full of firm, defined, and thoroughly consequential
    meaning.'
'Who, however, sees the supreme God live in all beings,
Who never vanishes, when they vanish, who sees him
Is really seeing. For he who sees the same God
Live in everything will not hurt himself,
Through himself, and thus walks the highest path.'

Some interpreters of Buddhism, such as F. O. Schräder,
Regard the 'Trishnâ' as a metaphysical centre-point
Of Buddhistic doctrine, and thus give it a position
Coinciding with Schopenhauer's will as the pith of every individual.
But this interpretation does not, in my opinion,
Correspond with the facts. But parallels can be adduced
With the Mahayana-Buddhism, as it comes very close
To the Vedanta in its doctrine, and has features in common
With Schopenhauer's morality of pity in his altruistic ethics.
Von Hartmann teaches the religion of the future
Will be a combination of the abstract pantheism
Of the Vedanta and the Judaeo-Christian monotheism,
And declares that in one place of the Vedântist 'Pancadashaprakarana'
His 'world-principle, the Unconscious,' is characterised
Better and more exactly than by any of the latest European thinkers.[1]

Nietzsche through Schopenhauer became acquainted with Indian
    ascetic philosophy,
But was afterwards a strong opponent of it, though he had always
A high regard for the social philosophy of the Laws of Manu.
We meet many Buddhistic ideas in Wagner's operas.
In 1855 he sketched a great musical drama, 'Die Sieger,'
The source of which was a story of the Divyâvadâna.[2]

[1] E. von Hartmann: *Die Philosophie des Unbewussten* (Leipsig, 1904).
[2] See Pero Slepčevič: *Buddhismus in der deutschen Literatur.*

E

Buddhistic subjects are treated in subsequent operas
– In Max Vogrich's 'Buddha' and Adolf Vogl's 'Maya.'
Michael Beer, Ferdinand von Hornstein,
Gottfried von Boehm, Leopold von Schroder,
Karl Gjellerup have based dramas on Indian themes.
But few German Buddhists yet have tried to go
'The path from home to homelessness,'
And as to Indian thought and literature generally,
It is still little more than a century
That Indian wisdom and Indian poetry
Have extended their 'Digvijaya' to the West.

Heine's words remain true: 'Portuguese, Dutchmen, and Englishmen
Have brought home from India the treasures in their big ships.
We were only lookers-on. But the spiritual treasures of India
Shall not escape us.' We cannot accept a divided world,
Or Max Müller's hemispheroidal classification of race characteristics,
As when he says: 'It is a problem worth considering whether,
As there is in nature a north and south,
There are not two hemispheres also in human nature.'

Yeats has advised young poets to go to the Upanishads,
And a greater interest in Indian thoughts and ideas
Exists nowhere in the world than in my mind
– One may see in this a spiritual sympathy and affinity
That keeps near to a friend also from afar
As is expressed in a Sanskrit verse of extreme beauty:

दूरसगोऽपि न दूरस्थ: सजनानां सुद्वज्जन: ।
चन्द्र: कुमुदखंडातां दूरस्थोऽपि प्रबोकध: ॥

Over a century ago the Collège de France
Had a Chinese chair, occupied by Abel Remusat
Who translated 'Ju Kiao Li' and delighted
Leigh Hunt, Thomas Carlyle, and John Sterling.
Théophile Gautier thought Chinese the most important language in
    the world

And secured a native tutor for his daughter.
A like enthusiasm is shared by Maspero, Pelliot, and Laloy;
And in the English-speaking world there is at least Ezra Pound.

It is not easy to enter into the soul of Chinese music
Which is a mere ting-yang monotone to most Westerners.
Yet Laloy thinks the union of the music of China and Europe possible
Because the scales are constructed upon exactly the same notes.

'Music imparts the same emotion to all those who listen to it:
It encourages humanity.'
'The points of contact do exist. To discover them
It would be necessary to know the history of music
Not only in Germany but in Europe
From the Middle Ages down to the present.'
He is right. And that is true not only of music
But of everything else in regard to the union
Of the East and the West. As Laloy says:
'The silence is only broken by a stream,
Falling in a series of waterfalls,
But invisible beneath the dark moss.
We are like those initiated into the mysteries,
Who hunt for the cloven mushroom,
Shining among dark undergrowth,
Which is said to prolong human life.'

England is Our Enemy[1]

The wrong that is as one with England's name,
Tyranny with boast of liberty, and shame
With boast of righteousness.

> FRANCIS ADAMS: Songs of the Army of the Night

How much knowledge of imaginative literature
Does it need to make a proper man?
It used to be said that a proper man was one
Who had built a house, planted a tree,
Begotten a son, and written a book,
And something else . . . played in a county cricket match, perhaps!
At any rate, the implication was
That a civilised human being should devote a fifth
Of his time and thoughts to the arts and the humaner letters.
That is more than enough
If the studies are pursued with intelligence.

---

[1] 'Our attitude to the literature of the past is almost invariably a kind of genteel idolatry. Instead of asking questions of our great writers we approach them with a pious irrelevancy that makes our reading of their works resemble a tourist's pilgrimage to Stratford-on-Avon. Their books lie on our shelves, to be respectfully neglected as so many cultural household gods, or invoked as totems to ward off the onslaught of history. We retire into the cosy warmth of Trollope's England or throw ourselves on the flat bosom of Aunt Betsey Trotwood to get away from the horrors of our day and age. At its best this kind of literary appreciation results in the sort of critical biography at which English men of letters excel. At its worst it leads to the arch parlour-game that we all know so well – the analysis of Branwell Brontë's influence on Charlotte, the discussion of the comparative merits of Jane Austen's heroines. . . . There is something almost indecent about the way in which we rediscover our great writers, remembering them in their centenary years, recalling their eccentricity and charm, their picture in the National Portrait Gallery, their niche in the columbarium of genius. The French re-discover their great writers all the time, but with them such rediscovery is a living intellectual process, a continual restatement of the moral "Great Debate" which has to be fought out in each generation. . . . Since I first read it, I have been haunted by a kind of parable in M. Sartre's *What Is Literature*, which I think expresses the peculiar danger facing English literary criticism today. "It must be borne in mind that most critics are men who have not had much luck and who, just about the time they were growing desperate, found a quiet little job as cemetery watchman. . . ."'

John Raymond on the B.B.C. Third Programme.

Eternity will be insufficient to civilise us
If we pursue our slipshod courses.

In the plastic arts, in music, in all foreign literatures
There are artists one calls axioms
. . . Not because they were supremely great by temperament,
But because they worked supremely
Along one or other technical line.
You may not like Whistler, but you have to accept him
As a prototype of a form of art
You may not like Jan Van Eyck, Dürer,
Holbein, Velasquez, Rubens, Rembrandt,
Ghirlandaio, Praxiteles, or even Raphael,
But you cannot ignore them
Even should Hokusai be your own master.
Similarly you may not like but cannot ignore
Bach and Palestrina.
It is the same, so far as all but the English
Are concerned, with literature.

No Frenchman can ignore, not the temperaments
But the technical skill,
Of Chateaubriand, Racine, Villon, Gautier,
Musset, Maupassant, Flaubert, and a great
Many other writers from Mallarmé back to Ronsard.
Indeed no human being can afford to ignore them.
. . . Or Heine, Goethe, Leopardi, Lope de Vega, Turgenev,
Chekhov, Dante, Bertran de Born, Boccaccio,
Catullus, Petronius Arbiter, Apuleius and many more.
To be ignorant – to be utterly ignorant –
Of the methods of any one of these writers
Is to be to that extent ignorant
Of some of the ways by which humanity
Can be approached, cajoled, enlightened,
Or moulded into races,
To know all the writings of Heine
Is not necessary, but not to know
How Heine mixed, alternated, or employed

Flippancies and sentiment is to have a blind spot
In your knowledge of how
A part of humanity may be appealed to.

Who among English writers is thus axiomatic?
Accepted thus by either the Anglo-Saxon
Or the foreigner of some culture?
You will say in your haste:
'But there are *hundreds*!'
After cursory reflection you will say:
'*But* . . . there are none.'

The name of Shakespeare jumps at once to the lips.
But when it comes to the methods of Shakespeare
We know nothing about them
And it is to be doubted
If the Germans know more.
And no other name at all jumps
Or comes ever so reluctantly to the lips.

Why should our Government never think
Of spreading broadcast amongst our men in the Forces
The works of Dickens, Thackerary, Tennyson,
. . . Or even those of Shakespeare?
Why do we not think it essential
That our lawyers and medical men
Should know the works of Meredith at least,
If not those of Henry James?
You will answer it is because Anglo-Saxondom
. . . And a very good thing, too, you will interject . . .
Has never suffered its Governments
To interfere with the arts.
But that is not the answer.

The Foreigner sees or feels that the national arts
Are a product of the national voice
And no Government on the continent of Europe
Can subsist without

Paying some attention to that voice.
So the German State makes axioms of Schiller and Goethe;
The French Republic produces the plays
Of Racine and Molière; Italy
Honours Dante, Tasso, and Petrarch
Whenever it has an opportunity.

We are accustomed to be told
That Anglo-Saxondom would not tolerate
Government interference with the arts;
That it would depose its kings,
Refuse to elect its presidents,
Revolt, erect barricades,
If the State had theatres in which Shakespeare,
Congreve, Vanbrugh, Robertson, and, say, Goethe
Were honoured by classical-minded renderings!
But Anglo-Saxondom wouldn't; Anglo-Saxondom
Does not know that it has any arts;[1]
Does not even know
That play-writing is an art.
If we did know we had arts and neglected them,
Or that the State neglected them,
We might, we should, revolt,
Refuse to pay our taxes
As did the Paris grocers, drink-shop keepers,
Paviors, and municipal slaughterers.

[1] '. . . the consummate diligence with which the moderns – the Anglo-Saxons, in particular – have ignored the strictly poetical works of the still living great of the slightly older generation. It is perhaps safe to say that comparatively few of Thomas Hardy's admirers really understand how much finer is *The Dynasts* than, say, *Tess of the D'Urbervilles*, or even *Jude the Obscure*. But a worse destiny has overtaken the great poets of foreign nations who have outlived their generation. If they are known at all to the English-speaking peoples, it is by their prose or dramatic works; their poetry is hardly read at all. Thus we know d'Annunzio chiefly as the author of *Il Fuoco*, the most unforgivably swinish novel ever written; Verner von Heidenstam by his *Folkungsträdet*, Rainer Maria Rilke by a treatise on Rodin, Hugo von Hofmannsthal by the libretto of *Der Rosenkavalier*, and William Butler Yeats by his discourtesy. Of Kostes Palamas, Endre Ady, Rubén Darío, Amado Nervo, Otokar Březina, Alexander Blok, Holger Drachmann, Antonio Machado, and a dozen other fine spirits, still living or but recently dead, we know, so to speak, little more than their names and quarterings.'
                    William A. Drake, *Contemporary European Writers*.

When the French Government tried to economise
By cutting down the subsidy to the Opera.

But the arts, and particularly the written arts,
Of Great Britain have been forced
By the 'highly refined imagination
Of the more select classes,'[1]
Have been so forced out of all contact with
Or inspiration from the masses
That, inasmuch as any human manifestation
That is taken in hand by any coterie
Or Class of the More Select
Must speedily die,
So literature in Anglo-Saxondom
Has, after growing
More and more provincial, died.

That is not to say that no one
Who writes to-day can write;
It means that the best writers of to-day
Can find only a handful of readers apiece
In the United States;
And only one handful for all the lot of them
In the British Empire . . . say 14,000.

The populations of the British Empire and the United States
Are, say three hundred millions; thus,
Mathematically put, the fraction of readers
For the best work to-day is:

$$\frac{14,000}{300,000,000.}$$

It means that in each 100,000 souls
Five are reasonably civilised.

[1] Shelley: Preface to *Prometheus Unbound*.

So our literature cannot be called
A very national or even racial affair.
Yet every inhabitant of Athens,
Slaves, helots, and all, must
In the age of Pericles, have had
At least a nodding acquaintance
With the works of Sophocles, Euripides or Pheidias.
Every one of them!

Literature of the imagination in Anglo-Saxondom then
Is not a very thriving national affair
Because it has lost touch completely
With racial life.

To distinctly English writers in England
Authenticity is never allowed;
The quality is perhaps
Not even known to exist.
There are too many vested interests.
In the United States Mark Twain
Could finally make headway
Against the Transcendentalists;
Poe could stand with his body starved
But his mind making its mark.
He had to fight many battles
Against many unscrupulous cliques,
And in the end his head became
Both bloody and bowed
But neither he, alive
Nor his reputation, he dead,
Have had to contend with the dead weight
Of dead, vested interests
And merely political disingenuousnesses
That have strangled
Most literary brightnesses
In England for a hundred years.
These tendencies work
Towards a wilderness of thumbs down.

It was Landor who first said
That every Frenchman takes a personal share
In the glory of his poets
Whereas every Englishman resents
The achievements of his poets
Because they detract
From the success of his own 'poetry';
And the remark was extraordinarily profound.
So the English literary world
Is an immense arena
Where every spectator is intent
On the deaths of those awaiting judgment
And every gladiator is intent
On causing the death of his fellow–combatant
By smiting him with the corpses
Of others predeceased.
The method, the mania, the typical
'Fair–play' of 'the sporting English'
Is really extraordinary in its operation.

Supposing, having no pet author of your own
Out of whose entrails
You hope to make a living,
No political bias,
No interest in a firm of publishers
Who make dividends out of other 'classics'
You timidly venture to remark
That Trollope, Jane Austen,
And the Mrs. Gaskell of Mary Barton,
Are English Authors
Authentic in their methods.

'*But*' you hear the professional reviewers
All protesting at once
'Trollope has not the humour of Dickens,
The irony of Thackeray,
The skill with a plot of Wilkie Collins.
Jane Austen has not the wit of Meredith,

The reforming energy of Charles Reade,
The imperial sense of Charles Kingsley,
The tender pathos of the author of *Cranford*.
And as for Mrs. Gaskell who wrote *Cranford*,
Well, she has not the aloofness of Jane Austen,
And Christina Rossetti had not
The manly optimism of Browning,
And Browning lacked the religious confidence
Of Christina Rossetti, or the serenity
Of Matthew Arnold. And who was Matthew Arnold?
Landor could not write about whist and old playbills
Like Charles Lamb.
(*Saint Charles, Thackeray murmured softly*!)

No one who has paid any attention at all
To official-critical appraisements of English writers
Can gainsay the moral to be drawn
From these instances of depreciation
Or the truth of the projection itself.
Literary figures should, of course,
As is said of race-horses, be 'tried high,'
But to attach a Derby winner to a stone cart,
And then condemn it as a horse
Because it does not make so much progress
As a Clydesdale or a Percheron
Is to try the animal
Altogether too high.
And not fairly.

English official criticism has erected
A stone-heap, a dead load of moral qualities.
A writer must have optimism, irony,
A healthy outlook,
A middle-class standard of morality,
As much religion as, say, St. Paul had,
As much atheism as Shelley had . . .
And, finally, on top of an immense load
Of self-neutralising moral and social qualities,

Above all, Circumspection,
So that, in the end, no English writer
According to these standards,
Can possess authenticity.
The formula is this: Thackeray is not Dickens,
So Thackeray does not represent English literature.
Dickens is not Thackeray, so *he*
Does not represent English literature.
In the end literature itself is given up
And you have the singular dictum
Of the doyen of English official literary criticism.
This gentleman writes . . . but always rather uncomfortably . . .
Of Dryden as divine, of Pope as divine,
Of Swift as so filthy
As to intimidate the self-respecting critic.
But when he comes to Pepys of course
His enthusiasm is unbounded.
He salutes the little pawky diarist
With an affection, an enthusiasm,
For his industry, his pawkiness,
His thumb-nail sketches.
Then he asserts amazingly:
'This is scarcely literature'
And continues with panegyrics that leave no doubt
That the critic considers the Diary
To be something very much better.
The judgment is typically English.
The bewildered foreigner can only say:
'But if the Diary is all you assert of it,
It must be literature, or, if it is not literature,
It cannot be all you assert of it.'
And obviously . . .

I once met a Peruvian who had come
To London to study English literature.
He said: 'Oh! but your writers, they pant and they pant;
Producing and producing! And then, as the type,
The Archtype, you have . . .

Charles Lamb *On Buttered Toast*!'
I said: 'Ah! That is because
You are not an Englishman!'

So our business men pretend to take pride
In the quite false assertion that they have no time
For reading books . . . And so we remain
A blot on the world, and our populations
Are regarded as more and more suspect.
That is a misfortune because our writers,
Hampered as they are by political necessities,
By hypocritical and crystallised moralities,
And by commercial pressures, have yet,
As it were between the blasts of these storms,
Produced a great body of beautiful and humane work;
Enough to entitle us to occupy a place
In the comity of civilised nations.

Suppose a British Cabinet Minister or an American high politician
Were asked to stand up in a Walhalla of the nations
And claim for their twin civilisations
Their place in the sun,
On what achievements would he base their claim?
He would talk about the steam engine, the spinning jenny,
The steam-hammer, the electric telegraph, submarine cables,
The gramophone, the 'movies,' wireless.
Being at this point probably coughed down
He would hazard, more dubiously, a new departure.
He would begin to talk of evolutions of freedoms
And moralities; of Houses of Representatives,
Of Congressmen, Commons, County Councils;
Of Colonial traditions, ballot-boxes, institutions,
Of perfecting the factory system,
Of modern industrial life which is nowhere so . . .
As for our favoured lands . . . the purity of . . .
In our great cit . . . initiation of legislation . . .
Against the White Slave Traf . . . Anti-Alco . . .
Non-Secret Dip . . .

His voice being drowned, puzzled and irritated
He would cease, and in the eventually resulting silence
A kindly Scandinavian would be heard to prompt:
'Speak about Mr. Shaw!'

'Oh! Ah, yes!' He would grasp at the proffered branch.
'There's Shakespeare . . . and . . . Shakespeare . . . and Lord Byron
. . . But perhaps he's a little too . . . And . . .
Of course Shakespeare . . . and . . .
Did someone say Herbert Spencer? Yes, yes.
There are few branches of human activities in which
By the temperate employment of non-sectarian religion
In social problems our favoured nations . . .'

And so our cases go by default!

It is not in that way that the rest of the world
Frames its *apologia*. In the forefront
Of *Toutes les Gloires de la France* are set
Not merely the names of Napoleon, the Great Condé,
Le Roi Soleil, or merely Pasteur, Robespierre,
Danton or Lafayette; it is not merely by the names
Of Bismarck, Moltke, Marx, or Ehrlich
That Germany claims pity from Europe;
Nor does Italy ask patience solely
Because of Mazzini, Garibaldi, Savonarola;
Nor Russia only because of Peter the Great,
Schuvalof, Bakunin, Kerensky, or Lenin;
Nor yet is it because of the names
Of Ginaclis, Thetocopoulos, or Venizelos
That the name of Greece survives among the nations;
Nor will the names of Rosebery, Haldane, Balfour
The Earl of Elgin, Sir James Lithgow, the present Lochiel,
Lord Bilsland, Tom Johnston . . . quicken a spark of life
In the once-great-name of Scotland again,
Nor the Duke of Buccleuch, the Earl of Strathmore, the Earl of Airlie
Or any of the famous fatheads . . . any name at all
Known to a fraction of 1 per cent. of the Scottish people,

Our blatant vulgarians of business men,
Our brainless bankers and lawyers
Our puerile Professors and dud Divines,
And all our other 'loyal Kikuyu'

(Call the roll of our M.P.s to-day,
All our peers and public men
. . . And public women too . . . of every kind.
A single little-known name outweighs the lot,
Is of infinitely more consequence
To everything worth calling Scotland . . .
The name of Father Iain of Barra!

Or think of Cunninghame Graham whose magnificent presence
And flashing wit these hoodlums hated like Hell
Because it showed them what sub-men they are,
How horribly infra-human in comparison;
Cunninghame Graham whose passing has left Scottish life
More mean and grey than ever before.

Yes, I still retain a little
Of the vehmic type of mind,
The 'raucle tongue,' and *Hohngelächter*
That has characterised my folk so long.

And weigh my friend Ruaraidh Erskine of Marr
Against all the massed battalions of those
Who know nothing of Gaelic civilisation and culture
And yet decry both
. . . Or against those others of whom as of the lady
Who wrote a book on the Lords of the Isles
It had to be said
'Tha cuid de'n sgrìobhadh anns an leabhar so bòidheach ri
leughadh, ach is mòr am beud nach robh na's fearr eolas aig a'
    bhan-ughdair air a' chùis.')

Indeed such names as these, of thinkers and of
Men of action in fields purely material

Are the names that separate Europe into nations . . .
They provide the separate glories of France, Italy,
The Alemannic peoples, Greece . . . but the others,
The glorious names of all the imaginative writers
From Homer to the Brothers Grimm,
From Flaubert back to Apuleius,
From Catullus to Turgenev,
All these form the glories of Europe,
Their works going together to make one whole,
And each work being one stone
In a gigantic and imperishable fabric.

It is possible that a change may come.
In the general revaluation that is taking place
All the commercial considerations, the moral greasinesses,
The Professors of Literature, *Vorschungen*, university curricula,
Honours examinations, all these phenomena commercial at base
Which stand in the way of the taste for
And honouring of literature
May be estimated at their true price.
To seek to abolish them is not much good,
For they are parts of the essential imbecilities
Of pompous men – of the highly refined imaginations
Of the More Select Classes.
They should be left isolated in little towns
But their existence should not be forgotten
Or they will come creeping in again.

Plaited Like the Generations of Men[1]

COME, follow me into the realm of music. Here is the gate
Which separates the earthly from the eternal.
It is not like stepping into a strange country
As we once did. We soon learn to know everything there
And nothing surprises us any more. Here
Our wonderment will have no end, and yet
From the very beginning we feel at home.

At first you hear nothing, because everything sounds.
But now you begin to distinguish between them. Listen.
Each star has its rhythm and each world its beat.
The heart of each separate living thing
Beats differently, according to its needs,
And all the beats are in harmony.

Your inner ear grows sharper. Do you hear
The deep notes and the high notes?
They are immeasurable in space and infinite as to number.
Like ribbons, undreamt-of scales lead from one world to another,
Steadfast and eternally moved.
(More wonderful than those miraculous isles of Greece
'Lily on lily, that o'erlace the sea,'
Than the marvellous detailed intensity of Chinese life,
Than such a glimpse as once delighted me of the masterly and
      exhaustive

---

[1] 'The gods having placed Vishnu to the East surrounded him with metres (*chandobhir abhitah paryagrihan*); saying "On the south side I surround thee with the Gayatri metre; on the west side I surround thee with the Trishtubh metre; on the north I surround thee with the Jagati." Having thus surrounded him with metres, they placed Agni on the east, and thus they went on worshipping and toiling. By this means they acquired this whole earth (*tena imam sarvam prithivim samvindata*).' – Satapatha-brahmana.

'When we have once penetrated the vaults of Nature's mysterious palace we can learn to speed our soul with the wings of speech, and it will chime away in ever more blossoming and sublime melody.' (With acknowledgments to Ferruccio Busoni.)

Classification of psychical penetrations and enlacements
On which Von Hartmann relied, giving here some slight dissection
Of the antinomies underlying ethical thought, discussing there the
    gradations
Of the virtues, the stratifications of axiology, with an elaborate power
And beauty – but there! – Oh, Aodhagán Ó Rathaille meets again
The Brightness of Brightness in a lonely glen
And sees the hair that's plaited
Like the generations of men!)[1]

All the knowledge is woven[2] in neatly
So that the plaited ends come to the hand.
Pull any of the tabs, and a sequence
Of practical information is drawn.

Each sound is the centre of endless circles,
And now the *harmony* opens out before you.
Innumerable are its voices, compared with which
The boom of the harp is a screeching,
The clash of a thousand trumpets a twitter.

All, all the melodies hitherto heard and unheard
Ring out in full number together, bear you along,
Crowd over you, sweep past you – melodies of love and passion,

[1] Aodhagán Ó Rathaille, Irish Gaelic poet, 1670–1726. The reference is to O'Rahilly's great *aisling* (i.e. vision poem), *Gile na Gile*.

[2] See also the third section of Professor R. B. Onians' *The Origin of European Thought* (London 1952), which is concerned chiefly with words connected with fate which can be interpreted as terms connected with spinning and weaving and the use of their product. The word *peirar*, often translated 'end,' means a bond or cord which the gods can put on a person or an army (and Ocean is the bond round the Earth, although here the bond is slipping over into the meaning of boundary and so end); the image of binding is often used to express the power of fate or the gods over men, and if we ask what these cords are with which fate binds men, Professor Onians answers that they are the threads which fate or the gods have spun, and that in certain phrases fate itself is thought of as a thread or bond which is put upon men. A further very important chapter deals with *telos*. *Telos* (which means 'end' in later Greek) in Homer 'covers a man's eyes and nostrils,' and so seems also to be some sort of bond. *Peirar* even in Homer already has the abstract meaning of boundary, but the boundary is doubtless still felt as a physical rope. See also Professor Onians' remarks on the words *thymos*, *psyche*, *moirai*, *phren* and *noos*.

Of the Spring and the Winter, of melancholy and abandon –
And they themselves are the spirits
Of a million beings in a million ages
Revealed as Krishna revealed his form
In the Udyoga-parva of the Maha-bharata
Or like the Vision of the Universal Form (visva-rupa darsanam)
Before which Arjuna bowed with every hair on his body bristling
      with awe[1]
(Or like the tremendous vision
Which came to Buddha under the Bo-Tree
Or to Socrates when he heard, or dreamt he heard,
The Sybil of Mantinaea
Discoursing on mortal and immortal love
Or like Descartes' dream of November 10, 1619,[2]
Near the environs of Ulm
When there were presented to him,
Coming as an enquirer after truth,
A Dictionary, representing knowledge,
And the volume of the Corpus Poetarum,
Which he took to be the symbol of inspiration,
Or like the 'sudden illumination' that came
To Benchara Branford one night in his fortieth year:
'At once was born into vivid and enchanting consciousness
A new metaphysical calculus of sixty-four
Inter-related cardinal categories, of which thirty-six
Were the transmuted forms of the Geddesian concepts.'[3]
Or like the moment (not like it – it!)
By which as Kierkegaard says in *Begrebet Angest*
The individual is related to eternity,
The moment St. Paul refers to when he describes
Our all being changed 'in the twinkling of an eye.'
Because in that moment the individual chooses himself
And thereby all may be changed.
The moment partakes of eternity:
It is then eternity penetrating time.

[1] In the Bhagavad-Gita. Compare also Matthew XVII. 6 and Luke V. 8.
[2] Chevalier, *Vie de Descartes*, pp. 40–47.
[3] i.e. the concepts of the late Sir Patrick Geddes, Branford's collaborator.

How the moment can be made eternity
For the individual Kierkegaard shows
In 'Gjentagelsen' – it depends on repetition,
Kierkegaard's substitute for Plato's theory of reminiscence).

If you examine one of them more closely you will see
How it clings together with the others, is conjoined with them,
Coloured by all the shades of sound, accompanied
By all the harmonies to the foundation of foundations in the depths
And to the dome of all domes in the heights.

Now you understand how stars and hearts are one with another
And how there can nowhere be an end, nowhere a hindrance;
How the boundless dwells perfect and undivided in the spirit,
How each part can be at once infinitely great and infinitely small,
How the utmost extension is but a point, and how
Light, harmony, movement, power
All identical, all separate, and all united are life.

Svaham aham samharami.[1]

Or like that moment in which Kassner assembles[2]
The scattered fragments of his personality
By identifying a strain of music
Heard through the walls of his cell
With the struggle of his comrades throughout the world
In the same cause.

'Kassner, shaken by the song,
Felt himself reeling like a broken skeleton.
These voices called forth relentlessly
The memory of revolutionary songs
Rising from a hundred thousand throats,
Their tunes scattered and then picked up again by the crowds
Like the rippling gusts of wind over fields of wheat
Stretched out to the far horizon.

[1] I myself will again bind the braid together. (See Bhatta Narayana's well-known drama, *Veni-samhara*, i.e. 'braid-binding.')
[2] Vide *Days of Wrath*, by André Malraux.

But already the imperious gravity of a new song
Seemed once more to absorb everything into an immense slumber;
And in this calm, the music at last rose above its own heroic call
As it rises above everything
With its intertwined flames that soothe as they consume,
Night fell on the universe,
Night in which men feel their kinship on the march
Or in the vast silence,
The drifting night, full of stars and friendship.'

Or is this, albeit language
Infected by positive vision,
Until, like that of Marlowe and the early Elizabethans,
It takes on vigorous new rhythms
And a fresh accretion of savagery,
Subject still to all the objections
Commonly raised against rhetoric?
– The reflection of ideas and values
Not yet wholly assimilated by the sensibility,
So that I seem to be resolving my conflicts
By a kind of verbal self-hypnosis
– Communicating an excitement that resides
Too much in a certain use of language
And too little in the ordering of materials?
Am I only fobbing myself off
With a few more of those opiate-like phrases
Whose repetition so readily operates
As a substitute for discovery –
Instead of realising the concept
Of an ultimate metaphysical scheme
Under which we have to suppose
A triadic movement of the Universe
In the course of which
We can think of the continuous
As having existed without a beginning
And of its coming to a close,
So that the discontinuous may safely begin
. . . And of the discontinuous coming to a dead end

As it is bound to do
And the continuous reappearing
So that it may continue for ever
And never end?

Have I failed in my braid-binding
At this great crisis
When the impending task of mankind
Is to help to bring to a close the 'conflict' stage
Of the present process of the discontinuous
And to usher in the 'harmony' stage
By means of an abandonment
Of the interlocking and proselytizing technique
Of 'Warfare' and 'persuasion'?
At this moment when braidbinding as never before,
The creation of the seamless garment,
Is the poet's task?[1]

(Even so we have seen a collection of papers
Seemingly multifarious nevertheless connected with a system
As well as entwined together
By their own μέρμις φαεινή
Yet, since the silver cord is often
Intricately knotted in a delicate disorder,
One need not apologise for defining
The author's purpose as embodying
'The doctrine that factors in our experience
Are clear and distinct
In proportion to their variability,'
That 'philosophical truth is to be sought
In the presuppositions of language
And is for this reason akin to poetry,'
And that 'rationalisation is the partial fulfilment
Of the ideal to recover concrete reality
Within the disjunction of abstraction.'

[1] 'The warp seemed necessity; and here, thought I, with my own hand I ply my own shuttle, and weave my own destiny into these unalterable threads.' – Herman Melville, *Moby Dick*.

– And yet it is none too easy to satisfy oneself
As to the role maximalized 'civilisation' can play
And however resolutely we try to speak
The language of pure metaphysics
We find ourselves wondering
Whether the apotheosis of successful appetition,
Concrete and transcognitive as it may be,
Will not represent an ultimate aestheticism
Little less exclusive
Than the intellectualism of Plato.)

The spiritual evolution from vile humanity
To authentic manhood and onward
To participation in self-universal
Is an operation which bases itself
On a full realization of the transiency
Of spatial and temporal conditions,
A permeability of spirit
To those mouldings from the unconscious
Abstractable from such conditions,
An appreciation of the fiduciary status
Of the self, and an ultimate capacity
For transforming the substance of these intuitions
From speculative belief to realized experience.
But what proportion of men are likely to be saved?
I do not agree that contempt of the simple-minded
Is a limitation that is destructive
Of any poise of the spirit.
Self learns that others in their vileness
(Even those Hollywood moguls for whom
Books are only 'story properties'
Or Horace Tograth, the Australian chemist
Who led the world-wide pogrom against poets
Or Mr. Furber, the Canadian dilettante
And all yahoos and *intellectuels-flics*)
Are not subjects for persuasion and alms
But are the appointed task
By which self is to achieve its destiny.

Is this a claim on the part of the self
Of my self – to feel itself superior to other selves?
Even if it is not, the element of rigoristic intellectualism
Present in my message goes beyond
That discoverable in Kant
Who was at least imbued with a conviction
Of the immorality of the idea
That oneself can ever be viewed
As metaphysically distinguishable in status
From another. Well. We have no means
Of deciding whether others *are* selves
And, if they are, the sort
That consists with self-universal.

Everlasting layers
Of ideas, images, feelings
Have fallen upon my brain
Softly as light.
Each succession has seemed to bury
All that went before.
And yet, in reality,
Not one has been extinguished . . .
The fleeting accidents of a man's life
And its external shows may indeed
Be irrelate and incongruous,
But the organising principles
Which fuse into harmony,
And gather about fixed pre-determined centres,
Whatever heterogeneous elements
Life may have accumulated from without,
Will not permit the grandeur
Of human unity to be greatly violated,
Or its ultimate repose to be troubled,
In the retrospect from dying moments,
Or from other great convulsions. [1]
It is with me now, surveying all life
From the heights of Literature and the Arts, as it was

[1] *Vide* Thomas de Quincey's *Suspiria*.

With Thomas de Quincey when he made
A symbology of the view he commanded
From the eminence of Everton.
Liverpool represented the earth,
With its sorrows and its graves left behind,
'Yet not out of sight nor wholly forgotten.'
The moving sea typified the mind.
Here was a respite, the tumult in suspense.
Here, cried de Quincey,
Are the hopes which blossom in the paths of life
Reconciled with the peace which is in the grave;
Motions of the intellect as unwearied as the heavens,
Yet for all anxieties a halcyon calm;
Tranquillity that seems no product of inertia
But as if resulting
From mighty and equal antagonisms,
Infinite activities, infinite repose.
(Even so am I now transformed on this plane
Into the semblance of those who in lower life
Deeming all philosophical systems heretical
Because they confuse the grammar of human expression
In language, logic, or moral estimation
With the substantial structure of things,
Finding the 'human orthodoxy' round which these heresies play
'The current imagination and good sense of men'
['This orthodoxy is largely erroneous, of course,
But it is capable of correcting its own errors,'
While Heresy is perverse, a 'rebellious partisanship,
A deliberate attachment to something
The evidence against which is public and obvious;
It is a sin against the light,'
Springing from 'dominance of the foreground,'
The attempt to use as the universal criterion of reality
Some immediate, obtrusive, and familiar aspect of experience
And proclaiming that the true philosopher who is content
To 'substitute the pursuit of sincerity for the pursuit of omniscience'
Will not, with the Pragmatists, ignore everything
But utility in relation to human affairs;

Or with the Behaviourists deny the fact of consciousness;
Or with some Idealists deny everything but consciousness;
Or, with other Idealists, everything except logic;
Or, with the New Realists,
Ignore substance and the essences which characterise it,
Or, like Croce, pretend that art is sheer expression,
Imagine that aesthetic experience
Discovers a peculiar kind of good,
In the estimation of which
All other interests are irrelevant.
– Forgetting that every genuine advance in 'human orthodoxy'
Must at first seem only a new heresy
To the blindly orthodox, and that 'human orthodoxy,'
May be in some important respect
Quite radically false,
Its correction involving concentration
On some unobtrusive but deeply significant set of facts
Ignored by the orthodox]
And facing at last the possibility
That nature may be but imperfectly formed
In the bosom of chaos, and reason in us
Imperfectly adapted to the understanding of nature.
Yet discovering the secret of peace though bereft
Of Spinoza's consolation – the bare rationality of the universe –
In the fact that mere existence is itself a miracle,
The spirit finds itself 'in the hands
Of some alien and inscrutable power,'
And, though that power may be destined to overwhelm us,
'It cannot destroy the joy we had
In its greatness and in its victory;'
This joy of contemplation being one of the most important
And radical of religious perceptions?)
(But it conflicts with our felt love
Of the creatures within the universe,
Each of which is seen to be striving
For its peculiar perfection,
'To love things as they are
Would be a mockery of things:

A true lover must love them
As they would wish to be')
Being in short as where literary art
Overpowers philosophical precision
And finding no intellectual solution
For this notorious conflict
Between the 'intellectual love' of the universe as it is
And the moral will that it should be other,
Concluding that perhaps the only solution
Lies in the faith, or the mystical perception,
That the welter of frustration in the parts
Is instrumental to some loftier perfection
In the universe as a whole?

Ah! no, no! Intolerable end
To one who set out to be independent of faith
And of mystical perception.
It does not after all seem certain
That the peace I have found is entirely
Free from mystical elements. Have I found
No salvation but only Santayana again?
Only *la plus funeste escroquerie à la paix*!
A universal Munich![1]

[1] M. Paul Hazard in *La Crise de la Conscience Européenne* asks *Qu'est-ce que l'Europe? Une pensée qui ne se contente jamais.* The Western peoples are immediately distinguished by a restless activity of mind, by boundless curiosity and insatiable idealism. M. Hazard does not assert that stability, certitude, serenity are qualities or states completely alien to the European genius; but he suggests that they are only attained by a sort of paradox, and that they offer a temptation to fall out in the march, to desist from that perpetual exploration which is the *dura lex, sed lex* of Europe. If Europe can accept Matisse and Picasso as great painters, in spite of the extensive break they have made with previous tradition, there is little reason why Indian art, also, should not come to be more widely recognised for its actual achievements; although such recognition does involve not merely a revision of purely aesthetic canons but also an acceptance as legitimate of an outlook on life, on the status of man and woman in the natural world, which is quite different from anything that has existed in Europe. That does not mean that Europeans and Indians need give their approval to everything that has occurred in the past, either in Europe or India. It means that we should prepare to share in feelings which are not those now current or those that have ever been current in our own civilizations. As Aubrey Menen says in his *Rama Retold:* 'There comes a time in the history of *every* civilization when, for the sake of human dignity, men turn their backs on it.'

Ah, Joyce, not a word, not a word!
I speak to you as if you are still alive.
Alive?
Your memory and your work will live
As long as there are men of letters in the world
And if your grave was here where I stand
(Equally far from all the world
That likes to imagine itself important!)
And I looking at the little hump of it
Through a *claire-voie* of iron spikes
I would be realising clearer than ever
– And knowing how greatly that's due to you –
That we are beginning more and more
To see behind, or through, things to something they hide,
For the most part cunningly,
With their outward appearance,
Hoodwinking man with a façade
Quite different from what it actually covers.
– An old story from the point of view of physics.
We know to-day what heat, sound, and weight are,
Or at least we have a second interpretation,
The scientific one. But I know now
Behind this there is another and many more.
But this second interpretation has powerfully transformed
The human mind and caused the greatest type-change,
In our history so far – literature in its own way
Must pursue the same course, the trail you blazed.

To-day we are breaking up the chaste
Ever-deceptive phenomena of Nature
And reassembling them according to our will.
We look through matter and the day is not far off
When we shall be able to cleave
Through her oscillating mass as if it were air.
Matter is something which man still, at most,[1]
Tolerates but does not recognise.

[1] With acknowledgment to Franz Marc (1880–1916).

'After all, what do we know of this terrible "matter," except as a
    name for the unknown and hypothetical cause of states of our own
    consciousness?'

And I know with Christian Morgenstern[1]
That the time will come soon when we will write
'From beyond.' I mean about much the same things
As always. But whose peculiar fascination now
Will be made transparent.
They will be characterised with entire belief
In their reality. Yet they will have
The effect of hallucinations. They will hold us
Spell-bound like some of the themes of poetry
As we have known it hitherto
But the awe experienced by him
For whom the old world has collapsed
(The change which takes place is not, in fact
An abandonment of belief seriously held
And firmly planted in the mind,
But a gradual recognition of the truth
That you never really held it.
The old husk drops off
Because it has long been withered
And you discover that beneath it
Is a sound and vigorous growth –)
Will be expressed in their portrayal too,
So that they will at once entertain
And excite a profound uncanny wonder,
Falling athwart
The tideless certainty of our disinterestedness.

All but an infinitesimal percentage of mankind
Have no use whatever for versatility and myriad-mindedness;
Erudition means less than nothing to them.
('Larvae, hallucinated automata, bobbins,
Savage robots, appropriate dummies,

[1] Christian Morgenstern: *Stufen, Eine Entwicklung in Aphorismen und Tagebuch-
notizen* (Munich: Piper Verlag, 1951).

The fascinating imbecility of the creaking men-machines,
Set in a pattern as circumscribed and complete
As a theory of Euclid – essays in a new human mathematic.')
Yet, as Gaudapada says, even as a bed,
Which is an assembly of frame, mattress, bedding and pillows,
Is for another's use, not for its own,
And its several component parts render no mutual service,
Thence it is concluded that there is a man who sleeps upon the
    bed
And for whose sake it was made; so this world
Of words, thoughts, memories, scientific facts, literary arts
Is for another's use. Ah Joyce, enough said, enough said!
Mum's the word now! Mum's the word!
Responsibility for the present state of the world
And for its development for better or worse
Lies with every single individual;
Freedom is only really possible
In proportion as all are free.
Knowledge and, indeed, adoption (*Aneignung*)
Of the rich Western tradition
And all the wisdom of the East as well
Is the indispensable conditon for any progress;
World-history and world-philosophy
Are only now beginning to dawn;
Whatever tribulation may yet be in store for men
Pessimism is false. Let us make ourselves at home
In *das Umgreifende*, the super-objective,
The final reality to which human life can attain.
Short of that every man is guilty,
Living only the immediate life,
Without memory, without plan, without mastery,
The very definition of vulgarity;
Guilty of a dereliction of duty,
The 'distraction' of Pascal,
The 'aesthetic stage' of Kierkegaard,
The 'inauthentic life' of Heidegger,
The 'alienation' of Marx,
The self-deception (*mauvaise foi*) of Sartre.

I believe it will be in every connection soon
As already in the field of colour
Where the imitative stage
Has long been passed
And coal tar dyes are synthesized no more
To imitate the colours of nature
Whether of autumn or spring.
The pattern cards of dye-stuffs firms to-day
Display multitudes of syntheses
That transcend Nature to reach
Almost a philosophic satisfaction
Of the aesthetic sense of colour.

Apart from a handful of scientists and poets
Hardly anybody is aware of it yet.
(A society of people without a voice for the consciousness
That is slowly growing within them)
Nevertheless everywhere among the great masses of mankind
With every hour it is growing and emerging.
Like a mango tree under a cloth,
Stirring the dull cloth,
Sending out tentacles.[1]
– It's not something that can be stopped
By sticking it away in a zinc-lined box
Like a tube of radium,
As most people hope,
Calling all who approve of it mad
The term they always apply
To anyone who tries to make them think.

For Schönberg was right. The problem involved
In mental vocalisation
Is not that the evolution of music
Must wait on the human ear
But that the human ear must catch up

---

[1] 'The history of literary expression should be regarded as part of the history of a vast, living organism directed in its manifestations by a definite, though obscure and inscrutable, law of growth.' – Ruth Z. Temple, *The Critic's Alchemy*, p. 223.

With the evolution of music.
As with Schönberg's so with your work,
And scant though the evidence be
Of progress here we have ample proof
(While yet the vast majority of mankind
Are but inching to close the infinite gap
And may succeed in a few billion years perhaps)
That the complicated is Nature's climax of rightness
And the simple at a discount. The Apocrypha is right
Of our Muse. 'She needs no simple man.'
We have learned the lesson of the Caddoan saying:
'When a woman grinds the corn with one hand
Don't let it in your belly.'
As in the clash between Red Indian and white man
Sophistication wars with simplicity everywhere
With only one possible conclusion. There can be no doubt
That the bed of which I have spoken will be filled,
All life's million conflicting interests and relationships,
Even as nerves before ever they function
Grow where they *will* be wanted; levers laid down in gristle
Become bone when wanted for the heavier pull
Of muscles which *will* clothe them; lungs, solid glands,
Yet arranged to hollow out at a few minutes' notice
When the necessary air shall enter; limb-buds
Futile at their appearing, yet deliberately appearing
In order to become limbs in readiness
For an existence where they *will* be all-important;
A pseudo-aquatic parasite, voiceless as a fish,
Yet containing within itself an instrument of voice
Against the time when it *will* talk;
Organs of skin, ear, eye, nose, tongue,
Superfluous all of them in the watery dark
Where formed – yet each unhaltingly preparing
To enter a daylit, airy, object-full manifold world
They *will* be wanted to report on. Everywhere we find
Prospective knowledge of needs of life
Which are not yet but are foreknown.
All is provided. As Aristotle says,

'To know the end of a thing is to know the why of it.'
So with your work, vastly outrunning present needs
With its immense complication, its erudition,
(The intricacy of the connections defies description.
Before it the mind halts, abased. *In tenuis labor.*)
But providing for the developments to come. . . .

Even so long before the foetus
Can have either sensation or motion,
When, in fact, its cellular elements
First begin to differentiate themselves,
The various nerves which are to govern
The perceptions and reactions essential to life
Develop, as they shape themselves, a faculty
For discovering and joining with their 'opposite numbers,'
Sensory cell 'calling' to motor cell
By a force we may call Cytoclesis.[1]
Nor is this mysterious 'call'
A phenomenon of the nervous system only.
Throughout the body cell 'calls' to cell
That the elaborate and intricate development
Of tissues may proceed aright.
Thus in the case of the kidney tubules
The myriad secreting tubules are formed
In one portion of the primordial embryonic tissue
Budded out from the ureter.
Nevertheless although these two entities
Are involved in the completion of all the kidney tubules,
There is the marvel that results in each secreting tubule
Meeting a collecting tubule

[1] 'Mankind's improved lot will be conceived in the laboratories of research scientists. From this womb composed of glass, nickel, physical and chemical elements, higher mathematical equations and philosophical thoughts, science will present the future with giant and resplendent children of the Hindu Gilgames legend. The reason our modern world ranks lower, particularly in a moral sense, than the age of Pericles or Saint Thomas Aquinas is that we have awaited the birth of a nobler future from sterile wombs, degenerate dynasties, ambitious and empty-headed statesmen with their Councils of Five, white-gloved military officers, and so-called constitutional parliaments with their motley cohorts of venal representatives.' - Lajos Zilahy in *The Angry Angel.*

F

Accurately end to end.
Each complete duct is composed of two sections
Preformed from different embryological elements
But guided to meet each other by a 'call,'
A 'call' so wonderful that each kidney tubule
Meets each ureteric tubule end to end
And so completes the canal.

Ah, Joyce! We may stand in the hush of your death-chamber
With its down-drawn blind
But those who were on the other side
When you passed over would find
It (despite the general view: 'Another queer bird gone')
As when – no! Not the Metaphysical Buzzard!
(*C'est un numéro! C'est marrant* – in both senses!)
But the peacock flew in through the open window
With its five-foot tail streaming out behind,
A magnificent *ek-stasis*[1]
Counterpart of your great *Aufhebung* here,
Der Sinn des Schaffens[2] completely seen at last.
– The supreme reality is visible to the mind *alone*.

And so I come to the end of this poem
And bid you, Joyce – what is the word
They have in Peru for *adios*? – *Chau*, that's it!
                         Well, Chau for now.
Which, as I remember it, reminds me too
Of how in Chile they use the word *roto*
To mean a peasant, a poor man,
In Guatemala called *descalzado*;
And how a man will leave an impression
By the way he mushes his 'r's'
Or buzzes his 'y's' or swallows his 'd's'
So that you automatically think
'Guatemala' or 'Argentina' or 'Colombia.'
They say '*bue-no*' in Mexico

[1] Breaking through to eternity.
[2] The Meaning of the Creative Act.

When they answer the phone.
You can tell a Mexican every time
If you hear him using a phone.
And in Guatemala they use '*vos*' instead of '*tu*,'
As they would say '*che*' in Argentina.
And so, like Horace long ago,
'*Non me rebus subjungere conor!*'[1]
Sab thik chha.

---

[1] Which the Hungarian novelist, Lajos Zilahy, glosses: 'I won't let things get the better of me.' The final (Gurkhali) sentence means 'Everything's O.K.' This indicates that the author shares Werner Bergengruen's conviction of what the German writer calls 'the rightness of the world,' despite all that may seem to enforce the opposite conclusion.

From
THREE HYMNS TO LENIN
(1957)

Third Hymn to Lenin[1]

FOR MURIEL RUKEYSER

None can usurp this height (return'd that shade)
But those to whom the miseries of the world
Are misery, and will not let them rest.

These that have turned the world upside down are come hither also.
ACTS XVII. 6.

The night is far spent, the day is at hand: let us therefore cast off the works of darkness,
and let us put on the armour of light.
ROMANS XIII. 12.

GLASGOW is a city of the sea, but what avails
In this great human Sargasso even that flair,
That resolution to understand all bearings
That is the essence of a seaman's character,
The fruit of first-hand education in the ways of ships,
The ways of man, and the ways of women even more,
Since these resemble sea and weather most
And are the deepest source of all appropriate lore.

A cloud no bigger than a man's hand, a new
Note in the wind, an allusion over the salt-junk,
And seamen are aware of 'a number of things,'
That sense of concealed but powerful meaning sunk
In hints that almost pass too quick to seize,
Which one must be won out of the abysses
Above and below, is second nature to them
But not enough in such a sink as this is.

What seaman in the history of the world before
On such an ocean as you sailed could say
This wave will recede, this advance, knew every wave
By name, and foresaw its inevitable way

[1] An alternative title would be 'Glasgow Invokes the Spirit of Lenin,' but, with slight alterations of local detail, it is, of course, equally applicable to any other big city under the Capitalist system.

And the final disposition of the whirling whole;
So identified at every point with the historic flow
That, even as you pronounced, so it occurred?
You turned a whole world right side up, and did so
With no dramatic gesture, no memorable word.
Now measure Glasgow for a like laconic overthrow!

On days of revolutionary turning points you literally flourished,
Became clairvoyant, foresaw the movement of classes,
And the probable zig-zags of the revolution
As if on your palm;
Not only an analytical mind but also
A great constructive, synthesizing mind
Able to build up in thought the new reality
As it must actually come
By force of definite laws eventually,
Taking into consideration, of course,
Conscious interference, the bitter struggle
For the tasks still before the Party, and the class it leads
As well as possible diversions and inevitable actions
Of all other classes. – Such clairvoyance is the result
Of a profound and all-sided knowledge of life
With all its richness of colour, connections and relations
Economic, political, ideological, and so forth.
Hence the logic of your speeches – 'like some all-powerful feelers
Which grasp, once for all, all sides as in a vice,"
And one has "no strength left to tear away from their embrace;
Either one yields or decides upon complete failure.'

As some great seaman or some poet grasps
The practical meaning, ideal beauty, traditional fascination,
Intellectual importance and emotional chances combined
In any instant in his particular situation,
So here there is a like accumulation of effects,
On countless planes of significance at once,
And all we see is set in riddling terms,
Making aught but myriad-mindedness a dunce.

How can the points be taken quickly enough,
Meaning behind meaning, dense forests of cross-reference;
How can the wood be seen for such a chaos of trees;
How from the hydra's mouths glean any sense?
The logic and transitions of the moment taken,
On the spur of the moment all the sheer surface.
And rapid narrative 'the public wants' secured,
How grasp the 'darker purposes' and win controlling place?

We are but fools who live by headlines else,
Surfriders merely of the day's sensations,
Living in the flicker like a cinema fan,
Nor much dedoped, defooled, by any patience.
Mere Study's fingers cannot grasp the roots of power.
Be with me, Lenin, reincarnate in me here,
Fathom and solve as you did Russia erst
This lesser maze, you greatest proletarian seer!

Hard test, my master, for another reason.
The whole of Russia had no Hell like this.[1]
There is no place in all the white man's world
So sunk in the unspeakable abyss.
Only a country whose chief glory is the Kirk,
A country with our fetish of efficiency and thrift,
With endless loving sentiment to mask the facts,
Has such an infernal masterpiece in its gift.

A horror that might sicken your stomach even,
The peak of the capitalist system and the trough of Hell,
Fit testimonial to our ultra-pious race,
A people greedy, lying, and unconscionable
Beyond compare. – Seize on this link, spirit of Lenin, then
And you must needs haul upwards to the light
The whole base chain of the phenomena that hold
Europe so far below levels worthy of its might!

Do you know the haunting slum smell? Do you remember
Proust's account of a urinal's dark-green and yellow scent,

[1] i.e. the slums of Glasgow.

Or Gillies' remark when Abelard complained
Of Guibert's horrible cooking, worse than excrement,
Yet he had watched him scour the crocks himself:
'He never washes the cloth he scrubs them with.
That gives the taste, the odour; the world's worst yet.'
But no! We've progressed. Words fail for this all-pervasive
Slum stench. A corpse beside it is a violet.

Door after door as we knocked was opened by a shirted man, suddenly and softly as if impelled forward by the overpowering smell behind him. It is this smell which is the most oppressive symbol of such lives; choking, nauseating; the smell of corrupt sweat and unnamed filthiness of body. That smell! Sometimes it crept out at us past the legs of the householder, insinuatingly, as if ashamed; sometimes it brazened out foul and pestiferous. Once in a woman's shilling boarding-house it leapt out and took us by the throat like an evil beast. The smell of the slums, the unforgettable, the abominable smell! – BOLITHO: *The Cancer of Empire,* describing the slums of Glasgow.

Ah, lizard eyes, how I would love to see
You reincarnate here and taking issue
With the piffling spirits of our public men,
Going through them like a machine-gun through crinkled tissue,
But first of all – in Cranston's tea-rooms[1] say –
With some of our leading wart-hogs calmly sat
Watching the creatures' sardonically toothsome faces
Die out in horror like Alice's Cheshire cat.
We, who have seen the daemons one by one
Emerging in the modern world and know full well
Our rapport with the physical world is safe
So long as we avoid all else and dwell,
Heedless of the multiplicity of correspondences
Behind them, on the simple data our normal senses give,
Know what vast liberating powers these dark powers disengage,
But leave the task to others and in craven safety live.

Normal, thanks to the determined blindness we possess
To all that might upset our little apple-carts,
Too cautious to do anything about it,
Knowing our days are brief, though these slum parts

[1] Well-known Glasgow restaurant, former resort of Glasgow Labour M.P.s and leading supporters.

Harbour hosts of larves, legions of octopuses,
Pulsing in the dark air, with the wills and powers.
To rise in scaly depravity to unthinkable heights
And annihilate forever all that is ours.

And only here and there a freak like me
Looking at himself, all of him, with intensest scrutiny,
Sees how he runs round like a dog, every particle
Concentrated on getting in safe somewhere, while he
With equal determination must push himself out,
Feel more at all costs, experience more, be shattered more,
Driven towards an unqualifiable upward and onward
That is – all morons feel – suicidally over the score.

Our frantic efforts go all ways and go none;
Incontinent with vain hopes, tireless Micawbers,
Banking on what Gladstone said in 1890
Or Christ a few centuries earlier, – there's
No lack of counsellors, of *die List der Vernunft*.
The way to Hell is paved with plenty of talk,
But nothing ever happens – nothing ever will;
The future's always rosy, the present no less black.

Clever – and yet we cannot solve this problem even;
Civilised – and flaunting such a monstrous sore;
Christian – in flat defiance of all Christ taught;
Proud of our country with this open sewer at our door,
Come, let us shed all this transparent bluff,
Acknowledge our impotence, the prize eunuchs of Europe,
Battening on our shame, and with voices weak as bats'
Proclaiming in ghoulish kirks our base immortal hope.

And what is this impossible problem then?
Only to give a few thousand people enough to eat,
Decent houses and a fair income every week.
What? For nothing? Yes! Scotland can well afford it.

It cannot be done. The poor are always with us,
The Bible says. Would other countries agree?

Clearly we couldn't unless they did it too.
All the old arguments against ending Slavery!

Ah, no! These bourgeois hopes are not our aim.

Lenin, lover of music, who dare not listen to it,
Teach us to eschew all the siren voices too
And get due *Diesseitigkeit*. Countless petty indulgences
– We give them fine names, like Culture, it is true –
Lure us up this enchanting side-line and up that
When we should stay in stinking vennel and wynd,
Not masturbating our immortal souls,
But simply doing some honest service to mankind.

Great forces dedicated to the foulest ends
Are reaping a rich victory in Glasgow here
In life stunted and denied and endless misery,
Preventible disease and 'crime' and death; and standing sheer
Behind these crowded thoroughfares with armaments concealed
Ready at any vital move to massacre
These mindless mobs, the gangsters lurk, the officer class, ruthless
Watching Glasgow's every step and lusting to attack her.

And Freedom's opposing forces are hidden too,
But Fascism has its secret agents everywhere
In every coward's castle, shop, bank, manse and school
While few serve Freedom's counter-service there,
Nor can they serve – for all but all men's ears
Are deaf to aught it says, stuffed with the wax
Of ignorant prejudice and subsidised inanity
Till Freedom to their minds all access lacks.

And most insidious and stultifying of all
The anti-human forces have instilled the thought
That knowledge has outrun the individual brain
Till trifling details only can be brought ·
Within the scope of any man; and so have turned
Humanity's vast achievements against the human mind

Until a sense of general impotence compels
Most men in petty grooves to stay confined.

This is the lie of lies – the High Treason to mankind.
No one but fritters half his time away.
It is the human instinct – the will to use it – that's destroyed
Till only one or two in every million men today
Know that thought is reality – and thought alone! –
And must absorb all the material – their goal
The mastery by the spirit of all the facts that can be known.

Instead of that we have a Jeans accommodating the stars
To traditional superstitions, and a Barnes who thrids
Divers geometries – Euclidean, Lobatchewskyan, Riemannian –
And Cepheid variables, white dwarfs, yet stubbornly heads
(Though he admits his futile journey fails to reach
Any solution of the problem of 'God's' relation to Time)
Back to his starting place – to a like betrayal
Of the scientific spirit to a dud Sublime.

And in Scotland a Haldane even, rendering great service to biological
    theory
In persistently calling attention to the special form of organisation
Existing in living things – yet failing greatly
Through his defeatist wish to accept
This principle of organisation as axiomatic
Instead of tracing its relation to the lower principle of organisation
Seen in paracrystals, colloids, and so forth.
Threading with great skill the intricate shuttling path
From 'spontaneity' to preoccupation with design,
From the realistic 'moment' to the abstraction of essential form
And ending with a fusion of all their elements,
At once realistic and abstract,

Daring and unblushing atheism is creeping abroad and saturating the working population, which are the proper persons to be saturated with it. I look to no others. It has been said to me by more than one person, 'Let us write in the style of Hume and Gibbon and seek readers among the higher classes.' I answer 'No'; I know nothing of the so-called higher classes but that they are robbers; I will work towards the raising of the working population above them.

RICHARD CARLILE

Or like Michael Roberts whose *New Country*
Is the same old country, and mediaeval enough his 'modern mind'
Confessing that after all he cannot see
How civilisation can be saved unless confined
Under the authority of a Church which in the West
Can only be the so-called Christian Church.
Perish the thought! Let us take our stand
Not on this infernal old parrot's perch
But squarely with Richard Carlile: 'The enemy with whom we have
    to grapple
Is one with whom no peace can be made. Idolatry will not parley,
Superstition will not treat or covenant. They must be uprooted
Completely for public and individual safety.'

Michael Roberts and All Angels! Auden, Spender, those bhoyos,
All yellow twicers: not one of them
With a tithe of Carlile's courage and integrity.
Unlike the pseudos I am *of* – not *for* – the working class
And like Carlile know nothing of the so-called higher classes
Save only that they are cheats and murderers,
Battening like vampires on the masses.

The illiteracy of the literate! But Glasgow's hordes
Are not even literate save a man or two;
All bogged in words that communicate no thought,
Only mumbo-jumbo, fraudulent clap-trap, ballyhoo.
The idiom of which constructive thought avails itself
Is unintelligible save to a small minority
And all the rest wallow in exploded fallacies
And cherish for immortal souls their gross stupidity,
While in the deeper layers of their ignorance who delves
Finds in this order – Scotland, other men, themselves.
We do not play or keep any mere game's conventions.
Our concern is human wholeness – the child-like spirit
Newborn every day – not, indeed, as careless of tradition
Nor of the lessons of the past: these it must needs inherit.

But as capable of such complete assimilation and surrender,
So all-inclusive, unfenced-off, uncategoried, sensitive and tender,

That growth is unconditioned and unwarped – Ah, Lenin,
Life and that more abundantly, thou Fire of Freedom,
Fire-like in your purity and heaven-seeking vehemence,
Yet the adjective must not suggest merely meteoric,
Spectacular – not the flying sparks, but the intense
Glowing core of your character, your large and splendid stability,
Made you the man you were – the live heart of all humanity!

Spirit of Lenin, light on this city now!

Light up this city now!

THE BATTLE CONTINUES
(1957)

The Battle Continues

PART I

Anti-Fascism is a bit out of date, isn't it?
All just yesterday's pancakes now?
And all the Spanish War newspaper clippings
Dried out like the lives of so many of my friends?
Forgotten – that's the way you would like it,
Calf-fighter Campbell, I have no doubt,
But there's an operation to do first
– To remove the haemorrhoids you call your poems
With a white-hot poker for cautery,
Shoved right up through to your tonsils!

Campbell, they call him – 'crooked mouth,'[1] that is –
But even Clan Campbell's records show no previous case
Of such extreme distortion, of a mouth like this
Slewed round to a man's bottom from his face
And speaking with a voice not only banal
                                    But absolutely anal.
Franco has made no more horrible shambles
Than this poem of Campbell's,
The foulest outrage his breed has to show
Since the massacre of Glencoe!

> *Sunk in tyranny – he who once was human,*
> *Abandoned by the Lord to slow corruption,*
> *He has driven from him like an evil thing*
> *His last resource of conscience.*
>   **MICKIEWICZ**

He turns on all that distinguishes
Man from beast with unbridled hate
And vaunts his contempt for all
That is not contemptible

---

[1] Translation of the two Gaelic words *caim* and *beul* which constitute the name, Campbell.

– All that is good and gracious
And seemly and of good repute
(In life or in death – for *de mortuis* . . .
Is a decency he disregards,
Along with respect for brave foes
And every chivalrous convention)
Butchered to make a Roman holiday
And a theme for his horrible doggerel.

One out of every 25 Spaniards dead,
And another one wounded;
A million lives lost in all,
A quarter of them civilians,
At a cost of 22 hundred million pounds
– (Enough to have given the whole population of Spain
Abundance in perpetuity
Instead of the terrible distress
That is all it has purchased).
And this stupendous agony
Moves one who thinks himself a poet
Only to witless bragging
And senseless laudation
Of the gangsters who brought it about
– Men not worth the least of the Republican fallen.
Insensitivity can hardly go further
Even in this Age of the Fish
When men's faces are becoming fixed,
Cold and hard and capable of anything
But anything decent . . .
Or the pretence that black is white
Or the hellish hatred of life
Developed beyond the termite stage.
This is the epic of the Clumsy Lout
Indulging his inferiority complex
And turning to revenge himself
On a civilisation for which
He was always constitutionally unfit
And on a literature that failed

To recognise matchless genius
In an unlicked cub
From the back of beyond
– Self-appointed laureate of a tentiginous cause
With no redeeming feature,
And crass celebrant of a system which deprives
Most folk of any chance of decent lives,
In helping with the strangulation of the Spanish people
He has won nothing
But gratuitous dishonour.

Spain, perfect example of the exclusive English virtues
Of Sportmanship and Fair Play! You always were a sportsman,
        Campbell,
Punctilious observer of the Raspberry Rules
Fishing, bull-fighting, and the rest (so you said). What a lovely treat
(Pursuing the 'degrading thirst after outrageous stimulation' of which
        Wordsworth spoke)
To have an indomitable great pain-blinded people
To torture in your bloody bull-ring for a change!
Fit subject for your vile veronicas!
Makes a chappie feel like a Roman gladiator, what!
For who can add insult to injury more deftly than you
Or salt an open wound to please the *aficionados* better?
You are indeed an honourable man,
As only the shootin' and the huntin' people
And officers and gentlemen can possibly be,
All bobby-dazzlers, all honourable men.
And I am perfectly entranced for my part
Not only with your expertise but even more
With your genial courtesy and largeness of heart,
Great Campbell, great Toreador, great reductio ad absurdum
Of Christianity, civilisation and what have you!
Whereas these reds – they've no traditions, these fellows.
They actually rushed into the ring to help the brute
And ease its wounds. Would you believe it!
                Bai Jove, the lousy cads!
The hellish anti-climax that behind the bland

Façade of these great names – Religion, Culture, and the rest –
Has been preparing all along to yawn asunder;
Since no real decency can co-exist
With the exploitation of man by man
And every high-falutin' claim with this abscess at its root
Must needs collapse like Non-Intervention and show
Its hideous true nature, Campbell, as you've now shown yours
– You and your fellow-Paladins, Yeats-Brown
And Douglas Jerrold, that very parfait gentle knight,
And Baldwin's Glory and Chamberlain's Charm
– The fine (and, we hope, final) flowers of the English Spirit!

Bullfighter? But it is not the Bull
He has modelled his personality upon,
But only that sour, surly, dogged animal
The Stot, which retains a most absurd resemblance
To a Bull – an absurdity augmented
By the fact he once absolutely was a Bull:
His forehead lowers and his eye is swarthy
But look him in the face and you discern
The malice of emasculation
And the cowardice of his curtailed estate.
(The malice and cowardice they all have
Who denying, and denied, full human stature,
Prefer class privilege and 'rights' of property
To human values in widest commonalty spread,
And deem Law stronger than life
And than men's desire to be free,
And lour in swarthy superstition still
– Like those ghastly women who walk about
Clad in their grave-clothes, insulting life! –
And are afraid of the rising people
Who shall take what these would not give!)

The people are always right in whatever they do
To break out of the bondage of ignorance and want
They are held in by the greed and power-lust of the few.
– All else is cowardice, crime, and cant!

No man or group of men has any right
To force another man or other groups of men
To do anything he or they do not wish to do.
There is no right to govern without
The consent of the governed. Consent is not only
Important in itself, and as a nidus for freedom
And its attendant spontaneity, (clearly valuable
As the opposed sense of frustration is detrimental), but the sole
Basis of political obligation. There is nothing
Supplemental to or coequal with consent itself
And even if we had not the lessons of all history
– The endless evidence of 'man's inhumanity to man'
And overwhelming proof that all power debases
And that no man is good enough to have it
Or can exercise it without doing far more harm than good –
The contention is utterly indefensible – sheer humbug! mortmain!
That 'so long as the exercise of certain powers is good in itself
Or a means to the good . . . these powers are right
Whether or not anyone is of the opinion that they are,'
The time-dishonoured formula that attempts to conceal or
        excuse
All the hellish wrong of human history,
The fraud and loss inherent in all Government,
That age-long monstrous distortion of the faculties of man
It is the great historical task of the working class
To eliminate today, no matter at what cost,
That human life no longer wrenched hideously awry
May spring up in its proper form at last.

In this cruel age he has not glorified Freedom
Nor invoked mercy towards the fallen.
Nor helped Hope, the faithful sister of Misfortune,
To awaken courage once again.
Nor sent friendship and love
With his free voice reaching through stone
Till chains are broken and prisons destroyed.
His denunciation of the Republican cause
Is only the angry barking of a dog, so long

Accustomed to his painful collar that at last
He turns against the man that would deliver him.

Woe on the poet who has seen
Without making protest, nay, with approval,
Everything noble and disinterested,
Everything that elevates the life of man
Crushed by inexorable egotism
And the passion for material satisfaction.

Nor is his mouth alone involved. His ear
Poetry from borborygmy cannot tell.
(Waiving the question if it ever could
– Its preferences were always horribly crude).
The same dislocation affects, it's clear,
His eyes and brain and so-called soul as well,
While if his rifle flowers it only bears
Such roses as in syphilis a penis wears.
Not a 'rod' Aaronic
          But only ironic,
And as the Drill-Sergeant said,
'A blooming disgrace on parade!'
And sentenced Roy Dunnachie[1] Campbell, the Warrior Bard,
– Lance-Private Campbell! – to seven days' hard.

But Campbell replied, 'It'll do, I suppose,
Well enough, at least against unarmed foes,
And I imagine that women and children
Will find death through a nosegay bewilderin'.
And I like to fire through a wreath.
My murderees get none after death!'

'Nobody else *could* have struck such a blow *in* verse.'[2]
A blunder, Blunden! The truth's not *in* but *to*,
Though your instinctive failure to immerse
Yourself in it sufficiently to see through
Its nature is excusable enough it's true.

          [1] Quaint old spelling of Donkey.
          [2] Edmund Blunden's praise of Campbell's *Flowering Rifle*.

And *could* should be *would*, of course, the blow being foul.
Two errors in one line! Blunden, chuck in your towel!
Let such slapdash be churned out by the acre.
A Left Jab soon disposes of such a Right Haymaker!

A 'poet' devoted not to composition
                    But to decomposition,
And if to the lyre, not
                    Spelled that way!
Exiled like Tristan da Cunha and severed from his race
By far more now than the cold ocean of his disdain,
He goes back to the howling void from which he came
And represented so well in Bloomsbury for a while,
Muttering to himself the bloody hosannas of Spain,
As who, in a padded cell, may his time beguile,
A naked Zulu doing his war-dance still,
Lost in his foul obsession like that island in the main
Or pathological abomination pickled in a phial,
Or bobbing merrily down a lavatory drain
– I'm thinking of the 'rhythm' of his 'poem' again!
Do not imagine, traitor to humanity,
That your 'frightful' position is unique.
Amaurosis can cut a creature off from humankind
Almost as completely as you have cut yourself,
Related to your fellow-men as to happy childhood
The bloody botch-work by which an aborteur earns his pelf.
There is a precedent for your plight.[1] Magellan flayed
A member of his crew as you have flayed yourself
And left him skinless on the Tierra del Fuegan shore,
His terrible cries long heard in his shipmates' ears.
You've cast yourself away on a far ghastlier coast.
Your cries have not a similar resonance,
And what has happened to the little gift you had
Is just what happens in quicklime to a felon's corpse.
Stillborn even among your comrades fall your songs,

[1] As there is one precedent for your doggerel too
– In the ancient Indian verse-form, so well-named
The *go-mutrika*, or stream of cow's urine, form.

Your tender lyrics of homicide and proud paeans of rapine,
Not moral but only Marquis de Moral at best,
And lovely as the Duke of Alba's or King Alfonso's face,
Their only purpose the Royal one – willing to share
His haemophilia if nothing else with all his people,
Till from that bloody flux to hear a song arise
– Even such a song as yours – is like hearing
A carcase in a butcher's shop burst into song,
Cadaverous ecstasy and lyric cry of offal!
Roses with the stench of putrefaction!
A bard of Blunden's pretentions should have seen
The way the dull mechanic lines betray
Campbell's loud claims that he has ever been
A champion of organic life – claims borne away
In the portentous Blimp-like movement of his verse
As in a hearse!
Le vers se venge!

The organic life – against the dead
Regime of the Robot Red! –
But there's no sign that he has loved
Or ever caught a glimpse of life at all.
I do not mean courage, cleverness, etcetera,
But the quintessence of life itself
Unspecialised into a set of virtues,
Indivisible, overwhelmingly real,
Submerging all calculation and every rule.

The goal will never be achieved by means of order, General, by means of sober-mindeded weighing of pros and cons, comparisons and probings. The solution to the problem must be a flash of lightning, a fire, an intuition, a synthesis. Looking at the history of mankind, one sees it is not a logical process of development, but rather something – with its sudden inspirations, the meaning of which only later becomes apparent – that reminds one of a poetic work!

ROBERT MUSIL: *Der Mann ohne Eigenschaften.*

That, welling up, has been the wonder and glory of Spain
While all he wanted, he who deems himself a poet,
Was to thrust it out of sight again,
Bury it in poverty and illiteracy,

All his 'divine afflatus'
Nothing but rigor mortis!

Our concern is human wholeness – the child-like spirit
New-born every day – not, indeed, as careless of tradition
Nor of the lessons of the past: these it must needs inherit,
But as capable of such complete assimilation and surrender,
So all-inclusive, unfenced-off, uncategoried, sensitive and tender,
That growth is unconditional and unwarped. – Ah, Lenin,
Life and that more abundantly, thou Fire of Freedom!
Firelike in your purity and heaven-seeking vehemence,
Yet the adjective must not suggest merely meteoric,
Spectacular, – not the flying sparks but the intense
Glowing core of your character, your large and splendid stability,
Made you the man you were – the live heart of all humanity!
Spirit of Lenin, light on this country now!
Light up this country now!

Nor has Campbell heard and weighed
The doctor's testimony,
(Only the protagonists of the people are healthy.
The rest are all sick with a loathsome disease).
Sure guarantee in the end
Of the Republicans' victory.
'We have practically no neurosis.
A "neurosis" is an escape from reality,
An attempt to avoid facing some unpleasant truth.
This disease was extremely common
During and after the Great War
But is almost unknown
Among the Spanish Republicans.'
Let those who have ears to hear
And minds to understand perpend
The significance of this great fact
– The forces of 'life and that
More abundantly' will triumph in the end.

And I think again of how most people accept
The impossibility of our outgrowing war

Or ridding ourselves of the major social ills
Just as folk recognise, with regret it may be,
Man's kinship with the most loathsome brute
Joggling his protruding sternum there
And letting his animal noises out,
The slack mouth and the goggling eyes,
    All they can have patience with,
    All they can pity,
All they can hide in their madhouses,
    In their gaols and hospital wards.
Fat hearts, thick ears, blind eyes,
All that's diseased, malformed, obscene,
    Mankind accepts and guards;
But when a higher type appears, in a man
Who looks just like themselves, a man
Infinitely superior to most men
As most men to apes, they howl with fear,
Or perjure their sight, and gibe and jeer
And deny that the like can ever appear.
And certainly not, like Christ, in the working class.

'L'extrême esprit est accusé de folie
    Comme l'extrême défaut;
Rien que la médiocrité n'est bon.
    C'est sortir de l'humanité
    Que de sortir du milieu.'

'Und wir, die an *steigendes* Glück
denken, empfänden die Rührung,
die uns beinah bestürzt
wenn ein Glückliches *fällt*.'

It is impossible that Franco can win
Since his victory would represent
The abandonment of all human hope,
The reversion of the masses of men
To the role of dumb beasts,
Subject to a lewd kakistocracy,

The degenerative subjugation
Of the superior by the inferior,
The denial of the illimitable
Creative powers of the people
For the sake of a ruthless few
Claiming as their rights the wrongs they do,
Ready to advance themselves
And secure the high posts and powers for which
No intrinsic merits qualify them
At no matter how great a cost
In the sacrifice of all human values
– A few whose only distinction
Is cowardice, cruelty, and greed,
Ill-gotten wealth, and empty titles they owe
To sires whose baseness is their fame,
'Degenerate descendants bred
In living evil from the evil dead,
Beslaverers of fortune, hearts of stone,
Greedy servility about the throne,
Hangmen of genius, liberty, and fame
Who hide behind the law's corrupted name'[1]
– A programme only grisly Death may choose
For the theme of its song
(Twin glories of Totalitarian Art,
Hitler the painter, Campbell the poet!
– And indeed, *Flowering Rifle* resembles the daubs
In the House of German Art at Munich
And has as little to do with true art,
The great protectress of the living,
The creative force which expands
The prison-house of our being
– Art, if it is to live, needs freedom.
It cannot flourish in the atmosphere of duress).
But no other Muse,
No matter from what *kraal* sprung,
In what howling-dervish fashion inspired,
Or how zebra-striped with sound and fury!

[1] Lermontov: *On the Death of Pushkin.*

The powers and principalities of darkness
May triumph for a while
But humanity will challenge them
Again and again – it is the very law of life –
As long as men harbour any decent instinct,
As long as hope springs in the human breast.
Better, Campbell, if you had stayed
In the Ham Yard club[1] than thrown in your lot
With such hams and shysters as these!

Poetry versus Animal Noises,
Our cause versus yours!
Your obscene taunts and jeers
Fit only for your friends the Moors.
Million-fold tragedy – indiscriminate slaughter.
All the widows and the orphans,
The young lives wrecked and high hopes blasted
Move this 'poet' to no just indignation,
No pity or noble passion,
But only to barrack-room bestiality
And nose-thumbing wit as though
It were not Roy Campbell we heard
But Queipo de Llano broadcasting
– And, indeed, you have made yourself
Only a ventriloquist's doll
For de Llano and his like.
(Not that the voice that comes from you now
Is much changed, Hottentot of Helicon!)
But if you had ever had
Any feeling befitting a poet,
Any magnanimity or milk
Of human kindness, you would
Have realised at the outset
That the working-class masses of Spain
Whatever they did deserved at the very least
Such exculpation as Manuel Quezon gave
To the driver of a buffalo cart,

[1] A London night-club Roy Campbell was sometimes seen at.

Earning 15 cents a day,
Arrested for making bombs.
'No wonder you are a bomb-thrower,'
Quezon said. 'No one can live
On 15 cents a day' – and he released the man.

But you, Campbell, stand for all
The hypocrisy, falsity, and callousness of the Law,
The infernal sadism that hauls to the scaffold
A poor woman sick at both ends, and places
A congenital idiot playing with his dolls
In the Electric Chair – yet kisses the bloody hands
Of mass-murderers like Hitler, Mussolini and Franco
And approves the professional expertise
With which the horror of Chamberlain's umbrella
Closes in
                    Berchtesgaden gamp
                    Like a tragic clamp
On helpless humanity like the walls
In Poe's story; symbol of the black circumscription
And lugubrious role Fascism gives mankind.
Felicity through homicide!
Every generous inspiration proscribed.
The only ambition regarded as worthy of men
The power of murdering each other
And grabbing all the loot they can.
Fit recruit to Christ's hellish levies!
You outrage the Muses after the way of your kind!
Bah! Any poet worth his salt would liefer die
With Lorca, Campbell, than survive with you.
And Fascism must needs treat any poet worth the name
As it treated Lorca – it is simply because
You are no true poet that they tolerate you.
No poet worth a damn is on your side.

'A fig for those by law protected!
Liberty's a glorious feast!

Courts for cowards were erected,
Churches built to please the priest.'
'Ye hypocrites! are these your pranks?
To murder men and give God thanks!
Desist for shame! – proceed no further;
God won't accept your thanks for MURTHER!'

Lorca! 'Pensive, merry, and dear to the people
As a guitar, simple-hearted and responsive as a child
– His whole life was helpful and inspiring to others
And he earned his people's deep and lasting affection.'[1]
Lorca's love for the people, clear in his writings,
Met with a passionate response. His songs and ballads
Were quickly caught up all over revolutionary Spain.
The Fascist henchmen could never forgive
His popularity and devotion to the people.
They shot him and made a bonfire of his books
On Carmen Square in Granada.
'Fear not! This debt we shall repay!'[2]
Lorca's poetry, however, can never be silenced.
It will continue to blow as free as the wind
Over the wide spaces of heroic Spain.
Lorca, dead, lives forever.
Campbell, living, is dead and rots.

The poet has been turned into earth and silence,
Yet every day he dies and resuscitates in the heart of Spain,
In the heart of the world, because today the world
Bleeds and throbs together with the people of Spain
– Ángel Lázaro is right when he cries:
'How was it that the murderers' bullets did not stop
Before that brow
Below which the angels of verse
Sang a matchless music?
I think of that head struck to the ground,
The black lock fallen as though it wanted to go,

[1] From Pablo Neruda's tribute to Lorca.
[2] From lines addressed to Lorca by Luis de Tapia.

With the last stertor,
To the thread of recondite water
Of his Andalusia.
I think of Lorca dead – he who stood upright
In the middle of life
Like a young bull in the middle of the fields.
I think of the last terror of his pupils,
Those pupils that had known how to see
Unique colours and foreshortenings of wonder,
And thinking of that
I cannot utter any word but this:
Murderers! Murderers!'

You were an accomplice in that murder,
Campbell, Nadir of English Literature,
A friend and associate of the unspeakable ruffians,
Traitors to the flag they swore to defend
And the country they swore to love,
Covered with opprobrium for ever
By having recourse to proceedings
Repulsive to all honest minds.
It did not suffice them to rend the soil of their land
And redden it with the blood and horror of war.
They fell so low in their infamy
That in order to carry out their criminal designs
They recruited from African villages
The most brutal type of Moor,
And let them satisfy their sensual desires
By violating the maidens and outraging
The women of Spain
While the degenerate aristocracy looked on,
Jeering and enjoying
The sight of such monstrosities.
And you, Campbell, are a cheerleader in this
And proud to have for fit audience
Honourless soldiers without a fatherland,
Mercenaries whose only ideal is booty,
Whose foul amusement is the epitaph

Of genius extinguished for a laugh,
Criminal lunatics who mutilate children and old people
For the monstrous crime – the only crime even you
Could accuse them of – the capital offence of being related
To men of democratic ideals.

Lorca sacrificed – Lorca of the *Romancero Gitano*,[1]
Of the folk songs of muleteers and shepherds, and of plays
Full of memories of the rustic people
In the village *granadinos* of his youth,
Lorca, poet of the genuine popular vein,
Butchered in the fulness of his genius,
And a rant like *Flowering Rifle* in exchange!
– Campbell, you have done literature dirt,
You have swindled the Muse!

Fascists, you have killed my comrades
And their wives and children!
You have killed them!
It were better that you all should rot in your vices
In the bottomless filth of damnation,
And that they should live!
What is the worth of your plague-spotted lives
That such a price should be paid for them?
But it is too late – too late!
I cry aloud, but they do not hear me.
I beat the doors of the graves
But they will not wake.
Take your victory – I fling it to you as a bone
Is flung to a pack of snarling curs.
The price of your banquet is paid for you.
Come then and gorge yourselves,
Cannibals, blood-suckers, carrion beasts,
That feed upon the dead!
This is the body that was given for you
– Look at it, torn and bleeding,
Throbbing still with the tortured life,

[1] Collection of Gipsy Ballades.

Quivering from the bitter death-agony!
Take it, Christians, and eat.
'All Spain,' it has been said of Goya,
'Is in the enormous range and volume of his work.'
– That is true. Even you are there,
But not in the Vendimia – only in the terrible painting
Of the Executions after the Dos de Mayo,
Napoleon's soldiers firing on a group of unarmed civilians.
That – and the people dead of hunger, guns, and pestilence;
The twisted zeal of the Inquisition;
The hag-ridden mythology of the peninsula;
And the pretty, distracting duchesses –
Is all that you know and have and are
Of Goya and of Spain.

Poet of the Right? Contradiction in terms!
The Right can have its Kings and Queens,
Its nobles, bishops, all its famous fatheads,
Nonentities all, rank and more rank!
But no creative artist has ever belonged
Or ever can belong to the Right.

Old hidebound Toryism being now openly cracking towards some incurable disruption . . .
long recognised by all the world, and now at last obliged to recognise its very self, for an
overgrown Imposture, supporting itself not by human reason, but by flunky blustering and
brazen lying, superadded to mere brute force.
                    THOMAS CARLYLE: *Life of John Sterling*, Part 1, Chapter 7

Poetry is a progressive art. No true poet today
Can worship superstition and defend false beliefs,
Or celebrate revenge and war,
As the primaeval poets did.
When we think of the ideal poet
It is not the champion of the middle class
Like Longfellow and Tennyson, nor one full
Of the early martial spirit, painting fighting heroes,

Like the author of *Beowulf*, or the *Nibelungenlied*.
The poetry of the future will sing like Amos of old
The beauty of social and economic equality,
Its hero the man who fights for social justice
For himself or the masses. The poetry of the coming age
Must come from the working class. In the upper ranks,
Poetry, so far at least as it represents their life,
Has long been worn out, sickly, sentimental.
Its manhood is effete. Feudal aristocracy,
With its associations, the castle and the tournament,
Has passed away. Its last healthy tones
Came from the harp of Scott.
Byron sang its funeral dirge. But tenderness, heroism, endurance
Still want their voice; it must come from the class
Whose observation is at first hand,
Who speak fresh from nature's heart.
What has poetry to do with our Working Class?
Men of work! We want our poetry from you,
From men who will dare to live
A brave and true life. But indeed
Poetry and the cause of the people are one
And in Spain the menace to the people
Menaced the entire national culture too,
For, from the *Cantos of El Cid*,
From the archpriest of Hita to Cervantes,
Lope, Quevedo, Gongora, Calderon,
All the classical literature of Spain
Is of the people's workmanship.
So also is their painting – Murillo, Velasquez,
Goya, El Greco, Zurbaran – as well as their music
And their theatre, synthesis of all these arts.
No wonder all the true creative artists of Spain
Were aware that not only Spain's present culture,
But also its future culture, depended
On the issue of this struggle
In which a savage attack,
Fiendish in its barbaric cruelty,
Was launched against the people.

It is in no way incidental
That an utter and absolute want of culture
Is typical of all the elements
Whose common denominator is fascism,
That is, of the insurgent militarists
Supported by foreign states and marching hand in hand
With the catholic church and the capitalists
Who always and everywhere defend
Their selfish and predatory interests.
Nor is there anything casual in the fact
That, following the 'renowned' traditions of world fascism,
The enemies of the people take aim and fire
At the very name of culture. For a whole century
The militarists boasted they knew nothing of Spanish culture.
And the corrupt ecclesiastics, rotten to the core,
Blessed this infamous ignorance.
Contempt for the people's culture
(And in Spain there is no other culture
Nor can there be)! Barbarism!
Shouting 'Death to the intelligentsia,'
Firing at culture they shoot at the people.
Shooting at the people crush all culture too.
You fought against Poetry, Campbell,
And against all intelligence and human worth!
With no deep sense of the tragedy
Not only of war's actual destruction
But of its defeat of beauty
And thought and spiritual values,
Its negation of civilisation,
Its terrible withering of life.

You have fought for a decrepit system
Which has lapsed into idiocy
And can produce nothing great;
Indeed, if the Fascist onslaught
Cannot be checked, your friends
May very well issue tomorrow
A decree of compulsory cretinization.

– Let us demolish those who want to stop thought!
No artist can choose as you have chosen, Campbell.
We cannot play the idiot game
Of Fascist underlings who have joined the apaches
And provocateurs for a war with lamp-posts.
We want to fight for a system
In which hope and happiness exist
Not merely as museum relics.
There is only one way out,
Immediate unification without phrases,
With no limitations,
Of all proletarian powers,
Of all defenders of human thought,
Against the Fascist onslaught!

The bourgeoisie is falling. Its feet
Are skidding in blood. It soon must die.
It is stupid, it is base,
It understands nothing of the new system
Which humanity so ardently desires
And on which it bases all its hopes.
The bourgeoisie is capable merely
Of murder, murder, and murder.
It is only capable of creating wars
And sending whole nations to be slaughtered.
The people are ardently demanding
A rational and just organisation of society
In which they can work in order to live.
The bourgeoisie, instead of granting this,
Continue stubbornly, absurdly, criminally,
To hold on to this ugly system
Under which all swindlers and their accomplices
Are the all-powerful.
While the workers die of starvation
The bourgeoisie is only capable
Of shooting down those who ask for bread.

Poetry does not become democratic
Because some poets dwell on the privileges

The workers of today have in contrast
With the workers generations ago
Or have discovered that common people even
Experience most of the emotions of the upper class.
Literature cannot be democratic
While poets write for the few who use them
As tools for their own interests, to defend a system
Courteously called competition, not exploitation.
Many wealthy and cultured authors take up
The cause of the labourer just as they would
That of caged animals. They suggest improvements
In the treatment of the captives, but not complete freedom.
To Hell with all that!
Poetry can have nothing to do with that philanthropy
Which only means the master throwing crumbs
To quiet the growling servant.
But Poetry shall cry 'Woe unto them[1]
That join house to house, that lay field to field,
Till there be no place, that they may be placed
Alone in the midst of the earth'
And Poetry shall cry: 'They are waxen fat, they shine:[2]
Yea, they overpass the deeds of the wicked:
They judge not the cause,
The cause of the fatherless,
Yet they prosper;
And the right of the needy
Do they not judge.'
The side that poetry is on
Is never in doubt for a moment,
And it is not the side
You have chosen, Campbell.
Not rhymes and rhythms constitute poetry
But only this passion.
Wherever it is, there is poetry.
Without it, no poetry is.

[1] Isaiah V. 8.
[2] Jeremiah V. 28.

The 'old soldier,' Skunk, unconsciously transposes
The properties of Poetry and of Mars,
Giving his gun a wreath of paper roses,
His verse an illiterate sergeant-major's roars
– And if the first sound markmanship debars
The second slays enough with halitosis
Yet like all gas impredicably wanders
And slays – but never where he proposes,
So while to belch upon his foes he's tried
He's choked himself and nauseated his own side.
Yet the only casualty when all was said and done
Was any little reputation he had ever won
(A flaming poetaster? – Well,
If all the irradiation is from Hell!
Nero *de nos jours*, while Guernica burns
He delights the yahoos with his Hyena turns,
A Bruno Mussolini bombing Parnassus,
And perpetuating a criminal assault upon the Muses!)
A negligible bag – and not to his gun
(But to the poison of his Hottentot lines
Ragtime as Karno–Franco's files where 'Christian' and Cannibal
        combines!
If indeed the cause is Christ's cause
The hands are the hands of Judas!)
In using which as in bull-fighting he
(A cowpuncher rather than a bullfighter
        – If only he'd had the punch!)
Was even a worse dud, incredible though it be,
            Than in the lists of poesy.
Witness the honours Franco showers upon him,
The general admission of the Rebel leaders
That but for this bogus Byron, this great Reichs-Marksman,
Moscow had won!
Single-handed almost,
This second Cid, this Robert Coates of the Theatre of War,
This Gun-Smoke McGonagall, this vest-
Pocket edition of the *Decline of the Wild West*,
Eddie Cantor Campbell in *The Kid from Spain*,

– Maximum of smoke and minimum of fire ! –
Routed the Bolshevik hordes and saved Civilisation !
This Sydney Horler of the English Muse
In Franco's wayzgoose is himself the goose,
Or bustard rather, that, when its foe comes nigh,
Cocks up its shitepoke and with that lets fly
– A better shot with that
                    Than with a gat !
(The truth is, Blunden, and well enough you know it,
He's poor shakes as a soldier and poorer as a poet !)

PART II

I DO not shriek for vengeance on the men
Who are the head and front of this offence
Since none the mind of man can comprehend
Can fit a *lusus naturae* so immense,
Cancel the wrong, bring back to life the slain,
Or give the bereaved and broken any recompense.
Yet in the perspectives that before me open
I know the evil will be undone and vengeance wrought
With a completeness beyond human thought.

We leave inhuman wrong to inhuman vengeance then,
Yet pending that we have our part to play.
Accessories before, nor in, nor after the act,
We must refuse any compromise and exact
All the interim vengeances within our power,
Agree to no truce whatever, and deny
Franco and his friends, and every neutral,
Any condonation, tolerance, or boon of intercourse,
Subject them in all connections to endless boycott,
Dedicate ourselves to eliminate from the earth
Every institution that favoured this Putsch or acquiesced,
Every thought that has anything in common with theirs,
Outgrow their psychological types in all respects
As most men have outgrown the original ape,

And hold them thus beyond the human pale
To meet the vengeance there that does not fail.
(And we've the right to make their passage short
By any means we can to that last Court!)
Remove them from the records of life, as operating theatre
Assistants remove malignant growths the surgeons have excised;
A pathological picture, Campbell, in which you figure
As no more than the minuscule contents of a teratoma cyst!

Campbell boasts he is the first English poet who has dared to give
Bleary old democracy a sock in the jaw.
He might as well brag of pinching errand money from a child
Or filching the coppers from a blind man's tin with his monkey paw.

Let him leave his base associates and go and live
Humbly and quietly for a change among the working class
And try to learn the ABC of their decency and honesty
Patience and diligence, and divine how it comes to pass

That denied the fruit of their labours and forced to endure
Endless drudgery and poverty and to forego
More than the tiniest fraction of the life that should be theirs,
The instant that they venture to show

Determination to secure a better life,
And a fairer share of the wealth they produce,
The worthless parasites who have battened on them,
Society, Church and all the ingrate rest, let loose

The mad dogs of war to drag them down again
Into the noisome dirt – spray them with mustard-gas,
Pepper them with machine-gun bullets – hesitate
At no infamy once more to enslave the mass

Heedless that this murderous myopia sacrifices
Ninety per cent of the potential glory of mankind,
Inhibits creative potentialities beyond the dreams
Of avarice, insists upon the leadership of the blind,
Those whose photographs adorn the *Tatler* and the *Bystander*.

This, Campbell, is the work you're busy with
– The insensate service of a modern Minotaur myth,
A racket ten million times worse than Cannibalism, run
By brainless blackguards – for what you deem fun!

And claim your infamy as ground for praise
Since you have nothing else to distinguish your days
Neither poet's laurels nor warrior's bays
But this sanguine and fecal halo in their place
That truly better fits your forcible-feeble face.

For all the good things in the Capitalist system
Like all the evil are founded on a gigantic crime
And need, as their hidden basis, preventible death
Disease and poverty, and hardship all the time
That a small class which never contributed to that good
But is responsible for almost all the evil
May lord it in lunatic luxury and power,
The ruin of mankind the wealth on which they revel.

Dulce et decorum est. . . . But the power to tell
When War is War and not brute murder is
A prerogative strictly confined of course
To those it affects least – the Upper Classes
– Those who have least judgment too in everything else,
Equally removed as those at the other end of the scale
From any interest in or contribution to
The arts or sciences; imposing and brainless as a whale.
Here, too, you've precedent, Campbell – and a rotten one!
In his 'Song of the English'[1] Kipling identified
The English with the mine-owners and the Government
As you identify all Right and Reason in the world
With the vile creatures of whom you are the natural agent.
And Sir John Fortescue[2] thought it would be a good thing
To flog the working classes back to work

[1] Contributed to the *Government Gazette* at the time of the General Strike, 1926.
[2] Letter to *The Times*, December 30, 1930.

Or – still better – to shoot them, Campbell, like you.
Be sure of one thing – we have taken your measure
Once and for all – cry up the hoary spells
Of exploitation, Campbell, as you will,
No matter what the workers' faults may be
At least they no longer lack the intelligence to see
The fraud under all the fine-sounding words and pious phrases,
The criminal character of your class-made Law
Pliant to the vile purposes of an inhuman system.
The dual standard we will tolerate no more
Of one law for the rich, another for the poor.
And when it comes to shooting or to flogging now
The workers' foes can no longer count on a monopoly of these
(Although in Spain the arms were on one side
As they still are in all industrial disputes,
Which is very convenient for men like you who need to know
Which side is best-equipped their 'bravery' to show!)
Knowing no country has ever had foes outside
A tithe as dangerous as its own ruling class.
Campbell, the gaff is blown once and for all
On all the old counters that you still employ
– They can no longer invoke respect or awe
In any but a viscero-tonic hobbledehoy.
And all the old confidence-tricksters are in the ludicrous position
Of a conjurer whose audience knows in advance how all his tricks
    are done.

POETS OF THE WORLD TO-DAY

*There is no longer any haven of refuge on five-sixths of this mad earth, for any poor
creature who wishes to escape from the horrors of capitalist civilisation. He must stand
his ground and fight it or go under. If he is barred by the collapse of capitalist finance from
being a wage slave, he must become a brigand, or sell his talents in some whorish way, or
die of hunger where he stands. Men of my profession generally take the choice of whore-
dom. While literature is still regarded as a noble art, those who pursue it are in the main a
spineless horde, grovelling before some rump-fed boor, who has made millions by selling
trashy newspapers, or else they are mouthpieces of the fantastic creeds that the mediocre
mob has invented in its war against the human intellect.*

                                                       Liam O'Flaherty

'Ní h-é lá na gaoithe lá na scolb.'
(When the storm is in its fury is not the time to make fast the thatch.)

THE ground on which the world has stood is cracking and sagging
    beneath it;
It was built in all its aspects on conventions once held true
Or at worst expedient, convenient; but these today
Are no longer believed – they have all been seen through.
No human action can proceed except on a belief,
A human organism must needs have sure ground for its feet.
It is impossible for that old world to continue then.
Its whole foundation is gone, its fall is complete.
In politics we think in terms of strategic reasons of State
That are echoes of a history that is *past*, a tale that is told;
Socially in terms of conditions only brute force holds together;
Economically with fictitious money no eye can behold;
Ethically with 'moral values' to which no human 'conscience'
Any longer corresponds; intellectually with a truth
Turned 'pragmatic'; and artistically with the self-expression
Of souls that no longer believe in themselves – and rightly forsooth!

No psychological conjuring can save such a world.
It is no use saying: 'Unless you bring yourselves to believe
In these expedient conventions the social fabric will crash.'
That ballyhoo is running like water through a sieve.
Belief can be produced neither by promise nor menace.
It depends on the quality of its foundations.

No manipulation of old formulas, no glib phrasing,
No amount of tied-Press eloquence and mendacity,
No amount of *professed* belief shouting itself hoarse,
Can substitute itself for the motive power of humanity.
Our religious, political, historical, social and ethical
Traditions are wholly disbelieved; and being discredited
Can neither move mountains nor the smallest cogwheel
Of the world's machinery any more than the dead.

It is no longer just matters of polite argument
Among well-bred people, but the very substance and status

Of our life and death issues, our most crucial concerns,
That have become shams and unveracities. That is
The appalling task that confronts us; not to find truth,
That monstrous and shocking opposite of the foundations of society,
Scandalous in its gross unfamiliarity, only to be faced
With girded loins and hearts of trebled brass – vainly.

We live in a world that has become
Intolerable as a subject of passive reflection.
What is our response to the unescapable reality?
Are we too like these miserable little cliques to turn
Because of theoretic inadequacy
From social causation, from the poetry of purgative action
And try to find form and significance
In pure feeling itself, transplanted and reimagined;
Seeking the meaning of experience in the phenomena of experience,
Pure sensation becoming an ultimate value
In the neurotic and mystical attempt
To give physicality an intellectual content,
In the sensitizing of nerves already raw,
– Meaningless emotion aroused automatically
Without satisfaction or education, as in melodrama?
Man can find his own dignity only in action now.
Most people live by a social discipline become intolerably artificial,
A constriction whose only merit is its security;
They feel that; they feel the pettiness and emptiness of a social form
Repeated beyond the day of its absolute necessity;
But they fear the possible chaos that always threatens those who break
        through a form;
They are right to fear it – for every creation risks being a
        destruction only;
Yet as long as there is strength for creation creation must be risked.

Young poets, the height and depth of your writings
Will be measured by the extent to which,
Sir Thomas Inskip permitting – or not,
The dialectics of our era find expression
In the artistic imagery – how widely, forcefully, clearly

The burning contemporary problems are expressed in it,
Class tendencies, the struggles and ideals
Of the proletariat, bent on changing the world,
And consequently on changing human nature.

The deathly obliterating breaths of wingless civilisationism
And frigid metropolitan snobbery are intolerable to a forward art
Time is confronting today with such majestic and responsible tasks
That no writer deserves the name save as his works impart
The motion of tremendous strata in history, the rough
Flaming beautiful language of popular spectacles, no
Superficial apologetics but deep artistic cognition of contemporaneity
– Young Poets, these are the sign-manuals that your poems must show.

The working class is the noblest of all classes judged alike
By its historic mission and the everyday relations that exist in it;
Its tremendous stores of good nature, solidarity, and comradeship.
The trouble is not with material want, life's maladjustments, and yet
These are primary factors, and one cannot rely
On spontaneity here – but art is a powerful means
Of communication, contact, drawing together; it must
Expel the poison, the contagion, of the old society and transform these
     scenes.

Wipe out the false word 'humanism'; our art is not to be
Misericordious, toothless, pacifist, but the art of full-blooded men,
Each in command of a full arsenal of feeling, including the feeling of
     social hatred.
No inertia, cowardice, quietism, weariness, apathy then.
(Even as sailors never want fair weather all the time
And have no savage exultation in the storm – no lust
Of life in their powers of endurance, their fighting strength, their
     desperate skill,
As all true sailors must.)
No hating by request but by oneself – vital images thrown in our
     way of life,
Grim selection of ideas and feelings, harsh opinions, intolerance,
     frankness – all

The red roaring life of Burns, Fergusson, old Scotland generally,
Hypocrites have whitewashed, emasculating us under their thrall.

The tide of tyranny and obscurantism
Is today at our garden's edge.
We are seeing and enduring events
Worse than which have not been seen and endured
Since man became himself.

The most terrifying spectacle the world has ever known,
Vast mobilised armies of maddened adolescents
And criminal leaders mouthing the foulest perfidies
Amid roars of loutish laughter and animal applause.

Young poets, remember above all today
(This darkest and longest day in human history)
The great imponderables of the world;
The power of courageous bearing,
The majesty of right action,
The comfort and stiffening to our friends
Of faithful words and counsel.

Young poets, here is your slogan.
            – Lorca, not Campbell!
                Christ, not Barabbas!

You ask whether the False-Hero ramp, with its cultures of contagion,
Simple Impudence and first surprising success,
Then Plotting Impudence, Lying Impudence, and Murderous
        Impudence,
Will not bring down the whole of humanity.

The recent political turn of the people
Against ramps, impudence, lies, intrigues, and banditry
Proves, however, the antique dictum:
Never has a whole nation been seen to act wickedly.
Perhaps the literary world will turn next.

. . . But people do not like to be freed of a clog,
Sentimental and intellectual,
And I am ready to hear the barbarous noise
(Preluded in Campbell's poem, Garvin's writings and elsewhere)
Of Milton's pack of 'owls and cuckoos, asses, apes, and dogs.'
There is nothing the Nazis and Fascists have done
That the English haven't done again and again
In the *name* of very different ideals, of course,
And are not repeating or trying to repeat
Continually. The horrors of Czechoslovakia
And China and Spain are the very stuff
Our Empire is founded upon. We have nothing to learn
From Hitler or Mussolini. We've forgotten more than they know
Of their stock-in-trade. Members of the House of Lords,
Judges, J.P.s, M.P.s, Clergymen, schoolteachers, ladies,
And retired Colonels and letters-to-the-Editor writers
Have said *ad nauseam* all that Roy Campbell says
(*This England* is full of it every week)
But – it is a curious fact – never a poet before,
Never a poet – not even Kipling!
The tongue that Milton and Shelley used
Is put to strange uses. Campbell is no exception
– Except in verse. He did well to write in English
– The language of the Power above all responsible
For the horrors of Abyssinia, China, and Spain,
And the base betrayal of Czechoslovakia.
Ah, the English are Christians – their whole life is based
On an innocent man put to death for their sake
A sacrifice they very graciously accept,
Never doubting they are worth it.

A man of genius must take life as he finds it;
The material of his art is the existence of his contemporaries;
English life presents him with nothing but money and sex
And with them he must do his best, for he will get no other.

Impossible with such impure material to create; the imagination
Becomes critical, finds nothing to criticise,

Sees the humour of the situation, and finds its material
Admirably suited for satire.

If it can start no pure idea nor joy
To disturb the stillness of the muddy flow
Yet it can send up the bubbles of laughter
To cause a stir in it.

It is simple enough. At the bottom of every genius
There is, as Stendhal said, a fund of good logic.
Nothing more is needed than its application
To the false ideas with which men's minds are beset.

Carry them to their logical extreme
And you arrive at absurdity
Just as when a pure idea is developed
It tops imagination, takes wings unto itself,
And reaches sublimity wherein to dwell
In harmony with all other ideas.

When that operation has been performed
Then money and sex will begin to exercise
Their natural instinct of gravitation
Towards all other facts,
Will establish connections with them once again,
And human energy will begin once more
Worthily to express itself
And incidentally English life
Will become dramatic
Instead of theatrical and hypocritical.

None, Campbell, are for being what they are in fault,
But for not being what they would be thought
– The English civilised, Christian, exponents of justice and fair-play;
And you for posing as a poet and thinker
And a fighter for decent values!

Well, there you have it.

Non Mollare![1] I sing of the Spanish Republic,
Of men who went to their deaths not with the hope of victory,
But in order to set up a principle and give
An example of faith, cost what it might – men who knew
That wrong, however strong, must be continuously challenged,
Since if even only a handful resist
The unanimity is broken.
Conscience resumes its rights.
Crying: 'We shall never surrender.
One period is ended, another begins.
But the struggle continues.'

In Britain up to now
The resistance has been fragmentary, the leaders passive or inept.
The masses have been left to themselves. The old parties,
The old cliques, have literally prevented us from fighting.
After two centuries of petty politics they still
Take shelter behind impotent moralising, boycott bold action,
And allow everything to be swept away
While they sit, contemplating
Their legalitarian navel.

British individualism and liberty have been able to survive to the extent to which they have survived because you make only very moderate use of them. You talk about the uniformization of Germany during the last four years, but on the other hand, if I were dictator of Britain, there would be very little to put you into uniform for. You are so used to living up to not State-imposed but convention-imposed *uniformity, that you can indulge in whatever individualism you desire – for you never go beyond those convention-imposed limits.*

DR. ABSHAGEN

THE world is fast bound in the snares of Varuna
– 'Cords consisting of serpents,' according to Kalluka
(*Pasaih sarpa-rajjughih*). The winkings of men's eyes
Are all numbered by him; he wields the universe
As gamesters handle dice. These are the unexampled days
Of false witness – a barbarous regime which gives power over life and
     death
To an oligarchy of brigands and adventurers,
Without security from vexation by irresponsible tyrants,

---

[1] Do not give in!

Without protection of the home against the aggression of criminal
     bands,
Without impartial justice, without dignity.
We are denied all the deepest needs of men who do not wish
To sink to the level of the beasts – condemned
To a life deprived of its salt.

Already, everywhere,
The speed-up, the 'church-work,' the lead poisoning,
The strain that drives men nuts.
The art of teaching fish by slow degrees
To live without water.
Men cheaper than safety
– Human relations have never sunk so low.

The British are a frustrated people,
Victims of arrested development,
Withered into cynics
And spiritual valetudinarians,
Their frustration due
To a social environment
Which has given them no general sense
Of the facts of life,
And no sense whatever
Of its possibilities;
Their English culture a mere simulacrum,
Too partial and provincial
To fulfil the true function of culture,
The illumination of the particular
In terms of the universal;
Beside the strong vigour of daily life
It is but an empty shadow.

Anywhere you go in Britain today
You can hear the people
Economising consciousness,
Struggling to think and feel as little as possible
Just as you can hear a countryside in winter
Crepitating in the grip of an increasing frost.

Like the termites we have our proletariat,
Army, pampered idle rich, exploited classes,
Tribal and inter-racial feuds – practise birth control,
Have crèches for the young, nurses, infant foods, etc.
Their armies are equipped with armour, sickle jaws,
Even cylinders of petrifying liquid.
Though stone-blind they manage to communicate,
Both by touch and by some sort of wireless,
And if they have no arts they are
Like the British people
Exceedingly versatile and accomplished craftsmen.
There is little they don't know about architecture,
Carpentry, drainage, ventilation,
Central heating and air conditioning.
Their skyscrapers rise thirty or more feet above the ground
And wherever they are not kept down by their enemies
They build over hundreds of square miles of territory.
They have no vision, they do not reason,
Blindly they carry out the injunctions
Of an Inner Voice – as the British people do.
And the Parliament at Westminster is to us
As the sort of will emanating from the queen
That organises and directs all the varied
And continuous work of a great termite colony
– This queen, a great bloated watery mass,
Safe in a dark cavity far underground,
With nevertheless a power so all-pervading
That, though limited by distance, it can pass
Unreduced through solid matter, even a steel plate,
The blind and deaf workers entirely dependent on it
For all direction and force of action.

Days of the general atimy of the human race,
Of greed that for the momentary frivolous advantage
Of a few nonentities exhausts the basic riches of the earth,
Of ῥᾳδιουργεῖν – reckless, unscrupulous, or knavish conduct,
(Plutarch used the word of 'false entries.' In the portion
Of a letter of Dionysius of Corinth to Soter

ῥᾳδιουργῆσαι is used of 'falsification of texts.'
Irenaeus seems to use this verb in the generic sense
Of 'garbling' – for 'distortion of *sense*' he seems to prefer
ἐφαρμόζειν or μεθαρμόζειν, implying 'adaptation,')
With Tarde I discover crime in all professions.
From the out-and-out criminal to the 'most honest' merchant
We pass through a series of transitions – the cheating tradesman,
The adulterating grocer, the upper classes reputed to be honest
Committing extortions and making doubtful bargains
Till, almost, like Peter Lavrov, one feels inclined
To champion the plain straightforward criminal,
And cry out against the whole commercial world
As Vanzetti cried: 'My father has many field, houses, garden.
He deal in wine and fruits and granaries.
He wrote to me many times to come back home
And be a business man. Well, this supposed murderer
Had answered to him that my conscience
Do not permit to me to be a business man.'
Campbell, I too am a Scot.
Not a Campbell, however, but a Murray
And, thinking of *Flowering Rifle*,
I remember my whole inheritance
Of Gaelic wisdom and pronounce
Against you, as mine too, the 'Hate of Cadoc':[1]
'I hate the judge who loves money
And the bard who loves war
And the chiefs who do not guard their subjects,
And the nations without vigour.
I hate houses without dwellers,
Lands untilled,
Fields that bear no harvest,
Landless clans,
The agents of error,
The oppressors of truth,
Lost learning,
And uncertain boundaries,
Journeys without safety,

[1] A Welsh saint of the sixth century.

Families without virtue,
Lawsuits without reason,
Ambushes and treasons,
Falsehood in council,
Justice unhonoured;
I hate a man without trade,
A labourer without freedom,
A home without a teacher,
A false witness before a judge,
The miserable exalted,
Follies in place of teaching,
Knowledge without inspiration,
Sermons without eloquence,
And a man without conscience.'

And I sing, too, in St. Cadoc's words:
'Without knowledge, no power.
Without knowledge, no wisdom.
Without knowledge, no freedom.
Without knowledge, no beauty.
Without knowledge, no nobleness.
Without knowledge, no victory.
Without knowledge, no honour.
The best of occupations, work.
The best of cares, justice.
The best of characters, generosity.'
And to every man in the world I cry
'Remember that thou art a MAN;
And that there is nothing like him
Who is king over himself.'

Because you have sided with the Beasts
Who leaped on a Decency, Campbell,

Because you have sided with those who drew the sword
And who carry the sole responsibility
For all this terrible time when fear and hate and cruelty and horror
And death untimely

And the maimings and the blindings and the chokings
That are worse than death,
Were loosed upon a world that should have been,
And may still be, secure.

Because when all the generous young genius of the world
Hastened to the assistance of the Spanish people,
You alone took the other side – the side no other
Poet of any reputation took, or could take,
The side the leading writers of every country
Denounced in the name of Freedom and Intelligence;
You alone bowed the knee to Baal

Because you have betrayed the cause of humanity
At a time when Fascism everywhere throws off its mask,
And we are faced with unequalled barbaric violence,
Murder, economic depression, growth of poverty,
Preparedness for war, and humiliation of the intellect!

Cervantes wrote on the escutcheon of Don Quixote, Campbell,
'Post tenebras spero lucem.' What a monstrosity
You will look in that clear shining to come!

What cretins and morons will follow *you*
Rather than Romain Rolland, André Malraux,
Hans Marchwitza, Gustav Regler, Ilya Erenburg,
Ludwig Renn, Ernest Hemingway, Ralph Bates, John Cornford,
And all the other anti-Fascist fighters?

All men of crystal-clear honesty, will power, talent,
Devotion to the great idea of the liberation of mankind,
The stuff of which real heroism is made.

Do you remember, Campbell, how the whole civilised world
Joined in the campaign for Renn's release?
His name was on everyone's lips,
Like the names of Ernst Thälmann and Karl Ossietski.
Your name will never be there, Campbell.
Even those who esteem some of your poems

– Or would do if you wrote a hundred times greater poems
Than any you have written yet –
Even in claiming so much for you will hang their heads.
You have committed the unforgivable offence.
You have sinned against the Light.

No, Campbell, you have made yourself one with those
Who murdered Mühsam and hounded Ossietski to death;
But you shall not gag us, nor stifle our love
For the working people or the flaming fire
Of our passion for the truth.
Ramón Sender, Ralph Fox, Christopher Caudwell,
And all the others who have given or risked their lives
For peace and human freedom,
For culture and the dignity of man!
You dare to spit upon the names
Of men such as these, Campbell,
And claim superior intelligence
And a clearer conscience –
> Tell that to your friend, Franco,
> Or whisper it in Goering's ear,
> But do not add to your incalculable offence
> By asking any Scotsman to believe you.

Scotland, thank God, gave scores of her sons
To the Republican cause in Spain,
Sent out her doctors and nurses,
Ambulances and foodships.
Ninety per cent of the Scottish people
Were whole-heartedly for the Republican cause,
– Hating like Hell all you have fought for and praised.
Are all these people wrong, Campbell,
And only you right?
You were always a braggart, Campbell,
But in the eyes of Scotland you rank
With Judas and Sir John Menteith
And the executioners of William Wallace
And the Judge who sentenced John Maclean.

Mental defectives, forward!

Campbell needs you!

Campbell expects every man to do his dirty!

See Life! Visit sunny Spain!
Mobilise the idiots!
Form fours, the insane!
Follow the Furor!
Field–Marshall Campbell leads the charge in person.
– The charge of the Gadarene swine!

Ah, Campbell, as Maxim Gorki said,
The philistines' fundamental slogan
Is 'Thus it was, thus it will always be.'
I understand the rhythm of your poetry now
– It reminds me of the automatic swinging of the pendulum.
You philistines are truly degenerating.
Like fish, your 'rotting starts from the head.'

Campbell, suppose for a moment you had been
A far greater poet than you are (yet with a kink, a blind-spot,
That made you take the side you've taken) and that your poetry
Were as great a service to world-fascism as it is
An insult to all democracy and decency!
Mussolini might have invited you to Rome
And Hitler to Berlin, and disciplined millions brayed your name,
While Ciano or Ribbentrop proclaimed your genius
– Honestly, Campbell, does *that* not give you pause?
Could you really associate with these creatures,
Accept their honours, listen to the infernal din
Of the Totalitarian *claque* applauding your great work?
– Greater than Goethe, or that damned Jew, Heine,
Greater than Dante, or D'Annunzio even,
Greater even than Baldur von Shirach.
Great Campbell, greatest poet the world has ever seen,
As Mussolini and Hitler are its greatest rulers,

(With Franco not far behind
But rather like a duck!)

No poet the world has ever known
Has risked a nightmare such as that before
– And the fair hands of Mrs Neville Chamberlain
In the sight of a hundred million conscript people
Would crown you Cheer-Leader of World Fascism
And encircle your brow with a garland of the best barbed wire!

Appalling vision! Fit to still
The Heart of Song for ever
And idiotise all mankind.

Campbell, like Hitler,
Mussolini and Neville Chamberlain,
One of the greatest men the world has seen
Since Jesus Christ!
Singing like the stars of the morning
The beauties of bloody Badajoz,
The fiery splendours of Guernica,
And all the rest of it.

Great Campbell! Great God!

No wonder you deride our vision,
The world seen, as Socialists have hoped to see
(Denouncing all the incidentals of Capitalism,
The low knavery, the ferocious cruelty,
The plotting and the lying and the bribing,
The blustering and bragging, the screaming egotism,
The hurrying and worrying) at last
(All the sham reformers self-stultified and self-convicted)
The radical Democracy left without a lie
To cover its nakedness, the rush that will never be checked,
The tide that will never turn till it has reached its flood.
Die Kunst ist überflüssig.
Sheer Communism!

Alight and alive with fundamental truth,
The rational mind, 'like water brimming in a crystal bowl,'
Reaching the utmost bounds of human thought,
The culmination of human intelligence,
The Idea of a World, purged by the artist's contempt
For all forms and kinds of furniture –
Furniture of conventions, of ready-made opinions,
Of 'thought' chawed up, vomited, and reassimilated a thousand times,
Furniture of family life,
Furniture of soul-aspiration,
Furniture of 'home,'
– A World (freed from 'civilisation'
With its tyranny of shams, its shoddy ideals)
With no room now save for fundamental authenticity,
Climbing out of the welter of confused thinking
A little nearer the stars of pure reason.

THE PARABLE OF CHAMBERLAIN

THE frightful vision I've conjured up
Of the triumph of Fascist Song
Reminds me, Campbell, of the following poem
By Count Alexis Tolstoy,
Which, I think, sums up
The present position splendidly: –

The infamous assassin struck with a dagger
            The great Delarue
In the breast: the other bowed, uncov'ring politely,
            And said: 'How d'you do!'
The villain again more deeply plunged the dagger,
            Far as he could:
And smiling still the stabbed man murmured: 'Your weapon's
            Remarkably good.'

The villain next the right of the other attacking
    Wounds him in the chest;
Delarue shaking a finger at him in fun says
    'Oh, naughty, naughty jest!'
And now in frenzy wild the villain all over
    With wounds terrible to see
Disfigures the other's body. Delarue: 'How time's flying!
    Will you stay to tea?'

The villain knelt and sobbed and cried, asking pardon,
    Disliking the scene.
'For God's sake, man, get up from the floor!' Delarue cries.
    'It isn't clean.'

The villain lies at his feet repentant and grieving,
    Confessing his wrong:
Delarue the prostrate man upraises with arms that
    Are loving and strong.
'I see you weep. For what? No use bewailing
    A trifle, my dear sir!
I'll speak to the Tsar on your behalf. He'll on you
    A pension confer.
The ribbon of Stanislaus shall deck your bosom soon –
    Does that make you vain? –
I can secure these things, as having the Tsar's ear,
    His chief Chamberlain.
Or would you care to wed my daughter, my Mary?
    If that is your desire
Ten thousand pounds in notes I will on you settle,
    A gift from her sire.
And now, I pray, accept from me this portrait here,
    If you'll be so kind!
A token showing love for you. It isn't framed –
    I know you won't mind.'

The villain's face grew evil now and sarcastic:
    'Is this then my fate
To owe my life and all I have to a man who
    With love repays hate?'

The lofty spirit thus the base aye discovers,
    Reveals this disgrace.
Assassins may forgive the gift of a portrait;
    Not pension and place.
The fires of envy smoulder in his vile heart's depths,
    Dark altars of shame;
And while yet the ribbon's new on his shoulder
    They burst into flame.
New filled with malice devilish he sets his dagger
    In venom to steep;
And from the back of Delarue he deals him
    A blow sure and deep.
His pains forbidding him to sit, on the floor low
    Poor Delarue lies,[1]

[1] 'Delarue is not a specimen of that "purified virtue" which one never meets in Nature. He is a real man with all the human weaknesses. He is vain ("I am a chamberlain," he says) and fond of money; whilst his fantastic immunity from the stabs of the villain's dagger is, of course, merely an obvious symbol of his infinitely good humour, invincible, even insensitive to all wrongs – a trait also to be met with in life, though comparatively seldom. Delarue is not a personification of virtue, but a naturally kind-hearted man, in whom kindness overpowered all his bad qualities, driving them to the surface of his soul and revealing them there in the form of inoffensive weaknesses. The "villain" also is not the conventional essence of vice, but the normal mixture of good and bad qualities. The evil of envy, however, rooted itself in the very depth of his soul, and forced out all the good in him to the *epidermis* of the soul, so to speak, where the kindness became a sort of very active but superficial sentimentality. When Delarue replies to a number of offensive actions with polite words and with an invitation to tea, the villain's sentimentality is greatly moved by these acts of gentleness, and he descends to a climax of repentance. But when later the Chamberlain's civility is changed into the sincere sympathy of a deeply good-natured man, who retaliates upon his enemy for the evil done, not with the seeming kindness of nice words and gestures, but by the actual good of practical help – when, I say, Delarue shows interest in the life of his enemy, is willing to share with him his fortune, to secure for him an official post, and even to provide him with family happiness, then this *real* kindness, penetrating into the deeper moral strata of the villain, reveals his inner moral emptiness, and when it reaches the very bottom of his soul it arouses the slumbering crocodile of envy. It is not the kindness of Delarue that excites the envy of the villain – as you have seen, he can also be kind, and when he cried, pitifully wringing his hands, he doubtless was conscious of this. What did excite his envy was the – for him – unattainable infinite vastness and *simple seriousness* of that kindness:

    "Assassins may forgive the gift of a portrait;
      Not pension and place."

Is it not realistic? Do we not see this in everyday life? One and the same moisture

The villain flies upstairs, and here poor Mary falls
        Despoiled as his prize.

The villain fled to Birmingham – as Governor there
        Is justly esteemed;
And, later, in London, as Premier, worthy honour high
        Is soon by all men deemed;
And soon he attains to an honourable membership
        In the Council of World Dictators;
Oh! what a good lesson this story teaches us!
        Oh, what a fate!

Fascism glorifies might; its battlecry
'Victory to the strong,
And subjection or annihilation to the weak.'
But – are *you* a strong man, Campbell?
Fascism reminds me of Wedekind's play *Hidalla*;
A man intoxicated with beauty founds a society
For the production of physically perfect human beings
Which only men and women specially selected
For their beauty could join.
When he himself appears on the stage
The audience is surprised to see a hunchback.
He is merely founder and secretary of the society
           – Not a member!

It is the same with Hitler. The apostle of racialism
Has no bearing, no natural assurance, no unconstraint,
No firmness or nobility of figure – in short,
Lacks all the distinguishing characteristics of pure race.

---

of vivifying rain causes the development of healing powers in some herbs and of poison in others. In the same way a real act of kindness, after all, only helps to develop good in the good man and evil in the evil one. If so, how can we – have we even the right to – let loose our kind sentiments without choice and distinction? Can we praise the parents for zealously watering from the good can the poisonous flowers growing in their garden, where their children play? I ask you, why was Mary ruined?' – (*War, Progress and the End of History*, by Vladimir Soloviev.)

He is a plebeian, 'formless and faceless,' of poor breed.
Who sees him first is appalled
At the startling insignificance of this man who has set the world agog.
So, Campbell, with the calibre of your ideas,
The petty stature of all your associates,
                    Your size – as a poet or soldier!

Fascism is strong, but not with the strength
Of a physically perfect man. Its strength
Is the incalculable spasms of strength of a maniac,
Or the hellish power of a plague
                    Carried by lice on rats.

Great ships are foundering everywhere, the watchman said,
And only their chamberpots come up, and sail instead!

And the great Leader, the Man-God, you worship
Is 'a man whose countenance is a caricature,
A man whose framework seems cartilaginous,
Without bones – a man inconsequent and voluble,
Ill-poised, insecure, the very prototype of the Little Man!'
Why did you not put your photograph in front of your poem,
        Campbell?

A lock of lank hair falls over an insignificant
And slightly retreating forehead. The back head is shallow.
The nose is large but badly shaped and without character.
His movements are awkward, almost undignified.
There is no trace in his face of any inner conflict
Or self-discipline. Fit generalissimo, Campbell,
            For conscript armies armed with flowering rifles!

And the Little Man spits his revilement at all decent citizens,
Even as you do – crying, 'Parliament bugs, ne'er-do-wells,
Sluggards, highwaymen, vagabonds, rabble,
Cheats, degenerate crew, wretches, stupid ignoramuses,
Chatterboxes, simpletons, empty-heads, sillies,
Deceivers, political Tom Thumbs, useless scoundrels,

Cowards, rogues, villains, villains, villains.'
You may not be a deliberate liar, Campbell,
But Fascism believes in exploiting
The weakness and bestiality of the masses,
And the Propaganda of the Lie.[1]
And a man is known by the company he keeps.
Birds of a feather flock together,
– And you consort with vultures and carrion crows!

The further society draws away, Campbell,
From the fundamentals of Christianity,
From peace, from love of one's neighbour, from charity,
The more receptive it becomes
To doctrines like Hitler's, Mussolini's, Franco's, yours.
– Doctrines which are a declaration of war
Against the basis of our intellectual and moral existence;
A crude, wild, outrageous attack on humanity
Before which the so-called conflict
Between Christianity and Socialism pales into insignificance.
– The flowering rifle only flowers in stinking smoke,
And all its fruit is wounds, and pain, and death.

No decent thing anywhere in the world today
Is unmenaced by the forces that have produced
In Italy, Germany, Spain – aye, England and France –
       Your infuriated imbeciles of friends.
And these poor people of Spain who have fought
So marvellously against such unconscionable odds,

---

[1] 'A man who thinks he can reconcile Christianity with National Socialism is neither a true Christian nor a true National Socialist.' – ERNST BERGMANN.

Hitler in *Mein Kampf* lays it down as a 'principle . . . that part of the secret of being believed lies in the size of your lie, since the broad masses of the people, in the deepest depths of their hearts, are probably corrupt rather than consciously and intentionally evil, and will therefore, in the primitive simplicity of their minds, more easily be taken in by a big lie than by a small one, for very likely they themselves sometimes lie in small things, but would feel too ashamed to indulge in a really big lie. . . . An untruth of this kind would never occur to them, and they will never be able to believe in the possibility of such insolent, scandalous distortion; even when it has been proved untrue, yet for a long time they will have their doubts and hesitate, or at least take some part of it as true; therefore however impertinent the lie, part of it will always stick.'

H

Fighting in their own land for the basic decencies of life
Against conscripts and foreign mercenaries
And denied the means of effective self-defence,
Forced to fight with pitiful makeshift weapons,
Aye, and with their bare hands, against the deadliest weapons of
    modern war,
Have fought not only for themselves – but for us,
And for all Freedom, Justice, and Peace,
All honesty and honour and friendship and love and truth,
Against the hellish baboonery you champion, Campbell.

No man with the heart and wit of a louse, albeit
His training, traditions and circumstances
May have made it difficult for him
To share the ideas of Socialists and Anarchists
And divided him from sympathy with
And understanding of the working class,
But feels his heart touched with silence and shame
And a terrible dread,
And knows that the fight is only beginning
And that the issue far outruns
The petty points you have put,
Goes down to the very foundations of life!
And whatever the outcome may be must sweep every landmark away.
– I'd rather have been Van der Lubbe,
        Campbell, than you
At this greatest turning-point in human history.

Anyone but a Fascist – a fellow like Campbell –
Among decent working men might well feel
Like a stockbroker at a distinguished medical society dinner,
Who said with a rare access to self-criticism:
'There's something *to* these chaps.
They're different from us business men.'
– But not a Fascist, a fellow like Campbell;
'Make the blighters toe the line,
Or mow them down with machine-guns!
We'll larn them! And their wives and children with them

Just for good measure! Human beings? Pooh!'
Theirs not to reason why.
Theirs but to do as they're told or die.
The peasants must be driven back to their former state
Of almost geological resignation; the workers cowed again:
The intellectuals given only a choice between
                    Becoming pariahs or state employees.
– And General Roy Campbell, *preux chevalier*,
With the courage, kindliness, modesty, sense of humour
                    Of the true English gentleman,
                    Feels like a dog with two tails!
I wouldn't give one Red Asturias miner
Or Asturias miner's wife or child
                    For him and all his kind!
If it had only been Spain Campbell's bluff might have held,
But the Hoare-Laval Pact, Abyssinia, China, Vienna,
And Czechoslovakia – the Peace Ballot,
Baldwin's cynical confession of how he tricked the electorate
And countless other examples – the game is up, Campbell.
Shame has struck deep to every clean heart in the world.
Everyone has felt the touch of the finger of death
                    And the horrible foretaste of corruption.
We know the truth about our own country too
– That we are in the grip of liars and ruffians
                    One with the G.P.I. that is Germany
                    And the *Folie de Grandeur* that is Rome.
And there is not a true heart in the world not dark
With full knowledge of the Hell we too must go through
– The terrible price we must ere long pay
                    For the perfidy you represent.
But it is always darkest just before the dawn.
I do not doubt the issue. Fascism is a foul disease
And if a man die of a disease it is no disgrace
Nor are the victorious bacilli to be praised,
Yet all the red corpuscles must rush to the rescue
And in the last resort Humanity will win through.
That Mankind should perish in such a plague
Would make lunacy of the whole creation.

But in the last analysis the fact is that the Fascists
Are conspiring against the very sense and meaning of human life
And that the instinct for self-preservation
Will compel mankind to throw off
The horrible incubus with which they have saddled it.
And if not – if Fascism wins – who would wish to live?
The victory of Fascism would be like the victory of Cancer
Which ends not only in the deaths of its victims
But *ipso facto* in the death of the disease itself.

Aye, Campbell, birds of a feather flock together,
And we have seen the interrelations of things at last
– Many elements some of us deemed innocuous
Or irrelevant to the Socialist Cause
Have come out unmistakably in their true colours now
Mouthing their ancient pretensions still
But shoulder to shoulder with Insanity, Murder, and
            Unspeakable Vice
– And Campbell, the White Hope of English Poetry,
Comes in at the tail of the foul procession.

All the bourgeoisie are alike in this,
Running the whole gamut of life from A to B,
University professors, lecturers, school-teachers,
Ministers, and all that awful gang of mammalia,
The high mucky-mucks.
They have all the same pettifogging spirit,
So narrow it shows little but its limits,
The same incapacity for culture and creative work,
(Capitalism, *arida nutrix* of hundreds of thousands of inhuman human
            beings,
Incapable of any process of spiritual growth and conquest,
Destitute of all rich and lively experience,
Without responsibility or honour,
Completely insensible to any of the qualities
That make for a life worth having,
Pusillanimous and frigid time-servers,

Idiots without ideas or feelings
                    (Full of caginess, that's all)
Who understand nothing and love nothing,
Devouring time as ducks gobble water, in order to live!
And, like ducks, finding nothing but a few insects for nourishment.

Only once in a lifetime a few of these hoodlums,
Embarrassed by some proffer of genuine affection
Or witnessing a personal friend die, may feel
Ashamed at being so poor and hard, so incapable
Of finding any place in their lives for the former, so lacking
In everything that might be of use in helping anyone to die,
And see, for an instant, that they have nothing inside them
Save things that serve the purposes of everyday life,
A life of comfort, one's own life, a damned insensitivity.
Campbell has not experienced one of these revealing instants.

'Wanna go home, baby?
Yes, for all that
(Suffer us not to mock ourselves with falsehood)
I am homesick after my own kind.
Home to many deceits,
Home to old lies and new infamy,
Usury age-old and age-thick
And liars in public places.'

These boobs don't know the answers!

Take another eyeful of the pulchritude!

What a pity they're not like Salome
Who threw a wild party and got up
With a real head next morning!

I, too, am heard as one 'whose armoury is full
Of hackneyed phrases – the class struggle,
The capitalist system, the bourgeoisie, exploitation,
Surplus value, wage slavery, and so forth; all stale stuff

Discussed and rediscussed a million times. There is nothing new
To be said about the theory of Marxism today.'
I am heard as the grass of the field is looked at.
'There it is. One has seen it all before.'
The journalists go by me like a tydinges of magpies
Munching vacuity and excreting lies,
– And leave me to confront the Medoysa's saxificous head.
But I am not like the Persian fatalist in Herodotus,
'Knowing the bitterest of griefs, to see clearly
And yet to be unable to do anything.' I am full
Of the violent energy of the minute electron
In the enormous atom, the thrilling vigour of the pentathlete.
My purpose is clear and irresistible within me,
As I look through my all-observing and half-shut eyes,
At the bridge of this All-Horror's nose,
The most exacerbating form of regard in the world.
WE HAVE WHAT IT TAKES.

The capitalist system can exist indefinitely
Without culture, morals, or religion – sans teeth,
Sans eyes, sans taste, sans everything, but,
When all these are swept away, the one thing left untouched
Of all that it ever had. Let us not bother then
With little local triumphs in culture, morals,
And so forth. No positive result can be achieved
Until that one thing is touched – that linch-pin
Removed – we must go for that and that alone
With that real and persistent purpose, that necessary fanaticism,
That unquenchable zest at that *atemberaubend* pace,
With that extreme pressure and blinding overwork
Only genius knows (resembling the intense
Activity of the brain to electrical impressions
So that a man who accidentally seized a telephone wire
That was grounded, said: 'Though the duration of the shock
Could not have been more than a couple of seconds,
A man riding by on a bicycle at good speed
Having only time to pass about 30 yards beyond me,
Before the operator got through talking and opened the switch

Yet I could see every spoke on the bicycle
And it barely seemed to be turning.
I could feel every reversal of the current
And these reversals occur at the rate of sixty complete cycles per
    second.')
So we – we artists – to do work worthy of our time
To write about contemporary things, to do work
Worthy of our art that is to say, is like trying
To keep pace with the four horses of the Apocalypse.
Our life is changing with so great rapidity.
'*Steht die Zunge selten ein.*' Seldom? Never!
Yet we must cope with it – master it – be armed with faith in
    victory
And with an exact and faultless knowledge of fact.

And no longer blame anything and everything
But the actual easily removable cause,
With a capacity for heterotopic pain, like the common
Reference of angina to the arm, or like the shoulder pain
In liver and diaphragmatic disease, or the attribution
Of the labour pains of childbirth to regions remote from the uterus.
All but a century ago – a century already –
Since Engels and Marx in London met with the members
Of the Fraternal Democrats, the League of the Just, and so on,
And the Communist Manifesto was drawn up,
And Heine admitted in an agony of fear
That the future belonged to Communism, crying:
'*Fiat justitia pereat Mundus*! This Communism,
So hostile to my interests and inclinations, yet
Exercises a charm upon me before which
I am powerless. A terrible syllogism holds me in its grip;
If I am unable to refute the premise
"That every man has the right to eat," then I am forced
To submit to all the consequences. A generosity of despair
Seizes me and I cry: For long this old society
Has been judged and condemned, let justice be done,
Let this old world be smashed in which innocence is long since dead,
Where egoism prospers and man battens on man.'

But there is no generosity of despair in you, Campbell,
And no concern for the things which made Heine pause.
Everyone knows that the future belongs to Communism
And that the present system is rotten from top to bottom
Yet their despair is lest it should not last out their time
And Communism belong not only to the future, but to now
(*Lead thou my feet. I do not ask to see*
The distant scene. One step enough for me.')
They are held in no terrible syllogism's grip.
'It is only the cyclical slump – the boom will come;
There are signs that we are turning the corner.'
– *Especially so now that the smart world*
Has revived the art of walking!

But then, Campbell, Heine's a poet,
That's where the difference is.
And so – the battle continues.

PART III

ONE loves the temporal, some unique manifestation,
Something irreplaceable that dies.

But one is loyal to an ideal limit
Involved in all specific objects of love
And in all cooperating wills.

Shall the lonely griefs and joys of men
Forever remain a pluralistic universe?
Need they, if thought and will are bent in common interest
In making this universe *one*?

All these things are clearer to me today than ever;
The ineluctable individuation of personality,
The importance of indefinables in life,
The moral urgency of definition if we are to make secure
For eternity the treasures of the moment
– As you, my Spanish comrades, have added

Its greatest chapter to the great story of Spain,
The crowning glory of all that long history
Defeat though it seem yet, aye, and added
One of the sublimest sagas of human courage
               To the whole history of mankind,
Shown again the individual is the only foundation
On which any social order may safely build,
That David can still stand up against Goliath,
That the individual can still
Be master of his fate, the captain of his soul,
That man is still the potential creator
Rather than the victim of his creations;
A creature of free will and untold possibilities,
Not the slave of environment,
His capabilities limited not so much
By heredity or poverty as by his own vision of himself.
I thank you – and the whole world has cause to thank you –
For the rediscovery of man and the powers
Of which he is capable when his mind has been freed
From fallacies about himself.
I thank you, my Spanish comrades, for this most timely
And invaluable reassurance –
For vouchsafing me so wonderful a spectacle
Of the movement of individual will
Towards a common beckoning good,
Always distant, yet always implicit
In love and in understanding,
And the only alternative to callousness and despair,
And for all the glimpses you have given me of the incredible beauty
Of those who give themselves while they are yet young
Selflessly, to a noble Cause.

Great tragedy leaves us with hope.
But it also gives us glimpses of the ideal good
Before the dénouement.
And I thank you for the men I have known
Who have heard that perfect harmony
Which no man – follow he the trumpets and the kettledrum

Never so loyally, follow he the clinking of gold
Never so honestly, follow he the whisper of scientific truth
Never so obediently – may hear
In the solitary prison of his own perplexities.
For out of that prison – even though a man's own strength
Wrench asunder the bars of it – only love and friendship,
Being one and indivisible, may deliver him whole,
The music that Kassner heard in the Nazi prison cell,
'It seemed to bind in a common bond all the voices
Of that subterranean region in which music takes man's head
Between its hands and slowly lifts it towards human fellowship.
It was the call of those who, at this very hour,
Were painting the red emblem and the call to vengeance
On the houses of their murdered comrades,
Of those who were replacing the names on street signs
With names of their tortured fellow-workers,
Of those in Essen who had been beaten down with bludgeons,
And who, as they lay there, limp like strangled men,
Their faces gory with the blood which streamed from their mouths
    and noses,
Because the SA-men wanted them to sing the "Internationale,"
Had shouted the song with such fierce hope ringing in their voices
That the non-commissioned officer had drawn his revolver and fired.
These voices called forth the memory of revolutionary songs
Rising from a hundred thousand throats,
Their tunes scattered and then picked up again
By the crowds like the rippling gusts of wind
Over fields of wheat stretching out to the far horizon.
. . . But already the imperious gravity of a new song
Seemed once more to absorb everything
Into an immense slumber; and in this calm,
The music at last rose above its own heroic call
As it rises above everything with its intertwined flames
That soothe as they consume; night fell on the universe,
Night in which men feel their kinship on the march
Or in the vast silence, the drifting night, full of stars and friendship.'[1]

[1] Vide *Days of Contempt*, by André Malraux, for this account of Kassner's reflections in prison.

Wonderful days!
'So General Mola had to stop the advance on Madrid.
For why? 'Cause he had to wait for his white horse,
So he could ride into Madrid in style.
But while he was waiting, the Internationals came in,
And the Anarchists from Barcelona,
And the Socialists from Asturias,
And the Communists from Guadarama,
And Mola's white horse turned out to be
A bloody white elephant!'
Have a ride on it, Campbell!
Yes, I am a Marxist, Campbell. And you hate
Marx for many reasons – perhaps the chief
Being that you'd like to think yourself a satirist
But know the Fates have given you no brief
– You wholly lack the terrific force and fire
Of Marx's brilliant and devastating satire.

You lack it because, among other causes,
Ideas are not to you, as to him, a highly personal matter,
Much more important than accidental personal relationships,
The intensely personal relationship to abstractions
Which expresses itself in violent hatreds and loyalties
And makes it impossible to separate one's disapproval
Of another's ideas from the person who utters them.
To persons like yourself who react less violently
To the stimuli of ideas, such characters are inexplicable
– But you hate Marx because of his great place in human history,
His world-wide and inextinguishable influence,
Compared with your own insignificance and impotence.

But, ah, there is a deeper reason, Campbell,
For your detestation of Karl Marx,
Not his ruthlessness and intolerance,
His unanswerable castigation of the worthy people
Who would fain offer their good-will as a substitute
For the proletarian class struggle. What you hate most
Is Marx the loving father, the deeply affectionate husband,

The man who inspired a friendship so unselfish
That it deserves to stand beside the famous brotherhoods
Of history and tradition; the glorious spirit we inherit
Which so infuriates your ingoble heart in Spain.

(I pay homage to Engels also. Learned,
Creative, generous, warm-hearted, gay,
It is not difficult to feel in him
The qualities of a great man.
Like Marx he, too, did not suffer fools gladly.
Unlike Marx he seems wholly free from vanity,
Owing probably to his more comfortable circumstances,
(Those who criticise Marx on this score
Must ceaselessly remember the tragedy of a man of genius
Almost the whole of whose life is passed in a bitter struggle
With a gnawing poverty which results
From his own supreme integrity.)
Engels' loyalty and devotion have become proverbial.
His courage was no less remarkable;
His integrity has never been called into question.)

No decent person who takes the trouble to learn the facts
Can possibly do so without turning,
In John Langdon Davies' words,
'In humility to the humble folk of Spain
– Republicans, Socialists, Communists, Anarchists –
Who are groping with their bare hands
To save the light from flickering out.'

Is it to be at the bidding of a foul defamer
Like Campbell that British people will make these feel
As a German friend of mine felt who wrote:
'After eleven months in a concentration camp,
A friend of mine escaped abroad. After he had been eight days in
       freedom
He shot himself, and left a note for us to say
He had not realised that the outside world
Was so indifferent – that ministers, men of honour, human beings

Shake hands with bloody murderers.'?
Do the martyred people of Spain have to cry in vain
Against the vile portrayal of them as fiends incarnate:
'We aren't "organised banditry" but ordinary decent people like
    (save the mark!) yourselves.
We've got wives and families; we are poor or not so poor;
We have colds just like you, and some of us
Wear spectacles and some don't.
We aren't superhuman; we aren't subhuman.
We are men with a belief.
We would like to see the English and the Americans
Treat us not as bogies to scare the bourgeois
But as people who represent a new revelation.
We do differ from you in that we dream
Of a definite happier future for our children.
We'll never attain it. But our children will
And so will the children of our enemies.
That's why we are ready to suffer.
Fight us if you will, but respect us,
             Really respect us.'

The Fascists picture them as dupes of Moscow,
A villainous good-for-nothing lot,
In order to destroy them with impunity,
Slaughter them like vermin,
Unembarrassed by the united aid
The workers of the world would bestow
If they were allowed to realise
That these Spanish revolutionaries
Were only decent people like themselves
Rebelling, after generations of incredible patience,
Against intolerable conditions
– Forced to rise to secure their minimum human rights,
Since these defenders of 'Law and Order'
Have set both at naught
As soon as the working class
Have won power by constitutional means.
– Since these patriots,

These gentlemen of the Right,
Do not hesitate to inflict
The deadliest injuries on the nation's interests
Of which they have always professed
To be the stoutest defenders
Now their class privileges are threatened,
Showing that despite the growth
Of Nationalism in the world today
Class interest comes first
And 'Patriotism' goes overboard
Immediately the workers seem likely to win
A tithe of their dues.

Campbell, we know your trick – Hitler
Expounds the whole technique in his book.
You simply impute all your own foulness
To these innocent people.
We are not deceived.
Such 'Patriotism'
Is 'the last refuge of the scoundrel'
And all the Right are just such scoundrels
Cheating the workers of the world
Like a military thug who rapes a girl
And having enjoyed her, gives her a Judas kiss
And plunges his bayonet into her guts.
That's all your patriotism, your love of country,
Your pretence of affection ever amounts to,
The moment your undue privileges
Are seriously challenged.
Scratch any of the workers' 'betters'
And you find a thief and a murderer.

When a primitive savage wants his enemy to die
He takes a strip of the enemy's clothing
And stuffs it in a dead snake's throat.
He hopes thereby that a real snake
Will bite the real enemy.
This is propitiatory magic and it has been

Part of man's wishful techniques
Since the beginning of history.
That is why you have to conjure up
    These lurid bogies, Campbell,
And dare not let the working men and women of the world
Realise clearly that these poor Spanish people
    Are just like themselves
– Dare not let them see a machine-gunner in a rebel plane
Flying over Madrid turn his deadly spray of bullets
Straight into a long line of women
Who had stood patiently for hours
Waiting for their turn to enter a butcher shop.
'After the planes passed,' said Dr. Norman Bethune,[1]
'I picked up three dead children from the pavement
Where they had been standing in line waiting
For a cup of preserved milk and a handful of dry bread,
The only food some of them had for days.'
The capitalist Press of the world,
Founded like Hitler's propaganda as he declares
On lying and fraud,
Dare not let its readers see
The women and children in these pitiful lines
While the supply of meat in the butcher shop dwindles,
While the bread grows scarcer,
And little children wait for milk that never comes;
Dare not let it be brought home
To the working men and women of the world
How in Spain one segment of humanity
Was passing through inhuman agonies of hunger and fear
While decent people the world over were prevented
From keeping that thinning stream of food flowing
To maintain life and proclaim
The continuity of simple human charity.
Where is the world which answered the call of Belgium?

---

[1] Roy Campbell may well think of himself in comparison with this great doctor of Scottish extraction, descendant of a great line of hereditary physicians in the Hebrides, who did magnificent work in Spain and in China, where his tomb is today the scene of great pilgrimages of grateful people.

Where is the humanitarian heart of the millions
                    Who go to Church and pray to God,
Or of the millions who call themselves idealists
Yet go about their business, signing letters,
Having manicures, seeing cinemas,
While a city of culture and beauty
                    Is being ground into dust?
The methodical bombing and extermination
Of the population of Guernica,
The daily murderous shelling of civilian Madrid,
Left Franco nothing to explain.
These utterly wanton and useless outrages
Explained more than any statements could.
They announced that he had no intention of governing Spain
With the consent of the governed. No Basques,
No Madrilenos, no decent-thinking Spaniards
Will ever forget or forgive
Franco's pointless wholesale cruelties.
He knows this, but he does not care.
There was pressure on the Republican government
To retaliate for the bombardment of Madrid
By similarly bombing Salamanca,
Seville, or some other large rebel city
The Republican army could easily have done this.
It is not difficult to drop bombs
On the immense target offered by a city
                    – And then run!
Yet despite the provocation, the Republican airmen
                    Do not attack civilians.
The secret of the struggle in Spain is hidden
In this distinction between Franco's action and the government's.[1]

[1] 'It is almost incredible that the entire French right should have thrown its support to the Spanish rebels. Even in England all the reactionary papers are openly pro-insurgent, though they must realise that a fascist Spain would mark the end of Britain's domination of the Mediterranean and possibly the dissolution of the Empire. That the extreme right, which has hitherto considered loyalty to country as its exclusive possession, should adopt a policy towards Spain which is clearly inconsistent with the national welfare is one of the most remarkable paradoxes of our time. It shows that despite the rapid growth of nationalism in

The Popular Front leaders want to rule all Spain
And have no desire to create
Unnecessary rancour and hatred of themselves.
They feel that the people are their people.
To Franco it does not matter.
If he dominates at all, it will have to be
With the aid of foreign bayonets
Or an unprecedented white terror,
Which will simply consist in massacring the masses.

The dictators make a cult of frightfulness.
When the Abyssinians didn't yield
Gas was used. The cultural level
Of the enemy is immaterial.
The people which produced Cervantes, Velasquez, Goya, and
    El Greco
Is treated with the same ruthlessness
As were Selassie's black warriors.
Britain and France must expect no better fate.
England and France *l'aveugle et le paralytique!*

Poor Campbell, who saw nothing in Spain,
But went through the War
Like a man walking in his sleep,
Having as little enthusiasm for the stern beauties of fact
And as little respect for its dynamics
As the textbook writers who teach
The mysterious *non-sequiturs* of elementary-school history
– That the American Revolution was caused
By dumping tea into Boston Harbour,
That the English turned Protestant
Because Henry VIII wanted another wife
And so on.
This is the stuff that Campbell is made of.

---

recent years, class interest has definitely come to transcend national interest, not
among the radicals, but among those who have been most fervid in the profession
of patriotism.'

'The true Spanish tradition,' Ralph Bates rightly claimed,
'The creative tradition, is in the keeping of those men
Who have gone out to battle, ill-armed, often literally unarmed,
Against the destructive machines of international fascism.
In the baptistry of a village church in the Pyrenees
An Anarchist militiaman said to me:
"This damned junk" – and he pointed
To the charred and tumbled mummery before the church –
"Is still *alive* in the minds of many of our people.
Once, perhaps, it comforted them.
Now it is just a lingering and shadowy fear."
He told me a legend from his own town, Arenys de Mar.
The people of Arenys commissioned a statue of the Virgin
From a famous image maker of Palma de Majorca.
A tremendous storm arose soon after
The statue-bearing ship had left Palma Bay,
And not all the prayers and entreaties of the crew
Could secure divine help against the storm.
Suddenly one of the seamen understood
What had happened – and rushing to the box
In which the image was packed, he turned it over,
Whereupon the storm went down.
The Virgin had been laid face downward
And to express her displeasure
Had raised the storm.'

How charming, you say, a fine, dramatic mediaeval legend!
No such thing. In Arenys the old women will tell you
The date of that storm. It was 1861.
Do you begin to see the truth in the Anarchist's statement –
That minds whose imaginations are controlled
By a culture of this type
Can never hope to live happily
In a world which has placed
New techniques and new responsibilities
       In people's hands? Gad, sir,
That seaman's 'understanding' of the trouble

Is precisely all Campbell's 'understanding,'
All the 'understanding' of the Right ever amounts to!

And so the Majorcans on the rebel side
Were continually stiffened by the promise
Of German and Italian help. Juan March,
The infamous Majorcan millionaire,
Owner of the Banca March, announced he would buy
German airplanes and present them to his country,
The population was heavily taxed for foreign planes,
And since payment had to be made in gold,
Gold articles were exchanged for dubious paper.
Every day the papers published lists of donors
With the amount of gold or jewels they had given.
The gifts were all holy.
The lists read like this:
For the immaculately conceived Mother of God
And for the continuation of the war – a gold chain;
For the Holy Friend of Children
And our courageous Blue Shirts – a gold ring;
For the Holy Trinity and the downfall of the heathen,
And so on. There were always numerous items about the heathen!
Holy! Holy! Holy!
Holy Campbell! Defender of the Faith!

No wonder the dupes of superstition hate the Reds
Who go under the fighting slogan of our era:
'Act as men of thought,
Think as men of action.'

It is too much to believe that the *Homo sapiens*
Who has brought forth a Leonardo, a Shakespeare,
A Beethoven, an Einstein . . .
Will allow fanatical obscurantism
To plunge him after a million years
Into the suffering darkness of the sub-man.

Even as we look into the Hell's Kitchen of Europe, however,
Let us be never unaware of the slow stream of history

On which these surface sensations –
The stock in trade of journalism and drawing-room
    conversations –
Are carried along and away.
We must not cherish the journalists' illusion
        That news makes history.

Only here and there we seize on and preserve
Out of all the Babel some revealing phrase
Like Hitler's
'Fetzen Sie aus Mussolini heraus, was Sie können!'[1]
Mr. Campbell defends the upper dog.
Some upper dog to need *his* defence!

THE INTERNATIONAL BRIGADE

Honour forever to the International Brigade!
They are a song in the blood of all true men.

The men of each nation showed qualities of their own.
The Swiss formidable for their dour obstinacy
And their concentrated, fretful impatience when not attacking;
The Poles kind-hearted, romantic, dashing, and absolutely fearless;
The English treat the war as a kind of job that has to be done
And they do it well (the pacifists from the English Universities
Making excellent machine-gunners). The Bulgarians
Have a preference for the hand-grenade. They resemble
The Spanish 'dynamiters' who storm machine-gun positions
With hand-made grenades. The French have the greatest number
Of deserters because it is easier for them
Than for any others both to come and go.
The French who remain are men of prodigious valour
And impetuosity. The Americans are an élite

---

[1] Austrian German: 'Rip out of Mussolini whatever you can.'

By reason of their sober courage
And their simple keen intelligence.
The Germans are the best that Germany can give,
(And that is saying much) many of them
Hardened by persecution and with much to avenge.

But if there had been a vote in the column
The Italians would have been shown as the favourites;
They combined a passionate chivalry and devotion
With supreme courage, resourcefulness and discipline.
There can be no doubt at all that the Italian
Is a first-rate soldier when he is fighting
                        For a cause he has at heart.

The battle of Guadalajara brought face to face
Anti-Fascist Italians fighting
For an ideal to which they had dedicated their lives
And Italians sent to Spain
To fight in a cause completely unknown to them.
Many of the latter had been deliberately tricked:
Signed on to be sent to Ethiopia
Where there would be work for them
And a livelihood for their families.
No interest of their country was at stake in Spain.
They had no reason to fight against the Spanish people,
Nor to shed their blood
For Spanish generals, bishops, and big landowners.
The alleged menace of Communism
Left them indifferent. What had they to lose
If Communism triumphed in Spain?
Or even in Italy? Wealth? They had none.
Liberty? They had none. To crown all
They found themselves fighting against Italians
Whose banner bore the name of Garibaldi.
No wonder they listened to their fellow-countrymen
And refused to fight in a cause
Which could never be theirs.

No man worth calling a man can deny
The wonder and glory of the International Brigade.

They will live in history for ever.

All the secrecy, sordidness, scheming, and lying of the Non-Interventionists
Was the fault of stuffy fools who are afraid of liberty.
                    The wide imaginative vision
Which touches the soul with the golden light of pity
Is hopelessly absent from every word they say

How could they possibly understand such men?
Ideals of duty and sacrifice, firmly grasped,
                    And faithfully followed,
Lead them to the starry heights where life
Becomes a divine adventure, and death
                    But an interlude leading
                        To yet more glorious achievement.

The soul of man became in them a dominant thing,
Its indestructibility in a world falling in ruins
Among scenes of indescribable horror
A thing to be held on to passionately.

They rang true. Is there more than one man
In a hundred thousand anywhere else
Of whom it is possible to say that
Courage and honesty
Are the foundations of his nature?

It is very rarely that a man loves
And when he does it is nearly always fatal.

The fire of life woke and burnt in these men
With that clear and passionate flame
That can only burn in those whose hearts are clean.

Britain and France may 'recognise' Franco.
                    History will never recognise him.

He is one of the countless petty military adventurers
Who figure in the news for a year or two
And have no real significance
And are soon forgotten.
We were transported into the flaming heart of the world;
We stood in a place to which all roads came;
In a light which made all riddles clear.

Love and Pain, Terror and Ecstasy,
Strife and Fulfilment, Blasphemy and Prayer
              Were one another's shadows,
Meeting and fading in a single radiance
              That was not light nor heat,
But a movement, a flowing, that carried us along
And yet left us steadier,
              More certain than we ever were before.

'It will take,' you say, 'a very good poet,
              And a very stable politician
To achieve the simplicity that accepts and subsumes
              All the complexities.'
But that is not our task – but to eliminate, to outgrow,
The complexities as the world of life has outgrown
The unwieldy statures and frightful shapes
              Of prehistoric life.

For the spirit is not given by measure!
              This, pro-Fascists, is the condemnation
– That light is come into the world
              And men loved darkness!

For you have seen honesty and virtue put to the shambles
And have abetted the deed when it was done!

It is no use saying to me
              That what we need
Is an imagination reaching out
To embrace the human reality
Which unites the combatants.

The other monkeys had their points
But man evolved from a particular kind
And humanity must outgrow our enemies here
As life in its various forms has outgrown
Many of the forms it took in earlier days
                    And which are now extinct.
So, Campbell, we are resolved
On the elimination from life
Of all that you stand for and are,
Knowing it is already an intolerable anachronism
With no more relation to us
Than the gorilla retains to man.

It is no more the poet's task
To reconcile the opposite beliefs
Which animate the Right and the Left
– To engender the recognition of one's foe
As in some sense a partner in a common struggle
Of which the issue is in the hands of 'God' –
Than it is mankind's task to undo
The circumstances which bred out the saurians
And bring them back into the world of life again,
Or the gardener's duty not to set aside
A plot for some particular flower or fruit
But to grow them all on the same patch of ground
And somehow reconcile and make them grow
With a certain harmony and mutual advantage side by side,
Or the animal lover's task
Not to keep doves in a dovecot and rabbits in a hutch
But rather leave them wild in a world
Which also contains snakes and stoats.
– I am not interested in a plea to 'live and let live'
When it means to abandon the right to pick and choose
Between the poison and the antidote
On the ground that they naturally grow alongside each other
And are both manifestations of life.

Nor are my withers wrung by the cry
That in fighting the Fascists

We needs fascisise ourselves.
That simply contends
That to kill men
And to kill rats
Is the same thing.

These considerations concern us no more
Than would a cry that it is the poet's task
While yet in the flesh
To write not as a man
But as the angel he might soon become
If the Christians' doctrine were right.

We will lose something in the process
– Some characteristics of brute strength,
Of stature and other primitive endowments;
For which, later, at a safe distance,
We may entertain some admiration,
But which life will never recapture, any more
Than it will recapture the size of the saurian monsters,
The proportions of mammoth and mastodon
– And any such 'loss' will be far more than made good
By what we gain.

People of Spain, would that my people,
The people of Britain, resembled you!
But, instead, we present a picture of old age
And it is necessary to indict
Without mercy or reservation
The caste system in England,
The failure of progressivism,
The refusal to educate the masses,
The disposition in powerful quarters
To follow the totalitarian states
In shedding liberty, tolerance, and integrity.

My friend Yeats is dead. In an age
When hardly any of the great roles

Are being played by the men to whom
They have been assigned – the role of king,
Of priest, of judge, of knight – he played
The roles of hero, freeman, human being,
Determined not to be held
In a sub-human part.
Not one man in ten thousand in Britain today
Stands in this respect with Yeats and you.
Is humanity to be like Leonardo da Vinci
Whose mortality defeated the grandest effort
Ever made by man to explore and interpret the universe;
A lifetime devoted to research in every field of knowledge,
One of the supreme intellects the human race has yet produced,
Ending without publication
Even of fragments of his conclusions,
Leaving mankind to discover afresh
The paths he had trodden and mapped,
To fall into his errors
After he had recognised them,
To struggle out of the paths
He had evaded?
A Leonardo to die unfulfilled
While lesser men 'succeed,'
The noblest conceptions and greatest efforts
To be frustrated and fail
While all that goes on in endless succession
Are the petty hearts and the empty heads,
The stupidity which alone is universal,
Men who are not men in any real sense at all,
And that ubiquitous basic bane of Bourbonism
Which learns nothing.

Is humanity to be like Leonardo da Vinci?
Even if it is, better a few such 'failures'
Than a million Hitlers, Francos, Mussolinis, Chamberlains,
And all the other 'successes' of modern life,
Even as Leonardo da Vinci himself

Counterbalances the nameless multitudes
Of 'human' rabbits and guineapigs.

Better to fail with Leonardo, and Spain,
Than 'succeed' with these and Italy, Germany, France, or Britain!
Better to fail with humanity
Than 'succeed' with a termitary!

Now, for the first time, we have the possibility of learning. I do not know how long this
possibility will last. I do not know how long the Capitalist Powers will give us the
opportunity of learning in peace and quietude. But we must utilise every moment in
which we are free from war that we may learn and learn from the bottom up. . . . *It*
would be a very serious mistake to suppose that one can become a Communist without
making one's own the treasures of human knowledge. It would be mistaken to imagine
that it is enough to adopt the Communist formulas and conclusions of Communist science
without mastering that sum-total of different branches of knowledge, the final outcome of
which is Communism. . . . Communism becomes an empty phrase, a mere façade, and the
Communist a mere bluffer, if he has not worked over in his consciousness the whole
inheritance of human knowledge, – made his own, and worked over anew, all that was of
value in the more than two thousand years of development of human thought. LENIN

You may keep people satisfied on a lower living standard, but only if you first make them
stupider. DR. HUGO ECKNER

We in Germany are moving rapidly toward a lower living standard, and I am glad of it.
WERNER SOMBART

Symbol of human freedom forever, you endured more
Than any other citizen army in history
– Even that which in June 1778
Marched on the heels of the retreating British
With William Billings, 'blind and slovenly,'
But full of fire, setting the key for the song:

> *Let tyrants shake their iron rods*
> *And Slavery clank her galling chains;*
> *We wear them not. . . .*

Neither legends nor lies are needed.
The truth is enough. It should stiffen the spines
Of all who fear for human liberty. The comrades
Who froze, and starved, and rotted in Spain
Were not superhuman; they merely preferred
Suffering and death rather than bend their knees
To persons and principles they (rightly) despised. . . .

Wherefore in every man and woman of you on the Republican side
I see that unconscious processes may be intelligent and aspiring,
Generating images and intuitions of moral import;
Solutions of conflict, desirable avenues of advance.
In presenting you thus, I function as a priest
But outside all systems of theology.
I see your War as an exciting drama
In which you are all platonic forms or archetypes;
Vast images that illumine, guide, and make significant
The most trivial occurrences.

Behind all this is an idea, suggested by indirection,
Of the human 'soul,' its creative evolution,
Its enlightenment, its fulfilment in relationship,
Not with some imaginary deity, but with
The boundless potentialities of other creative individuals;
And your story is thus a revealing mirror
That will instigate a resurrection from the dead.

You will be remembered when your foes are forgotten.
On the one side the People; on the other
The vain titles and vicious wealth
Of a worthless few. Chartres versus Versailles!
Versailles, symbol of the 'model of kingship
In our civilisation' – vast, ornate,
Magnificent, overpowering, wholly unconnected
With the real life of the nation, sterile always
As it is silent and empty now,
Trivial, ephemeral, dead.
Nobody remembers what kings reigned in France
When the people of the Beauce were building their cathedral,
And their days, like all *life*,
Knew poverty and ignorance and oppression and suffering.
But the living force and beauty in the minds and souls of many men
Created in their work a vital beauty.
So today hope lies in the free and many-sided
Spirit of humanity against any one-man domination.
Beyond the meaningless dead splendours of Versailles

The glowing beauty of Chartres
Speaks imperishably through the ages.
And even so will the future see
The Upper Classes versus the Working Class;
The defrauded, dauntless People of Spain on the one side;
Monarchy, Wealth, Superstition, and traitor soldiery on the other.
– The glowing beauty of Democracy;
The meaningless dead splendours of Despotism.
Franco, to the true glories of the Spanish people, is like
The horrid intrusion of Woolworth's in Princes St., Edinburgh.

Franco, cool as a fish and smiling!
And Campbell, with his *Flowering Rifle*,
That is English poetry's most atrocious *bloomer!*
Fit ornaments both of the charnel house!
English poetry's nadir – Campbell here,
And Auden, Spender, Allott, Grigson,
The Woolfs, the *New Statesman* clique,
All Left Fascists, so very pointedly unrevolutionary,
Writing nothing any 'intelligent' Fascist
Might not equally well write. *Flowering Rifle* like these
Is another product of *Blooms*bury indeed.

I prefer the forthright brutality and aggression of Hitler
To the smug double-crossing and sanctimonious hypocrisy
Of Britain's umbrella-bearer.

Ah, Spain, already your tragic landscapes
And the agony of your War to my mind appear
As tears may come into the eyes of a woman very slowly,
So slowly as to leave them CLEAR!

Spain! The International Brigade! At the moment it seems
As though the pressure of a loving hand had gone,
(Till the next proletarian upsurge!)
The touch under which my close-pressed fingers seemed to thrill,
And the skin to divide up into little zones
Of heat and cold whose position continually changed,
So that the whole of my hand, held in that clasp,

Was in a state of internal movement.
My eyes that were full of pride,
My hands that were full of love,
Are empty again . . . for a while.
                    For a little while!

Fools need not trouble to call me a Red,
A Bolshie, an Anarchist – for none of these terms
              Really describes my position at all.
I believe *thoroughly* in the philosophy
Of equality of opportunity, and know of nothing
That is more radical.

Democracy must always be on the attack,
Always on the side of social change
Against the forces of 'law and order.'
The Socratic search for truth is the principle
Which seeks to undermine the dogmatism of inertia,
To break down the rational defences of prejudice,
And so to allow human personality to grow
And to adapt itself to new conditions.
                    Its innate humility
Is the deadliest enemy of absolutism in all forms.
Thus Socrates was compelled by his creed
To attack Athenian democracy,
Jesus to expose the Pharisees. And you, my friends,
To serve in the International Brigade in Spain.

The ideas for which my comrades fought
Will win though my comrades themselves are slain
And the opposite ideas to theirs may seem to have won
And to sit secure in the saddle again.

At a time when civilisation
Appears to be headed for the grave
The chances of progress may well seem slight.
But so might the chances of progress have seemed
During all previous evolutionary crises. Danger and hardship

Are the traditional roads to achievement.
There has never been any advance guarantee
That danger would not lead
Merely to destruction,
And hardship merely to death.
There can be no such guarantee now for man.
There can only be the presumption
That if security and new life are to come to him
They are likely to come,
As they have always come,
In the guise of doom.
At least man is beginning to realise
That he must raise his axe
Against the tragic framework of existence.
At least he strikes,
And therein lies his hope.

You, Campbell, with your brainless juggling
Of Left and Right, Right and Wrong!
(Which reminds me, indeed, of the old French song,
'Le Saint-Père l'avait rougi,
Le roi, la reine, l'ont noirci,
Le Parlement le blanchira.
              Alleluia!')
– Even the programme of the Falange
And the officially adopted Charter of Labour,
By proposing revolutionary reforms, recognises
That the Republic was justified in seeking
A drastic transformation of Spain's economic life!
Thus the Insurgents, who style themselves Nationalists,
Have in effect agreed with Salvador de Madariaga
That 'left is right, for Spain must change!'

Even Señora Sanz Bachiller has cried:
'All this is quite new. If we had done it earlier
We might have had no revolution.'
Even among Franco's supporters
It is widely recognised

That the revolution had its roots
In the social life of Spain
With almost half the people still illiterate,
Many peasants extremely poor, rigid feudalism
Lingering on in the twentieth century.[1]

Eager young Falangistas have worked out schemes
For redistribution of land
Which would have pleased
The Republicans on the other side of the fighting front
As much as they displeased
Certain diehards on the Franco side.
Neither they nor General Yague
Hate the Republicans;
They regard them as potential associates
In a forthcoming modernisation of Spanish economy
And objected to their leader's policy
Of holding Left supporters in prison.
Their *dream* is not a restoration
Of the old pre-Republican Spain,
But the creation of a brand-new Spain,
Inspired by its sixteenth-century greatness
But with a social foundation of a type
Many would deem socialistic.

In this day when in Britain too
Every third man and woman we meet in the streets
– Almost all the leaders in society, in business, in the Church –
Are enemies of the people, ready to commit murder,
Available for every vileness of repression and cruelty.

[1] See Dionisio Ridruejo's *The Victors are Vanquished: A Spanish Testament: 1957*, e.g. 'My reasons for withdrawing (1942) were nevertheless "Falangist," deriving as they did from what I have called the "hypothetical Falange," which must not be confused with the actual and historical Falange. I considered that the civil war had ended in a fraud, by merely turning upside down, as it were, the elections of February, 1936, from which the Popular Front had emerged triumphant. It was certainly the right-wing elements who "won" the war. I considered that the national revolution was thereby left in suspense, and I expressed that view, with a wealth of details, in a critical letter addressed to Franco – a letter which, I might add, produced no result.'

I confidently believe that the day is near
When Capitalism will be abolished here
And Labour will rule the British Isles.
But make no mistake – it won't come without a fight,
And a bitter one! The workers have no choice.
Look at the way employer and capitalist ranks
Close in our midst at the least annoyance,
When there is not even a minor crisis.
When their privileges and property are actually threatened
By some sort of popular front movement
And the onward sweep of Labour they won't hesitate
To go all the way to fascism.
There's no use kidding ourselves.
All these pillars of British society
– All these fine ladies and rich gentlemen –
Are ready to turn their machine-guns
On the British people at a moment's notice.

The army will betray us as it betrayed
The Spanish people; the Church will betray us;
All that holds high position in our society,
All that we have been trained to honour and respect,
Is masked murder, biding its time,
And ready for every imaginable evil
That can be let loose on a people
The moment 'constitutional means'
Favour us in any real way.
Law, Order, Religion, and all the rest of the nonsense
That masks the real state of these criminals
Will be thrown off them in Britain as in Spain
And in place of these notable citizens
We'll see Cain and Iscariot again.

Religion, Literature, Patriotism, all
Surrounded by masses of victimised human beings,
As Mr. Reuben Galgenstein, the 'Phosphorus King,'
During the strike of the Galgenstein Lucifer Match
      Company,

I

Had his palatial residence on Fifth Avenue surrounded
By a parade of strikers, men and girls, all
Afflicted by the terrible industrial disease
Due to the process employed in Galgenstein's works
– Necrosis; phossy jaw; a dreadful thing;
The poison gets into every nerve, then into the bones,
The skin peels, the flesh rots, the bones, especially the jaw bones,
Crack, break, splinter, become pulp
– All because it costs a few cents a pound
To convert white phosphorus into red,
To stop that disease – *White* into *Red*,
The cure for all diseases!

The idea of Roy Campbell and the *Times*
That Poetry cannot be salved
From coexistence with, and dependence on, such horrors,
Is enough to make a glacier shake till it calved!

Do you remember Glencoe, Roy Campbell,
Fit panegyrist of Franco's abominations;
History repeats itself – the evil spite of Breadalbane and Stair
You walking inferiority complex!
Is identical with yours. 'Enraged that so many
They had hoped to enmesh in their pride and so ruin
Should have escaped by stifling that pride
They vented all their evil fury upon the few
A legal technicality left at their mercy.
Vile as this was, viler still
Was the method employed to execute their will,
The treachery, the abuse of hospitality.'
So here again, in regard to Spain
All true men, as all true Scots
In regard to Glencoe, swear an oath
To take no rest nor thought for their own concerns
Till the authors of these abominations shall have been brought to
        account,
To spend themselves without stint to accomplish this,
And shrink from nothing that shall forward the sacred task.

And so we call over the great battle-roll of Spain
– Guadalajara, Jaen, Viver, Bilbao,
Brihuega, Durango, Guernica,
The Red Cross hospital at Josefinas
And a thousand more.

'Twenty-two German bombers accompanied by six chasers
Raided Galdcano village this afternoon.
The 'planes stayed for half-an-hour,
Dropping several large high explosive bombs. . . .
The chasers machine-gunned the inhabitants,
Including women and children,
As they fled from the burning village to the fields.

'I saw 10 Junker three-engined 'planes swinging from the east
Over the valley wherein lie Zamudio and Derio.
They dropped a couple of dozen heavy bombs on Zamudio,
Smashing houses and killing the occupants.'

Pines on the summit of Mount Solube
Are still ablaze tonight,
And the valleys are filled with smoke.

Names! It is to youth above all that I commend
These Spanish names – names such as youth demands,
Which make you clench your fists and at the same time laugh
With that light laugh of exaltation
Which is so close to tears, but which bears
The idea of victory!

For this terrible tale of the Spanish War
Will be to all true men in the years to come
As to us the sombre history of the Commune,
That terrible echo of past years that rang again in our ears
In the days of the Reichstag fire, in the days of Vienna,
And since the October of Asturias
Is today haloed with light.
Without the experience of the Commune

Would the workers of Russia have marched
To the Soviet Victory?
To what victories will the workers of the world
Not yet march in the immortal light of Spain?

The lesson to be derived from Spain,
Black as history makes it,
Is it a lesson of despair?

Is it the dismaying moral
Of other love stories
Which finish on a tomb?

    The shots of Galliffet did not truly kill Marie-Rose.[1]
    They pierced but one Marie-Rose.
    Marie-Rose is immortal like the class,
    A thousand times decimated, which carries
    The standard of humanity into the light of the future.

    Marie-Rose is the youth of this youth
    Which I recommend to find its own reflection
    In the story of the Commune, in the story of Spain,
    And to draw from this reflection
    A new lease of the enthusiasm
    Which makes it unconquerable,
    The enthusiasm of Gavroche and Vuillemin.

    Thus the poet who is a true poet, Campbell,
    Finds in the very life of the proletariat
    The flame which transforms him, and which, in his turn,
    By dint of his poet's gift, he renders back
    To the class which incarnates all poetry,
    The living and animating poetry of struggle.

Campbell, you have written for those involved
In what Garratt well calls 'England's Betrayal'[2]

      [1] *Vide* Jean Cassou's *Massacres of Paris*.
      [2] Vide *Mussolini's Roman Empire*, by G. T. Garratt.

– Business and press magnates, land-owners
Of families who have long lived on unearned incomes,
Unimportant peers,
The shades of great names in our history,
With, below them, the army of jackals
– Sir Timothy Tadpole elbows out Mr. Taper,
A crowd of second-rate publicists
Struggling for recognition by the leaders.

'Time has its revenges. Nearly a century ago
Flaubert was laughing at the socialists
Who wanted "to drill humanity in barracks
        And divert it in brothels."
Now we have a far more potent danger from the right,
The Fascists who would drill humanity in labour camps,
        And educate them in seminaries.

'Mass suggestion has already reached a stage in England
At which the control of opinion is at least comparable
With that in the totalitarian states.
This typically English fascism depends less
On active force than upon the force of inertia.
The new fascism becomes gradually accepted
As representing order and religion in a shifting world,
Though the ultimate control will not be
In the hands of Catholics, whose beliefs are sincere,
But of hard-bitten men whose religion, at most,
        Is that "of all sensible men."

'Hypocrisy is likely to play a large part
In the new internationalism.
Dante would probably have disliked Signor Mussolini
Only a degree less than he would
Have despised his English supporters.
His verdict upon them must surely have been
That most damning phrase –
"Hateful to God and to the enemies of God!"

'Democracy will fail and deserve to fail
Unless those people in Western Europe and America
Who still have the free use of their intelligence
Will insist on being told the truth by their rulers,
Will throw those rulers out of power when their Governments
Wilfully and systematically deceive them,
And will keep vividly in mind
Their responsibilities abroad.'

We must face the facts:
The League of Nations deserted by nation after nation;
Democracy derided by its foes
And doubted by many of its friends;
The ideal of collective security yielding
To an intensified reliance upon national self-sufficiency;
Hate, greed, persecution, and war
Erected into boasted national policies;
Instead of a world safe for democracy,
Democracy desperately seeking
To make itself safe in the world.

Let us face the worst.
What has been done is irrevocable.
Not a line of the past can be erased.
Manchuria, Ethiopia, Spain,
China, Austria, Czechoslovakia
– The appalling record is there.
But it is because of the ignorance,
Timidity and faithlessness of men
That we are afflicted by our present evils,
And we shall be delivered from them
By the wisdom and courage of men.

If the prospect for peace looks dark
There is all the more call
For redoubling the efforts for peace.
If our complicated economic and social structure

Puts a heavier strain on the girders of democracy,
That is no reason for abandoning democracy,
But the most cogent argument
For strengthening the girders.

We believe that with all its faults
Democracy is the best form of government
That the world has known
And the only one that holds the promise
Of the free development of human personality
And the realisation of the 'great society'
Of peaceable and progressive nations.

Certainly we are not going to abandon
The noble experiment of democratic government
At the impudent call of Mr. Roy Campbell.
Or at the bidding of bullies
Who have no more understanding
Of what democracy really means
Than to call it, as Hitler does,
'A ludicrous chicken farm
Where everybody cackles'
Or to shout with Mussolini that 'the plain truth is
That men are tired of liberty'
And that the hardy youth of today
Want to 'pass over the decayed corpse of Liberty'
To 'order, hierarchy, war and glory.'
That is not 'the plain truth' but an outrageous lie,
Devised to throw dust in the eyes of the multitude
So that they may blindly follow
'The pied pipers of hysteria,' and support
The inordinate ambitions of tyrants.

No country enjoying a fair amount
Of economic prosperity and security
Has given itself over to the dictators.
They are the product of misery,
Jealousy, bankruptcy, and desperation

– Adventurers whom civil disorder and social confusion
Have thrown to the top
To strut for a brief time
As heaven-sent deliverers.
If history has any lesson at all
It is that their day will be short.

Even wise Thales, more than twenty-five centuries ago,
Declared that one sight the world would never see
Was 'a tyrant growing old.'

Napoleon, with more political and military genius
In his little finger than today's 'sawdust Caesars'
Have in their whole bodies, lasted about twenty years.

Drunk with power,
Which breeds ambition for more power,
He had dared to challenge the historic process
Of the emergence of political, religious and economic liberty.
For all his great gifts he failed.
And are we to believe his feeble imitators
Fighting with the noble weapons
Of purges, pogroms, confiscations,
Concentration camps, castor oil, castrations
And rubber truncheons will succeed where he failed?
Histrionics against the majestic march of history!

Not till Roy Campbell is rightly accounted
A greater than Shakespeare and Goethe, Pushkin and Dante,
And all the other poets of the world put together.
– Roy Campbell, like Jonah, swallowed by a whale;
Fit mate for Queipo de Llano, the 'Lion of the Subway'
With his Kaiser Wilhelm moustache and his bottle,
Swaying uncertainly, foul-mouthed, before the microphone,
And for Don Tadeo Bergante, 'un fascista repugnante.'

But concerning culture, Christianity,
Or any decent human interest,

Campbell, keep a still tongue in your head.
Or your sphincter in order!
If indeed you are sphincterate!
You know nothing of these things at all.

What prompted the criminal and stupid murder
Of Garcia Lorca who took no part in politics
And made rather a point of avoiding assemblies
Where political argument was rife?
Was it because the fascists made a pretext,
Either through illiteracy or wilfulness,
Of misinterpreting certain letters;
Or was it the fact that his sister resided in a house
Owned by the Popular Front *alcalde* of Granada?
More probably the fascists' instinct
Was sounder than their reasons:
They recognised in him the kind of person
They are eager to get rid of –
Lorca who, affirming his Spanish character,
Yet execrated the man
Who would sacrifice himself
For an abstract national idea,
And who insisted on loving his country
With a bandage over his eyes;
And declared that he preferred any day
A good Chinese to a bad Spaniard;
Lorca who knew how to write
Both simply and subtly at the same time,
Wherefore minority and masses
United in his praise
– Lorca, with his universal interests
In music and painting as well as in letters,
Collaborating with Falla and Zuloaga
In developing the *Cante Hondo* fiesta
– Scrupulous insight, technique and force:
Garcia Lorca was popular deservedly,
Not because he had the wish
But because he had the power.

What could fascists do with a man like this
But butcher him?
Nothing worth having in life
Can co-exist with the fascists.
They must destroy it.
And all your poem means, Campbell,
Is approval of that destruction,
Since, like your masters, you
Are void of everything else.

The absence of neurosis among the Spanish Republican soldiers
Was simply due to the fact
That they had fewer delusions about the nature of the struggle
They were engaged upon
Than soldiers in any previous war.
During the Great War men were sent to the front
With a complete outfit of false illusions
And newspaper sentimentalities, which were revealed
As so much cheese to lure the unsuspecting mouse.
The Spaniards knew what they were fighting for.

MAJOR ROAD AHEAD

THE workers of Spain have themselves become the Cid Campeador.
A name whose original meaning is 'to be in the field,
The pasture.'
It has the further meanings of
'To frisk in the field,'
And so 'to be in the field of battle,'
And, especially, 'to be prominent in the field of battle,'
And so it came to mean 'surpassing in bravery'
And, in the mouths of their detractors,
'Men of the field, yokels.'
The word went from mouth to mouth among the timorous

Who had no better defence than their irony;
It slipped glibly from lips unctuous with envy.
'We are men of the field,' they cried,
Catching the jesting word like a ball hard driven,
Accepting the nickname with pride,
And launching it into the firmament,
And on their lips
The jesting word assumed a dignity
And sparkled and shone and flashed
And became a blazon and a star

Who was the first to say it?
No man can tell. None of them knew.
It found itself suddenly upon all lips.
Was it born from the earth?
Did it fall from the sky,
From stones and trees,
From the dust and the air,
It was born from everywhere
At the same time.
It filled all space like light.

The heart of Spain expanded at the name
And embraced the world.
The name rose up,
Rose up into space,
Was charged and condensed
And fell again in a heroic rain.
A flight of swallows flying overhead
Caught up the name on the wing
And carried it to all the corners of the world.
The swallows sang it as they flew
And Spain grew by leagues
As it heard the name.

So their name issued suddenly
From all the pores of the earth,
And found itself upon all tongues,
Singing like a tree in the sun.

It was born and grew and ascended into Heaven,
Multiplied and was one with the forests,
Invaded the plains, crossed the mountains,
Covered Spain, leapt the frontiers and seas,
Filled all Europe,
Burst the boundaries of the world,
And grew and ascended,
And stayed only at Hope's zenith.

History and geography
Were obsessed with the name.
To the north, to the south,
To the east, to the west,
It was borne by the wind like a rose.
It passed above all banners and all birds
With a noise like a thousand banners,
A thousand birds,
While, beneath, a multitude
Weeping for joy,
Followed its passage on their knees
– Millions of heads
Raised in a branch of offering.
That heroic name is an eagle's nest
On the highest peak of History,
Sending through History a surge of song.
And there it remains through all eternity
Nestling on the strings of a lute

You come to me shining from beyond the bourne of death,
You come to me across life,
Over a wide sea beneath a sky of doves.
The tide of the battle surges upon the gleaming shore of your eyes.

Your eyes are two bas-reliefs of your glory.
Your hands are folded to offer up your heart.
Clothed in a comet,
You soar above Spain,
Above human history,
Into the infinite.

Your fury of love and faith
Planted four crosses to the wind
The garland of the four corners of the compass.
The hurricanes of God conjured you above your battles.
I saw you dedicate yourself
And arise out of your flesh
In a divine frenzy
Drawn up towards the infinite
In a mystic ecstasy,
A celestial drunkenness.

You are a tree which climbs and climbs
To bear up once more the Christ
Who came down to visit souls.

Bent over a flight of thunderbolts,
With your eyes fixed upon a journey,
Whither are you going?
In an immense sweep you soar resplendent
Up to the kingdom that is within yourself.
He who would now seek to follow the march of your thoughts
Would lose his reason in dismay,
Would go astray in abysses of vertigo.
There are no limits to your soul.
Whither are you going?
How can I follow you?

The courses of the seven planets
Are reflected in the mirror of your shield.
Go your ways, go your ways,
Leave your flesh behind and go your ways
Clad in Epic.
I will watch beside you
As you roam the spaces of the stars
Without form and void,
As you circle the ellipse of God
I will keep vigil at the foot of your memory.
Your heart leaves a wake of spreading deeds
And perhaps I can follow you with my eyes.

They are gone.
Before my eyes
Their sword gleams and twists in a sudden blaze
And sprouts wings – two great wings of fire and flaming feather.

The sword moves, it is lifted up,
It soars, soars above my head, above the world.
I hear a hecatomb of planets falling into chaos.
I hear windows opening in space.
I hear eternity rushing in my ears.
Where am I? What is happening to me?
A whirlpool of light sucks me into its centre
And I fall down, down, down. . . .

I have returned to earth,
To Spain.
I have come back to myself.

They were the people of destiny.
Of destiny, not fate.
Destiny went tied to their saddle-bow,
Linked with them in some mysterious fashion.
I do not know why.
In presence of the fact
There is nothing to do
But bow the head.
As in a pack of cards
There is one ace of trumps,
So it is the habit of life;
Suddenly there emerges a man, a people,
Who is life's ace of trumps.

They were people of more than genius or than talent.
They were people of electricity.
Genius may fail of inspiration,
Talent may fail in calculation,
But the electric man
Does not fail in current.

Higher than the inspiration of genius
And a nicety of calculation
Is the discharge of a high potency,
The current of irresistible voltage,
Which a people can make pass
From one pole of the world to the other.

They were faith,
Ardour transfigured by faith,
The unconsciousness of faith,
The madness of faith which multiplies strength
And know no possible barrier.
Wherever they passed there sprang behind their footprints
Mystic signs – I put it to the wisest
To reveal the mystery, to solve the problem.

The truth is that the problem has no solution.
They regarded themselves, they contemplated their work,
And they saw themselves escape from all laws
And enter into that region of the imponderable
Where things cannot be reduced to logic
So they were – and that was all about it.

Their bodies were a stupendous factory
Which manufactured the imponderable.
It was a factory
Which created the supernatural out of the natural,
Which created excess out of proportion,
Because all this factory worked
In the service of an exaltation
And this exaltation made them sublime
And made them illogical.

It was not logical that the Spanish workers should fight one against ten
Against World Fascism. – But so it was.
It was not logical that they should contend
Against superior numbers, superior armaments, superior civilisation.
But it was so. And in the end

It will be seen that they have won,
And are consubstantial with all that has ever really lived
And lives forever as part and parcel
Of the very meaning and purpose of life.
An imperishable honour to Man;
One of the great glories of human life,
At the greatest turning point in human history
When mankind was faced at last with the sign: MAJOR ROAD AHEAD.

The Battle continues.

For the spirit knows no compromise.

But now, if we'd let it (which we won't)
Silence would crack down on Spain with all
The hostile suspicions of a peace conference,
You hope – being always original
As a B.B.C. comedian's gag-book.
Never mind, Campbell, I'll be seeing you one of these days
In the old soldiers' home that Nell Gwynne built
Out of the orange business perhaps.

Men like you in the world today, Campbell,
Are simply human phagocytes
– Wandering cells such as we find
Eating bacteria in the pus of an abscess
Or pullulating in a fissure of the *Anus Mundi*,
With Mosley's Blackshirts, Joyce's National Socialist League,
Arnold Leese's Greyshirts, the Link, the German-American Bund,
The National Gentile League, McWilliam's Destiny Party,
Pelley's Silver Shirts, and all the rest.
And your poetry is the sort of stuff one expects
From a mouth living close to a sewer
And smelling like a legacy from Himmler.

Ah, Spain, already your tragic landscapes
And the agony of your War to my mind appear
As tears may come into the eyes of a woman very slowly,
So slowly as to leave them CLEAR !

Campbell, clutch a little longer at the slippery plank
Of your perfidious friends', and your own, praises,
In vain – you will scrabble and plunge into the tank
And drown there in the world's collected *faeces*.

'I shall undertake to bury his errours, which are published in his so-much admired, yet unworthy, booke; and happy would it be for the world if this booke and all its fellows could be buried, that they might never rise more, unless it were to a confutation. . . . Get thee gone then, thou cursed booke, which hath seduced so many; get thee gone, thou corrupt, rotten booke, earth to earth, and dust to dust; get thee gone into the place of rottennesse, that thou maiest rot with thy Author, and see corruption.'[1]

'With those who took this part I have only in a formal sense a common humanity. They have so radically removed themselves from the human sphere, so transposed themselves into a sphere of monstrous inhumanity inaccessible to my power of conception, that not even hatred, much less an overcoming of hatred, is able to arise in me. And who am I that I could here presume to "forgive"?'[2]

[1] Thus Francis Cheynell refused to bury the body of William Chillingworth (who died in 1644) but agreed to bury his book instead.

[2] Martin Buber.

THE KIND OF POETRY I WANT
(1961)

The Kind of Poetry I Want

A POETRY that never for a moment forgets
That if we study the position of the foetus
As it appears in about the ninth month
Of its development, we see the tiny body
Curled up with its head bowed over,
The hands crossed, and the knees drawn up
To permit the whole structure
Of bones, muscles, nerves,
And arteries to fit comfortably
Into the cage or matrix.
As it was in the beginning
So it is again at the end of life.
Think of the decrepit old human being,
Bent over, head bowed,
Seated in a weary, curled-up position
Exactly similar to the unborn babe's.
The cycle of life begins and ends
In the same design. Only the proportion,
Size, and shape of the human being
Change as he passes through the stages
Of babyhood, youth, maturity, and old age.
The eternal oval, the egg itself.
A poetry therefore to approach with two instruments
– Which, being mutually destructive,
Like fire and water, one can use
Only one at a time
– Even as one may attempt to describe
The relative positions of the Imperial Palace,
Hagia Sophia, and the Circus, in Constantinople.
On the one side the Palace was connected,
By open arcades and paradoxical gardens,
With the Golden Egg of Hagia Sophia;
On the other side an intestinal system
Of passages and winding stairs

Led to the Circus. But as regards
Byzantium in especial, these things are merely
The elements which combine to form
A stupendous life pregnant with symbolism.
Because the theme of that life
Was the world-embracing mystery
Of God and man
It stands supreme
Above its ingredients.
The ingredients resemble the things
For which a woman with child longs.
Like the juice of the oyster,
The aroma of the wild strawberry,
The most subtle and diversified elements
Are here intermingled to form
A higher organism.

A poetry concerned with all that is needed
Of the sum of human knowledge and expression,
The sustaining consciousness,
The reasonable will of our race,
To produce this super-individuality, Man,
In whom we all even now participate
Is the immediate purpose of the human race.

The only alternatives we can envisage
Are intolerable prospects of biological disaster,
Chronic war, social deterioration, diseases,
Specific differentiation generation after generation
Of distressed existences with extinction looming at the end.

Either we take hold of our destiny, or, failing that,
We are driven towards our fate.

Cyclopean prejudices, innate misconceptions,
Oceans, mountain barriers, limitless space,
The protean blind obstructions of nature
Within us and without, will not prevail
Against the crystallizing will; the ordered solvent knowledge,
The achieved clear-headedness of an illuminated race.

Amidst the fear and lassitude and ugly darkness
Of our world today I can believe *that*,
Believe that the specific man in us
Has the power to assimilate, utilize, override, and fuse
All our individual divergencies.
The rarity and value of scientific knowledge
Is little understood – even as people
Who are not botanists find it hard to believe
Special knowledge of the subject can add
Enormously to the aesthetic appreciation of flowers.
Partly because in order to identify a plant
You must study it very much more closely
Than you would otherwise have done, and in the process
Exquisite colours, proportions, and minute shapes spring to light
Too small to be ordinarily noted.
And more than this – it seems the botanist's knowledge
Of the complete structure of the plant
(Like a sculptor's of bone and muscle)
– Of the configuration of its roots stretching under the earth,
The branching of stems,
Enfolding of buds by bracts,
Spreading of veins on a leaf –
Enriches and makes three-dimensional
His awareness of its complex beauty.

I dream of poems like the bread-knife
Which cuts three slices at once;
Of poems concerned with technical matters
(Poems braced by Carducci's 'cold bath of erudition'
– As befits one of the new '*Gli Amici Pedanti*' –
Knowing Sotomayor's[1] essay on poetic erudition too
And all the other manifestations
Of *cultismo* and *concettista* through the ages,
Since of course everything depends on providing the divining power
With the preparatory bath of practised concentration
We roughly call 'an interest in the subject to hand')
Which, as masterpieces of intricate lucidity

[1] Luis Carrillo y Sotomayor (1583–1610).

(The power to penetrate as with the lens of the X-ray
Into the interior and exterior of a solid
Free from the distortion of perspective)
Or in cut-gem clearness surpass even Huxley's
Prose account of the endophragmal system of the crayfish
And his *Anatomy of the Vertebrata*;
Crystal-clear as Joule's first full exposition
– Given to a popular audience, a church-reading-room audience,
Of no special knowledge – of the central doctrine
Of modern science, that of the Conservation of Energy;
Or beautifully acute as Moritz Geiger's
Fragment über den Begriff des Unbewußten und die psychische Realität;
Or like the way in which the Pada text
Is converted by a process of euphonic combination into the
    Samhita,
Or like the more than six-score synonyms of Gāmāti he gives
Which include all forms and varieties of motion;
Or like Fred Astaire, who has combined
All forms of dancing into one perfect whole
– Endowed his work with all the intricacies,
Incorporated all the things that make dancing difficult,
But developed them to such a point that they seem simple
– So great an artist that he makes you feel
You could do the dance yourself – Is not that great art?
A poetry in which the disorder and irrelevancies
Of the real world are seen
As evidence of the order, relevance, and authority
Of the law behind, so that what
Is misleading (private or untidy) becomes
By its very irrelevance significant of a reality
Beyond the bewilderment of external reality;
And a brain and an imagination that takes
Every grade without changing gears.
Like glancing at the rev-counter, partially closing the throttle,
And gliding down to make a fine
Three-point landing into the wind.
For this is the poetry I seek
– The vividness of the orchestra in the cobbling song,

The unbelievable control of the crescendo of the fight in the street,
Then the decrescendo, the watchman's horn and call,
The lovely modulation to the lyrical,
The peaceful and the miniature,
(The performance's shape and life-giving forms
Never forced before us after the opening
Concentration on clarity in the preliminary unfolding of the argument)
To the end – where the banner of song is opened
With a width and nobility which cause
Happiness and sadness, laughter and tears,
To express one and the same pride in life
– After the prelude,
The running waves of song to the finale,
The heart-wounding cry of adoration,
The reconciliation of all things gay and sad in the quintet,
The colour and Shakespearian love of all sorts and conditions of
       humanity
In the meadow scene, the swelling heart of the music
In the homage to Sachs – all brought
To a high noon of love of life.

Swift songs, in keeping with the ever-expanding
And accelerating consciousness Březina has sung so nobly,
Sdrucciola – swift and utterly unEnglish,
Songs like the transition from the *ùrlar* to the *crunluath*,[1]
Those variations which suggest hidden reserves
Of strength, of ingenuity, to follow,
Of undreamed-of gracenotes hidden in the fingers,
Then into the *crunluath breabach*,
Before the merciless variety, the ranting arrogance of which
Even the wonders of the *crunluath* pale to insignificance,
And finally into the fourth and greatest movement of the
       pìob mhòr,
The most fantastic music in all the range of the pipes,
The *crunluath a-mach* – where miracles of improvisation
Form themselves of their own volition under the fingers;

   [1] The italicised words in this verse are Scottish Gaelic terms for different tempi
in pipe music.

The expert ear may trace the original melody
Of the *ùrlar* weaving its faint way
Through the maze of gracenotes
But the very gracenotes are going mad
And making melodies of their own
As the player conceives new and ever louder diversions.

Ah, sweetheart, what a pool! Broad, deep, strong, silent, and sedate!
The foam-patches spinning round in the eddies and then
Hurrying onwards betray the speed of the current.
A sturdy Norsk-Murdoch spinning-rod, a 4-inch Silex reel,
A steel trace, and a box of artificial minnows
– A selection essentially for a big water.
(Very unlike the dainty but deadly outfit
Used when the streams are at summer level.)
Indeed, the river is a gorgeous colour,
Golden in the shallows, black in the depths,
Foam-flecked over all the pools.
For the initial attempt I choose a 3-inch anti-kink minnow,
      brown and gold.
– First, one or two casts downstream, to make sure
The tension of the reel is correctly adjusted to the weight of the bait,
That the line is well and truly wound,
Then out goes the minnow at the correct angle,
To drop on a circle of foam possibly 50 yards away.
Minnow, line, and rod are in one straight line.
The rod-point, dipping low almost to the surface,
Is slowly moved around, the minnow is bravely spinning its way across,
When a vicious tug sets the reel screaming.
A salmon is on; it makes no attempt
To increase the distance between us.
After I persuade it out of the full strength of the current
And get on terms with it
I keep it moving to a speedy end,
A perfect picture of a fish of 17 lb.
With the silver of the sea undimmed.
Oh, surely, the due attendance of the lying-in Muse
Always calls for *scodelle da donna di parto*

Of at least nine single pieces so made
That placed on one another they form
A vessel with the outline of a fine vase;
And all the world must visit her
Abrogating all restrictions like the 1537 Naples Senate's.
Then let the branch of pandanus be hung up,
My house be in the power of the Phong Tong,
And give me trumpeters whose trumpets are adorned
With wide hanging cloths bearing coats of arms
Betokening most august rank.

A poetry – since I was born a Scottish Gael
Of earth's subtlest speech, born with a clever tongue,
Moving one's tongue and lips and throat
In bird-sounds, mocking the cheewink of the joree,
The belly-hoot of the great horned owl –
To put the skids under the whole of modern consciousness,
Not unaware of our great crisis of opportunity nor unfit fully to seize it,
Nor ignorant like those who prate of 'empty air',
Unaware of its ceilings and vaults, the Heaviside Layer and the
    Appleton Layer,
Along which the sound-waves run as tho' along vaults of stone,
And against which we can throw things and have them bounce back,
Our shelter also from the torrent pelting outside;
A structure so strong and sound it throws back waves
Which, if they got through, would sweep away
All life from the surface of the earth;
A structure sturdier than Earth's horrendous stone
And strong almost as this poem even.

A poetry like the hope of achieving ere very long
A tolerable idea of what happens from first to last
If we bend a piece of wire
Backwards and forwards until it breaks.
'Toute l'industrie de l'homme,' disait Bacon,
'Consiste à approcher les substances séparées
Les unes des autres, ou à les séparer;
Le reste est une opération secrète de la Nature.'

Nor insensitive to any difference such as that between
The earlier Kajanus interpretation of Sibelius's Second Symphony
And that of the Boston Symphony under Kussevitsky,
The latter scrupulously faithful, though the glow and fire
And inner passion of the performance may make it doubted,
Thanks to the common prepossession that a sound performance
Like a sound man inevitably predicates one
Utterly without imagination, insight or sympathy.
– Poems of prodigious observation and alarming chic,
Couched in a language so adroit that at no matter how
Deep levels the introspective exploration
Of the inner essence of the self proceeds, the thought
Can never break through it and escape.
And with an exquisite finish that redeems them
From the appearance, if not from the reality,
Of obscurity – a language *serré*, quick with Ithuriel's spear,
With no thought *sine mucrone*,
And all its sword-play with a *ricasso* edge
To let my thumb rest on the blade,
A language like '*mar léine-chneas aig a bràthair*'
– The true form, the 'garment next the skin'.
Such poems as might be written in eternal life if there
By such a steady vision of God as in the present life
Is altogether beyond our reach we are relieved
Of the intolerable burdens of temporality,
– Its rude interruptions, and tragic endings, but no less
Its *Langweiligkeit*, its ennui, the irksomeness of its petty pace,
Yet retain a certain form of successiveness.

A poetry that goes all the way
From Brahma to a stock,
A poetry like pronouncing the Shemhameporesh,
Unremitting, relentless,
Organised to the last degree.
Ah, Lenin, politics is child's play
To what this must be.
(If I have evolved myself out of something
Like an amphioxus, it is clear

I have become *better* by the change,
I have risen in the organic scale,
I have become more organic.
Of all the changes which I have undergone
The greater part must have been
Changes in the organic direction,
Some in the opposite direction,
Some perhaps neutral – but if
I could only find out which,
I should say that those changes which have tended
In the direction of greater organisation
Were good – and those which tended
In the opposite direction bad.
The words good and bad belong
To the practical reason, and if
They are defined it is by pure choice.
I choose that definition of them which must,
On the whole, cause those people who act
Upon it to be selected for survival.
The good action, then, is a mode of action
Which distinguishes organic from inorganic things
And which makes organic things more organic.)

A poetry with the power of assimilating foreign influences
As in the wonderful flowering of the Golden Age in Spain
– The exceptional receptivity due to no poverty of inspiration,
No *Mangel eigener Begabung*, but rather
To the strength and fervour of the indigenous character and
          genius,
Der unerhörten formalen Begabung des eigenen Landes,
The absorbing power irresistible because collective;
A poetry finding its universal material in the people,
And the people in turn giving life and continuity
To this poetry by its collective interest.
An extraordinary breadth of material that can only
Be coped with and confined within the limitations of art
By great subtlety, sense of proportion,
And delight in concrete expression.

Or, like that mile-long gallery, broken
By open bridges roofed with a flutter
Of thousands of municipal flags, the *Hohe Weg*,
In which, by means of relief maps, revolving globes,
Moving herds, and armies of Noah's Ark figures,
And occasional gigantic frescoes, the history,
Geography, industry, engineering,
Agriculture, and defiant Chauvinism of Switzerland
Are displayed to, by, and for the people,
With a Scotswoman (married to a Swiss architect)
Who acted as official interpreter during the Lord Mayor of London's
     visit
To Zurich in July, as my guide sometimes
And sometimes a Nazi woman – a lady
Once as intelligent and well-mannered as she had been dark-haired,
But now a peroxide blonde (*vernordert* is the word for this)
With plucked eyebrows and a bright pink make-up
That only enhances the desperate artificiality of her hair.
 – The vine-wreathed wine-bars, the attractive
Alkohol-frei restaurants, the téléférique cars
Swinging across a wire looped three hundred feet
Above the surface of a lake,
And all the rest of it,
And at night the *Sechseläuten* again.

A poetry in short in which, as in Spain
With the Roman, Germanic, Catholic Church, and Jewish elements
As the unifying influences, and the Iberians,
Berbers, Greeks, Phoenicians, and Carthaginians
As the disintegrating elements, in the wavering balance
Between unity and great achievement on the one hand
And particularism and chaos on the other,
By the end of the fifteenth century the whole nation was a great group
The component parts of which remained individual and distinct
Like the blades of wheat in the sheaf
Which was the emblem of the Catholic Kings,
And the Nation could thus express itself
In a form at once genuine and universal.

A poetry like the character of Indian culture
Which is and always has been its universal contacts.
Motifs flood in from Iran and Persia,
Nestorian monks colour the practice
Of Tibetan devotees, and in the Court
Of the rude Mahmud of Ghazni is a Moslem scholar
Acquainted with Plato. A wonderful panorama
In which, though its strength is rather
In arts and thought and race
Than in social structure and growth,
Innumerable reflections and parallels
For European culture strike us,
In the types of wergeld and feudal fief,
Land custom, paternal justice, and the bards;
A vast picture in which we see
The furious passage of Tamerlane or Zinghis Khan,
Or the great conquerors who have left hardly a wrack behind,
Taxila, with its memories of Alexander,
The Greek king who reigned in Sialkot,
And thousands more – with everywhere
The impression of universality,
Of the million grains of sand and gold
Which have rolled to the delta.

A poetry at the worst adept
In the artful tessellation of commonplaces
Expressed with so exact a magnificence
That they seem – and sometimes are – profound.

A poetry the quality of which
Is a stand made against intellectual apathy,
Its material founded, like Gray's, on difficult knowledge
And its metres those of a poet
Who has studied Pindar and Welsh poetry,
But, more than that, its words coming from a mind
Which has experienced the sifted layers on layers
Of human lives – aware of the innumerable dead

And the innumerable to-be-born,
The voice of the centuries, of Shakespeare's history plays
Concentrated and deepened,
'The breath and finer spirit of all knowledge,
The impassioned expression
Which is in the countenance of all science.'

Finally, a poetry such that if someone asks
As of the forest by the river Kundalini
'Of what nature is the monk
Who adds glory to this forest?'
The reply, like Dhammaasenapati's must be,
'It is the monk who is of his own mind the ruler;
His mind does not rule him!
At the opening of each day he considers,
In what state of mind shall I spend
Each hour until night falls?
As a king with a box of many robes,
Of many and varying colours,
In the first watch of each day decides
What robe he will wear, and at noon
Changes to the robe which he then chooses,
And so also at night – so here;
The ascetic, Moggallana, adds glory
To this forest by Kundalini.'
So here, in this poetry of one who knows
An ontological system behind physics
In which a past event has no finality
Of being absolute past,
And has a Philosophy of Art
That throws light on the unphysical question
As to whether there are other perspectives
In which the factual status of the past
Is transformed into an actual appearance;
Nothing guaranteeing that event is an ultimate category
Which may not be expressed in terms of as yet unknown
But more basic entities –
Robes worn by the Master of my Art!

A language like the magnetic needle,
The most sensitive thing in the world, which responds alike
To Polar light in the north, electric currents
Flowing round the equator, the revolutions
Of the earth on its axis, the annual course
Of the earth round the sun, the revolution of the sun itself,
And the mysterious processes in sunspots,
And hence we shall have a poetry in which,
As after Schwabe's discovery that the number of sunspots
Occurring within a given time reaches a maximum
Every eleventh year, led to efforts
To see whether this eleven-year cycle appeared
In any other terrestrial phenomena until now
Schostakowitsch in *Gerlands Beiträge*
Examines the statistics of North Atlantic air temperatures,
Nile flood levels, wheat prices, winter in Europe,
Tree-rings, sedimentary layers and lake deposits,
The dates of the sprouting and bloom of hawthorn,
Of the first cuckoo, of the beginning of harvest,
Of cattle products, herring and salmon catches, diphtheria,
Typhus and measles epidemics, prices of Consols,
Workers' wages, coal production, discount at the Bank of England,
British export trade, American wheat production,
Suicides and lynchings – and finds the eleven-year cycle in them all
And shows the connection between them.
Or as through the influence of *buddhi*
The whole of the subtle body is affected by dispositions or conditions
In the same manner as a garment is perfumed
By contact with a fragrant *champa*[1] flower
Or like the *akūta* by which organs
With defined and separate functions act upon each other
Or like any *linga paramarsa*,
Or like the specific elements, the supports, without which
As a painting does not stand without a frame
Nor a shadow without a stake,
The *linga-sarira*, vehicle of the *linga*

---

[1] The *Bauhinia variegata* of Linnaeus, called *kovidara* in the *Asiat. Res.* (IV, 285)
'a leguminous plant'; 'flowers chiefly purplish and rose-coloured, fragrant.'

K

Whose substance is like light, does not exist
– The *linga* which enters into the womb and forms the inner frame
Over which the bodily form, derived from the mother,
Is gradually wrought.
A speech, a poetry, to bring to bear upon life
The concentrated strength of all our being
(Eloquent of victory in the stern struggle for self-conquest
– Real freedom; life free, unhampered, unalloyed;
A deep religious impulse moving us, not that
Interpreted by others through systems of belief and practice,
But the craving for the perfect synthesis of thought and action,
Which alone can satisfy our test
Of ultimate truth, and conception of life's purpose.)
And not like only the 8 per cent of the fuel
That does useful work in the motor-car – the bare 2 per cent
The best incandescent lamp converts of the energy received
Into radiation, visible to the human eye,
– Against the glow-worm's 96 per cent efficiency.

Is not this what we require? –
Coleridge's esemplasy and coadunation,
Multeity in unity – not the Unity resulting
But the mode of the conspiration
(Schelling's *In-Eins-Bildung Kraft*)
Of the manifold to the one,
For, as Rilke says, the poet must know everything,
Be μυριόνους[1] (a phrase I have borrowed
From a Greek monk, who applies it
To a Patriarch of Constantinople),
Or, as the *Bhagavad-Gita* puts it, *visvato-mukha*.[2]

Or as when the track of the excavator
Has been advanced about 26 feet
The first conveyor is slid sideways,
The second conveyor runs at right angles
To the first and finally rises
At 1 to 3 to enter the tower.

---

[1] Myriad-minded.   [2] Facing in all directions.

The structure is flexible in elevation and rigid in plan.
It is light to move and entirely protects the return belt.
The upward curve of the conveyor can be so sharp
Without the belt's lifting off the idlers
Because the idler friction is extremely small.
So we can rise to any height.

A poetry like Pushkin's in the morning sky of Russia,
Prédestiné, lumineux, et insolent de bonheur;
A poetry as when Pierina Legnani
Walked into the middle of the stage
And took an undisguised preparation.
The conductor, his baton raised, waited.
Then came a whole string of vertiginous pirouttees
Marvellous in their precision and brilliant as diamond facets.
Academically, such an exhibition of sheer acrobatics
Was inconsistent with purity of style,
But the feat as she performed it had something elemental and heroic
In its breathless daring. It overwhelmed criticism.
Or like seeing Diaghilev at work
– I saw a Japanese performer once
Exhibiting feats of quadruple concentration.
I failed to be impressed by him.
I had seen Diaghilev at work.
And again, a poetry of which it may be said,
As of Plato's position in relation to the culture of the race,
That it is unique, and he owes it
Not to the closeness of his reasoning,
Not to the extent of his knowledge,
Not even to his great passion for truth
Or any specially firm grasp of it,
But to the unparalleled fecundity of his thought,
That is, to the breadth and length of his view.
A poetry full of *cynghanedd*,[1] and hair-trigger relationships,
With something about it that is plasmic,
Resilient, and in a way alarming – to make cry
'I touched something – and it was *alive*.'

[1] A complicated device in Welsh poetry.

There is no such shock in touching what
Has never lived; the mineral world is vast.
It is mighty, rigid, and brittle. But the hand
That touches vital matter – though the man were blind –
Infallibly recognizes the feel of life, and recoils in excitement.
See how from all the points of the compass
My subject-matter races to me now,
A race magnificent beyond description
With in it all the elements of greatness
– Wonderful speed, wonderful tactics, constant fluctuation,
And all the romance of the great race
These matters have been running in modern times
Through which they have been making history.
But this is X's day. His mood is on him.
He is running in a rapture. No rival
Can live with him today. Y takes the lead,
But at the bell X and Z (X going so exquisitely
That we suspect the truth already)
Pass him unhurriedly.
And now at the top of the back straight
With 300 yards to go, the smouldering fire
In X bursts into blinding flame – as though he cried
To the rest of the field, 'No cleverness or trickery today.
Here I am; come and beat me if you can.'
And away he comes – one's memories
Of that delirious last lap are a little incoherent.
Climax remains in the mind – Z falling
And seeming to drift backwards, as letter after letter
Passes it, W tearing through the field with giant strides,
V coming from nowhere to pass the flagging W in the straight,
U, steady as a rock, never gives up the chase,
Never won a victory so glorious as this defeat.
T's bitter spirit drives it round the last lap.
The two great runners fall greatly. S fights its way
Into sixth place, like the grand old warrior it is,
And does the fastest time of its career. But none of them
Could catch X – winning by five yards,
And the freshest of them all.

A poetry full of erudition, expertise, and ecstasy
– The acrobatics and the faceted fly-like vision,
The transparency choke-full of hair-pin bends,
'Jacinth-work of subtlest jewellery' poetry *à quatre épingles* –
(Till above every line we might imagine
A tensely flexible and complex curve
Representing the modulation,
Emphasis, and changing tone and tempo
Of the voice in reading;
The curve varying from line to line
And the lines playing subtly against one another
– A fineness and profundity of organisation
Which is the condition of a variety great enough
To express all the world's,
As subtle and complete and tight
As the integration of the thousands of brush strokes
In a Cézanne canvas),
Alive as a bout of all-in wrestling,
With countless illustrations like my photograph of a Mourning
      Dove
Taken at a speed of 1/75,000 of a second,
A poetry that speaks 'of trees,
From the cedar tree that is in Lebanon
Even unto the hyssop that springeth out of the wall,'
And speaks also 'of beasts, and of fowl,
And of creeping things, and of fishes,'
And needs, like Marya Sklodowska at her laboratory table,
For its open-eyed wonderment at the varied marvels of life,
Its insatiable curiosity about the mainspring,
Its appetite for the solution of problems,
Black fragments of pitch-blende from Saxony and Bohemia,
Greenish-blue chalcolite from Portugal and Tonkin,
Siskin-green uranium mica from France,
Canary-yellow veined carnotite from Utah,
Greenish-grey tjujamunite from Turkestan,
Pinkish-grey fergusonite from Norway,
Gold-tinted Australian monazite sand,
Greenish-black betafite from Madagascar,

And emerald-green tobernite from Indo-China.
And like my knowledge of, say, interlocking directorships,
Which goes far beyond such earlier landmarks
As the Pujo Committee's report
Or Louis Stanley's 'Spider Chart';
And everywhere without fear of Chestov's 'suddenly',
Never afraid to leap, and with the unanticipatedly
Limber florescence of fireworks as they expand
Into trees or bouquets with the abandon of 'unbroke horses',
Or like a Beethovian semitonal modulation to a wildly remote key,
As in the Allegretto where that happens with a jump of seven
    sharps,
And feels like the sunrise gilding the peak of the Dent Blanche
While the Arolla valley is still in cloud.
And constantly with the sort of grey-eyed gaiety
So many people feel exalted by being allowed to hear
But are unable to laugh at – as in the case of the don
Who, lecturing on the First Epistle to the Corinthians,
In a note on the uses of ἀλλά mentioned ἀλλά *precantis*
Which an undergraduate took down as *Allah precantis*.
In photographic language, 'wide-angle' poems
Taking in the whole which explains the part,
Scientifically accurate, fully realized in all their details,
As Prudentius's picture of the gradually deputrefying Lazarus,
Or Baudelaire's of the naked mulatto woman,
Or Pope's most accurate particularities
In the Epistle to Lord Bathurst,
Or like a magic of grammar, a syntactical magic,
Or the relations of thought with thought whereby
By means of the syntax a whole world of ideas
Is miraculously concentrated into what is almost a point.
No mere passive hyperaesthesia to external impressions,
Or exclusive absorption in a single sense,
But a many-sided active delight in the wholeness of things
And, therefore, paradoxically perhaps,
A poetry like an operating theatre,
Sparkling with a swift, deft energy,
Energy quiet and contained and fearfully alert,

In which the poet exists only as a nurse during an operation,
Who exists only to have a sponge ready when called for,
Wads of sterilised cotton wool – nothing else
Having the smallest meaning for her.

A poetry not for those who do not love a gaping pig
Or those made mad if they behold a cat
And least, those who, when the bagpipe sings i' the nose,
Cannot contain their urine.

The poetry of one the Russians call 'a broad nature'
And the Japanese call 'flower heart'
And we, in Scottish Gaeldom, '*ionraic*'.
The poetry of one who practises his art
Not like a man who works that he may live
But as one who is bent on doing nothing but work,
Confident that he who lives does not work,
That one must die to life in order to be
Utterly a creator – refusing to sanction
The irresponsible lyricism in which sense impressions
Are employed to substitute ecstasy for information,
Knowing that feeling, warm heart-felt feeling,
Is always banal and futile.
Only the irritations and icy ecstasies
Of the artist's corrupted nervous system
Are artistic – the very gift of style, of form and expression,
Is nothing else than this cool and fastidious attitude
Towards humanity. The artist is happiest
With an idea which can become
All emotion, and an emotion all idea.
A poetry that takes its polish from a conflict
Between discipline at its most strenuous
And feeling at its highest – wherein abrasive surfaces
Are turned upon one another like millstones,
And instead of generating chaos
Refine the grist of experience between them.
The terrific and sustained impact
Of intellect upon passion and passion upon intellect,

Of art as a vital principle in the process
Of devising forms to contain itself,
Of germinal forces directed
Not upon a void or an ego,
But upon living materials in a way
That becomes physically oppressive
To almost everybody,
Recalling the figure of Aschenbach 'whose greatest works
Were heaped up to greatness in layer after layer,
In long days of work, out of hundreds
And hundreds of single inspirations.'

And a poetry in which as in a film
Pure setting – the physical conditions
Under which action takes place – is extremely important,
So important, in fact, as to make us sometimes impatient
With a tale that is but crudely attached to it.
A poetry, in short, like that great Sheep Dog Film[1]
Whose setting is in my own native countryside;
The landscape and the people match perfectly.
The slow roll of the Border valleys,
The timeless fells and the ledges of rough rock,
The low dark sky and the hard going of the ground
Are an environment for no other human beings
Than those seen in this film. The first sequence
Brings men and stones together in one meaning.
After that we would watch with fascination
Anything whatever that happened, and believe it.
Then, of course, there are the dogs which introduce
The ripple of movement into an otherwise rock world.
They are the spirit of the place, not only
When they streak after their sheep at the trial
– The high moment, naturally, of the film –
But at all times.
They have the freedom of the mountains,
And it is their movements,
Even when they are miles away,

[1] 'To the Victor' (Gaumont British).

That the minds of the people follow.
It is through the dogs that the men become alive,
And again it might not matter too much what the dogs did,
Or whether what they did was intrinsically interesting.
We are committed to them from the moment
We see them as part of this world
And understand their rôle in it.
The film has won us long before
We know it has a story to develop.
This is something that can only happen
In the movie art. I want a poetry
In which this happens too,
In a poetry that stands for production, use, and life,
As opposed to property, profits and death.

A poetry throwing light on the problems of value
– Deriving its stimulating quality, its seminal efficacy,
Not from the discovery, as old as the Greeks,
That moral codes are relative to social factors,
But from the nice and detailed study of the mechanisms
Through which society
Determines attitudes in its members
By opening to them certain possibilities
By induction into objectively recognised statuses
While closing quite effectively other possibilities
– A poetry, not offering a compromise between naïve atomism
Giving an utterly unrelated picture of social phenomena,
And the unrealistic conception of a mystical social *Gestalt*,
The defining quality of which is intuited by transcendental means
(That growing danger, as a reaction from the bankruptcy
Of the atomistic approach, of a mystical
Organismic approach instinct with anti-rationalistic obscurantism),
But seeking to do justice to the discrete
As well as to the organically integrated aspects of society,
To the disruptive as well as to the cohesive forces.
– A poetry that men weary of the unscientific wrangling
Of contemporary social and political dogmatists
Will find a liberating experience

– Rich in its discoveries of new problems,
Important questions so far unsuspected,
For which field research does not yet supply
The data necessary to answer them.

A poetry that is – to use the terms of Red Dog[1] –
High, low, jack, and the goddamn game.

Or like riding a squealing *oscuro*
Whose back has never held saddle before

Or a *grulla* with a coat
Like a lady's blue-grey suede glove

Or a bayo coyote in the red morning sun,
His coat shining like something alive,

A poetry wilder than a heifer
You have to milk into a gourd.

A force reaching out as an electric current
Leaps a gap between two opposing nodes,
Charged with a power that only needs
The throwing of a switch to let loose
A devastating power.

The poetry of one like a wild goat on a rock.
You may try to rope him on one crag.
He leaps to a still more dangerous perch,
Where, flirting with death, he waggles his beard
And fires you an ironic ba-a-a. . . .

A poetry in which the images
Work up on each other's shoulders like Zouave acrobats,
Or strange and fascinating as the Javanese dancer,
Retna Mohini, or profound and complicated
Like all the work of Ram Gopal and his company.

      [1] Red Dog – American pastime.

Or, again, like Sohan Lal's 'Hunter's Dance' in Kathakali style,
Overwhelming in its concentrated force and vertiginous rhythm,
Showing the astounding acrobatic technique
Formerly practised in Malabar by the Nayar warrior-caste
Now the chief practitioners of the Kathakali dance-drama.

Poetry of such an integration as cannot be effected
Until a new and conscious organisation of society
Generates a new view
Of the world as a whole
As the integration of all the rich parts
Uncovered by the separate disciplines.
That is the poetry that I want.

A poetry abstruse as hedge-laying
And full as the countryside in which
I have watched the practice of that great old art,
– Full of the stumbling boom of bees,
Cuckoos contradicting nightingales all through a summer day,
Twilight deepening with a savage orange light,
Pheasants travelling on fast, dark wings,
– Or like a village garden I know well
Where the pear-trees bloom with a bravery of buds,
The cydonia blossoms gloriously against its wall,
And roses abound through April, May, and June,
– And always with a surprising self-sufficiency
Like that of almost any descriptive passage of Mary Webb's[1]
– The fact that she was not wholly herself in all she wrote
Creating a sort of finality and completeness
In each part of any given whole,
The integrity of her experience revealing itself in many ways,
In the fulfilment of rare powers of observation,
In the kind of inward perception which recognised
'The story of any flower' is 'not one of stillness,
But of faint gradations of movement that we cannot see,'

[1] Several of the verses given here are inspired by the fact that Mary Webb, author of *Precious Bane* and other novels, was a personal friend of the poet's.

The outer magic and the inward mystery imaginatively reconciled,
Her deep kinship, her intuitive sympathy with leaf and flower
Extending without a break into the human kingdom,
And flowering there in an exquisite appreciation
Of the humours of single characters,
And a rare power to make them live and speak
In their own right and idiom.

There are few writers who can so capture
The elusive spirit of a countryside.
Alive and deeply felt in the mind
It dies on the pen,
Slain by the cold winds of propaganda,
The mists of exaggeration,
The warm fog of sentimentality.
The very desire to pin it down is in itself
Almost sufficient to ensure its doom.
It dies, and its corpse,
Pinned to each page by the unwitting writer,
Becomes overwhelmingly offensive to the sensitive reader.
To capture it alive and undamaged,
To display it with unfaded colours,
Is a miracle – only to be achieved
By humility, simplicity,
A sharp sense of humour,
And a practical working knowledge,
Subtly concealed, of country matters,
With decoration that clarifies,
And raises to heights of imagination,
The bare facts – literary graces concealing
No poverty of context, lack of virility, emptiness of thought,
But, held in perfect control,
Contributing the substance of poetry
To subjects 'with quietness on them like a veil',
A manifold of fast-vanishing speech,
Customs and delights,
– Cussomes, wivetts, short and long bachelors,
Short and long hag-hatters,

Rogue-why-winkest-thou,
And Jenny-why-gettest-thou. . . .[1]

A poetry, since I am writing of the country,
That like a wrestling bout on a village green
Divides the people and wins only those
Who are honest, strong, and true
   – Those who admire the man
     Who has the faster mind,
     The faster, suppler, better-governed body –
For there is not only a class war
But a war in the working-class itself
Between decency and self-respect on the one hand.
And a truckling spirit, seeking self-gain, on the other.

A poetry fully alive to all the implications
Of the fact that one of the great triumphs
Of poetic insight was the way in which
It prepared the minds of many
For the conception of evolution,
– The degree to which the popular mind
Was sensitized by it to the appeal of Nature,
And thus how poetry has progressed
Until, for example, flowers
Can never be thought of again
In a generalised way.
Chaucer's 'flowers white and rede'
Gave way in Spenser's April eclogue
To pinks, columbines, gillyflowers,
Coronations, sops-in-wine, cowslips,
Paunce and chevisaunce.
Bacon's *Of Gardens* is as much a formal plan
As a Loggan print of a Jacobean Great House;
Conceived as a whole, the garden is thought of
As a generalised form of beauty.
It is the whole that matters, not the parts.

[1] These unfamiliar terms are references to old English rural customs and expressions.

And where they were considered separately
The parts still tended to be
Such lesser exercises in design
As a topiary. But the flower regarded as a symbol
Rescued our forefathers from these horticultural patterns
And brought man and flower
Into a new relation. By poets like Herbert and Vaughan
Tree and plant were recognised as having a place
In the same economy of which man was a part.
They obey the inner law of their being
And it is for man to emulate them.
'In the beauty of poems,' as Whitman said,
'Are henceforth the tuft and final applause of science
. . . Facts showered over with light.
The daylight is lit with more volatile light.
The poets of the cosmos advance
Through all interpositions and coverings,
And turmoils and stratagems
To first principles. . . . Beyond all precedent
Poetry will have to do with actual facts.'
'The true use of the imaginative faculty of modern times
Is to give ultimate vivification
To facts, to science, and to common lives.'
A poetry, therefore, that like William Morris
In his *News From Nowhere* will constantly show
'How the Change Came'[1] – how far more clearly
The poet may see into the nature of political reality
Than can the practical men of his day.

A poetry which in all connections will constantly render such services
As the protest of the nature poetry of the English poets
Of the Romantic Reaction on behalf of value,
On behalf of the organic view of nature,
A protest, invaluable to science itself,

[1] The chapter in which, at the time when the Fabians thought Socialism would be achieved by a process of cumulative reform, 'at once,' as John Strachey says, 'so gradual that the capitalist class would never resist it, and so thorough that nothing of Capitalism would remain,' Morris gives a most acute forecast of the rise of Fascism.

Against the exclusion of value
From the essence of matter of fact.[1]

Not only then a progress of poetry in relation to flowers
From Marvell's tribute to 'that sweet militia'
Whose order and variety he deemed the twin pivots
About which human welfare revolves
To myself debating 'whether the old eschscholtzia
Is any better for the scarlet, carmine, and vermilion
Which have invaded the sunny golden-orange
Of its pristine splendour'[2] – a progress
I'd fain see it equal and far surpass
In regard to every branch of nature.

And thus a poetry which fully understands
That the era of technology is a necessary fact,
An inescapable phase in social activity,
Within which men are to rise
To ever greater mental and emotional heights,
And that only artists who build on all that men have created,
Who are infused with a sympathy and sensitive appreciation
Of the new technological order
And all it may mean for their art,
Can play their role with any certainty
That their work will survive historically
And in so doing they will also make
Their contribution to the New Order.

And above all a learned poetry, knowing how
Taliesin received the hazel rod
From the dying hand of Virgil
Who in his turn had taken it from Homer
– A poetry full of milk,
'Milk rising in the breasts of Gaul,
Trigonometrical milk of doctrine,'
In which it is more than fancy

[1] *Vide* A. N. Whitehead's *Science and the Modern World.*
[2] Quotation from the long poem, *Once in a Cornish Garden.*

That brings together the heroes of Arthur,
The founders of Rome and of New Rome,
Moslem and Manichean,
Joseph of Nazareth and Joseph of Arimathea,
Lupercalian and Lateran rites,
The pagan and the Christian,
And groups them kaleidoscopically
Around Taliesin, our 'fullest throat of song'
– A poetry covering 'the years and the miles'
And talking 'one style's dialects'
To London and Omsk.

A learned poetry, rich in all such historical and linguistic knowledge
As can constantly educe and use such a fact
As that the ruin of a Dominant Minority
(As we discern in ranging all human history)
Takes the form of the sequence κόρος, ὕβρις, ἄτη.
(Subjectively κόρος means a psychological condition
Of being 'spoilt' by success; ὕβρις means
The consequent loss of mental and moral balance;
And ἄτη means the blind headstrong
Ungovernable impulse that sweeps an unbalanced soul
Into attempting the impossible).
There is the formula for all the great catastrophes of history
From 480 B.C. to A.D. 1939.
  – A learned poetry wholly free
    From the brutal love of ignorance;
     And the poetry of a poet with no use
    For any of the simpler forms of personal success.

This is the testament of a man who has had
The supreme good luck ever since he was a lad
To find in himself and foster a vast will
To devote himself to Arts and Letters, and still
(Constantly in 'devout prayer to that eternal Spirit
Who can enrich with all utterance and knowledge')
Is happily in middle age insatiable yet,
An omnivorous reader and passionate lover
Of every creative effort the whole world over,

A poet who might take Bourget's lines as his war-cry:
'Malheur au lâche à qui sa chair fait oublier
La seule vie humaine et sainte: la Pensée,'
And a Scot who thinks of the English as Rimbaud did:
'Leur . . . est un idiot, leur . . . un âne,
Et toutes leurs enterprises une suite insensée
D'absurdités et de déprédations.'

How long is it now since my lips were taught to stammer
The Aleph Beth, and Homer and Virgil stood side by side
On my boyish bookshelf with the Mishnah and the Midrash,
While before I entered the Academe of Plato and his friends
It was deemed well to steep my mind for a time
In that ocean called the Talmud, and to teach me fierce dialectics
In the discussions of Rabina and Rab Ashi,
Before I learned to contrast the fierce lightnings that shook
The rafters of Sara and Pumbeditha
With the mild, serene, ironically smiling lips of Socrates?
Then the arena of classic Hellas was opened to me,
Making the *eistoe mystica* become clear revelations
And simultaneously I was taught Horace
By the light of Herman and Heine.
And to open my eyes for the greater features of human strivings
– How out of barbarism grew the light and glory of the Renaissance –
And thence to the presence of our own day – and to show the bright
　　　germs
Of those goodly trees of freedom under whose shadows
The peoples of Europe came to dwell, was there not Ranke?
While Ritter took me from Greenland's icy mountains
To Sahara's burning sands, and spoke of all plants
From the cedars of Lebanon to the hyssop
That grows in the ruins of Visagapatam
And so on, and on . . . Enough of those days and feasts
Spread before me: feasts of tradition, wisdom, and grace
Within which, as the Talmud has it, the mother of the calf
Was yet more anxious to give suck
Than was the calf always to drink.
The evenings passed, while the mind was too overwrought

For midnight study, in sitting entranced
Before the noblest sons and daughters
Of Goethe, Schiller, Shakespeare, Sophocles.
Thus for nigh twenty years all the glories of the past
Were at my beck and call, all days, all hours,
– Alexandria, Rome, Carthage, Jerusalem, Sidon, Tyre, Athens . . .
The last man in the world then to say with Congreve
'I beg you will look upon me
Not as an author but as a gentleman'
And receive the rebuke of Voltaire
('Très choqué de cette vanité si mal placée')
'If you had had the misfortune to be simply a gentleman
I should not have troubled myself to wait upon you,'
And accordingly one who judges all men,
As Voltaire wrongly deemed the English did,
By the homage they pay to intellectual eminence.
'The portrait of Walpole is to be seen only in his closet
But portraits of Pope in half the great homes in England.'
And like Voltaire I pursue my studies in all directions,
Absorbing and assimilating all that has been achieved
In politics, in philosophy, in letters, and in science.
(And, above all, my life is full of men like Theocharis Dadichi
Who could abruptly announce himself 'the countryman of Homer' !)
And far from indifferent to 'life' though like Voltaire at the races at
      Newmarket
I remember how even as a boy I watched
The courting couples go out the Ewes road – the girls
Walking along so neat and ladylike
While coming down the street but as soon as they got in the dark
Siding up like heifers, or coming back
Stop (where I stood hidden) to fix up. I soon tired of the show,
Especially after a night when I saw Jean Scott come back.
It was the first time she'd gone out. Her people were strict too.
I had no desire ever again to see a scared girl
Coming home from her first kick at the whiffle tree.

But above all things, poetry always.
I have known all the poets of the world, I think.

Akhtal, Mutanabbi, and Maari.
Stars of song like Assamasal Suba, Asraby, Garid,
Rab ben Alasraf . . . Or the songs which saw the light
At the foot of the Sierra Morena or in the valleys of the Indian
     Caucasus,
And yet reached the extreme ends of the Islamic dominion
Carried thither by pious pilgrims or well-equipped caravans
As surely as the literary productions of the present day
Fly from one corner of civilisation to the other
– Songs in which stanzas like the 'Muwashaba' and the 'Zadshal'
Were grafted almost unchanged upon Spanish and Provençal poetry.
– Oh, I too have sat at the feet of Ibn Chaldun and Ibn Roshd and
     Ibn Bessan
And been in Toledo when, after its capture by Alphonso IV,
It became the centre of Orient and Occident,
Toledo where young Germans learned the black art
Under Caesarius of Heisterbach, and where
Gherardo of Cremona and Michael Scott and hosts of others
Went to study Avicenus, Averröes, and Aristotle
                              Done into Arabic.
Arabic! . . . Cutting fine figures on horses which only
A few experts notice are not thoroughbreds. . . .

The following section is supplementary to those passages in In Memoriam James
Joyce *where to effect certain communications the poet says that 'the way is the way of
Kierkegaard's "indirect impartation" or Rozanov's Solitaria,' and the other passages in
which he deals with the utmost limits of human expression.*

Or the way of Martin Buber's
Moi et toi, or, six years later, his *Dialogue*,
'Car là où régnait le forcené (Rückhaltlosigkeit)
Même muet, la parole dialogique est devenue sacrée.'
(Pour Buber, comme pour les hassides,
Comme pour ceux par la bouche de qui
Parle aux hommes dans la Bible
Le mystérieux Créateur du monde
Rien n'est plus inacceptable et plus haïssable
Que ce 'Es' (on) impersonnel
'Qui règne dans l'univers dit réel,

Quels que soient les couleurs brillantes
Et les vêtements splendides
Dont le pare notre culture moderne'
Buber 'sait combien grande est la tentation
Qui guette tout homme parvenu
Aux limites de l'être.')

Trouver et proclamer 'le dernier mot,'
Même si ce mot définitif il fallait l'obtenir
Au prix d'une conclusion fausse et mal fondée.
Like Buber's way, or like the way by which
The 'moi originaire' enters into relation
With the 'moi objectif' by 'les 14 *keiraku*.'[1]
(Voies idéales qui sillonnent le corps vivant,
Mais qui échappent à l'anatomiste;
Equivalent de la circulation du *prâna* chez Yogins)
And by 'le rythme respiratoire.'
Or like *prajñâ-pâramitâ* (climax of wisdom)
Meaning not that nihilistic literature which
Towards the beginning of the Christian era
Laid the foundations for the great mahâyânist systems
But the life of the Buddhas according to the Yogâcâra philosophy,
And *abhisamaya* connoting a form of intuition
Superior to the relativity of subject and object.
'Le système complexe et mouvant des stages ou stades
De la connaissance chez les êtres plus ou moins éloignés
Du salut; leurs rapports avec les "subjects" (padârthâli)
Et les "topics" (artha) selon Maitreya[2]
Donnant, pour être élucidés,
L'occasion de préciser la valeur
D'un vocabulaire tout de subtile préciosité.'

I love this most of all
And rejoice in this world in which

[1] *Vide* Shoseki Kaneko, 'Über das Wesen und den Ursprung des Menschen' (Osaka, Mishima-Kaibundo, 1932).

[2] Obermuller: 'The doctrine of *Prajñâ pâramitâ* as exposed in the Abhisumayâ-tamkâra of Maitreya' (from Acta Orientalia, XI) 1932.

'Les trois cents manières d'expliquer le monde,
Les milles et une nuances de Christianisme,
Les douze douzaines de positivisme,
Tout le spectre de la lumière intellectuelle
A étalé ses couleurs incompatibles.'
Une certaine diversité des œuvres de l'esprit
Est pour nous un signe de santé,
De vigueur dans la vie spirituelle.
A une condition, cependant:
C'est que cette diversité ne menace
Et ne désagrège point
Les bases mêmes de notre civilisation;
La liberté d'examen philosophique
Et de recherche scientifique,
C'est-à-dire cela même
Qui rend cette diversité possible.

. . . Mais comment tenter de définir les limites de la pensée
Sans, de quelque façon, les outrepasser?
I remember how Senart, translating from the Chândogya,
Has remarked 'qu'il vaut mieux conserver
Les noms sanscrits, car les conceptions mêmes
Dont ils s'inspirent ne sont rien que limpides.'
I remember how in Heidegger 'à tous les points culminants
De son œuvre on trouve un jeu de préfixes';
I remember Hoffding's remark: 'Il y a quelque chose de tragique
Dans le fait que pour un motif de terminologie
L'œuvre puissante d'Avenarius n'obtient pas l'accueil
Qu'elle mérite auprès du public.'
And I do not forget
The old Red River dialect,
That curious patois born
Of the union of Scots pioneer with Cree,
Now dying out, with *apeechequanee*
Meaning head over heels, and *chimmuck*,
The sound of a rock falling perpendicularly into a lake,
. . . Or loch!

From
COLLECTED POEMS
1962

Coronach for the End of the World

MONY a piper has played himsel'
    Through battle and into daith,
And a piper'll rise to the occasion still
    When the warld is brakin' faith!

A trumpet may soond or harps be heard
    Or celestial voices sweet,
But wi' nocht but the cry o' the pipes can Earth
    Or these . . . or silence . . . meet.

The pipes are the only instrument
    To soond Earth's mortal hour;
But to greet what follows, if onything does,
    Is no' in even *their* power.

Glasgow, 1960[1]

RETURNING to Glasgow after long exile
Nothing seemed to me to have changed its style.
Buses and trams all labelled 'To Ibrox'
Swung past packed tight as they'd hold with folks.
Football match, I concluded, but just to make sure
I asked; and the man looked at me fell dour,
Then said, 'Where in God's name are *you* frae, sir?
It'll be a record gate, but the cause o' the stir
Is a debate on "la loi de l'effort converti"
Between Professor MacFadyen and a Spanish pairty.'
I gasped. The newsboys came running along,
'Special! Turkish Poet's Abstruse New Song.
Scottish Authors' Opinions"– and, holy snakes,
I saw the edition sell like hot cakes!

[1] First printed in the *London Mercury*, 1935.

Bonnie Birdie, A' Aflocht

BONNIE birdie, a' aflocht!
What's in me to gar ye dreid
Till affward frae the earth it seems
Your wings athwart the sun maun spreid?

Aswaip the lift ye drap again
To tak' anither keek at me.
Or was't the sun I dinna fleg
That smilin'ly encouraged ye?

I wad that like the sun and you
I had a' Space for awmous tae,
And wore it wi' a gallant cant
In sic a bricht astalit way.

Adist, ayont, you come and gang
Inerrand in abandon.
Men say that God's awhaur at aince,
Then you're his imitation!

Ah, no! blithe bird, man's thocht is that,
Invisible as God himsel!
Wad else 'twere mair like you or him
– Or baith, you aefauld miracle!

The Glass of Pure Water

In the de-oxidation and re-oxidation of hydrogen in a single drop of water we have
before us, truly, so far as force is concerned, an epitome of the whole life. . . . The burning
of coal to move an iron wheel differs only in detail, and not in essence, from the decom-
position of a muscle to effect its own concentration.

JAMES HINTON

We must remember that his analysis was done not intellectually, but by an immediate
process of intuition; that he was able, as it were, to taste the hydrogen and oxygen in his
glass of water.

ALDOUS HUXLEY (of D. H. Lawrence)

Praise of pure water is common in Gaelic poetry.

W. J. WATSON: Bàrdachd Ghàidhlig

HOLD a glass of pure water to the eye of the sun!
It is difficult to tell the one from the other
Save by the tiny hardly visible trembling of the water.
This is the nearest analogy to the essence of human life
Which is even more difficult to see.
Dismiss anything you can see more easily;
It is not alive – it is not worth seeing.
There is a minute indescribable difference
Between one glass of pure water and another
With slightly different chemical constituents.
The difference between one human life and another
Is no greater; colour does not colour the water;
You cannot tell a white man's life from a black man's.
But the lives of these particular slum people
I am chiefly concerned with, like the lives of all
The world's poorest, remind me less
Of a glass of water held between my eyes and the sun
– They remind me of the feeling they had
Who saw Sacco and Vanzetti in the death cell
On the eve of their execution.
– One is talking to God.

I dreamt last night that I saw one of His angels
Making his centennial report to the Recording Angel
On the condition of human life.

Look at the ridge of skin between your thumb and forefinger.
Look at the delicate lines on it and how they change
– How many different things they can express –
As you move out or close in your forefinger and thumb.
And look at the changing shapes – the countless
Little gestures, little miracles of line –
Of your forefinger and thumb as you move them.
And remember how much a hand can express,
How a single slight movement of it can say more
Than millions of words – dropped hand, clenched fist,
Snapping fingers, thumb up, thumb down,
Raised in blessing, clutched in passion, begging,
Welcome, dismissal, prayer, applause,
And a million other signs, too slight, too subtle,
Too packed with meaning for words to describe,
A universal language understood by all.
And the angel's report on human life
Was the subtlest movement – just like that – and no more;
A hundred years of life on the Earth
Summed up, not a detail missed or wrongly assessed,
In that little inconceivably intricate movement.

The only communication between man and man
That says anything worth hearing
– The hidden well-water; the finger of destiny –
Moves as that water, that angel, moved.
Truth is the rarest thing and life
The gentlest, most unobtrusive movement in the world.
I cannot speak to you of the poor people of all the world
But among the people in these nearest slums I know
This infinitesimal twinkling, this delicate play
Of tiny signs that not only say more
Than all speech, but all there is to say,
All there is to say and to know and to be.
There alone I seldom find anything else,
Each in himself or herself a dramatic whole,
An 'agon' whose validity is timeless.

Our duty is to free that water, to make these gestures,
To help humanity to shed all else,
All that stands between any life and the sun,
The quintessence of any life and the sun;
To still all sound save that talking to God;
To end all movements save movements like these.
India had that great opportunity centuries ago
And India lost it – and became a vast morass,
Where no water wins free; a monstrous jungle
Of useless movement; a babel
Of stupid voices, drowning the still small voice.
It is our turn now; the call is to the Celt.

This little country can overcome the whole world of wrong
As the Lacedaemonians the armies of Persia.
Cornwall – Gaeldom – must stand for the ending
Of the essential immorality of any man controlling
Any other – for the ending of all Government
Since all Government is a monopoly of violence;
For the striking of this water out of the rock of Capitalism;
For the complete emergence from the pollution and fog
With which the hellish interests of private property
In land, machinery, and credit
Have corrupted and concealed from the sun,
From the gestures of truth, from the voice of God,
Hundreds upon hundreds of millions of men,
Denied the life and liberty to which they were born
And fobbed off with a horrible travesty instead
– Self righteous, sunk in the belief that they are human,
When not a tenth of one per cent show a single gleam
Of the life that is in them under their accretions of filth.

And until that day comes every true man's place
Is to reject all else and be with the lowest,
The poorest – in the bottom of that deepest of wells
In which alone is truth; in which
Is truth only – truth that should shine like the sun,
With a monopoly of movement, and a sound like talking to God . . .

Happy on Heimaey

MEANWHILE, the last of the human faculties
To be touched by the finger of science,
Still unanalysed, still immeasurable,
The sense of smell is the one little refuge
In the human mind still inviolate and unshareable
Because communicable in no known language,
But some day this the most delicate of perceptions
Will be laid bare too – there will be
Chairs of osmology in our universities,
Ardent investigators searching out, recording, measuring,
Preserving in card indexes
The departing smells of the countryside.
Hayfields will be explained in terms of Coumarin,
Beanfields in Ionone, hedge-roses in Phenyl-Ethyl-Propionate,
Hawthorn as Di-Methyl-Hydroquinone.
(But will they ever capture the scent of violets
Among the smoke of the shoeing-forge, or explain
The clean smell of a road wet with summer rain?)
Until that day, on Heimaey, 400 miles due North-West
Of Rona in the Hebrides, I am content to walk out
Into an unreal country of yellow fields
Lying at the foot of black volcanic cliffs
In the shadow of dead Helgafell,
And watch a few farmers scything
(Careful of the little birds' nests,
Iceland wheatear, snow bunting, white wagtail, meadow pipit,
And leaving clumps of grass to protect them)
A sweet but slender hay-crop
And tell its various constituents to myself
– White clover, chickenweed, dandelion,
A very large buttercup, silverweed, horsetail,
Thrift, sorrel, yellow bedstraw,
Poa, carex, and rushes –
Or look out of my bedroom window

In the farmhouse near Kaupstadur
On a garden planted with angelica,
Red currant, rhubarb, and the flower of Venus,
Or at midnight watch the sun
Roll slowly along the northern horizon
To dip behind the great ice-caps
And jokulls of distant Iceland.
'Mellach lem bhith ind ucht ailiuin
    for beind cairrge,
Conacind and ar a mheinci
    feth na fairrci.'[1]
Ah me! It is a far better thing to be sitting
Alive on Heimaey, bare as an egg though it were,
Than rolled round willy-nilly with yonder sun.

Listening to a Skylark

ARE you, bricht sangbird, o' the earth or sun?
Or baith? and tell me, gin the last, O! can
A like sublime duality – in life,
No' daith! – no whiles be won to by a man?

For when, as noo, you soar in silence 'gainst the clear
Plate o' the midday sun I only ken
You're there gin you ootshine its licht
Wi' some quick move, syne melt into't again.

Yet when your gowden sang comes glitterin' doon
I ken at aince that oor puir human clay
Can whiles, unlike a' ither mortal life but yours,
Tak' fire and soar and sing divinely tae.

[1] From an ancient poem ascribed to Colum Cille, meaning: 'Pleasant, methinks, to be on an isle's breast, on a pinnacle of rock, that I might see there in its frequency the ocean's aspect.'

Even as, O bird! your fedderome can tak' on
The *haill* sun's licht, shine ane wi't, or ootshine,
Oor lourd flesh, God, has poo'ers to mak' oors tae
Maist o' the glory that else 'ud still be nocht but Thine.

Of My First Love

O MY first love! You are in my life forever
Like the Eas-Coul-aulin[1] in Sutherlandshire
Where the Amhainnan Loch Bhig burn
Plunges over the desolate slopes of Leitir Dubh.
Silhouetted against grim black rocks
This foaming mountain torrent
With its source in desolate tarns
Is savage in the extreme
As its waters with one wild leap
Hurl over the dizzy brink
Of the perpendicular cliff-face
In that great den of nature,
To be churned into spray
In the steaming depths below.
Near its base the fall splits up
Into cascades spreading out like a fan.
A legend tells how a beautiful maiden
In desperation threw herself
Over the cataract – the waters
Immediately took on the shape
Of her waving hair,
And on moonlight nights she is still to be seen
Lying near the base of the fall
Gazing up at the tremendous cascade
Of some six-hundred feet!

[1] The beautiful Fall of Coul – the highest waterfall in Scotland – its name meaning, in Gaelic, tresses of hair.

O my first love! Even so you lie
Near the base of my precipitous, ever lonelier and colder life
With your fair hair still rippling out
As I remember it between my fingers
When you let me unloosen first
(Over thirty chaotic years ago!)
That golden tumult forever!

Audh and Cunaide

Two women I think of often.

Audh, the deep-minded, mother
Of Hebridean chiefs,
Who, widowed, went to Iceland
And sleeps in one of its cold reefs.

And Cunaide, a spinster of thirty-three
Buried fifteen centuries ago near the west end
Of the railway tunnel at Hayle in Cornwall
– Cunaide, no more unapproachable
In death than she was in life,
In Eternity than she was in Time.

Oh, the cry might be found even yet
To bring Audh back to life again,
To quicken that resourceful heroic old body
Lying there like a cameo under glass.
A cry might be found to bring back
Audh, wife and mother, whose intrepid blood
Still runs in far generations
Of her children's children.

But Cunaide?... Who can imagine
Any appeal that would stir Cunaide,

Who died, a virgin, so long ago
She might have been the sole inhabitant of another star,
Having nothing to do with human life
And Earth and its history at all?

Audh lies like a cameo under glass.
Cunaide is an unmined diamond.

There is hope for one buried in ice,
But by a railway viaduct? No!

Audh had the sense to choose
A reasonable grave.

'Come back to life, Cunaide!' we cry,
But if the answer comes: 'To life? What's that?'
How could we tell one who doesn't know
What life is? What is it anyway?
. . . Audh knew!

Glasgow

It is not every poet who has the inner authority for remarking that Glasgow contains a million slaves.   THE LISTENER

In a city like Glasgow, all the upper class well-to-do, and professional people are nothing more than so many phagocytes feeding on the pus of an abscess.

> *Nothing in Nature is unserviceable,*
> *No, not even inutility itself.*
> *Is, then, for nought dishonesty in being?*
> *And if it be sometimes of forced use,*
> *Wherein more urgent than in saving nations?*
>   MARSTON

WAGNER might call Berlin a city
Of sordid spaces and pretensions to greatness;
Berlioz write down Paris 'the infernal city
That thinks itself the home of art' – Glasgow

(Though Cazamian praises its *originalité puissante*
– A phrase I too might use; but only as Villon in his hymn
To the Blessed Virgin the triple invocation to Dian-Hecate!)
– Glasgow, the great city that has never had
A single poet of the slightest consequence! –
Glasgow thinks nothing, and is content to be
Just what it is, not caring or knowing what.

Crowded with *Grundformen*, incommunicable as hand-writing,
It is beyond all human knowing indeed,
And that's the only knowing there is, alas!

'Let a Colgate smile get you out of it.'

The houses are Glasgow, not the people – these
Are simply the food the houses live and grow on
Endlessly, drawing from their vulgarity
And pettiness and darkness of spirit
– Gorgonising the mindless generations,
Turning them all into filthy property,
Apt as the Karaunas by diabolic arts
To produce darkness and obscure the light of day.
To see or hear a clock in Glasgow's horrible,
Like seeing a dead man's watch, still going though he's dead.[1]
Everything is dead except stupidity here.

Where have I seen a human being looking
As Glasgow looks this gin-clear evening – with face and fingers
A cadaverous blue, hand-clasp slimy and cold
As that of a corpse, finger-nails grown immeasureably long
As they do in a grave, little white eyes, and hardly
Any face at all? Cold, lightning-like, unpleasant, light, and blue
Like having one's cold spots intoxicated with mescal.
Looking down a street the houses seem
Long pointed teeth like a ferret's over the slit

---

[1] 'Is it possible that all realities are nothing to them, that their life runs on, unconnected with anything, like a watch in an empty room?'
                                                              – RAINER MARIA RILKE

Of a crooked unspeakable smile, like the Thracian woman's
When Thales fell in the well, a hag
Whose soul-gelding ugliness would chill
To eternal chastity a cantharidized satyr;
And the smell reminds me of the *odeur de souris*
Of Balzac's Cousin Pons. All the strength seems
To leave my body as I look, and a deadly
Grey weariness falls over my thoughts like dust.
A terrible shadow descends like dust over my thoughts,
Almost like reading a *Glasgow Herald* leader
Or any of our Anglo-Scottish daily papers,
Smug class organs, standardized, superficial,
Unfair in the presentation of news, and worse than useless
As interpreters of the present scene or guides to the future,
Or like the dread darknesses that descend on one
Who, as the result of an accident, sustained
In the course of his favourite recreation, tricycling,
Suffers every now and then from loss of memory.

'And she thought she had been so careful. . . .'

The very thought of hurling myself once more
Against the obstacles raised by the crass stupidity
Of my opponents . . . ah, no! I am too old,
Too old, too old, too old, and as for Scott[1]
The only other 'whole and seldom man' I know here,
Feeling independently the electricity in the air,
The cabal of his foes gives all this insensate welter
Of a city an expression of idiot fury.
All the fools whose jobs impinge on music here
Howl: 'If *he* becomes popular, where
Will *our* compositions be – our arrangements, rather?'
(Scott popular? – Scott whose work is *di essenza popolare?*

[1] 'I do not hesitate to say that no finer work than these songs has been done in these islands in our time. . . . In rhythmic flexibility and elasticity these songs recall the finest specimens of Hugo Wolf. In fact, for highly organised unity of shape, style, vocal line and expression, I should not hesitate to place them, worlds asunder though they are spiritually, in the same rank.' – Kaikhosru Sorabji, of the *Scottish Lyrics* of the contemporary Glasgow composer Francis George Scott.

This popular not meaning plebeian or poor in content,
But *sano, schietto, realistico,*
e religiosamente attinente al profondo spirito della razza?
Scott popular? – in Glasgow?)

What a place for bat-folding!

Whenever the faintest promise, the slightest integrity,
Dares to show in any of the arts or thought or politics
At once the jealous senile jabber breaks out
Striking with sure instinct at everything with courage and integrity
('There's nothing too cowardly for Glasgow's spokesmen
To have the courage to do.')
'Confound it all! If once we let these young folk in
What is to become of us?' An ant on a hot brick
Is a study in repose compared to these leading citizens
When any new talent's about – Haydn of Beethoven,
Grétry of Mozart, Handel of Gluck, Rossini of Weber,
Out-Haydnd, out-Grétryd, out-Handeld, out-Rossinid,
By mannikins a million times pettier still
Than any of these were to their hated betters.
Scott, I say . . . but who knows in this broth-like fog
There may be greater artists yet by far than we,
Unheard of, even by us, condemned to be invisible.
In this Tarnhelm of unconscionable ignorance
Where 'everybody is entitled to his own opinion.'

Open Glasgow up! Open it up. It is time
It was made sun-conscious. Give every house
Ceilings and roofs of iridescent glass, windows for walls,
Let great steel-framed windows bring the blaze
Of the sky into every room; half partitions
And low divisions of polished shining wood break up
The entire sweep of the main constructions and give
A sense of great space and air; waxed floors
Reflect the window vistas. Have chairs of chromium steel
    (And never ask where the money's coming from,
    It's there all right, and doing nothing else.)

Let metal ornaments and glass shelves
Catch and multiply the floods of light everywhere.
Let the eye be bewildered trying to identify
The new aspects of familiar materials, 'bravely coming out of the
　　ether.'
– But this is modernism, Bolshie art? In other words
Those hateful things, common sense and efficiency!
('Brilliant common sense' as Orage used to call it,
In which all the essential elements of life
Are fused like the contradictory components of a lens.)
And do not fear to use new materials too. I do not fear
So much black and white and shining steel will give
A chilly effect – for colour will be everywhere,
Strange subtle colours hard to name,
– Schooner, terroco, graphite, matelot,
Sphinx-like fawn and putty, string and carbon blue –
The most utilitarian objects unrecognisable
But none the less useful, every room will be enlarged
To huge dimensions by the windows; the rippling foliage
Of the trees will dapple your tables
– Albeit a simplified forest calling for no such formula
As, say 150Ad ab (30) Fsd (2) oo Gx.
'These trees have no zeal of tragic glory, breathe
No life, no death, in their cool dusky sprays.'

The Caledonian Antisyzygy

I WRITE now in English and now in Scots
To the despair of friends who plead
For consistency; sometimes achieve the true lyric cry,
Next but chopped-up prose; and write whiles
In traditional forms, next in a mixture of styles.
So divided against myself, they ask:
How can I stand (or they understand) indeed?

Fatal division in my thought they think
Who forget that although the thrush
Is more cheerful and constant, the lark
More continuous and celestial, and, after all,
The irritating cuckoo unique
In singing a true musical interval,
Yet the nightingale remains supreme,
The nightingale whose thin high call
And that deep throb,
Which seem to come from different birds
In different places, find an emotion
And vibrate in the memory as the song
Of no other bird – not even
The love-note of the curlew –
                    Can do!

The Aerial City

From the Russian of Afanasy Shensin-Foeth

AT the peep o day in the lift forgether
    Bonnie cloods like a steepled toun,
Wi mony a dome like a bubble o gowd
    And white roofs and white waas blinterin doun.

O yon is my ain white city –
    Or I cam to the earth I bade there!
Abune the derk warld quhile it sleeps
    In the reid lift skinklan fair.

But it hauds awa to the North,
    Sails saftly, saftly, and high –
And a voice is fain that I'd join it –
    But gies me nae wings to try.

Crystals Like Blood

I REMEMBER how, long ago, I found
Crystals like blood in a broken stone.

I picked up a broken chunk of bed-rock
And turned it this way and that,
It was heavier than one would have expected
From its size. One face was caked
With brown limestone. But the rest
Was a hard greenish-grey quartz-like stone
Faintly dappled with darker shadows,
And in this quartz ran veins and beads
Of bright magenta.

And I remember how later on I saw
How mercury is extracted from cinnebar
– The double ring of iron piledrivers
Like the multiple legs of a fantastically symmetrical spider
Rising and falling with monotonous precision,
Marching round in an endless circle
And pounding up and down with a tireless, thunderous force,
While, beyond, another conveyor drew the crumbled ore
From the bottom and raised it to an opening high
In the side of a gigantic grey-white kiln.

So I remember how mercury is got
When I contrast my living memory of you
And your dear body rotting here in the clay
– And feel once again released in me
The bright torrents of felicity, naturalness, and faith
My treadmill memory draws from you yet.

The North Face of Liathach

THE north face of Liathach
Lives in the mind like a vision.
From the deeps of Coire na Caime
Sheer cliffs go up
To spurs and pinnacles and jagged teeth.
Its grandeur draws back the heart.
Scotland is full of such places.
Few (few Scots even) know them.

I think of another
Stupendous wall of rock
On the west coast of Foula
Rising eleven hundred feet from the sea.

Keep all your 'kindly brither Scots,'
Your little happinesses,
Your popular holiday resorts,
Your damned democracy.
This is no place for children
Or for holiday dawdling.
It has no friendly sand or cove.
It is almost frightening
In its lack of anything in common
With Dunoon or Portobello or Aberdeen.
It has no modern conveniences at all
– Only its own stark magnificence
Overwhelming the senses.
Every Scot should make a pilgrimage here
Just once, and alone.

And thereafter pick shells at Montrose,
Or admire our rich Hebridean rock pools,
Or go to 'the island that likes to be visited'
In the Loch of Voshimid in Harris

Or seek like Selma Lagerlöf
For 'the butterfly changed into an island'
And 'pervaded ever since with an intense yearning
To be able to fly again
And go with the birds beyond the horizon.'
And so regain the proper holiday feelings
The proper human feelings,
Surprised at no wildness of belief among
A people who can swallow the Incarnation theory,
The Christian feelings of those of whom Meredith said
'If you can believe in a God
You can believe in anything.'

Seen through a murky patch of fog,
Violent, ruthless, incalculable.
I have seen a head blood-drained to this hue.
But this cliff is not dead.
It has an immense life of its own
And will loom, as if it could come rushing
To beat, to maim, to kill
(Damned anti-climax of a notion!)
Just as it looms to-day
After every human being now alive
Has returned, not to rock but to dust.

What does it remind me of?
Why since extremes meet,
Of the life of a great city perhaps,
The compelling sense of the *vécu ensemble*
The *zusammenerlebt*,
Any of man's great *unanimes*
And their place in the history
Of human stupidity.

No flower, no fern,
No wisp of grass or pad of moss
Lightens this tremendous face.
Otherwise it might remind me of my mother.

> The education she gave me was strict enough,
> Teaching me a sense of duty and self-reliance
> And having no time for any softness.
> Her tenderness was always very reserved,
> Very modest in its expression
> And respect was the foremost of my feelings for her.
No. Not of my mother.
But of many other women I have known
As I could not know her.
It is with them I have found the soul most exposed,
Something not of this world,
Which makes you tremble with delight and repulsion
When you see it so close.

To a Friend and Fellow-Poet[1]

IT is with the poet as with a guinea worm
Who, to accommodate her teeming progeny
Sacrifices nearly every organ of her body, and becomes
(Her vagina obliterated in her all-else-consuming
Process of uterine expansion, and she still faced
With a grave obstetrical dilemma calling for
Most marvellous contrivance to deposit her prodigious swarm
Where they may find the food they need and have a chance in life)
Almost wholly given over to her motherly task,
Little more than one long tube close-packed with young;
Until from the ruptured bulla, the little circular sore,
You see her dauntless head protrude, and presently, slowly,
A beautiful, delicate, and pellucid tube
Is projected from her mouth, tenses and suddenly spills
Her countless brood in response to a stimulus applied
Not directly to the worm herself, but the skin of her host
With whom she has no organised connection (and that stimulus
O Poets! but cold water!) . . . The worm's whole musculocutaneous
   coat

[1] Ruth Pitter.

Thus finally functions as a uterus, forcing the uterine tube
With its contents through her mouth. And when the prolapsed uterus
    ruptures
The protruded and now collapsed portion shrivels to a thread
(Alexander Blok's utter emptiness after creating a poem!)
The rapid drying of which effectually and firmly
Closes the wound for the time being . . . till, later, the stimulus being
    reapplied,
A fresh portion of the uterine tube protrudes, ruptures, and collapses,
Once more ejaculating another seething mass of embryos,
And so the process continues until inch by inch
The entire uterus is expelled and parturition concluded.
Is it not precisely thus we poets deliver our store,
Our whole being the instrument of our suicidal art,
And by the skin of our teeth flype ourselves into fame?

Reflections in a Slum

A LOT of the old folk here – all that's left
Of them after a lifetime's infernal thrall
Remind me of a Bolshie the 'Whites' buried alive
Up to his nose, just able to breathe, that's all.

Watch them. You'll see what I mean. When found
His eyes had lost their former gay twinkle.
Ants had eaten *that* away; but there was still
Some life in him . . . his forehead *would* wrinkle!

And I remember Gide telling
Of Valéry and himself:
'It was a long time ago. We were young.
We had mingled with idlers
Who formed a circle
Round a troupe of wretched mountebanks.

It was on a raised strip of pavement
In the boulevard Saint-Germain,
In front of the statue of Broca.
They were admiring a poor woman,
Thin and gaunt, in pink tights despite the cold.
Her team-mate had tied her, trussed her up,
Skilfully from head to foot,
With a rope that went around her
I don't know how many times,
And from which, by a sort of wriggling,
She was to manage to free herself.

'Sorry image of the fate of the masses!
But no one thought of the symbol.
The audience merely contemplated
In stupid bliss the patient's efforts.
She twisted, writhed, slowly freed one arm,
Then the other, and when at last
The final cord fell from her
Valéry took me by the arm:
"Let's go now! *She has ceased suffering.*"

Oh, if only ceasing to suffer
They were able to become men.
Alas! how many owe their dignity,
Their claim on our sympathy,
Merely to their misfortune.
Likewise, so long as a plant has not blossomed
One can hope that its flowering will be beautiful.
What a mirage surrounds what has not yet blossomed!
What a disappointment when one can no longer
Blame the abjection on the deficiency!
It is good that the voice of the indigent,
Too long stifled, should manage
To make itself heard.
But I cannot consent to listen
To nothing but that voice.
Man does not cease to interest me

When he ceases to be miserable.
Quite the contrary!
That it is important to aid him
In the beginning goes without saying,
Like a plant it is essential
To water at first;
But this is in order to get it to flower,
And I *am concerned with the blossom.*

British Leftish Poetry, 1930–40

AUDEN, MacNeice, Day Lewis, I have read them all,
Hoping against hope to hear the authentic call.
'A tragical disappointment. There was I
Hoping to hear old Aeschylus, when the Herald
Called out, "Theognis, bring your chorus forward."
Imagine what my feelings must have been!
But then Dexitheus pleased me coming forward
And singing his Bœotian melody:
But next came Chaeris with his music truly
That turned me sick and killed me very nearly.
And never in my lifetime, man nor boy,
Was I so vexed as at the present moment;
To see the Pnyx, at this time of the morning,
Quite empty, when the Assembly should be full'[1]
And know the explanation I must pass is this
– You cannot light a match on a crumbling wall.

[1] Aristophanes, *The Acharnians.*

The Bobbin-Winder

N O T even the fine threads in a lace factory,
Coming, like rays from the sun, towards the woman
Winding the bobbins, can vie
With that miracle now on the river.

Look! Where the bowls of yon water-lilies
And the threads they send down to the depths
Are so elfin it seems only a chord struck
On a piano could have given them birth.

Esplumeoir

He's chain lightning. Brains count in this business.

*It was an amazing discovery, like the inside of your head being painlessly scraped out.
There was an amazing clarity, like the brilliant moon falling into it and fitting it neatly.*

B U T shairly, shairly, there maun be
Or sae, of course, it seems to you –
Some instinct o' black waters swirlin'
And dangerous images juist oot o' view
Ettlin' to spoil happiness and pu' apairt
Dreams that ha'e become realities?

I tell you, No! There's naething – naething o' the kind.
Nae ootward things, shapes, colours, soonds, or memories o' these
To strike in on and move and muddle the mind;
Nae *sombra do tempo* cast
By comin' events or present or past,
And least o' a' ony *Scheinprobleme* here!
I ken fu' weel for a man like you
To think o' this maun be as when

On the wa' abune your heid
Shiftin' prisms o' licht frae the water
May dance a fandango
Unutterably free and airy
In a squalid wee ship's-cabin
While you couldna hit the wa'
If you were locked in a wardrobe, you fool.
But as for me I canna mind a time
When the mere thocht o't didna mak' me
Licht up like a match!

'Aloof as a politician
The first year efter election'
You grumble, 'There's naething to see.
It's a' expressionless as tho' it micht be
Enamelled wi' an airbrush that tawnish grey
Nae-colour sae common on motors – wasn't only yesterday? –
Yet bricht as when the stars were glowin'
Wi' sic a steady radiance that the lift
Seemed filled to overflowin' – I wadna hae't in a gift.
It mak's me feel upon my word
Like a fly on the edge o' a phonograph record.'
(A phrase divertin'ly *vergeistigt* here)

The Leisure State! Fell dreich, you think? Intelligence is characterised
By a natural lack o' comprehension o' life
But here intelligence is a', and a'thing devised
To favour 'life' and its expense excised,
Naething left in human nature cybernetics
Can ever delegate to electronic tricks;
Tint, clean tint, as gin it had never been
A' that could be touched or tasted, heard or seen.
Wi' nae mair expression than a china settin' egg.

The utter stillness o' the timeless world!
The haill creation has vanished forever
Wi' nae mair noise or disturbance than a movie fade-out,
The expression o'blankness which sae often
Distinguishes the profound thinker.

Naething to see – you sudna ha'e far to gang
For an analogy frae your Earth experience tho',
Sin' at winter's edge when a'thing's gone sere
Emptied o' a' Simmer's routh and bare as a bane gey near
Bacteriologists say the soil's teemin' mair thrang
Wi' life than at ony ither time, yet wi' nocht to show.
Like cricket's deceptive impression o' slowness
Tho' the split-second decisions sae often required
Ha'e to be made quicker than in ony ither game;
Or like the sleepy een o' a great detective
Wha misses nocht and canna be fooled
But's aye maist, when he looks least, alert.
Or as a day that was gaen to be
Oppressively het wi' thunder later
Used to stimulate a'thing to live
Brimmin'ly afore the cataclysm
Till a'thing that ran or flew or crawled
Abune or aneth was filled pang-fu' wi' life
Like yon cicada shrillin' piercin'ly
Try'in to stert up the haill chorus.
He'd been underground an 'oor ago
And micht be doon a bird's throat by nicht.
That he was alive richt then was reason eneuch
For singin' wi' a' his micht.
Eternity's like that – a'thing keyed up
To the heichest pitch as if
A cataclysm's comin' – only its' no!

Eternity is like an auld green parrot
I kent aince. Its conversational range was sma'
Yet when it tilted its heid and cocked
A beady eye at you, you got the feelin'
That, if it chose, it could tell you a thing or twa;
That, as the French pit it,
Il connaît le dessous des cartes.
Eternity is like an obstinate jellyfish
That comes floatin' back as soon as you've scared it off

But, if you try to seize it, reverses its tactics
And jouks awa' like a muckle dawd o' quicksilver.

Or pit it like this – Eternity's
Twa doors frae the corner a'whaur
A sma', demure white biggin'
Wi' shutters and a canopy.
The canopy's royal blue
And it says *Eternity*
In discreet soap-glass letters
On ilka-side. Under the canopy
You walk up and the front door
Is a' mirror wi' a cool strip
O' fluorescent light on top.
You push the pearl button,
And listen to the delicate chimes
And adjust your tie in the mirror
And fix your hat – but the guy
Ahint the bullet-proof mirror
Sees a' that too,
Only you canna see him.
The guy ahint the mirror
Is Tutti-Frutti Forgle,
A muckle nigger wi' fuzzy-white hair
Wha kens his business.
Aince past Tutti, you check your hat
In a quiet soft-lit anteroom,
Syne the haill place is yours.

Sae cool and sculptured in its lack o' detail,
Its quiet reserve, its expensive simplicity,
Sae couthily different frae earth's nerve-frayin' emotionalism,
Coolness, stillness, nae silly vivacity,
Nae spillin' owre and showin' feelin's here,
Like a wumman wha's daurk hair disna reflect the licht,
Tho' her grey een reflect far mair than their share o't.
Yon cauld snake. Yon *nymphoea tuberosa!*

Water-lillies hae sic a strong urge to live
They can get unco teuch wi' obstacles in their way.

Aye, dreich eneuch, at first sicht – I ken fu' weel
Hoo efter pursuin' his quarry furiously
Mony's the keen hunter feels his spirit unaccoontably
Sag when at last it's wi'in easy reach;
Staleness clamps on him syne like a muckle leech.
Staleness? – the Deil!
Juist as intense desire whiles mak's a man
Impotent at the richt (or wrang) minute!

That's why a poet like Valéry tried
Frae his poetry to haud a' 'life' ootside
'You're deid. You've nae mair to dae wi' the warld again.'
It's neist to impossible for onybody to be
Circumcised frae the warld like this,
Hyne away frae its pleasures, sorrows, comforts – free
O' the haill damned thing as a corpse is.
Of course you canna understand, canna grasp the connection
For *this*, you fool, *this* is to ken the resurrection!

Old Wife in High Spirits

In an Edinburgh Pub

AN auld wumman cam' in, a mere rickle o' banes, in a faded black dress
And a bonnet wi' beads o' jet rattlin' on it;
A puir-lookin' cratur, you'd think she could haurdly ha'e had less
Life left in her and still lived, but dagonit!

He gied her a stiff whisky – she was nervous as a troot
And could haurdly haud the tumbler, puir cratur;
Syne he gied her anither, joked wi' her, and anither, and syne
Wild as the whisky up cam' her nature.

The rod that struck water frae the rock in the desert
Was naething to the life that sprang oot o' her;
The dowie auld soul was twinklin' and fizzin' wi' fire;
You never saw ocht sae souple and kir.

Like a sackful o' monkeys she was, and her lauchin'
Loupit up whiles to incredible heights;
Wi' ane owre the eight her temper changed and her tongue
Flew juist as the forkt lichtnin' skites.

The heich skeich auld cat was fair in her element;
Wanton as a whirlwind, and shairly better that way
Than a' crippen thegither wi' laneliness and cauld
Like a foretaste o' the graveyaird clay.

Some folk nae doot'll condemn gie'in' a guid spree
To the puir dune body and raither she endit her days
Like some auld tashed copy o' the Bible yin sees
On a street book-barrow's tipenny trays,

A' I ken is weel-fed and weel-put-on though they be
Ninety per cent o' respectable folk never hae
As muckle life in their creeshy carcases frae beginnin' to end
As kythed in that wild auld carline that day!

A Moolie Besom

Wi' every effort to be fair
And nae undue antagonism
I canna but say that my sweethert's mither
Is a moolie besom, a moolie besom,
    Naething but a moolie besom!

Am I no' feart Jean'll turn the same?
Her mither was aince as bonny as her.
Sae what's mair likely she'll become in turn
Her vieve een dull, face lourd that's noo kir,
    Naething but a moolie besom?

POEMS TO PAINTINGS BY
WILLIAM JOHNSTONE 1933
(1963)

A Point in Time

NOW you understand how stars and hearts are one with another
And how there can nowhere be an end, nowhere a hindrance;
How the boundless dwells perfect and undivided in the spirit,
How each part can be infinitely great and infinitely small,
How the utmost extension is but a point, and how
Light, harmony, movement, power
All identical, all separate, and all united are life.

Wedding of the Winds

HENCE here we can perceive contentedly,
Abreast of the attempt to synthesize
Work on the soil sciences with that
On the ductless glands,
The fact that sexual selection was originally directed
Mainly by the need to economise iodine,
The whole development, physical and mental, of our race
Dependent on the supply of certain minerals in the soil,
And all our instincts closely associated with
The unconscious desire for particular forms of food,
And face without fear the future phosphorus shortage
That will not immediately reduce our numbers, but at first
Swell them to well-nigh Oriental proportions.

Conception

I HAVE reached the stage when questioning myself
Concerning the love of Scotland and turning inward
Upon my own spirit, there comes to me
The suggestion of something utterly unlike

All that is commonly meant by loving
One's country, one's brother man, not altruism,
Not kindly feeling, not outward-looking sympathy,
But something different from all these,
Something almost awful in its range,
Its rage and fire, its scope and height and depth,
Something growing up, within my own
Separate and isolated lonely being,
Within the deep dark of my own consciousness,
Flowering in my own heart, my own self
(Not the Will to Power, but the Will to Flower!)
So that indeed I could not be myself
Without this strange, mysterious, awful finding
Of my people's very life within my own
– This terrible blinding discovery
Of Scotland in me, and I in Scotland,
Even as a man, loyal to a man's code and outlook,
Discovers within himself woman alive and eloquent,
Pulsing with her own emotion,
Looking out on the world with her own vision.

Composition (1934)

SCOTLAND! Everything he saw in it
Was a polyhedron he held in his brain,
Every side of it visible at once,
Of knowledge drawn from every field of life.
Polyhedrons everywhere! He knew
There was a way of combining them he must find yet
(Like the movement, almost too quick for the eye to catch,
The no-meeting . . . but only change upon the instant . . .
Of spirit and sense; the agile leaping
From the sensual plane to the spiritual,
This straddling of two universes,
This rapidity of movement and back again.

The change is instantaneous, it is dizzying.
Will it stop – stand out like a star,
This gale of crystalline mockery?)
Into one huge incomparable jewel,
Like knowing the sunlight as a living thing
(For no man sees anything, save in proportion
As he sees everything, clear and complete)
An ultimate Brooch of Lorne
To hold his plaid on his shoulder
(Though when that happened, of course,
Everybody would say it was just one-sided!)
Scotland! How he hated all those
Who said 'Scotland' when they only meant,
When all they knew was only,
In their rich slug-like carneying voices,
Like some gimcrack abstraction,
Some Pisgah-vision down a city cul-de-sac
Of that made-in-England specialty, the Proletariat,
Some owl-blink of an anthropocentric routineer,
Some cheap glass-bead of a single-track mentality,
Some wretched little worm-cast of their own casting!
Babes feeding a lion with spoonmeat!
Scotland – like a copy of Greek prose without accents!
As different from the glorious complex reality
As some tittuping iron railing from the sounding walls of Paradise,
The sounding walls of soaring Paradise.

Knight

VOLCANIC laughter streamed like lava from his mouth.
In the depths of his being this man,
Terrible, phantasmagorical,
Had kept much of the child.
His soul had preserved itself pure,
Primitive and clean,

As a precious stone fallen from another star.
Nothing was more extraordinary about him
Than that he should have kept his soul fresh
In all its intrinsic worth,
Unsullied by contact with a life so tumultuous.
In the midst of the most awful battles
He had raised his soul on high
Above the seething mass,
So that nothing could reach it,
As the bard of Portugal[1] bore his poem
Above the waves of shipwreck.
Faith held this man to a plane so lofty
That his soul was ever ready to soar above his body
And dwell in the upper ecstasies.
There was something of the mystic about him
As about all exalted men.
He was a visionary – with his feet
Planted solidly on the ground!

A visionary, a lover of facts,
Not such, however, as might cry
'We are all conscious of facts
And we are all conscious of values
But a fact which has no value is not a fact
And a value which is not a fact has no value,'
And make no more of it than a weak argument
For the collaboration of church and science,
Not seeing the real significance of it.
. . . *A fact that has no value is not a fact.*
It means that when the scientist has discovered a fact
Which is a fact, he has therefore discovered a value.
That is sufficient to gainsay all the nonsense
That is being talked about 'blind forces.'
If a force is real it is also important.
If it is blind its blindness has value.
Why are so many people clamouring for free will?
Because they cannot see that fact has value,

[1] Camoens' *The Lusiads.*

They cannot see that will as a fact
Has any significance. To give it value
They must divorce it from fact,
Remove it from causation. Why are there so many people
Rejoicing today in the supposed overthrow of the atom?
Because they value fact? No. Because they are afraid of it!
And because they hope to find
That what they feared was fact
Is just a bubble floating on the surface of Mystery!

Of William Johnstone's Art

SCARCELY anybody has really seen Scotland before
– Let alone understood such facts,
That a bright colour (a cadmium, say)
Vibrates more strongly in angular or pointed forms,
And a blue would be made more profound
By being confined in a rounded space,
A circle or full ellipse,
Or that, as Kandinsky has shown,[1]
A triangle of colour, whether it be
Acute-angled, obtuse-angled, or equilateral,
Is an entity with a spiritual perfume
Proper to itself alone.
In combination with other forms
This perfume becomes differentiated,
Acquires accompanying nuances,
But remains radically unalterable,
Like the smell of the rose which can never
Be mistaken for that of the violet.

It was difficult for his work at first
To secure the reception it deserved
Among such sentimentalists as the Scots.

[1] Vide *Über das Geistige in der Kunst,* by Wassily Kandinsky (1914).

They did not realise he had
Already put such emotion and feeling
Into it that all *they* had to do
Was to accept it straightforwardly,
Directly and simply, and that the emotion
Would liberate itself like a volatile vapour
Of its own accord,
Without any efforts on *their* part.

What happened was often like what happens
When, in Mahler's VIIIth Symphony
That very lovely solo passage given to the soprano
In the first part, in D flat major,
'*Imple superna gratia*' – full to the brim
Of all possible intensity of passionately devout feeling
– Is sung 'expressively'
And ruined and vulgarized
In a way that hurts.

The Scots were always devils
For adding rouge to a rose
And whitewash to a lily
And prone to the pet vices of many Liedersänger
– Scooping, and unnecessarily marked dynamics.

Though simple in the sense of single,
Of unified in aspiration,
His work of course is not 'simple' in any way
Any more than life itself is.

Ode to the North Wind

I AM not one who longs
For perpetual sunshine
And would fain dispense
With rain and snow and cold winds,

Or craves eternal light
And would forgo
The morning and the evening twilights,
Darkness and moonlight and starlight
Any more than I am like the modern aesthete
Who expects a 'kick' from a picture
And does not wait for any emotion.
That is not my attitude. . . .

But the external aspect of Nature
Does not permit us sufficiently
To penetrate its sudden depths.
It is only the superficial part,
The skin of its immense body,
And only conforms to the obvious
And petty side of our impulses
And is not qualified to manifest
The most essential and vital subsistence.
Our task is not to reproduce Nature
But to create and enrich it
By methods like musical notes, mathematical tables, geometry,
Of which Nature knows nothing,
Artifically constructed by man
For the manifestation of his knowledge
And his creative will.

Of William Johnstone's Exhibition

Any commonplace acceptance of the visible world was due, not to the importunacy of mere occupations, but to sheer grossness of perception, men, women, and children going to the grave in groups, unaware, unawakened.

LLEWELYN POWYS

So, now, instead of a world, a Scotland,
Which always and in all its parts remains the same,
Instead of a process of development,

Instead of the idea of transforming
All that is important into the imperceptible,
Which is so imperceptible that it cannot be seen,
We will live like eagles
And grow new forests of humanity:
Now before our eyes arises a Scotland, a world,
Of sudden, wonderful, and mysterious transformations,
Each of which means more than the whole process
Of today and its natural development
(Even as, by becoming collective, poetry in the era of communism,
Will not become less individual but more so,
The world of ideas behind language expanding for poetry
In the same way as it did in the Elizabethan era.)
Such a world, it is true, cannot be 'comprehended.'
But such a world *need* not·be comprehended.
In such a world comprehension is superfluous.
Comprehension is necessary for the natural world
From man, who came in natural wise into it;
But in a world of wonderful transformations
In an eternally unnatural world,
Comprehension is only a meagre and wretched gift
From the pauper world of limitation.

From
THE COMPANY I'VE KEPT
(1966)

Scottish Universal[1]

SCOTTISH Universal – but not Hugh Fraser's.
My theme's a better one in every way, sirs.

One of the few decent politicians in Britain today!

That does not prevent a man having enemies.
On the contrary, the more unswervingly upright
The more powerful the hatred he arouses,
The deadlier the enmity combining against him.
So we have had it here – a man indefatigable
In his attention to affairs, serving his electors
With sustained ability and scrupulous devotion,
A genial man, exemplary citizen, and loving husband.
Not many men tested in the acrid fires
Of public life come through so intact and unsullied,
Pure gold thrice refined. I remember as a boy
Searching a wide Border moor, acres of purple heather,
Looking for white heather – and suddenly
I saw it, hundreds of yards away,
Unmistakable – so in the hosts of men I've known
Willie Gallacher shines out, single of purpose,
Lovely in his integrity, exemplifying.
All that is best in public service – distinct,
Clear-headed and clean-hearted,
A great humanist, true comrade and friend.
Without variableness or shadow of turning,
Eighty years young in his sterling spirit
And the immaculate courage of his convictions.

A sprig of white heather in the future's lapel,
A wave and cheerful handshake for all mankind!
But surely he has some fault? Yes, of course.
The worst of all, the unforgivable knack of being always right.

[1] Scottish Universal, the combine headed by Sir Hugh Fraser, the millionaire draper.

From
A LAP OF HONOUR
(1967)

By Wauchopeside

THRAWN water? Aye, owre thrawn to be aye thrawn!
I ha'e my wagtails like the Wauchope tae,
Birds fu' o' fechtin' spirit, and o' fun,
That whiles jig in the air in lichtsome play
Like glass-ba's on a fountain, syne stand still
Save for a quiver, shoot up an inch or twa, fa' back
Like a swarm o' winter-gnats, or are tost aside,
              By their inclination's kittle loup,
              To balance efter hauf a coup.

There's mair in birds than men ha'e faddomed yet.
Tho' maist churn oot the stock sangs o' their kind
There's aiblins genius here and there; and aince
'Mang whitebeams, hollies, siller birks –
                            The trees o' licht –
                            I mind
I used to hear a blackie mony a nicht
Singin' awa' t'an unconscionable 'oor
Wi' nocht but the water keepin't company
(Or nocht that ony human ear could hear)
– And wondered if the blackie heard it either
Or cared whether it was singin' tae or no'!
O there's nae sayin' what my verses awn
To memories like these. Ha'e I come back
To find oot? Or to borrow mair? Or see
Their helpless puirness to what gar'd them be?
          Late sang the blackie but it stopt at last.
          The river still ga'ed singin' past.

O there's nae sayin' what my verses awn
To memories, or my memories to me.
But a'e thing's certain; ev'n as things stand
I could vary them in coontless ways and gi'e
Wauchope a new course in the minds o' men,

The blackie gowden feathers, and the like,
An yet no' cease to be dependent on
The things o' Nature, and create insteed
                    Oot o' my ain heid
                    Or get ootside the range
                            O' trivial change
Into that cataclysmic country which
Natheless a' men inhabit – and enrich.

For civilization in its struggle up
Has mair than seasonal changes o' ideas,
Glidin' through periods o' flooers and fruit,
Winter and Spring again; to cope wi' these
Is difficult eneuch to tax the patience
O' Methuselah himsel' – but transformations,
Yont physical and mental habits, symbols, rites,
That mak' sic changes nane, are aye gaen on,
Revolutions in the dynasty o' live ideals
– The stuff wi' which alane true poetry deals.
Wagtail or water winna help me here,
(That's clearer than Wauchope[1] at its clearest's clear!)
Where the life o' a million years is seen
Like a louch look in a lass's een.

Diamond Body

In a Cave of the Sea

WHAT after all do we know of this terrible 'matter'
Save as a name for the unknown and hypothetical cause
Of states of our own consciousness? There are not two worlds,
A world of nature, and a world of human consciousness,
Standing over against one another, but one world of nature

---

[1] Wauchope is one of the tributaries of the River Esk, which it joins at the little Dumfriesshire town of Langholm, the author's birthplace.

Whereof human consciousness is an evolution,
I reminded myself again as I caught that sudden breathless glimpse,
Under my microscope, of unexpected beauty and dynamic living
In the world of life on a sliver of kelp
Quite as much as the harpooning of a forty-two foot whale shark.

Because, I reminded myself, any assemblage of things
Is for the sake of another, and because of
The existence of active exertion
For the sake of abstraction,
In like manner, as Gaudapada says,
As a bed, which is an assemblage
Of bedding, props, cotton, coverlet, and pillows
Is for another's use, not for its own
And its several component parts
Render no mutual service,
Thence it is concluded that there is a man
Who sleeps upon the bed
And for whose sake it was made
So this world, which is an assemblage
Of the five elements is for another's use,
And there is another for whose enjoyment
This enjoyable body of mine,
Consisting of intellect and all the rest,
Has been produced.

And all I see and delight in now
Has been produced for him –
The sand-burrowing sea urchins with shells
Delicate as those of hen's eggs,
Burrowing by movements of long backwardly-directed spines;
And the burrowing star-fish which settle into the sand
By rows of pointed 'tube feet',
Operated by hydraulic pressure,
On the under-side of each of the five arms;
And the smooth-bodied sand eels and the shrimps
And sea-weeds attached by broad hold-fasts
– Not roots! – to the rocks or boulders,

Brown masses a host of small animals
Grow on or shelter amongst, protected here
From the buffeting of the sea when the tide is in
Or kept moist under the damp weight of weed
When the tide is out. And high up the shore
The limpets wandering about
Grazing on fine encrusting weeds,
And the acorn barnacles, the dog-whelks
Grey-shelled unless they have mussels to feed on
When the change of diet puts brown bands on the shells;
And, in a rock pool, 'crumb of bread' sponge,
Hydroids red, green, purple, or richly patterned
Like the dahlia anemone, yellow sea-lemon, and now and again
A rapidly moving snail shell which shows me
It is inhabited by a hermit crab
Much more active than its original occupant.
Countless millions of creatures each essential
To that other, and precisely fashioned
In every detail to meet his requirements.
Millions upon millions of them
Hardly discernible here
In the brilliant light in which sea and sky
Can hardly be distinguished from each other
– And I know there are billions more
Too small for a man to see
Even though human life were long enough
To see them all, a process that can hardly
Be even begun.
Our minds already sense that the fabric of nature's laws
Conceals something that lies behind it,
A greater-unity. – We are beginning more and more
To see behind them something they conceal
For the most part cunningly
With their outward appearances,
By hoodwinking man with a façade
Quite different from what it actually covers.
I am convinced that behind this too
There is another and many more.

Today we are breaking up the chaste
Ever-deceptive phenomena of Nature
And reassembling them according to our will.
We look through matter, and the day is not far distant
When we shall be able to cleave
Through her oscillating mass as if it were air.[1]
Matter is something which man still
At most tolerates, but does not recognise.
Here in the brilliant light, where the mandala[2] is almost
    complete,
The circumference of a blinding diamond broken
Only by a few points and dashes of darkness yet,
The shapes and figures created by the fire of the spirit
Are only empty forms and colours. It is not necessary to confuse
The dull glow of such figures with the pure white light
Of the divine body of truth, nor to project
The light of the highest consciousness into concretized figures,
But to have the consciousness withdrawn, as if
To some sphere beyond the world where it is
At once empty and not empty,
The centre of gravity of the whole personality
Transferred from the conscious centre of the ego
To a sort of hypothetical point
Between the conscious and the unconscious,
The complete abolition of the original
Undifferentiated state of subject and object;
Thus through the certainty that *something lives through me*

---

[1] *Vide* the Aphorisms of Franz Marc.

[2] In 'The Secret of the Golden Flower', symbols having the form of mandalas are reproduced. Mandala means circle, specifically 'magic circle': (Jung has published the mandalas of a somnambulist in his *Collected Papers on Analytical Psychology*). Magic, because the protecting figure of the enclosing circle is supposed to prevent any 'out-pouring', that is, to prevent consciousness being burst asunder by the unconscious, or by partial psychical systems – complexes split off from the whole. At the same time, the mandala gives form to the transformation of inward feeling, such as Paul, for instance, has in mind when he recognizes that 'it is not I who live, but Christ who lives in me' – Christ being here the symbol of the mystical fact of transformation. The inner conversion, the assumption of a unique individuality, is described by the Chinese as the production of the 'diamond body' or the 'sacred fruit'.

Rather than I myself live[1]
A man bridges the gap between instinct and spirit,
And takes hold upon life, attacks life,
In a more profound sense than before.
In the reconciliation of the differentiated
And the inferior function, the 'great Tao
– The meaning of the world' is discovered.

Crossing the island I see the tail of my coat
Wave back and forth and know
It is the waves of the sea on my beach.
And now I am in the cave. A moment ago
I saw the broad leather-brown belts of the tangleweed,
And the minute forms that fix themselves
In soft carmine lace-stencils upon the shingle,
The notched wrack gemmed with lime-white bead-shells
Showing like pearls on a dark braid,
And minute life in a million forms.
And I saw the tide come crawling
Through the rocky labyrinths of approach
With flux and reflux – making inch upon inch
In an almost imperceptible progress.
But now I know it is the earth
And not the water that is unstable,
For at every rise and fall of the pellucid tide
It seems as though it were the shingle
And the waving forest of sea-growth
That moves – and not the water!
And, after all, there is no illusion,
But seeming deception prefigures truth,
For it is a matter of physiographical knowledge
That in the long passages of time
The water remains – and the land ebbs and flows.

I have achieved the diamond body.

---

[1] See 'The Secret of the Golden Flower', a Chinese *Book of Life*, translated into German and annotated by Richard Wilhelm with a European commentary by C. G. Jung.

Whuchulls[1]

Il ne peut y avoir du progrès (vrai, c'est-à dire moral), que dans l'individu et par l'individu lui-même.   CHARLES BAUDELAIRE

GIE owre your coontin', for nae man can tell
The population o' a wud like this
In plants and beasts, and needna pride himsel'
On ocht he marks by a' he's boond to miss.
What is oor life that we should prize't abune
Lichen's or slug's o' which we ken scarce mair
Than they o' oors when a' thing's said and dune,
Or fancy it ser's 'heicher purposes'?
The wice man kens that a fool's brain and his
Differ at maist as little 'gainst a' that is
As different continents and centuries,
Time, station, caste, culture, or character –
Triflin' distinctions that dinna cairry faur –
And if at ony point he stops and says:
'My lot has fa'n in mair enlightened days,
I'm glad to be a European, no' a black
– Human, no' hotchin' glaur' ahint his back
Let him forehear as foolish a future set
Him in a class as seemin' laicher yet,
Or ten pasts damn him for a graceless get.
Original forest, Whuchulls, public park,
Mysel', or ony man, beast, mineral, weed,
I clearly see are a' aside the mark.
The poet hauds nae brief for ony kind,
Age, place, or range o' sense, and no' confined
To ony nature can share Creation's insteed.
First speir this bowzie bourach if 't prefers
The simmer or the winter, day or night,
New or forhooied nests, rain's pelts or smirrs,
Bare sticks or gorded fullyery; and syne invite
My choice twixt good and evil, life and death.

[1] Local pronunciation of Whitshiels, a wood near Langholm.

What hoar trunk girds at ivy or at fug
Or what sleek bole complains it lacks them baith?
Nae foliage hustle-farrant in windy light
Is to the Muse a mair inspirin' sight
Than fungus poxy as the mune; nae blight
A meaner state than flourish at its height.
Leafs' music weel accords wi' gloghole's glug.
Then cite nae mair this, that, or onything.
To nae belief or preference I cling,
Earth – let alane the mucklest mountain in't –
Is faur owre kittle a thing to scho ahint.
I'll no' toy wi' the fragments o't I ken
– Nor seek to beshield *it*, least o' a' men! . . .
Yet here's a poem takin' shape again,
Inevitable shape, faur mair inevitable
Than birks and no' bamboos or banyans here,
Impredictable, relentless, thriddin' the rabble
O' themes and aspects in this thrawart scene.
O freedom constrainin' me as nae man's been
Mair constrained wha wasna, as I'll yet be, freer! . . .

'Clearlier it comes. I winna ha'e it. Quick
And gi'e me tutors in arboriculture then.
Let me plunge where the undergrowth's mair thick.
Experts in forestry, botany – a' that ken
Mair than I dae o' onything that's here.
I ken sae little it easily works its will.
Fence me frae its design wi' endless lear.
Pile up the facts and let me faurer ben.
Multiply my vocabulary ten times ten.
Let me range owre a' prosody again.
Mak' yon a lammergeir, no' juist a wren.
Is that owre muckle for a Scotsman yet,
Needin' a soupler leid, great skills, he lacks?
Is he in silence safer frae attacks?
Yet wha can thole to see it cavalierly choose
In God's green wud – tak' this and that refuse?
Yon knoul-taed trees, this knurl, at least 't'll use!

Gar memory gie the place fower seasons at aince.'
The world's no' mine. I'll tak' nae hen's care o't.
'Is that Creation's nature you evince,
Sma-bookin' Whuchulls to a rice or twa
Sae arbirtrarily picked, and voidin' a'
The lave as gin it wasna worth a jot?'

There is nae reason but on unreason's based
And needs to mind that often to hain its sense,
Dodo and Mammoth had the same misplaced
Trust in their *données* – and ha'e lang gane hence.
Why fash sae muckle owre Nature's present stock
In view o' a' past changes and to come?
Its wipin' oot 'ud be nae greater shock
Than mony afore; and Poetry isna some
Society for Preservin' Threatened Types,
But strokes a cat or fiddles on its tripes,
And for inclusions or exclusions, fegs,
Needna apologize while a'e bird's eggs
Are plain, anither's speckled, beasts ha'e legs,
Birds wings, Earth here brairds trees, here nocht but seggs.
'Troth it's an insult for a man to seek
A'e woman owre anither. A' women hae
Their differences and resemblances, but whatna freak
Thinks, frae the latter, ony ane'll dae
Or, frae the former, fain 'ud sair them a'?

The world o' a' the senses is the same.
Creation disna live frae hand to mooth
Juist improvisin' as it gangs, forsooth,
And there's nae meanin' in life that bode to da'
Until we came – or bides a wicer day –
'Yont brute creation, fools, bairns, unborn, deid.
I'd sing bird-mooth'd wi' ony ither creed,
No' wi' Creation's nature and its aim;
Or sing like Miffy – wheesht, world, while he speaks.
In English – hence, the Universal Speech.
He has nae wings; let birds pit on the breeks.

Nae fins. Fish, copy him! And sae let each
O' Nature's sorts be modelled upon him
Frae animalculae to Seraphim.
He is nae poet, but likes the Laureate best.
What, write like that? – Ah! here's the crucial test!
I ha'e the courage to be a Scotsman then
(Nae Scot 'll e'er be Laureate we ken!)[1]
Divided frae ither folk to Eternity's en',
And, if I hadna, ken it wadna maitter.
I'd be it still. Exclusive forms are nature.
It means to be and comes in Nature's way.
– In its ain nature's, as a' in Nature does.
Supersessions, innovations, variations, display
Nature, no' hide; and Scotland, Whuchulls, us
Interest me less for what they are than as
Facts o' the creative poo'er that, tho' they pass,
'll aye be qualified by their ha'en been.
It is nae treason then to stell my een
No' on their fleetin' shapes but on their deep
Constituent principles destined to keep
A mystery greater than the sight o' eels
Kelterin' through a' the seven seas reveals.
These to a'e spot converge, but we gang oot
Aye faurer frae oor source – ne'er back, I doot.

'*I like to see the ramel gowd-bestreik,*
And sclaffer cuit-deep through the birsled leafs.
Here I dung doon the squirrels wi' my sling
And made the lassies brooches o' their paws,
Set girns for rabbits and for arnuts socht,
Herried my nests and blew the eggs, and lit
Fires o' fir-burrs and hag in tinker style.
Hoo faur the interests o' progress warrant
Meddlin' wi' Whuchulls' auld amenities,
And their dependent livelihoods and ploys,
I'm no' to say; I'm glad to see it still
Temporarily triumphant against control.

[1] 'There are poets little enough to envy even a poet-laureate.' – *Gray.*

It's pleasant nae doot for a woman to dream
O' yieldin' hersel' to some buirdly man
Wha kens what he wants and willy-nilly'll ha'e't
But when the time comes she'll aye find, I think,
Guid reasons for no' yieldin' – bless'her hert!
Sae wi' the Whuchulls. May the Lord be praised.'
Nae doot primeval beasts felt juist the same
Aboot the place – tho' different frae this
As ony change that's still in store for it.
Hauf saurian-emeritus, hauf prentice spook,
You'll never see the plantin' for the trees,
This Eden where Adam comes fu' circle yet.

There is nae ither way. For weel or woe
It is attained. Tho' idle side-winds blow
In on me still and inferior questions thraw
Their crockets up, a' doots and torments cease.
The road is clear. I gang in perfect peace,
And my idea spreids and shines and lures me on,
O lyric licht auld chaos canna dam!
Celestial, soothin', sanctifyin' course, wi' a'
The high sane forces o' the sacred time
Fechtin' on my side through it till I con
This blainy blanderin' and ken that I'm
Delivered frae the need o' trauchlin' wi't,
Accommodated to't, but in my benmaist hert
Acknowledgmentless, free, condition or reform,
Or sunny lown or devastatin' storm,
Indifferent to me; where the Arts stert
Wi' a' else *corpore vili* – 'God's mercy-seat!'

The Terrible Crystal

TO SADIE MCLELLAN (MRS. WALTER PRITCHARD)

CLEAR thought is the quintessence of human life.
In the end its acid power will disintegrate
All the force and flummery of current passions and pretences,
Eat the life out of every false loyalty and craven creed
And bite its way through to a world of light and truth.

Give me the open and unbiased mind
Valuing truth above all prepossessions to such an extent
As to be ready to discard them all
τό κατ' ἀνθρωπόν, and, furthermore,
Is content to approach Metaphysics through Physics,
In the Aristotlean sense in so far
As it recognises that empirical factuality
Can best be attested in that domain,
And is therefore impelled to recognise in the cosmos
A dynamic and teleological character

And by virtue of that recognition
Stands not far from religion
– A teleology essentially immanent,
God's relation to the world being in some general way
Like the relation of our minds to our bodies.

This is the hidden and lambent core I seek.
Like crystal it is hidden deep
And only to be found by those
Who will dig deep.
Like crystal it is formed by cataclysm and central fires;
Like crystal it gathers into an icy unity
And a gem-like transparence
All the colour and fire of life;
Like crystal it concentrates and irradiates light;
Like crystal it endures.

Since only those who have looked upon tragedy
Can dare to behold it.
It is terrible to uninitiated eyes.
 Yet in this white stone
Those upon whom tragedy and catastrophe are come
May find their cure and their redemption,
For it has been formed in tragedy
And calcined in catastrophe
I have seen refractions of its purity
In the facets of seers past and present –
Virgil's day-star dawning over ruined Ilium;
Kierkegaard's 'arousal broad awake'
Out of his 'dread and trembling';
Barth's 'horizon light' breaking through the dark obscure;
Brunner's lightning flashes in the midnight of 'eclipse';
Heim's 'two infinitudes' beyond the boundary of dimension,
– Visions of a transcendental country
Stretching out athwart the temporal frontiers;
The sacrificial 'salutation of the cleanness of death'
On the part of Joan the Maid
– All, indeed, but broken lights,
Partial gleams reflecting each in their degree
Some aspect of the white intensity
Of that single central radiance,
But all carrying the same gospel:
'When consciousness is crucified upon circumstance
Give praise!'

The poetry I seek must therefore have the power
Of fusing the discordant qualities of experience,
Of mixing moods, and holding together opposites,
And well I know that the various facets
Of sensibility, sensuous, mental, and emotional,
And its alternating moods
Cannot be fully reconciled
Save in an imaginative integrity
That includes, but transcends, sensibility as such.

Our time opposes such integrity
As much as it demands it
And to struggle through complexity to simplicity
Is therefore as necessary as it is difficult.

A Vision of Scotland

I SEE my Scotland now, a puzzle
Passing the normal of her sex, going erect
Unscathed through fire, keeping her virtue
Where temptation works with violence, walking bravely,
Offering loyalty and demanding respect.

Every now and again in a girl like you,
Even in the streets of Glasgow or Dundee,
She throws her headsquare off and a mass
Of authentic flaxen hair is revealed,
Fine spun as newly-retted fibres
On a sunlit Irish bleaching field.

Larking Dallier

UP frae the sea the trusting rocks
You had nae suner wiled than you
Let oot a laugh and 'neth the wave
    Hid your ain sel' frae view.

The cheated rocks nae faurer cam'
Yet couldna to the deeps return
And day by day maun thole to watch
    Your same toom promise burn.

Tho' by the moon at second-hand
You drag the waters still you'll see
Nae mair dry land come snoovin' oot
    This side Eternity.

You conjure the larks, no continents,
And gar them soar and sing – but ah!
You'll no' even hear the burdies oot
    Afore you jouk awa'.

Men keep their feet upon the grun'
Tho' whiles their thochts the larks ootsoar,
For sense frae life's nae ither ploy
    Than light frae night afore.

Tho' subtler forms o' life emerge
They still maun cry: 'Nicht sune obscures
What profit's in ootsoarin' yet
    A' ither larks but yours!'

In Talk with Donnchadh Bàn Mac an t'Saoir[1]

After making an English verse translation of his Moladh Beinn Dobhrain

It is very difficult for an active mind stuffed with the matter of 'Education' to play its part effectively in stalking wild animals.
F. FRASER DARLING *in* A Herd of Red Deer: A Study in Animal Behaviour (1937)

> *The Muse of old Maro hath pathos and splendour,*
> *The long lines of Homer in majesty roll;*
> *But to me Donnchadh Bàn breathes a feeling more tender,*
> *More akin to the child-heart that sleeps in my soul.*
> Principal SHAIRP: *Aspects of Poetry*

He seemed to know, by personal experience, what it was like to be a tree or a daisy or a breaking wave or even the mysterious moon itself. He could get inside the skin of an animal and tell you in the most convincing detail how it felt, and how, dimly, inhumanly, it thought.
ALDOUS HUXLEY (of D. H. Lawrence)

N o t the speech of ordinary city folk (with their air
Of elaborate superciliousness which testifies
To ages of systematic half-culture. They seem
To utter that hopeless word *connu*). But in such wise
As Doughty found in the poorest Arabians – the bird-like ease
Alacrity and perspicuous propriety of speech
United with quick significance – since words must reach
To the heart of the matter, like Abdullah of Kheybar's
'Round kind of utterance, with election of words,
And dropping with the sap of human life,'
Or the young man of Shuggera's, who put life in his words
As a juggler impresses his will on his properties:
An art learnt not from books but from life – tales of men
Unlettered like you, yet wise in speech, and practised, like you,
(Aye, even to the mental grasp of a Rob Donn
Whose *Òran a' Gheamhraidh* is an exact counterpart,

[1] Donnchadh Bàn Mac an t'Saoir (Duncan Bàn MacIntyre), 1724–1812, one of the greatest of Scottish Gaelic poets, was a deer-stalker, unable to read or write, who carried all his poems in his head until towards the end of his life he dictated them, amounting to several thousands of lines, to a minister friend.

Line by line and phrase by phrase,
Of Alexander MacDonald's Òran an t-Samhraidh,
Tho' he could not read the original on which he wrought!
– Greater even than Su Tungp'o's feat of writing
A complete set of poems on the rhymes used
By the complete poems of T'ao).
Not town-folk's speech, flat like the rest of their natures,
But the power that can speak to the heart of others
With that faculty of sheer description
Which not only tells *what* a thing is, but at least
Incidentally goes far towards telling *why*.
– But beyond this how? The speech of one neither man nor animal –
    or both –
Yet not monster; a being in whom both races meet
On friendly ground – all the pleasantness of sylvan life,
All the genial and happy characteristics of creatures
That dwell in woods and fields, seeming mingled and kneaded
Into one substance with the kindred qualities in human nature,
Trees, grass, flowers, streams, cattle, deer and unsophisticated man,
Like a poet's reminiscence of the time
When man's affinity with nature was more strict
And his fellowship with every living thing more intimate and dear,
Like the Faun of Praxiteles – not supernatural,
Just on the verge of nature yet within it.
Nature needed, and still needs, this beautiful creature
Standing betwixt man and animal, sympathising with each,
Comprehending the speech of either race, and interpreting
The whole existence of one to the other.
– How happy such a life, enjoying the warm, sensuous,
Earthy side of Nature, revelling in the merriment of woods and streams,
Living as our four-footed kindred do – as mankind did
In its innocent childhood before sin or sorrow
Or mortality itself had been thought of! How difficult to make out
A genius such as yours. So full of animal life as you were,
So joyous in deportment, so handsome, so physically well-developed,
Giving no impression of incompleteness, of maimed or stinted nature,
Yet in literary intercourse how we
(Educated chimpanzees, O thou Gaelic Mozart!)

Habitually and instinctively allow for you
As for a child or some other lawless being,
Exacting no strict obedience to conventional rules,
Hardly noticing your eccentricities enough to pardon them
Because of the indefinable characteristic that sets you outside our
     bounds,
(You who were writing superb descriptions
Of wild scenery for its own sake
When the English were still complaining
Of the 'frightful irregularity' of Highland mountains,
'Most of all disagreeable when the heather is in bloom'
And making pained contrast of them
With that truly 'poetical mountain', Richmond Hill!
It was not until the success of Scott and Wordsworth
Your attitude could be conceived of by the South of England.
In an age of brilliant Gaelic poetry, Scottish Lowlanders even
Regarded the Highlanders as illiterate savages
And the sad history of Highland education
In the three centuries after 1560
Reveals they did their best to make them so)
– The Faun – twenty-five centuries old, to judge by the date
Praxiteles carved on this statue; oh, Donnchadh Bàn,
A century and a half by Scottish literary history,
You look as young as ever; you have nothing to do with time,
But have the look of eternal youth in your face. . . .

It would be relatively easy to write the history
Of a pair of nesting dab-chicks or of a day in their life,
With a continuousness and exhaustiveness that might challenge
     comparison,
Without breaks, a seamless garment,
With the most accomplished and most dangerous works of modern
     fiction,
Differing from them only in not pretending to know
The birds' minds from the inside out, but hoping at best
To get at their nature from their movements and write their odyssey
By working from the outside in; but the red deer are more difficult
     subjects

Than any species of birds, since there is in their existence
No period of helplessness – nothing to correspond
To the nesting season and its ties. – Even the new-dropped calf
Needs little or no attention from its mother,
In its first days of weakness, she suckles it
But twice in twenty-four hours, and as soon as it needs her more
It is already able to follow her wherever she goes.

How can we expect ever to know with accuracy then
The life and movements of individual deer? – At the best a man
Who has seen an immense number of typical incidents
Might nigh to the end of a long life get near telling us
What the probable main outlines of the story would be.
Without intuitional divination all the tests and checks
Of science avail nothing. The desire to be with them,
Near them, among them must be a controlling passion.
Your long life was a more or less continuous stalk.
This brought you nearer to their life than any other poet
(Even we who have pursued everything appertaining to deer
So closely that we have not even missed
The fact that in the Gospel of Teliau,
Now commonly known as the Book of St. Chad
There is a stab in St. Matthew xii, 48,
Between *bo* and *nos*, and in this hole
The deer's hair from the original skin can still be seen.
Even the photostat shows the mark
Where the hair is in the stab).

The whole threshold of awareness was raised; the whole organism
Worked with unheard-of co-ordination. It is almost
As if to know the life of a deer one must become a deer
And live among them; and as your life showed
That is not so impossible as it may sound.
You got near enough to such an imaginative identification
To know that your life and theirs were part of one plan.
The deer are more than the material of a scientist's paper.
Indeed the nobility of their beauty has been
Among the major motives of poetry since time began,

And the mere sight of a stag in its wild freedom still
Means more to many of us than to hear the nightingale's song.
– But only in *your* poetry can we feel we stand
Some snowy November evening under the birch-trees
By a tributary burn that flows
Into the remote and lovely Dundonnell river
And receive the most intimate, most initiating experience,
When three hinds and a stag approach where we stand,
Rise on their hind legs, and browse on the twigs above us.
We could touch them; their breath comes into our faces.
Many more of the herd are within a few yards of us.
We have the feeling of having reached that state
All watchers of animals desire
Of having dispensed with our physical presence.
Or is that it? Is not really the bottom of our desire
Not to be ignored but to be accepted? . . .

Once in a Cornish Garden

For Valda

A spray of red rose berries flung against the blue
Cornish sky – what more does man want here below?
                                        Stephen McKenna

Even as St. John could not depict
The glories of the New Jerusalem without
Recourse to gold and precious stones, so we
Our spirits' perfect state in terms
Of Cornish geology.

Il y a deux sortes d'élaborations géologiques: L'une qui est un procès de désintégration: le granit, par exemple, qui devient argile. L'autre – et c'est comme le philosophe qui, par le brassage d'une multitude de faits, arrive au concept, au joyau abstrait d'une définition irréprochable – est une espèce de création ou de parturition, quelque chose à quoi aboutir qui échappe à la décomposition par la simplicité. Les entrailles de la nature en travail ont enfanté ce bézoard. Il a fallu la presse cosmique, l'action qui est passion d'un monde en révolte contre sa propre inertie, l'épreinte tellurique, le vomissement du feu intérieur, ce qui de plus central est capable de jaillir sous une main inexorable, l'écrasement millénaire de ses-couches qui se compénètrent, tout le mystère, toute l'usine métamorphique, pour aboutir à ce brillant, à ce cristal sacré, à cette noix parfaite et translucide qui échappe à la pourriture du brou. Parfaite, pas encore! Il faut que la main de l'homme s'ajoute à ce caillou qui l'invite. Il faut qu'un lent polissage vienne dissiper l'obscurité inhérente, effacer la rugosité adventice, accentuer le clivage, éliminer le défaut, éveiller l'œil secret, compléter la rose ébauchée. Il faut que la facette multiplie le prisme. Il faut user le refus. Il faut que naisse ce prodige minéral qui est un nombre solide; il faut qu'apparaisse enfin sous la main de l'ouvrier ce soleil minuscule qui doit ses rayons à la géométrie. (Ainsi cette pierre merveilleuse dont parle Buffon, et que j'aime autant ne pas identifier, et qu'il appelle la girasol.) *Non plus un miroir seulement, mais un foyer.*

PAUL CLAUDEL, *La Mystique des Pierres Précieuses*

THERE is no outline of the landscape here.
No element in the objective world,
You have not vitalised for me,
(*Spyrys Kernow*,[1] be with me now!)
At every turn establishing some original confrontation
Of Cornwall and myself as pure and as immediate
As on Creation's day.
And how you suit your setting at every point!
Cornwall incarnate, costumed by Aage Thaarup,
With your little nigger felt cap, its forward poke
Accentuated by fringed grosgrain ribbon;
Dress and coat in the new Persian brown,
The coat generously trimmed with lamb to tone,
And with large antique bronze buttons
To finish the draped neckline of the dress.
Or, at night, in 'Nitchevo', the little Ardanse black crepe dress,
Its intricate and unusual cut blazoned by
A waistcoat-bodice of white and gold lamé.
These are your colours – sultan-red, rich gold, gold brown,
Black, scarlet, nut-brown and sunrise pink,
Copper glance, purple, peach, and cream,
Cherry, geranium, coral flame, and blush,
Wheat gold, sun-orange, and harlequin red,
Just as the right cosmetic chart for your type is this –
Carmine rouge, used high on the cheeks and skilfully shaded;
Brown eye-shadow; black eyelash make-up;
Black eyebrow pencil very carefully applied
Not to give a harsh line;

[1] Cornish, meaning 'Spirit of Cornwall'.

A rachelle powder, dusted lightly over
To soften the whole make-up; carmine lip-stick,
And a rachelle make-up blender for your arms and neck:
And for the evening under artificial lights
You'll change your powder to the flesh colour
And your eye-shadow to a glorious violet
And use vermilion lip-stick.
Even as in our garden all the flowers have
Colours like these and look
Like isolated moods of yours, particular memories of you,
Gestures and smiles of yours that have somehow taken root
And flourish here for ever.
Oh, all the colour in this golden moment
Seems to flow from you!
– The brilliant red supergiant El Monte asters,
Double petunias in fringed, ruffled, and laciniate forms,
Rose of Heaven and Little Star petunias,
And, among the roses, the flaming yellow
And copper-toned Feu Pernet-Ducher, the coral-petalled
Carrie Jacobs Bond, the orange-overcast
Carillon, and the brilliant deep-red Dickson's Centennial.
Then the sweet-scented Golden Gleam nasturtiums,
The great clusters of glorious fiery red Russian lilies,
– Like the reflection of my own heart's blood –
And the rainbow show of giant zinnias
Burnt orange, deep salmon, rose and purple
(And these be your words, beloved),
In so far as earth-speech may avail,
That sight or sound of you always
May conjure up without fail –
Coinnealta, solasta, croidhearg, cunbhalach,
Eireachdail, taiceil, glòir-ghleusta, fìonfhuil, gnìomh-luaineach,[1]
And for the phrase that matches you best
'The mile-great sheaf-like blast of purple-glowing and red flames'
Or Meredith's 'her pomp of glorious hues, her revelry of ripeness,
    her kind smile',

[1] These Scottish Gaelic words mean bright, brilliant, blood-red, constant,
handsome, staunch, of tuneful speech, of deft deed, and 'wine-blood' (i.e. noble).

The 'radiance rare and fathomless'
That Hardy won in Cornwall too
(Doughty loved Cornwall and spent his honeymoon here,
And W. H. Hudson, and Stephen McKenna,
The translator of Plotinus – even as I!)
Best of all the little knit play-suit you made yourself
Of peau d'ange yarn, shorts of corn yellow,
Striped short-sleeved jumper blouse of corn yellow and brown,
And brown knit overskirt to button on to the shorts
When you want to be less informal,
Or that other one, dusty pink flannel skirt,
Matching high-necked sweater blouse,
And prune-coloured knitted finger-tip jacket,
The belt of the blouse prune suede.
Or your Tahitian *paréo*, with its gay printed shorts and brassière,
And skirt open down the front
– A new high note in hilarity!
Caprice Espagnol earrings of little carved red roosters,
Or, again, lattice sandals of black satin
Studded with mirror baguettes,
A tiny black felt jockey cap with huge bunches of black aigrettes
Jumping out at unexpected places at the front and sides;
And the house things you have chosen
(Ah! The blond wood, and pistachio and rose-red upholstery,
And great vase of crimson-black Nigrette hybrid tea-roses!
– Rare examples of Swedish sloyd, beautiful
Hand-beaten pewter-ware and delicately blown
Mountain glass so frail that it looks
Like curly white smoke, and peasant rugs
From Dalecarlia, striped in orange and red and purple!)
Or on windy promontories or in the autmn lanes
In your wine-red suit of rough soft woollen
With a mushroom-collar of beaver, blouse and coat-lining
Of a wool shell-knit fabric in a shade of blue
That looks shimmery because two different tones are used.
I have a million memories of you, all fitty and suant.[1]
From waters like the Dancers of Huai Nan,

[1] Cornish words meaning appropriate and sweetly satisfying.

(Chang Hang's famous poem . . . 'So dance to dance
Endlessly they weave, break off and dance again
Now flutter their cuffs like a great bird in flight,
Now toss their long white sleeves like whirling snow')
And the dark-green rocks with bands of grey felspar or yellow epidote,
(Scryfer meyn,[1] be with me now!)
Through all the intensely plicated, compressed, cleaved series
To the 'Delabole Butterfly', the clear blue topaz at Cligga and
    St. Michael's Mount,
The wolfram openworks at the north end of Bodmin Moor
(Not Wolfram's – von Eschenbach's – too little opened works,
Which, though lip-service is occasionally paid
To the conventional *amour courtois*, find
The true relation between man and woman in the married state
– In this a marrow of the *Song of Winifreda*
A kindred spirit wrote two hundred years before.
Poets of happy married life are few, and none,
Not even Patmore, meets the case for me –
And portray a Parzival not as a lad who wins
By reason of his utter purity and innocence
To the beatific vision but a boy who, brought up
In complete ignorance of life, is driven
By his innate force of character to go out
Into the world to carve his career and achieves
Success only after many misadventures due
To his lack of experience and failure to grasp
The true spirit of chivalry; I too have failed
The suffering Amfortas more than once,
And, proving incompetent in Grail Castle,
Been driven out into the world again
And spent much time in Trevizent's company
– Excuse a parenthesis like Wolfram's own!)
The Tremore elvan spangled with purple fluorspar
(Which Derbyshire workers call Blue John),[2]
The pinitiferous elvan at Goldsithney,
The Prah Sands elvan, and the flow-banded
Quartz felsite of Tregonetha.

---

[1] Cornish, meaning writer of the rocks.   [2] John, i.e. Jaune.

And we are with the Cornish miners and we know
'Horses' from 'vughs', 'peach' from 'capel' or 'gossan' from 'iron hat',
The 'pigs' eggs' of the clay-workers, and whether China stones
Are 'hard purple', 'mild purple', hard white' or 'mild white'.
The Goss Moors and the Luxulyan valley,
St. Nectan's Kieve, the Rocky Valley, Lydford Gorge and Lustleigh
    Cleave
Are all known to us, and we have loved to note
The grey and purple fine-grained compact basalt
Of the Dunchideoch type, and where the red Iddingsite occurs,
Dolomitic conglomerate in the Keuper Series,
Metamorphic aureoles round the granite masses
And subangular stones of quartzite, grit and quartz
In a dark red matrix of sand, and the peculiar
Red quartz-porphyry in the breccias between Dunchideoch and Ide,
And all the herring-boned or chevroned pegmatite dykes
And those inclusions of the iron front driven by potassium,
And later, silica, into enclaves (like the Cornish people themselves)
That form the dark ovoid patches the quarrymen
Call 'furreners' in the coarse granite.
And changes of volcanic rocks abutting on granite
Into calcareous hornfels, showing the minerals
Axinite, vesuvianite, and garnet.
Extensive sheets of spilitic lava and of tuff
With beds of radiolarian chert, the large
Amygdaloidal and pumiceous masses of Brent Tor,
The horneblende picrite of Polyphant ornamental stone,
And, in the albite-diabases, augite fresh and purplish hued
In ophitic enclosure of the albite laths,
And all the upward sequence of lithological types
Extending from Lewannick to Trevalga.
White quartzite *schuppen* of Gorran Haven
Connected with the Breton and Portuguese fauna,
Networks of ilmenite and prisms of apatite,
Lenses of dark blue limestone, groups of sheared dolerite sills,
Shining plates of enstatite or bastite, facaoidal masses
Of pink and grey gneiss in the serpentine, north-west of Kennack,
Dykes of gabbro in the serpentine near Coverack,

And flaser structure developed as at Carrick Luz.
The meneage rocks of the Lizard and the Start and Bolt,
The Ordovician rocks at Manaccan, Veryan, and Gorran Haven,
The Mylor and Portscatho Beds – we know them all,
And every scovan, every stannary, and all
The greywethers of Cornwall, the sarsden-stone,
And piles of attal-Sarsen, Jews' leavings,
And stringers and stockwerks, greisens and gangue,
'Black shell' and 'stent', 'grizzle' and 'growder',
The Cretaceous Overstep, the Cowstones, and the Foxmould sands,
Horneblende, in the extreme stages of contact alteration,
Pale-brown with large crystals or entirely acicular,
With needles so fine that they are referred
To horneblende only by analogy.
Or the decomposed mica-lamprophyres of Newquay Headland and
    the Gannel,
And fresh biotite-orthoclase traps like the Hicksmill and Lemail dykes,
We know them all, all bathed in the glow of unison
Or in the frail effulgence of eternity.
Hence here we can perceive contentedly,
Abreast of the attempt to synthesize
Work on the soil sciences with that
On the ductless glands,
The fact that sexual selection was originally directed
Mainly by the need to economise iodine,
The whole development, physical and mental of our race
Dependent on the supply of certain minerals in the soil,
And all our instincts closely associated with
The unconscious desire for particular kinds of food,
And face without fear the future phosphorus shortage
That will not immediately reduce our numbers, but at first
Swell them to well-nigh Oriental proportions.
And as the theory that the foliation of the Lizard rocks
Was due to injection foliation in a metasomatic rock
Was followed by that of dynamism and orogeny
Till it was found that these structures could only be created
By *both* these agencies acting concurrently,
So through the whole range of possible experience

In our intelligence, intuitions, thoughts and beings
We know we are able *récompenser* each other
– *Récompenser* in French philosophy's use of the term,
Or as a watchmaker would use it of his wheels and escapement!
(Though if our relation like that between body and mind
Is not described as one of interaction
It is mainly because that word does not express
Adequately the intimate character of the relation) –
Without fear, although we clearly realize
Perpetual mental progress is neither impossible nor inevitable.
Clear thought is the quintessence of human life.
In the end its acid power will disintegrate
All the force and flummery of current passions and pretences,
Eat the life out of every false loyalty and craven creed,
And bite its way through to a world of light and truth.

EARLY LYRICS
(1968)

Tryst in the Forest

WITH starry eyes she comes to me
Between the dim trees there.
Love is the rosebud at her breast
And Time the ribbon in her hair.

On cloudcool breasts she'll cradle me
In the long darkness there
With Dust the rosebud at her breast
And Death the ribbon in her hair.

Ennui

I HEAR what the bird sings
(Cuckoo! Spring comes in!)
And know what the bell saith
(Ding! Dong! The worms win!)
And tire but of two things
– Life and Death!

She Whom I Love

SHE whom I love hath many eyes
Since with the waters and the skies
She watcheth me: and openeth
Light after light within my heart.
Naught in my secret dreams hath part
Save 'It is good' she saith
With a clear eye
That shineth by.

In Memory

ONLY the rosebud I remember
Only the rosebud and the one green leaf
And lest these fail me too I make
The little summers of my spirit brief.

Only the rosebud I remember:
Only the rosebud and the one green leaf
My fearful heart to breasts of dust
Restores between the winters of my grief.

Only the rosebud I remember,
Only the rosebud and the one green leaf
– Beneath the gravestone of the sky
At last I lay them – a sufficient sheaf!

To Margaret

As from a hedge
Wild roses do
So from my dreams
Spring dreams of you.

And thoughts of you
In my thoughts are
As twixt dark clouds
A thrilling star.

Truth

Lo! Youth!
In the heart of the world
Like a knife
Quivers this truth.
All that lacks love
Lacks life!

Two Gods

The present moment is a powerful Deity.
GOETHE

Now is a mighty God,
Then an unknown.
The One shall have my heart,
The Other own
The dreams I dare
Not let my own heart share.

From
A CLYACK-SHEAF
(1969)

The Ross-shire Hills

WHAT are the hills of Ross-shire like?
Listen. I'll tell you. Over the snow one day
I went out with my gun. A hare popped up
On a hill-top not very far away.

I shot it at once. It came rolling down
And round it as it came a snowball grew,
Which, when I kicked it open, held not one
But seventeen hares. Believe me or not. It's true.

To Those of My Old School who fell
in the Second World War

ONE loves the temporal, some unique manifestation,
Something irreplaceable that dies.

But one is loyal to an ideal limit
Involved in all specific objects of love
And in all co-operating wills.

Shall the lonely griefs and joys of men
Forever remain a pluralistic universe?
Need they, if thought and will are bent in common interest
In making this universe one?

All these things are clearer to me today than ever;
The ineluctable individuation of personality,
The importance of indefinables in life,
The moral urgency of definition
If we are to make secure for Eternity

The treasures of the moment,
– As you, comrades of my old school,
Have helped to add
One of the sublimest sagas of human courage
To the whole history of Mankind!
Shown again the individual is the only foundation
On which any social order may safely build;
That David can still stand up against Goliath,
That the individual can still
Be the master of his fate, the captain of his soul;
That man is still the potential creator
Rather than the victim of his creations;
A creature of free will and untold possibilities,
Not the slave of environment;
His capabilities limited not so much
By heredity or poverty as by his own vision of himself.
I thank you – and the whole world has cause to thank you –
For the rediscovery of man and the powers
Of which he is capable when his mind has been freed
From fallacies about himself.
I thank you, comrades of my old school,
For this timely and invaluable reassurance
– For vouchsafing us so wonderful a spectacle
Of the movement of individual will
Towards a common beckoning Good,
Always distant, yet always implicit
In love and understanding,
And the only alternative to callousness and despair;
And for all the glimpses you have given us
Of the incredible beauty
Of those who give themselves while they are yet young
Selflessly to a noble cause.

Symbol of human freedom forever,
You endured more
Than any other citizen army in history,
Even that which, in June 1778
Marched on the heels of the retreating British

With William Billings, 'blind and slovenly'
But full of fire, setting the key for the song:

> *Let tyrants shake their iron rods*
> *And Slavery clank her galling chains;*
> *We wear them not . . .*

Neither legends nor lies are needed,
The truth is enough. It should stiffen the spines
Of all who fear for human liberty. You, comrades,
Who froze and starved and rotted in this War,
Were not superhuman; you merely preferred
Suffering and death
Rather than bend your knees
To persons and principles you rightly despised.
Wherefore, in every man and woman of you on the Allied side,
I see that unconscious processes may be intelligent and aspiring,
Generating images and intuitions of moral import,
Solutions of conflict, desirable avenues of advance.
In presenting you thus I function as a priest
But outside all systems of theology.
I see your War as an exciting drama
In which you are all Platonic forms and archetypes;
Vast images that illumine, guide, and make significant
The most trivial occurrences.

Behind all this is an idea,
Suggested by indirection,
Of the human soul, its creative evolution,
Its enlightenment, its fulfilment in relationship
Not with some imaginary deity
But with the boundless potentialities
Of other creative individuals;
And your story is thus a revealing mirror
That will instigate
A Resurrection from the Dead!

You will be remembered when your foes are forgotten,
On the one side – the People,

On the other – the vain titles and vicious wealth
Of a worthless few. Chartres versus Versailles!
Versailles! symbol of the 'model of kingship
In our civilisation' – vast, ornate,
Magnificent, overpowering,
Wholly unconnected with the real life of the nation,
Sterile always,
As it is silent and empty now,
Trivial, ephemeral, dead!
Nobody remembers
What kings reigned in France
When the people of Beauce were building their cathedral;
And their days like all life
Knew poverty
And ignorance and oppression and suffering,
But the living force and beauty
In the minds and souls of many men
Created in their work a vital glory.

So, today, hope lies
In the free and many-sided spirit of humanity
Against any one-man domination.
Beyond the meaningless dead splendours of Versailles
The glowing beauty of Chartres
Speaks imperishably through the ages,
And even so will the future see you,
Little group of comrades from my old school,
Who went out
Against the Powers and Principalities of Darkness.

Hail and farewell, my friends!
At the moment it seems
As though the pressure of a loving hand had gone,
The touch
Under which my close-pressed fingers seemed to thrill
And the skin divide up into little zones
Of heat and cold whose position continually changed
So that the whole of my hand, held in that clasp,

Was in a state of internal movement.
My eyes – that were full of pride,
My hands – that were full of love,
Are empty again – for a while,
For a little while!

For Daniel Cohn-Bendit

*On the occasion of his candidature in Glasgow
University Rectorial Election, 1968*[1]

No man or group of men has any right
To force another man or other groups of men
To do anything he or they do not wish to do.
There is no right to govern without
The consent of the governed. Consent is not only
Important in itself, and as a nidus for freedom
And its attendant spontaneity (clearly valuable
As the opposed sense of frustration is detrimental)
          But the sole
Basis of political obligation. There is nothing
Supplemental to or coequal with consent itself
And even if we had not the lessons of all history
– The endless evidence of 'man's inhumanity to man'
And overwhelming proof that all power debases
And that no man is good enough to have it
Or can exercise it without doing far more harm than good –
The contention is utterly indefensible – sheer humbug! mortmain!
That 'so long as the exercise of certain powers is good in itself
Or a means to the good . . . these powers are right
Whether or not anyone is of the opinion that they are,'
The time-dishonoured formula that attempts to conceal or excuse
All the hellish wrong of human history,

[1] The author was one of Cohn-Bendit's sponsors on this occasion.

The fraud and loss inherent in all Government,
That age-long monstrous distortion of the faculties of man
It is the great historical task of the working-class
To eliminate today, no matter at what cost,
That human life, no longer wrenched hideously awry,
May spring up at last in its proper form.

Good-bye Twilight

FOR NEIL M. GUNN

BACK to the great music, Scottish Gaels. Too long
You have wallowed as in the music of Delius.
Make a heroic effort now to swing yourselves round
To the opposite pole – the genius of Sibelius.
(Out of the West Highlands and Islands of Scotland now
What a symphony should come, more ghastly and appalling
Than Sibelius's gaunt El-Greco-emaciated ecstatic Fourth!
Far beyond *Squinting Peter's Flame of Wrath*
Or *Too Long in This Condition*[1]
But like the great jigs, whirling electrons of musical energy,
Like *The Shaggy Grey Buck* or *The Baldooser*,
Fantastic, incredible, all but impossible to human fingers.)

It is impossible perhaps to imagine two men
More utterly unlike in temperament than these.
Sibelius lacks wholly the rather morbid preoccupation
With what is vaguely termed 'Nature' Delius possesses,
An obsession that does not allow of any very clear
Spiritual vision or insight into the true inwardness of the thing
That is the obsession. Delius looks upon 'Nature' and promptly
     becomes
Doped, drugged, besotted – my countrymen, even as you.

[1] Titles of two of the great *piobaireachd*.

Sibelius, on the other hand, keeps all his very fine
Acute Northern wits – not a commodity to be found
Growing on blackberry bushes here in the North, you know –
Very well on the alert; he knows
That that aspect of the matter is an aspect only,
That there's much more to it than only that,
And the magic of his Finland is in his very nerves and bones
As the magic of our Scotland should be in ours.

If and when he does indulge in a specific piece
Of 'nature' writing, as in the *Oceanides*, one has the feeling
That in those parts at least it is felt and he too feels
That the outward aspect of the thing vaguely called 'nature'
Is itself a magical manifestation as much as
Any transportation, materialisation, or like phenomenon might be.

Delius merely exclaims, with a catch of his breath,
'Oh, how lovely! – and how sad it must all come to an end!'
And promptly dissolves into tears. Sibelius
Does not think or feel it sad at all for he knows
That one piece of magic is as good as another
And the conclusion of one piece of magical evocation
By no manner of means means the end of anything at all.
Anyhow, what about the magician? The contrast in outlook and
        temper
Makes itself vividly felt in a prolonged listening
To the two. A long spell of Delius
Is enervating and relaxing like a muggy winter day in London,
While Sibelius charges his hearer with nervous energy
Almost as if he had performed some operations of *Prana* with him.
Back to the great music, you fools – to the classical Gaelic temper!
Out of the Celtic Twilight and into the Gaelic sun!

In portions of his writings Franz Kafka deals
With the material of his own obsessions,
The sub-conscious mechanisms are never allowed
To throw up fantasy uncriticised, but continually
Put through a checking process . . . whereas you
With the best intentions in the world get nowhere

Because your sub-conscious nature, which, apparently,
You know nothing about, is manipulating you from the start.

Out from your melancholy moping, your impotence, Gaels,
(You stir the heart, you think? . . . but surely
One of the heart's main functions is to supply the brain!)
Back into the real world again – the world once of *The Barren Rocks of
     Aden,*
The 79th's Farewell to Gibraltar, The Burning Sands of Egypt,
The Taking of Beaumont Hammel, Kantara to El-Arish,
And, now, the world of Barke's *Scottish Ambulance Unit in Spain*
– For the true spirit is still living here and there, and perhaps
The day is not far distant when the Scottish people
Will enter into this heritage, and in so doing
Enrich the heritage of all mankind again.

When the Birds Come Back to Rhiannon

ONCE more a man cried
(Passionately identifying himself
With the whole of Scotland
From top to bottom,
Surveying entire Scotland with his mind's eye
– To hear his phrases was like watching a fog rise;
We saw great tracts of country, roadless, unvisited,
Rare flowers and birds in inaccessible places,
Rocky formations, currents, soils,
Weather conditions, caves, legends, antiquities.
He sang the whole song of Scotland
With a marvellous gift for seizing the mood of Nature,
A profound animistic understanding,
A lyrical genius giving a sense of revelation,
Conjuring up an open country, ploughed all over,
Surging like the sea, its horizons sleeping under a misty haze.
Its landscapes were filled with life

– Alive as these old woodcuts in which we see
Men, animals, and birds all going about their business,
Each completely in character,
As if they had just stepped out of the Ark.
He painted not outside time and space,
But rather in a time and space
Enlarged by the force of emotion
– A comprehensive poetic grasp of appearance)
Quoting from the breastplate of St. Patrick:

> 'I bind to myself today
> The power of Heaven,
> The light of the sun,
> The whiteness of snow,
> The force of fire,
> The flashing of lightning,
> The velocity of wind,
> The depth of the sea,
> The stability of the earth,
> The hardness of rocks.'

His indeed was the eloquence
Elusive at shape-shifting as the Mor-rigu,
A power of the word in the blood,
By virtue of which as Plato says,
He conformed his soul
To the motion of the heavenly bodies.
He had been given to drink of Conndla's Well,
Where grew the hazels of wisdom and inspiration.
(Had his quest been for wisdom only he had
Like Sinann been overcome by its waters
And verily tasted of death!)
Pure of heart and aright with nature
And having read the runes and rubrics of the spirit,
Cliadna Fairhead, of the race of Gods,
Had bestowed on him the Cuach of emerald
Which translates water into luscious wine,
Along with the three duo-coloured birds
Of infinite comfort and beguilement,

He brought the notes from the deeps of time
And the tale from the heart of the man who made it,
Knew the colour of Fingal's hair, and saw
The moonlight on the hoods of the Druids.
He had visited the Golden Tree
Which reaches the clouds for height.
And the words being in his heart for a song
And the beat on his pulse for rhythm,
As Caoilte had it in his foot for running,
He got the notes for the tune
In the music of the branches which,
Says the Filidh with the artful thought,
Guards the eloquence and judgement
Of the children of Gaeldom.

The rede is for the wary.
Druidical tenets demanded and received
Purity of thought and material chastity.
And out of the wonderful artistry
Of the illuminated manuscripts of Celtic art
And the age-laden Sagas
He had seen emerge, and understood,
Anaglyphs of ethnic fusions
– A struggling of the spirit for permanent possession,
And by the antennae of this provective spirit
Vanishing epos reappeared
And for this and many such cognate epos
He had rediscovered the alumni of Dagda;
Amairgen the just; Medb of the Sithe;
Merlin or Merwyden; Oengus Mac ind Oc,
The wisest and most cunning of Tuath de Danann;
Ossian in Tir nan Og;
The Fianns in their last convulsions;
And the magic darts of Cuchulain
Defending the royal harp of Tara;
And well he knew the word-magic of the bard, MacCoise,
Who, for the purposes of his art,
Could invoke and receive from Elathan (Skill)

The panegyrics of MacLonam;
The tales of Leech Liathmhuin;
The proverbs of Fitheal;
The eloquence of Fearceartais;
The intellect of the bardess Etain;
The brilliance of Nera,
And the clear truths of Mor-Mumhan.
Having traced and found the footmarks
Of Gael and Cymric from the shadows of the Himalayas,
The mystic regions of Irak,
Across the trails of continents
To the Isle of Saints and to Barra,
He knew from his childhood days
The world must yet seek
Further spiritual creations
From the awakened Celt
Ere the last of the race passed
To join his deathless kin in Tir nan Og.
And discovered in himself 'the word of knowledge'
With which Amairgen 'fashioned fire in the head'
And set himself to master 'the marvel of honey verse
With lines of long alliterative words
And sweet compacted syllables, and feet
Increasing upon feet' – and to learn
Enchantments such as Aefi played
On the De Danann children.

And in due time
He raised the wizard horn of the Fingalian heroes
And the voice of bards was tuned in his song.
His was the 'beguiling song of far-off voices',
The spirit-tongued Echo of Prometheus Unbound,
Showing the Coolins of Skye,
The Scurr of Eigg, and the Bens of Jura
As the Crom-Sleuchd of the bard's confessional,
– The beacon-heads from which the shades of the Druids
Transmit the secrets of their Pherylt

To those selected of our race
Who inherit the gift of song.

No longer then need Cathmor transmit
His despairing monody from the Hall of the Winds.
The choristers in the Palace of Enchantment are again astir.
Magnetic clouds raise high the Silver Shield
That it may re-echo the song of joy.
An Deo-Greine, Fionn's banner, cracks crisply all over the world.
The birds have come back to Rhiannon,
The rainbow of promise hangs resplendent over Gaeldom today,
The mysterious prophecies of Merlin
Are being fulfilled in our generation.
Now that the solemn but chivalrous practices
Of the Celtic peoples of history are applied
In the light of modern knowledge
To soften international and individual asperities,
Humanity, with a 'pulse like a cannon'
Will co-ordinate in faith and charity
And swing its aspirations forward
Towards peace and goodwill to men.

An English War Poet[1]

IN another respect the Spanish War
– Fought on the Republican side
Not by doped conscripts, foreign mercenaries, professional soldiers,
And Moors and worse than Moors,
But by men who passionately believed
In the cause for which they fought –
Has stamped all the men I know
As members of the International Brigade

[1] This poem, and the next, while not included in *The Battle Continues*, were written at the same time and deal with the English reaction to Spain and to war in general.

With a different bearing altogether
Than even the best, the most anti-militarist, gained
Of those who fought against Germany in the first Great War.
There in a man like Siegfried Sassoon, for example,
Despite the undeniable honesty, the little literary gift,
What is *Sherston's Progress* but an exposure
Of the eternal Englishman
Incapable of rising above himself,
And traditional values winning out
Over an attempted independence of mind?

Second-lieutenant George Sherston went on strike against the war.
But his pacifism led him, not before a court-martial,
But into a hospital for the 'shell-shocked'.
There a psychiatrist, as clever as calm,
Coupled with plenty of good food and golf,
Restores Sherston to sanity.
He decided finally to return to the front,
Did so, found the job not too awfully awful don't you know,
Was wounded, and ended up
In a rather nobler type of hospital
Where members of the royal family stopped by his bed
To offer forty-five seconds of polite sympathy,
And there the narrative ends, with Sherston as muddled as ever,
And given to rather vague – and glib – interrogations
That may be taken to express
His partial dissatisfaction with the universe.

As a transcript of a young man's actual emotions in war
The book is convincing enough. You must, however, regard
The young man as extremely average,
With no real self-knowledge
And no fixed scale of values.
He is anybody who has seen the blood and horror of war
Which is a great deal less than we are supposed
To take Sherston to have been. Furthermore,
Seeing that almost twenty years lie
Between Sherston's experiences

And the writing of them down
One looks for a sense of perspective,
A revision of values, a growth of understanding,
One nowhere encounters.
This is what happened to Sherston
And so far as the book is concerned
Nothing ever happened afterwards.

There is possibly an argument in favour
Of presenting things simply as they were,
Of leaving them inclosed
Within their own time and place,
Without hindsight, without revaluation;
Though it is not easy to put it forward here,
Since the Sherston of today constantly and pointedly
Keeps interjecting himself into the picture.
But what is really wrong with the book
Is the portrait of Sherston as he then was:
A man so quickly able to accommodate himself,
After one flare of defiance,
To prevailing sentiment.
It is not that Sherston was either
A weak or a cowardly person.
It is rather that his rebelliousness was only
Superimposed on his profoundly English nature.
It would be unfair to say that, after coming out
Against war and all it signified
He traduced his principles. Rather he changed his mind,
Regained the national disease of 'seeing things through',
Saw them through, and ended up, pleased
That the royal family should stand by his hospital bed
And confer its verbal largesse. In other words
Sherston rebelled under stress of feeling
Then conformed again under stress of feeling;
Throughout the ordeal he was altogether
The victim of his emotions.

This is not the stuff the members
Of the International Brigade were made of.

This is not enough to create for me,
A provocative book.
Set against any of the better narratives of the war
By Continental writers, *Sherston's Progress* seems
Not only confused, but confused
In an immature and childish way.
In Mr. Sassoon's book there is simply no evidence
Of a thinking mind; there is neither
Psychological nor philosophical substance.
There is only a young man who lets himself in
For a bad quarter of an hour, and then,
Not because he lacks courage,
But because he lacks conviction,
Falls back into the ranks.
His real interests are golf,
Chasing the fox, reading poetry;
Is it too cynical to think at times
That his real objection to the war
Is its interfering with these pleasures?

But the members of the International Brigade
Were made of different stuff,
And will never fall back into the ranks.
And the war in Spain – and everywhere else –
Will never end till they win it,
Since they fight for Spain and not
                                        Just for castles in Spain.

England's Double Knavery

THE recent political turn of the people
Against ramps, impudence, lies, intrigues, and banditry
Proves, however, the antique dictum:
Never has a whole nation been seen to act wickedly.
Perhaps the literary world will turn next!
. . . But people do not like to be freed of a clog.

Sentimental and intellectual,
And I am ready to hear the barbarous noise
(Preluded in Roy Campbell's poem,[1] Garvin's writings and elsewhere)
Of Milton's pack of 'owls and cuckoos, asses, apes and dogs',
There will also be some grieved sighs,
And, I hope, some honourable amends.
But already every writer of any account is on our side;
Only Campbell, de Montalk,[2] and a few others,
Negligible scribblers, have gone the other way.
But with John Bull, the enemy of enemies,
The perfidy goes to infinitely greater depths
And passes through allotropic stages
Taking forms ill to connect with the first.
Among the unintelligent, who desire someone's disappearance,
Simple satisfaction of spite and rage is enough.
But no *plotter* ever yet aimed
At the mere downfall of his victim.
Although spite is ever the heating passion,
With Codlin as with Pecksniff, with Iago and all
There is always a cold passion down below.
Codlin wreaked his spite on Short as the real,
Though invisible, showman, but when he whispered
That Codlin was the Friend, not Short,
He heard the coins already rattling in his pocket
And saw himself honoured at the feast
And Short out in the cold.
Pecksniff not only manœuvred *de bon cœur*
To embroil the young Chuzzlewit with his friends;
He also stole the credit
For the design of the grammar-school.
Iago plotted
'To get his place and to plume up my will
In double knavery.'
This double knavery works so smoothly
It is hard to detect which half works first,
But it is certain that a cold passion lives with a man

[1] *Flowering Rifle* by the late Roy Campbell.
[2] Count Geoffrey Potocki de Montalk, Editor of *The Right Review*.

And enters into *all* his behaviour,
Whereas spite needs special circumstances to make it active;
This double knavery is so difficult to unmask
That dramatists and novelists are mostly driven
To call in coincidence and confession
To make a fair-play ending.
The victim is rarely in any sort of position
To defend himself, since only the unsuspecting
Can be victimised, and be his own character good,
Or even middling, and his brain a busy one,
Warning will fly past him,
So history of successful and glorified plotters.
There was only a stage-play slip
Between the cup and the lip of Iago
And, if he had *succeeded*, he would have heard
As many *Evvivas* as Mussolini
While forgotten Othello rotted in the earth,
And Cassio cooled his exiled heels in some Libya.
Hitler's June 30th hand finds many of the world's high folk
Willing to shake it.
But for the gift of the gab, neither Hitler nor Mussolini
Might ever have attracted any attention.
In England, though aspiring leaders still need to collect their crowd
By offering honey (with, of course, opportune threats of vinegar)
Inconvenient colleagues can be put out of the way
By that most discreet of poisons, the boycott.
(They do these things better in France . . . when a well-known
    officer tried
To organise a campaign of boycott
Against his former *amie* and colleague
Paris laughed – and someone crushed
The business with untranslatable wit:
'Mais ce coquin érige en juge litteraire
Son lingam dépite!'
But, also, the woman was on the spot,
Knew all the ropes, and fought like a lioness.)

It is very simple; you just say nothing.

The method is not vulgarly to bleed your victim
But to dry up his blood
(Though England prefers victims who begin by being restive,
They taste better afterwards – like birds
Cooked while their blood is still warm).
England, every now and again, achieving
A larger subjugation of truth than ever before,
And delighted with the cleverness of her Cabinet ministers
When they show themselves most cynically dishonest,
Openly betraying all they simultaneously profess,
Building up incredible lies into self-congratulatory virtues!
England! – Can we cut out of our hearts that absurd old loyalty,
That half-shamed admiration which makes us feel
How clever it is of her always to be able
To get away from the disaster? She is so unscrupulous,
So selfish, so wilful, and so arrogant – and yet
Somehow or other she never has to pay for it.
But she is going to have to pay for it now
At compound interest, and to the uttermost farthing!
Most of the great social forces in the world today
Are like some quiet woman all her neighbours respect
And can imagine no ill of – yet she holds
Her husband under with hellish cruelty,
And may well drive her long-suffering family
To murder her at last. Well, murder's murder,
And society exacts the penalty, of course,
But let one of the family cry 'she deserved it'
And instantly the neighbours will denounce
The vilifier of the innocent dead (as they deem)
And defender of murder (no deed less deserved).
The family must suffer in silence to the end
And preserve the decent fiction, generally believed,
Obloquy and ostracism their portion if they don't.
– This is the age-long tyranny Campbell supports
(Royalty, Religion, and all the other quiet old women
Hocussing humanity with their old wives' tales,
And hiding infernal cruelty behind their quiet looks,
The remnants of the ancient Matriarchal system

That delayed the coming of civilisation for thousands of years
And still poisons it through and through!)
And conjures up in defence a fantastic picture
Of left-wing politicians stampeding with ill-got gold!
How much of the stolen wealth of the workers
Has ever found its way into left-wing pockets?
What tiny percentage of the bloody horror of war
Has ever been caused by the left? Every word of his poem
Has twenty tons of beef or mutton behind it,
He says – He is wrong.[1] The dead weight is neither beef nor mutton
But pork – sheer swinishness! And the several thousand tons of wheat
Is wrong too. The backing is nothing but hay-wire.
Left-wing poetry represents a rise in the price of bread,
And starving workless peasants, a bread queue, a stricken field.
Represents is right, i.e. *Protests against!* – not *causes*.
That is the proud prerogative of Right-wing poetry
And since in Britain and America at least
The latter outbulks the former by ninety-nine to one,
Surely it could nullify the one per cent,
If there were any truth in the ludicrous charge?
How does Campbell explain its impotence?
His logic is as rotten as his poetry
And all his precious harvest can possibly produce
Is an epidemic of pellagra – the true
Harvest of the Right in very fact. Poor opisthocoelian Campbell,
The hollowest of all the hollow men, and so
Fit champion of his wholly indefensible cause,
Which, if it had been good, his bonehead gaucherie
Would have let down and ruined in any case!
Not that his typical reader would have known!
– A stout man, walking with a waddle, with a face
Creased and puffed into a score
Of unhealthy rolls and crevices
And a red and bulbous nose;
A rich man who fawns his way through life,
With a thick husky voice, naturally coarse,

---

[1] *Vide* Roy Campbell's letter in *The Times Literary Supplement* of 25 February 1939.

Through which with grotesque insistence runs a tone
Of mock culture – a man whose fat finger
Ticks off the feet in Campbell's lines
'Left, right! Left, right!' and whose aesthetic sense
Delights to hear the recurrent crack
Of the hippopotamus hide whip or to note
The sibilance as of rubber truncheons every here and there.
So you went for a soldier, did you,
Campbell? – a soldier in Spain?
The hero of a penny novelette
With the brain of a boy scout!
All soldiers are fools.
That's why they kill each other.
The deterioration of life under the régime
Of the soldier is a commonplace; physical power
Is a rough substitute for patience and intelligence
And co-operative effort in the governance of man;
Used as a normal accompaniment of action
Instead of a last resort it is a sign
Of extreme social weakness. Killing
Is the ultimate simplification of life. And while
The effort of culture is towards greater differentiation
Of perceptions and desires and values and ends,
Holding them from moment to moment
In a perpetually changing but stable equilibrium
The animus of war is to enforce uniformity
– To extirpate whatever the soldier
Can neither understand nor utilise
(And the most degraded soldier is the policeman
– The perpetual civil war in our midst!).

From
MORE COLLECTED POEMS
(1970)

Why

CONCERNED as I am with the West Highlands and Hebrides
Instantly to my hand is the fact
That the two greatest social and religious reformers
Of modern India – Dayanandi and Gandhi –
Were both born in the small peninsula of Kathiawar.
Gandhi was born at Porbunder.
It is on the sea-coast, jutting out into the sea,
And has all the infinite variety and charm
Of the expanse of ocean around it.
Mists of extraordinary beauty
Constantly rise from the sea
And encompass the land,
The sea itself is usually a brilliant ultramarine
With liquid green where the shoals lie.
The little town where Gandhi was born
Rises almost out of the sea
And becomes a vision of glory at sunrise and sunset
When the slanting rays beat upon it,
Turning its turrets and pinnacles into gold.
Morvi, where Dayanandi was born, lies inland
Not far away from the desolate waste
Of the Rajputana Desert which stretches to the north
Unbroken for hundreds of miles.
The land at Morvi is rocky
And the country is rugged,
The differences of their birthplaces are clearly seen
In the differences between Dayanandi and Gandhi.
We have Porbunders and Morvis enough
In Scotland: but they produce
No such outstanding characters
As Dayanandi and Gandhi.
Why?

My Songs are Kandym in the Waste Land

ABOVE all, I curse and strive to combat
The leper pearl of Capitalist culture
Which only tarnishes what it cannot lend
Its own superb lustre.

Somewhere in its creative faculty is concealed
A flaw, a senseless and wanton quality
That has no human answer,
An infernal void.

Capitalist culture to the great masses of mankind
Is like the exploitative handling in America
Of forest, grazing, and tilled lands
Which exaggerates floods and reduces
The dry-season flow of the rivers to almost nothing.

A hundred million acres, which might have maintained
A million families, utterly destroyed by water erosion,
Nine million acres destroyed by wind,
Hundreds of millions of acres more
Yielding rapidly to wind and water erosion,
Forests slashed to the quick
And the ground burned over,
Grazing lands turned into desert,
The tragic upsetting of the hydrologic cycle
Which has turned into disastrous run-off
The water that should have been held in the soil
To support vegetation and percolate
To the lower levels and feed wells and springs,
Till now the levee builders try to race
The Mississippi and set it up on stilts
Whence sooner or later it must stumble.

Problems of erosion control, regulation of river-flow,
Flood control, silt control, hydro-electric power.

I turn from this appalling spectacle
Of illimitable waste; and set myself, they say,
Gad im ghainimh (putting a withy round sand).
The sand will produce a vegetation itself
If it is not interfered with. It will be a slow growth.
Nevertheless the vegetation manages to get a start
In the course of thousands of years,
And my poetry will be like the kandym
That doesn't advance step by step
But goes forward on the run, jumps through the air.
The little nut jumps along like a ball.
The sand comes along after, but the sand is heavier
And cannot catch up with the little nut
And bury it. But when the seed takes root
And the little shrub starts, the shrub
Cannot jump along like the seed ball.

How is it going to save itself
From the encroaching waves of sand?
It is not so easy to bury the kandym.
It doesn't have branches like those
Of the apricot and peach tree – its branches
Are slender and there are no leaves on them.
When the sand comes on the kandym doesn't try to stop it
But lets it go right through its branches,
Gives it right-of-way.

But sometimes the sand waves are so big
They bury the kandym nevertheless.
Then a race begins – the dune grows and the plant grows.
The dune grows fast but the plant grows faster still
And by the time the sand dune has attained its final height
The plant is found to have outstripped it.
Its little green bristles are waving in the wind
On the crest of the sand dune.
It has not only grown in height but has branched out too.
The whole dune is perforated with its branches.
The wave passes on, leaving behind
A good half of its sand.

So the little kandym has stopped the advance of the sand,
Turned the dune into a little hillock
Covered with vegetation.

But is there not one last danger?
The wind may blow the sand away
And leave the roots bare?
But the kandym knows how to fight with the wind too.
Lying flat on the sand it sends out extra roots
And holds the sand down with them.
In this way it gathers up the soil
And makes a foothold for itself.
My songs are kandym in the Waste Land.

From
SELECTED POEMS
(1970)

Kinsfolk

From Work in Progress (*The Modern Scot, July* 1931)

Gin scenic beauty had been a' I sook
I never need ha' left the Muckle Toon.
I saw it there as weel as ony man
(As I'll sune prove); and sin syne I've gane roon'
Hauf o' the warld wi' faculties undulled
    And no' seen't equalled.

But scenic beauty's never maittered much
To me afore, sin poetry isna made
O' onything that's seen, toucht, smelt, or heard,
And no' till lately ha'e the hame scenes played
A pairt in my creative thocht I've yet
    To faddom, and permit.

Gin there's an efter life hoo can I guess
What kind o' man I'll be wha canna tell
What's pairted me here frae my kith and kin
In a' airts mair than Heaven is frae Hell
(To bate the question which is which a wee)
    As't seems to them and me,

Nor tell what brings me unexpectedly back
Whaur't seems nae common thocht or interest's left.
Guid kens it wasna snobbery or hate,
Selfishness, ingratitude, or chance that reft
Sae early, sae completely, ties that last
    Maist folk for life – or was't.

I bein' a man made ither human ties
But they – my choice – are broken (in this case
No' a' my choice) as utterly as those
That bound me to my kin and native place.
My wife and bairns, is't tinin' them that thraws
    Me back on my first cause?

Foreseein' in Christine's or in Walter's mind
A picture o' mysel' as in my ain
My mither rises or I rise in hers
Incredible as to a Martian brain
A cratur' o' this star o' oors micht be
       It had nae point o' contact wi'.

Daith in my faither's case. I ha'e his build,
His energy, but no' his raven hair,
Rude cheeks, clear een. I am whey-faced. My een
Ha'e dark rings roon' them and my pow is fair.
A laddie when he dee'd, I kent little o'm and he
      Kent less o' me.

Gin he had lived my life and wark micht weel
Ha' been entirely different, better or waur,
Or neither, comparison impossible.
It wadna ha' been the same. That's hoo things are.
He had his differences frae some folks aroon'
      But never left the Muckle Toon.

He had his differences but a host o' freen's
At ane wi' him on maist things and at serious odds
In nane, a kindly, gin conscientious, man,
Fearless but peacefu', and to man's and God's
Service gi'en owre accordin' to his lichts
      But fondest o' his ain fireside o' nichts.

Afore he dee'd he turned and gied a lang
Last look at pictures o' my brither and me
Hung on the wa' aside the bed, I've heard
My mither say. I wonder then what he
Foresaw or hoped and hoo – or gin – it squares
      Wi' subsequent affairs.

I've led a vera different life frae ocht
He could conceive or share I ken fu' weel
Yet gin he understood – or understands
(His faith, no' mine) – I like to feel, and feel,

He wadna wish his faitherhood undone
      O' sic an unforeseen unlikely son.

I like to feel, and yet I ken that a'
I mind or think aboot him is nae mair
To what he was, or aiblins is, than yon
Picture o' me at fourteen can compare
Wi' what I look the day (or looked even then).
      He looked in vain, and I again.

Gin he had lived at warst we'd ha' been freen's
Juist as my mither (puir auld soul) and I
– As maist folk are, no' ga'en vera deep,
A maitter o' easy-ozie habit maistly, shy
O' fundamentals, as it seems to me,
      – A minority o' ane, may be!

Maist bonds 'twixt man and man are weel ca'd bonds.
But I'll come back to this, since come I maun,
Fellow-feelin', common humanity, claptrap (or has
In anither sense my comin'-back begun)
I've had as little use for to be terse
      As maist folk ha'e for verse.

My wife and weans in London never saw
The Muckle Toon that I'm concerned wi' noo
(Sittin' in Liverpool), and never may.
What maitters't then, gin a' life's gantin' through,
Biggit on sicna kittle sands as these,
      Wi' like haphazardries?

My clan is darkness 'yont a wee ring
O' memory showin' catsiller here or there
But nocht complete or lookin' twice the same.
Graham, Murray, Carruthers, Frater, and faur mair
Auld Border breeds than I can tell ha' been
      Woven in its skein.

Great hooses keep their centuried lines complete.
Better than I can mind my faither they
Preserve their forbears painted on their wa's
And can trace ilka tendency and trait
O' bluid and spirit in their divers stages
   Doon the ages.

To mind and body I ha' nae sic clue,
A water flowin' frae an unkent source
Wellin' up in me to catch the licht at last
At this late break in its hidden course,
Yet my blin' instincts nurtured in the dark
   Sing sunwards like the lark.

I canna signal to a single soul
In a' the centuries that led up to me
In happy correspondence, yet to a'
These nameless thanks for strength and cleanness gi'e,
And mair, auld Border breeds, ken I inherit,
   And croun, your frontier spirit.

Reivers to weavers and to me. Weird way!
Yet in the last analysis I've sprung
Frae battles, mair than ballads, and it seems
The thrawn auld water has at last upswung
Through me, and's mountin' like the vera devil
   To its richt level!

Bracken Hills in Autumn

THESE beds of bracken, climax of the summer's growth,
Are elemental as the sky or sea.
In still and sunny weather they give back
The sun's glare with a fixed intensity.
      As of steel or glass
      No other foliage has.

There is a menace in their indifference to man
As in tropical abundance. On gloomy days
They redouble the sombre heaviness of the sky
And nurse the thunder. Their dense growth shuts the narrow ways
      Between the hills and draws
      Closer the wide valleys' jaws.

This flinty verdure's vast effusion is the more
Remarkable for the shortness of its stay.
From November to May a brown stain on the slopes
Downbeaten by frost and rain, then in quick array
      The silvery crooks appear
      And the whole host is here.

Useless they may seem to men and go unused, but cast
Cartloads of them into a pool where the trout are few
And soon the swarming animalculae upon them
Will proportionately increase the fishes too.
      Miracles are never far away
      Save bringing new thought to play.

In summer islanded in these grey-green seas where the wind plucks
The pale underside of the fronds on gusty days
As a land breeze stirs the white caps in a roadstead
Glimpses of shy bog gardens surprise the gaze
      Or rough stuff keeping a ring
      Round a struggling water-spring.

Look closely. Even now bog asphodel spikes, still alight at the tips,
Sundew lifting white buds like those of the whitlow grass
On walls in spring over its little round leaves
Sparkling with gummy red hairs, and many a soft mass
       Of the curious moss that can clean
       A wound or poison a river, are seen.

Ah! well I know my tumultuous days now at their prime
Will be brief as the bracken too in their stay
Yet in them as the flowers of the hills 'mid the bracken
All that I treasure is needs hidden away
       And will also be dead
       When its rude cover is shed.

Facing the Chair

    HERE under the radiant rays of the sun
    Where everything grows so vividly
    In the human mind and in the heart,
    Love, life, and all else so beautifully,
    I think again of men as innocent as I am
    Pent in a cold unjust walk between steel bars,
    Their trousers slit for the electrodes
    And their hair cut for the cap

    Because of the unconcern of men and women,
    Respectable and respected and professedly Christian,
    Idle-busy among the flowers of their gardens here
    Under the gay-tipped rays of the sun,
    And I am suddenly completely bereft
    Of *la grande amitié des choses créées*,
    The unity of life which can only be forged by love.

From
THE HUGH MacDIARMID ANTHOLOGY
(1972)

Talking with Five Thousand People in Edinburgh

God forbid that I should justify you: till I die I will not remove mine integrity from me.
JOB XXVII.5.

TALKING with five thousand people in Edinburgh yesterday
I was appalled at their lack of love for each other,
At their lack of ecstasy at the astounding miracle
Of being alive in the flesh and together with one another,
And amazed that men and women each superficially so different
Should be so obviously the product of the same temperament,
Dyed in the same vat to a uniform hue.
In each the mood, the atmosphere, the peculiar nature
Of the tension produced, all the intangibles in fact,
Were almost identical – the same unresolved discords,
The same sultry hates, the same murderous impulses
Below the surface of decorous lives, the same
Hopeless struggle against an evil no one dares name
– The same growing understanding that the substitute names
They use for it are wide of the mark, that the name must be spoken,
That it will be impossible soon not to speak it out plump and plain,
The whole five thousand of them, as with a single voice.

But yesterday I listened to the mutual criticisms,
The sneers, the belittlings, the cynical acceptances,
Misunderstandings, indifferences, looking down their noses,
Pursing their mouths, giving meaning looks, till I saw all these people
As specialists in hates and frustrations, students of helpless rages,
Articulators of inarticulate loathings, and suddenly understood
That the trouble was no one knew where the centre lay
Of the system of discontent in which they were pent,
All emotionally suspended and dubious
(Saying all sorts of things with the single exception
Of what they ought to be saying – what they needed to say;
Their powers of speech all hopelessly misapplied)
Because their talk evaded, deserted, their real theme.

They expressed themselves in despairs, doubts, grumblings and fears.
None of them had yet made clear contact with the sources of his or her
    power.
They were all fascinated by their hatred of something – but of what?
The passion of that nameless hatred got itself partially expressed
By seizing on this or that – on anything – in lieu of its true object.
These were occasions for the rages but not the causes.
Edinburgh produces and sustains agonising tensions of life
– Edinburgh, a blinded giant who has yet to learn
What the motive spirit behind his abilities really is.

So that as I spoke with these five thousand people
Each of us was more or less lost
In the midst of the events so powerfully presented.
All who should help to open the way for true expression
– The teachers, the ministers, the writers – are living like maggots
On dead words in an advanced state of decomposition,
Big words that died over twenty years ago
– For most of the important words were killed in the First World War –
And Edinburgh has not given birth to new words yet
In which it can say anything worth saying, make anything but animal
    noises.

Edinburgh – But Edinburgh is no worse than anywhere else;
All the big centres of mankind are like thunder-clouds to-day
Forming part of the horrific structure of a storm
That fills the whole sky – but ere long
Will disappear like the fabric of a dream.

Perhaps Edinburgh's terrible inability to speak out,
Edinburgh's silence with regard to all it should be saying,
Is but the hush that precedes the thunder,
The liberating detonation so oppressively imminent now?
For what are its people standing in their own light,
Denying life infinitely more abundant,
Preferring darkness to light, and death to life?
Edinburgh is capable here and now of a human life
As illimitably greater than any it has yet known,
As any human being's is to the lowest order of animal existence.

All they need to do is to lift up their hearts
And conceive nobler conditions of life, acquire
The feelings which will give forms to such a life, and at once
The necessary organs of these will appear,
Just as life at first put out arms and legs.
All they need to do is to be true to themselves
And not like some foolish woman who cries
There's thunder in the air and stuffs her ears with cotton wool
And goes to bed and hides herself under the blankets
Afraid of the thunder and lightning – the bridegroom who enters in.

There is no one really alive in Edinburgh yet.
They are all living on the tiniest fraction
Of the life they could easily have,
Like people in great houses who prefer
To live in their cellars and keep all the rest sealed up.

There is nothing to prevent them except themselves
Having all that the mind of man can know
Or the heart of man conceive.

Total strangers to all the events
Taking place around and in and through them.

No one with either the scientific training
Or the courage and desire to learn
What is going on beneath the surface of life.

Few, if any, of life's collisions here
Are on the purely individual plane.
There is no general scheme behind it,
No real general purpose,
No genuine fighting spirit.
Is there no one to fight this decline of honour,
This hypocrisy, meanness, and boredom?

Let the demagogues denounce me,[1] and betray me too
As Burns was betrayed and Bakunin and Maclean;

[1] 'Au milieu de douces imbéciles, c'est l'homme d'esprit qui est une bête.'
Maria Star.

Serve me as Utin served Marx, with vile slanders to expel
Bakunin and James Guillaume. *Veritas odium parit.*
Friends, you know. I am guilty of it. Let it rest.
At the worst, *in magnis et voluisse sat est.*
I stand to my position, do what I can,
And will never be turned into a 'strong, silenced man,'
For I am corn and not chaff, and will neither
Be blown away by the wind, nor burst with the flail,
      But will abide them both
      And in the end prevail.

For I am like Zamyatin. I must be a Bolshevik
Before the Revolution, but I'll cease to be one quick
When Communism comes to rule the roost,
For real literature can exist only where it's produced
By madmen, hermits, heretics,
Dreamers, rebels, sceptics,
– And such a door of utterance has been given to me
As none may close whosoever they be.

Let a look at Edinburgh be called
Just an educational film then
Such as we see any day on the screen.
'The Abortion,' say, or 'Why Does It Rain?'
Or 'How Silk Stockings Are Made,' or, finally,
'What Is the Difference Between A Man and A Beaver?'

It's far too late in the day
    For a fellow like this
Trying to organise a conspiracy of feelings
    In Edinburgh of all places.

Let us fall in with the wishes of Authority,
Hush to treasonable rubbish like 'The Red Flag';
Let us study – and in the end be content to be
Each of us no better than a carted stag.

A Change of Weather

Scotland: February 1966

Even the cauld draps o' dew that hing
Hauf-melted on the beard o' the thistle this Februar day
Hae something genial and refreshin' aboot them
And the sun, strugglin' airgh and wan i' the lift,
Hauf-smoored in the grey mist, seems nane the less
     An emblem o' the guid cause.

It's like quality in weather, affectin' a'thing
But aye eludin' touch, sicht, and soond,
Naething o' the Earth sinks deeper noo
Aneth the canny surface o' the mind
Than autumn leaves driftin' on a lochan.

Yet thinkin' o' Scotland syne's like lookin'
Into real deep water whaur the depth
Becomes sae great it seems to move and swell
Withoot the slightest ripple, yet somehoo gi'es me
An unco sense o' the sun's stability
And fills me, slowly, wi' a new ardour and elasticity.

It's like having – hashish, is it?

DIREADH
(1974)

Dìreadh I[1]

FOR HELEN B. CRUICKSHANK

'I turn from the poetry of beauty to the poetry of wisdom – of "wisdom", that is to say, the poetry of moral and intellectual problems, and the emotions they generate.'

'The need for a new kind of Scottish literature, one which will touch on politics as well as poetry, philosophy as well as fiction.'

> *Is it not nauseating*
> *Always to hear the hackneyed chime*
> *That everyone, up there,[2] is a prophet,*
> *And all of us down here misbegotten idiots?*
> *To hear everywhere, in the schools,*
> *Heads and assistants, all the crew*
> *That we have to pay out of our pockets,*
> *Cast in our teeth, like a blemish,*
> *The speech that binds us*
> *To our fathers and our land? . . .*
>
> *. . . Oh! those fools, those gulls,*
> *Wanting to wean their children from it,*
> *To gorge them with vainglory,*
> *Overweeningness and emptiness!*
> *Let them be drowned in the mob!*
> *But thou, my Alba, do not trouble*
> *About thy sons who deny thee*
> *And cast off thy speech;*
> *Though they live, they are but still-born,*
> *Reared on sour milk!*
>
> MISTRAL: *Espouscado*

CUT, cleft, sheer edge, precipice,
Bearradh (from *bearr*, clip or shear)
With here a *beithe* (a birch wood)
And there a *bad* (a clump of trees)
Basdalach (cheery) with birds
(The point is 'not one bird, but a lot of birds,'
As the violinist said of Francesco da Milano's
'La Canzone De Li Ucelli')
Each giving their *aideachadh*
(Act of confession, declaring aloud,

---

[1] *Dìreadh*, act of surmounting.   [2] i.e. in London.

Clear utterance) – their *ard-ghaoir*
(A clear, thrilling sound),
Ardghuailleach, high-bowed like a ship,
Lifting its *àrbhuidhe* (gold-yellow) light
In the door-way of Heaven, *anail a' Ghaidheil*
Air a' mhullach,[1] that to-day
As in yon school in Colonsay
Has a *sgathach fhraoich*
(Heather substitute for door),
Where towering, full-eyed, we stand
At *ceann réidhte gach facail*
(The head that makes every expression clear
Or every problem plain)
– Standing, freed of mortality's *dallbhrat*
With the *móramh* (the longest note in music)
Behind us, and before us
The *brasphort* (swift-going tune)
Of every river in Scotland;
Looking, *cromadh*, at all Scotland below us,
Airgbhraiteach (clad in finely-wrought mantles),
And *storach, tomanach, cuireideach, tromdhaite*
(Rugged, bushy-haired, intricate, vividly-coloured),

[1] 'The Gael's breathing-place – on the summit!'

dallbhrat, blinding bandage.

cromadh, act of swooping down like a hawk.

fuar-ghreann, coldhue (i.e. apathy, sullenness).

creachann, bare wind-swept spot on summit.

cuaicheineachadh éilidh, act of rolling, or folding the breacan (lower part of plaid) below the waist so as to form a kilt.

'*fraighean failmhe d'a bus!*', empty shelves to her gab! (a North Uist imprecation).

briosg-ghlòireach, of lively speech.

ràbhartach, uproarious talk.

neo-fhàilteamach, without flaw, perfect.

réis etc., when the fingers are at full stretch.

comhruith, act of racing together.

sruth-tràghaidh, ebbing tide.

goic, toss of the head.

gradcharach, quick-turning.

beurla, English language.

siùdan (Gaelic), *showd* (Scots vernacular), swing.

ruaim, angry red flush.

leus, a light, a torch, a blister.

sgiath, wing.

rag mhéirleach, arrant thief.

riadh, interest on money.

neo-éisleanach, healthy.

ge b'oil leis, though it should be a pain in his eyes (i.e. in spite of him).

gaiseadh, shrivelling, withering, defect.

dh'aon ghuth, with one voice, unanimously.

fìon 'ga leigeadh, cask of wine newly broached.

Àirigheach, bàtannach, crotach, conaltrach
(Rich in shielings, rich in boats, rich in curlews, rich in conversation),
No *fuar-ghreann* in it from top to bottom,
With an *ursgeul* (Fenian tale) here
And with many a *ròd nan cliar* (anchorage of poets)
And a *blaoghan* (a fawn's cry) there,
And, note, the *creachann* of Ben Nevis,
Brang-shrònach (of wrinkled snout) like a badger,
Picked out in the tail of my eye
As thin and sharp and small
As cheeks of branks.
– A look like a cosmic *cuaicheineachadh éilidh*,
A *cuairt* (circuit, of bards) indeed,
A look like *laghadh, ragachadh, tàileasg*
– Like the act of putting in order or playing (strings),
Or the act of tightening fishing lines,
Or playing a game of chess –
And a glimpse of England down below
– 'Fraighean failmhe d' a bus!'
While through the *biothfhuaim* (unceasing sound),
A *brothluinn* with no *buige* in it
(A boiling with no flatness – of music – in it),
Stagh dìonach dualach
(A stay-rope firm and plaited),
Pìob as dìonach nuall (a music without breaks,
Continuous, fluent) I distinguish still
The friends *briosg-ghlòireach* I love best,
(Hating as I do all mumblers, manters, mealy-mouths,
And all of Schleswig ancestry whose lips
Meet like the two halves of a muffin),
The *ràbhartach* of my boon companions of old,
Here where I see the *breacan-an-fhéilidh* of the end of the world.
Neo-fhàilteamach,
Éileadh sguaibe (gathered up in sweeping folds),
Like spanning the full *réis* between the extremities
Of the *òrdag* and the *lùdag*.
Scotland at last *neo-ghloiceil, neo-liotach, neo-lomarra*
(Not silly, not stammering, not stingy),

While, our seeming *comhruith* over, I hear
The *sruth-tràghaidh* of the English pretensions,
Something, with a *goic*, *gradcharach*,
We turn our backs on forever,
Heedless of all the cries in the *beurla*
Over Scotland's *siùdan* – its sudden showd on high,
And John Bull glowering with a *ruaim* like Hell,
Fain to be a *leus* under our *sgiath* now,
The old *rag mhéirleach* roaring for his *riadh* still
After a Scotland happily at last
Too *neo-éisleanach* – *ge b'oil leis* –
To be plagued with such a gaw.
(As Taine said the *gaiseadh* of the English
Is their lack of bonheur.)
All the rest of the universe *dh'aon ghuth*
Praises the New Scotland, *f'ion 'ga leigeadh.*

Basto! per iéu, sus la mar de l'istòri,
Fuguères tu, Alba, un pur simbèu,
Un miramen de glòri e de vitòri
Que, dins l'oumbrun di siecle transitòri,
Nous laisso vèire un eslùci dóu Bèu.[1]

Free Scotland! The Golden Eagle
Looking into the eye of the sun
As at its own reflection in the eyes of its mate.

Au pur soulèu que lis inoundo,
Sènton flouri si tèsto bloundo;
E coume la mouié qu'en plen amour councéu,
Eli, sèns fin apadouïdo.[2]

---

[1] *It is enough. For me, upon the sea of history,*
Thou wast, Alba, a pure symbol,
A mirage of glory and victory,
That in the dusky flight of centuries,
Grants us a gleam of the Beautiful.
                              MISTRAL: *Lou Parangoun (The Archetype)*

[2] *In the pure sunlight that floods them,*
They feel their yellowing heads flower.
Like the spouse conceiving in the full flush of love,
Endlessly luxuriant.
                              MISTRAL: *Calendau*

Zoology, botany, and geology
Contribute to my work;
Without the least self-consciousness
I achieve the ideal of so many poets,
The union of poetry and science,
My theme being nature *in solido*,
That mysterious presence of surrounding things
Which imposes itself on any separate element
That we set up as an individual for its own sake.
All the destinies of my land are set before me
– All the elements of its complex history –
Like the lines on the palm of my hand;
All the conflicting elements reconciled,
Each seen as contributory to the whole,
And my own nature that for a while gave way
Before a complete historical summary,
Immersed in the countless difficulties of my task,
(To choose what is easy is an act of infidelity,
An evasion of life, a withdrawal from the scene of action.
Our concern is essentially with what is difficult.
Elsewhere I have quoted in this connection
MacCrúitin, O'Heffernan, O'Hosey and other Gaelic bards,[1]
We must adhere to what is difficult
If we would make any claim to having a part in life.
Irreparable wrong has been done to life
– And nowhere more than in Scotland here –
Because men have been cowardly in this sense.)
Returns and crowns the whole,
Scotland seen entire,
Past, present and future at once.
I am the primitive man, Antaeus-like,
Deriving my strength from the warm, brown, kindly earth,
My mother.[2] For now, like my brothers in the lower planes
    of evolutionary life,

[1] See notes to *To Circumjack Cencrastus* (p. 293). See in this connection also Rainer Maria Rilke's *Briefe an einen jungen Dichter*, pp. 23f., 37 and 46, and *Briefe 1902–06*, p. 195.
[2] The theorists of the new Scottish Movement, Mr. MacDiarmid and others, have written a great deal about the Caledonian Antisyzygy and that has become

The fowls of the air and the beasts of the field,
Sun, wind, and rain are but adjuncts to my physical needs,
Not enemies of my body.

To subordinate my Muse to a cause
So remote from literature
Was to court failure as a poet,
To risk having but one string to my lyre,
And turning single-mindedness into obsession.
Yet, to begin with, the very object of my song
– This marvellous land of Scotland,
Rich in natural beauties
And historical and literary associations –
Was a microcosm. On a theme so fruitful,
So diverse in its unity,
He would have been a dullard indeed
Who failed to bring to bear
A rich and varied personality;
Whose 'fitness for life' proved insufficient
To give his work points of contact
With all his readers, above all, who failed
In addition to enumerating and extolling
The beauty and glory of his land
To raise his theme to a higher level
And transform it into a philosophic ideal
In successive poems, realistic, idealistic, historical,

---

one of the quintessential principles of the Movement. It has been less frequently recognised how related that is to the distinctive character of the Scottish landscape. 'The outline of the country is irregular to a degree; plains are almost unknown; and the asymmetry of the landscape is reflected in the arts and affairs of the people. A sense of perspective seems foreign to their spirit. Visitors, brought up in the Graeco-Roman cult of straight lines, and simple curves of thought, and art, and action, find themselves brought up short by a new, strange, different atmosphere. Everything they have been carefully trained to think correct is reversed – their entire sense of values is repudiated. The startling thing is to find that the Scots are not wrong, that they are often very, very right, that their line of evolution is as complete as, perhaps even more complete than, any other. One so readily slips into an inelastic way of thinking there is only one line of progress, that evolution can only occur in one direction, that the discovery of the contrary comes as a distinct mental jar.'

And, finally, triumphantly, all three combined,
Like the clear, sharp, changing looks of the Shetland Islands
That gain by not being a separate fact.

Scotland! Coigeach in Wester Ross
And Assynt and Edderachilis in Sutherland,
Eigg with its great cock's-comb of rock,
Emerald-green Canna, the hills of Harris
That have been so long above the sea
As to make parvenus of the Alps,
Skye, with the Quirang, among the seven wonders of Scotland,
A rowboat from Fionnphort to Iona,
Breasting the tide the way it has been breasted
A thousand years and more.

A great inheritance! The tale is scarce begun.
The outer and the inner Hebrides,
The Dungeon amid the dark Merricks,
Cairnsmuir and the Cruives of Cree,
Lone St. Mary's silent lake,
Broomy Bemersyde, Flodden Field,
Lincluden, Ellisland, Penpont,
Drumlanrig, Durisdeer, Enterkin Pass,
The Bullers of Buchan, the Laich of Moray,
The enchanted land of Drumalbain,
Kintyre, Crinan, Lorne, Inverness, Scone,
Dunfermline, Edinburgh, Perth, Stirling
– The successive stages of the Scottish Kingdom;
I see them all, an innumerable host,
As Mistral saw the 'lou regard pacifi de mis Aupiho bluio,'
'L'inmènso Crau, la Crau peirouso . . .
La mudo Crau, la Crau deserto . . .'
Singing not of particular deeds and persons,
But of a whole land and a whole people,
And beginning with his native region
Ended by embracing all nations
In one *amphictyoneia* – a vision *in parvo*
Of the labours of all mankind.

Every form of work appears,
Be it for a second only,
In *Mirèio*. Up and down the Rhone
Pass all aspects of humanity,
Pope and Emperor, harlot and convict,
And the manifold elements are grouped together,
In one final hubbub,
At the fair of Beaucaire.
So I hold all Scotland
In my vision now
– A Falkirk Tryst of endless comprehension and love.

In the wonderful diversity and innumerable
Sharp transitions of the Scottish scene,
The source of our Scottish antisyzygy,
Grundvorstellung des mannigfaltigsten Umschlags,
I who used to deplore the incredible shallowness
Of all but all of my fellow-countrymen,
So out of keeping with the Scottish mountains
Far more of them surely should have resembled,
Each with a world in himself,
Each full of darkness like a mountain,
Each deep in his humbleness,
Without fear of abasing himself
And therefore pious,
People full of remoteness, uncertainty and hope,
People who were still evolving,
Suddenly (my master Shestov's *suddenly!*)
See now the reconciliation of all opposites,
das Offene, das Ganze, das Sein, der Weltinnenraum,
And understand how '– der reine Widerspruch des kosmischen Seins
– die Tatsache, dass das, was dem Menschen nur im Umschlag
　　　zusammen kommt
im Kosmischen immer schon zusammen ist.'

Scotland small? Our multiform, our infinite Scotland *small?*
Only as a patch of hillside may be a cliché corner
To a fool who cries 'Nothing but heather!' where in September
　　　another

Sitting there and resting and gazing round
Sees not only the heather but blaeberries
With bright green leaves and leaves already turned scarlet
Hiding ripe blue berries; and amongst the sage-green leaves
Of the bog-myrtle the golden flowers of the tormentil shining;
And on the small bare places, where the little Blackface sheep
Found grazing, milkworts blue as summer skies;
And down in neglected peat-hags, not worked
Within living memory, sphagnum moss in pastel shades
Of yellow, green, and pink; sundew and butterwort
Waiting with wide-open sticky leaves for their tiny winged prey;
And nodding harebells vying in their colour
With the blue butterflies that poise themselves delicately upon them;
And stunted rowans with harsh dry leaves of glorious colour.
'Nothing but heather!' – How marvellously descriptive! And
      incomplete!

Was it only yesterday I cried 'Our life is like
Some sour silly substance of which every human being
Is given more than he can handle,
So that he is always in a state of semi-exhaustion,
Always on the point of being suffocated by it;
It is like being put to work in an enormous hayloft,
With dozens of carts bringing in hay at a gallop,
Until at last one dies. . . .
Life is life in all its forms and the only absolute
In relation to it is that it has to be lived'?[1]

Was it only yesterday I was struggling still
With frames of reference, patterns of culture, cyclical phases of
      causation,
And crying 'the unpredictable or fortuitous elements
Are so much vaster still (than the irrational elements
Even the best historians insensibly import)
That no conceivable formulae can ever deal
With the past or present in any spirit of certainty'?
– I have fully explored all the 'habitual assumptions' now
(An enquiring sceptic tirelessly applying

[1] With acknowledgments to Finland's greatest living writer, F. E. Sillanpää.

The Socratic elenchus to my own assumptions
And never proclaiming myself the possessor
Of the 'higher ideal,' of absolute certainty)
And in the twinkling of an eye arrived
At knowledge of the whole and absolute truth,
(Attach no religious interpretation, reader, to this,
Least of all one that in any way
Identifies Volksgemeinschaft with religion
And adapts existential philosophy
To that revaluation. Remember, I speak
Never of the representative individual man as man,
But always of the artist as the great exception
To the whole human order of things)
Stripped of all question of 'individual bent,'
'An invisible hand,' 'the natural order'
And all other such preconceptions at last.
For Man in his diversity has need of many gods,
But though 'one god debateth this, and another answereth this,'
Man alone knoweth, and with him lies the issue.

Scotland seen, as Socialists have hoped to see
(Denouncing all the incidentals of Capitalism,
The low knavery, the ferocious cruelty,
The plotting and the lying and the bribing,
The blustering and bragging, the screaming egotism,
The hurrying and worrying) at last
(All the sham reformers self-stultified and self-convicted)
The radical Democracy left without a lie
To cover its nakedness, the rush that will never be checked,
The tide that will never turn till it has reached its flood.
Die Kunst ist überflüssig.
Sheer Communism!

Alight and alive with fundamental truth,
The rational mind, 'like water brimming in a crystal bowl,'
Reaches now the utmost bounds of human thought,
The culmination of human intelligence,
The Idea of Scotland, purged by the artist's contempt

For all forms and kinds of furniture –
Furniture of conventions, of ready-made opinions,
Of 'thought' chawed up, vomited, and reassimilated a thousand times,
Furniture of family life,
Furniture of soul-aspiration,
Furniture of 'home,'
– Scotland (freed from 'civilization'
With its tyranny of shams, its shoddy ideals)
With no room now save for fundamental authenticity,
Climbing out of the welter of confused thinking
A little nearer the stars of pure reason,
An experience refreshing as rare.
And thence – since the earth is not all of nature,
And there are instincts within us that lead elsewhere,
And it is part of the art of living
To use naturally all those instincts –
In so doing, behold, the spiritual burdens
Which the ages have laid upon us
Glide away into thin air.
Organize. Organize. Organize.
Everything is a matter of organization,
Not of primal substance.
(And always at the furthest remove from some humbug of a
      Glasgow welfare worker
Who assumes that there must be those
Who have more and those who have less,
Those who have power
And those who must serve,
Those who have wisdom, and those
Who must depend upon others;
That the 'better class' is an economic-social concept,
And also impute to it
Superiority in moral standards and stamina,
Associating indolence and shiftlessness
With poverty, poverty with squalor, and using 'the poor'
Not only as description but as judgment too,
And deeply resenting any injection of basic economic principles
Into a study of social work!)

The one thing needful is to seek wisely
The fullest organic satisfaction.
It is quality rather than quantity of life
Which finally counts.
Civilization was immortal
Long before the first Englishman was born.
The races that have given the world
The chief examples of fine living have never
Save sometimes in their decay
Sought quantity rather than quality of life.
So, we scale the summit and leap into the abyss,
And lo! we have wings.

Ansin, bèl estrambord qu'as empura ma vido,
Pousquèsses, quand sara ma lengo enregouïdo,
Sus li nible faurèu longo-mai dardaia![1]
Like Durandal, the sword of Roland, with which the hero
In his dying hour drew forth fire from the rocks.

Direadh II

THIS is the full, the immarcescible flower
I divined long ago in the bud
When I first trod the rough track that runs
Along the Allt na Bogair
Up to the shoulder of Meall a Bhuic,
And turning found myself looking
Over the blue waters of Loch Rannoch
To the whole snow-capped range
Of the Grampains and Cairngorms
– One of the most stupendous views
In all Scotland, and only to be seen

[1] *Thus, noble enthusiasm that has kindled my life,*
Mayest thou, when my tongue shall lie stiff,
Over the devouring birds of prey irradiate for ever!
                                    MISTRAL

By the airman, rider, or walker,
Being far beyond the reach
Of car or tram.

And there as I found myself
Topping the glen, in the presence
Of scores of stags almost indistinguishable
From the moorland on which they fed,
And, overhead, black specks in the sky,
Saw, wheeling, falling,
Circling at tremendous heights,
The golden eagles, safe
In their empyrean liberty,
And knew squadrons of bomber planes
Would never fly there instead,
I cried: Here is the real Scotland,
The Scotland of the leaping salmon,
The soaring eagle, the unstalked stag,
And the leaping mountain hare.
Here, above the tree-line, where the track
Is the bed of an amethystine burn
In a bare world of shining quartz and purple heather,
Is the Scotland that is one of the sights of the earth
And once seen can never be forgotten.

This, not Edinburgh and Glasgow, which are rubbish,
The Scotland of the loathsome beasties climbing the wall
And the rats hunting in the corners
Which it is next to impossible to believe
Coexists with this, and men value – *Men?*

And now as I look at the whole of Scotland
I feel as though I had Furmanov[1] with me
And am discussing it all with him
In an atmosphere very similar

[1] D. A. Furmanov, first Secretary of the Moscow Association of Proletarian Writers, and, in reality, the creator of this fighting organization, which gathered under its wing the overwhelming majority of the growing proletarian cadres of Soviet literature.

To that crystal-like, serious, and thrilling attention
Which characterized the creation of *Chapayev*,
Furmanov, with that special quality he had
Of being able to see himself objectively,
To weigh himself in the scales of the Communist Cause
As I here my devotion to Scotland
In the balance of the whole world's purpose
With a like amazing sincerity, pitilessly truthful criticism
Of my political and cultural activities,
And painstaking and critical analysis
Of my emotions.

I have come to this height as of old
In Berwickshire I thridded the 'Pass of Peaths',
'So steepe be these banks on either syde
And so depe to the bottom
That who goeth straight downe
Shall be in danger of tumbling
And the comer-up so sure
Of puffyng and payne; for remedy whereof
The travellers that way have used to pass it
By paths and footways leading slopewise';
And fortified against the English at the East Lothian end
By Scottish trenches, 'rather hindering than letting'.
It was a difficult passage to put into prose
For an invader sworn not to step one foot
Out of his predetermined course.
But the part of Scotland brimful of life at the full
Into which it gave was the only part
Of Scotland in the past that was ever fulfilled
Like the whole of Scotland in my vision now.

Unlike any other part of Scotland
And more unlike, needless to say, any region of England;
No lush hedgerows, no flowery lanes,
No picturesque unkempt orchards, no crooked lines;
A garden of twenty- or thirty-acre fields
Geometrically laid out and divided

By well-built walls or low-clipped thorn fences
Upon either side of which no foot of space
Was given to the unprofitable or picturesque in nature.

This is the cream of the country – probably
The cream of the earth, the famous Dunbar red lands.
These red loams combine a maximum of fertility
With friable easy-working qualities of unequalled perfection.
Potatoes, a level sea of lusty shaws and flowery tops
From fence to fence in summer-time,
Then wheat, going to eight quarters an acre,
And then the swedes and turnips
Flickering strong and lusty
In the wind over the large fields
And much fitter to hold birds
Than many a southern rootfield in early September.

No waste ground here – nor open ditches,
Nor rambling fences, nor tousely corners,
Nor ragged headlands, nor hedgerow timber
To draw the land and obstruct the sunshine!
The crop pushes stiff and level
Up to the stone wall or trim thorn hedge
Which, in the growing and maturing season,
Subside – as all over Scotland
In my vision now –
Into thin faint lines hardly discernible
Amid the lush abundance.

How different Berwickshire and Wales! The comparison
Suggests itself, because just such tracts of moorish country
In the counties of Cardigan and Carmarthen,
Sloping away as these do from the hills,
Are more or less reclaimed.
But how different custom and tradition affect the landscape
Of a tract of country in the making!
Instead of these great fields geometrically traced
By the stone walls that here take the place of hedges,

And the large substantial homesteads with their hinds' cottages
Standing on ridges far apart, we should have
A patchwork of little white- or pink-washed homesteads
In a clump of trees, each surrounded
By a network of small fields;
There would be
Irregular patches or straggling belts
Of moorgrass, heath, gorse, or rough pasture,
The small man's more diffident plough had flinched from,
Straggling everywhere in and about.
The little streams too would claim
Their ample margins of copse and bracken.
– But ah! there are no half-measures here,
No little corners or odd patches of waste-land,
No inconsequent straggling thickets of birch or alder,
And broom and gorse. – The symmetry is tremendous,
The treatment thorough to the last degree.

Nor can I forget that the material development
Of English life between the accession of George III
And the death of George IV, great as it was,
Becomes almost as nothing compared
To the transformation of Scotland in the same period.
It is curious how little this sensational chapter
In British history is known, which sets forth
How completely, within the span of a single long life,
The Northern Kingdom turned the tables
On her more favoured Southern neighbour
– How the once-accepted, nay, the eagerly sought
Teachers of agriculture became the taught,
And the once-jeered-at microscopic rent-rolls of the North
Swelled to figures that became the envy
Of Norfolk and Lincolnshire in their proudest days.
The majority of folk, Scots or English, care nothing at all
For the past, certainly not for a past
Of mere, unembellished fact, though
They may owe their present condition to it.
And, alas for the interest, this dramatic revolution

That had in great part its origin
In a timely enthusiasm for lime
And Swedish turnips and subsoil-draining,
Sounds like bathos beside the theological strife
Which prolonged poverty and misery,
And the gorgeous pageants which accompanied
The truculence of Whig and Jacobite and made
Things extremely unpleasant for everybody.

Now I remember in particular an inn near Coldingham.
Mine host was a man after my own heart,
A veteran of character and long memory,
A sportsman, a farmer, and, among other things,
A master-hand at a 'crack',
And when a Scotsman shines in this,
And he very often does, he is hard to beat.

So far as I have known both upon their native heath
Along the Border, he is more efficient in this particular
Than his ancient enemy, the Northumbrian.
His Doric is richer and even racier; he has also
The undoubted advantage of his Rs in emphasis,
When, that is to say,
There is life and character behind them.
And men with a twinkling eye have always seemed to me
More abundant upon the left than upon the right bank of Tweed,
– Around the Lammermoors than along the Cheviots –
Dour as is the average hind
In the low country of either.

Now I see all my land and my people
As I saw Berwickshire and East Lothian then,
With every potentiality completely realized,
Brimming with prosperity and no waste anywhere,
And note once more as I cast my eyes this way and that
How the healthy well-fed flickering turnip breadths
Are more vivid in their green between the woods,
And even that homely article, the potato,

When clustering over a thirty-acre field
With the slanting sun upon it,
Contributes a characteristic note.
And how every one of the streams of the Merse
Brings the spirit of the mountains and the wild
Into the rich low ground, and retains the buoyancy
Of its clear amber waters until its voice
Is ultimately silenced in the wide swish of the Tweed.
With fine disregard for the well-ordered landscape,
Its pride of timber and its pride of crop,
See how the impetuous Whitadder churns
In the deep twisting valley its chafing waters
Have cut in the course of ages
Through the sandstone ! Narrow breadths of green meadow
Serve to set off the glitter of its rapid currents
And take no great injury from its floods.
Chafing always upon a rocky bed
The river gathers round it
All that fine tangle of foliage
You see only upon impetuous streams.

And so to the Berwickshire Bounds, these few thousand acres
Of cornland windswept from the North Sea
– Surely 'but scant counterpoise
For sunny Aquitaine and Guienne,
Opulent Bordeaux and the Pas de Calais,
All lost to the Crown of England
In the Hundred Years' War
– Part of the price
Paid for the lesson
That Scotsmen may never be coerced.'

And now I am where, upon Hardens Hill,
After trailing between fine avenues of beech and ash,
And mounting higher into wind-swept pine woods,
The road sweeps out at last
Into the glorious heaths of Lammermoor.
The drubbing wings and vocal plaints

Of restless peewits close overhead,
The song of rejoicing larks
In the air far above them,
And the call of distant curlews
Mingle with the faint bleat of sheep.
These edges of great moorlands, which open wide
Upon the one hand into sweeps of solitude,
And on the other over vast distances
Where rural life is thickly humming,
Are seats for the gods indeed!
And I am indeed of the Daoine Sidhe[1] today.
The heather is just touching with its first faint flush
The folding hills that heave away
Towards a far horizon that looks down
Upon East Lothian. Below,
The Merse glimmers far and wide
With its red fields, its yellowing cornlands and mantling woods,
Its glint of village church spire or country seat.
Beyond the line of Tweed spread the fainter
But yet clear-cut hills and valleys of Northumberland.
I can follow up the windings of the Till
From Flodden and Ford Castle to Wooler,
And from Wooler to the woody spur
Beneath which the wild white cattle
Of Chillingham have their immemorial range.
The Cheviots roll their billowy crests
From the 'Mickle Cheevit'
Looming large and near upon the Border line
To fade remotely into the more rugged heights
That embosom Rothbury
And the upper waters of the Coquet.

And in fancy I drink once again
– A final toast to Scotland fulfilled,
Every promise redeemed –
With one of the many hundreds of splendid men
With whom I have so drunk in days gone by.

[1] Gods of the Earth.

Not drinking whisky and soda
As an Englishman does, which is very dull,
But with all the splendid old ritual,
The urn, the rummers, the smaller glasses,
The silver ladles, and the main essentials.
The whisky toddy is mixed in a rummer,
A round-bottomed tumbler on a stem,
And transferred at intervals with a silver ladle
Into an accompanying wine-glass
By way of cooling it
Sufficiently for consumption.

And with me men like Henderson of Chirnside
– Admirable people, so fashioned that their native district
Provides an inexhaustible mine
Of affectionate interest and study of its people,
Its customs, antiquities, scenery,
Birds, beasts, flowers.
Every countryside has happily a few
Who have eyes to see and ears to hear
In this sense, and ask for nothing better,
And what could be better, than to use and enjoy
These too-rare faculties and this happy temperament
Upon the soil that bred them and for love of it?

Time which has brought such prodigious changes
In the world below and the world at large
Has here at least stood absolutely still.
The same old cry of curlews and wail of peewits,
Whistling of golden plover, call of anxious grouse,
Plash of waters, and bleat of far-scattered sheep
Still sound the same unchanging music of the wild.
Black peat-hags, glistening mosses of emerald green,
Tawny moor-grasses flecked white with the wild cotton-flower,
Scaurs of red sandstone, and vivid patches
Of sheep-nibbled turf,
All add their note.

This is the full, the immarcescible flower,
Scotland, known like the music of a moorland stream
To which poets and musicians pay conventional tribute,
But which few can approach with an understanding
Of what it means to an old fisherman
Who knows its infinite varieties of chord and melody
With an intimacy of a thousand day-long recitations.

Known, as often old gardeners and farm-hands
Understand the personality, as it were,
Of individual fields and gardens
To which they have ministered since boyhood
And their fathers perhaps before them.
For the constitution of a piece of land
Is more than skin-deep and draws
Some of its peculiar characteristics
From geological depths.
Pedology may tell us *why* a soil
Behaves as it does,
But only the rustic knows exactly *when*,
And, familiar with a tract of land, can often say
Without going to it
When the day has come to find it
In a humour to respond
To the caress of a harrow
Or when it will be found
As obdurate as iron.
But this is a kind of knowledge
Scotland has lost almost altogether,
Blighted in the shadow of great institutions
Of learning designed
For the depotentization of free intelligence,
The Fascist barracks of our universities,
The murder machine of our whole educational system,
And far gone towards that Naziism
Which is at bottom
A revolution of black-coated workers,
Multiplied in number by social conditions,

Striving for jobs they feel suitable
To their training and dignity;
Scotland drowned under a percentage of clerks
That is rising by leaps and bounds!
And it's O for the Berwickshire bondagers[1]
And the country folk and fisher folk of old,
And many a great day I had with them
Thirty years ago now!
– *Ah! quam dulce est meminisse!*
– We have fallen upon lean days.
Would Burns have sparkled upon small ale
And how would the Ettrick Shepherd
Who took his whisky in a jug
Fare in a time like this?

All the clerks in Scotland are not worth one glimpse
Of an East Lothian bailiff I knew then
With a voice that could carry nearly all over
The six hundred acres of his farm
And a whistle that would carry
Even further than his voice
And not a tree or a bush in the whole place
To break the force of either
(Just as there is no higher ground between us here
And the Ural Mountains in the East!)
When he appeared at the gate of a thirty-acre field
The subdued cackle of the bondagers ceased abruptly
And twenty poke bonnets, bent over their Dutch hoes,
Pushed with renewed zeal along the wheat drills,
And the ploughman halting for a moment on the headrigg
Started and swung his pair of horses round
And geehawed away for his life
When he heard that voice two fields away.

Across the heavy-laden grainfields;
Over the great broad rectangles of potato land,
Thigh deep in their dark green covering of shaws:

    [1] Women field workers.

Beyond the flickering blue-green tops of the thickly-clustering swedes
Or the paler pastures, where heavy Border Leicesters
Or their crosses are lazily grazing the rye grass and clover ley
And tramping it hard for the autumn ploughing,
And between the woods the indeterminate line of the shore
And the gleam of the sea beyond,
Fading into the far-spreading woods of Tynninghame
... The sudden unfolding of the greatest of agricultural counties
Girt about with wide waters and shadowy mountains.
If a vista of plain and mountain appeals solely
To his artistic sense, a man is obviously incapable
Of reading any deeper into it, or of responding
To any other appeal, and there is nothing more to be said.
No undervaluing of the elevating influence of nature,
Unilluminated by anything but its own form and colouring,
On the senses is intended here; yet this is not
To 'feel' a country, but only its physical surface,
Which might be occupied by negroes
Without the least disturbance of the emotions engaged.
But the great thing is to be able to drop at once
Into terms of intimacy with the local *genii*
Till, whether it be the Tees, the Greta, the Trossachs, or the
    Welsh Border,
All the rivers for you sound their tales, the woods shake out
    their secrets.

Direadh III

'So, in the sudden sight of the sun, has man stopped, blinded, paralysed and afraid?'

I AM reft to the innermost heart
Of my country now,
History's final verdict upon it,
The changeless element in all its change,
Reified like the woman I love.

Here in this simple place of clean rock and crystal water,
With something of the cold purity of ice in its appearance,
Inhuman and yet friendly,
Undecorated by nature or by man
And yet with a subtle and unchanging beauty
Which seems the antithesis of every form of art.

Here near the summit of Sgurr Alasdair
The air is very still and warm,
The Outer Isles look as though
They were cut out of black paper
And stuck on a brilliant silver background,
(Even as I have seen the snow-capped ridges of Hayes Peninsula
Stand out stark and clear in the pellucid Arctic atmosphere
Or, after a wild and foggy night, in the dawn
Seen the jagged line of the Tierra del Fuego cliffs
Looking for all the world as if they were cut out of tin,
Extending gaunt and desolate),
The western sea and sky undivided by horizon,
So dazzling is the sun
And its glass image in the sea.
The Cuillin peaks seem miniature
And nearer than is natural
And they move like liquid ripples
In the molten breath
Of the corries which divide them.

I light my pipe and the match burns steadily
Without the shielding of my hands,
The flame hardly visible in the intensity of light
Which drenches the mountain top.

I lie here like the cool and gracious greenery
Of the water-crowfoot leafage, streaming
In the roping crystalline currents,
And set all about on its upper surface
With flecks of snow blossom that, on closer looking,
Show a dust of gold.
The blossoms are fragile to the touch
And yet possess such strength and elasticity
That they issue from the submergence of a long spate
Without appreciable hurt – indeed, the whole plant
Displays marvellous endurance in maintaining
A rooting during the raging winter torrents.
Our rivers would lose much if the snowy blossom
And green waving leafage of the water-crowfoot
Were absent – aye, and be barer of trout too!
And so it is with the treasures of the Gaelic genius
So little regarded in Scotland today.
Yet emerging unscathed from their long submergence,
Impregnably rooted in the most monstrous torrents[1]
– The cataracting centuries cannot rive them away –
And productive of endless practical good,
Even to people unaware of their existence,
In the most seemingly unlikely connections.

I am possessed by this purity here
As in a welling of stainless water
Trembling and pure like a body of light
Are the webs of feathery weeds all waving,
Which it traverses with its deep threads of clearness
Like the chalcedony in moss agate
Starred here and there with grenouillette.

[1] See John Ruskin's description of the spring at Carshalton.

It is easy here to accept the fact
That that which the 'wisdom' of the past
And the standards of the complacent elderly rulers
Of most of the world today regard
As the most fixed and eternal verities –
The class state, the church,
The old-fashioned family and home,
Private property, rich and poor,
'Human nature' (to-day meaning mainly
The private-profit motive), their own race,
Their Heaven and their 'immortal soul' –
Is all patently evanescent,
Even as we know our fossil chemical accumulations
Of energy in coal, peat, oil, lignite and the rest
Are but ephemeral, a transitory blaze
Even on the small time-scale of civilized man,
And that running water, though eminently convenient and practicable
For the present, will give us a mere trickle
Of the energy we shall demand in the future.

And suddenly the flight of a bird reminds me
Of how I once went out towards sunset in a boat
Off the rocky coast of Wigtownshire
And of my glimpse of the first rock-pigeon I saw.
It darted across one of the steep gullies
At the bottom of which our boat lay rocking
On the dark green water – and vanished into safety
In a coign of the opposite wall
Before a shot could be fired.
It swerved in the air,
As though doubtful of its way,
Then with a glad swoop of certainty
It sped forward, turned upward,
And disappeared into some invisible cranny
Below the overhanging brow of the cliff.

There was such speed, such grace, such happy confidence of refuge in
        that swoop
That it struck me with the vividness of a personal experience.

For an instant I seemed to see into the bird's mind
And to thrill with its own exhilaration of assured safety.
Why should this be? It was as though
I had seen the same occurrence,
Or some part of it, before.

Then I knew. Into the back of my mind had come
The first line of the loveliest chorus in *Hippolytus*,
That in which the Troezenian women,
Sympathizing with the unhappy Phaedra,
Who is soon to die by her own hand,
Sing of their yearning to fly away from the palace
Whose sunny terraces are haunted by misery and impending doom.
They long to escape with the flight of the sea-birds
To the distant Adriatic and the cypress-fringed waters of Eridanus
Or to the fabulous Hesperides,
Where beside the dark-blue ocean
Grow the celestial apple-trees.
It is the same emotion as filled the Hebrew poet
Who cried: 'O for the wings of a dove,
That I might flee away and be at rest.'
'ἠλιβάτοις ὑπὸ κευθμῶσι γενοίμαν'
The untranslatable word in that line
Is the ὑπό. It includes more
Than a single word of English can contain.
Up-in-under: so had the pigeon
Flown to its refuge in 'the steep hiding-places,'
So must Euripides have seen a sea-bird
Dart to its nest in the cliffs of Attica.
For an instant, sitting in that swaying boat
Under the red rocks, while the sunset ebbed down the sky
And the water lapped quietly at my side,
I again felt the mind of the poet reaching out
Across the centuries to touch mine.
Scotland and China and Greece!
Here where the colours –
Red standing for heat,
Solar, sensual, spiritual;

Blue for cold – polar, bodily, intellectual;
Yellow luminous and embodied
In the most enduring and the brightest form in gold –
Remind me how about this
Pindar and Confucius agreed.
Confucius who was Pindar's contemporary
For nearly half a century!
And it was Pindar's 'golden snow'
My love and I climbed in that day.
I in Scotland as Pindar in Greece
Have stood and marvelled at the trees
And been seized with honey-sweet yearning for them;
And seen too mist condensing on an eagle,
His wings 'streamlined' for a swoop on a leveret,
As he ruffled up the brown feathers on his neck
In a quiver of excitement;
Pindar, greatest master of metaphor the world has seen,
His spirit so deeply in tune
With the many-sidedness of both Man and Nature
That he could see automatically all the basal resemblances
His metaphors imply and suggest.
Scotland and China and Greece!

So every loveliness Scotland has ever known,
Or will know, flies into me now,
Out of the perilous night of English stupidity,
As I lie brooding on the fact
That 'perchance the best chance
Of reproducing the ancient Greek temperament
Would be to "cross" the Scots with the Chinese.'[1]
The glory of Greece is imminent again to me here
With the complete justification his sense of it
In Germany – his participation in that great awakening
Taking the form of an imaginative reliving,
On behalf of his people, of the glory of Athens –
Lacked in Hölderlin. I see all things
In a cosmic or historical perspective too.

[1] Sir Richard Livingstone.

Love of country, in me, is love of a new order.
In Greece I also find the clue
To the mission of the poet
Who reveals to the people
The nature of their gods,
The instrument whereby his countrymen
Become conscious of the powers on whom they depend
And of whom they are the children,
Knowing, in himself, the urgency of the divine creativeness of Nature
And most responsive to its workings in the general world.
'Wer das Tiesfste gedacht, liebt das Lebendigste.'

And remembering my earlier poems in Scots
Full of my awareness 'that language is one
Of the most cohesive or insulating of world forces
And that dialect is always a bond of union,'[1]
I covet the mystery of our Gaelic speech
In which *rughadh* was at once a blush,
A promontory, a headland, a cape,
Leadan, musical notes, litany, hair of the head,
And *fonn*, land, earth, delight, and a tune in music,[2]
And think of the Oriental provenance of the Scottish Gael,
The Eastern affiliations of his poetry and his music,
'. . . the subtler music, the clear light
Where time burns back about th' eternal embers,'
And the fact that he initiated the idea of civilization
That to-day needs renewal at its native source
Where, indeed, it is finding it, since Georgia,
Stalin's native country, was also the first home of the Scots.

The Gaelic genius that is in this modern world
As sprays of quake grass are in a meadow,
Or light in the world, which notwithstanding
The *Fiat Lux* scores of thousands of years ago,
Is always scanty and dubious enough
And at best never shares the empery of the skies
On more than equal terms with the dark,

---

[1] Sir James Crichton-Browne.
[2] Macfarlane's *English and Gaelic Vocabularly* (Constable, Edinburgh, 1815).

Or like sensitive spirits among the hordes of men,
Or seldom and shining as poetry itself.
Quake grass, the 'silver shakers,' with their glumes shaped and corded
Like miniature cowrie shells, and wrapped
In bands of soft green and purple, and strung
(Now glittering like diamonds,
Now chocolate brown like partridge plumage)
On slender stems and branchlets, quick
To the slightest touch of air!

So Scotland darts into the towering wall of my heart
And finds refuge now. I give
My beloved peace, and her swoop has recalled
That first day when my human love and I,
Warmed and exhilarated by the sunny air,
Put on our skis and began
A zigzag track up the steep ascent.
There was no sound but the faint hiss and crush
Of the close-packed snow, shifting under our weight.
The cloudless bowl of the sky
Burned a deep gentian. In the hushed, empty world,
Where nothing moved but ourselves,
Our bodies grew more consciously alive.
I felt each steady beat of my heart.
The drawing and holding of my breath
Took on a strange significance.
Nor was I merely conscious of myself,
I began to be equally aware of my love;
Her little physical habits
Sinking into my mind
Held the same importance as my own.

How fragrant, how infinitely refreshing and recreating
Is the mere thought of Deirdre!
How much more exhilarating to see her, as now!

'She said that she at eve for me would wait;
Yet here I see bright sunrise in the sky.'[1]

[1] From a Chinese eight-line lyric, twenty-seven centuries old.

Farewell all else! I may not look upon the dead,
Nor with the breath of dying be defiled,
And thou, I see, art close upon that end.

I am with Alba – with Deirdre – now
As a lover is with his sweetheart when they know
That personal love has never been a willing and efficient slave
To the needs of reproduction, that to make
Considerations of reproduction dictate the expression of personal love
Not infrequently destroys the individual at his spiritual core,
Thus 'eugenic marriages' cannot as a whole
Be successful so far as the parents are concerned,
While to make personal love master over reproduction
Under conditions of civilization is to degrade
The germ plasm of the future generations,
And to compromise between these two policies
Is to cripple both spirit and germ,
And accept the only solution – unyoke the two,
Sunder the fetters that form time immemorial
Have made them so nearly inseparable,
And let each go its own best way,
Fulfilling its already distinct function,
An emancipation the physical means for which
Are now known for the first time in history!

Let what can be shaken, be shaken,
And the unshakeable remain.
The Inaccessible Pinnacle[1] is not inaccessible.
So does Alba surpass the warriors
As a graceful ash surpasses a thorn,
Or the deer who moves sprinkled with the dewfall
Is far above all other beasts
– Its horns glittering to Heaven itself.[2]

[1] Of Sgurr Dearg, in Skye.
[2] See *Volsungakvida en forna*, 41 (*Saemundar Edda* Jónsson).

HITHERTO UNCOLLECTED POEMS
CONTRIBUTED TO BOOKS AND PERIODICALS
(1920–1976)

La Belle Terre Sans Merci[1]

HATCHMENTS of houses multitudinous
Shine starry-white, and Eden-green
Glimmer the cypress groves innumerous
That sit between,
And many a slender spire
Of silver fire
Shoots heavenward. Over the foothills run
The tides of stone and leaf in terraces
Full on the toppling towers of Yedi-Coule
Worn by th' imponderable sun
To shadows dun,
One scarce distinguishes
From lion-coloured shapes of far great peaks,
Where streams the East in many a sapphire pool
And silence speaks –
Speaks with the voice of War,
Thundering afar!

The broad seas are a mesh of quivering gold
Full of a haul miraculous,
Of sailing ships and warships bold
And fruit-boats odorous.
See where Olympus sounding soars
Like Heaven's walls! –
Where dark the Vardar pours
And sorrow calls –
And all the blue-grey hills of Thessaly
Stand to the sea.
High in the throbbing skies
Twinkles an aeroplane

[1] Salonika.

Dim as an early star,
Flashes and fades afar,
Swims into sight again,
And swoops and springs enormous in our eyes!
And when night falls – Psathoura's gleam
And pyramidal Athos starred,
And Lemnos sleeping there
And Mitylene dim in dream!
The young moon swings up slim and fair
And all the bay is silver barred –
But now the sleeping soldiers are
In Cornwall or in London Town
Or Donegal afar,
Or where the Gaelic hills look down
On Gaelic villages,
Heedless that still the trembling breeze
Murmurs with every breath
That some one perisheth!

By every silver minaret
In emerald cypress set,
By the incomparable bay
Whereby the city stands,
By all the memoried battlements
That still the centuried storms defy
And lift into the equal sky
A mighty monument to Time
Unbroken yet.
And by the incommemorate hands
That shaped them so, but long to dust returned,
While still the sunlight burns like wine
Where their strong faith is urned;
By all the fire in Eastern eyes,
By all the light in Eastern skies,
By colour and the coloured breeze,
By music and the choiring seas,
By sorrow and the endless graves,
By life and all the human waves,

I deemed the scene miraculously fair
With glory golden in the air,
And blessed the fate that gave my eyes
To light on Paradise.

O Siren of the wrecking shores,
O Mirage of the desert lands,
Mother of whores
With leprous hands –
'Unclean! – Unclean!'
O prostituted skies,
Worthy of Paradise,
O luring hills whose glory is a lie,
The calm crystalline light that on Olympus lies
The alabaster is of Death embalmed,
A lantern for the damned
To light their orgies by!

Death gives the ball
And sets the pace withal.
Syphilis in silver hides
Her running wounds and rotting bones.
Fever is clothed in gold.
Gaily-caparisoned War rides
And on the pointed stones
The dervish Dysentery whirls
Attenuate,
While all in pearls
And gleaming rubies hung,
She who devours her young
Insatiate!

By all the apple cheeks have here been blanched,
By all the shining eyes have here been dimmed,
By all the wounds unstanched,
By all the dead unhymned,
By every broken heart
And every ruined mind –
The eyes are opened that were blind,
And know thee for the murderess thou art!

Allegiance

Written on the Mediterranean

'THE ancient chorus of the rich blue flood,
  The mystic sundance of the Middle Seas,
What have you in your heart, Scots Borderman,
  Prithee, that can compare with these?'

'A brown stream chunners in my heart always.
  I know slim waters that the sun makes dance
With splendid subtlety and suppleness,
  And many a green and golden glance.'

'See by the Spanish and the Afric coasts,
  The sailing vessels go with precious freight,
Of silk and costly oil and coloured fruit,
  And treasures of the antique great!'

'I see: but in my treasure-chest I have
  Chimes of the red bell-heather, green fir-fans,
And moorland mysteries and mountain hopes
  That are no other man's.

'Praise give I freely to the mighty Queen
  Who passes now in splendour and in state,
But ah! – my heart is hers whose shy, light eyes
  And small, swift smile elate

'Sealed me the servant of a cause forlorn,
  Whose dream and whose desire I cannot tell,
Where timeless silence in the far blue hills
  Hangs like a ready bell!'

Mountain Measure

Les Hautes-Pyrénées, June 1919

AND now Aldebaran in the keen dawn dies,
Vega and Althair from the kindling zenith pass,
The valley mists
Blush and dislimn
And ancient peaks like fabulous statues stand,
Shining like roses and athrill with song,
Where morning burns them with apotheosis.

Breastplate of Judgment, here
The planes of man-wrought fields
The sapphire and the agate are,
Jasper and beryl, and their glory shines
Like living rainbows hung about
Th' imponderable mystery of the graven world!

The barrier vast and inoppugnable,
Ordained to give
Through all the guessless course of time
Difference to man, –
To set 'twixt eye and equal eye
Commensurate spaces as 'twixt star and star,
Convert like blood
To currents that contend incessantly,
And sever tongue and tongue in pentecosts perpetual, –

Lifts sheerly in the staring light
To the unknowledgeable skies
Bastions of ivory and jet,
Vivid with ice and black with antique fire,
That have withstood the whirling suns and storms
Of countless centuries
Whereunto they were vibrant cymbals once,

Instant with black and scarlet chords,
Frenzying the stars.

And all man's thoughts are but as winds
That in the valleys still
Spin gravel!

To a French Girl Friend

Cirque de Gavarnie, Les Hautes-Pyrénées, June 1919

YOU named the mountains in your eager way,
Singling each cloud-bound peak along the chain,
As if you called them and they came to you
And knew your hand upon their heads again,
And I, the stranger, who had been afraid,
Was taken into friendship too.

And in the unfamiliar fields you lifted up
The blue face of a flower, and then the red,
And I, who else had passed with lonely eyes,
Saw sudden welcome through the grasses spread,
Returning gaily between blade and blade
Greetings that glittered starrywise!

To M.G.

WHETHER you are fairy or flesh
I may now know never.
A shimmer of rose in my eyes
And a song in my ears for ever,
You and the haze of my dreams
I cannot dissever.

With a rattle and whirl of drums
You carry the heart of me,
Or lure me with elfin pipes
The ends of the world to see, –
In batlight and noonday blaze
My mistress and mystery!

Edinburgh

Midnight

GLASGOW is null,
Its suburbs shadows
And the Clyde a cloud.

Dundee is dust
And Aberdeen a shell.

But Edinburgh is a mad god's dream,
Fitful and dark,
Unseizable in Leith
And wildered by the Forth,
But irresistibly at last
Cleaving to sombre heights
Of passionate imagining
Till stonily,
From soaring battlements,
Earth eyes Eternity.

Playmates

O THOU upon whose breasts
The pale skies dangle
Show me your heart!

Children we were together
And playmates long ago.

Do you remember
That funny old spare star
On which we kept pet nations?

The frantic little things!
But they were always fighting
And killed each other out at last

All except America,
Poor old America!
Which went wrong in the head!
You took pity on it
And killed it too.

You were merciful then.

O Thou upon whose breasts
The pale skies dangle
Show me your heart!

Sonnets of the Highland Hills

I Courage

SINCE when I see a mountain my own heart
Is lifted mightily upon the dawn
And I am inoppugnably updrawn
And in the centuries take a founded part,
Let me recount my courage in the world
– With Slioch, and Ben Airidh a Char,[1] and Ben Lair,
Marscodh's twin peaks, and to the westward there
The javelins of Scuir na Gillean hurled!

[1] Pronounced 'Ben-achar.'

I name no more. Such are the moods I lift
Heedless into the troubled skies of Time,
Whence, see, how deviously slide and shift,
Gleaming, the songs I gather for my own
– And loose, in ecstasy, that so their rhyme
May rounded be by faithful seas unknown.

II Heaven

IF, scaling skies precipitous, we reach
The gates we deem should give on Paradise
And pick their locks and find a void of skies
– A skyey void again! – and still have speech:
If thought be but a cranny in the wall
Where through we briefly glimpse the dazzling world
And straight to endless dooms again are hurled
And blindly borne away, and that is all –

Let us give praise that unto us is given
To see on Blaven's and on Marsco's heads
The wild stars spill (and know it for our Heaven,
Seeking no cranny but the Scalpay view),
The timeless magic of their greens and reds,
Nor further climb in search of wonders new.

III Rivals

To M.G.

THE multitudinous and various hills
Court thee. Shyly at dawn attending thee
Or bending in the twilight tenderly
They vie to pleasure thee, and my heart fills
(In silence there beyond each dawn whereon
Your eyes with passion seize, beyond each night
That thrills you with enchantment and delight)
With mingled pride, and grief for dreams foregone.

You do not greet me as you welcome these,
Though kind your smile and intimate your nod,
I know too well with what bright mysteries
Your eyes on Braeriach turn: and how you run
To where Schiehallion standing like a god
Turns me to dust and ashes in the sun!

IV The Wind-bags

Gildermorie, November 1920

RAIN-BEATEN stones: great tussocks of dead grass
And stagnant waters throwing leaden lights
To leaden skies: a rough-maned wind that bites
With aimless violence at the clouds that pass,
Roaring, black-jowled, and bull-like in the void,
And I, in wild and boundless consciousness,
A brooding chaos, feel within me press
The corpse of Time, aborted, cold, negroid.

Aimless lightnings play intermittently,
Diffuse, vacant, dully, athwart the stones,
Involuntary thunders slip from me
And growl, inconsequently, hither, thither
– And now converse, see-saws of sighs and groans,
Oblivion and Eternity together!

V Valedictory

PARNASSUS and Schiehallion are one,
But one hill is that any life may climb,
One Pisgah from whose summit lies sublime
The land of Promise in the morning sun.

But all bones whiten ere the goal is won.
Parnassus or Schiehallion – each song
The grateful echoes for a time prolong,
But silence falls before the song is done.

Schiehallion and Calvary are one.
All men at last hang broken on the Cross,
Calling to One who gives a blackening sun.
There is one hill up which each soul is thrust
Ere all is levelled in eternal loss,
The peaks and plains are one. The end is dust.

Sonnets of the Highland Hills

VI High Over Beauty

NEVER a cuckoo ghostlike in the Spring
Troubles this unbelieving solitude
Whose eyes shine blank beneath their misty hood
And scan the world with endless questioning
While still across the naked stones flash on
The urgent centuries and the waters take
Unchangingly the suns and moons they make
And like a wing life glitters – and is gone!

No rose diverts the mind, nor any wind
Entices to a maze the baffled sense.
No song beguiles the heart that beats behind
This mystery to forget and hail a face
Lifted in invitation – but immense
Silence encompasses the patient place!

VII Within that Week

THIS ancient place was God without mankind.
The stones and light were there, waters and trees,
And 'thwart the skies befell the mysteries
Of dusk and day and dusk again. The wind
Was ceaselessly employed to register
The miracles that everywhere beset
The place with shadows and with stars – and yet
The eyes of God were disenchanted there.

But how they lightened when He dreamt His dream
And on the hill-line 'gainst the dawn foresaw
Your slim white form exult, your white arms gleam

Cast passionately round the neck of Time!
Ah! still I feel God's lonely heart updraw
And keep His triumph trembling in my rhyme!

VIII Eden Regained

Un seul instant d'amour rouvre l'Eden fermé
                                    VICTOR HUGO

YOUR flesh was kindred to the Daffodil,
To that cold mood you stood, as to the grey
Forbidding sky of a late winter's day
The flower opposes the fairness that will
Instantly capture wind and trembling wind
And carry sunlight to the heart of Time
Waking, therein, the lost eternal rhyme
– *Eden! Rejoice! Thy lovers have not sinned.*

I come, O Garden, from life's wilderness
And, lo! your gate is wide and no sword there.
Less than a dream the ancient doom is less,
No flower has fallen in the centuries
And all the old fruits brighten on the air.
Eternity, my fawn among the trees!

IX Acme

LET God remember when the world of men
Is like a dream that He can ne'er recall
The mode or meaning of – when Earth's grey ball
(O Force Creative, fail within Him then!)
Drifts shadowily between succeeding stars
That keep Him still omnisciently employed
– A vague reminder from some outer void
Of how His will illuminates and chars,

Studding Oblivion with globes of ash,
World after world!... Let him remember then

How aeons earlier when His heart was rash
He set you rapturous upon a peak,
A glory He shall not achieve again,
– A dream He lost and must forever seek!

X The Outer Night

I AM her memory of me who now
Lies one with Him who won her from my side.
Their souls are but a single light. Astride
The bed whereby I desolately bow
Might stand Oblivion or Eternity
And they would never know. The centuries
Are but the shining gestures each one frees
As each constrains the other ceaselessly.

I stand in darkness and I watch them climb
Quick light by light into their unity
And Love and Life and Death and Truth and Time
Are shadows fleeing from that ruthless light
That find a refuge in my memory
– My memory that is the Outer Night!

XI Funeral

SOFTLY ye winds! Blow soft, ye winds, and low,
Between the skies, upon the lifted clouds,
Where hush unmovingly the starry crowds,
Columnar shapes go evenly and slow
Bearing the corpse of Time. Naked he lies.
No rose of any dawn bedecks his bier,
Empty his hands. Void of their radiance clear
And closed, th'ubiquitous and kindly eyes!

Softly ye winds! Blow soft, ye winds, and low,
Commit they now their trust to the profound.
The vast cords slip out evenly and slow

And God himself is standing at the head
And silently the stars are gathered round
While through the endless void descends the Dead!

The Blaward and the Skelly

THE blaward and the skelly
Are bonny as of yore
But bonnier far was Nelly
Whom I shall see no more.

The gowden hair that glamoured
To wan weeds turned the skelly
And bluer than the blaward
Were your eyes, Nelly.

The blaward and the skelly
Are bonny as can be;
The blaward and the skelly
Are Nelly's ghost to me.

The Universal Man

TO LADY ASTOR

HELEN's white breasts are leaping yet,
The blood still drips from Jesus' feet,
All ecstasies and agonies
Within me meet.

Centurion and Pilate I,
Cyrenean and Thief and Christ,
Still in a thousand shapes with Time
I keep my tryst.

Aphrodite, I rise again;
Eurydice, am drawn from Hell;
And lean across the bar of Heaven,
The Damozel.

Yea, and I sit in Parliament
For Portsmouth and the Sphinx
Who am what every newsboy shouts
And what God thinks.

From *Water of Life*

I

EXULT, one with the Bridegroom, in the plight
Of the virginal year, O Soul,
Opening her robe in the nuptial night,
Gaining the lubric goal.
Feast your eyes on the light
Of hair of gold
And body white
– Yea, till you hold
Earth, as a bridegroom holds his swooning, bare,
Impregnate bride,
Pleat your wild shivers on the quivering air,
Insatiate tide,
While in your seminal shower
Dead wombs reflower.

I sing
The innumerable King
Who enters in exceeding strong and glad
In plenitudes of passion clad
To Queens no longer sad.
His golden groins vibrate
And in the womb of space

A sound of silver throbs.
Shed are the robes
That hid the visibility
Of myriad love.
Rhythms of lifted breasts cry unto me
As to a lover's face
Their nakedness above.
O female world, receive again
Th' immortal rain! . . .

II

Pool of the Holy Ghost
In tides of light expand.
Let each diffamèd land
Rejoice – for naught is lost,
While quiring skies with starry breath
Proclaim, divinely bright,
'Behold a victor over Death
Stirs in a virgin's womb to-night.'

Thy name is Legion, Son of Man,
And every day is Christmas Day
And every morn is Easter Morn.
Where'er the Tides of Life are borne
You tread upon the waters still.
You speak to them and they are wine.
You crave them in Your agony
And shameful vinegar is Thine.
Born and reborn upon their way
Life's waters serve the hidden will
Of Him Who turned away from Thee,
Yea, water, wine and vinegar
We in our changeful courses are
According to His plan.
'Father,' You cried, 'Thy will be done.'
So we who into darkness run
Beneath the all-eclipsèd sun!
You rose again, as we shall rise,

O Christ, and we, as with Your eyes
Shall mirror God in Paradise.
Our crystal depths shall Heaven hold
As pealing Ys was held of old.
Nay, we shall be to God in bliss
As blood unto the body is. . . .

Spring, a Violin in the Void

SPIDERS, far from their webs, with trembling feet
Assemble on the ceiling, a charmed group,
While the grey bow with many a swing and swoop,
Draws from dim strings a music crying-sweet.
Hard by the doorstep shelving to the street
A fascinated lizard swells the troop
Of mean hearts taken in the magic loop,
From terror freed, and given a cosmic beat.

Even in the loft's profound behold a bat,
But half-awakened from its winter sleep
And hanging there head-downwards by a claw,
In its small brain th' insidious tune has caught,
And, swinging to the rhythm, has a deep
Sense of at-one-ment with an unknown law.

The Last Chord

THAT carefully-shaded sevenfold Amen
Vibrated still, he said, within his soul.
A wonderful performance on the whole!
The lightening of the orchestration then
He instanced and the visible magic when

A thin unharmonied melody rose sole
Above the prayerful chorus' murmurous roll
– A Lily of Malud in bloom again!

Of brassy stresses he had much to say,
Discordant sequences of startling chords,
But ever and again in reverent way,
This little fluttering man, this human wren,
Would breathe once more these enigmatic words,
'That carefully-shaded sevenfold Amen.'

The Litany of the Blessed Virgin

THE Mystic Rose with petals of great rubies
'Twixt towers of ivory and davidica
Statelily moving through his dream he saw.
Processional had passed what mysteries! –
Titles of quality in their degrees,
Sanctas in green and gold; Maters in awe
Of crimson lit with gems that had no flaw,
Virgos in cloth of silver following these.

Then came the Mystic Rose, – moment sublime
In which his heart rang with the cosmic rhyme! –
The Golden House, the Ark of the Covenant,
The Door of Heaven at length, whence glory fell
Straight on his naked heart, all palpitant
With ecstasies no earthly tongue can tell!

The Rhythm of Silence

On Seeing a Lonely Bird in Space

O BIRD whose flight the rhythm of silence is,
Sole melody of earth that soars so high!
Songs that the sun pursue from sky to sky
Like mermaids chant below a vast abyss.
Life lies beneath the seas of space like Ys.
See you no gleam of gold with earthward eye,
No Siren Soul that with a wondrous cry
Invites the lonely Universe to bliss?

Nay, the Circean hopes of Man are vain.
The faring Universe will port not there.
O bird that poiseth in the grey Inane
Thou knowest that no song is heard above
Save thy dumb hymn: and can'st returning bear
No olive branch to my soul's ark, O Dove!

Vanitas

HE wha bides at hame maun aye
Dream o' lan's he's never seen,
Sittin' in his ingleneuk
Hauntit by the micht-ha'-been.

He wha waunners far an' wide
Has he fun' the lan' he socht?
– Na! the auld hame far awa'
Draws his vain regretfu' thocht!

He wha waunners far an' wide
An' the man wha bides at hame,
Langin' for each ither's shoon,
Gi'en them still wad crave the same.

J. K. Huysmans

Pauvre bougre,[1] who yet such singular secrets knew,
Folantin of the Church who did'st divine[2]
In what disgust of the thin raisin wine
And wafers of potato-flour withdrew
God from mean altars lest His Soul should spew;
And in the broad fields of the Church with fine
Sure eyes saw every tare that did'st entwine
The gilt grain that so perilously grew.

'En route' you sped with power beyond all praise
From phrase unto inimitable phrase,
O Thou, whose beautiful embittered speech,
Radiant and effortless, made such war on
All topics that your tireless tongue could reach
In endless evenings at the Café Caron.

Amiel

On the occasion of his centenary in 1921

THE octave of your century's consciousness
Is sounded in your soul. In minuscule
You mirror there the dread and beautiful
Ranged peaks of all desire and all distress.
Let whoso seeks to climb them first address
Him duly to his task, and his soul school,

---

[1] As Flaubert called him.

[2] Gourmont says: 'Il aimait à dénombrer les frauds des matières sacramentelles, à énumérer les tares qui entachaient la beauté et la sincérité des cérémonies religieuses. Cela l'excitait. ... Il exposait gravement que, le pain et le vin du sacrifice étant adultérés, Dieu se refusait absolument à descendre désormais sur les altars, dégoûté du vin de raisins secs et des hosties en fécule de pommes de terre.'

As on a table-land that they o'errule,
Where you their stature in defeat confess.

Ah! few there be who win to your plateau
Flat though you lie colossal peaks below,
And untraversable save to how few
The way to your horizon whence uprear
The forms of Nietzsche and his Russian peer[1]
Whom scaling not none may the future view.

Introduzione alla Vita Mediocre[2]

To Arturo Stanghellini

THE youth called straight from school to soldiering
What sense of destiny and solitude
Possessed! Lonely in all his world he stood
His boyhood like a dream evanishing.
Nights in the train, then the long-suffering
On marsh-cinct hills of limestone bald and rude[3]
Routines of trench-life, fitful, futile, crude,
With Time, an epileptic, captaining!

He is demobilised and meets old friends,
The *imboscati* who now that War ends
Jealously hate the soldiers who regress
To these strange worlds of merchants who must vent
Their crazy Lilliputian littleness
On souls in Brobdingnagian memories pent.

[1] Dostoevsky.
[2] An Italian war-novel by Arturo Stanghellini (London: Messrs Truslove and Hanson).
[3] The Carso.

Science and Poetry

To Sir Ronald Ross

To me, as to Galileo, crying
'Earth is a star, a star,'
Many the Jesuits are
And bitter their denying.
I look within – and, lo! my heart
Spins mote-like in a blinding ray
Of Earth's fair day.

All-conscious Earth serenely swinging
In its appointed place
Is flawed by no least trace
Of chaos to it clinging;
And all that all men are and have
Is one green-gleaming point of light
In infinite night.

Modern Poetry

What's Poetry noo when a's din
But a puir bern-windlin?

Outline of a Fear-Complex

'I AM afraid of being afraid,'
The lonely little lady said;
'How so?' I asked, 'that's very queer,
You fear – and yet you fear to fear?'

'Yes, in a way!' the lady said,
'I'm not afraid of being afraid
Of being afraid, of course – but yet
I fear that doesn't help a bit!'

'Then I'm afraid I cannot aid
Your complicated case,' I said;
'Your fear of fear will die away
If fear of fear of fear gains sway.'

The Pathetic Fallacy

CAN I convey the truth
  Of hill or sea?
Nay, if I speak, they turn
  To parts of me.

But facets of myself
  Can I present
Ev'n to myself, and hence
  My discontent.

Pathetic Fallacy,
  None thee escape
To see things other than
  Their own thoughts shape!

It is a monstrous thing
  That Earth can be
No more to me than what
  My thoughts decree,

And that I must depend
  On my own wit
To dream a Heaven too
  And win to it.

Woe for the Heavens then,
  Or hills or sea,
Of all poor folk who have
  Less brains than me!

Les Mammuques

KNOW ye the wingless birds
  From no eggs come
That in the heaven's height
  For ever thrum?

So light their bodies are,
  Feathers so long,
They can no more descend
  Than a sung song.

But feed upon the air
  Eternally,
And like these mammuks seem
  The Dead to me!

Approaching an Unknown Island at Sea

From the Japanese of Doppo Kunikida

FROM th' unknown isle see larks ascend!
　　Where there are larks there must be fields,
Where fields, then folks, you may depend,
　　Where folks, then love the island yields!

Gildermorie (October)

THE panorama is suffused
With motionless eternity
And with that melancholy
That weighs on perfect things.

I see the world as the Gods may,
Like a grey boulder drowned beneath
A shining pool of Space
Whereon no shadow falls.

The Bees

THEY perfected their complex social life
　　Millions of years ere man or his remote
Progenitors evolved; and have 'progressed'
　　Through all the generations since no single jot.

And aeons hence if life on earth survives,
　　Though mankind still 'progress towards the Divine,'
Unchanged their fungus gardens they will tend,
　　Still keep, for milk, their herds of aphid kine.

Of any industry which man pursues
    Or any human community dare we
Anticipate a similar permanence
    To that assured, while earth lasts, to the Bee?

To Duncan McNaught, LL.D., J.P.

President of the Burns Federation

HONOUR to him who hath establishèd
A means to realise Burns' noblest dream
And haste the time whereof he caught the gleam
– He of the grey indomitable head
Whose service followed where the great song sped!
Like Moses now on Pisgah doth he seem
To stand and gaze upon the plains that teem
With all fulfilment. Thus far hath he led.

Burns International! The mighty cry
Prophetic of eventual brotherhood
Rings still, imperative to be fulfilled.
M'Naught, who follows you must surely try
To take his stand where, living, Burns had stood
Nor save on this foundation can he build.

Lament

MA hert unsocht to a laddie I gied
But alas, an' alas, I need crave nae mair for'm
Sin' he's wedded noo wi' the betherel's spade
To the clod o' the valley an' the slime-worm.

MONY's the likely loon
An' bonnie lass
Maun ha'e their honeymoon
Aneath the grass.

An' be weel-twined at last
Wi' quilts o' stanes
For rowth o' coverin's cast
Aboun their banes.

SWEET be the milk o' the breist
O' the wumman I lo'e
An' canny her hands an' her een,
An' may I be true!

Bonnie her bairntime be
An' bonnie the weans,
An' may I be weel-eneuch pleased
Wi' my days an' dae'ins.

The Test

'YE maun wrestle a fa' wi' me
Gin ye'd ken yer chance wi' Jean.'
– O' a' the wooers that's speired her
Nane's bin twice seen!

He's fun' the backsprents o' a'
The loons o' the countryside.
– It'll be a lang day, I'm jalousin',
Or Jean's a bride!

Der Wunderrabbiner von Barcelona[1]

To Else Lasker-Schüler

Outwith the walls of Barcelona dwelt
A wonder-Rabbi humbly and alone
Whose eyes with radiance unearthly shone,
Whose holiness through all the land was felt.
The hearts of all he met a glance would melt.
The Jews adored him as their saintly own
And Christians, swift to throw the hostile stone,
Towards him at all times deferentially dealt.

There came a pogrom of the Jews at last
And naked corpses in the streets were cast.
The Rabbi deep in meditation came
Oblivious of the blood in which he trod.
Unseen the murderers stood beneath the flame
Of eyes that shone remote as th' eyes of God.

Miguel de Unamuno

(*On reading* The Tragic Sense of Life in Men and in Peoples)

Unamuno the dark night of the soul
Pierces with owlish eyes.[2] What sees he there?
His lonely heart that cannot know despair!
The tides of doubt illimitable roll

[1] Else Lasker-Schüler's book of this name (Berlin: Paul Cassirer, 1921).

[2] Madariaga refers to the fact that a caricaturist has represented Unamuno as an owl – 'a wonderful thrust at the heart of his character.' 'His reason can rise no higher than scepticism, and, unable to become vital, dies sterile, his faith, exacting anti-rational affirmations and unable therefore to be apprehended by the logical mind, remains incommunicable. From the bottom of this abyss Unamuno builds up his theory of life. . . .'

In vain. Th' impermeable rocks are whole
No coast erosion can his will impair.
Incapable his faith of wear and tear.
A Diamond Spirit! A Magnetic Pole!

On the survival of his Will-to-Be
Unscathed by self-assaults of criticism
He founds his faith in Immortality.
Only upon the floor of the abyss
Is rooting ground to rear through seas of schism
A soul of living adamant like his.

Deidman's Gait

THEY hear a Heilantman's ling
On the heel o' the twilicht
As they sit i' the cheek o' the gushack.

'Is't Angus hame frae the war?
– Angus, the licht o' the glen,
A hule amang the lassies!'

Like ane to their feet they spring
An' gae glowerin' into the nicht.
– Wae's me, a's goustrous an' black.

'He'll hame nae mair frae the War
But his ghaist for a' that we ken
I' the cauld win' passes.

'When we hear a Heilantman's ling
On the heel o' the twilicht
As we sit i' the cheek o' the gushack.'

The Deid-Bell

I HEAR a deid-bell jowin'
I' the deasie dayligaun.
The worms 'll sune be chowin'
Anither braw man.

I hear a deid-bell jowin'
I' the deasie dayligaun
– An' gowans 'll sune be growin'
Frae this auld harn-pan.

Funeral

'THERE's waur things than a guid funeral,'
Quo' the gutcher grey an' bent.
Sic a deid-auld man maun shairly ken
A' that there is to be kent.
Foolish an' young tho' I be mysel'
I ken – I ken what he meant.

Love an' success an' fame are ferlics for fools,
A diet for worms at the end.
By-produc's o' dirt, a' things gae back
To naething but dirt again;
An' what but a'e lang braw funeral
Is a' that is seen by men?

In Autumn

THE windfall apples blacken in the grass:
Dishevelled are the trees: the sun's last rays,
Corruptly coloured, ripple like slow snakes
Through all the orchard ways.

Ah, Life! Shall my eyes also bitter-bright
Their careless glances through corruption send,
And find but rotten fruit and ravaged trees
At all the long days' end?

Exodus

NOW in a violent flood of sunlight
The sea shines with dark metallic gleam,
And with uncanny cries
Dream follows dream.

Dream follows dream in the wild gold light,
Black fall their shadows on the vibrant sea.
Yea, with uncanny cries,
My dreams leave me!

The Pool

INTO the pool
The shadows cast
Their faces of silence.

Their faces of silence
Which are old and vague
And pitiful.

Now in my heart the wondrous wave of night
Rises and swings to its star-crested height.

Well Hung

You shall be, my dear,
One of El Greco's holy figures,
Lithe and undulating
And bluishly spiritual,
And I one of Ribera's
Wrinkled black heads,
Ferocious with torture,
And we shall hang
On opposite walls
Of a small private gallery
Belonging to an obese financier
Forever
And ever.

L'Enfant Terrible

'I am just a little girl,
And my head's in *such* a whirl.
Jesus has sent word to me
That He will be here for tea.

'I will lay it on the lawn,
Don't you think that *that's* the plan?
Underneath the chestnut tree
Surely He'll enjoy His tea.

'I will use my white and blue.
Don't you think that it will do?
I am sure He *can't* be given
Prettier cups and plates in Heaven.

'But one thing has got me beat.
What can I give Him to eat?
I must ask Mamma her view.
She'll know how to feed a Jew.

'I am just a little girl,
And my head's in *such* a whirl.
Jesus has sent word to me
That He will be here for tea.'

In Memoriam, J.B.N.

KNOWEST now the mockery of Paradise
O Thou, from out whose hollow eyes flies thin
The light that on the verge of night may win
All that remains of what at least we prize?
I see thee with a single sickle seek,
On banks forlorn where now a star strikes red,
Sparse stems, that stand ev'n yet unharvested,
Of loves foregone wherewith your store to eke,

And know how pitifully at the last
My eyes shall gaze upon your emptiness,
No little dust of any rose thou hast!
No withered wisp of all the green and gold
Your starveling fingers in the Night may press!
And Life's a wind that 'twixt your bones blows cold.

The Drum of Death

THE drum of death is booming in the hills,
The grey light trembles, and its furtive eyes
Know that ere dawn a man amongst us dies,
And dare not face us up – since unfulfils
This stern tattoo, whereunto granite shakes,
And the slow-moving hearts of mountains leap
The promise with which morning broke our sleep
      – *Now to the sunlight only man awakes!*

For morning smiled and spoke us goldenly.
Well may the false light tremble thus between
The hills, and hillmen gathering fearfully,
Listing the drumstick beat upon the drum
For one of us – but which? unknown, unseen,
Save in a lonely heart the drum says 'Come!'

On a Lone Shore

Sea – Boomflapswirlishoo.
          Boomflapswirlishoo.

Bird – Weewee. Weewee.

Sea – Boomflapswirlishoo.
          Swirlishoo. Swirlishoo.

Bird – Weewee. Weewee.

   '*An' the sky looks on*
   Wi' a'e muckle white e'e.
   It's the tither, I'm thinkin',
   I'll be ha'in' on me.'

The Dying Earth

PITMIRK the nicht: God's waukrife yet
An' lichtnin'-like his glances flit
An' sair, sair are the looks he gies
The auld earth as it dees.

Pitmirk the nicht: an' God's 'good tell
I' broken thunners to hissel'
A' that he meent the warl' to be
An' hoo his plan gaed jee.

He canna steek his weary lids
But aye anither gey look whids
Frae pole to pole: an's tears doonfa'
In lashin' rain owre a'.

On an Ill-Faur'd Star

FAR aff the bawsunt mount'ins jirk
Their kaims o' ribie trees.
Like howlets roostin' roon' aboot
Are a' the seas.

Ae rimpin' i' the riach lan'
Glowers at the lift revure:
An' yont its muckle ringle-een
Time scuds like stour.

Braid Scots

An Inventory and Appraisement

To Edwin Muir[1]

[The poem 'Gairmscoile' (see pp. 72–75), printed in *Penny Wheep* (1926), is a revision of the Prologue, Section I, and all but the last stanza of Section II of this fragment of a long poem which was to have contained twelve Sections, each consisting of four or five eight- or ten-line verses, with a Prologue and an Epilogue.]

II

.　.　.　.　.

Wergeland, hoo weel I ken amid sair tews
What gar'd ye claut yer wee bit mawkin up[2]
An' peerin' in its dosky een, fin' views
O' new warls the Creator micht lat slup.
Ill-tethed like you, an' prone to tellyevies,
Midst men like dowf nits or like fozie neeps,
My trauchled hert, set free, to Eden flies
Whene'er I see the truth a beast's e'e keeps.
. . . . As the mune moves the seas but leaves the wells
Unstirred, only a poet's hert to poesy swells.

III

The auld rime-kennars fired to doughty deeds,
Wrocht i' their warl' an' manfully ser'd their day,

---

[1] Written extempore on receipt of a letter from Mr. Muir suggesting that 'a long poem in the language you are evolving would go tremendously.'

[2] At the time when he was toiling with studies Wergeland might fling the book into a corner, snatch up his little tame rabbit, and, gazing into its dim eye, would see the creation of worlds in vista deep and far. See *Den Förste Sommerfugl* (1837), vol. I, pp. 194–197.

Maisters o' dreams, they dreamt to bring aboot,
An' sang accordin' to the benmaist needs
O' a' their folk. Theirs was nae passment play.
The warl' a clod through which they ran a root,
Their sangs were prophecies – they lived afore the times
They helped to bring to be wi' their undauntoned rhymes.

Ah, Gudlaugsson,[1] my cry is e'en as thine.
Great thochts, great dreams, my country tae has borne
Thoro' the nicht o' Time – gied the divine
Licht that it had to ithers, an' noo' forlorn,
By Time forgotten, it lies sunk i' gloom.
Still frae the sea it rises as o' auld,
The race is still the same – as thro' oor cauld
Gray earth flo'ers brak', oor herts strive still agen' the doom.

Come, let us lift oor land towards the sun,
Up frae the dank mists – brithers, gie your strength!
Soon can the goal we a' desire be won
An' Scotlan' to its place restored at length.
Lift it we can gin we a' heeze at aince.
Lang ha'e we been unable to rejoice
But let's win' back oor freedom tined lang since
An' whan we get oor freedom back we'll soon get back oor voice.[2]

Strang an' deep-suckin' are the roots I rin
Into my race; an' a' its misery
I'll raise into mysel' – an' towards the sun!
Let whasae may lament the poverty
O' mind an' saul they say aboonds to-day,
An', coorin' frae reality, fin' bield
For craven wits whaur cynicism hauds sway.
– *Oor tree's nae daised wud yet but's routh o' fruit to yield.*

END OF FRAGMENT

[1] Cf. the modern Icelandic poems of Jonas Gudlaugsson.
[2] Cf. Aasmund Vinje's *Dolen*, vol. 1, no. 1 (1858).

Hooch-Aye!

A DOWIE ill-faur'd life they lead
An' dourly haud it's planned by God
Wha naturally gi'es his chosen folk
The heaviest load an' rouchest road.

They warsel on, wi' fixed belief,
That they sall be eternally
The opposite o' what they are
– An' turn to sang an' ecstasy!

The things that are nae use on Earth
Rejectit an' despised o' men
'Ull be the corner-stanes o' Heaven
An' much appreciated then!
          Hooch-Aye!

Puir Gowks, gin sic a Heaven c'd be
E'en sae sma' wish I'd ha'e to harm ye
– I'd spend Eternity inflictin'
Verlaine upon ye, an' Mallarmé!

A dowie ill-faur'd lot they are
An' glibly hint their brutish taste
Is God-devised to hide the fac'
That they luve luvely things the maist.

(Fer mair than a' the heighbroos wha
Mak' sic a sang o' Art an' Letters
Yet rin doon Burns an' Annie Swan
An' aye gae hectorin' their betters!)
          Hooch-Aye!

Why hide it? – 'Weel the reason is
That Heaven an' Earth maun different be.
Ye michtna ken Heaven when ye saw't
Gin Earth improved owre much, ye see!

'Or Heaven can ha'e its corner-stanes
It's necessary they s'ud be
Rejectit an' despised on Earth
– Hence oor contempt o' *Poesy!*

'Sae on their sins an' latter-end
Wi' due solemnity
Let brood the wanton crew wha waste
This life i' sang an' ecstasy,

'An' mair especially Hugh M'Diarmid,
A Scotsman like unto oorsels,
Wha says: "To Hell wi' this your Heaven.
I hope to Heaven ye've better Hells!"'

.   .   .   .   .

Puir gowks! wha's shallow herts are still
Wi' sic preposterous notions rife
– God gi'e ye never learn the truth,
Insensible in death as life!

The First Thing

ARE there folk on Mars an' the Mune
An', yont sayin', what ither starns?
– Nae doot, but wi' that it's owre sune
To gae fashin' oor harns.

The first thing's to fathom the eild
Lear o' oor aulder brithren there
– The beasts o' the flood an' the field
An' the birds o' the air !

Apology

ECH, Muse, hoo I ha'e fa'en short!
Twine the thrissel wi' the laurel,
Since I turn frae payin' thee court
Wi' gowks an' gomerils to quarrel!

Peace

From the Dutch of Pieter Corneliszoon Hooft[1]

THIS warl', wi'ts muckle mount'ins, twined wi' streams;
Speckled wi' cities ringed aboot wi' to'ers;
Wha's face wi' hill an' lauchin' valley gleams,
Wha's darksome wuds are sawn wi' canny flo'ers;
The birds; an' gangrel beasts aneath the mune;
An' even the puir pridefu' stock o' man
Are a' alike haud'n in by luve, an' sune
Withouten love 'ud lapse frae nature's plan.

I' nowt but luve earth's cities can be reared
An' ha'e guid growth an' flourish: strife's their daith.
Thro' civil wars they pech wi' waesome braith.
Dissension gnaws the roots o' ony State:
I' luve alane the seeds o' joy can braird,
An' peace at hame mak's little countries great.

[1] Pieter Corneliszoon Hooft (1581–1647), the celebrated Dutch poet and historian, who first imitated Petrarch and introduced Italian poetry to the attention of his countrymen, after his famous journey to the South of Europe in 1599. His Castle of Muiden was for nearly forty years the centre of literary and artistic activity in Holland.

Sorrow and Song

Suggested by the Polish of Mickiewicz[1]

THE black seas lounder doon upo' the san's
An', ebbin', leave them bricht wi' shells.

Sae aye the onrushin' o' dule's black tide
A routh o' bonnie sang foretells.

The Day Before the Twelfth

Caretaker of Highland Shooting Lodge Loquitur

IN come sic a rangel o' gentles
Wi' a lithry o' hanyiel slyps at their tail
That the hoose in a weaven is gaen
Like a Muckle Fair sale.

Ye canna hear day nor door
For their tongues a' hung i' the middle
Like han'-bells: an' ilk ane squeakin' an' squealin'
Like a doited fiddle!

I wish that the season was owre
Afore it's begun: an' the haill jingbang
Awa' sooth again: an' the hurley hoose
Like a deid man's sang,

Like a deid man's sang i' the white birch wud,
A lanely sang in a toom domain,
While the wutherin' heather lies on the warl'
Like an auld bluid-stain!

[1] Adam Mickiewicz (1798-1855), the greatest of Polish poets.

Glasgow

WHAT leeroch is't Glesca mak's
For the waugh white starns,
Leesin' the haill nicht through
The plies o' its harns?

Gin I were a wan white starn,
Ilka wearifu' soun'
Wad be like a muckle black craw
That cam' clourin' doun,

Craw efter scunnersome craw
Till ma licht was dung oot,
Leavin' a carfuffle o' craws
An' a starn turnt soot!

—————————◦❰◦—————————

The Flowing Bowl

FIERCE as rich cordials
   Are the sharp hill airs
In the land that I know
   Will cure all my cares.

The roar of the wind,
   The roar of the sea,
And the great roar of the silence
   My tonics shall be.

In the land that I know,
   My cares to eclipse,
I'll lift the whole world
   Like a bowl to my lips.

The Crown of Rock

IN bitter and uproarious winds,
   Where naught can stand but stone,
I lift my life that it may be
   Blown clean as bone.

Let whatso may be blown away.
   The like I would not own,
But to myself by what remains
   Contented I'll be known.

And what if all be blown away?
  So be it – 'tis well gone.
More than most men he sees to whom
  What nothing is is shown.

The sight would please me, but perchance
  I'll be a pipe played on
By subtler players than Nescience yet
  Alone here with th' Alone.

Eyes

THE frost lies glumpin' i' the pool. . . .
But my ain hert that mirrors a'
The haill braid warl's delight an' dule
Deeper than its reflections fa',
Hauds sic anither pair o' een
Lyin' toom 'yont a' that plies atween.

Creation

CELLS o' my brain are trauchelt yet
Wi' daiths o' airmies an' the birth
O' wild floo'ers owre their burial pit.
For ilka heid has a' the earth,
Its past an' future, for its load.
Wha fin's himsel' fin's Man an' God.

Death

IT was as wild a sunset yon
As 'twere the hinder-en' o' Licht
Wi' nae mair days to shine upon.
An' so, I think, Daith's awesome sicht
'Naith ither skies nae mair may mean
Than's common a day as this has been.

'Pop Goes the Weasel'

LIKE a futrat bobbin' in a bourachie o' scrogs,
Is the glory o' God i' the herts o' men.
It pops oot here, an' it pops oot there,
An' it's nae sooner scansed than it's tint again,
Like a futrat bobbin' in a bourachie o' scrogs.

Like a futrat bobbin' in a bourachie o' scrogs,
That the gamey traps an' nails to a tree,
As sodjers did wi' the Son o' Man
When he 'good t'unsettle little auld Judee,
Like a futrat bobbin' in a bourachie o' scrogs.

Back Bedroom

THE dirty licht that through the winnock seeps
Into this unkempt room has glozed strange sichts;
Heaven like a Peepin' Tam 'twixt chimley-pots
Keeks i' the drab fore-nichts.

The folk that hed it last – the selfsame bed –
Were a great hulkin' cairter an' his bride.
She deed i' child-birth – on this verra spot
Whaur we'll lie side by side.

An' everything's deid-grey except oor een.
Wi' wee waugh jokes we strip an' intae bed. . . .
An' suddenly oor een sing oot like stars
An' a' oor misery's shed.

What tho' the auld dour licht is undeceived?
What tho' a callous morn oure shairly comes?
For a wee while we ken but een like stars,
An' oor herts gaen' like drums.

Mony's the dreich back bedroom whaur the same
Sad little miracle tak's place ilk' nicht,
An' orra shapes o' sickly-hued mankind
Cheenge into forms o' licht.

At Heaven's Gate

KNOW you not full many a star
  Is bigger than the sun;
That you should cleave to the lesser light,
  And all the others shun?
At noon, and when your song pours out,
A star with silence girt about
  Our universe appears,
Caught in the rays of many a star,
Beyond the sun ten times as far,
  And black out a million years.

Sky-lark and Aeroplane

MANY a lovelier bird than you
Flaunts on earth a vivid hue
While you sit obscurely by
Cherishing the secret might
That can blot it out of sight.
Man and beast are left behind
In a turning of the wind.

Tell me, have you never seen
On your pinnacle serene
Upstarts of the human race
Void of meaning as of grace,
In a sudden great machine?
Did the engine's dreadful noise
Quench awhile your glorious voice?

Did you start your song again
With the old assurance then?

A Soaring Bird

EARTH may dwindle 'neath your flight
  Till it is seen no more.
Fly on, fly on, you've far to fly
  Before your flight is o'er;
If in the sun's clear pool you'd see
Your body like a memory.
. . . Despite your distance from the earth
  The sun no nearer seems
But in the endless sands of light
  A phantom water gleams,
– And yet once more you start to sing
As though you glimpsed your mirrored wing!

The Question of Leadership

I DO not ask to lead, but when at last
The time I work for comes then must I have
A holiday from pen and paper (that labour past)
Though only from my study to my grave,
Those graves that more than leaders we will need
Ere anyone has anything worth while to lead!

I do not ask to lead, but let me be
Forcmost amongst the led, and let me see
Thought flower to action, let me hear
My own words speak like rifles in my ear,
And show there is no issue to my work
That I myself will for an instant shirk.

Scotland's Noblest?

This brave and rugged land which gave him birth now waits with loving welcome to receive his dust to its dear embrace, and Scotland will never boast a nobler name than that of Douglas Haig

Very Rev. CHAS. L. WARR

Earl Haig ranked with the greatest names in all history and as an example of all that was best in British humanity he has not been excelled.

Brig.-Gen. Sir WM. ALEXANDER, M.P.

SCOTLAND cares not, Cæsar, clown,
Whoso in it lays him down,
Far from noblest tho' he was
(Albeit greater than his cause)
Haig had worth and honours high –
No need to shroud him in a lie!

A Scotsman's Heaven

HE'LL ca' nocht else a Heaven if he'd fain
Hae's fit insteed upon the heathery miles,
Or wi' the lobster-fishers sail again
To Fladda Chuain and the Ascrib Isles.

If there's to be a Heaven it maun vie
Wi' this auld land o' his wha's hillsides lirk
Like elephant skins as he gangs by
Aince mair 'twixt John o' Groats and Maidenkirk.

A Laverock in the Lift

A LAVEROCK in the lift forgets
A'thing except his sang
– A thoosand years o' history I
The Gaelic hills amang.

Feudalism, Calvinism,
Can never bc undune?
– Hoots they're as they'd never been
In ony simple tune!

The Celtic Sunrise

THE lands o' black and yellow men,
And ploys that mak' white folk like them,
He tines in mony a caller glen
    As gin they'd never been,
And when he clims his hills again
The sea's sma' boukit to a gem
    And naething else is seen.

Sae in his mind he wanders a'
Laich forms o' thocht and ugsome life.
A wind that whistles aff the snaw
    Is mair than they can thrive in.
He mounts, and wi' an extra blaw
It severs Earth as wi' a knife
    Frae the sun that he's alive in!

The Kelpie in the Dorts

THE kelpie in the dorts owre lang has lain
Drooned in the heedlessness o' men,
Owre idle or owre ignorant to ken
The glories that it micht ha' ha'en,
Till in its hingin' fupple's dreich lines nane
Can weel be blamed for dootin' they remain,
Nor lippen to see't uncurl its blazin' train
And, louch nae mair, through a' the lift be gane.

There is nae height that ony leid can gain,
You canna match wi' ferlies o' your ain,
Nae height unreached but you may first attain;
Faurer than the laverock's soars your sweeter strain.
Only to earth the laverock sinks again,
But you plunge deeper faur than ony brain
'S yet gane, or aiblins can till you unchain
            Poo'er's yours alane.

Then up and skail your maikless fires again,
And multiply new shades o' joy and pain
Kittle and mony-shaped as licht or rain.
Tak' nae fixed shape. Nae suner kyth in ane
Than to anither 'yont belief you're gane
Until you show in sicna sequence plain
A' that we'd tine if you s'ud halt and hain
This form or that, that silly folk are fain
To fix – oh!, *recta ratio factibilium* reign
            In a' we're daen'.

Banish oor beliefs for they are a' in vain,
Whummle oor sanctities in quick disdain,

Licht vulgar words wi' glories that contain
Nocht that to human life can appertain,
Glories denied, or understood, by nane,
Like new stars lyin' in the faur inane,
Brichter and bigger and to ootlast oor ain,
Or glorify oor beliefs afore they've gane,
Honour oor sanctities, let laich life feign
New stature frae you – shed on us bliss or bane;
But oot and aboot; nor in the dorts be lain
But wax a hundred-fauld abune your wane.

The Graves of My Race

A' OWRE the Borders lie the unkent graves
   O' oor coontless hosts.
Only their ghosts micht find them – and we're no'
   A folk that's gi'en to ghosts!

Fatherless in Boyhood

YOUR bike-wheels ga'en like bees-wings doon the road,
Or, your face scarlet frae the icy wind,
Openin' your big broon bag and showin' in'd
Cakes, apples, oranges, a wondrous load,
Frae hogmanayin' a' the way up Ewes,
Or 'mang your books, as queer a lot to me
As ony library frae Mars might be,
Or voicin' Trade Union and Co-operative views
Or some religious line, as 'twere the crude
Beginnin's o' my ain deep interests there,
Or gien' me glimpses, fleetin', unaware,
O' feelin's that noo I micht ha'e understood,

Or jokin' mither (a ploy you aye were at),
Then suddenly deid, wha'd never ailed afore.
Ah, no' your death, but memory's trivial store,
The tragedy – o' no' bein' even that!

At a Humble Grave

YET gin by speakin' o't as tho'
It was a maist distinguished grave,
That folk in croods 'ud flock to see't
My braith I'd save.

I'll no' pretend that it moves me
To thochts profounder than I ha'e;
Nor credit to anither grave
– Even Nihum-Nahum's, say!

Gin I invent sic sentiments
An empty plot o' grund 'll ser'
– Yet where on Scottish soil the fraud
Or the gain elsewhere confer?

Water of Life

WHA is the fool that disna ken
    The aneness that's betwixt,
Through a' the divers forms in which
    They're temporarily fixt,
    The ocean and the dewdrop,
    The river and the cloud?
Water is ane, and man is ane,
Nae maitter what shapes they've ta'en.

Speak o' your lives and principles,
　　　Your tastes and hopes and fears,
And a' you think is you indeed,
　　　Still plainly it appears
Water accommodates itsel'
To the vessel in which it's put,
And so do you; and when it's broke
Joins again the common stock.

The Dog Pool

OOT o' the world and into the Langholm!
There's mony a troot in the auld Dog Pool
Livelier, praise be, than ocht you can write.
Lean owre as you used to ga'en to the school
And see the broon shadows and ivory beaks
　　　Bonnier than ony book bespeaks.

Or when there's a spate and the water's as black
As Maxton's hair and as noisy as Kirkwood
Wha'd no watch it withoot wantin' to think?
Tech, ony man that isna a stirk would.
It'll be time to think when the Esk rins dry.
　　　Watch it noo while it's still ga'en by.

Catch it noo – for even as I speak
The fish may be gaspin' on dry land there
And the hindmaist wave o' the Esk gang roon'
The curve at Land's End to be seen nae mair
And a silence still waur for a sang to brak'
　　　Follow the row the waters mak'.

To Any Scottish Laird

YOUR land? You fool, it hauds nae beast
Or bird or troot or tree or weed
If they kent you as owner but
'Ud leave it empty as your heid.

The Key to the Situation

Scotland, Autumn, 1932

WHA prates o' unity here in the changin' scene,
Cryin' for tolerance, sympathy, and goodwill?
– No' *a good will*, but goodwill, that bastard thing!
Oh, the fools 'ud hae us cuddle in brotherly love,
Like cattle-breeders makin' their livestock mate.
I ken maist o' the notions fleein' noo
(*The Daily Record* – Beaverbrook – MacDonald –
The Cathcart Tories – *The Scots Observer*)
A' airts like fleggit birds, and tremble for what
Even my picked freends may fancy important
'Mang sae mony emergencies. The feck
O' folk are hopelessly lost in the Caledonian Wud.
– But, a' at aince, there's a rent in the green-black mists,
And, look, a shaft o' sunlicht irradiates
The glade in this primeval forest of fists,
The crown and centre of the bayonets!

Potted Reviews

The Archer in the Arras.   (Lewis Spence)

YOU say beyond illusion and probability goes
Spence's tale of the tapestry archer who
Kills a young man by an arrow shot there
Blatantly impossible? I think so too.
But Spence himself in very truth this is.
'Stuffed shirt' who shoots – but always misses.

The Laburnum Tree   (Orgill Mackenzie)

FAIR is the blossom as all may see
Of the none-the-less poisonous laburnum tree.

Hatter's Castle   (A. J. Cronin)

BUT why did Cronin leave the adjective out?
It's a mad-hatter's castle without a doubt.

Allelauder

Ramsay MacDonald to Sir Harry Lauder:
*'For fifty years you have been making us happy, and the art you have employed has not
had a tinge of the degrading in it. You have dealt with the great fundamental human
simplicities, and have taught us to find joy and inspiration in qualities and feelings which
belong to the good things in human life.'*

THE curly nibby has put to flight
The legions of despair.
A flap of Sir Harry Lauder's kilt
And our woes are no longer there.
To God, our help in ages past,
There is no need to pray
When the softest of the family
Presents an easier way.

Most of us may lack the cash
To hear Lauder in person – yet
If we're too poor for the music halls,
Through gramophone disc or radio set,
The little man with the enlarged heart
Can make us wholly forget
All the horrors of war and peace
With which mankind's beset,
Every so-called crisis disappears
– *'He's made us happy for fifty years!'*
Honour to Ramsay MacDonald who
Sees and proclaims this fact,
Knowing that pawky patter does more
Than an Ottawa or O-to-Hell pact.
Dire necessity and foul disease
Are vanquished by a variety act.
Unemployment, poverty, slums
Can be cured by a fatuous song
(If Lauder receives a suitable fee!) –
Then the Government policy's wrong.
Abolish all social services,
Hand Lauder the dough instead,
Give all other public men the sack
And put him alone at the head.
With a waggle here and a wiggle there
The world will soon be rid
Of all its troubles and doubts and fears
– *Happy for good as for fifty years!*
Allelauder, Allelauder,
Let the grateful millions raise
Their starving mouths and helpless hands
In great Sir Harry's praise,
Happy as the dead who went
Blithely to graves in Flanders fields
(Lauder's son too) to the seemly strains
Of the ineffable songs he yields.
Lest we forget of our own accord
Let Lauder do it for us

And end all the ills to which we're heir
With an imbecile chorus.
– But even his stupendous powers
May cure life's every loss and want
Save his or MacDonald's brainlessness,
Or stop their ghastly cant.
Oh, Lauder is bad enough, but we
Might have been happier still
If MacDonald every now and again
Hadn't figured too on the bill
– The cross-talk duo, it appears,
Toplining these fifty filthy years.

The Feast is Spread

THE feast is spread yet helplessly they fast,
Aye win an Irishman's rise wi' unco strife,
Cast oot frae a' their dues by the silly fear
That hauds them in habits o' poortith still,
While by them brim the torrents . . .
The vast way-drawing that denies mankind
Or pairt or paircel in science or in art
Till bare as worms the feck o' them we find.
Each generation at zero still maun start
And's doomed to end there . . .
Or pairt or paircel in science or in art –
Or even in life! Hoo few men ever live,
And what wee local lives at best they ha'e.
Sirse, science and art micht weel rin through the sieve,
If maist folk through nae elf-bores dribbled yet,
But in some measure lived to a' life is.
Wad that their latent poo'ers 'ud loup alist,
Kyth suddenly a' their wasted past has missed,
And nae mair leave their lives like languages,
Mere leaks frae streamin' consciousness as if

Thocht roond itsel' raised wa's prohibitive
O' a' but a fraction o' its possible sway –
But rax in freedom, nocht inhibitive,
In fearless flourishin' amidwart,
Fed by the hail wide world and feedin' it.

My Sense of the Greatest

My sense o' the greatest man can typify
And universalise himsel' maist fully by
Nocht ta'en at second-hand and nocht let drift,
Nae bull owre big to tackle by the horns,
Nae chance owre sma' for freedom's sake he scorns,
But a' creation through himsel' maun sift
Nor possible defeat confess,
Forever poised and apt in his address,
Save at this pitch nae man can truly live.

The Noble Seventy-four

We did nothing as long as we could
   But condemned whoever tried,
And the facts we admit at last
   Are those we've always denied.
But the Movement's grown despite us,
   And we can't have that, you know,
So we thank the fools for their labours,
   And sail in and take over their show.

No pioneer effort for us,
   For we have the wit to sleep
Till the harvest is ripe, and then,

Tho' we did no sowing, reap.
We just sit and twiddle our thumbs
Till it's time to pounce on the plums.

For we are the wonderful seventy-four,
    Scotland's élite – the Duke of Montrose,
Kevan M'Dowall, and W. F. Stewart,
    And a score or more nobody knows,
Fit chums for his Grace, unheard of before,
    Least of all in a Scottish connection,
But the Movement has reached the stage
    When it needs distinguished direction.

It wouldn't have begun
    If we had had our way,
But now it has, of course,
    We must impose our sway.
Our brains are a certain bar
To keep it from going too far.

Our names'll go down to history
    With Wallace, Bruce, and the rest,
General Carruthers and Colonel McLean –
    There's no doubt we've Scotland's best.
Paisley Mitchell and Roberton Hew,
    The Dean of Glasgow morticians,
Ex-Provosts, ex-Bailies, X-all –
    Nobody can vie with 'ishuns'!

Cathcart Tories, Cathcart Liberals,
    Scotland's in the cart all right.
Just let Will Fyffe and Lauder
    Their forces with ours unite,
And Rothermere and Beaverbrook,
And we'll win by hook – or crook!

For what's a mere Compton Mackenzie
    To a Miss Marnie of the Empire Guild,

A Cunninghame Graham to a Bosomworth –
   The National Party has filled
Its ranks with mere nonentities,
But we know better than that,
And soar superior to these.

With a Love Mackay
   And a Marshall Love,
Each of us coo
   Like a turtle dove,
And mere poets go down to a peep
As soon as we stir in our sleep.

The Scott Centenary

No poet did you honour, Scott,
No master of your craft, and you
Are welcome to the royalty and rubbish
Who saw your dud centenary through.

Donald Sinclair

Recently Dead

I HAVE been blessed in having many poets
– Yeats, Eliot, A. E., Sturge Moore – for friends.
You were so little known that having you too,
Their unfamed peer, a heightened wonder lends.
I could not know Ó Rathaille or MacMhaighstir,
Of all dead poets I would most have known,
But knew one of Gaeldom's greatest since, knowing you,
And being in that of living poets alone.

At the Grave of William Livingston

Janefield Cemetery, Glasgow

Hater of England and all things English who
(But not your poetry) suffered cruelly for it,
The Anglophiles are on the run – your grave
Will be a hallowed spot in Scotland yet.

The Object Lesson of the Scottish Coinage

In truth the golden age is past,
At least in Scotland, all may see
Who in the Royal Scottish Museum
Our coins' show perpend with me;
And note the rich array we had
Before the English Union and
The woeful anti-alchemy since –
A lesson all may understand!

The Scottish National Yo-Yo Contest

All the dud men
On Scotland's chest.
Yo-ho-yo – it's certainly rum.
Our political Yo-Yo champions
Are giving their dazzling displays;
The 'Daily Record' and 'Daily Express'
Spin Scotland in countless ways.
Dalziel has won his Spinner's Badge,

Beaverbrook's busy with a '33,'
But Joe Young's nothing to the Duke of Montrose
At Tweedledum and Tweedledee.
            All the dud men
            On Scotland's chest.
        Yo-ho-yo – it's certainly rum.
Poor Joe only knows a hundred tricks,
    That's nothing to wizards like these,
To whom 'Over the Falls' and 'Skinning the cat'
    Is easier than pulling a wire through cheese,
But 'Diddle the Public' and 'Grab the Plums'
    And 'St Vitus Visits the North Again,'
The National Party reels as it watches
    Trying to see how they've 'done' – in vain!
    Yo-ho-yo – we chortle and sing
    Poor old Scotland's once more on a string.

The Teaching Profession

To A. S. NEILL

I've little to say aboot the school,
    And the question o' teachers shelve
By sayin' they're lucky to earn a livin'
    Wi' what they'd learnt at twelve.

Dante and Douglas

Nature and Art – by these two powers, if thou hast rightly read, 'tis meet the nations should in life's true course be led; and since the usurer elsewhere turns his feet. . . . Vergil to Dante; The Inferno.
How can it be that a good when shared shall make the greater number of possessors richer in it than if it be possessed by a few? – Dante to Vergil; The Purgatorio.

To nurse indignation and horror
Is nae langer possible – here
A' that is past; the haill thing,
And way oot, at last are clear.

Dante was richt in his judgments
And their several places in Hell
Suited his trimmers, traders, and traitors,
Barrators and usurers well.

The number's increased since he wrote
O' the crood that watches the fecht
To tak' whichever side wins.
They're mony times multiplied.

Let them join the useless angels
Wha' stood 'for themsel's' alane
– Nor for God nor against; but *say*
Nae mair o' them – a'e glance and on!

'Why holdest thou?' 'Why spendest thou?'
The vain coonter-cry continues
– Neither avails; and the haill lot
Even their names and identities lose.

The abuse of intellectual gifts,
Violence to Nature and Art – of late
Phlegethon, the red river of Hell,
The river of blood's aye in spate.

A' fruit o' capital that comes
To wha sit still and tak' it and gi'e
Nae real work to the world – *and hoo mony*
Dae that? – is frae the Deid Sea.

Let Scotland abune a' remember
Calvin was the first Kirkman o' note
To defend the takin' o' interest
– And ponder its shamefu' lot.

Times ha' changed? – Shopkeepers,
Bankers, Clerks, and the mony-rangin'
Servants o' Mammon are respectit noo?
Times ha' changed – but no' the unchangin'!

To Hell wi' the lot o' them? – No!
Coals to Newcastle! They're there as it is.
To Hell wi' Hell? At least nae mair
Need swell some circles o' th' Abyss.

'*The sempiternal effluence streams abroad,*
Spreading wherever charity extends,
So that the more aspirants to that bliss
Are multiplied, more good is there to love,
And more is loved, as mirors that reflect,
Each unto other, propagated light.'

The Eighth Wonder of the World,
A Douglas at rest? – aye, in truth;
Certain o' the ultimate issue
And set abune wrath and ruth.

The New Makars

A. COME, let us sing of Scotland
   The land that we belong to.
B. Till it belongs to us
   – The end we set our song to.

C. Nay, not the end, but something
   We incidentally do.
A. All it is and how much ours
   Depends on our poetic powers.
D. What others than poets make of it
   Is Scotland, too, we must admit.
E. There is no Scotland –
F. There are too many –
B. And too few worth having –
D. I'm happy with any.
B. I want the best.
D. Best? By what test?
A. And what have you done
   To deserve it, son?
C. That's what's wrong. We Scots are given
   Too much for which we have not striven
   To value't rightly and strive for more
   As what we have was striven for,
   While all we have, be it understood
   Is nothing to what we could and should.
A. Not could and should; if we're poets at all
   The words we use must be can and shall.
D. Is Scotland nothing then
   But the will of certain men?
A. And dead men's thoughts forgotten
   – By us – and men's still unbegotten.
D. It makes these thoughts as much
   As it is made by such.
A. We'll argue later; first let each
   Prove he's a poet true
   And sing of something Scottish
   At last as is its due –.

The Vital Fact

A. GORDON o' Straloch's Map o' Badenoch
   Spreids oot in my heid again –
B. I ken a hill in Ross-shire but forget its name,
   They say it means 'the hill o' the dog's hole.'
   What 'ud the Gaelic be for that, d'ye think?
C. *Think?* There's nae need to *think.* What kind o' hill?
   Big, sma', sharp, roond, bare, green or what?
   Gaelic has ony amount o' words for hills,
   A different name for ilka different shape.
   No' like oor thowless speech that canna seize
   The essential fact in as mony sentences
   As Gaelic placenames in a soond or twa.

   Wha looks at Scotland through anither leid
   Goams through a wa' o' fog. If we'd gane on
   And thocht o' a'thing else as sheerly as
   Oor forbears did in gi'en places names
   Cleavin' to the vera core o' a' they saw! . . .
   Ten thoosand names cry shame upon oor minds
   And are to maist o' oor thochts as stars to mud –.

Homage to Dunbar

WHA wull may gang to Scott's or Burns's grave
But nane to yours, in your lost Scotland, lost
Neth this oor Scotland as neth the ocean wave
Atlantis lies, and haud'n a greater host
Than Brankstone's deidly barrow ten times owre
To reckon nane but men o' wit and worth.
The floo'ers o' the Forest wede in Flodden's earth
Were nocht but weeds to you, Scotland's best floo'er.

Still, like the bells o' Ys frae unplumbed deeps,
Whiles through Life's drumlie wash your music leaps
To'n antrin ear, as a'e bird's wheep defines
In some lane place the solitude's ootlines
(As a sculptor the form frae the marble
A greater silence's you wi' your warble
– A' th' auld Scotland abandoned, unexplored,
Brocht oot vastly, waesomely, in your a'e word!)
And wee wings shak' the immobility
And ootshine the vera sunshine suddenly
– Oh, in your unkent grave there's mair life yet
Than Scotland's had else or's like to get!

Balmorality

NAE statue to Prince Charlie, while the haill
Land's fu', as wi' some great grey vermin,
O' tombstones even uglier than themsel's
To this, that, or the other German!

Hoo could a country wi' sic hills as these,
Sic wuds and streams, breed forms o' human life
Content to see its brawest plaid thrawn roond
The boolie shouders o' yon dreich auld wife?

As Edinburgh shopkeepers glowered upon
The lad wi' the gowden hair, sae Scots folk yet
Are doomed to glower on a'thing that micht mak'
Their mean lives for their country's beauty fit.

Verlaine in the Forest

IT's not the German soldiers
    But the hosts of Heaven pass,
Tho' all their bright accoutrements
    Turn to shadows on the grass.

Ride on, you starry squadrons,
    When in the forest here,
There's always a ditch to shelter in
    If you should come too near.

The tangle sheets above me
  In plies no light can pierce,
And I lie soft and dark and warm –
  With your music in my ears.

Taureau

R o y Campbell needna ha' gane
For bull-fechts owre to Spain,
Nor Hemingway the same airt ta'en
    That Campbell took afore'm,
Nor Villalón wrecked his pen
On *La Toriada* when
In England *Deus, a' men ken,*
    Est anima brutorum.

Let us be toreadors
In this *corrida* then
Where the greatest bull on earth's
The sport o' a' true men,
For he that's worth bein' ca'd a
Real *aficionado*
'Ud find ocht less 'ud bore'm
Than you, agog to 'shor'm,'
    Carissime Taurorum.

O Tullochgorum's auld delight
Ne'er gar'd us a' in ane unite
Like this exhilaratin' fight
    Wi' John Bull in the forum.
A reid flag's a' we need.
To waggle aboot his heid.
At aince he gethers speed
    To storm his form enorm
Like a whiz-bang roond the ring,

Roarin' to raise the deid.
The beast o' the Apocalypse
To him's a slug insteed,
Tho' nae man worth his saut
'll care a haet for that,
But seek the medicine for'm,
Nor rest till he can lower'm,
    Carissime Taurorum.

Slow come the *coup de grâce*
And may mony a bonny pass,
Navarros and *veronicas*,
Develop as we harass
    The brute wi' due decorum,
But gralloch him at last
And a' his bowels cast
Roond Colonies aghast
    Wi' the inside story o'm,
Syne stuff him wi' *The Times*
And mount him in a case
– In the Scottish War Memorial
As the maist appropriate place! –
That bairns in efter ages
Tracin' history's foulest stages
May see the Sassenach norm
And wish they'd helped to floor'm,
    Carissime Taurorum.

In the Langfall

For Valda

The path is lost in tanglewood,
    I go towards the light
But how fair the bracken tops are
    And lower leaves to-night.

I would that I had time to stay
    And study them aright,
It is the light that cannot stay,
    They do – but not in sight.

And round me now the sombre trees
    Each of a different black,
Weld into one their various shapes
    Tho' here and there a crack
Lets in a line of silver light
    About the unseen track,
A line that lacks no less than I
    The kind of light I lack.

Yellow Belly

An ardent Scottish Nationalist
    Cam' fu' o' the Cause the day.
– But the world's aye fu' o' movements;
    What need for anither, pray?

A greater than Christianity
    'Ud alane be worth fashin' aboot,
But this that you're thrang wi, laddie,
    Is haurdly that, I doot.

It's time we had something, ocht,
    That we may vie wi' the rest.
– Juist as I thocht; your slogan is:
    Ilka worm lo'es its ain wriggle best.

Daur you ca' that a Scottish Cause?
    Yellow Belly, hearken to me,
It's a lang worm that has nae turnin'
    – And ane I'd leifer see!

North and South

The vigour of the Northern brain
Shall nerve the world outworn
                    WHITTIER

SINCE Northern plants in Southern lands
    At Southern plants' expense
Must multiply – what weeds were these
    That have been taken hence?
Since England is as English yet
As there were ne'er a Scot in it.

The folk at home are weaklings too.
    The natural law's annulled,
With Sassenach importations now
    The whole of Scotland's dulled.
The plagues that waste the North at times
Are always born in Southern climes.

Letter to R.M.B.

From the Island of Bruse Holm

O, that men's ears should be
To counsel deaf, but not to flattery!
                    TIMON OF ATHENS

MY dear R. M. B., I was still a bit feart
O' madness, o' livin' in a 'warld o' my ain,'
Afore I cam' back to Scotland last time.
Noo that's hailly and forever gane.
And withoot hesitation I'd choose
The grave or the madhoose cell than share
A single 'idea' but twa-three Scots hae –
And wi' these twa-three scarce share ony mair.
Scotland nae mair exists for me

Than it does for ony ordinary suicide.
I've come ti this uninhabited isle
And wi' it and the sea and sky I'll bide
And o' my life here can tell even you
Naething whatever – nae human speech
Can describe a life sae completely foreign
To a' that's wi'in onybody else's reach.
But as a last letter afore I forget
The past as if it had never been
I'll pen my verdict on Scotland here,
Since you're still there, and I hope, my freen',
That you may manage to get clear o't tae
As weel as me – in as different a way
As mine frae Daith's or the Man-in-the-Moon's
          Or ony clean-gyte loon's.

                    .   .   .   .

The lie men worship hasna gi'en them much
And yet they winna abandon it –
Hae less pooer to dae't than ever may be;
The lie that there are truths that a' men fit
To judge canna but be agreed upon,
That naething ever happens withoot a cause,
That reason is the same in a' men and remains
Aye the same itsel' – that there are laws
That sanctify the obvious and justify
The bannin' and denial o' a' that is
Irrational – a' that denies that there
Is grun' for men's feet, no' juist th' abyss.

                    .   .   .   .

Scotland shares this false doctrine to the full,
But unlike ither European lands
Narrows doon reason tae to the grooves
In which the business man or golfer moves
Or politicians like Elliot and Horne
Wha's existence thraws doots on Christ's been born,
And save what sic a man-mole understands
Condemns, as ithers condemn the irrational,

A' the high forms o', sic as they are;
Nay, as the warld at large treats lunacy
And glozes owre daith the sumphs in Scotland gar
A' Art and Poetry and Philosophy
Keep lepers' distance lest they smit
The swinish stupidity that's Scotland's ain
In which nae ither country rivals it
Or seeks to yet – although America
'S no' faur ahint and may level draw
At present progress in a century or twa.

.   .   .

Scotland'll never change. Tho' the deid weight
O' a' these wrang ideas be yet removed
On ither lands, and whasae hauds them still
Be, as their foes are noo held proved,
Regairded as insane – or as the senseless brutes –
Scotland'll bide impervious forsooth,
Pent in a dullness that nae licht can pierce,
Devoid o' sensibility and ruth
On its insensate championship o' a'
That's mindless, mean, and sordid,
A' a Ramsay MacDonald canna preach
Or, ower it, a Harry Lauder lord it.
There is nae ither country 'neath the sun
That's betrayed the human spirit as Scotland's done,
And still the betrayal proceeds to the complete
Dehumanisin' o' the Scottish breed.
Oh, R. M. B., I looked frae Arthur's Seat
On a waur Hell than ony God decreed.

.   .   .

Nae man, nae spiritual force, can live
In Scotland lang. For God's sake leave it tae.
Mak' a warld o' your ain like me, and if
'Idiot' or 'lunatic' the Scots folk say
At least you'll ken – owre weel to argue back –
You'd be better that than lackin' a' they lack.

Bedtime

A little epithalamium for David and Margaret Orr,
Broch Schoolhouse, Island of Whalsay, May, 1933

SHE's like a pond in the woods
   Destined to lie
Reflectin' a circle o' leaves
   And short tract o' sky.

Kennin' nocht o' the vastity
   That surroonds and weighs on it,
A' the firmament and the forest;
   Where nae ither man can gaze on it.

The Scots Renaissance

IT was in these wowf places in years gane by
That the Scots Renaissance had its origins
And bred the unco spirits wha breenged through
Oor douce conventions – Tarras Moor, the Rhinns
O' Galloway – did what Rimbaud socht to
Wi' 'des secrets pour changer la vie' brocht
Frae the lang road that leads to the Hill o' Nocht.

Mim as a may-puddock was the whale
That swallowed Jonah, but less mim than Sime,
The shark o' civilisation swallowed him haill,
But he cam' through't diodon-like in time,
And, safe on the Wauchope side o' Europe, spoke
Things different as Christ frae ither folk.

And Oliver's world in which daylight's abolished
And vocabularies afore then unkent
Spring up like whirlwinds lies next to 'Geele,
Whaur a' body's insane' – by which he meant
The haill world no' whummled i' the New Dark Age
He invented thocht's horrors to assuage.

And here Armstrong lifted a blotchy leaf
Like an umbrella 'twixt his heid and the sun,
And sat under't like Blok's wee Priest o' the Bogs,
Prayin' for each bacillus in the grun'
Singly, by name, and for the White Rose Prince o' Wales,
On the spider-faced song that, if ocht, prevails.

And Blacklock's work like an auld peel-too'er stands
Strang, dour, but if men add useless, toom
– Aye, tomb o' mair than ever they'll jalouse,
It'll stand until the haill earth has nae mair room
For the deid bodies o' nonentities,
Ane wi' the end that naebody foresees.

The Kernigal

A THOOSAND people in this a'e kirkyaird
I kent, and suddenly a' the memories laired
'Neth these green sods, o' looks and ways
And a' the freends an' foes o' my young days
Encompass me – hoo could it be
That ocht could change sicna diversity?

Daith's gi'en nae added stature to them then?
In this vain resurrection they seem to rise
Juist as they were, and sae belittle Daith;
And there is naething in the haill wide world
That is the better for a repeat supply

O' ordinary folk; and so it is
Wi' a' Earth's graves and memories.

O wad they micht rise up afore me noo
Like the auld Kernigal on Warblaw there,
Firs ranked in gloomy corridors,
Tall too'ers each drilled to its straight height
By its close neighbours' command – stern, bare;
– And no' this chaos o' weeds and waste again,
This human scree wi'ts artificial floo'ers.

Scotland, My Scotland!

WHAT have you lain fallow for?
              Scotland, my Scotland,
And why do you waken now, if you do?
It cannot be just to endorse
What the others have done without you?

What have you lain fallow for,
If we still glean more from the fields
That have been under continuous cultivation
Than yours after its long rest yields?

What have you lain fallow for?
How can you once more claim
On the strength of a trivial echo
The proud right of a separate name?

I'd rather you lay fallow forever
Than take what the others provide,
But rise to insist on a quibble
– It was not for this that you died.

It was not for this that you died,
Scotland, my Scotland,
Nor for this that you'll rise again
To challenge other nations' stewardship
In all men's, and God's, eyes again.

The Difference

THE difference between MacCormick and his friends and I
Is this – that they
Constitute the National Party of Scotland,
I am Scotland itself to-day.
They have dared to stake less than the highest
In Scotland's name.
Scotland will shine like the sun in my song
While they vanish, like mists, whence they came.

Lines for a Gaelic University

TO THE HON. R. ERSKINE OF MARR

IGNORANT as the oak is of the elm
And the lily of the rose,
Beautiful like each of Earth's beautiful things
That nothing but God and its own self knows
– Nay, sith, kindred-wise, that knowledge they lack,
Beautiful as the unconscious beauties of those,
As a bird had a spiritual joy in its song
Or a star in the light it shows, –
At last on this Hebridean isle
Where no other culture throws

Confusion on its perfect integrity
Our Gaelic University grows.

As well cry to a lonely bird that flies
As its spirit bids it: 'Whither away
Over lands where other birds happily nest?
You cannot do better. Come down and stay.
O brave the perils of sea and night,
No more in your strange instinctive way
Beating to an unknown shore where at best
You cannot fare other than they,'
As cry that 'Culture no frontiers knows.
We are interdependent to-day.
There can be no sense in holding aloof.'
Gaeldom flies on: 'They say? – Let them say!'

Even as it is with trees so it is
With our Gaelic University,
Each rooted in its own place and keeping
Inexchangeable identity,
Open to the sky and what winds may blow,
Fulfilled in its own form, complete and free,
And knowing nothing else and none the worse
For that, for what could a tree
Learn from aught else? It teaches life nothing
To know other forms of life can be.
Let us lead our own and leave other men's
As the elm leaves the oak, the rose the lily.

The sea that encircles this small isle
Is of our spirit a symbol fit,
For it is one with the ocean that flows
To the ends of the Earth and yet
It rings us off from the whole world here.
So united and severed alike by it
We seem in physical fact, as we are
In spirit, specific and infinite,

Where with nothing between them and the skies
Our candid buildings sit,
And kin to the sun and the moon and the stars
Our lovely lamp of learning is lit.

Wallacetown

TO THE DUKE OF MONTROSE

GUID sakes, your Grace, you shouldna ettle
To draw yon wabblin' length o' metal
For fear your unpractised hand insteed
Should wabble waur and sned your heid.

I doot if a' your martial race,
Wha fell in this or anither place,
Could see your gest, they'd strauchtway dee
A second daith o' hilarity.

But Wallace wight was a sterner cratur;
I doot he'd think it nae lauchin' maitter
For sicna fribble o' a lord
To mock Scotland's cause wi' a museum sword,
And to pit you in your place juist let you feel
A tickle or twa o' the genuine steel.

Epistle to the Philistines

HONOUR your empty Royalty and vicious nobles,
Your great divines, professors, all the lime-lit
Circle of your vain and negligible figureheads. At last
These will not suffice you. You will hunger for the opposite.

And turn to us who knew all these for fools
And laughed all their pretensions – and all yours! – to scorn,
And only by the grace of we isolated Philistines
Obtain your most sorely needed oil and corn.

And speaking for myself, but I think I voice
The feelings of the others, I would fain,
When at last you come, treat you as you have treated us
And deny you the least drop or grain.

Rhymes for the Times

To the Man in the Street

'I DON'T understand economics.'
My dear man, you haven't to.
Who does? Whoever's responsible
For this mess does less than you!
Simply insist on tip-top living
Is all you've got to do
And get rid in quick succession
Of rulers who fail to give it
Till you find someone who does –
And then do your best to live it!

The Root of the Trouble

THERE couldn't be any war
If nobody went;
There couldn't be any poor
Without their own consent.

The Real Snag

THE Problem of Quantity's solved.
There is abundance for all.
But the Problem of Quality now
Confronts us with an insistent call –
    And who can blame the countless host
    Who would fain dodge *that* at any cost?

The Legal System

PEOPLE may learn in course of time
The law exists to make the crime.

Edinburgh Castle

BROODING again on Edinburgh, that unparalleled
Provision for noble functions all unfulfilled,
Mere factor to London now, and Jewry, for the land
That would have been its own if it had rightly willed,
I watch the Castle huddled above the stinking slums,
And see in it the symbol of Scotland's state to-day,
Where between the sunbeams and the shadows slip
The dung-beetles of Empire infesting the esplanade,
The lice-like jewels of Scotland's Crown in foul parade,
Mindless little mercenaries of murder, as is fit
In shapeless uniforms that are the colour of shit,
The excremental interests that have us in their grip,
Would it were boiling made the scum rise this way,
Not cold corruption that from stagnation draws
This impenetrable filth, fastness of lawless laws.

In Memoriam Vladimir Mayakovsky

O WOULD your nature now from Russia gone
Might reincarnate in a Scottish bard;
Some influence from you, some knowledge of your life
By genius's intuition be bestowed usward;
For there are thousands inarticulate here
In Glasgow in the worst slums that Europe knows
That could they speak, with poet's power endowed,
Of your great voice would ring like echoes.
Alas! By your suicide far more is lost
Than Scotland's ever had of what it needs the most,
Or's ever like to have save so by death transferred
A man's tones are at last among our toy-angels heard.

Ode for the 350th Anniversary of Edinburgh University

NOW let Ramsay MacDonald and Lauchlan Maclean Watt,
Harry Lauder and Morton of the 'Rangers'
And all the other 'great Scots' of to-day
(Like the sands of the sea for number they be)
With a bevy of notable strangers
Lift up their voices in pride and praise,
        In congratulation and glee,
For the continued progress (to put it sum-wise,
Since to strike a suitable note one tries)
During the past 350×365 days
        Of Edinburgh University,
And let all the students who won't get jobs
And the thousands whose jobs are not worth having
And the hundreds of thousands who are unemployed
        Stop their untimely laughing,

And the women all busy
With contraceptives to see
That the number of these won't increase
(Without letting that boon activity cease!)
Join in the national – the world-wide – chorus
On the great occasion that is now before us
That pleases Sir Thomas Holland may be
(But is certainly double-dutch to me),
   That notable Scot
   Sir Thomas, but not
A poor aborigine like me!

 Come listen to the Muse of History
 Here where Bruce got his LL.D.
 And Wallace scraped through with a bare M.A.
 And the Deity was 'ploughed,' they say.

It stands to reason that where we have had
An institution like this in our midst so long
We've grown continually in wisdom and power,
Ensued the right and eschewed the wrong,
And that accounts for our state to-day,
The glorious influence the University's had
In every phase of our national being.
You've only to give a casual look round
In any direction the choice fruits to be seeing.
A century ago we had a mediocre place
In the arts – and now we have none at all;
Other nations have stuck to their national culture –
We wouldn't be subject to any such thrall,
But cast our language and literature away
In favour of English – with the blessings you see;
And for that of course the main thanks are due
   To Edinburgh University.

 You must judge an institution like this
 By its alumni who have soared to the highest
 Places in Church and State, the Services, Business –
 And not by a 'stickit minister' like Christ.

Let professional etiquette be maintained
And the honour of the Alma Mater;
And any concern with anything else
Can come later, of course – much later!

And now like our culture we're shedding fast
Our basic industries, all trekking south.
Fools may think that's wrong but they'll hear
A different tale from the sapient mouth
Of every distinguished person here.
They know the benefits that – gradually – accrue
(Gradually, for three hundred and fifty years
Aren't long to such a Godlike place it appears)
And aren't dismayed by such obvious things
(Blessings in disguise if you only knew –
For you mustn't judge by appearances
Any more than you did by the Highland Clearances)
As increasing difficulty, destitution, disease –
Such a general predicament only clings
Like mud from a 'bus to the outer walls
      Of such great academic halls;
And if Scotland's strange centrifugal policy,
      So seemingly suicidal,
Is the opposite of all other nations, why, that
Is due to the superior *savoir faire*
      (Trust them to guide all!)
Of those in this ancient building taught.

O don't worry about the Crisis! –
Hasn't ex-Principal Ewing
Dealt with it in terms that should have set
All decent people spewing?

And it doesn't matter in any case
What happens to the Scottish race, you see.
There will always be plenty of Chinks and Japs,
And English, in this University!

The greater the Crisis the greater the need
For all our peculiar 'Varsity services.
Who can beat us at breaking strikes
And bringing the *canaille* to their knees?
Who can man more ably than we
The cute little steel-boxes that all around
The police are establishing just in case
The crowd's misled by the fools at the Mound?
Who would supply if it wasn't for us
The young officers always ready to throw
Their own lives – and other people's – away
For no good cause so far as they know
Since the University never has taught
Discrimination in details like that?
O we've plenty to do and no mistake
What with black-legging, snobbery, sport and so on.
Let others worry over serious affairs.
We're the Fascisti who think of ourselves alone,

> The mercenaries
> Of money yet,
> The cadets better described
> Without the 'et.'

> *Let common people but us no buts,*
> *And think no more of their empty guts*
> *But just gape round adoring their betters*
> *And crying how they are all our debtors.*

> *Come all you blue-eyed cherubim*
> *With a proper Nordic stride*
> *And gay girl-students with golden hair –*
> *And leave the dirt outside!*

It's true of course that we can't produce
A creative artist worth a damn;
Poets, dramatists, and wild-fowl like that,
Are sadly to seek to swell our psalm,

And always have been ever since Burns
Failed so cruelly in his entrance-exam.
It's equally true none of the big noises
In science, etc., in the world to-day –
And least of all in Finance – belong here;
But of second-rates we've a rich array –
The men who do the super-donkey work,
The slave-drivers, the factors for the rulers, –
And hordes of expert parasites,
Sinecure-holders and mob-befoolers.

> For we are the incubi,
> The careerists, the toadies,
> The distinguished lickspittles,
> And Honours degree nobodies.

> Oh, Edinburgh University
> Can still hold its head
> Up proudly enough –
> In the slums round it spread!

O well may the Medical Faculty flourish
For everything is conspiring well.
The infant mortality statistics
And insanity figures continue to swell,
But it's certainly a privilege to die
In an Edinburgh-trained doctor's hands
And go to the Heaven specially prepared
By our flourishing Divinity graduands –
For nothing thrives better of course
On decay than Christianity.
So all things work together for good
And behind our doctors and parsons stand
Our Science Departments with armaments,
Mustard gas and what not all planned
For all the civil and other wars needed
To ensure the due continuance
Of Religion and Social Hygiene and lead

The ignorant masses a fine old dance
In the future as in the past, for the glory
Of Edinburgh University's priceless story.

So we'll go on as we've always done
In complete indifference to the common-weal,
And praise each other for our noble work
And bring the crowds like curs to heel
By ballyhoo where that will serve
And when it won't – why then, by steel!
And leave Scotland's condition more and more
Our remarkable worth to reveal.

You might think a University in
A declining land like Scotland would be
Small beer too, but that's where you're wrong
As a great occasion like this lets you see.
I remember the late Conan Doyle describing
How a glorious cancer like marble compared
With the miserable carrion it battened upon.
Edinburgh University a like rôle has shared
To poor old Scotland's woeful condition.
And will flourish the more Scotland sinks to perdition.

Sir Harry Lauder

YOU'VE played England's game and held Scotland up
    To ridicule wherever you've gone,
Yet it was a different ladder behind the scenes
    You crawled to knighthood on.

We all know the tale of the clown who completes
    His turn though his heart is breaking,
But what of the clown who sugar-coats cannon-balls
    For his dupes with the fun he's making,

What of the clown who debauches the minds
  Of the workers from their real concerns
And serves their betrayers with lying propaganda
  For the filthy lucre he earns?

The workers have not too much fun in their lives
  And gladly they paid you well.
You took their cash; and double-crossed them then
  And sold them into Hell.

Who told of the Black Watch men kept standing
  Naked all night at the salute
By their German captors; then forced to run back
  Over No-Man's-Land for the brutes to shoot?

You did, you liar! The Order of Knighthood
  Is mostly made up of knaves and fools,
But you are the lowest it's come to yet –
  The basest of murder's tools.

Durchseelte

FOR MRS. HERBERT READ

I THOCHT when I saw it first
There was neist to nae need
For a'e bird to kyth in a world
Where a' else seemed deid.

But I saw when I heard it cry
It had juist to begin it
For a' else to crowdle itsel'
And be, silently, in it.

Riding in a Fog

FOR PROFESSOR HERBERT READ

MEN o' action dinna need
A course set clear afore them.
Gi'e me the men wha feel blin' fog
To poo'ers like God's restore them.

Wha ride wi' a' forgotten
Except what they love best
And *that* – shapeless like the wind,
Openin' nae way through the rest.

Something vaguer, deeper, commoner,
Than ony form, they choose;
And exult that ithers canna
Ken hoo deep are their views.

Breaking the Ice

IT stood there by the frozen loch,
    A ghaist o' a bird,
And watched me wi' een I couldna mak' oot
    Till I cam' wi'in reach. It stirred,

Silently opened its grey wings and gar'd
    The haill world shift,
And the sun was a ring roond ane o' its legs
    Hyne awa' in the lift.

Scots Dyke

MONY's the time hereaboot I've
Seen a foumart I've happened to gliff
Chark in its anger as if
A bit o' the dyke cam' alive.

Or ane o' the English breed
Wha' looked, on the point o' daith,
As if they'd twal sets o' teeth each, tho', faith,
Ane amang them was sune mair than they'd need.

Jesusina MacDonald: or, The Only Way Out

THE whole thing has been settled. Christ
Will return as a woman you know
And he – she – won't be born in a manger
This time, but – let me whisper low –

In Number 10 Downing Street no less;
And of a man – yes, of course, Ramsay!
He'll be suddenly seized at the postponed meeting
Of the World Economic Committee.

And whisked into bed in the nick of time
For the Second Advent to occur
In far better circumstances than the first
Which was badly arranged – but trust Ramsay and her!

What'll happen then? The most I can say
Is just look at the world and see
All Christianity has done. The she-Christ
Cannot do less than the he one surely!

God hadn't meant it to be so soon
But Ramsay's getting on and nobody else'd do.
When approached he agreed it was his duty
– And modestly admitted he'd thought of it too!

In Dury Voe

WHAT are men taught by ane o' the millions
O' the sma' stars they see set faur oot o' reach,
Like an arrested snawstorm there in the sky?
As much as my poem'll ettle to teach.

What could men learn o't if it chanced that the haill
O' the warld at aince lay open to discern?
As little's a' lear put thegither can tell,
Nae mair than that o' my poem they'll learn.

The Northern Muse

AWA' here where nae wumman has been
And where noo nane ever can be
I thocht for a meenut my Muse
Had come in the flesh to me.

I'm still apt to think in the terms
O' the human life I fashed wi' owre lang,
The swish o' the Northern Lichts
Misled me – yet I wasna faur wrang.

Shibboleth

IF the sangs I sing here
　　To men were wafted alang
There's at least a'e thing they'd ken
　　O' the source whence they sprang.

They'd cry a' at aince
　　As I whiles dae mysel'
'Guid kens where they come frae
　　– But they've a fell fishy smell.'

They come frae the source
　　O' a' life, sparklin' wi' saut
– Forerinners o' the Flood
　　In which Earth'll sune be recaught.

Two O'Clock in the Morning

NOO the rest o' Scotland's asleep, but I walk here
　　And brood wi' a lanely mind
On the stars in the heavens, and the poets
　　Sae faur awa' frae mankind.

A Mountain of Music

A MOUNTAIN of music
　　Comes up frae the sea,
In whiter wings hidden
　　In white mist frae me.

Merrily, merrily
  It rings in my ears
– 'Happy who hears not,
  Happy who hears.'

The Catch from Above

IT is wi' poetry as it is wi' herrin' fishin' when
The catch doesna enter the net frae below
But frae abune, and sinks it to the sea-flair then
And even the buoys gang faddoms deep; and the herrin' show,
Shinin' solid, ten cran in ilka net, fu' raxed frae the buoy tow
Doon to the bush-raip – it's then the fishers ha'e to tyauve, I trow,
Yet as they heave on them the nets cant and skail.
A lot o' ony divine gift's lost without fail.
Aye, and it is wi' poetry as it is wi' herrin' withal;
There's never a guid market for owre guid a haul.

To Charles Doughty

Ev'N eild wi' creation
Till a century back
– And that's added little
Eneuch to it, alack! –

Watchin' the cauld clutch
O' a warld aff its eggs
You spent your days; and what mair
Could a true man, fegs?

Hauf-men flew heidlang
Wi' the doited cratur.
You stood fast; Doughty
By name and by natur'.

And slow as the movements
O' continents in the sea
Risin' and fallin' again
Is your influence in me.

Let the warld tak' its eind
In your noble pages
– Abune a' Europe, puir aizle ! –
And wi' God be ages.

Coronach for the End of the World

FOR FIONN MAC COLLA

LIKE them or no' you canna deny
If you think the maitter owre
The Pipes are the only instrument
To soond Earth's mortal hour.

They should be keepit for that you think?
The joke may pass but yet
A fittin' fareweel to a' that's been
Is nae ither wise to get.

Mony a piper has played himsel'
Through battle and into daith,
And a piper'll rise to the occasion still
When the warld is brakin', faith !

A trumpet may soond or harps be heard
Or celestial voices sweet,
But wi' nocht but the cry o' the Pipes can Earth
Or these – or silence – meet.

The Pipes are the only instrument
To soond Earth's mortal hour;
But to greet what follows, if onything does,
Is no' in even their power.

The Frontier: or The War with England

HIS first thocht when he fund that he was lost
And didna ken which country he was in
– Scotland or England – was: 'Gin this leaks oot
Then my political career is din.

'I couldna meet in Cranston's tearooms syne
And pop my pow up wi' the lave and crack
O' which o' us'll tak' this job and that
Aince Scotland gets its national Parliament back.

'Is that a lost sheep yammerin' in the dark
Or the Nationalist M.P. for Auchtermuchty
Makin' his maiden speech in Parliament?
– A maiden speech, wi' nae virginity!

'Is that a lost sheep yammerin' in the dark
Or just the Nation's voice or my ain soul's?
Hyuch, caulder than the wund the thocht o' a'
The press'll say the morn aboot me rolls.

'"Poet's intuition baffled by peats.
Nationalism whummled on Border moor.
Countries Indistinguishable in Dark.
Daily Record's Competition – Midnight Tour.

'"Scottish Party trains reid herrin' as guides.
Novelist suggests a phosphorescent line.
Where is it? Pictures. Prizes for Replies.
MacDiarmid denies he'd owre muckle wine."

'And caulder still the thocht I still can think
Ocht o' they say; and that the Movement's built
Upon foundations open to the like
And that I share the Glesca coterie's guilt!

'No' that I ever let them trust me – quite.
They felt I wasna ane o' them at heart
And never planned as glibly wi' me there
Wha'd play or this or that word-shakin' part.

'A cleckin' o' ambitious naebodies
Foreseein' each ither in sic and sic a post
– Prime Minister and Chancellor and sae on –
Owre cups o' tea and dominoes o' toast.

'No' ane o' them wi' harns abune contempt
(Best o' oor race in some respects albeit)
Tho' that's nae bar in ony country noo
But vera passport to a Cabinet seat.

'A country capable o' Jimmy Thomas
Is capable o' ocht; I wadna wonder
But McWhapple and the rest o' them are richt
And I'll triumph yet by sinkin' faurer under. ...

'The influence I've had's been mainly due
To knowledge o' spheres o' Scotland maist men ha'e
Less o' than I o' where the Line lies noo.
I aye could fa' on them like nicht or day.

'Aye, coup upon their tittlin' thochts the dark
O' kennin' a billion times better than the lave
The relation o' the little that we ken
To a' we dinna. Like Death on Life I pressed

'(Or thocht I did – this teaches me) on folk
Content to play wi' ready-made ideas,
Newspaper paragraph conceptions o' oor land,
That 'ud gar the bluid o' ony true man freeze.

'Quicker than ony wund that ever blew
In Polar regions – or Edinburgh even;
The untholeable guff that mak's it ill
To tell deid folk in Scotland frae the leevin'

'If ony's really leevin' but mysel'
If in nocht else in intuition ane
Wi' what made Scotland (Men made little o't
And still less o' themsel's) – Nicht, Wund, and Rain!

'My intuitions'll be clearer still
If I survive this nicht, for Scotland's here
To a degree that fain I'd see breenge through
The N.P. roof, and change the atmosphere.

'They wadna recognise you, Scotland – 'phone
The weel-ca'd Sillytae to pit you oot;
A roarin' torrent wi' nae delegate caird,
A howlin' void – in Bolshie pay, nae doot.

'A swatch o' forest, flappin' in the blast
Micht gar them think my heid was in the plot.
"*A point o' order*" – Wha the Devil's that?
Tip a bit landslide doon the puir nyauf's throat!

'Guid sakes, *that* Oliver Hope? The dainty man!
His kilt's sair slarried. What's that in his cheek?
His tongue? Or just the Scotland he's tryin' to use
As Demosthenes the pebble in learnin' to speak?

'It's easier for him to swallow that
Than for us to swallow his pretensions, fegs!
Chirpin' o' Scotland in the nit-wit terms
O' Kelvinside! – Up, Chaos, how awa' his legs!

'Owre wi'm! Never mind his pocket lookin'-glass,
Mak' a Pompeii o' his pomposity.
Gi'e what he says the wecht it's time it had,
Nocht solid agrees wi' maist folk till they dee . . .

'Och, damn it! I've forgotten efter a',
I dinna ken if 'ts Scotland here or no'.
I'll hae to think the maitter thoroughly oot.
– No' juist clap Cumberland owre Hope and Co.!'

Welcome to the PEN Delegates

GENIUS of Europe, welcome to the land
Fit least of all your gifts to understand,
Yet happ'ly, so unable to perceive
Its incapacity you'll needs receive
A greater, if a queerer, welcome here,
Despite the absence of a single peer
To midwife you to our insensate mob,
Who, therefore, must themselves take on the job
And give you the unspeakable sensation
Of being mothered by a Yahoo nation. . . .
Genius of Europe, welcome to a land
That best of all your gifts can understand,
If you are not too nice to nuzzle-nuzzle
Like any pig and with us guzzle-guzzle.

As if this Muse or that had suddenly found
Herself transported from her sacred ground
To some Defectives' Fête or Highland Mod
– Nay, you would find even these a sight less odd,
Or Wet Review, Assembly Levée even,
Than this lewd spectacle beyond conceiving,
Crémieux and Benda here at Holyrood
Convened with Annie Swan and Harvey Wood
And Däubler and Čapek exchanging views
With 'Riff-Raff' of the *Scotsman* and the *News*.

Pye on 'The Drama' shows how drink and whores
Are 'awfa' coamic' when a padre snores.

The Spaniel fawns, and Wooden beats his name.
Even Bella Millar squirms in hopes of fame,
Till inch by inch you find yourselves o'ercome
By the rank weeds that deck Lord Darnley's tomb
Fed by the wells of all inanity.

Was it for this you braved the raging sea?
– To feel a deadlier sickness on dry land,
Till in your gorge the whole damned island
Crew makes you spew! If you have genius, friends,
You'll need it all before this business ends.

For hark! The Joy Bell rings! And who survive
Channel and Holywood at last arrive
At the *chef d'œuvre* of all the week's events.
The Congress as a final treat presents
The Caledonian Hunt! The privileged few
Who witness this their visit ne'er can rue
If they outlive the ardours of the chase
O' the Golden Stag, the pride of Scotia's race,
Arranged on a titanic scale for you,
With high and low combing the country through.
All other sports are bagatelles to this,
Whose range, whose vehemence, you must not miss
Else you miss all that's quintessentially Scots,
For little else is ever in our thoughts.
It would indeed be very funny
If we thought aught of aught but money.

Well may our noblest rite upon us act
Like those pipenotes upon the rats that packed
Old Hamelin Town. See how it holds us all,
Playwrights, essayists, nondescripts, in thrall.
As when tempestuous Nature in a torment
Pours out her prodigies and Heaven is rent
With fearful glories, Scotland here emits
In speedy sequence to your gaze her wits
(Nitwits!) and seers, lords, priests, and business men,
And women too, unheard of until then,

Thrust into low relief by this tense game,
Nonentities in everything but name.
And, above all, the potent *pisseurs d'encre*
Who, subs. and copy-boys, rank on (more) rank,
Thunder in cubby-holes and make Earth quake.
Do not commit the pardonable mistake
Of slighting them, for, though you know them not,
Their backstair powers must never be forgot.
Their weasel minds the least of them quintuple
By underhand intrigue and lack of scruple,
And like a weasel pack they always go
Wriggling like one though twenty form the row.
Full worthy members of the Pen are they;
We'd have no Centre left were they away.
– And none will welcome you as you will see
More royally – or more egregiously.
Brains, looks, etcetera, cancel out. They prize
Only their mercenary expertise,
And over every precipice profound
Pursue Earth's nimblest quarry to the ground.
Culture, and art, and fame are not their quest,
Louse-skinning for the leather with the best.

The great day dawns. The glorious sport's begun.
We sally forth with shepherd, bark, and gun.
You'll crookshank on these moors, but have a care
– Is that the sun or sixpence shining there?
It seems as though the very heavenly light
Winks from a bottle labelled Black-and-White.
Behold! Yonder is power indeed. No goat
More nimbly leaps from peak to peak of thought.
He ranges wanton over all the arts,
Displaying at every turn his hinder parts,
While islanded in his own tallow see
An ex-divine who like the Deity,
Lives in a lighthouse lit by his own wick
Round which old spinsters' fancies flutter quick.

And still they come. The changing shapes of clouds
Before a gale are nothing to the crowds
Of novelists who, in huge remainders, now
Stampede the scene behind Blake's beefy brow,
Buck and bestride, like bullock (or bull-calf)
In lusty style – the only style they have,
While kilted Tearlach, standing cap in hand,
Cheers on the dirty work from Barra's strand.
– But mind your step lest from its lair you wake
On these high hills the dreaded Tartan Snake!

And whose th' amorphous form that looms afar,
Veiled prophet sitting on a tinsel star,
Biding his time in dudgeon, proof to sense,
Dabbler in mummeries? – the bald-faced Spence!

And whose these weirdest forms of all you ask,
Each like some old witch-doctor in his mask?
These are the Business Men, who run the show.
The rest are but their fatuous tools you know.
These pay the piper – call the tune you hear,
Which, liked or not, at least is ne'er too dear.

And ah! the ladies! What is any cause
That lacks the final imprint of their claws?
The Game! They'll run the Game to death all right.
What's lost by day they always find by night.
And so the outcome of this high occasion
May be a profit to the Scottish nation.

Since Scotland's welcome to the Pee Ee En
Is simply this: 'In with your gruntles!' then
Accept, my friends, the Order of the Trough,
Enough for us for you is more than enough.
With haggis, singed sheep's head, and potted meat
You'll find us stranger than the foods we eat.
There is no meeting-ground save on this level.
It's Hobson's Choice. Come on – or go to the Devil!

Nekrasov

ONLY a spirit such as yours will serve;
Thousands of verses in one continuous jet of gall,
Acrid dissolvent of hypocrisy and spiritual oppression
And all the treacheries that hold mankind in thrall.

The generous aspiration of the young give way
To apathetic acquiescence in the order of things.
Nihilism dies down and ceases on maturity.
– To you alone time's flight a sterner passion brings.

Personal prosperity did not serve to change
Your attitude to society nor yet
This petty seeming triumph or that prevail
From its first savagery to soften it.

So may it be with me; I too would run
In deepening channels of the darkest ire;
The only modification of my wrathful gloom
The lesser darkness mine when I expire.

Nemertes

NOT much to look at many of these business men,
But they remind me of Nemertes, 'bootlaces' as he's called;
A shrimper turning over a boulder may pass him by
As just a bit of red-brown stone, but would be appalled
To see his real nature – put him in a rock-pool then,
Introduce a shrimp, the 'stone' at once proves to be
A worm of seemingly unlimited length. So with these drab
And undistinguished men in our economy!

T

Veuchen

THE sun that has lit the world a' day
Its last beam here is content to lay,
No' on a hill but on this laich sod,
No' on a tree but on this puir weed.
Earth sprang frae less. It wadna be odd
If ocht mair to be lies here in seed.

Look at it! Look at it! Awa' wi' your greed!
It's less, no' mair, ony poet can need.
Look at it! Look at it! For a' you ken
You may never set een on ocht again.
The sun's content tho' a' else is away.
I feel as tho' I had waled it tae.

Art and the Workers

I COME away with a heavy heart
From these fellow-workers' homes. My sadness can be
Best illustrated, I think, by the fact
That each of these houses has two or three
Framed pictures of the grocer's calendar type
.... The antithesis, the foe, of all art.

I wonder how men like these
With a knowledge of the dynamics of pitch
In propellor blades, say, or the distribution
Of forces in a ball-bearing, which
Enables them to share imaginatively
In the action of mechanical functions,
Can endure such monstrosities.

I want no pictures of the King or Queen,
General Haig or Christ or the Madonna,
Shaggy cattle knee-deep in a mountain tarn,
Or pretty rural scene. Photography is the art
Of super-reality, essentially mechanical, essentially human,
But the converse of Humanistic. Then give me
Good photographs of a line of high pressure
Oil switches in a grid station, of turning
An insulator base to size, and the like,
That I may to some extent participate imaginatively
In the marvels of machinery still beyond my ken,
The extension of my, and my fellows', day's work,
Day's work and life's work, in endless range and precision and power,
The inexhaustible delight of my eyes.
Religion, exploitation, Kings and Queens, Nature
Are unthinkable anachronisms – museum pieces – here;
Reinforcing tungsten steel with chocolate,
Eking out arc lamps with 'the inner light.'
Function indicates form in a general way
But does not dictate it; the artist's task
Is to choose from a variety of forms,
Each equally adequate functionally,
The one æsthetically most satisfying.
Never too much concerned with form in the abstract or not enough
With form in relation to the means by which it is produced,
I compare all the forms I can see. I try to think
Of at least as practical but far lovelier forms.
I revel, among my photographs,
In the æsthetic of the moment
In all three senses of the word.
We are concerned with the here and now,
The day to day conditions, the particular job,
Experimenters, always ready to scrap old plant.
Let others rejoice – it is not for us –
That humanity keeps growing in omnitude
Like a teratoma cyst in a eunuch.
We do not believe in autonomous values
Set over us, unaffected by temporal change,

Or that differences are only evolved to be
Resumed into undifferentiated oneness again.
Philosophy is not the enhancement but the denial of life.
There is something decadent, even something depraved,
In an attempt to achieve a completely coherent world of experience.
But fancy engineers with stuff on their walls,
In their minds, as if they were yokels,
Or old women, or ministers! Ugh!

My Sailor Son Comes Home

After the German of Stefan George

MY muckle son has grown sae faur awa' frae me,
Oot o' this warld into anither a'thegither,
That lookin' at him, bearded, sunburnt, back frae the sea,
I find it hard to feel I'm really still his mither.

Sae infinitely faur awa', and yet my ain,
O look he's back a giant wha gaed to sea a loon!
And, fegs, he's faurest frae me noo he's come hame again
Wi' a sinfu' rowth o' growth owre sudden and owre soon.

His een are fu' o' secrets that are no' for me to share.
It's no' his mither's lips cleave sweestest to his taste.
Losh me! To hae a bairn's an unco queer affair,
And me wi' airms owre airgh to gang roond the critter's waist.

Personalities and the Machine Age

Personality crushed out? Slaves to machines?
What personality ever had they then?
The sight, with knowledge, of any great machine
Games still, alas, to all too few men.
They are fearing something they know nothing about
Out of blind funk in case they lose
Something they never had – a base deception, a myth,
Created by their exploiter, an enslaving ruse.

No man who has the cleanness and efficiency
Of any great machine and the ability
To run it is taken in by this piffling cant
Of loss of precious personality.
Scottish people, Glasgow people, should be the last
To deceive themselves or to be deceived
By rubbish of this sort. What is there
In religion or the past to be believed
– What else is there to Glasgow's credit,
What else is any future founded on
Worth having it can have – if not the power, the beauty
Of great machines? Let poetlings moan
About primroses and skylarks and the Lord knows what;
Not the matters of crucial concern to most folk
Any poet worth a rap would be hammering at.
The only poet of value Glasgow ever had, Livingstone,
Knew better – he sang not of himself but of a cause,
Not of personal ambition, regret disillusionment,
And held in contempt the weak yearnings of love,
Concerned with the great historical forces.
Personality? Watching the tinpot wheels
Of twopence-ha'penny souls going round,
The whole damned human Woolworth's! – In Glasgow
Something infinitely more worth seeing can be found
In crank-heads flashing rhythmically between
Twin columns hiding flying crossroads and thrusting silver rods;
The starboard shaft oiled and shining in the blaze of the electric
    lights
Turning its eighty revolutions a minute. My sympathies
Are with the workers, not the country clods.
Just look at the difference today
Between most professional painters and the photographers.
The camera men show far more enterprise and true originality.
They are far more closely in touch
With the ramifications of modern life.
Light and shade mean everything to them.
They must have an infinite capacity
To wait hours, and days if need be,

For the right moment. This would exhaust
The patience of most painters.
Corrugated iron, cotton reels, steel rods,
A net over a capstan on a quayside,
A study of taxicabs seen under two arches!
The artists think too much of themselves,
Take the phenomena of the outer world
Too much for granted, and concentrate
On self-expression – and have nothing to express.
Happy practitioners of a younger and newer craft
The photographers still look out on the world
With eyes of inquiry and wonder; they escape
The narrow environment of their petty personalities,
Lose themselves in the fascination of all the marvel
That light reveals to a zealous observer,
And in losing themselves they find themselves.
– So will all men yet in the Machine Age!

The Glen of Silence

πέφρικα τὰν ὠλεσίοικον
θεόν οὐ θεοῖς ὁμοίαν

AESCHYLUS: *The Seven Against Thebes*

By this cold shuddering fit of fear
My heart divines a presence here,
Goddess or ghost yclept;
Wrecker of homes. . . .

G. M. Cookson's translation, *vide*
Four Plays of Aeschylus, p. 142

Where have I 'heard' a silence before
Like this that only a lone bird's cries
And the sound of a brawling burn today
Serve in this desolate glen but to emphasize?

Every doctor knows it – the stillness of foetal death,
The indescribable silence over the abdomen then!
A silence literally 'heard' because of the way
It stands out in the auscultation of the abdomen.

Here is an identical silence picked out
By a bickering burn and a lone bird's wheeple
– The foetal death in this great 'cleared' glen
Where the *fear-tholladh nan tighean*[1] has done its foul work
– The tragedy of an unevolved people!

A silence burdening two-thirds of Scotland now!
While, in our belt of mining-towns and the like,
There is an awful sense of the presence of death.
Poverty? – Ah, but the difference must strike

[1] The Destroyer of Homes.

Whoever knows Spain, where the poverty's far worse
Yet under it life still springs fresh and alert,
Whereas over Scotland an appalling weight hangs
And everything is morbid, hopeless, and inert.

Half a millenium ago in adamantine verse
Proudly utilising a wealth of historical truth
George Buchanan celebrated in the Scottish people
A cat-like vitality, through many centuries forsooth
Like that amazing vigour, vitality, strength
Of the common people of Spain, which saw unexhausted
Romans, Visigoths, Moors, Napoleon
– That '*Improvisación creadora ibérica*'
The indefinable quality which astounded Napoleon and Wellington.

– It is gone, forever, incredibly, gone.
Fain would I cry again today
'My faith is in the Commons of Scotland'
But alas! it is gone, it is a' wede away.
Scotland is in the last stages of the fell disease
ἀβουλία; and in its glens there is only peace – peace?

The peace indeed that passeth understanding!
For Scotland – Scotland! – has thrown her hand in!
And Alba[1] produces a wretched alibi
At the bar of human history.

The people crawl about – decaying things,
Their clothes like damp mould on trees, their faces green,
Beyond all doctoring – ghosts, we gaze at each other
As though the River of Oblivion ran between;
Vitality, mentality, spirituality, sociality
All sucked away – and on dumps round our ghost towns laid
A rusting wreckage of machinery, like hopes betrayed.

A dynamic spirit like me? No. I can do little or nothing.
This terrible apathy cramps my style.
I am doomed to sing as though I were a blind deaf mute.
Eutrephelia has no effect on an imbecile.

[1] Ancient name for Scotland, pronounced 'alaba.'

Let this be Scotland's epitaph when at last she lies
In the unconsecrated ground where the abortions are hidden:
'Which do you think should have won the prize
'Mong all Europe's nations to Time's contest bidden?
Scotland here, undoubtedly,
Scotland was by far the best.
Why she had as many hills and dells,
Almost, as Mae West!'

Set in golden letteris then this ressoun:
'Pride of Earth's landis, Scotland, Europe's croun,
Sumtyme countit the floo'er of Nationheid
Under this stane, late lipper, lyis deid.'

Three Wars

I TOO fought simultaneously in the Three Wars;
The official War, and the secret, bitter, and desperate War
By which most men forced themselves to carry on from day to day,
And the Third War – of rising hatred against those at home
Or safely behind the line, making profit or glory out of it,
The War Makers, the War Profiteers, and all the morons by whose
    consent
Such swine could be. Henceforth I fight in the Third War only.

Under the Hallior Moon

Hoo odd it seems on a nicht like this
When the shadows come walkin' oot frae the rocks
That God should ha' gien us nae greater size
When he finally made up his mind to mak' folks!

The Black Rainbow Over the Minch

A black rainbow owre the Minch
Needna mak' onybody flinch,
It means juist aboot the same
As gin the usual colours came.

The Auld Houff

The Houff that stood here's
Vanished drap and drain.
I'd leifer a' else
In creation had gane,

And let us sit on,
A pack o' auld scamps,
Smokin' like chimlies
And drinkin' like lamps.

The glint o' the whisky
'Ud ha'e ser'd us for licht
And the blue reek hidden
The lack o' ocht else frae oor sicht.

Wha's unbiggit the Houff,
And left – the sun, is't? or mune?
Lichtin' the world like a toom pipe
When the last fill's dune?

What Has Been May Be Again

(*Timely footnotes to famous passages in George Buchanan's* Epithalamium *for Mary Stuart and the Dauphin of France and in Corneille's* Horace.)

As long ago the never-conquered Scots
Stopped the extension of the Roman Empire
So may it be their proud role again today
To prevent the power to which the Fascists aspire.

As long ago almost alone among the nations
When barbarian invasions shook the power of Rome
Scotland gave refuge to the banished Muses,
So now, more direly menaced, may it prove again their home.

And as through many centuries Scotland stood
Shoulder to shoulder in unbreakable alliance with France,
Today when perfidious England favours Germany
Let Scotland to break from England seize its chance,
And reuniting with its immemorial ally
Foil the foul plot and their joint glory once more enhance.

Just so, every decent man in the world today
Must launch against the new Italian infamy
Corneille's great curse again, brought up to date:
'Rome, l'unique objet de mon ressentiment!

Rome, à qui vient ton bras d'immoler mon amant !
Rome, qui t'a vu naître, et que ton cœur adore !
Rome, enfin, que je hais parce qu'elle t'honore !
Puissent tous ses voisins ensemble conjurés
Saper ses fondements encore mal assurés !
Et si ce n'est assez de toute l'Italie,
Que l'Orient contre elle à l'Occident s'allie ;
Que cent peuples unis des bouts de l'univers
Passent pour la détruire et les monts et les mers !
Qu'elle-même sur soi renverse ses murailles,
Et de ses propres mains déchire ses entrailles !
Que le courroux du ciel allumé par mes vœux
Fasse pleuvoir sur elle un déluge de feux !
Puissé-je de mes yeux y voir tomber ce foudre,
Voir ses maisons en cendre, et tes lauriers en poudre,
Voir le dernier Romain à son dernier soupir,
Moi seule en être cause et mourir de plaisir !'

In the Slums of Glasgow

A LOT of the old folk here – all that's left
Of them after a lifetime's infernal thrall
Remind me of a Bolshie the 'Whites' buried alive
Up to his nose – just able to breathe, that's all.

Watch them; you'll see what I mean; when found
His eyes had lost their former gay twinkle.
Ants had eaten *that* away; but there was still
Some life in him – his forehead *would* wrinkle.

And if most of the working-class could be made
Like that from birth onwards, the bosses, by jings,
– Still as genial and Christian personally, of course! –
Would say, even believe, it was just in the nature of things!

A Poet Rejects a Right-Wing Plea

WE are transported into the flaming heart of the world;
We stand in a place to which all roads come;
In a light which makes all riddles clear.

Love and Pain, Terror and Ecstasy,
Strife and Fulfilment, Blasphemy and Prayer, are one another's
      shadows,
Meeting and fading in a single radiance that is not light or heat,
But a movement, a flowing, that carries us along
And yet leaves us steadier, more certain than we ever were before.

'It will take', you say, 'a very good poet, and a very stable politician,
To achieve the simplicity that accepts and subsumes all the
      complexities.'
But that is not our task – but to eliminate, outgrow
The complexities, as the world of life outgrew
The unwieldy statures and the monstrous shapes
Of prehistoric life.

It is no use saying to me
That what we need
Is an imagination reaching out
To embrace the human reality,
Which unites the combatants.
The other monkeys had their points
But man evolved from a particular kind
And humanity must outgrow our enemies here,
As life in its various lines has outgrown
Many of the forms it took in earlier days
And which are now extinct.
So, pro-Fascist, we are resolved
On the elimination from life

Of all that you stand for and are,
Knowing it is already an intolerable anachronism
With no more relation to us
Than the gorilla retains to man.

It is no more the poet's task
To reconcile the opposite beliefs
Which animates the Right and the Left
– To engender the recognition of one's foe,
As in some sense a partner in a common struggle,
Of which the issue is in the hands of 'God,'
Than it is mankind's task to undo
The circumstances which bred out the saurians,
And bring them back into life again;
Or the gardener's duty not to set aside
A plot for some particular flower or fruit,
But to grow them all on the same patch of ground,
And somehow reconcile and make them grow
With a certain harmony and mutual advantage side by side!
Or the animal lover's task
Not to keep doves in a dovecot and rabbits in a hutch
But rather leave them wild in a world
Which also contains snakes and stoats.
– I am not interested in a plea to 'Live and let live,'
When it means to abandon the right to pick and choose
Between the poison and the antidote,
On the ground that they mutually grow alongside each other
And are both manifestations of life.

These considerations concern us no more
Than would a cry that it is the poet's task
While yet in the flesh,
To write not as a man
But as the angel he might soon become
If our Christian doctrine were right.

We will lose something in the process
– Some characteristics of brute strength,

Of stature and other primitive endowments,
For which, later, at a safe distance,
We may entertain some admiration,
But which life will never recapture, any more
Than it will recapture the size of the saurian monsters,
The proportions of mammoth and mastodon.
– And any such 'loŝs' will be far more than made good
By what we gain.

1944

The Fall of France

TO MY FRIEND PROFESSOR DENIS SAURAT OF L'INSTITUT
FRANÇAIS, LONDON

... THIS terrible tale of the Fall of France
Will be to all free men in the years to come
As to us the sombre history of the Commune,
That terrible echo of past years that rang again in our ears
In the days of the Reichstag fire, in the days of Vienna,
And since the October of Asturias
Is today haloed with light.
Without the experience of the Commune
Would the workers of Russia have marched
To the Soviet victory?
To what victories will the workers of the world
Not yet march in the immortal light of Spain?
– And in the darkness of fallen France?

The lesson to be derived from the Fall of France,
Black as history makes it,
Is it a lesson of despair?
Is it the dismaying moral
Of other love stories
Which finish on a tomb?
The shots of Galliffet did not truly kill Marie Rose,[1]
They pierced but one Marie Rose.
Marie-Rose is immortal like the class,
A thousand times decimated, which carries
The standard of humanity into the light of the future.

[1] *Vide* Jean Cassou's *Massacres of Paris.*

Marie-Rose is the youth of this youth
Which I recommend to find its own reflection
In the story of the Commune, in the story of Spain,
In the story of the Fall of France,
And to draw from this reflection
A new lease of the enthusiasm
Which makes it unconquerable,
The enthusiasm of Gavroche and Vuillemin.

Thus the poet who is a true poet
Finds in the very life of the proletariat
The flame which transforms him, and which, in his turn,
By dint of his poet's gift, he renders back
To the class which incarnates all poetry,
The living and animating poetry of struggle.

And already it is with France as when from a ship
One sees the coast astern blotted out by the night,
But the compass starts shining
Within the helmet of its binnacle.

So I hold my faith in France today
As a binnacle holds a ship's compass,
Rocking under and around it, but holding it
In miraculously isolated suspension.

The Bourgeoisie, 1939-1943

THE bourgeoisie is falling. Its feet
Are skidding in blood. It soon must die.
It is stupid. It is base.
It understands nothing of the new system
Which humanity so ardently desires,
And on which it bases all its hopes.

The bourgeoisie is capable merely
Of murder, murder, and murder.
It is only capable of creating wars
And sending whole nations to be slaughtered.
The people are ardently demanding
A rational and just organisation of society
In which they can work in order to live.
The bourgeoisie, instead of granting this,
Continue stubbornly, absurdly, criminally
To hold on to this ugly system
With no deep sense of the tragedy
Not only of war's actual destruction
But of its defeat of beauty
And thought and spiritual values,
Its negation of civilisation,
Its terrible withering of life.

Lamh Dearg Aboo

To Stalin

STALIN, when we Scottish Gaels salute you
It is, like all else, by no mere chance
That an old battle-cry of our people at last
Wins on our lips to its full significance
      – Lamh dearg aboo![1]

Suddenly we know what one meant who cried
'Montrose fought for more than his king – he fought for all men,'
And see the underlying meaning of 1645
And 1745 leap up in us again
      – Lamh dearg aboo!

We know now why our Gaeldom had to fall for a while
Under the English, Money, the Church and the Law
And see fully at last what our kin through the ages
Only at their best in fleeting glimpses saw.
      – Lamh dearg aboo!

1645, 1745 – and now in the midst
Of history's greatest and final war
We believe by 1945 the true sense
Of all our tangled tale will shine out like a star.
      – Lamh dearg aboo!

Ah, Stalin, we Scots who had our first home
In Caucasian Georgia like yourself see how

[1] Battle-cry of the Scottish and Irish MacDonalds under Alasdair MacDonald and Montrose at Tippermuir, Inverlochy, etc. Means 'The Red Hand to Victory.'

The processes of history in their working out
Bring East and West together in general human triumph now.
          – Lamh dearg aboo!

The very centre and lifeblood of Scotland is here,
Misprized and distorted for hundreds of years.
Now there fluent Gaelic sunshine floods through at last
And all the fog of oppression and cant disappears.
          – Lamh dearg aboo!

Scottish history – ah, indeed, a strange woman,
Incomprehensible creature, full of faults to the brim,
And yet of a curious twisting tenderness! Scottish history – good?
Fools laugh – as some chucklehead might at one of the Seraphim.
          – Lamh dearg aboo!

'Ask your red-faced friend at Scotland Yard.
He has no illusions about me, I know.
Morally I am in the depths. But to you – to you,
What falls grey in London is still pure as Schiehallion's golden
          snow.'[1]
          – Lamh dearg aboo!

It is to-day as when Montrose and his men
Struggled up out of the bed of the Tarff through the night.
Came a shaft of red through the blackest clouds and suddenly
The whole vast scene took shape and colour round them, and
          bright,
Up behind the Monadhliath Mountains broke the dawn
– Not a Five Year's this, but a Millennium's plan.
          – Lamh dearg aboo!

Red and snow-white?[2] Have these startling colours
Ever flared in such high conjunction before? – Aye, so they sprang
When from the highest mountain in Britain's three kingdoms
Suddenly in the white and scarlet air Montrose's trumpets sang.
          – Lamh dearg aboo!

[1] Golden snow, i.e. snow in sunlight. Pindar's phrase.
[2] The poet is coupling here the Red Flag of Russia and Scotland's Silver
Saltire.

Fifteen hundred men and a body of horse
Without food and without rest for thirty-six hours
Scaling the inaccessible mountains of Lochaber in midwinter!
– So all the meaning of our history suddenly flowers.
           – Lamh dearg aboo!

Away with the word 'impossible.' Here surely
Was no trip for anyone not of the bird clan.
Bifrost Bridge, sharp as a sword-edge, which stretches to Valhalla?
Straiter still is the way of all true greatness in man!
           – Lamh dearg aboo!

To see this is as when in a great ship's engine-room
Through all the vastness of furnaces and clanging machinery is
        found
The quiet simple thing all that is about – a smooth column of steel,
The propeller shaft, in cool and comfortable bearings, turning
        round and round with no sound
– All the varying forces, the stresses and resistances,
Proceeding from that welter of machinery,
Unified into the simple rotation of this horizontal column,
And conducted calmly along its length into the sea.
           – Lamh dearg aboo!

In the Gangs

       GANGS of louts at every street corner
       Full of nothing but *ochiania*

       True, they are keenly aware of their sensations
       But is not this sensory awareness
       The most elementary form of consciousness.

       On the other hand they cannot be said
       To think at all, and their feelings are rather
       Sharp transitory reactions

Than long-continued dominant emotions.
Above all, they are devoid of will and purpose,
Helplessly impelled hither and yon by the
    circumstances of the moment.

They have no strength of resistance. They are weak
As the very core of personality . . . the power to choose,
Freedom of choice may be an illusion
But if so it is an inescapable one.
When the mainspring of choice is weakened or left out
The conflicts and contradictions of character
Lose their virtue and significance
And personality almost disappears.
They are hardly persons enough to sustain
Real relations with one another
Any more than billiard balls do.

1946

———————◦⋈◦———————

The Path of the Old Spells[1]

RICH is the peace o' the elements the nicht owre the Land o' Joy
And rich the evenness o' the calm's music roond the Isles o' Love,
Ilka wing plies urgently in obedience to nature
While the path o' the auld spells winds inexorably westwards.
Rich the breist o' the hills wi' memories o' bygone days,
Serene the face o' the seas wi' dreams o' the times that are gane.
O seilfu' days, your pride, your nobleness, your love!
O white days o' love wi' your clean and kindly ways!
O times o' joy wi' your lauchter, your cheer, and your music!
O warld o' grace, lit by rays o' knowledge and art!
Why ha'e you gane and left hardly a trace
        o' the noontide o' your glory?
Is it a wonder desire and hope seek to follow eftir you,
Fain for the secrets that aince cled your lap wi' esteem?
Is it a wonder the elements sing o' your time and poo'er
And the curved lid o' ilka eye is weak frae the fire o' jewels?
O yon days that ha'e gane wi' the shinin' load o' the wisdom o' my race,
Why did you want to strip awa' ilka last ear o' maist worthy
        excellence?
Nae wonder the western lift is noo sae illustrious wi' licht
And that your dwellin's in the distance are alowe wi' an everlastin'
        flame!
Nae wonder the bareness o' ilka flat bespeaks the fullness o' your story!
Nae wonder the hills haud the words o' twilicht in their mooths!
Nae wonder the harp o' the sangs is silent under the belly o' yon clood
And the voice-of-song o' the bards without spell or excellence o' art!
Nae wonder the kirkyaird o' my folk, by the sea, is dumb!
Nae wonder the breists o' the graves are a' hoven wi' the worth o'
        what's gane!

[1] From the Gaelic of Donald Sinclair.

O Warld! It is a woe that no' an 'oor that has gane can ever come back,
Nor can my desire, tho' lastin', draw a single word frae the sleep o' the
   deid!

Bizerta[1]

WHILE I'm standin' guard the nicht I see
Awa' doon yonder on the laich skyline
A restless lowe, beatin' its wings
         and scatterin' and dimmin'
A' the starns abune wi'-in reach o' its shine.

You'd think, tho' it's hine awa', there 'ud be heard
Wailin' and lamentation pourin' oot frae't,
That roarin' and screamin', and the yowlin' o' mad dogs,
   'Ud come frae that amber furnace
         a' the noises o' fear and hate,
And flood the haill lift – insteed o'
         which the foul glare
Juist rises and fa's alang the horizon
         in ghastly silence there.

What are the names the nicht o' thae puir streets
Whaur ilka lozen belches flame and
         soot and the screams o' the folk
As hoose eftir hoose is rent and caves
         in in a blash o' smoke?
And whase are the voices cryin' on
         Daith the nicht
In sae mony different tongues to come
         quick and end their plight
Or screamin' in frenzy for help and
         no' heard, hid
Under yon muckle heaps o' burnin'
         stanes and beams,

[1] From the Gaelic of George Campbell Hay.

And payin' there the auld accustomed
    tax o' common bluid?

Noo reid like a battlefield puddle, noo wan
Like the dirty pallor o' fear, shootin' up and syne
Sinkin' again, I see Evil like a hammerin'
    pulse or the spasms
O' a hert in the deidthraw aye rax up
    and dwine
The fitfu' fire, a horror on the horizon, a ring
O' rose and gowd at the fit o' the lift
    belies and denies
The ancient hie beauty and peace o'
    the starns themselves
As its foul glare crines and swells.

The Auld Hunter[1]

EILD comes owre me like a yoke on my craig,
A girn roon' my feet, the lourd and the chill.
Betwixt my sicht and the licht it comes,
It comes betwixt the deed and the will.

This is the thing that warps the sapling
And sets its knife to the aipple's root,
But the warst deed o' a' its spite has been
To filch the hill frae under my foot.

My narrow gun and the paths o' the cruach
Eild has stown, wha's deef and heeds nae grief;
My hand and my foot, this Blear-eyed's stown them
And a' my cheer, like a hertless thief.

[1] From the Gaelic of George Campbell Hay.

But gin Eild were a man that hauns could grapple
And I could come on him secretly
Up there on the hill when naebody passes
Certes ! grass 'ud be trampled or he gat free !

Nearer, My God, to Thee

WHATNA peety it is, an auld Scot said,
Maist folk canna see mair o' oor country.
Nae man can be an atheist wha spends his life
'Mid the glories o' the mountains, believe you me !

To associate sport and the things unseen and eternal
– Sae close to the auld sportsmen – soonds nonsense noo, may be.
Yet there's really naething like shootin' a wheen grouse
For pittin' a man in touch wi' the Deity.

Boon Companions

To sit with them and drink with them night after night
Gives me a rough pass into the kingdom not
Of their minds, their souls, their emotions, but rather
Of a kind of diffused being they have then got
In common. Different in appearance and personality
As in age, nevertheless in the social hour
There is an elemental commonalty between them
As between leaf and grass and wayside flower.

Die Grenzsituation

WAS *this* the face that launched a thousand ships?
No! But it frightened one right smartly down the slips
When – while the whole world held its silly breath –
She gave it her own hóly name – as sure as death!
Deeming *that* the greatest compliment that she,
After a profound spell of Queenly secrecy,
To duty nobly yielding her notorious modesty,
Could pay this miracle of Clydeside industry,
And everybody (almost!) hastened to agree
And marvelled how she'd got the great idea,
Perfect, sublime, the very peak of poetry,
An epic in three words, *The Queen Mary*,
And not one honest soul in Glasgow, or Christendom, laughed!
It seemed – and was – as though she'd stricken all mankind daft.

To James Fergusson, the Inventor of 'Plastic Scots'

NOW you'll be needing all the plasticity that'll
Be going yourself, and no mistake!
– For it's always unwise to try to sell the rattle
Before you catch the snake!

From 'In a Cornish Garden'

FOR VALDA'S BIRTHDAY

IF the beauty in our lives seldom seems so
And is still much mixed with ugliness, my dear,
Let us not regret that we are far too young yet
For the beauty in us to shine out complete and clear.

Let us remember that most flowers are loveliest
When the sun is low and can shine through their petals,
And have no fear of our present faint impure foreshowings
Of the glory that against that hour within us settles.

Nor forget no man can delight in Nature save
For reasons similar to Cowper's playing with pet hares,
Rarely though the tranquil surface lets be seen
The black foundations of such innocent affairs.

Like our happiness in this garden now, my dear
So a river runs smoother and deeper
With no fleck or ripple upon it, before the waterfall;
So arches a wave, green and crystalline,
Before the plunge and smother of foam!

Glasgow

(AND constantly in the eyes of these keelies
We see an experience which contains a criticism of modern existence
That cannot be parried by observing that after all
These keelies are cowardly, untrustworthy, and lascivious
Since we cannot declare our most prominent citizens
Less monstrous and inhuman,
Or any razor-slasher different in kind
From a bold knight of old or modern V.C.
'Then they should be all in the army' – learning like beasts
To make movements when they hear a shout!)
The only difference is they have some patter-off, class shibboleths
– But Berlioz, Wagner, Heine, Nietzsche, Orage,
Beethoven, Mozart, Gluck, Weber – it is hell
To think of men of such stature in Glasgow,
To think of any man at all that is more than a louse!

A patter like the endless denunciations of war
Or all the blither of social democracy
(*Grandes hystériques*, always about to give birth to
The New Order, the celebrated 'phantom tumour'
That comes to nothing; just words – words without works.)
So here in all matters of spiritual significance
There is nothing but words, high-sounding impotent words,
Words like a parrot's, words with nothing else behind them,
The unflagging and nauseating garrulity
Of professors with the minds of keelies,
Of teachers who know nothing but what they impart
To children who in turn learn no more
From an educational system designed above all
To prevent attention to anything that matters.
(I do not merely mean they've never taken part
In the Kneipen at Heidelberg or learned
The composition of Zuppa di peoci or anything about
Aryballoi and figurines from Rhitzona in Boeotia

Or read the hero saga of Gesser Khan
And millions of similar things I'd loathe not knowing
Who am an off-showing intellectual hated by those
Sweet simple souls more eager still
To show off since they've nothing to show off.
They do not even know why Lothian and Border folk
Differ as greatly as Volnay and Pommard do
And in fact know less of Scotland altogether
Than of Chirico's *Les Muses Inquiétantes*,
Oblivious to all those intranational differences which
Each like a flower's scent by its peculiarity sharpens
Appreciation of others as well as bringing
Appreciation of itself, as experiences of gardenia or zinnia
Refine our experiences of rose or sweet pea.

Must a true poet be like a human pincushion,
Have a habitual criminal's insensitivity to pain,
A social hypalgesia, an extensive indifference,
To the problems of his fellows? Is poetry
A product dependent upon a local cerebral lesion?
(Probably situated near the left supramarginal gyrus).
Not a 'loss' of sensation, however, since even Glasgow's rhymesters
Still respond to certain milder stimuli, and in its distribution
Their disability does not correspond with that found
In cases of focal damage to the sensory pathways.
The defect is a higher one in the sense that it entails
Factors of inattention, not only imperception.

Orage said that 'of the hundred million people in America,
Not more than a hundred are using their brains
To the fullest capacity.' Of Glasgow's population not one!
– Not one! Even such poor brains as the best of them have,
Not one of them knows – not one of them tries –
That the hardest thing in life and the most valuable
Is to control congested energy till one gets exactly the right line.
They are all on wrong lines in every relation of life.
They are faced with devastating problems – and shirk them.
But the problems do not shirk *them*, the Gadarene swine!

And we – we artists – to do work worthy of our time,
To write about contemporary things, that is to say,
To do work worthy of our art, is like trying
To keep pace with the four horses of the Apocalypse.
Our life is changing with so great a rapidity.
'Steht die Zunge selten ein.' Seldom? Never!
Yet we must cope with it – master it – be armed with faith in victory
And with an exact and faultless knowledge of fact.

Glasgow – the capitalist system – can exist indefinitely
Without culture, morals or religion – sans teeth,
Sans eyes, sans taste, sans everything, but,
When all these are swept away, the one thing left untouched
Of all that it ever had. Let us not bother then
With little local triumphs in culture, morals,
And so forth. No positive result can be achieved
Until that one thing is touched, that linch-pin
Removed. We must go for that and that alone
With that real and persistent purpose, that necessary fanaticism,
That unquenchable zest at that *atemberaubend* pace,
With that extreme pressure and blinding overwork
Only genius knows (resembling the intense
Activity of the brain to electrical impressions
So that a man who accidentally seized a telephone wire
That was grounded said: 'Though the duration of the shock
Could not have been more than a couple of seconds
A man riding by on a bicycle at a good speed
Having only time to pass about thirty yards beyond me
Before the operator got through talking and opened the switch
Yet I could see every spoke in the bicycle,
But it barely seemed to be turning;
I could feel every reversal of the current
And these reversals occur at the rate of sixty complete cycles per
          second.'
– Yet, of course, it is the element of surprise
That is disastrous in cases of electrical shock
And genius is like a shock which being completely anticipated
Has no ill effects) which no one in Glasgow

u

Is pursuing in any direction – or could pursue
Save only in this (not even in preserving this old order,
Since there is no necessity there as with us) –
Idiots without ideas or feelings
                    (*Full of caginess, that's all*)
Who understand nothing and love nothing,
Devouring time as ducks gobble water, in order to live!
And, like ducks, finding nothing but a few insects for nourishment.

The one thing untouched! Eighty years ago
(All but a century now – a hundred years already –
Since Engels and Marx in London met with the members
Of Fraternal Democrats, the League of the Just, and so on;
And the Communist Manifesto was drawn up!)
Heine admitted in an agony of fear
That the future belonged to Communism, crying
'*Fiat justitia, pereat mundus!* – This Communism,
So hostile to my interests and inclinations, yet
Exercises a charm upon me before which
I am powerless. A terrible syllogism holds me in its grip.
If I am unable to refute the premise
That "every man has the right to eat", then I am forced
To submit to all the consequences. A generosity of despair
Seizes me and I cry: for long this old society
Has been judged and condemned; let justice be done,
Let this old world be smashed in which innocence is long since dead,
Where egoism prospers and man battens on man.'

I thanked the bozo for you but told him 'nerts.'

For there is no generosity of despair in Glasgow.
And no concern for the things which made Heine pause.
Everyone knows that the future belongs to Communism
But they are only anxious the present order
Should last out their time.

Glasgow has good cause for fear – for fear of the dentist's bright
        weapons,
And all efficiency. Poor Glasgow, imprisoned

Behind its mask of fraud
And the filth that goes with it,
What a marvellous new thrill frankness would be for it!
– Like Bleuler's carious tooth which ached when he heard music!

'Efficiency! Efficiency!' I was so much
Wound up with my theme as I walked up Buchanan Street
That I felt as if I were saying to the crowds of girls
I met on the pavement, 'You girls know what that means
In some little thing. What then in everything?
In some little thing. Say stockings. No wrinkled ankles,
Twisted seams or slipping heels. No strained-up tops
To cause garter-runs. No lumpy double-over hems
Beneath smooth gowns – Perfect! Designed
Not only in footsize, but in width and length as well
For every individual woman.
The footsize has a number, the leg-size has a name.'
– Or more intimately still, ('*Do I dare
Disturb the Universe*'?) 'welcome aids for difficult days.'
'When I think of the days I lost' – These don't pull or twist,
Bind, curl, irritate or slip. They conform to the body,
Readjust themselves to fit, no matter how active you are.
No chafing or rubbing, secure, smooth-fitting, snug,
'*White light folded, sheathed about you, folded.*'

Help yourself to happiness!

I am consumed with love for the people I detest;
And as to my kind of poetry it is not
The high-souled pretensions of orthodox verse
The fashion for high-moulded busts demands
To give the necessary bosomy effect
Like those brassières for the flat-chested that have
Cunning little net-rosettes tucked inside them!

Foul chaos! People of Glasgow, you have done so much
And worked so hard, yet life is undigested.
Now shape it into proportions you can handle!
Feel that you have life here, in your hands!

That you can evoke from it pretty much what you will!
But no! You are afraid. You do not seem to know
How to receive the gifts that might be yours.
Life passes through Glasgow too.
Glasgow is the reverse of Charlie Chaplin – of his superb skill
In combining the ridiculous comedy of his make-up and antics
With a hint of tragedy. Tragedy is so much
Part of Glasgow's nature; it over-emphasises its effects,
And here and there in order to 'take the bumps'
Develops a sense of humour, enough
To make the bluest nose among them
Glisten with righteous satisfaction!
Stooges for real live people,
A human look just won't jell on them.

. . . . .

Omniscience. A world of simple, free,
Ungrudging comprehension in which all human feelings
Are now real and genuine and not to be bought.
Dynamic, nervous, but laconic. Positive,
Without the human faults and blemishes, and cockroaches
No longer looking out of the crevices, and no beating
Of any however-muted witch-doctor's tambourine;
But reflecting the great wisdom and heroism
Of the Communist Party.
For 'there are in the experience of great poets
Features of such naturalness it is impossible,
Having tasted them, having ascertained
One's relationship with all that is
And being familiar in life with the future,
Not to fall ultimately,
As into a heresy
Into an unheard-of simplicity.'[1]

Steelworkers, why don't you have a steel-made wit to match
That can lick its weight in M.P.s?

They wouldn't be in the picture if it wasn't for your votes.

[1] Pasternak echoing Tyutchev's famous masterpiece, *Silentium*.

These boobs don't know the answers!

Take another eyeful of the pulchritude!

What a pity you're not like Salome
Who threw a wild party and got up
With a real head next morning!

I too am heard as one 'whose armoury is full
Of hackneyed phrases – the class struggle,
The capitalist system, the bourgeoisie, exploitation,
Surplus value, wage slavery, and so forth; all stale stuff
Discussed and rediscussed a million times. There is nothing new
To be said about the theory of Marxism today.'
I am heard as the grass of the field is looked at.
'There it is. One has seen it all before.'
The journalists go by me like a tydinges of magpies
Munching vacuity and excreting lies;
– And leave me to confront the Medoysa's saxificous head.
But I am not like the Persian fatalist in Herodotus,
'Knowing the bitterest of griefs, to see clearly
And yet to be unable to do anything.' I am full
Of the violent energy of the minute electron
In the enormous atom, the thrilling vigour of the pentathlete.
My purpose is clear and irresistible within me
As I look through my all-observing and half-shut eyes
Straight *at the bridge* of this All-Horror's nose,
The most exacerbating form of regard.

WE HAVE WHAT IT TAKES.

To Mrs. Walter Pritchard

née Sadie McLellan

You remind me, young, lovely, a wife and a mother,
And capital artist to boot,
Of orange groves seen with their simultaneous burden
Of leaves and flowers and fruit.

Choice

Audh the Deep-Minded
Is MacDiarmid's muse;
For Auden the cheap-minded
He has no use.

Royal Wedding Gifts

It is unfortunately understandable enough
That gifts should pour in from all over the earth:
Not so the greed of the girl who accepts so much
And so monstrously overrates her own scant worth.

The daughter of a base and brainless breed
Is given what countless better women sorely need,
But cannot get one ten-millionth part of tho' they slave and save
Relentlessly from the cradle to the grave.

Rope in the shameless hussy – let her be
Directed to factory work or domestic service
Along with all the other spivs and drones –
Our life-stream's clogged and fouled with all these damned
   conservas.

For St. Andrew's Day 1947

ST. ANDREW is your patron saint?
Oui, Monsieur,
But remember, St. Andrew
Of Scotland – and of Russia!

1948

The Poet and the Angler

Nor can I doubt what Oyl I must bestow
To raise my Subject from a ground so low.
                    Dryden's translation of Virgil's 'Georgics'.

IT sud be wi' the guid poet as it is
Wi' the practised angler wha loves to see
Trout feedin' seriously and quietly
Wi' nae heich jumps efter air-borne flies,
Nae playfu' frisks that can only excite
The novice.

        And gin he sees here and there,
Cooried laich by the burn as tho' in prayer,
Floatin' doon like wee ships wi' a' sails set,
The flies causin' the rise he blesses the sight,
And gin ane comes close eneuch in to the land
May weel scoop it up wi' a hollowed hand
As when frae amidst the dampness the fine weather kyths
Hesitatin' like a young ear o' corn.

A trig wee insect, fearless on his loof upborne,
Licht as the thocht o' death in a soond man's heid,
For water-flies ha'e nae sense o' dreid.
Twa tall veined wings the colour o' thunder clood
And langer than the segmented jade body
Like hillsides atour a sma' glen road
Or yon bipetallous floo'er o' earth and sky
The horizon hinges. And twa setae
Wavin' gently in the air, noo sideways,
Noo up and doon. Syne suddenly
The critter flutters and tak's flight
Like the white flash o' a thrown switch

When a new circuit's formed and the current
Flows invisibly through anither channel.
Sae, profitin' by what he's seen he cheenges
To anither waled frae his box the fly on his cast
And touches the new ane wi' a drap o' thin, colourless oil
– To gar it float – and is ready at last.

But a poet may see perched thus on his hand
(Gin scientific accuracy is o' nae mair concern
To Poetry than ultimate or absolute truth
Is to Religion, since these are attempts
At union wi' the infinite no' mainly on the side o' thocht
But mainly on the side o' will in the a'e case
And Imagination on the ither, and perfectly true ideas
Are neither essential for that, nor is it essential
To either Religion or Poetry to believe
That its ideas are perfectly true)
Less a fly than a challenge to gaze
On a hieroglyph o' the end o' ane
O' the great αἰῶνες o' the human race,
The queasy glory o' life-and-death – as a man may get
Sight in snell air o' his breath, like reek frae a cigarette.
Or, allied to nightmare, deem it again
Nocht but a vulgar weakness o' the brain,
The shairp edge o' madness made starkly plain,
The human need to inflict, and suffer, pain.
Gaunt, sallow wings, still, stormy, unpredictable,
Like a' ither wings the minified wings o' Death's Angel,
(Tho' glowered at lang eneuch they can swell to full size)
And wi' something in them like the alternation
In a poet's nature o' vanity and humility,
Delight and desolation,
Lust to exhibit and shrinkin' secrecy,
Like flashes o' his auld vulgarity
In a man that seemed to ha'e been born again.

Study them aince mair afore they flit
(This horrid wraith come into your life frae naewhaur,

This carrion by-product suddenly becomin'
The total o' everything!)
And note the brimmin' sense o' life
Shot through wi' tragic intimation
That mak's a man in a schizophrenic way
See in them as in a greasy mirror
His dooble character – spectator and actor tae,
Till like Piero di Cosimo he sees a'thing
Salvatico like his ain nature.
Or, abjurin' thocht and intuition baith,
Wins clear o' a' imagery and achieves
The peculiar delight o' the empathetic experience
– A love that raxes oot longin'ly
Faur ayont the grasp o' knowledge,
A love that's no' only a delight
But a nostalgia and a desolation . . .

Even in the height o' simmer
It's cauld by the waterside,
Engagin' no' sic trout as an angler can
But naething less than Leviathan.

My Heart Always Goes Back to the North

THERE are few better things in the world, I think,
Than to recognize what crops are coming up
At a stage when that is a mystery to the unskilled eye
– Knowing that wheat has a deeper green,
Barley a twisting blade that gives it a hazy look,
Oats a blue, broad blade.
The beans blossom and the cloverfields also.
Now the valley becomes clothed as with diverse carpets
– Red clover, white clover,
The yellow of mustard and lucern,
The silver blue of beans,

And, occasionally,
The wine-glow of a field of trifolium.

Meanwhile, the last of the human faculties
To be touched by the finger of science,
Still unanalysed, still immeasurable,
The sense of smell is the one little refuge
In the human mind still inviolable and unshareable
Because communicable in no known language,
But some day this the most delicate of perceptions
Will be laid bare too . . . there will be
Chairs of osmology in our universities,
Ardent investigators searching out, recording, measuring,
Preserving in card indexes,
The departing smells of the countryside.
Hayfields will be explained in terms of Coumarin,
Beanfields in Ionone, hedge-roses in Phenyl-Ethyl-Propionate,
Hawthorn as Di-Methyl-Hydroquinone.
(But will they ever capture the scent of violets
Among the smoke of the shoeing forge, or explain
The clean smell of a road wet with summer rain?)
Until that day, on Heimaey, 400 miles due northwest
Of Rona in the Hebrides, I am content to walk out
Into an unreal country of yellow fields
Lying at the foot of black volcanic cliffs
In the shadow of dead Helgafell,
And watch a few farmers scything
(Careful of the little birds' nests,
Iceland wheatear, snow bunting, white wagtail, meadow pipit,
And leaving clumps of grass to protect them)
A sweet but slender hay-crop
And tell its various constituents for myself
– White clover, chickenweed, dandelion,
A very large buttercup, silverweed, horsetail,
Thrift, sorrel, yellow bedstraw,
Poa, carex, and rushes –
Or look out of my bedroom window
In the farmhouse near Kaupstadur

On a garden planted with angelica,
Red current, rhubarb, and the flower of Venus,
Or at midnight watch the sun
Roll slowly along the northern horizon
To dip behind the great ice-caps
And jokulls of distant Iceland.
'Mellach lem bhith ind ucht ailiuin for beind cairrge,
Conacind and ar a mheinci feth na fairrci.'
Ah, me! It is a far better thing to be sitting
Alive on Heimaey, bare as an egg though it were,
Than rolled round willy-nilly with yonder sun.

I in myself a Cordoba, cultural centre of Europe,
A university town where intellectual tolerance
Scepticism and rationalism flourished when they
Were unheard of throughout the rest of Europe,
– A focal centre, where Persian, Babylonian,
Egyptian, Grecian, Roman, Byzantine, and Christian cultures
Merged and fructified each other, the point where medicine and
    mathematics
(Arabic numerals, the zero, the local value of numbers, algebra)
Classical philosophy and jurisprudence and certain elements
Of poetry and rhetoric entered and re-entered Europe.
I too loving such unfamiliar and most complex prospects
As in that enormous scene of Indian culture
– The coming of the Aryans, and the wars of the Heroes,
The rise of Buddhism and Jainism,
Alexander and the infiltration of Greek influences,
Asoka and Vikramaditya and Harsha,
The development of Hinduism and extirpation of Buddhism,
Intercourse with the Far East, the inroads
Of Muslim invaders, and, finally, of Muslim conquerors,
And last of all the arrival of the Europeans,
Portuguese, Dutch, French, and British,
And dwelling particularly on such episodes
As the struggle of the Rajputs and Muhammadans,
The Empire of Vijayanahar, Akbar,
The culmination of the Mogul Empire and its decline,

The Vaishnava and Sakta poets of mediaeval and Mogul India,
In the South the *Kural* and Manikkavasahar,
In theWest Tukaram and the other Marathi poets,
In Bengal Chaitanya and his companions
(And rejoicing in all those intranational differences which
Each like a flower's scent by its peculiarity sharpens
Appreciation of others as well as bringing
Appreciation of itself, as experiences of gardenia or zinnia
Refine our experiences of rose or sweet pea)
Yet always I turn back to 'l'Europe aux anciens parapets,'
('I doe love these auncient ruynes:
We never tread upon them, but we set
Our foote upon some reverend History.')
Turning from the rhodomontades of Mussolini, Hitler,
    Churchill
To the steely brevity of Iceland nine centuries ago
And the recurrent contempt for loquacity there
– 'No longer silent than the cuckoo.'
'Tall in talk as a fox's tail is long' –
Such peerless things as Bergthora's reply
To the burners of Njal's home – unparalleled
Except by some moments in the Bible
And in Greek poetry – as in, for example,
The whispered half-line with which Odysseus
Ends the story of the last agony of his comrades lost at sea
– 'And God took away their homecoming,'
Or the proud brevity of Einar Tambarskelvar's prophetic words
When his bow is snapped by a hostile arrow at Svold,
And King Olaf shouts: 'What broke there so loudly?'
And Einar answers, 'Norway from thy hand, O King!'
– Ah, yes, all the wealth and wonders of human utterance,
But my heart always goes back to the North
With its mingling of fire and ice, of black lava, green fell, blue
    firth,
'When all that ever hotter sprites expressed
Comes bettered by the patience of the North.'

Repelling a Poultryman's Advice

YOU council me 'not to count
My chickens before they're hatched.'
But I've given a fair amount
Of thought to the matter and watched
How racehorse owners – and especially those
Interested in raising their own blood-stock –
Conduct their affairs. Since everyone knows
Entries for the most valuable events must be made
At least eighteen months before they are run,
And Produce Stake nominations entered
Before the time of foaling. So I mock
At your metaphor drawn from the hen-run.
That's not where my interests are centred!

Glasgow is Like the Sea

A Hebridean Speaks

GLASGOW is like the sea; a greater sea
Than that which surges about my native isles,
Less calculable and more cross-currented.
A man could know those waters like his hand,
But who gauges Glasgow's endless wiles,
        Who understands?

Nor are we fixed Hebrids here ourselves,
But waves, each of us, that in this ceaseless tide
Change shape and colour in countless ways and yet
Keep our identity through all;
Our lives in this vast whirlpool ride
        Well-reined withal!

It is one thing to gauge the waters
And know the set a sailing boat must have
And all the bearings of the wind and weather.
We islanders never weary of such lore
– But another to be oneself a wave
    And know no more.

And yet the figure scarcely further serves;
For even as the islanders in their blood
Have inarticulate fathomless sea-knacks
So we far more in this great human sea
Our unplumbed inklings that can thrid the flood
    With surety.

The watery wave no memory has
Of what the sea has been nor any dream
Of what it yet will be; we human waves
Like mirrors somehow image all the past
And of the future too hold many a gleam
    Howe'er we're cast,

No single wave at once the surface knows
And the profounds; but these are every man's
Albeit in greater measure or in less;
No wave its neighbour knows, or lifting bright
Or smashed in spray; our sea Life plans
    With such lore dight.

And here where Glasgow all Scotland gathers
As a sea its rivers my chief delight
Is to companion now this wave, now that,
And know the course it's taken, where it rose,
Glimpse, share, its interpenetrations, note the sleight
    It keeps itself through those.

Even as I recall the eddies round the isles,
This aspect and another of the waters there,
So here I am filled with subtle knowledge

Of ways more intricate human lives possess,
Forms and effects more subtle and more rare,
        More fugitive – and less.

I'd lack this in another city perhaps;
Here I can place almost all the shapes,
Knowing the course, the tempo, of every element sent
Hither from all over Scotland and further afield,
And seldom a sound or a colour escapes
        My informed judgment.

The sea is always water, Glasgow life;
And yet life changes each ten years or so
Out of resemblance in a million ways
To what it ever was or can be yet,
And in a different medium we flow
        And match with it.

Glasgow was freer in the old days, of course;
Less mim-mouthed, puritanical, controlled;
Individual and typical oddity have gone
Or at least their outward shows; it has lost
Most of its colour; truth, scarce can hold
        More than a ghost.

Great forces plough through us to unknown ends;
We plunge to brief glimpses of the ocean floor,
And in a moment are babbling idly
In a sunny current, or towering high
In glittering peaks, or lapping a golden shore,
        Or spraying the sky.

Filled with a whale, a mackerel, a gannet,
Or dark tangle in a rocking mass;
All marvels whirl in us – all chances run;
But through all occupations and all forms
Beyond shape and sound and hue we pass
        Lost in the sun.

Largely compenetrant we flow
And yet we double every clarity
We have deeper opacities yet,
And are content to have it so
Nor sacrifice ignorance, surprise, and mystery
    Omniscience to get.

The diverse sea-growths and curious shells
Folk exclaim on their sea-side holidays,
All joy of exploration and romance
Of sunken wrecks and buried treasure
Here in a more complex medium meet your gaze
    In greater measure.

The blood has far more marvels than the brine;
In these amazing torrents of it here
How few adventure! – preferring to keep
Some notion of humanity like a map
To go by, and not the living haemosphere
    For fear of mishap!

The difference of water and life understood,
My concern with life is as a wave's with the sea;
Save as a spectacle – or for some instant end –
The ups and downs, storm and shine, of the rout
Trouble me no more. Above the battle I've no wish to be
    To know what it's all about.

It is a mighty maelstrom. That I know,
No matter to what purpose it is spun;
And whatever may be my personal share
In this vast jumble with the rest, I relish;
Not anxious from it ever to be won,
    Gasping like a landed fish. . . .

The Nature of a Bird's World

I'm like Mussolini – fond of birds.
ETHEL LINA WHITE

I HAVE spoken of a pair of courting cuckoos;
Of the history of a pair of nesting dabchicks
And of a continuous and exhaustive account of a day in their life.
But let us take nothing for granted.
Allen Upward used to warn us to learn
From things themselves, not from words about the things.

 How do you know but ev'ry Bird that cuts the airy way,
 Is an immense World of Delight, clos'd by your senses five?
BLAKE

If one thinks of the reproductive instincts in birds
One has a clear, conventional picture of what happens.
This instinct causes them at certain seasons
To do certain things – to claim territory,
To do battle with rivals for it and for a mate,
To find such a mate, to breed,
To build nests and bring up the young.

It is a pretty story and broadly speaking true.
These things manifestly happen, but watching real birds
Shows that our concept of the process
Does not fit the facts.

Our error lies in conceiving
Some mythological agent outside the bird,
We call an 'instinct,' which causes
The process to occur – like clockwork.

But observing actual birds
One gets a different impression.
Here is a cock which gets sexually excited
Without any female being present,

And goes on to build a nest
Without any eggs.
Another, while in the act of chasing a rival,
Chances to pass his hen,
Strikes a sexual posture,
And then goes on to deal with the enemy.
A third accomplishes coition,
And then immediately turns
And attacks the hen.

Or consider the behaviour of the hen.
The development of the reproductive process
In a hen of the Tree Pipit species
Has three stages.

In the first she is sexually excited
But cannot accomplish the sexual act.
She also picks up material but cannot build.
In the second she finishes her nest and lays her eggs
But loses sexual excitement,

These facts do not tally with a definite instinctive pattern
Set to accomplish itself like clockwork.
Yet the various reactions
Must have some relation to each other,
And, indeed, have all a common physical basis
In the enlargement of the generative organs
And the secretion of hormones.

These reactions form an organised whole
Any part of which *may* react
Apparently at random – yet at any particular time
One reaction is master of the others,
Which one is evidently determined
By the needs of the external situation.

Thus, when the cock has an actual rival to meet,
The fighting reaction is the master one.

The reaction of striking a sexual pose
May be activated by some process of association,
But it is not allowed to take command
Or seriously to interfere with the master reaction.
Thus we see any reaction in the pattern
May awake any other, which may attend it
Without either helping or hindering it,
And may, indeed, follow it as the master.

The master reaction is awakened
By stimuli from the bird's environment,
But the bird is only sensitive to these
When the 'threshold' is lowered
By the action of the reproductive organs.
There is possibly a biological value here,
Whereby false reactions may be activated
Along with true, since, in a rapidly changing environment,
These false reactions may more speedily become
Master reactions should a real need arise.

But the problems posed by direct
And careful observation multiply quickly.
Nor always is the master reaction
An appropriate one. Move a Yellow Bunting's nest with young
Four inches from its site in a bank.
Returning with food for the youngsters
The hen is puzzled. She goes to the original site,
Hesitates and flies away. Later she comes back
And feeds the young, but still goes
To have a look at the site. Finally
She settles down to the new arrangement.
But how differently she behaves if you place
Another nest with blown eggs in the site.
Now she sits and broods the eggs
And nothing the youngsters can do
Can attract her attention away from the eggs.
But the cock now comes and feeds the youngsters.
She sees him but seems uninterested.

As soon, however, as he also feeds her,
She flies to the young
And feeds them by regurgitation.

Obviously the bird lives in two different worlds
– A 'brooding' world whose object
Is the nest with eggs,
And a 'feeding' world whose object
Is the nest with young.
And while she is in one
She is oblivious to the other.
The eggs hold her spellbound
In the 'brooding' world
Until by the cock's action
She has food inside her
Ready for feeding the young.
Then and not till then
Is the spell broken.
Yet in neither of these worlds
Can her behaviour be explained
Entirely by reflex action,
Either simple or conditioned.
Knowledge plays its parts.

How does the bird acquire knowledge?
Without the power of retaining experience
– Memory in some sufficiently broad sense –
Learning is impossible. Does a bird
Learn as we do, by repetition?
Does it form habits? Certainly it does.
Routines are formed with regard to feeding,
To paths of travel, to entrances to the nest.
And these routines often enslave the bird.
But again observation provides a problem.
Such routines are not always formed
Even in the most favourable circumstances.
And when they are formed
They are frequently broken with ease.

And so the whole question of habit-formation
Is opened anew.
Why should the mere repetition
Of an action make it easier?
At first the answer seems easy.
A pathway of lessened resistance
Is formed through the nervous system,
So that the same stimulus
Naturally results in the same action.
But this is a mere restatement of fact.
It is not an explanation.
The question is – is there a compelling mechanism formed
Which enslaves the individual?
Even in ourselves we may observe 'dreamy states'
In which habitual actions become
No easier to perform than any others,
In which familiar objects
Lose their familiarity,
In which the mechanism of habit
Simply does not work.
There is no real evidence
Of such a mechanism at all
And the formation of habits,
Which is undeniable,
Remains a mystery.
Yet nearly all the psychological
Theories of learning
Depend on the assumption
Of some such mechanism.

But the bird does not apparently
Learn as we do.
The experiments which we frame to try
To test the bird's power of learning
Are all very artificial, and so we reach
The paradoxical conclusion
That sometimes the bird is extremely stupid
While at other times it seems extremely quick.

For in the natural state it can learn
And has also the power of choice.
With regard to its territory,
The size, duration, and type of locality
Are fixed by its species, but the shape
Varies from bird to bird, and is fixed
By the bird's own choice of boundaries.

Thus we reach the conclusion that a bird's behaviour
Is in part determined by physical changes,
I.e. by heredity, and in part
By mental activity on the bird's part.
But this is illusion.
There is one bird – one agent only.
And the final result may be expressed:
'No matter how much we learn
Of sensory experience, of retention, of reminiscence,
We cannot rebuild behaviour.
Behaviour is always something more,
Something which expresses itself
In continuity and persistent change
– Which raises some pretty problems
For the psychologist and the metaphysician.
It may even turn out after all
That Blake's guess was inspired.'

Shadows from the Ship

I STUDE in the heich efternune by the rail,
The sun bleezin' ahint me, silent, wi' the ship to mysel',
And on the foam o' oor bow-race
Fower ventilators' shadows, and mine, were cast,
A' aboot the same height and shape,
Rigid, and silent, and motionless.

The centre-castle's was in the lead,
The funnel's ahint, the derrick's owreheid.
On we gaed. And on gaed the shadow-show,
Motionless yet movin', ephemeral,
Yet, in its way, as lang as the sun shone
And the foam fermented, eternal.

Aince the sun was tint in a clood and we
Were tint tae. Aince the foam failed in odd sea
And we failed ana'. This, I thocht, is life,
A shadow on the foam o' a wave
That lasts only as lang as the foam abides
Or till a wanderin' clood obscures the sun.

A Plea for the Reopening of a Unique Howff

This vacance is a heavy doom
On Indian Peter's coffee-room,
For a' his china pigs are toom . . .
                                        ROBERT FERGUSSON

E CH, sure it seems if we wad drink
In Scotland Scotch Drink warth the name,
When a' oor gizzened pubs to poother shrink
Ane maun reopen no unkent to fame
Wi' this restored inscription roond its lintel curled:
'Peter Williamson, vintner frae the Ither Warld.'

Nae doot the landlord's cellar, like his sel',
'll come frae some great bond in Heaven or Hell.
It cheers me up juist tae imagine this,
Oor ae hope noo o' preein' ancient bliss!
Aye, Reid Indian Peter's oor last chance, I doot,
And, failin' his ghostly aid, Scotch Drink'll peter oot.

Two Scottish Boys[1]

Not only was Thebes built by the music of an Orpheus, but without the music of some inspired Orpheus was no city ever built, no work that man glories in ever done.

THOMAS CARLYLE

For the very essence of poetry is truth, and as soon as a word's not true it's not poetry, though it may wear the cast clothes of it.

GEORGE MACDONALD

Poetry never goes back on you. Learn as many pieces as you can. Go over them again and again till the words come of themselves, and then you have a joy forever which cannot be stolen or broken or lost. This is much better than diamond rings on every finger . . . The thing you cannot get a pigeon-hole for is the finger-point showing the way to discovery.

SIR PATRICK MANSON

Science is the Differential calculus of the mind, Art the Integral Calculus; they may be beautiful when apart, but are greatest only when combined.

SIR RONALD ROSS

THERE were two Scottish boys, one roamed seashore and hill
Drunk with the beauty of many a lovely scene,
And finally lost in nature's glory as in a fog,
Tossing him into chaos, like Bunyan's quag in the Valley of the
    Shadow.
The other having shot a lean and ferocious cat
On his father's farm, was profoundly interested
In a tapeworm he found when he investigated
Its internal machinery in the seclusion of his attic room,
– A 'prologue to the omen coming on' !

For while the first yielded nothing but high-falutin nonsense,
Spiritual masturbation of the worst description,
From the second down the crowded years I saw
Heroism, power for and practice of illimitable good emerge,
Great practical imagination and God-like thoroughness,
And mighty works of knowledge, tireless labours,
Consummate skill, high magnanimity, and undying Fame,

[1] 'Fiona Macleod' (William Sharp) and Sir Patrick Manson.

A great campaign against unbroken servility,
Ceaseless mediocrity and traditional immobility,
To the end that European reason may sink back no more
Into the immemorial embraces of the supernatural . . .
Sainte-Beuve was right – the qualities we most need
(Most of all in sentimental Scotland) are indeed
'*Science, esprit d'observation, maturité, force,
Un peu de dureté,*' and poets who, like Gustave Flaubert,
(That son and brother of distinguished doctors) wield
Their pens as these their scalpels, and that their work
Should everywhere remind us of anatomists and physiologists.

Poet and therefore scientist the latter, while the former,
No scientist, was needs a worthless poet too.

On the Asportation of the Scone Stone

SINCE David with a pebble in his sling
Goliath slew, now with this heavier stone
A little nation marks the opening
Of a like unequal battle for its own
And splits the atom of Earth's greatest throne.
This though perchance it prove like David's fling
But 'juvenile deliquency' yet may bring
A like result – the giant overthrown!

Scotland knew better than to ask for bread
Merely to get (but took!) a stone instead,
England's stony response full well foreknown.
Far more, O England, than the Scone Stone's gone,
And all the King's horses and the King's men
Cannot set up your Humpty Dumpty again!

Flamenco

THERE can be nae true Scot wha disna ken and lo'e
Rain in a thoosand forms, tho' floods o' rain destroy
The significance and quality o' rain. Draps are needit for that,
Aiblins mony, mony draps, undeemis draps gin you will,
Still and on, separate draps tho' yont coonts,
Blae draps, or broon, or whitey-grey, as lang's you get
The rain-smell, rain-taste, and rain-secret
That distinguishes rain frae juist water.

Look at her owre the hills yonder noo!
Whaur else in the wide world could you see
A dancer to manage hauf sae weel as yon.
Her trailin', frothin', mony-tiered skirt
Wi' serpent-like movements, explosive claps, sudden
    twists o' her haill bouk,
And ever and again a diamond-bricht shake,
A' keyed to the clatter and stamp o' her feet?
The infinite variety o' her fit-wark
Passes through a' the gradations
Frae a faint purrin' to a dynamo throbbin'
That gars the haill earth shake,
Syne – O look at her noo! – boundin' sae lichtly
And fetchin' her feet thegither in mid-air
To land as saft as an india-rubber ba'!

Oh, watch the prood pillar o' her neck,
The intense fixed fire o' her een,
The upright kist that seems to scorn
The agitation o' her laicher limbs!
Syne listen to the changin' sang o' her feet
And marvel aince mair at the prodigal ootpoorin'
O' dance efter dance sae varied in rhythm and fitwark,
And at a' the possibilities inherent
On this a'e form o' a Nature's coontless forms.

Beyond Argument

IT is now the duty of the Scottish genius
Which has provided the economic freedom for it
To lead in the abandonment of creeds and moral compromises
Of every sort, and to commence to express the unity of life
By confounding the curse of short-circuited thought
Circumscribing consciousness, for that is the thought
Of compromise, the medium of the time-server.
This must be done to lead men to cosmic consciousness,
And, as it cannot be quick, except on occasion,
And that the creative instant, the moment of divine realization,
When the self is lit by its own inner light,
Caused in the self by its intensity of thought.
Possibly over a long period, it must be thought of as a craft
In which the consummation of the idea, not in analysis, but in synthesis,
Must be the subject of the object – life.

The Unicorn

What matters most in the unicorn
Is unquestionably the horn.

What a pointer this is to the way
Man has evolved to the present day.

Just so the frontal lobes of his brain
Their salient significance gain

Till cortical understanding stands out
Pre-eminent beyond a doubt

But the unicorn's one horn can only point
Pointlessly in a world out of joint

While what minds men yet have painfully won
Still point in all directions – and none!

Yet a dehorned unicorn would be
A 'lusus natura': so, dehorned, are we!

Napalm Sunday

A Calendar for Cannibals

THE Christian calendar
You can see at a glance
Is oot o' date a' thegither
To gie you an instance.

It's silly this year to ca'
The Saxt o' April Palm Sunday. It should
Shairly be styled Napalm Sunday noo,
To gang wi' 'civilisation's' mood.

The calendar should never ha' been changed, you see.
The fact is we're a' still deep in B.C.
– If that's no libellin' pre-history!

A New Scots Poet

IT was difficult for his work at first
To secure the reception it required
Among such sentimentalists as the Scots.

They did not realise he had
Already put such emotion and feeling
Into it that all *they* had to do
Was to accept it straightforwardly,
Directly and simply, and that the emotion
Would liberate itself like a volatile vapour
Of its own accord,
Without any efforts on their part.

What happened was often like what happens
When, in Mahler's VIIIth Symphony,
That very lovely solo passage given to the soprano
In the first part; in D flat major,
'*Imple superna gratia*' – full to the brim
Of all possible intensity of passionately devout feeling –
Is sung 'expressively'
And ruined and vulgarised
In a way that hurts.

The Scots were always devils
For adding rouge to a rose
And gilt to a lily,
And prone to the pet vices of many Liedersänger
– Scooping and unnecessarily marked dynamics.

Though simple in the sense of single,
Of unified in aspiration,
His work of course is not 'simple' in any way.

Bringing Scotland alive in people's blood again
Rather than in their minds at first,

Through their instinctive actions and sense perceptions,
Through their sight, touch, smell and hearing,
Making them vividly aware
Of every element in the Scottish scene.

He was like the Pìob mhòr, or Great Highland Bagpipe,
The only instrument extant whose manual is derived
In enharmonic concord with a fixed fundamental bass.
Pìobaireachd is derived from the upper responses of the human
      heart
To the fundamental sequence of the elements.

Snollygosters[1]

I DON'T know whether the word
Snollygosters is English or Yankee
But wherever it comes from
I can only say 'thank'ee.'

For it conspicuously denotes
The great majority of Anglo-Scots,
'Quisling' is a word that doesn't
Half so well define the unpleasant
Types the Union fosters
As does Snollygosters.

Wherefore I'm inclined on balance
To think the word Post-Union Lallans.

[1] Mr. Malik's definition of the word is 'people who in the field of political struggle are false, hypocritical, and indiscriminately use any method and make any promises.' H. L. Mencken's definition is 'fellows who want office, regardless of party or principles, and who, whenever they win, get there by sheer force of talk-nothical assumacy.'

A Poem for Christmas 1952

A BAIRN disna lead us noo, for at length
We've learned the secret o' Peace through Strength.
Oor trust is in Collective Security
And no in Christianity,
Wi' the Atlantic Pact as the fount
O' wisdom – no' the Sermon on the Mount.

Providence waled unco weel
Baith the time and the place
For Christ's birth. Twenty centuries later
Micht hae sairly altered the case
And Bethlehem suddenly been
Like Hiroshima's hellish scene.

Yet born in the Twentieth Century
Christ micht hae been a conscript or conchie
Or singled oot in a loyalty check
By M.I.5 maybe as a Commie
While (Glasgow or Daily) Herald angels sang
Peace on earth to the tune of Whizz Bang.

'Peace on earth, goodwill to men,'
But naebody had the technique then,
Praise be we're in a better position
Thanks, of course, to nuclear fission,
And Ike and Monty, no' Jesus,
Financed by ilka Wall Street Croesus,
Proclaim the way that truly frees us.

Goodwill to men, but not of course
To Russians, Chinese, Bulgars, Poles,
Or Czechs or Malays or Kikuyu
All of whom are minus souls,
Not to be named in the same breath
As citizens of the Atlantic Powers
Those highly spiritual beings whose faith
In Freedom Science and Finance so richly endowers.

Faugh-a-Ballagh

To the S.R.A.

'FLEGGIN' shopkeepers, bombin' a wheen windas,
Daubin' oot the damned English numbers.
Dinna fash. It's naething. Juist a pack o' laddies
    Dreamin' they've a noble mission.
Ninety per cent o' Scotland still safely slumbers,'
    Said the Westminster politician.

'Huh! Ye mind me,' a true Scot replied,
'O' 31st January last. A blash o' rain,
A puckle breeze, a risin' sea. Nae sensible man
Gied it a second thocht. Juist a bit storm again.

'But the folk in Holland and doon the East Coast
Kent better when the mornin' cam' roond
And they saw the result o' what had begun
Sae simply that maist folk still sleepit soond.
Ye'll see the haill o' Scotland pourin' oot yet,
    The flood you've lang disdained,
    Fierce and unrestrained,
Howin' doon like water frae a breached dam!'
Faugh-a-Ballagh, Faugh-a-Ballagh!

Edinburgh's Tattoo Culture

CULTURE? Dinna gar me laugh.
The Edinburgh Festival's blawn the gaff
Aince for a' on that highbrow rot.
Juist look at the facts. It's not
Music, ballet, paintings and dramas
That sell it to the typical ignoramus,
And that's whaur the money comes frae.
It's plain eneuch naething else 'ud pay.

Bach and Beethoven and a' the rest
Are useless when it comes to the test.
Poetry readings and lectures juist a deid loss,
Ceilidhs Gaelic or Lallans no' worth a toss.
In the words o' the Bible a joyfu' noise
Alane gars the feck o folk rejoice
And only a guid-gaen military tattoo
Appeals to the taste o' ilka yahoo.

The Festival 'ud hae been written off
As a failure lang syne, a mock and a scoff,
If the promoters had lippened to the sae-ca'd arts.
But as in Africa and ither similar parts
Edinburgh kent fu' weel success only comes
When stupid mobs hear the beat o' the drums
And the blare o' the brass, and ony braw uniform
Can cairry the fat hert o' ignorance by storm.

Chamber music. Opera. Fiddle-dee-dee
It's the Castle Esplanade for fules like me
For a Ghurka band's worth mair
Than a' the nine muses there!

Nuts in May

I SAW twa items on
The T.V. programme yesterday.
'General Assembly of the Church of Scotland'
Said ane – the ither 'Nuts in May.'
I lookit at the picters syne
But which was which I couldna say.

The Royal Visit

A CINEMA star, a fitba match,
Dinna tell me that we can attach
Mair value to a Royal display
Than to sic affairs maun be paid.

The masses o' the people are drawn
To onything in inverse proportion
To its real significance, but to Thocht,
Art, Science, they show nae devotion.

Genius could never draw sic a crood
As follows a crack golfer. Is public taste,
Unspeakably bad in a'thing else
In this alane wi' true judgement graced?

Nonsense! It's juist the same idiot rush
To enthuse owre tripe that marks this occasion
As gethers for a murder trial, a bargain sale,
A dog-fecht, or any rotten War's declaration.

The Poet as Prophet

The Man for whom Gaeldom is waiting

Au fait with the whole range of European arts and letters
As few have ever been, he proudly proclaimed himself
A barbarian, in the sense that the art
Of the Celtic lands and of Scandinavia
Were both on the edge of the world
Wherein classical art progressed
Through Carolingian, Ottonian, Italian and Byzantine phases,
And neither was strong enough
To stand aside from the main stream of European art.
They aped it, and, whenever they did,
They fell from grace, as is the way with barbarian art.

Lowland Scotland is a battleground
Between Europe and Gaeldom and the work
Of European civilisation in this 'march'
– As in England and Russia –
Has always had to be pursued
Under hard conditions and given
Unstable and precarious results.
He discussed this a great deal
With his friend Eugenio d'Ors,
The Catalan writer (of Catalan and Cuban descent)
And successor of Prat de la Riba in the great work
Of intellectual and political renovation
Initiated by that industrious and particularist race.
Later, d'Ors dissociated himself from Catalanism
And thereafter wrote only in Castilian,
But it was Catalonia in the first place
That inspired him with the intellectual concepts
Out of which he built up his Europeanism,
By a movement inverse to that
Which led Barrès from the contemplation of the world

To practical and self-centred Lorraine.
He did not follow d'Ors or Barrès
Though he learned much from both.
But in the terminology d'Ors used,
Deriving from Alexandrian neo-Platonism
The concept of *eons* – by which is meant
A category in progress, a category on the march,
An idea which makes history – when it was claimed
That just as there is a sempiternal opposition
Between the *eon* of Pan and the *eon* of Logos,
Between the *eon* of unity, and the classical *eon*,
That of geometry, of reason, of the mind,
And the baroque *eon*, that of dispersion,
Of restlessness, of 'Nature,'
So in the interpretation of history
There is an opposition between
The concept of the European *oecumenos*
– The *oecumenos* of which England, Russia, and Spain
Alike stand on the periphery –
And the concept of barbarism
Which we derive through Rome from Greece.

'I am opposed to Rome, the religion of law and social contracts,
Assuring the development of material existence without satisfying the
    spiritual needs
Of humanity; to the bastard Christianity of State religion;
To the division between Church and State, and State and People,
    which leads
To classes hostile to each other's interests; I am in favour of all
That remains remote from centralisation – preserving
Its spiritual vigour and independence; not falling like Rome to the
    barbarians,
But inviolable, preferring death to any barbarian's or infidel's yoke,
Accepting nothing forced on them from without, nothing not issuing
From the innermost recesses of their spiritual life,
Independence, peace, and goodwill . . .
Give me a genius like a placid sheet of water
Whose surface is broken into circles that touch and interlink,

Each ring representing some sphere of external influence
Which widens and vanishes as it grows more remote
From its centre – reticulations all superficial,
Never disturbing the depths of my individuality.'

He claimed to stand outside both
In a distinct world altogether,
The separate and sovereign world of Gaeldom;
But if there are three Europes on the political map
– A Communist Europe, with a hold
On Europe and a hold on Asia,
Whose centre is Moscow and whose prophet is Karl Marx,
A liberal and parliamentary Europe
Whose prophet, Rousseau, may be French,
But whose centre is 'the English tradition,'
And, finally, a federative, corporative Europe
Whose centre is Rome, not necessarily
In the religious Catholic sense,
But certainly in the culturally oecumenical sense;
Not necessarily in the politically Fascist sense,
But certainly in the sense that the problem
Of the twentieth century is not freedom but cultural authority,
A Europe whose prophet is Proudhon –
His sympathies were wholly with the first of these
Which alone, he knew, had anything of value
To say to Gaeldom, and under which alone
Gaelic independence and the Gaelic languages
Would be respected and encouraged,
A view in which alone the disastrous split
Between Highlander and Lowlander might be healed
And a united Scotland arise in the world
– A view in which also the unnatural
Symbiosis of Gael and Gall might be severed
And Gaeldom detach itself from the sub-fusc Sassenach
As the golden moon swings free from a cloud again.

The reason was that he rose
Out of the category of men

And entered the category of the elements.
He was the wind, the sea, the tempest, the hurricane.
He was the marvellous embodiment
Of the complete identification
Of the Celtic mind with all nature and all life
That before his emergence had been long
Totally beyond the comprehension
Of the vast majority of modern Gaels,
Who had been in full retreat for over a century,
Fearing reality, passion, tragedy, communal assertion,
Fearing even the imputation of sadness
And blind and deaf to the things of the mind
And the intricate high arts of their ancestors;
In love with graceful and melodious ghosts,
Dancing to their own shadows
On the edge of the Imperial scheme of things,
From which they were being pushed off.
– He changed all that.

For the real Gael has something which the old Greeks had,
Which the French had in great measure,
Which the Swedes have acquired,
Which even the English have possessed now and then
– He has an ideal, a plan of life,
Transcending the mere means and apparatus of living.
Feverish immersion in secondary and ancillary matters
Leaves him unsatisfied.
He has a craving for essentials.
The miracle of literature,
Of culture, in racial history
Is that it is at once the bow and the mark,
The inspiration and the aim.
'In the beginning was the Word,'
But the Word is also
'The last of life for which the first was made.'
The seed and the flower are one.
The Gaels are among the peoples
Who have always taken that mystery for granted.

But in Scotland under the blight
Of the English influence
They have grown blind
Or indifferent to it.
The Celts with all their follies, weaknesses, and savageries
Never fell into that cardinal blunder
Of mistaking means for ends.
The ends they pursued, often blindly and wildly,
Were the fostering of individual dignity,
And of the spiritual imagination,
And the maintaining of a spiritual orchestral harmony
Between man and the universe.
His mission – his triumph – was to redirect
The vast dynamic and mechanism of modern life
To such aims again.

Suddenly, splitting the sky
Was heard a great voice
Which echoed round the firmament.
'Stand fast for Scotland!'

The whole nation felt itself shaken
As by an electric shock
Into one great sob which burst forth
In a flood of jubilation over the miracle.
An indomitable ardour blazed in all hearts
Until each man had the strength of four.

In him were incarnate at that moment
The liberties and the rights of man asserted in the face of power,
The independence of the spirit which demands
That conscience be satisfied
Even against one who ranks himself higher than its claims.
Scotland felt at that moment
That no man ever personified her,
Ever would represent her,
As he did,

And she grew in glory
And was transfigured with pride.
It was not a Scottish moment;
It was a universal moment.

Miracle in the Horribals

The law exists to make the crime.
LEO SHESTOV

It is the legal crimes of modern States, involving no sanction on the executioner, that are the ultimate abomination, for they abolish the only value that can make sense of human existence.
The great terror and danger of northern peoples, M. Camus observes, is that they lack the appetite for life and consequently any respect for it.

WHEN the Horribals, that jam-packed slum quarter o' Glesca
On 5th October '53 gaed dry as Cripps' speeches
And crime o' ilka kind ceased in't, and a'
The kirks and religious and charitable bodies
Were treated by the folk as if they werena there,
And even the polis on their beats could nae mair
Win a cheery word or nod frae ony man or wumman
Or lad or lass, gosh, it didna seem human!

A' Law and Order, Religion, Guid Citizenship,
Had ettled to want was suddenly gained.
The writers in the newspapers tried in vain
To explain hoo the miracle had been attained,
Nor were they pleased aboot it! No, by goy!
For hoo could the publicans and bookies enjoy
Seein' their haill trade vanish as it had never been
And a' the muckle hive eident, douce, and clean?

Letters to the editors swore it couldna last.
It was against a' nature. Some fell deep-laid plot
Maun be at the bottom o' this byordinar change.
Days passed, lang days. Yet nae clue could be got.

Syne in the city pulpits a' the ministers spoke
Stressin' the difference atween the Horribals folk
And sic true converts as only *they*, by the Grace
O' God, could mak', sae singly and seldom in sic a place.

Croods frae a' the ither pairts o' Glesca poured in
To see the ferlie for themsels, and feelin' that they
Wi' pubs, bookies, and thrang polis courts still
Infestin' their areas, were shown up in a way
Cursed and jeered and socht to bait the Horribals men
But wi' nae success, for they keepit indoors then
And were dubbed cowards, Pharisees, and what not
– Wild words that didna fash them a jot !

Some say the polis were inclined to provoke
The folk, yet nae law or even bye-law was broke
For the stricken month the 'Conversion' lasted,
And mony a worthy lawyer and beadle said 'Blast it !
Noo there's nae mair crime or drink, kirk-gaen or vice,
Oor cushy jobs are gane. It's yont endurance
To hae oor livins snatched awa' like this
By sic an incredible, unprecedented chance.'

Bitterest o' a' were the Salvation Airmy,
Licensed victuallers, health visitors, nuns, and charity agents,
And it became clear as glaur that a'thing in life
Hings thegither, and a' Society's pageants
Need a' the auld elements if they're to gang on
As they've dune in the past. Whaur there's nae crime
Lawyers, court officers, polis'll ha'e a thin time
And wi' them a' the thoosands that to them hang on !

Pity a' the respectable folk wha canna learn
A true ethic despises ethic or discern
Hoo servile, frightened, and egoistic the attitude is
O' a' wha dinna juist obey the law
But punish, and enjoy punishin', them wha canna;
And sufferin' frae their self-inflicted rules o' Good

Aye need folk like the Horribals folk for scapegoats
To load wi' the sins they're tempted to themsels,
And thus create and keep and live on the Myth o' Crime.
Freedom as the Foundation o' Value's a concept
Alien or hostile to traditional morality
And pressed to a logical conclusion as here
Blaws the gaff on a' Law and Order haud dear.

It ended in the way it began, and a muckle sigh
O' relief the haill civilised world let fly
Since if it happened in a'e place it could onywhaur neist,
And, lastin' a month aince, might be permanent sune,
And respectable citizens feel badly let doon
When sic unlooked-for competition comes
Frae the vera elements in contrast wi' whom
Their virtues hae aye been like select suburbs to slums.

Owre muckle virtue's no' for the Horribals denizens,
Let them stick to their lusts and continue to gie
Guid jobs to barmen, bookies, and bobbies
And sic-like essentials o' true humanity,
Wi' scouth to a' the busybodies wha dae guid
To the unfortunate, but canna if there's nane!
– Certes, there was cause eneuch for national rejoicin'
When the Horribals became the Auld Horribals again!

A Coronation Dream

For a rag and a bone and a hank of hair
                              KIPLING

A' THAT's left o' the Coronation noo
Are a puckle memories o' the hullabaloo
Like somebody sookin' in vain through straws
At the bottom o' a toom ice-cream glass.

Shairly naebody can hear sic a raspberry
And no' be whummled by a very
Tidal-wave feeling o' sinfu' 'idiocy'
In the Athenian sense. Fegs, no' me !

For the Coronation for a wee like a toposcope
Displayed a' the rhythms o' human thocht and hope
In the form o' sparklin' lichts, sune slain
By oor dowf fatuity again.

The presentation o' the Bible to the Queen
May no' be a thing Scottish ministers want
Broken into as in America
By a plug for a deodorant.

Yet the interventions o' Providence
Can be nae less disconcertin',
God shows nae consideration ava'
For Earl Marshall's arrangements, that's certain.

The pomp and glory last a wheen 'oors,
Syne if ony trace can be seen it's
In lumps o' sodden papers on the pavements
And cherry stanes and husks o' peanuts.

It minds me o' a fearsome dream I had aince.
I dreamt I was at a muckle Fair
Whaur a' the things folk think they need
Were laid oot roond me like the things frae a loon's pockets there.

Yin 'ud think it 'ud tak' hunders o' years
For a man to get used to this world, brim fu'
O' millions o' things, into which he is born
An endless complexity to adjust himsel' to.

But in fact he gets used to 't sae incredibly fast
It's almaist as tho' he had expectit
A' thing to be as it is. Wha kens? Folk are sae quick
To tak' in what they see and come to terms wi' it,

As tho' the idea o' a'thing existit
Ready-made in their heids, a kind o' conjurer's trick.

Weel, there I was at that super-Fair
Wi' croons and coronets, the sceptre, the orb
And a' the rest o' the paraphernalia,
An endless museum for a'e glance to absorb.

I turned clean dizzy in my dream, for I kent
I was seein' a' thae things for the first time, sent
Up oot o' the void yince-yirn to see
A' this nonsense cluttered aboot me!

What fleggit me was that naething o't
Astonished me in the least. I'd got
The feelin' o' kenin't a' sae weel
I was fair at hame in that endless reel.

Yet hoo could *I* ken what the Cap o' Maintenance was
Or the Gowden Ampulla frae wha's beak oil fa's
Or the Armills, and a' the rest o' the junk.
Flotsam frae which History's tides ha'e shrunk.

Syne in my dream a'thing hardened to stane,
Ilka trumpery gadget seemed to attain
Eternal status. A' that rubbish till then
Hadna maittered muckle. Noo to my hert it cam' ben,

Suddenly different and somehow sublime.
I felt nae human being until that time
Had reckoned wi' sic a possibility
And wondered why *that* had been left to *me*.

Forenenst me noo was a' this hocus-pocus;
A'thing superfluous, a' that's gane sour
Or run to seed, made into a memorial to mock us
Everlastin' as God Himsel' in this dreidfu' 'oor.

A' petrified, preserved for the haill o' Eternity!
But what's Eternity? What's God? Is He
Juist anither idea o' Man's, no' made concrete
Because no' seemin' worth while? Albeit

Like a' the perishable rubbish that had taen
Eternal form in my dream sae suddenly
God micht ana'! The idea lowed in my brain
Like a terrible tantalisin' possibility.

Archangels gaed by this way and that
In the midst o' that unco masquerade
And gutchers wi' lang beards and God himsel'
– Or Churchill – as tho' a' the Abbey statues joined the parade.

Syne an angel came and comfortin me
In my horror and led me oot o' my extremity
– And I saw nocht but toom beer-bottles and banana skins attour
And was mortal glad sicna Coronation was owre.

Music Not for Me

With compliments to Duncan Robertson, Mary Dawson,
Richard Hardie, etc.

O BETTER surely to die at once
Than lie in a Scottish hospital
Forced to hear the Scottish Home Service
And Jean Taylor Smith's love call.

O better to be on the D.I. list
With no chance of recovery again
Than listen to another such programme
For the hopelessly inane,

Ending (God, how she knows her onions!)
With some hackneyed hymn or psalm
– O better to be in a coma than suffer
This eternal service of 'ham'!

1954

Like Millefiori in Clear Glass

Through little stones hills sprang into existence
And in the brier trampled underfoot
Loud was the sound of forests with black arms.

NICOLAI TIKHONOV

It is not enough to be an Aeolian harp
that trembles with every wind; one must onself be
the wind and call the tune.

JOHN GUEST

A Y E mind, ye poets, wha seek the Muse's boons,
Nor curlew's spring flute nor passionate sang
O' nichtingale bowered in the may
Fa's as pleasurably and lingers as lang
       On the inward ear
As the saft gay chatter o' a menzie o' sandpipers
Flyin' invisible owre the dunes
       In the end o' the year.

Covet that syne, or the wee sillery pieces
O' the lintie in Spring that are haurdly mair
Than a perfection o' the sough o' the flock
On the way to roost. Some sic apotheosis, shair,
Or aiblins juist an inklin' subtly aware
O' the bent o' hosts o' folks herts maun be
(Like millefiori in clear glass he sees,
Or those incomparable *éloges*
Compressing into a few shining lines
The manifold existences o' men;
Ilk ane o' the varna set in the whiteness
Like a star that shivers wi' its ain brightness)
       A poet's purpose and gree.

Sib to the illumination won oot o' the brooding darkness
When in a man's ingyne, nesh to the signs
And indications o' the hidden truth, a quick flame
O' incandescence loups oot and like lichtin' refines
A'thing in its momentary but eternal gleam,
Till his gifts eindoon charismata seem,
Their function to reveal and acclaim
The miraculous nature o' the miracle. Nae less!
The fertilising o' an impersonal 'given,' it's true,
By a personal 'life' which 'mak's a' things new,'
Since the 'given' is capable o' sic revivings
Bein' itsel' the product o' coontless previous personal strivings,
　　　And by genius kissed
　　　Can come suddenly alist!

1955

The All-Scotland Salvation Stampede

*The brash illiteracy – the use of the Bible as a rag-bag of texts, to be learned by heart,
the preacher who brandishes a wheel on whose hub and circumference 'Christ' is written,
and spells out the word c–h–u–r–c–h, saying 'Take U away, and it's meaningless: this
means U are needed.'*

*Survey most nations and most ages. Examine the religious principles which have, in
fact, prevailed in the world. You will scarcely be persuaded that they are anything but
sick men's dreams. Or perhaps will regard them more as the playsome whimsies of
monkeys in human shape than the serious, positive, dogmatical asseverations of a being
who dignifies himself with the name of rational.*

DAVID HUME

WHAT about Dr. Billy Graham and all
The 'Tell Scotland' parsons today who call
Our fatuous folk back to the Bible story
Equating ignorance and superstition with glory?
What about the hordes of mindless fans who tryst
In the same way with a crooner, a film star, Churchill, Attlee, or
    Christ?

By every movement of their facial features,
By every word and gesture, these creatures
Declare their ardent and boundless devotion
To the great ideas and interests that reach their lug
With precisely the same emotion
As Persian camomile inspires in a bug![1]

[1] With acknowledgments to Dmitri Pisarev (1840–68).

King Over Himself

HOW he loved to survey the lands of Scotland
From some nest of eagles in a cloud of stone
– To let his soul pasture in her valleys
And frolic on her mountains,
Roam from her Northmost to her Southmost point,
Watch her skies, drink her waters,
Breathe her forests and her fields!
All the flowers of Scotland grew in his soul,
And he felt that savour of his own soul rise to his head.
All the people of Scotland once more
Were timeless, aflame, and virile.
Their speech rang like steel.
They talked in poems and their words
Held echoes of miracle.
Miracle followed the man like a domestic animal.

Ere the great day on which he declared himself
Had he not looked at Anglo-Scotland and understood and judged,
Here there was no justice, or love of justice, he thought,
No reality or love of reality.
Here there was only expediency and love of expediency.
Here all was venal, and to feign worth
Was better than to possess it.
There was too much outward showing,
Too little inward meaning,
Too much appearance,
Too little reality.

And instantly, summing up in himself
The whole range of Gaelic wisdom,

He pronounced as his, too, the 'Hate of Cadoc',
The Welsh saint of the sixth century:

'I hate the judge who loves money
And the bard who loves war
And the chiefs who do not guard their subjects
And the nations without vigour.
I hate houses without dwellers,
Lands untilled,
Fields that bear no harvest,
Landless clans,
The agents of error,
The oppressors of truth,
Lost learning,
And uncertain boundaries,
Journeys without safety,
Families without virtue,
Lawsuits without reason,
Ambushes and treasons,
Falsehood in council,
Justice unhonoured;
I hate a man without a trade,
A labourer without freedom,
A home without a teacher,
A false witness before a judge,
The miserable exalted,
Follies in place of teaching,
Knowledge without inspiration,
Sermons without eloquence,
And a man without conscience.'

And he sang, too in St. Cadoc's words:

'Without knowledge, no power.
Without knowledge, no wisdom.
Without knowledge, no freedom.
Without knowledge, no beauty.
Without knowledge, no nobleness.
Without knowledge, no victory.

Without knowledge, no honour.
The best of occupations, work.
The best of cares, justice.
The best of characters, generosity.'

And to every man in Scotland he cried:

'Remember that thou art a man,
And that there is nothing like him
Who is King over himself.'

The Poetic Faculty

WHEN a person is greatly interested in a problem
This problem is often worked upon and solved
By processes which are unconscious
Relatively to that part of the mind
Normally in control of the body.
Intuition has a superior process
(Which is not above being tested)
To our reasoned efforts. An added element
Comes into the extra-conscious mind
To reinforce the given material
On which the intuitive faculty is set to work.
We know definitely what it is,
There are vast stores of memory
Unavailable to the conscious mind,
Intractable to the conscious will,
Containing details and items
Unlikely ever to appear in full consciousness,
And probably some vital details
Forever forgotten by us,
Shreds of truth thrown on the waste-heap
By our foolish and careless consciousness
And forever and ever irrecoverable
Except by the marvellous capacity of intuition.

Nicolas Kostyleff in 'Le mécanisme cérébral de la pensée'
Reporting the outcome of his interviews
With contemporary French poets and novelists
Stresses their care to document themselves,
Saturate themselves in the subject-matter of their work,
And to enrich their verbal associations.
Such documentation eventuates,
According to his theory of poetic inspiration,
In the formation of chains of associations
Which, when a discharge is once set off,
Results in an unravelling of verbal reflexes.
Transition from one chain of verbo-motor associations
To another may be mediated
By the most subtle connections between them,
So that first drafts of poems
Frequently exhibit apparently unrelated ideas.

So there were times in the early stages
When it was difficult to follow his doings.
During a space his way was sown with obstacles
And twisted and turned so swiftly
Among a thousand difficulties,
From a mountain to a plain,
From a plain to a forest,
From a forest to a river,
That it was impossible for us to keep up with him.

But, as he himself said later,
Suggesting how we might utilise biographical material
In discovering how to energise ourselves,
To tap the reservoirs of talent
That most of us never utilise:

'The West Highland Railway Company
Was formed with the sole object
Of opening up a lonely depopulated countryside.

'There were scant prospects of a remunerative traffic
For many years to come, and in consequence

The line had to be built as cheaply as possible.
Speed was of no consideration whatever.
Accordingly not the slightest attempt was made
To obtain a smoothly graded course.

'The engineers went ahead almost regardless of hill and dale,
And where the mountain sides are seared with deep clefts
So the railway winds in and out
Following the profile of these indentations.

'The earthworks have been reduced to such a remarkable degree
That where the line climbs open hillsides
It is often well-nigh impossible to detect its course
When looking from the glens below.

'But it is this very form of construction
That gives the West Highland line   -
Its own unique character.

'Had the railway been planned as a fast express route
We should never have enjoyed
These bewildering twists along Loch Lomond and up Glen Falloch.

'There would never have existed
That astonishing switchback from Glenfinnan and Arisaig
Where the changes of gradient are so abrupt
That they can be plainly felt in the carriage.

'Only the scenery would remain
And even then a fleeting glimpse of Ben Dorain
From a streamlined express
Bucketing up Glen Orchy at 70 m.p.h.
Would be a poor substitute
For the ever-fascinating perambulation
Of the Horseshoe Bend.'

(He was the last man in the world
To be glad that many of our famous gradients

Have been either flattened a little
Or their hairpin bends widened,
And have, as a result,
Lost some of their sporting qualities
– But are definitely easier for the visitor
Who cannot be expected to know,
As it were, what is round the corner.)

'Over so severe a route the loading restrictions
Are very strict, and the slightest excess
Over the maximum tonnage laid down for each type
Of engine used on the route
Makes the use of two engines imperative.
(And neither a really old-fashioned engine
Going *Scotia, Scotia, Scotia,*
On a little local line as from Riddings to Langholm!)

'At the summit of the long climb is Glen Douglas station
For a moment there is a vista eastwards towards Loch Lomond
And then the line swings round to the West.

'At Garelochhead climbing begins in real earnest
And by this time the engine has developed
A full-throated exhaust something akin to gunfire,
She is going practically "all out"
And yet with a load of only six coaches
The speed is barely 25 m.p.h.

'A 1 in 15 gradient takes its toll.
Higher and higher the line rises
Until, almost unexpectedly,
As the train swings round through Whistlefield station,
One finds that the railway has come out
On the edge of a steep hillside.
300 feet below is Loch Long
Winding among the mountains
And right opposite is the entrance
To a still narrower fjord, Loch Goil.

The very suddeness of its appearance
Makes the scene leave a feeling of exhilaration and excitement
Whether it be on a still summer day
When the hills are mirrored in the Loch,
Or in early Spring when the highest peaks
Are still snow-clad and the water the colour of steel.

'Framed in a V of the hills are the crags of Ben Arthur's summit,
The Cobbler,
And remembering the nearness of Loch Long
It seems this dive through a rock cutting
Must surely take one over the edge and into the loch.'

He did not break down.
His frequent changes, his vertiginous speed,
Were in keeping with the true nature of the Scot
Almost wholly lost in Anglo-Scotland.
The polymath tradition – Burns's delight
In 'intermingledons' – is more than seven centuries old;
Intricately, even abstrusely, literary work
With little or no parallel in English work
Has had a strong grip on Scots as long.
Scots prosody and music through the ages
Is characterised by that headlong speed
Or giddying subtleties of movement;
'There is one general principle
Which informs and pervades all Gaelic artistry
– The principle of precision, definiteness, completeness,
Admirably exemplified in the extraordinary meticulousness
And symmetry of the Brehon Laws,
Seen not less strikingly in the native Gaelic art
Of Scotland and Ireland as applied
To the illuminated manuscripts
And the sculptured stones.
(The work of the illuminations in the Book of Kells
Is so fine it has to be studied with a microscope.)
There is the tendency to attempt to exhaust
The details of a description

By piling up of descriptive adjectives.
In England it was tried by Southey
In his description of the cataract of Lodore.
In Gaelic it was a well-recognised form.
In him it is a leading feature.
A piling up not of adjectives, however,
– The completed effect of the piling up of details
Is one of movement, suggesting the action
Of a concerted dance, or the centre of a squadron.
We have gone astray if we call this art merely meticulous,
A pedant's or cataloguer's vanity in words.
The whole is not always lost in the parts;
It is not a compilation,
Impressive only because it is greater
Than any of its contributory elements,
But often single in result,
And above all things lively.

To My Friend the Late Beatrice Hastings[1]

(Who expressed the fear that a Communist anti-religious line might yet provoke a great swing back into the arms of the Church unless some substitute is provided, perhaps from Indian religious thought; and also to a friend in Manchester, who asks me to assist her young son in the preparation of a script on: 'What for youth today, if anything, is taking the place of the religion that so profoundly influenced former generations?')

CAN historical materialism, which is only a historical method,
Be an adequate substitute, to the proletariat, for philosophy,
Always taken in its traditional meaning
As a universal and closed *Weltanschauung*
Into which all the currents
Of the natural and material sciences flow?

[1] A brilliant contributor under the pseudonym of Alice Morning to the *New Age* in its heyday, and authoress of *Defence of Madame Blavatsky*.

One meets here the well-known 'need for metaphysics'
Which rises up everywhere;
And it cannot be denied
That such a need exists
In the masses of workers.
Workers often develop a remarkably deep
Interest and understanding of philosophic problems,
The deeper, indeed, the greater the poverty
Out of which they labour to raise themselves.
Nor can it be doubted that the satisfaction of this need
Is a powerful and essential means
By which the working class makes itself more efficient and skilled
For the fulfilment of its historic tasks.

However, this 'need for metaphysics'
Has nowhere metaphysical roots.
And it would remain dissatisfied
Even though a new philosophy
Was brewed out of the holiest and costliest
Surrogates of the old philosophies.

It has, in every case, only historical roots
By means of which it is nourished
And with which it dies.

These roots, on one side, are the 'metaphysical stuff'
With which the brains of proletarian children
Are oppressed in the public schools
In the brutal and vulgar form
Of incomprehensible Bible texts
And hymns from the hymn books;
And, on the other side, the soulless character
Of modern mass-production, mechanical labour,
Which, by its eternal monotony,
Even anticipates the spirit of the worker
And leads him to philosophise
Over the meaninglessness of this existence

Which from infancy has been impressed upon him
As the work of a supernatural power.

A worker who has worked his way up
Out of the lowest depths of the proletariat writes:
'I wish to be free from the dogmas of dualism
Dictatorially commanded, free from servility.
My philosophy is the autocracy of the spirit. . . .

'Is this civilisation, when the intelligence
Dies physically a horrible death?
Is this humanity
When the soul goes hungry?
When its desires thirst
Languishing for beauty and power.
I demand a remedy.
The plough, the chisel,
The trowel in the sinewy fist
– But this fist belongs to a man!
Watch over it!
The pen, the lyric, the telescope
Belong to the cycle of the spirit.
Do not forbid these!
For the suppressed talent bitterly avenges itself. . . .

'Thought, in my world, is a cause of suffering,
Because through thought I know
How needy and unfortunate I am.
Were the veil of ignorance
Still over my spiritual eyes
Truly my heart would feel only half as much
The travail of my earthly suffering.
I have entered completely into the Marxist idea
That economic poverty is just as much
A basis for the degeneration of the spirit
As of the body of a people
And that only a life half-way free from worry
Will allow man to blossom
Into complete personality.

'How else could it happen that until now
Only the materially secure
(I will not say absolutely, but relatively)
Have formed the circle of the artistic élite,
Whilst much valuable talent has been murdered
Under the base pressure of economic calamity,
Or, better said, remained in embryo?
Man is matter, stuff; his spirit exists
In a material organisation,
And wherever physical nourishment
Necessarily has to be obtained
Only through externalised power,
Claiming everything, there falls away
The spirit-enlivening element which fructifies the soul.

'Such a person, naturally, is absorbed entirely
With the struggle round the ordinary problems of the stomach.

'He is, and remains, considered
From this point of view, the animal
In whom the spiritual personality is a farce.

'Here is found the great,
Ignominious and cardinal flaw
In the multitude of mankind today.'

One sees from this that modern workers
Understand how to philosophise very well,
But they wish to know nothing
Of a single philosophy
Whether it be the 'dualism' of philosophical idealism
Or of the 'ordinary problems of the stomach'
Of philosophical materialism.

What they have 'completely absorbed'
Is the 'Marxist idea' – historical materialism –
Which can in fact fully satisfy their 'metaphysical needs,'
Not through a new philosophy,
But through a history of philosophy
Written in accordance with the historical-materialist method.

It would not be difficult to write that history,
For, as Schopenhauer correctly says,
All previous philosophy revolves
About certain fundamental ideas
Which always return.
But *how* they return, out of what causes,
In what form and under what circumstances,
To determine this requires
An ever more precise scientific instrument,
And we will not be able to count on this
For a long time to come.

Therefore all the more
Ought we to avoid
Bringing philosophical speculation and playthings
Into the proletarian class struggle,
Whose metaphysical need,
In its dark impetus,
Knows much better the right road!

The Girl on the Vertical Capstan Lathe

O MAGGIE Mackay was the quean for me
I kent as sune as I saw her first
Daen' something I'd thocht that haurdly a man
Let alane a bit o' a lassie durst.

She was gaily drivin' a muckle
Automatic vertical capstan lathe
Performin' owre a hunner operations
On aucht steel projectiles in a cycle, faith!

Cigarette in mou', she was rinnin' the robot
Syne flickin' the levers lowsin' the job,

Insertin' anither in its place, and guidin'
The flow o' the oil while her bonny flock nob
Ootshone the smokin' coils o' new-cut steel
As she rakit the deidly swarf awa'
That, gif she'd pit a haund wrang, 'ud hae left her
Shorn o' her fingers in nae time at a'.

It was a richt cordial to my hert
To watch her eident unerrin' way,
Sae quick and clever, yet leavin' her
Aye free for a routh o' byplay tae.

I stood and gapit wi' admiration
And wi' a sklent o' her een she saw me
And weaved, without stoppin' her skilly darg,
And 'Cooee, cooee' I heard her ca' me.

Noo I've nae doot she'll manage me
As lichtly and successfully
Wi' never ony airgh o' spirited fun
Kittler faur tho' this new job'll be.

Artistic Developments in Scotland

I. Painter

NOTHING had been seen like this in Scotland before
– No realisation that the elements of a visual art
Such as lines, colours, shapes,
Possess their own forces of expression
Independent of any association
With the external aspects of the world;
That their life and action
Are self-conditioned psychological phenomena
Rooted in human nature;

That these elements are not chosen
By convention as words and figures are –
They are not merely abstract signs
But they are immediately and organically
Bound up with human emotions.

Scarcely anybody had really seen Scotland before
– Let alone understood such facts
That a bright colour (a cadmium, say)
Vibrates more strongly in angular or pointed forms,
And a blue would be made more profound
By being confined in a rounded space,
A circle or full ellipse,
Or that, as Kandinsky has shown,[1]
A triangle of colour, whether it be
Acute-angled, obtuse-angled, or equilateral,
Is an entity with a spiritual perfume
Proper to itself alone.
In combination with other forms
This perfume becomes differentiated,
Acquires accompanying nuances,
But remains radically unalterable
Like the smell of the rose which can never
Be mistaken for that of the violet.

II. Composer

IT was difficult for his work at first
To receive the reception it required
Among such sentimentalists as the Scots.

They did not realise that he had
Already put so much emotion and feeling
Into it that all *they* had to do
Was to accept it straightforwardly,

[1] See *Uber das Geistige in der Kunst* by Wassily Kandinsky (1914).

Y

Directly and simply, and then the emotion
Would liberate itself like a volatile vapour
Of its own accord,
Without any efforts on *their* part.

(Though simple in the sense of single,
Of unified in aspiration,
His work of course is not *simple* in any way!)

What happened was often like what happens
When, in Mahler's VIIIth Symphony,
That very lovely solo passage given to the soprano
In the first part, in D flat major,
'*Imple superna gratia*' – full to the brim
Of all possible intensity of passionately devout feeling
Is sung 'expressively'
And ruined and vulgarised
In a way that hurts.

The Scots have always been holy terrors
For adding rouge to a rose
And gilt – guilt – to a lily,
And prone to the pet vices of many Liedersänger
– Scooping and unnecessarily marked dynamics.

1958

The Burnet Rose

FOR M. PAUL LORION, FORMER FRENCH CONSUL-GENERAL IN
EDINBURGH

I THINK in the Burnet or Scots rose
All that's best in my people shows.

Ideal for a poor starved soil or windy place
– Surely that's true too of our Scottish race.

They bind a loose surface staunchly together
Yet underground run hither and thither,

With their dense root-system, and everywhere
Their stout little thorny thickets uprear

Keeping the weeds away. And so they thrive
Where less tough things could never survive.

One drawback they have. They only flower
Briefly once a year – save the kind whose power

Hybridisation with a *Gallica* may nourish
– Scotland and France again! – to season-long flourish.

And in that fact I am sure, my friend,
There is a moral all Scots should perpend.

Tropaeolum Speciosum

THE thistle is a handy thing
If a barefoot foe comes trampling.
Else, being a worthless weed, it's not
A fitting symbol for a Scot.

The flame-coloured nasturtium, *Tropaeolum speciosum*,
Which does so brilliantly in Scotland and so poorly
In England, should be adopted now
As our national emblem surely.

And not for that reason only, but also
Because it buries itself so deep in the ground
It is impossible to dig it up. Even so
The true genius of our country is found.

It has the pleasant habit of rambling about
Through anything planted near it,
And coming up in unexpected places
In all ways our symbol most fit.

The Bog in Spring

HERE in the evening an artist would find the inspiration
For the trick of evolving colour in shadow
– Producing colour for the sake of light
Rather than light for the sake of colour.
For the colours of Spring's livery are not emphatic,
Unlike those of winter and summer, here,
But more toned, far subtler in the blending,
Baffling in their quick transitions from saffron to silver,
And from silver-grey to white when the evening 'sokes'
Steal up the 'deeks.' Clumps of reeds waving dark-brown tassels
And green-blue irises of marshland suddenly
Become spectacular with the magic touch of Spring's sun
Just as when artfully coloured lights are cast
On a theatre's bits of symbolic scenery.
This is the charm of the bog in Spring –
The sudden emergence of the landscape with vital colour.
Only yesterday the scene was but a poor shrivelled composition
– The reed-beds a dead-wood colour as if left over
From last year. To-day the process of a new birth's complete.
The slow river and meandering waterways move
With the mysterious throb of life. The forlorn marsh farm,
Starkly rectangular to the eye, is now
Peeping transfigured from some proscenium
Of alder and sallow. – Summer's herald's trumpeting.
O look! O look! Two or three days ago
There were nothing but formless wastes
Of yellow reed and slate-blue waters
Gleaming flatly beneath the hard March sunshine.

The yellow has turned to a pale amber now
The water is a silvery-grey,

And a vague wreath of mist hangs over the lush grassland
Giving the illusion of immense translucent distances.
The air is heavier, as if awaiting with more certain expectancy
The unmistakable voice of early Summer.

The empty sky of March is replaced by a sky
Full of light and faery shapes, feathery clouds
Floating or drifting lazily, enchanting
The somewhat mournful tranquility of the soft grey wastes of the
    lagoon.
Now you can hear the earliest short sleepy-like croak
Of the erstwhile torpid frogs. They hop from their holes
Feeling their way into the warming waters, influenced
By the thrill of the universal burgeoning of Spring.
They'll come out in platoons to-morrow, shiny, black-stained,
Growing ever more venturesome until at night
If you go down to the 'deeks' you'll hear
Their quaint orchestration, their croaking Serbonian lullaby,
Down below in the very bowels of the marsh.

Burns's Salute to King Homer I

THE stooka Burns in Glesca's George Square
Cam' alist for a wee while yestreen
And spak to me aboot the self-coronation
Earlier in the day there he'd seen.

'King Homer the First o' Scotland,' he cried.
'Weel, weel! Juist let the mannie be,
He'll mak' at least as worthy a king
As ony in monarchy's history.

'Dinna lichtlie his shoddy pink silk robe
Or his onion-polished gowd-leaf croon
Or the fauldin' aluminium throne
– It'll be easier if need be to tak' doon.

'For what ha'e ony o' the ithers had
But sic flashy gauds as to fools appeal?
The bubblin' guid nature o' this wee Yank crank
Is a welcome change in Royalty I feel.

'Let him annex his saxty-odd thrones.
That'll ha'e yae advantage if nae mair
– Gettin' rid o' the present incumbents I mean.
Yae nonentity's better than saxty I swear.

'And if Scotland maun ha'e a King ata'
And a native Scot it canna be
I'd as lief ha'e Mr. Tomlinson here
As ony ony established Royal line can gi'e.

'Kings and Queens are a puir lot at best.
Certes Homer at warst's nae waur than the rest.
Hiya, Homer, slainte and skol!
I pledge you wi' the haill Clyde in a bowl.'

The mair I lookt at Burns's sculptured face
The mair o' jokin' in't I saw nae trace
And the mair I thocht o' his words forsooth
The mair I kent they were nocht but truth.

Goal

With acknowledgments to Søren Kierkegaard

OH, in the days of youth,
Of all torments the most terrible
– Not to be like others,
Never to live a single day
Without being painfully reminded
That one is not like others,

Never to be able to run with the crowd,
The pleasure and joy of youth,
Never to be able to abandon oneself freely,
Always, as soon as one would venture on that,
To be reminded of the chains,
The isolation of separateness,
Which with a pain close to despair
Divides one from all that is called
Human life and cheerfulness and joy.
One can, it is true, by the most frightful efforts,
Endeavour to conceal what one at that age
Regards as his disgrace,
That he is not like others.
This may perhaps succeed up to a certain point
But nevertheless the torment is in the heart,
And the success is assured
Only up to a certain point.
With the years, certainly,
This pain disappears more and more,
For in the measure one becomes
More and more spirit.
It is no longer painful
Not to be like the others.
Spirit is just this –
Not to be like the others.

Montrose

WHERE better could a town be placed than here?
Peninsular Montrose has everything
With water on three sides, while, beyond
Rich farmlands, the hills upswing.

It has the right size too – not a huge
Sprawling mass, but compact as a heart,
Life-supplier to a whole diversified area
Yet with the economy of a work of art.

So small that it is possible to know
Everyone in it, yet it still radiates
In ties not broken but strengthened
To successive generations of expatriates.

So small and yet radiating out
Not only in space but in time, since here
History gives permanence of distinction
And dignity to each succeeding year.

'Guid gear gangs in sma' book' and fegs!
Man's story owes more to little towns than to great,
And Montrose is typical of Scotland's small grey burghs
Each with a character of its own time cannot abate.

Model of the preference of quality to quantity
Montrose set here between the hills and the sea
On its tongue of land is a perfect example
Of multum in parvo – Earth's best in epitome.

The Chinese Genius Wakes Up

THE Yellow Peril you say,
But how do you spell pearl, pray?
I spell it E A R, not E R I.
That's much the better way.

'When the Chinsese genius wakes up . . .'
Napoleon used to say.
Well it's wakened up now all right,
Must we turn our faces away?

Ex oriente lux we've been told,
But if the light blazes out too bright
Or a different colour from what we expected
Must we hide our eyes from the sight?

And like ostriches bury our heads
In black prejudice till we get
Nothing in our eyes but Formosa
Or some such bit of nasty grit.

If the light blazes out too bright
And quite different from what we expected
It won't blow out again just because
We shut our eyes and reject it.

It's always been agreed the Chinese
Are at least good laundrymen.
Why should we shrink like poor quality clothes
When they wash our dirty linen then?

It's always been agreed the Chinese
Are excellent cooks. Then why be sore
When they're giving good meals to millions
Who never had one before?

It's always been agreed the Chinese
Have a wonderful sense of humour.
Why shouldn't they laugh, and we with them,
Now Capitalism bursts like a tumour?

Such a tumour has drained the life
From half mankind under the white man's sway.
Surely nobody is going to deny
That turn about is fair play.

Who that has seen millions of empty bellies
Filling out, and millions of faces wizened
By inhuman suffering plump again, to our cries
Of Western alarm has listened?

Look, look, like a brilliant torch passed on
To the runners in a vast relay,
Hope, Confidence, Peace at last light up
Hundreds of millions of eyes today.

Eyes ten years ago no one would have thought
Would sparkle with joy and courage again.
Who can doubt a miracle's been wrought –
What'll happen in twenty if that's taken just ten?

Isn't the very sunshine yellow itself?
Why then fear if health's golden hue
Sheds its blessing on the future of all mankind
Instead of the pallor we're used to?

The West has always had the myth
Of the hero asleep in a cave
Who will come again in due course
His people's fame and fortune to save.

Now a greater hero than the West
Ever dreamt of has risen again
To play a decisive part
In all the affairs of all men.

The United Nations without China
Is ludicrously incomplete
And amounts to little more in truth
Than the tailors of Tooley Street.

I am asked for a poem about China
But I've been there and seen with my own eyes
Infinitely more than any single poem
Can hold – no matter how hard one tries.

To incapsulate in verse even a tithe
Of the Chinese People's Republic I'd need
To write something like the Anthology
Of Tang poetry indeed.

And that you may know, runs into
Nine hundred volumes and gives
More than 48,000 poems
By 2,300 poets, and China lives.

A many-fold greater land now
With all its industrious millions intent
On making up for the wasted centuries
In a few years properly spent.

A vast density in unity
And not a drab uniformity
With scores of national minorities
Working joyfully in full fraternity.

And all bringing their separate gifts
To the common pool – gifts they didn't know
They had till life-giving Communism came
Their hidden wealth and power to show.

You say you believe in democracy,
Then don't try to keep it to yourself,
Put it right in the window for all mankind
Not hidden away on your own back shelf.

For it's not the colour of your skin
Any longer that's going to matter,
It's the colour of your politics –
And the Chinese are right with the latter.

Why shouldn't the majority of folk count?
They're going to now without a doubt.
And your reckoning is certainly haywire
If you try to leave the Chinese out.

If you can't see that you should ask
The N.H.S. to test your sight,
For when it gets as dull as Dulles
It urgently needs putting right.

Black, yellow, white – just being human's
The thing. And nothing now could be finer
Than the rest of the world clapping Mao's back
And crying: 'What ho! my old China!'

The Hoang-Ho that for centuries
Caused rack and ruin has now been tamed.
So they'll tame many another torrent of ill
Of which the West should be black ashamed.

Though East is East and West is West,
Now the world's so small they're bound to meet
And everything that's decent in either of them
Will get on with each other a treat.

But the first thing I think that China will do
Since the West has been so slow
Is simply to make a great big pagoda
And stick it . . . where? . . . well, U.N.O.?

In the dawn of history the Chinese
With their arts and inventions glorified Man.
Now at this crisis in human affairs
It's good to see them again in the van.

Militarism, Imperialism, Superstition,
Exploitation, Oppression – heck!
This is the great Pay-Off at last,
Who'll square it – with a phoney Chiang Kai-shek?

A Poet in Glasgow Today

TELL Scotland! Tell Scotland what?
Just at this time when Scotland
Is being drenched once again
With the woozy goodwill
Of men with all the fittings,
Gold-rimmed spectacles, dog collar,
Neat grey trousers
Beneath a neat black overcoat,
All looking as if they'd just come
From a church soirée
(You can almost smell
The bread-and-butter they've been eating!).

And He gave them their request; but sent leanness into their soul.
PSALM CVI. 15.

To have the opposite effect surely
Should be a live theatre's rôle,
Wherefore give thanks our Citizens' hecht
To Scotland at last this play by Brecht.

No subtle means of self-indulgence here!
Are you afraid it'll blow up in your face?
It's explosive enough, but smug complacence
Will be the only casualty in this case.

It's true the good wife of Szechuan
Hardly resembles your better half or mine.
She's a new experience altogether, but who
Off 'cauld kail rehet' would always dine?
Dogs no doubt return to their vomit
But wise folk keep well away from it.

If a theatre today is not a live theatre
It's because the public's just such a gross eater.
That's why, conventional bad taste to correct,
This play is one you cannot neglect.

So here's to Citizens' and here's to Brecht
And all playgoers who love a good mental fecht.

The Poet We Hope For

HIS hearers were attacked on three sides simultaneously.
They saw pictures, heard music,
And a certain incantation of words
Moved on their minds. Any one of these things
Would have been incomplete,
Perhaps unintelligible, by itself,
And any two of them without the third
Would have still left something to be desired.
The three accomplished an enormous result. They recited
The physical history of the Highlands of Scotland,
Analysed its economic geography,
Exposed in full the tragedy of its waste,
Announced a programme whereby its wealth could be restored,
And they did all this in a rhythm
Irresistible, exciting,
And, however sophisticated its source,
Transparent.
The pictures went from mouth to mouth,
And from glen to glen,
To the rivers, the crofts, the deer forests,
The aluminium works, bridges, new roads, afforestation areas,
And water-power plants,
While the music ranged with variations
Over the universe of our folk music,
And meanwhile too the voice was saying
A poem that went on down hundreds of names
And through hundreds of ideas,
All of them chanting at us while we heard and saw
Two-thirds of Scotland on the move.
The vastness of the theme, the speed and brevity
With which it was handled, and the apparent lightness

– These in their combination achieved an effect
More moving than anything his audience had heard before,
Not merely the power melodiously to arrange words
But the power to suggest human values. . . .

What he did for Scotland, by a brilliant operation,
Of almost inconceivable complexity,
Was akin to what evolution had done
With regard to the pineal body.

He concentrated on the one special projicient sense of right
Whose peculiar privilege it is to carry the self
Outward to meet surrounding and distant objects.

Our eyes are either glorified warm spots
Or they may be organs developed out of small areas of skin
Peculiarly sensitive to pressure
And registering a greater and greater delicacy
To the touch of the finger of light.

We may characterize the pineal body
As an organ of exceeding impressionability,
Functioning on the upper surface
Of the sensitive brain mass,
As a register of pure pressure from light,
And becoming so efficient and supersensitive
That it needed special protection.
So in the plesiosaurus
It may have been a third parietal eye
As the beast fumbled about with his nose in the marsh
Half-in and half-out of the water.
We can imagine it surviving in primitive creatures
Like hag-fish and lampreys, as an eye or pair of eyes,
With suitable lens of water above them.

But descending for protection into the skull
In crocodiles and lizards, and finally coming to rest

In the safest place in the centre of the head
Between the two cerebral hemispheres in man,
And above the medial nucleus of the thalamus,
Where its sensitive soul must rest in peace,
Because there is no safer place.

In Scotland it had failed to develop normally,
It was not in the right place
(Or perhaps Scottish heads were far too thick
And it had sunk too deeply in
And become as safe as the buried dead)
It remained rudimentary and diseased to boot,
And had, indeed, become little more
Than, as he called it,
The 'wandering abscess' of the English influence.

As for the elaborate arrangements with crossed and uncrossed fibres
(As in the lower mammals all fibres are crossed
So it was with most Scots, whereas in more highly developed men
A quarter of all fibres are direct)
For overlapping the fields of vision and centring the sight,
For focussing both eyes on varying distances,
For adaptation of scotopic vision in the dark
Or for photopic vision in the light
And for perceiving colour vibrations
Space fails me to indicate them here,
But – probably through the comparatively small group of optic fibres,
Dispatched to the pulvinar in the lateral nucleus of the optic thalamus,
The eye can pull the whole body about and adjust
Hands, trunk, and position of head
For their purpose of preparing the frame and active muscles
For instantaneous motor action in connection with light.

Scotland had not developed or had lost
This provision or allowed it to become atrophied.
It could not move its own members about
But it was hypnotically controlled from London.
Thanks to him it has regained its own outlook

And power of immediate appropriate action.
It can act off its own bat now.
It has got the thing clear once and for all.
It can see for itself.
It can see as well as can be seen anywhere,
Its sight is properly centred
And it can focus both eyes perfectly
On all the distances there are
Including, as was least of all the case before,
Even those nearest to it.

The Highlanders are not a Sensitive People

THE Highlanders are not a sensitive people
But exactly the opposite; I am all
For the de-Tibetanisation of the Hebrides.
It is perfect humbug to imagine
There is a reservation there for fine forms of consciousness,
Where the natives cultivate rare soul-states,
Handfed principles and choice spiritualities
Much as the Sassunach tenants of the deer forests, grouse-moors,
    and lochs,
Rear and tend the young stalk of their sports.

Yet, beloved, as who upon the Cornish moors
Breaks apart a piece of rock will find it
Impregnated through and through with the smell of honey
So lies the Gaelic tradition in the lives
Of our dourest, most unconscious, and denying Scots.
It is there, although it is unnoted,
And exerts its secret potent influence.
That a spiritual ideal of life
Could revive among us is largely due
To its subtle emanation.

1964

'Virgilium vidi tantum . . .'

On Shakespeare's Quatercentenary

HENRY IV:

> God knows . . .
> By what by-paths and indirect crook'd ways
> I met this crown.

HENRY IV, Part 2, IV.v

CANTERBURY:
> . . . Which is a wonder how his Grace should glean it,
> Since his addiction was to courses vain,
> His companies unletter'd, rude and shallow,
> His hours fill'd up with riots, banquets, sports;
> And never noted in him any study,
> Any retirement, any sequestration,
> From open haunts and popularity.

ELY:
> The strawberry grows underneath the nettle,
> And wholesome berries thrive and ripen best
> Neighbour'd by fruit of baser quality.
> And so the Prince obscur'd his contemplation
> Under the veil of wildness, which no doubt
> Grew like the summer-grass, fastest by night,
> Unseen, yet crescive in his faculty.[1]

HENRY V, I.i

To view a mountain its peak's no good stance.
Best off from the foot over flat ground perchance.
Although but one aspect's visible then,
That may as fully represent the whole
As can be encompassed by the eyes of men
(Close scrutiny may yield even less than a glance.

[1] *Vide* Hazlitt's 'On Posthumous Fame – whether Shakespeare was influenced by a love of it'.
'This at least is as probable an account of the progress of the poet's mind as we have met with in any of the Essays on the Learning of Shakespeare'
HAZLITT, *Characters of Shakespeare's Plays*

Though when there's but one mountain to climb, the feat
Means the climbers must at the summit meet!)
Happy who from no more, or less, take toll.
Shakespeare, did *you* see more? You could not hope
To comprehend your work's incredible scope
Towering over literature's multitudinary sphere
Through history to this quatercentenary year
Or guess all Time could not bring you a peer.
Yet as in through the gold blaze of its light
The sun is sometimes seen a penny-size pool
Of quicksilver or clear water welling full,
So we may see the simple genius at the core
Of your vast fame and all its attendant lore!
Others abide our question . . . You are free
– For endless fond questioning happily!

Poets' Trouble

As not the stored and capped honey in the comb
But the discovery of a fresh honey flow
Gives a contented hum to a hive
So it is with a poet, I know.

Thus, too, with the tapping of the maples,
A run of sap must be refreshed by a nightly frost.
But how bitter a night may follow and precede
A flow of poetry, we know to our mortal cost.

1965

Ingenium Omnia Vincit

The stream has suddenly pushed the papery leaves!
It digs a rustling channel of clear water
On the scarred flank of Ben Bulben,
The twisted tree is incandescent with flowers.
The swan leaps singing into the cold air . . .
A. J. M. SMITH

What are the words on that stone? Pilate's words which are the finest
rejoinder in all literature to the captious and disputatious: *What I have
written I have written.*

EARTH has nowhere any grave so deep
As the power of utter withdrawal
Into yourself you had, and Death
No power to restore to life again
Like your power, still and forever, to come back
Full of *brio* as if never away
And laughing like a better Lazarus.
(You who knew if Christ had made even one
Joke about sex what vast good He'd have done!)
What is the secret? You never breathed her name
But the old woman in Euboea was your Muse
Whose lesson to man is not to abstract himself
From immersion in present experience.
So out of death arises fresh life, even as Kenelm's corpse
Touched off springs where it rested. So you practised her rites
That ward off the menace of death
And ensure that life be strong and vigorous
And no song ever a swan-song.

1966

Three Poems for Austin Clarke

I

Thinking of the corpus of Austin Clarke's work set against the entire production of contemporary English poetry known to me.

THE Muse to whom his heart is given,
Historia Abscondita,
Is already working like a leaven
To manifest her law.

The Gaelic sun swings up again
And to itself doth draw
All kindling things, while all the rest
Like fog is blown away.

II

As a Scotsman I envy Austin Clarke's secure background of Irish scholarship, and wish my own mind was equally undivided.

WOULD that I held Staoiligary
And the four pennies of Drimisdale,
And had never seen a news-sheet,
Not even 'The Daily Mail'.
The fifteen generations before me
Could trust me not to fail
Into the darkness of alien time
To carry my song and sgeul
As the duck when she hears the thunder
Dances to her own Port a' Beul!

III

The programme I would have hoped to provide for him if he had come to spend a holiday with me in Scotland.

I TOOK him to the islands
Where the wells are undefiled
And folk sing as their fathers sang
Before Christ was a child,
Then by gask and laggan and coul
To Aigas in Strathglass
Where he heard a port on the golden chanter
That can never be heard by a fool,
      And lastly to Lochan na Mna
That will respond, I believe,
To us, if we want her,
As Lake Saima couldn't to Soloviev.

The Borders

THIS is the land I love
Whaur I was born and bred
And I come back to it noo
As a man micht come back frae the dead.

No' to escape frae life – to escape
Into a faur fuller and richer life
The Borders had when I was a lad
And ha'e still surpassin' rife.

There's nae wee stretch o' land on Earth
– Nor ony a hundred times its size
'S gi'en birth to sic a routh o' sang,
And prose, and great inventions likewise.

No' England, the United States, or the haill
British Empire even at its apogee
Has ha'en like Scotland at the yae time
A Burns and a Scott to croon its poetry.

The glory o' the Borders has aye been
Ilka noo and again doon the centuries
The combustion o' the placid wi' the intense.
Certes, *that* hasna ceased and downa cease!

The lang lines o' thae bleak hillsides
Like whippets streekit oot in a race
May gar an ignorant incomer speir
What mair can come, as frae naewhaur, in sic a place?

But we ken it's no' folk wi' the deepest feelin's
That show their emotions maist obviously.
Sae here – the toom dales, nigh peopleless,
Ha'e secrets hidden frae the mere e'e

A miracle o' sang can be made
Oot o' a mouthfu' o' empty air.
The Borders ken that's a miracle
Every noo and again fund here.

The ballads o' Europe are ferlies in which
Sangs and tales frae mony lands blend
But whaur save in the Border ballads
Dae the words tak' wing and to Heaven ascend?

The journalism o' their day thae ballads were
Aboot local feuds and forays and auld wives' tales
Yet a' at aince they soar up frae doggerel
To heichts that only sheer genius scales.

Wha doots the spirit o' the Borders lies here
May weel ask why Yarrow's dowie glen
Has inspired great poets in a way that maist
O' the warld's big rivers may ettle in vain.

The Volga, the Danube, the Thames,
And Mississippi are mighty waterways.
Beside them Yarrow's but a wee burn
Yet ootranks them in its poets' lays.

Sae it's still frae the lanely places,
No' the croodit centres o' mankind yet,
The treasures o' human ingyne emerge
And oor inspiration is aye relit.

What guid can come oot o' wee Nazareth?
Fules sneer – and a' history replies.
There's nae majority rule in this
Ettrick Forest, or Ayr, no' London's the prize.

The hert o' mankind is naked here
As naewhaur else and access gi'es
To the haill range o' human passions,
Joys, sorrows, triumphs, tragedies.

You meet them at ilka turn – there's no'
A bend in the road that disna disclose
A glimpse o' King Arthur yet, or the soond
Some horn o' Elfland blows.

Flodden aye and mony anither field
Whaur Borderers lie wha fell in auld wars,
Yet this land o' Annie Laurie and Kirkconnel's Fair Helen
Still belangs mair to Venus than to Mars.

Yet tell me, gin you can
Hoo peerless sangs cam' frae wee wars then
But nane their equal frae the great World Wars
That took faur sairer toll o' Border men.

Oh the Border scene's a wonderfu' drama
Wi' endless variety and sudden changes.
Look at the Esk, hoo saftly and sweetly
Through its pastoral valley it ranges.

Look at it again – and realise
Hoo a' at aince it roars doon in spate
Whirlin' deid sheep and torn-up trees
Heids-owre-gowdy in its heidlang gait.

Aye, quick as that is the Border temper
And no' to meddle wi' lichtly.
Ane o' the best o' the auld ballads
Expresses the haill thing richtly.

'A' the bluid that's shed on Earth
Rins thro' the springs o' this countrie.'
I wot that's been since the warld began
And will to the warld's end be.

Sae a' the moods o' human nature
Are seen in ilka Border lad and lass
Ev'n as the quick clood shaddaws there
On the lown hillsides pass and repass.

Look at the Forestry Commission's rich plantings
And tell me if it isna true
Mony a bonny tree here seems to grow
Less here than in Heaven's ain venue.

While doon in the croodit valleys still
The Border folk still gang their ways
In the mills and streets o' their eident toons
Ev'n as the Lindsays flew like fire in ancient days.

Here whaur the Romans were halted
And the Angles thrawn oot
The bulwark o' Scots independence
Is still as pooerfu' and resolute.

The Border rins through the quick o' my hert
And the herts o' a' my kind
And as lang as ane o' us is alive
Well' ha'e nae blurrin' o' that line.

Sae ev'n the cauld draps o' dew that hing
Hauf-melted on the beard o' the thistle this February day
Hae something genial and refreshin' aboot them
And the sun, strugglin' airgh and wan i' the lift
Hauf-smoored in grey mist, seems nane the less
                    An emblem o' the guid cause.

It's like quality in weather affectin' a'thing
But aye eludin' touch, sicht, and soond.
Naething o' the Earth sinks deeper noo
Aneth the canny surface o' the mind
Than autumn leaves driftin' on a lochan.

Yet thinkin' o' Scotland syne's like lookin'
Into real deep water whaur the depth
Becomes sae great it seems to move and swell
Withoot the slightest ripple, yet somehow gi'es me
An unco sense o' the sun's stability
And fills me, slowly, wi' a new ardour and elasticity.

It's like having – hashish, is it?
Huh? Nae mescalin quickens and expands the spirit
As the quiet-seemin' Borders dae to folk
Prood o' the glories they inherit and transmit.

Ask yoursel' why on the a'e side
O' the Border line you've sic splendid traditions
– And haurdly ocht on the ither side
Shaped by nearly the same conditions.

The official frontier has whiles been changed.
Frae the Mersey to the Humber it s'ud be.
But the haill warld kens it hauds in twain
Twa neighbour folk wha differ utterly.

And weel may it be remembered
England's doon there but as true Tammas fund
To the Nor' East the Borders slide into Fairyland.
There's nae divide 'twixt Scottish and magic grund.

Sae woe to them wha'd shift oor landmarks.
Tho' the Borders may be an imaginary line
Yet it's a' the mair real for that, of course,
And deeper than Ordnance Surveys divine.

The column atap Whita's hill marks the way
Malcolm and Leyden yoked us wi' the East
And Bruce and Mungo Park through Africa scored
The Border line in a way Time's never erased.

Syne woe to ony comin' up frae the Sooth
Wha dinna ken at aince when they come
Frae England into Scotland tho' there's nocht to tell
The ane frae t'ither – gin their ain herts are dumb.

O it's naething oot o' the common here
If a barnyaird hen to Heaven's yett
Beats eagle or skylark and syne sings there
A sang that has the nightingale's bett.

Here we can deny a'thegither
The notion that value's on the side
O' the big battalions, and ken a Dauvit yet
Wi' a sling-shot can whummle ony giant's pride.

Sae come wi' me and we'll rove again
To Ettrick Heid and doon Eskdalemuir
Or into Liddesdale to Hermitage
Whaur Bothwell's heart was stieve and dour.

Or dourer still at Ecclefechan feel
The volcanic spirit o' Tammas Carlyle,
Or through Sweetheart Abbey's shattered fanes
Steep in Eternity's licht awhile.

Or in Dumfries at the Globe Inn mind
A' the ardour and anguish o' Rabbie Burns,
Or hoo Roger Quin frae his lodgin' winda
By Devorgilla's Brig drew eels frae Nith's currents.

Look! Yon's ane o' the gairden wa's I climmed
To fill my wame whiles wi' honey-blobs,
No' carin wha's gairden I riped providin'
It belanged as it did to ane o' the nobs.

And there are the hills and moors
I gathered the blaeberries on
And the ploughed fields whaur I used to look
For peesie's eggs in the days lang gone.

And a' the rivers, the Esk, the Ewes,
The Wauchope, the Nith, I dooked in and fished,
Guddled and girned – the hert o' a loon
Nae better playgr'und could ever ha'e wished.

And the wuds o' the Langfall and Kernigal
Whaur we picked the hines and got oor conkers
And dung the squirrels oot o' the trees
In the happy days when we were younkers.

Aye, and later trysted oor lassies there
And cut oor initials on muckle tree-boles,
Cut them sae deep they maun still be seen
No' to be grown oot while on Time rolls.

Whitadder, Teviot, Leader and Jed
Wauchope, Kirtle and hundreds mair
The names ring oot like a pccl o' bclls
In jubilee or lamentations there.

O dinna fear the auld spirit's deid.
Gang to Selkirk or Hawick or Langholm yet
At Common-Riding time – like a tidal wave
It boils up again, and carries a' afore it.

Or in the seven-a-side Rugby games
Translated into terms o' skilfu' rivalry
The keen combative spirit o' the Borderers still
Races and chases as aince on Canonbie lea.

Able for ocht in War or Peace,
At Work or Play, or in the Arts,
The Borders bide as they've aye been
– Ane o' human nature's favourite parts.

We dinna ken what horrors waur
Than ony in history we yet maun face
– But seein' yon atomic lums at Chapelcross
Mortal concern, ev'n terror's, nae disgrace.

And yet, if the warst s'ud come to the warst
I wadna pit it past
The Borders to rise like a phoenix again
Even frae sic a holocaust.

1968

———— ◦⊨◦ ————

'Cranks never make good democrats'[1]

In Memoriam Duncan Macrae

EVERY movement of the lanky lean
Don Quixote-like figure
Was a revelation that made one smile
But never inclined to snigger.

For there was keen intellect in the fun,
A great comedian but no fool,
Measuring everything precisely
With movements like opening a joiner's rule.

His voice, the faces he made,
Every least antic, like a surgeon's knife
Intent on removing the ramifying tumour
That was poisoning Scotland's life.

The brainless clowning, the sheer fatuity,
Of the 'Scotch coamics' whose psyche
In all its vulgar ignorance he laid bare
With masterly skill, by Crikey!

Duncan Macrae was a true Scot, a great Scot
And as such must not be forgot.
But whether we'll ever see his like again
On that, alas! I'd not wager a groat.

A wonderful operator, every gesture
An accurate, if perilous, cut,
Deflating the foul complacency,
The Philistine idiocy and chortlin' 'wut.'

[1] Cranks, i.e. people with exceptional artistic and intellectual gifts, particularly
if dedicated to Scotland.

He made the matière d'Ecosse
A little less impervious to sense
Than for several centuries, a single-handed
Triumph, against huge odds, for intelligence.

All the ubiquitous false Scottishness
He alone, it seems, could expose
With one thrust of an elbow or knee,
Turn of a bony wrist or poke of his nose.

If ten just men sufficed
To save a city long ago
We may well to Duncan Macrae alone
The salvation of the Scots genius owe.

Most theatregoers are morons, you said,
But why did you, dear Duncan, limit it
To theatregoers – it's true of all here.
There's no replacement now for your wit.

Contrite

From the Italian of Giuseppe Ungaretti

I GANG prowlin' roon'
My sheep's body
Wi' the hunger o' a wolf.

I am like
A wallowin' barge
On a tumultuous ocean.

Weep and Wail No More

From the Italian of Giuseppe Ungaretti

STOP killin' the deid. Gi'e owre
Your weepin' and wailin'. You maun keep quiet
If you want to hear them still
And no' blur their image in your mind.

For they've only a faint wee whisperin' voice
Makin' nae mair noise ava'
Than the growin' o' the grass
That flourishes whaur naebody walks.

The Difference

I AM a Scotsman and proud of it.
Never call me British. I'll tell you why.
It's too near brutish, having only
The difference between U and I.
Scant difference, you think? Yet
          Hell-deep and Heavenhigh!

Earth is Enough

WHY must I go to another world
(If indeed I must) to enjoy eternity,
When it would take twice eternity for all
This world's delights to be savoured by me?

Most of My Contemporaries

I HATE them because like animals
They have no comparisons to make,
Because they cannot see beyond his or her own life.
They have no mental ability
To make any worth-while choices.
They know only what appears on the surface.
They can see the bees swarm, but
They do not know when the old queen dies.

This Scotland is not Scotland;
These People are not Scots

On approaching my 80th birthday

'I don't think you belong
To any particular country when you're old.'

'Oh, surely, more than at any time.'

'No. When you're old you live somewhere
But I don't think you belong
To anything as big as a country.'

'Scotland is small enough to hold a Methuselah.
I'm old enough to fit in there.'

'Nonsense! Just look at Edinburgh or Glasgow.
They are full of folk who are nobody and nowhere.
How on earth does anyone know them apart?
Nevertheless, I'd believe I belong to Scotland
If only Scotland and I were really there.'

I have said: 'My native land should be to me
As a root to a tree. If a man's labour fills no want there
His deeds are doomed and his music mute.
This Scotland is not Scotland.'

Like my comrade Mayakovsky
'I want my native country to understand me.
And if it doesn't, I will bear this too;
I will pass sideways over my country
Like a sidelong rain passes.'

This Scotland is not Scotland
But an outsize football pitch
Filled with nothing
But an insensate animal itch.

The Goal of all the Arts

A tribute to Sacheverell Sitwell in admiration and gratitude

WHERE the Paneubiotic Synthesis is grasped in its totality,
Omnilateral aristology obligatory on everybody,
Each having five hundred ethnohistorians within reach,
A thousand philosophies, and being well-acquainted
With the universal masterpieces of literature and the fine arts,
And enjoying the perfect vitality that only comes
Through mastering the synthesis and duly welcoming
All the higher thought-currents of love!

This is what our lives have been given to find,
A language that can serve our purposes.
A marvellous lucidity, a quality of fiery aery light,
Flowing like clear water, flying like a bird,
Burning like a sunlit landscape,
Conveying with a positively Godlike assurance,
Swiftly, shiningly, exactly, what we want to convey.
This use of words, this peculiar aptness and handiness,
Adapts itself to our every mood, now pathetic, now ironic,
Now full of love, of indignation, of sensuality, of glamour, of glory,
With an inevitable richness of remembered detail
And a richness of imagery that is never cloying,
A curious and indescribable quality
Of sensual sensitiveness,
Of very light and very air itself
– Pliant as a young hazel wand,
Certain as a gull's wings,
Lucid as a mountain stream,
Expressive as the eyes of a woman in the presence of love,
Expressing the complex vision of everything in one,

Suffering all impressions, all experience, all doctrines
To pass through and taking what seems valuable from each,
No matter in however many directions
These essences seem to lead.

Civilised being is bound up with values
Unaffected by the destruction of *ce qui ferme*
Because the only *résistance au temps*
Relevant to them is a resistance
Having nothing to do with survival in time.
The objects of an endeavour acceptable
In the light of these values are alone
Invulnerable to the decay of time
Or the disappointment of imperfection;
By their means alone may we approach
The idea of self-possession and self-coincidence
And become 'changed into ourselves by eternity'.

Responsibility for the present state of the world
And for its development for better or worse
Lies with every single individual;
Freedom is only really possible
In proportion as all are free.
Knowledge and, indeed, adoption (*Aneignung*)
Of the rich Western tradition
And all the wisdom of the East as well
Is the indispensable condition for any progress;
World-history and world-philosophy
Are only now beginning to dawn;
Whatever tribulation may yet be in store for men
Pessimism is false. Let us make ourselves at home
In *das Umgreifende*, that super-objective,
·The final reality to which human life can attain.
·Short of that every man is guilty,
Living only the immediate life,
Without memory, without plan, without mastery.
The very definition of vulgarity;
Guilty of a dereliction of duty,

The 'distraction' of Pascal,
The 'aesthetic stage' of Kierkegaard,
The 'inauthentic life' of Heidegger,
The 'alienation' of Marx,
The self-deception (mauvaise foi) of Sartre.

I believe it will be in every connection soon
As already in the field of colour
Where the imitative stage
Has long been passed
And coal tar dyes are synthesised no more
To imitate the colours of nature
Whether of autumn or spring.
The pattern cards of dye-stuff firms to-day
Display multitudes of syntheses
That transcend Nature to teach
Almost a philosophic satisfaction
Of the aesthetic sense of colour.

Apart from a handful of scientists and poets
Hardly anybody is aware of it yet
(A society of people without a voice for the consciousness
That is slowly growing within them)
Nevertheless everywhere among the great masses of mankind
With every hour it is growing and emerging
Like a mango tree under a cloth
Stirring the dull cloth
Sending out tentacles.
– It is not something that can be stopped
By sticking it away in a zinc-lined box
Like a tube of radium,
As most people hope,
Calling all who approve of it mad,
The term they always apply
To anyone who tries to make them think.

For Schönberg was right. The problem involved
In mental realisation

Is not that the evolution of music
Must wait on the human ear,
But that the human ear must catch up
With the evolution of music.
As with Schönberg's so with your work
And scant though the evidence be
Of progress here we have ample proof
(While yet the vast majority of mankind
Are but inclining to close the infinite gap
And may succeed in a few billion years perhaps)
That the complicated is Nature's climax of rightness
And the simple at a discount.

Celebratory Ode for the 200th Anniversary of the Speculative Society of Edinburgh

Two hundred years – not a bad innings!
What other Edinburgh body with its beginnings
Around then flourishes to the present day?
There have been hundreds but these floo'ers
Or weeds of the forest are all wede away.
Almost. But not quite. Since *we're* here still
Determined to carry on or excell in their stead.
What then accounts for the Spec's longevity?
Our sapient founders were at pains to see
We had the right foundations. They made siccar
By giving us a triple indestructible basis,
Knowing who's given an inch often takes an ell
They took three L's and founded us well
On Law and Literature and Liquor.
Devouring time can't blunt such a lion's paws.
Nothing is lost if as now the case is
Literature and Learning are no longer one,
Since both are L's it doesn't matter
And anyhow the Spec has always had
Its interdisciplinary feet in both, by Gad!
And when they weren't just synonymous
Performed a most adroit strabismus.

The great register of our membership you'll find
Names many men who have left behind
Them nothing really memorable, but there
Are kinds of genius of whom one never *feels* that,
And no end of men of the first ability.
Think of them – all the professors and judges,

The *Kunsthistoriker*, the Ministers of the Crown,
The top civil servants. No one grudges
After such great careers the lack of permanent renown,
Since here's another reason for the Spec.'s staying power
Its elitism and exclusivity.
Had it demanded enduring fame
Of its members it would not have been the same
And its membership would have been rather less.
The best available was good enough,
A sound principle when the going's rough
(So long as it is always understood
That the enemy of the best is the good)
Wherefore the Spec. has never been caught
By any Gadarene stampede, and has taught
Succeeding generations through the centuries
The sense of *contra nando incrementum*.

Where are these others now? Fallen into oblivion.
The Bautherwhillery Club of which
Bumperquaich was toastmaster and croupier,
The Chirruping Club, the Helter Skelter Club,
The Killnakedly Club with its ingoings
In the Cleikum Inn, the Select Society,
The Theological Society, the Griskin and Poker Club,
The Soaping Club and even the Cape
– All withered on the vine! How utterly absurd
Because they omitted Literature and Law – and just relied on the Third.

Let us not forget that throughout human history
All the arts and sciences that constitute
What is called civilisation were the work
Of an infinitesimal proportion of the people,
Went all against the understanding and often
In the teeth of the vicious hostility
Of the many-too-many. And that tiny percentage
Has been, and remains, a constant
In all countries and in all ages.
The significance of the Spec. is just

That it is part of that infinitesimal element
Which, if it were excised from the mass of mankind
The remainder could never do anything whatever
To re-establish and further civilisation.
I wish I could have a composite
Photograph of all the members
Of the Spec. since its inception.
That would show a face
Everybody would needs turn to look at
Since it would be so distinguished
From the faces of all the general run
Of mankind – and yet, I am sure,
Would closely resemble many of the Spec.'s members
Of the past, the present, and the future.

Gone is the old Edinburgh with its lands
Ten and twelve storeys high in the Royal Milc
And branches in wynds and closes where
The people were crammed cheek by jowl
And the great gutters were full of filth and refuse
In which pigs rooted for scraps – the city
With its evening stench of urine and excrement
Paralleled by that of burning brown paper
Supposed to deodorise it; and its roistering social life
Passed in taverns and oyster cellars. . . .
Oh, there's a certain amount of drinking
In Edinburgh yet – but in how many pubs
Can you converse with friends in the hubbubs
Of juke boxes, radio and T.V.
And louts capable only of animal noises,
Hippies and their floozies – not conducive in part or whole
To any feast of reason or flow of soul?

We here in the Spec. never forget
That twenty-eight centuries ago in the Med.
Our ancestors astonished the Greeks
By their strange habit of drinking their wine neat

Not watered down, a tradition we still do our best
Piously to maintain. Not here the sort of fellow
Who comes into a bar and calls for a whisky without
Specifying the precise whisky he wants.
Such creatures should be at once debarred – and forever.
If then we stand secure on our three-fold basis
There is an old phrase about another trinity
We've never entertained – Wine, Women, and Song.
Women *have* their place, perhaps – but not among
The male chauvinist pigs of this Society.
Women's lib may be all right – so long as they don't libb us!
For us Wine and Song suffice. The Third
Would only induce anxiety or perhaps satiety
Or – horrible thought – impose sobriety.
We swim against the tide – only fish
Bellies up and gone bad in the head
Should be carried along helter skelter
In a common indiscriminate welter.
In that spirit then, *and not that spirit alone*
The Spec. confronts more centuries than it's yet gone
Resolved never to sacrifice quality
For the current mania of equality
Nor to share the brutal love of ignorance,
The degenerative preference for the inferior
And the hatred of intelligence we view askance
Rampant everywhere else but here.
So be it then for a still longer career,
For if we've done our duty
And fathered the right successors
There is no need to fear
Provided strong drink doesn't become too dear,
A point it's already appallingly near.

In any case I earnestly hope
That I do not live
To find parched throats and dry as dust minds
In the Speculative.

Since they can have little love of life
Who fear licence, so
Immune from that inhibiting fear
Gaily onward let us go.

For the Hundred and Fiftieth Birthday
of the Royal Scottish Academy

A CENTURY and a half ago
A group of keen naturalists
Founded in London a society
To 'introduce new and curious examples
Of the animal kingdom'
And house them in its gardens in Regent's Park.
The public soon gave the collection
A name. It became the Zoo.
The first of its kind in the world.

Coincidence is a profound and wonderful thing.
The danger is to read too much into it.
But there must be some significance
In the fact that while these Londoners
Were collecting rare wild animals
Other people were busy in Edinburgh
Establishing the Royal Scottish Academy.
It would not do to infer too much
About the respective value of the two enterprises.

The first exhibition of Scottish art
At Burlington House earlier this century
Was declared by the President of the Royal Academy
To be an eyeopener. He had had no idea
That Scotland had had such a wealth
Of indigenous artists. But if that were so

He and most of his kind soon shut their eyes again.
While lesser spirits derided the idea
That Scotland could have any art of its own
Worthy of being placed alongside
The national art of other countries
And found the display not an eyeopener but an eyesore.

It is perhaps time for a more catholic
Opening of eyes to the treasures
Created by members of this Academy
And to reflect on what their successors
May well produce today or in the future
To the continuing glory of God and honour of Scotland.

Then Regent's Park may complete itself
By caging a few wild Scots who have no use
For the R.S.A., if such there still be.
They will be in good company there
Especially if they are in cages
Next to a few English know-alls and smart alecs.

Knowing how to handle dangerous animals
Snakes, scorpions and the like – is a speciality of the Zoo
But they have been – and remain – very chary
About handling even the tamest Scots artist
Unless perhaps one of the freaks
Of the B.B.C.'s Salon des refusés
Of whom W. Gordon Smith makes so much,
So much too much!

They say. What say they? Let them say. I dare say
Their blethers'll never fash the R.S.A.

GLOSSARY

a', all
abaw, abash, appal
abies, except
ablach, dwarf
abordage, the act of getting on board
abstraklous, outrageous
abune, above
abuneheid, overhead
aclite, awry
acresce, increase
adhantare, phantom
adreigh, distant
a'e, ane, one
a'efauld, single
afflufe, extemporary
afore, before
aftergait, outcome
aft'rins, the remainder, off-scourings
agley, off the right line, wrong
ahint, behind
aiblins, perhaps
aidle, foul slop
aidle-pool, midden-dub
aiglets, points
aiker, motion or break made in water by fish swimming rapidly
ain, own
aince, once
airels, musical notes of any kind
airgh, lack, or what anything requires to bring it up to the level
airt, direction
alist, alive
alist (to come), to recover from faintness or decay
allemand, orderly
allevolie, volatile
allryn, weird
alluterlie, utterly
alow, below
alunt, blazing

amows, disturbs
amplefeyst, animosity, contrariety
ana', also, as well
ane, one
antrin, occasional, rare
appliable, compliant
archin', flowing smoothly
areird, troublesome
arnuts, earth-nuts
aroint, clear away
arrachin', tumultuous
arrears, goes backward
arselins, backwards
ashypet, scullery maid
aspate, in full flood
assopat, drudging
Atchison, old Scots coin
atour, around, out from
attercap, spider
auchimuty, reduced to a mere thread
aucht-fit, eight-foot
aumrie, cupboard
austerne, austere
averins, heather-stems
avizandum (to tak' to), to defer decision
awa', at all
awn, own, owe, owning
awte, grain
aye, always
ayont, beyond

backfa', side sluice of a mill
back-hauf (worn to the), practically worn out
backlands, Glasgow slum tenements
backsprent, spine
baggit, enceinte
bairn, child
bairnie, baby
bairntime, a woman's breeding-time

bait, grains
baith, both
balapat, a pot in a farmhouse for the family but not for the reapers in harvest
balk, ridge in ploughing
barkin' and fleein', on the verge of ruin
barley bree, whisky
barmy-brained, wanton
barritchfu', troublesome
barrowsteel (to tak' my), to co-operate
ba's, balls
bauch, dull, sorry
bauld my glead, stir up my fire
bawaw, an oblique look of contempt or scorn
bawbees, half-pennies
bawsunt, with a white stripe
beanswaup, the hull of a bean, anything of no value
bear-meal-raik, fruitless errand
bebbles, tiny beads
beddiness, silly importunacy
beek, show, shine brightly
begane, decorated
begood, began
bellwaverin', uncertain
belly-thraw, colic
belth, sudden swirl, whirlpool
ben, through
ben (gang), go in
benmaist, inmost
bensil o' a bleeze, a big fire
bern-windlin, a ludicrous term for a kiss given in the corner of a barn
beshacht, crooked
betherel, gravedigger
bide, stay, await
biel, shelter
bien, complacent
big, build
bightsom, ample
bike, nest
binna, except
birks, birch trees
birsled, scorched

births, currents
blackie, blackbird
blainy, blemished
blanderin', babbling
blash, sudden onset
blate, bashful, cautious
blauds, fragments
blawp, dull, yawning look
blebs, drops
bleezin', blazing
blether, bladder
blethers, havers, nonsense
blin', blind
blinnin' stew, storm through which impossible to see
blinterin', gleaming
Blottie O, a school game
bluffert, squall
bluid, blood
bobby, policeman
bobquaw, bog
boddom, bottom
bodily sicht, to see entire
bogle, scarecrow
bood, should
bool, bowl, curve
boon, excellent
boot, matter
borne-heid, headlong
boss (of body), front, torso
bouks, hiccups
bourach, cluster
boutgate, roundabout way
bowzie, misshapen
bracks, interstices
brade-up, with address
brae-hags, wooded cliffs
brairds, grows
bratts, scum
braw, handsome
breeks, trousers
breenge, burst
breist, breast
brenn, burn
brent, wrinkled
brent-on, straightforward

brod, table

brough, ring round moon

broukit, neglected

bubblyjocks, turkeys

buddies, folks

buff nor stye, one thing or another

buik, trunk (of body)

buirdly, stalwart, well-made

bumclocks, flying beetles

'bune, above

burn, stream

burnal, strip of barren land

burnet, brown

bursten kirn, difficult harvest

buss, bush

byordinar, extraordinary

byous, wonderful

byre, cow-shed

byspale, precocious, a child of whom wonderful things are predicted

ca' o' whales, drove, school

caber, a pole or tree for hurling

ca-canny, go slow

cairn, pile

cairney, hillock

camsteerie, disorderly, perverse, unmanageable

canny, cannily, gentle, quietly

cantles, summits

caoin, edge

cappilowed, forestalled, outdistanced

carle, man

carline, old woman, witch

cauld, cold

cavaburd, heavy snowstorm

cay, jackdaw

chafts, jaws

channel, gravel

chauve, black and white

cheatrie, deceit, fraud

cheek o' the gushack, fireside

chests, breasts

chief, very friendly

childing, child-birth

chitterin', trembling violently, shivering

chouks, jaws

chow, chew

chowl, twist, distort

chuns, sprouts, germs

claith, cloth

clanjamfrie, collection

clapt, shrunken

claught, grab at

cleg, gad-fly

cleiks, the merest adumbration

cleisher, monster

cleisher o' a whup, a fine big whip, a dandy 'cracker'

climmed, climbed

clints, cliffs

clout, cloth

clyre, tumour, gland

clytach, balderdash

cock-lairds, empty braggarts

cod, pillow

coinyelled, pitted

come-doon, degradation

connached, abused, spoiled

coom, comb

coonter, counter

cooried, crouched

corbaudie comes in, that is the obstacle

cordage, tackling of a ship

corn-cockles, corn-flowers

corneigh, enough (lit. coeur ennuyé, internally disquieted)

cornskriech, corncrake

corrieneuchin', murmuring

cottons, cottar houses

coup, overturn, upset

courage-bag, scrotum

couthie, comfortable

coutribat, struggle

crack, converse

craidle on the ca', cradle being rocked

crammasy, crimson

craturs, creatures

craw, crow

cray, pigsty

cree legs wi' (no' to), not safe to meddle with

creel, in a state of mental excitement or confusion or physical agony, influence
creesh, fat
crine, shrink
crockats up, on one's dignity
crockets, tresses
croon, crown
cross-brath'd, braided
cross-tap, mizzen-mast
crottle, crumble away
croud, murmuring
cuckold, hoodwinked, diddled
cude, barrel
cuit-deep, ankle-deep
cull, testicle
cullage, genitals
cundy, drain
cushie, cushat dove
cwa', come away

daberlack, leek-like lengths of seaweed
dackered, searched, gone into, worn away
dae, do
daffin', playing
dally, stick used in binding sheaves to push in ends of rope
dander, temper
danders, cinders
datchie, sly, secret
daunton, intimidate, overawe
daur, dare
dayligaun, nightfall
deasie, raw, cold, uncomfortable
deed, died
deef, deaf, unimpressionable
deemless, countless
deil, devil
deltit, pampered
depert, divide
derbels, eyesores
derf, taciturn, cruel
dern, hide
din, done

ding, bang down, knock
dirlin', throbbing
dishielogie, tussilago
doited, mad
donnert, dazed, stupefied
dooks, ducks
doonfa', downpour
doonhaudin', holding down
doonsin', dazzling
dorbels, eyesores
dorty, petted
dottlin', maundering
doup, backside, end
dour, intractable, sullen
dowed, faded
dowf, hollow, gloomy, inert
dowless, feeble, imponderable
downa, unable
dowse, quench
doze, immobilisation through great speed
dozent, stupid
draiks (i' the), in a slovenly neglected condition
draughtin', delineating
dreich, dreary, tedious
drings, wretches
drites, drips
drob, prick, fall like hail
drochlin', puny
drodlich, a useless mass
drookit, soaked
drumlie, troubled, discoloured
druntin', whining
drush, smush, refuse
drutlin', piddling, incontinent, slow
duds, clothes
dumb-deid, midnight
dung, knocked
dwamin', overpowering
dwine, decline, diminish, dwindle

eel-ark, breeding ground for eels
eel-droonin', ludicrously vain
eelied, vanished

eelyin', vanishing
eemis, ill-poised, insecure
een, eyes
eerned, clotted
egg-taggle, act of wasting time in bad company
Egypt herrings, old name for Saury Pike
eident, busy, eager
eisen, lust
eisenin', lustful, yearning
elbuck, elbow
elf-bones, hole in a piece of wood
emerauds, emeralds
emmits, ants
eneuch, enough
ettle, aspire, attempt, hope, expect, reckon
ettlin', eager

fa', fall
faburdoun, faux bourdon
faddom, fathom
fair, completely
fairin', deserts
fanerels, accessories
fank o'tows, coil of ropes
fankles, becomes clumsy, traps
fantice, imagination, whimsicality
farle, oat-cake
farles, filaments of ash
farlins, fish troughs
fash, trouble, worry
fauld, fold
fause, false
fause-faces, masks
feck, great deal, majority
fecklessly, impotently
feech, exclamation of disgust and contempt
feery-o'-the feet, nimble
fegs, faith, truly
fell, clever (*adj.*), very (*adv.*)
ferlie, wonder, marvel, surprise
fey, fated
fidge, move
fidged, worried

figuration, harmony, musical structure
fiky, fastidious, troublesome
filed, dirtied
flauchters, flutters
flaught, abased
flaught, flame
flech, flea
flee, fly
fleerin', flaring, gibing
fleg, frighten
flegsome, frightening
flense, cut blubber off a whale
flet, flit
flype, turn inside out
flytin', railing
fochin', turning over
fog-theekit, moss-thatched
fordel, progressive
forenenst, in front of, opposite, over against
forenicht, early evening
forfochen, exhausted
forgaed, gave up
forgether, meet
forhooied, abandoned
fork-in-the-wa', means of diverting share of labour pains to husband
fotherin', supply
fou', drunk
foudrie, lightning
fousome, disgusting
fower, four
foziest, most stupid
fozy, rotten
fraise in ane anither's witters, run through each other
fratt, fretwork
fraucht, cargo
freaths, plumes of foam or froth
fremit, strange
fremt, friendless, isolated
fu', full
fug, moss
fule, fool
fullyery, foliage
fushionless, dispirited

gaadies, bloomers, howlers, gaffes

gad, fishing-rod

gaed, went

gaff, hook for fish

gair, small patch

galliard, rapid dance

gallus, callous, indifferent, reckless

gammons, feet

gams, gums

gane, gone

gang, go

gangrel, wanderer

ganien, rodomontade

gansel, nonsense talk

gantin', yawning

gantrees, planks for putting barrel on

gar, make, compel

garded, covered

gausty, ghastly, ascetic

gaw (to have a), to have a catch upon

gealed, congealed

geg, trick, deception

gell, on the gell, on the go

gemmell, double harmony

get, illegitimate offspring

gey, very

geylies, very much

gie, give

gi'en, given

Gillha', pub of all weathers, hostelry of life

gin, if

girds, hoops

girles, thrills with horror

girn, snare

glaur, mud

gleg, eager

gleids, sparks

glisks, glances, glints, coups d'oeil

glit, slime

gloffs, dark patches appearing denser than other parts of atmosphere

gloghole, deep hole

glower, gaze at, glare

goam, gaze stupidly at

golochs, earwigs

gorded, frosted

gorlin', fledgling

goustrous, frightful, tempestuous

goves, comes angrily

gowd, gold

gowd-bestreik, gold-streaked

gowden, golden

gowk-storm, storm of short duration (sub-sense of foolish fuss)

gowls, hollows (opposite of gloffs)

gowpenfu', fistful

gowpin', gaping

graith, tackle, equipment

grat, wept

gree (bear aff the), carry off the palm

grieshuckle, embers

grue, revulsion

grugous, ugly

grun', ground

gruntle, pig's nose

guid, good

guisand, thirsty

guisand cude, a barrel whose staves have sprung apart owing to drouth

guisers, maskers

guissay, pig

gundy, violent

gurly, savage

guts, bowels

gy, spectacle

ha'e, have

hag, peat

haik, drag, hoist

haill, whole

hain, keep, preserve

hair kaimed to the lift, on the go

hairst, harvest

haliket, headlong

hanlawhile, a moment

happit, covered

harn-pan, brain box

harns, brains

harth, lean

haud, hold

haud their row, be quiet
hauf, half
hauflins, adolescent boys
haw, hollow
hawdin', holding
hazelraw, lichen
heels-owre-gowdy, head-over-heels
heich, high, height
heich-skeich, crazy, irresponsible
heidstrang, head-strong
henree, hen-run
herried, plundered
hert, heart
hesp, hasp
hinds, farm-labourers
hines, rasps
hinny, honey
hod'n, hidden
holine, holly green
hoo, dog fish
hotchin', restless
houk, hulk
how'd, shorn down
how-dumb-deid, the very dead of night
howe, bottom, hollow
howff, public-house
howkin', digging
hule, mischief
hullerie, with ruffled feathers
hustle-farrant, clad in tatters
hwll, ululation

ilka, every
ingangs, intestines
ingles, hearths
inklins, intuitions

jag, prick
jalouse, guess
jaup, splash
jizzen, straw, child-bed (*lit.* in the straw)
jouk, dodge
jow, surge, swing

kaa, drive
kail-blades, cabbage blades
kaim, comb
kebbuck, cheese
keeks, looks slyly or suddenly
keethin' sicht, sight of the 'keethin's' or disturbances caused by the movements of fish
kelter, undulate
keltie, bumper
ken, know
kilted in a tippit, hung in a noose
kindle, light
kine, cows
kink, bend or twist
kirk or mill (to mak' a), to do the best one can
kist, chest, breast
kite, belly
kittle, tickle, (*adj.*) ticklish, difficult
knedneuch, sour
knool, pin, peg
knoul-taed, swollen-toed
knurl, knob
krang, hulk of a whale after the blubber has been removed
kyths, appears, becomes known, emerges

lade, mill stream
laich, laigh, low
lammergeir, great hooded vulture
langsyne, long ago
lapper-milk, sour milk
laroch, hole in the ground, foundation
lauchs, laughs
lave, rest, remainder
laverock, lark
lear, learning
leed, strain
lee-lang, live-long
leid, language
leuch, laughed
liddenin', going backwards and forwards
liefer, rather

lift, sky
lig, lie
ling, gait
linns, rocky stairway
lint, flax
lippen, trust
little-bodies, fairies
loan-soup, see white
lochan, little loch
lo'e, love
loof, palm of hand
loon, lad
loonikie, little boy
loppert, coagulated
losh me, goodness me
louch, come-hither, downcast
loup, jump
lourd, heavy, overcharged, cloudy
loutit, curtsied
lowe, flame
lown, hushed, quiet
lowse, loosen
lowsin'-time, stopping-time
lozen, window
luchts, loose locks
lugs, ears

maik, partner
maikless, matchless
'mang, among
mant, stammer
mapamound, map of the world, earth's surface
mappiemou'd, rabbit-mouthed
marrow (winsome), a creditable limb
maun, must
mebbe, perhaps
mell, mix
minnie, mother
mirlygoes, dazzle
mocage, sardonic humour
mochiness, closeness
moniplied, manifold
moniplies, intestines
mools, earth, soil for a grave
moosewob, spider's web

mou', mouth
muckin', cleaning
muckle, big, much
Muckle Toon, Langholm in Dumfries-shire
mudgeons, mocking motions
mum, silent
munk, imitate
munkie, rope with noose at end
munks, swings away
murgeons, mouth movements
mutchkin, liquor measure, half-bottle

nae mowse, perilous
natheless, nevertheless
natter, rant
neb, nose
neist, next
nesh, full of awareness, nervous
'neth, beneath
neuked, crooked
nicht, night
nocht, nothing

ocht, anything
on-ding, downpour
oolin', crouching
oon, shell-less, addled
oorie, weird
ootby, outside
ootcuissen, outcast
ootrie, outré
or, before
orra, odd, nondescript, not up to much
Overinzievar, Perthshire place-name
owre, over
owt, anything

paddle-doo, frog
panash, Fr. panache.
pang-fu', crammed full
pap o' the hass, uvula
partan's tae (literally crab's toe), cutty pipe

peepy-show, cinema
peerie, spinning-top
peerie-weerie, diminished to a mere thread of sound
penny wheep, small ale
pickle, small quantity
pirn, reel
pitmirk, complete darkness
plaited, pleated
plat o' shairn, cow's dung
ploys, games, amusements
plumm, deep pool
pokiness, congestion
poortith, poverty
port a' beul, mouth-music
powsoudie, sheep's-head broth
prick-sangs, musical compositions
puir, poor
puslock, dung

quean, lass, woman
quenry, reminiscences of dealings with women
quither, quiver
quo', said

raff o' rain, a few streaks of rain
ragments, odds and ends
raim-pig, cream basin
ramballiach, tempestuous
ramel, branches
ratt-rime, incantations for killing rats, doggerel
raw, row
rawn for the yirdin', frightened to death
rax, stretch
recoll, reminiscences
reek, smoke (*There was nae reek i' the laverock's hoose*, it was a dark and stormy night)
reek forth, stream out
reid e'en, according to tradition, the one night in the year when harts and hinds mate, in November
reishlin', rustling
reistit, dried

renshels, beats
ressum, particle
revelled, ravelled
revure, dark, gloomy, contemptuous
riach, dun, ill-coloured
ribie, stripped of leaves like a bird that is plucked
rice, branch
rimpin, lean cow
ringle-een, eyes showing a great deal of white
ripe, pillage, search
rippit, rumpus
ripples, diarrhoea
rise, bough, branch
risp, grass
rit, scrape
rived, torn
rizzar, currant
rooky, misty
roon, round
root-hewn, gnarled, twisted, awkward
rouch, rough, plentiful
rouchled, ruffled
rouk, smoke, mist
row'd, rolled, wrapped up
rowin', rolling
rowth, abundance
rowtin', roaring
royat, unmanageable
rude, bold, stubborn
rugs, rives
rumgunshoch, rough
rumple-fyke, itch in anus
runkled, wrinkled

sabbin', sobbing
sae, so
sae-ca'd, so-called
sair, serve
sair, sore
sall, shall
samyn, deck of ship
santit, swallowed up in sand
sauch-like, willow-like
sauls, souls

savin'-tree, sabine, said to kill foetus in womb
scaddows, shaddows
scaldachan, chattering
scansin', glinting
scaut-heid, scrofulous, disfigured
scho, vacillate
sclaffer, shuffle
sclafferin', slovenly
sclatrie, obscenities, scandal
scoogie, apron
scorlins, tangles of seaweed
scount, small example
scouth, scope
scrats, hermaphrodites
scrauchin', screeching
scunner, disgust
scunnersome, disgusting, repulsive
scut, fud
seggs, insignificant plants
seil o' your face, fortune favour you
seilfu', blissful
send, convoy to fetch a bride
sentrices, scaffolding
ser', serve
shairest, surest
shasloch, loose straw, litter
sheckle, wrist
shog, swing, rock
shoon, shoes
shot, freed
shouders, shoulders
sib, blood relations, related
sibness, relationship
sic, such
siccar (to mak'), to make certain
siller, silver
simmer, summer
sinnen, sinew
sirse, exclamation of surprise
skail, come out
skarmoch, scrum-like
skime, gleam
skimmerin', glimmering
skinklan', shining, gleaming
skirl-i'-the-pan, fried oatmeal

skrymmorie, frightful and terrific
slee, sly
sliggy, cunning
slorp, lap up, slobber over
slounge, sharp fall
sma'-bookit, reduced to small proportions, minified
sma'er, smaller
smirrs, drizzle
smoored, smothered
sneith, smoothness
snell, bitterly cold
snod, neat, tidy
snood, see *tint*
snoovin', sneaking
socht, sought
sonsy, contented
sook, suck
sook-the-bluids, little red beetles
soon', sound
soupled, accelerated
soupler, suppler
spales, melts, runs down
spalin', burning away
spatrils, musical notes (as printed) (Used in *Ex vermibus* to denote visual effects of a bird singing)
spauld, backbone
speir, ask
spiel, climb
splairgin', spluttering
stang, blast, paroxysm
starnies, *starns*, stars
sta'-tree, pole for tethering cattle to
steek, shut
stegh, glut
stell, fix
stented, appointed
stert, fright
stertle-a-stobie, exhalations
stilpin', striding
stishie, rumpus, hullabaloo
stoichert, bedizened
stound, throb
stour, dust
stow, stole

stramash, noise, rumpus
stramulyert, panic-stricken
straucht, straight
strawns, strings, chains
streek, stretch
streekit, stretched
sud, should
sumphs, blockheads
sune, soon
swack, active, supple
swallin', swelling
swaw, ripple
swee, jerk, sway
sweetie-pokes, bags of sweets
swippert, active, lively
switchables, earwigs
swith, swift
swith wi' virr, vehement
swither, hesitate
syne, afterwards, since, then, thereafter

tae, too
taed, toad
taigled, entangled
tak's tent, takes care
talla, tallow
tapsalteerie, topsy-turvy
tash, destroy
tassie, glass
tethered splore, adventure within pre-
  scribed limits
teuch, tough
thae, those
thaim, them
thegither, together
thieveless, impotent
thole, bear, endure
thorter-ills, paralytic seizures
thow, thaw
thowless, handless, useless, impotent
thrang, busy
thraw, throw
thrawart, perverse
thrawn, contrary, stubborn
thraws, convulses
threidin', *thridden*, threading

thring, shrug
thringin', hoisting
tine, lose
tint, lost
tint her snood, dishonoured herself
tirls at the pin, rattles at the door-handle
toom, empty
toories, pom-poms
tossils, tassels
toukin', distorted
tousie, rumpled, untidy
toves, moods
trauchlin', troubling
trig, trim
turn-gree, winding stair
twaesome, the two of them
twa-neukit, two-horned
tyauve, struggle

ugsome, horrible, repulsive
ullage, deficiency in contents of barrel
unco, strange (*adj.*), very (*adv.*)
undeemis, countless
unkennable, unknowable

vennel, lane, narrow street
vieve, vivid
virr, stamina, force, vigour

wab, web
wae, *waesome*, woeful
waesucks, alas
waled, selected
wame, belly
wanchancy, unfortunate
warl', world
watchet, dark green
watergaw, indistinct rainbov
waun'ert, confused
waur, worse
wecht, weight
wee, small
weel, well
weet, wet
weird, fate
weirdless, worthless

wheen, few
wheengin', complaining
wheesht, be quiet, hush
whigmaleerie, trifle
whiles, sometimes
white as a loan-soup, pallid, as thin and weak as charity soup
whuds, dashes, thuds by or down
whummle, overturn, upset
whummlin', tumbling
whup, whip
whuram, crotchet, quaver
wi', with
wice, wise
widdifow, perverse
widna, would not
windlestrae, straw
winnock, window
wizened, shrunk
worm-i'-the-cheek, toothache
wud, wood

wud, would
wunds, winds
wuppit, winding, wound round

yabblin', gabbling
yammer, jabbering
yank, throw
yett, gate
Ygdrasil, Celtic Tree of-Life
yince-yirn, once-errand, on special purpose
yirdin', see *rawn*
yirdit, buried
yon, further
'yont, beyond
yowdendrift, counter-swirl of snow from the earth, gale driving down, opposite of earth-drift
yowlin', howling
yow-trummle, ewe-tremble (cold spell at end of July after sheep-shearing)

INDEX OF TITLES

[1] The unpublished third volume of the huge poem of which *In Memoriam James Joyce* and *The Kind of Poetry I Want* are the first two volumes.

INDEX OF FIRST LINES

APPENDIX

As the poet explained in his Author's Note, the *Complete Poems* reprinted only poems already published in books or periodicals; there was no thought of printing poetry from manuscripts. The poems in this Appendix have come to light or have been printed for the first time since the *Complete Poems* were collected for publication in 1978. Seven were included in the anthology of MacDiarmid's poetry and prose, *The Thistle Rises*, edited by Alan Bold (London: Hamish Hamilton, 1984); the poem now reprinted from *The Red Poppy* (1959) was discovered by J. K. Annand; and the two poems from the first issue of *The Scottish Nation* (1923) were identified by Bill Herbert, who reprinted them in *The Gairfish* (Autumn 1983). These poems are not included in the indexes of titles and first lines.

It is known that other poems still unpublished are to be found in the poet's papers and notebooks.

W.R.A.

What Will God Do?

(After the German of Rainer Maria Rilke)

What would God do if I should die.
I am his jar (if I should break?),
His fountain (if I should run dry?),
I am His consciousness, and make
All that he knows His Own Self by.

I am the sandals he must wear
Or with bare feet crave wearily.
If I should die and go not there
His Heaven would his prison be.

From my barr'n bones his cloak would drop,
His glance that on my cheeks depends,
As a tired head a cushion befriends,
Will founder if old Death extends
Dust for the comfort my life lends
Naught but a void where He may grope!

What will God do if my life ends?

(*The Scottish Nation*, 8 May 1923)

A Pretty Prospect

(*We can no longer be fortified like Clough, by the thought
that 'though I perish, Truth is so.'*)

Not that we perish but that all
That all men living now deem true
Must share our funeral
And perish too. –

Save that some anthropologist
May disinter in far-off years
The monstrous tangle of
Our hopes and fears,

Or some remote descendant write
'Not till the thirtieth century can
We draw a definite line
'Twixt beast and man,'

And question even if there was
Ere then much difference between
Mankind and plants! – 'at least
They both were green!'

(*The Scottish Nation*, 8 May 1923)

An October Nightfall

LEAFS that ha'e scrauched in the wund a' day
Hing forspent on shaddaws o' trees.
Birds ha'e gane as gin they'd been nocht
But fleetin' ferlies a dream can gie's.

Deasie sheep in the haar are fankled,
Horses dow wi' their heids thegither,
And I'm fell feared that it's Life itsel'
And no' juist Licht that's aboot to wither . . .

O whatna cry can I reeze that'll gar
The warld haud hard by its colours and shapes
Or a' thing's tint in the gantin' dark
Like my bonny hen that gaed wi' the gapes?

It'll heist its feathers in whustlin' licht
Nor jouk wi' its eident neb again.
There's nocht but nocht whaur its gleg een glinted
– Maun I tine the warld as I tint my hen.

(*The Glasgow Herald*, 14 October 1925)

On the Island of Little Linga

That which appears most real to common consciousness has the least existence.
— PLOTINUS

It's a' vera weel
   On an island like this,
To lack for a while
   Sae muckle, and no' miss.
But what 'ud I dae
   If I lived here lang,
And never mair mixed
   Other people amang!

Hoo lang could I live
   On the store I had yet,
Frae my previous life,
   At a new store get?

If I'd naething to dae,
   No even work to eat
– The Past gane frae memory,
   And the Future wi't.

That's what'll happen,
   That's why I cam' here
– I'll sune no be able
   Even to think, that's clear.

What'll happen then
   Is juist what I seek
–– The communion it's impossible
   To think o', or speak.

(*The Broughton Magazine*, Summer 1933)

The Stone of the Dog, in Glen Lyon

THIS is the Stone of the Dog,
With a neck that comes up to my knee
And a clumsy spatulate head
Going out horizontally,

The stone by which the women believe
They can tell, from the ease with which they can go
Stooping under the head when they're heavy with child,
If their time is to be easy or no'.

(Undated manuscript in Edinburgh University Library)

The Wild Swan

SEE, Scotland, see how in these desolate days
When all your other birds to kinder countries fare
One wild swan in your freezing waters stays
And strives to keep an open channel there!

But now the encroaching ice is clutching at its feet
And soon in vain its whirling wings may beat!

(Undated manuscript in Edinburgh University Library)

The Terns

NOW all about us the terns
Make gestures of incredible grace
– But in human intercourse surely
Only lovelier shapes should ever have place.

Stupid slack girl with a silly sense
Of your human superiority to these,
The lifted wings of any of these little birds
Should suddenly bring you to your knees.

Man with the fat dull eyes just taking for granted
Or indifferent to all this lovely display,
If the sky were like your look it might do for you,
But these snowy wings would go a dirty grey!

(Undated manuscript in Edinburgh University Library)

The Boon of T.V.

I USED to be a drucken coof –
    A rantin' rovin' deil-ma-care;
But noo, my freens, I haud aloof
    And gang to the public hoose nae mair.
Farewell my harum-scarum freens,
    Fareweel to spongin' at the bar,
Fareweel, ye soul-degradin' scenes,
    Owre lang I've waddled in the glaur.

Nae mair I mean to 'shoot the craw,'
    Nae mair ye'll see me rollin' fou,
A bleared and blusterin' 'Johnnie Raw,'
    To meet me sober something new.
Nae mair ye'll laugh at me wi' scorn
    And at my silly antics gape;
My elbows oot, my trousers torn,
    My hat in concertina shape.

My chums hae dragged me up the stairs
    And left me at my mither's door,
A sicht that maun hae grieved her sair
    And stung her auld heart to the core.

But noo my wife, my bairns, and I
   Spend ilka night roon my T.V. set.
Ye'd be surprised hoo time whids by
   Noo John Barleycorn his match has met.
It has anither advantage tae:
   I buy my whisky by the bottle noo
And hae my gless or aiblins twae
   And enjoy't the mair noo I dinna get fou!

           (*The Red Poppy*, 1959)

'The Unholy Loch'

'CAN you account for it? The Scottish people
Are all opposed to the Polaris base, it's said.'
– It must be some sort of half-forgotten
Self-respect at last raising its ugly head!

The term 'military intelligence', of course,
Is an outsize oxymoron
But for the criminals running Polaris
The first two syllables of the word must be shorn.

The Swedish poet, Harry Martinson,
Has asked in one of his inspired flashes:
'Will Man banish himself from the Paradise of Earth
And crown himself "The King of Ashes"?'

Or will he be able to control his urges
And see the Earth as the only orb where life can find
A land of milk and honey? None will be left
If these maniacs poison Mankind.

Earth is the only ground of human hope, showing now
Unprecedented perspectives for happy fulfilment
Against which only purblind prejudice launches
Its tentiginous genocidal intent.

Some half-forgotten self-respect? By God,
It's high time *that* surged up and prevailed
Before morons, with none, make the whole world
Enurn a humanity that has failed.

Nowhere in Scotland, Europe, America even
Is there a fit place for such a base.
If it must be located anywhere at all
Then Hell itself is the only place.

It's nothing, fools think, to destroy
The population of Glasgow in a second.
That's it – it's *nothing they think* – that's the fact
With which it's high time we reckoned.

Nay, Hell itself it would disgrace,
For a Polaris base there is NO PLACE!

(*Peace Campaign*, January/February 1961)

On the Fishing Grounds

I AM a poet
And beliefs are to me
No more than the sunlight
Is on the deep sea.

Fishers know it's at night
Their harvest is got.
Daylight's only of use
For disposing of the 'shot'.

(Undated manuscript reproduced in *Hugh MacDiarmid: a Festschrift*,
edited by K. D. Duval and Sydney Goodsir Smith (Edinburgh 1962))